DON'T CALL IT MURDER!

MOCKINGBIRD PUBLISHING
CHIPLEY, 2021

Jeremy A. Mutz

For Amanda.

**In memory of Cooper Donley—
Detective.**

PROLOGUE

It's always loud in True Fulton's house. Like the surge of the river in flood season, the grown-up voices course through the thin walls. Speaking. Cussing. Hollering. Crying.

There's the rattle and scrape of Momma fixing something to eat. The sudden crash of Daddy breaking things. New notes, then, are improvised to a familiar drumbeat, one which repeats itself whenever True's Old Man gets mad, like a record player stuck on one little piece of a song.

The sounds of cleaning up and putting away. The sounds of the little ones, hungry. The hushed tones of apologizing and a new 'discussion' hastily commencing.

It's as if Mother and Daddy thought the roof would fall in if they didn't hold it up by talking, filling every nook and cranny of the little house with words. The nervous, sharp, frightened, sounds of hard times. The distraction afforded them by reminisces of their younger years.

True, eleven years old, just does his chores quietly. Tries to stay out of the way. He tucks in his younger siblings. He closes his eyes in the darkness with a mind to drift off to sleep, those sounds like the explosions of war to his little, sponge-like mind. It's a barrage never relenting not even for the span of a heartbeat.

He likes the sounds of the shore. Of Apalachicola Bay. He knows them all like friends. The gentle splashes of raindrops dripping from the eaves by the window. The bullfrogs. The whistle of the ferry boats late at night. The rustle of the wind from the Mexican Gulf that relieves the stifling July heat. There's comfort in such 'quiet noise.'

Part I

ONE

Bloodstains covered a child's pair of blue jeans and a peculiar little straw hat. The clothes were evidence—of murder.

Bill Ledbetter dropped the items into a paper sack. He set it on the desk and folded himself into his chair. *Hell—what now?* he wondered

Ledbetter is the High Sheriff of Leon County. He knows his duty. He ought to telephone the circuit judge. He ought to get word to the Sheriff down in Apalachicola. That was the right thing to do—Ledbetter knew that the clothes belonged to the little boy from Franklin County who disappeared four years ago.

But he didn't pick up the phone.

He was startled by a tap at the door.
"You're working late."
It was one of his deputies, Jim Mealer. "Oh, hiya, Jim."
Jim plopped down in a chair. Looked over at the bag sitting between them. "What's doin', boss?"
Ledbetter leaned back and grinned. "Oh, just tyin' up some loose ends. Don't want anything to interfere with our huntin' trip."
"No, sir! Nothin' had better interfere! Already cleared it with the 'better half.'"
"Right, Jim."
"Well, speaking of your sister, I best get home, 'fore she starts to worry."
"Sure, Jim! See you for dinner after church?"
"Yes, sir! Goodnight, Sheriff."
"Goodnight, Jim."
Mealer gone, Ledbetter's attention returned to that bag. *Damn it, why does it have to land in my lap? I've got to do something about it, though.* He leaned over and looked through the blinds, out the back window of the courthouse. Calhoun Street was dark as sin. His brother-in-law's headlights flashed over the window like magnesium powder—as the younger man drove away.

The family, down there in Apalachicola—or, was it Eastpoint? Anyhow, they'd suffered. I could end that suffering.
Bill Ledbetter reached for the phone but stopped himself.

He stared at that bag, silently cussing it. *No, I gotta get rid of this. I've no choice.*
He felt bad. He hated to do it.
By getting rid of the bag he'd be deciding this wasn't a murder. He'd be taking to himself the powers of coroner, prosecutor, and jury. He'd be ensuring someone would get away with the vilest of crimes. He knew the kid's parents would be left to wonder, forever, what happened to their boy.

That sickened Ledbetter. But when someone in a certain family kills, that family gets to tell you *they* will take care of it. When a certain *daddy* calls you, when he tells you it would hurt the whole town, you listen. Ledbetter looked at the backwards letters on the other side of the glass door. They spelled his name. He wished to keep it there. As much as he felt for the Birches, for *that family*, he had to do this for *his family*.

He picked up the phone. But not to ring the judge or his counterpart on the coast. He gave the operator a different number. "Okay. I'm takin' care of it. Yeah. Goodbye."

He crossed Calhoun. Climbed into his new Ford. Mashed the starter and flicked on the lights. They seemed to spar with the darkness, shadows dancing on the pale back wall of the courthouse.

Ledbetter turned onto a deserted Pensacola Street. The gloomy windows of Culley's funeral parlor made him shiver. He sped up, heading toward the Capitol—which sat on "Rascal's Hill." The rascals were relaxing at home at this hour. He crossed Monroe Street, proceeding toward the Women's College.

Small bungalows lined Pensacola Street, in the quiet neighborhood that looked uphill to Westcott Hall. He was thankful everyone was indoors. When he passed the last house he breathed a little easier. Pensacola Street turned into a quiet country road. *No witnesses.*

He slowed.
There's the field—the old wagon ruts.

He turned the wheel—the car bouncing along the unpaved surface. He knew this farm. Last month, he'd served foreclosure papers. Helped the family load up their belongings. He shut off the motor. Stepped down. It was pitch-black out in the old cotton field. Thankfully, he no longer felt like he had eyes on his back. The glowing windows of the women's dormatories were distant, far-away dots. Just a short ways from the college, Tallahassee became rural and lonesome.

He turned around with a start! Something jingled by the fence! His heart nearly came out of his chest. *What the hell was that!* His eyes adjusted. *Hell—just a milkcow!* Silently, she watched him.

That heifer can't testify—get on with it! He pulled the little pair of jeans and the crumpled hat from the bag. He doused them in gasoline from the can he carried in his Ford.

But then it startled him, and he nearly dropped the can. *That scream! Sounds just like a scream! That damned train whistle!*
He laughed at himself. *Sure am jumpy! Hell, that train comes through here every night. None of those men, riding along, smokin' their cigars can see me! Let's get this over with and get the hell outta here!*
But, the engineer kept on and Ledbetter couldn't move. *Damn, I wish he'd quit!* The *Florida Limited's* whistle was more mournful than he'd ever heard it, a long wail as jarring as a baby's cry out there in the open field.

He worked up the nerve to strike the match. Though his hands were shaking, he got the match lit. He prayed it would go fast! The dried blood on the Levi's seemed so unnaturally red in the little flickering light. The gasoline flashed. The paper burned up. The flames spread out over the denim. The train kept wailing. He cussed it.

Maybe I oughta stop—stomp out the fire! he thought. But he didn't.
He lit a cigarette. Watched. For what felt like an eternity. Finally, it was gone. He felt bad. *But it's done! And supper's waiting.*

TWO

True likes his uncle, who's quiet like him. A tall, lanky man, Pratt Harlowe looks like a Civil War soldier. Like the "battle-scarred" lead soldiers some of the boys play with, but the Fulton's can't afford. On his forehead, Harlowe has a real scar. Some say it came from a real bullet. True heard folks say Harlowe reminded them of Harry Carey, the cowboy star. The way he grinned. Drawled. The way his bangs fell on his forehead, and the quick turn toward gray he'd taken.

True "took to" Harlowe ever since he was an infant. He, from the first, looked up at Harlowe with those blue, clear eyes fixed on him. True's mother, Lexie, had commented on it. *"See how* Truitt *looks at you, Pratt, like he's already known ya for years! Like there's some deep bond theah. Look at 'im stare into your eyes!"*

It was Harlowe that first took to shortening the boy's name—to True. This summer, True started working for Harlowe, commencing a new pattern of sounds. He'd listen for Harlowe's Model T truck. When it rattled, he'd run to the mailbox and climb in. They'd drive down to meet the ferry boat—called the *Save Time.*

Captain Andy Wing ran her. He blew the whistle when they rolled aboard as he always did. The ferry is little more than a barge with a pilothouse and smokestack in back, a ramp for automobiles in front. She takes an hour to cross the Bay.

Her engine chugged. They broke free from Eastpoint. For True, it was like escaping from the county jail! As much a relief as the breezes that refreshed them on the way over.

Today, True's new routine started the same as every morning, ever since the one-room school in Eastpoint let out. It's a good routine! The *Save Time*'s engine throbbed and churned water with little urgency. Cap'n Wing shared his coffee and recounted the county's 'goings-on' to Harlowe. And True could breathe easy.

He watched the oystermen on the water, yonder, 'tonging' with long poles as they did every day until the sun cycled from *hot*—to *full blowtorch.* Some of the men were kinfolk.

True looked back at that little settlement of forty souls. He could still see one rooftop—his house—among the pines that covered the shore. He watched the house shrink to a dot. Then he turned the other way, toward Apalachicola. At first she was just a few tiny dots, herself—the oysterhouses and canning factories along Apalachicola's waterfront. As she came into sharper focus, the dots separated into white and tan brushstrokes, the outlines of individual buildings, tin roofs, her "Tin Man" water tower poking up over the trees.

The new paved roads brought more automobiles through "Apalach" and True's attention turned to a yellow De Soto that rode lashed down ahead of Harlowe's truck. Something besides a Ford, and a color other than black, was a real treat! True's parents talked of 'the Depression' and how no one had any money except folks coming down from Tallahassee or Georgia they called 'tourists.' It didn't sound nice, the way Daddy said the word, almost the same way he might pronounce *banker* or *carpetbagger*. True reckoned the people who owned the automobile were such 'tourists,' but they seemed real nice! They told him they'd come from Atlanta. Shyly, he answered their questions about where he lived, what he was doing this early in the morning. The woman noticed his workclothes and toolbelt that was a few sizes too big for him.
"You like the roadster?" asked the man.
True nodded. The hood was a slide-to-second-base in length. The headlights were as big as drums in a marching band. The other men, aboard, appreciated it to. "They done polished 'er shinier'n a Chattanooga fire engine," remarked Wing.

The couple dressed well, the way rich folks dressed for church—and it wasn't even Sunday! The lady sure was fancy, her hair and the feathers in her hat, like a gal in a picture show. True took in every detail. True and his uncle wore simple workclothes, Harlowe's typical gray shirt, his gray fedora. True wore a blue workshirt, overalls, a straw hat. True felt no sense of deprivation or envy seeing the 'tourists.' He was simply interested in the new things he saw, as he might be of a bird or fish he'd never seen before.

The woman asked True what kind of bird it was diving to the water with such a flourish. "Oh, he's an ol' *oss-spray,* ma'am."
"So pretty!" the woman exclaimed.

True looked up, watching the bird circle around. True tried to see if he could tell where the water stopped and the sky began—he couldn't. Water and sky were one, where a fellow floated in it as free as that osprey, and it was all a pale, silvery blue that even the best painters in the world might struggle to match. The water was smooth as glass, and a little mist remained, before the sun burned it off. Apalach seemed to float, ahead, at the edge of this heavenly blue space.
"My, it *is* pretty here!" declared the woman.

True nodded. He was proud she'd say that. Franklin County people were proud of their section. They were taught so—after all, this was *Paradise.*
"Good fishing here, son?" asked the man, the ferry chugging ever closer to town.
"Yessir," True replied. He was too bashful to tell them about the fishing he'd done on this Bay, in the flats, where the redfish liked to feed. He thought how his friend Gibby would have told them all about a forty-pound Red' he'd caught all by himself and nearly sunk the skiff trying! He'd have

worn their ears out—all the way across—with that story. True nearly smiled at that. The fish got bigger, and the waves rougher every time Gibby told that story! It probably started with a ten-pound fish, True couldn't remember, and now it really didn't matter. It was *forty pounds* as far as everyone in Eastpoint was concerned!

Cap'n Wing reversed his engine. The *Save Time* ground to a halt at the foot of Avenue E, "Uptown" Apalachicola.

"You really build houses, then? A little fella like you?"
"Yes'm. Well, I don't really build 'em. I he'p my uncle's all."
"Where? We might like to see after we've had breakfast."
"Down yonder. Bay Avenue."
Harlowe told them, "Y'all stop by and see us—any friends of my nephew are welcome to walk through the house. We'll be there all day—if it doesn't rain!"
"Why, that's very nice of you," said the man. "We just might do so." Cap'n Wing had tied off the ferry and dropped the ramp by this time. There being no such thing as a stranger in Apalachicola, the subject turned to the best place for breakfast.
"Why, there's none better than the Fuller *Hoe-tell*," said Harlowe. He pointed to a menagerie of wooden gables and dormers three blocks distant. "Over yonder."
"We never woulda known that," the woman declared. "Thank you!"
Harlowe and Wing took the ropes off the roadster. "It was swell meeting you, young fella!" said the "Tourist man."
True reached up. Shook his hand like a gentleman.
The woman offered her gloved hand, likewise.
The man started the motor. True said goodbye to the couple, again. He kind of hated to see them go. But he was equally interested in watching the man ease the fine automobile down the ramp. *How smoothly it pulled away!*

Now, before him were all the sights of a big town! *Everything a fella could dream of!* Department stores—where you could buy anything from a suit-of-clothes to an outboard motor! Stores that sold automobile parts, shoes, geehaws and sundries, you name it! Two drugstores with long soda fountains! The bank stood yonder. True reckoned the most interesting were the Automobile dealerships—'Apalach' had *three of 'em!* While every little town in the Southland had a Ford dealership, here you could buy '*Mr. Willys' cars'* and '*them big Buicks,' brand new!* And at night the town was all lit up with electric lights, the brightest at the picture show—the *Dixie* theatre! People came here from miles and miles upriver, on the train, to do their trading!

Saturday morning was the busy 'shopping day.' Consequently, a line of black Model T's strung out along Market Street—clear to Huff Hardware and Gorrie Furniture. Sidewalks bustled with folks who'd '*gone to town'* to do their trading. Neighbors stopped to talk to neighbors. Storekeepers propped their doors open and set out their stock.

True took in all that activity from the cab of the Model T. The automobiles. The faces. The sacks of goods. The workings of the waterfront. The oysterhouses they passed down Water Street.

A boy, toting a cane pole, waved to them, heading for the dock.
The town sparkled and jingled like Christmas, the stores and characters enough to make Norman Rockwell take notes!

Harlowe pulled to the curb on Commerce Street, beside the Post Office. They walked around front.
An oysterman's wife, pushing her baby along the sidewalk, waved. "Mornin,' Mister Pratt!"
Harlowe squeezed the rim of his hat. Gave a grin. "Mornin,' ma'am."
A buggy, drawn by a speckled horse, approached, the animal's bridle jingling as he trotted along at the hands of a colored houseman. A lady with silver hair under her ostrich-feathered hat nodded, formally. "Good Morning."
"Mornin,' Miss Ruge!"
Harlowe knew everyone in the county, it seemed. *Wasn't a person they passed on the street he didn't know!* thought True. Pretty ladies stopped. Said, 'Good Morning!' to him. *Even the one that Momma said was 'bad,' and whispered to Daddy about.* Harlowe spoke to her like she was anyone else, squeezed the rim of his hat just like he'd done when the other ladies went by!

Harlowe paused a moment, watching a car maneauver into a parking space. The same thought kept repeating in his mind. *Collis Hutto has left town and not come back. Why?*
Half-way up the front steps, Harlowe turned to True. "Ready, son?"
True nodded.
He liked going in the Post Office. Polished wood paneling and brass. That ornate window that the clerk, Merle Herring, sat behind. The man just finished giving a gal change for a two-cent stamp when they came in. "Howdy!"
"Oh, hiya, Pratt!" Herring reached into a bin, retrieving a folded paper. "I wrote down the information you asked for. Here." He passed the note through the window. He squinted over his reading glasses at True, whose head just reached the counter. "Good Mornin,' young man!"
"Mornin,' Mister Merle!"

While Herring asked of the boy's mother, Harlowe glanced over the paper. He read it like it was something important, True noticed. Harlowe didn't say what it was. Tucked it in his shirt pocket. Said, "Thanks, Merle. I'll see ya later."
"See ya, Pratt. True, you tell your momma I said hello!"
"Yessir."

Harlowe wound his watch. He was expecting someone on the train tonight. True noticed his uncle winding, but didn't ask what he had on his mind, didn't know about the train.

13

Harlowe drove up Commerce Street to Demo George's general store. George—a friendly man with dark eyes and a full mustache—barely waited for Harlowe to cut off the motor before bounding over to shake his hand. "Well, hello, Pratt!"

"Howdy!"

George patted True on the shoulder, happy to see the boy also. "Hello, son!" he exclaimed in his accented English. George was a Greek—many of the latter had settled in Apalachicola, bringing with them their way of sponge-diving and boatbuilding. Most agreed, George built the best shrimpboats on the Gulf. He was not often in the "Uptown" store, rather spending the time at his workshop on Water Street. He enjoyed talking to Harlowe whenever he saw him.

The doors were open, catching the breeze. They went inside, Harlowe choosing a brush, a wallpaper pattern, other things. He seemed to be in a good mood, grinning and listening to what the Greek was saying, one story after another, as they paid, and True helped load the truck.

"You don't say very much?" asked George.

True shook his head. "No, sir." He was looking at the saws and other tools on the wall, taking them in one at a time.

"I was the same way when I was his age," stated Harlowe, picking up the last bundle.

Harlowe looked back at his nephew, scratching his chin, thinking about what he just told the Greek. *That ain't exactly so, now*, Harlowe realized. The boy had grown more taciturn lately. True hadn't said much at all since his friend Gibby Birch went missing. His only friend. And True's parents had their own problems, Harlowe knew, too many to notice that the boy was retreating more and more to the quiet of the woods, or the creeks—or the solace offered by 'Uncle Pratt.' Harlowe knew that could only take the boy so far. While all boys had some job or other in Franklin County, little True had stopped playing and being a child. No baseball. Nothing. That wasn't right, Harlowe thought. "True, did you see them new toy automobiles, Mr. George has?"

"Yes, take a look at this one." George handed the boy a jaunty roadster made of tin.

"Why, it's jus' like the one on the ferry!" True declared.

"It sure is!" replied Harlowe.

True admired it, surely a car a movie star would own if it was real! It was a very lucky boy who'd have this little one to play with. Then, he wiped his smile away and put it back, knowing he wouldn't be allowed to have it.

"Just a minute, True. You've been workin' so much that—well, I reckon you're due for a little raise 'n your wages."

"But--."

"Don't talk him out of it!" said George, winking. "Here, I'll wrap it up for you."

"Thankya, sir!" said True.

"Don't mention it."

"Thankya, Uncle Pratt!"

Harlowe gave his Harry Carey grin. "Not a'tall, you earned it! You've done a 'jam up' job workin' with me!"

"That's so good to hear!" said George. "I might want to hire him to work with me next year!"

"You hear that, son?"

True blushed—he wasn't used to such talk.

They said goodbye. Climbed into Harlowe's Ford. People commented that Harlowe seemed more like a daddy than an uncle. Even now as they chugged by in the truck. Harlowe proceeded down Bay Avenue. He turned into the yard of the new house, a perfect thing that True saw rise from a clearing covered with goosegrass to how she stood now. A pretty thing, with dormers looking out over endless blue water.

True liked this summer job better than shucking, though he could barely lift the two-by-fours, or the buckets of nails, he was so little. He'd struggle some and Harlowe, with his easy-going grin, would come down the ladder and help the boy with his loads.

As he always did, Harlowe looked over the work from the day prior, before preparing his brushes and setting up the ladder. If anything was amiss, he'd notice it and patiently correct it, True had learned. This was only the second house they'd built. Harlowe didn't rush them.

True opened the can of blue paint. Stirred it. The water, the air were still and quiet, away from the noises of "Uptown." The rooftops of big houses poking over the trees and the view from the bluff, spelled *"High Cotton,"* as Daddy would say. It just seemed real pretty to True.

Harlowe got to work, silently brushing, until bare lap-siding became the color a sailor wore on his uniform.

THREE

Harlowe could go all day without saying more than a few words.

Funny thing, it was as if he could just give a look and True knew his thoughts without their being spoken, knew when to hand him cans and things, the hammers, whatever needed done when the boy was helping him.

Whatever was on his mind he kept to himself. That didn't bother True; he was just the same. But today Harlowe was even more reticent, to the point True couldn't help notice something was *bothering him.*

Harlowe looked up when he heard the noon churchbells. But True saw Harlowe open his watch not long after! The sun went to its hottest, the cicadas their loudest, then the shadows begin to cover them with welcome shade. The day passed and they'd painted the entirety of the house—and Harlowe hadn't spoken at all.

True wondered what it was. The house was coming along well. True had painted neatly. Hadn't spilled a drop from the buckets. What could it be? He watched Harlowe come down the ladder and stir a new can. He looked up to his uncle's full, six-foot-height, Harlowe like a giant to an eleven-year-old boy, even when he climbed down. His gray workshirt by now soaked a darker shade in sweat, his face was red, blank.

True hoped he hadn't done something wrong. He liked working with his uncle, and the peace and quiet of being with him. Fishing with him was the same, where the sounds of mullet bobbing up or the osprey guarding her nest or the silence out in the Big Bay were the loudest things around you and provided all the stimulation a boy could want.

Harlowe never caught much when they fished, but the boy loved it just the same. Harlowe often said he couldn't catch a bass in a bathtub, and it was a bit of a running joke in Franklin County that he had no luck as a fisherman, even with a nice rod-'n-reel. People commented on how he paid attention to the boy, taking him out on his boat when True's old man didn't. True heard these things and remembered them. He heard people talk about his uncle. He took it all in like somehow it would teach him how he should be. Things like, 'Mister Pratt don't say much, but he hears and remembers damn near everything.' People commented on that, 'you think he ain't payin' attention, watch out, 'cause he's soakin' it up like a sponge, every damn detail tucked under that gray hat 'o his.' And, 'look at his houses. There ain't the smallest thing he missed. I keep lookin' for something wrong, ain't found it yet!' said one client. And Franklin County people reckoned all that added up to a damn good lawman—because besides building houses, Harlowe was the *Sheriff.* 'Ain't no one better at catchin' men 'at needed catchin.' True heard the people say that too. It all stuck with him.

And so True knew something was troubling Harlowe. Was it the case that wasn't talked about? The one case that bothered his uncle? The only one he hadn't solved in all the years he'd been a lawman—nearly twenty. True didn't know what it was about. *'But I reckon it must be real bad!'*

It was just after six o'clock. *Two more hours,* thought Harlowe.

The sun felt like a blast furnace on True's cheek and there was no cooling off in sight. But the house was gleaming in its fresh coats of paint. They went inside, painting long strips of wood for the baseboards. *Uncle Pratt's real quiet—still,* True realized. *Distraught.* He'd heard that word once. It seemed to fit!

True wondered what it was! There wasn't much that went on in the county Harlowe didn't know about. *Reckon somebody's sick? Somebody thieven'?* "Son, you did a good job in *heah.* We get these brushes cleaned and we can knock off early. How's that sound?"
"Fine!"
They cleaned them. Silently they packed up, loading the empty cans and things on the truck.

Harlowe hadn't said a word. But, finally, he spoke. There seemed to be considerable purpose behind his words. "True, I reckon since we finished early, you and me can go over to Buzzett's. Buy you a coke-cola. Whachya think?"
"Sir? R-Really?" True was glad Harlowe wasn't mad at him, and surprised by the promise of a Coca-Cola—a rare treat! But even the excitement over that was nothing in comparison to knowing Harlowe was about some matter of importance.
"Yeah, son. There's a fella I wanna talk to." Harlowe wiped his forehead and put his hat back on—adjusting it. His look was serious. True knew this was sheriffin' business fixin' to start right now!
True nodded. Any way you sliced it, it sounded good to him! It would be daylight for a while. If he went home he'd just be in the way. Daddy expected him to work, not lay around the porch like one of *"them cur dogs,"* is what he'd say. If he was with Harlowe, then he was doing that— working—and he knew that's how Harlowe would tell it. Harlowe was taking him along on this lawman business, almost like a real gun-hand!

They got in the truck.
Harlowe wished it wasn't so serious. What he'd been thinking about all day.
But it was.
The train had something to do with it.
Then there was that box under the seat. *True saw it. Noticed it had 'a mess' of postage stamps on it. The boy, otherwise, hadn't gone near it nor mentioned it.*

17

How could I mention it? When you open a package and realize it contains a human skull, you didn't show it to a young'n.

To say it was unusual, morbid, and ominous, to describe the shock of unwrapping it could hardly begin to convey the feelings he felt in looking down at what *was* someone's face. Someone's smile. The holes where someone's eyes had been. Anger and helplessness and horror washed over him in waves, like a drunk lying on the shore, unable to feel his way out of the surf. When you realized the size could only mean that this was a *child,* you only felt those things more deeply.

The morbid surprise had come in yesterday afternoon's mail.

FOUR

Buzzett's Drug Store, at the corner of Market Street and Avenue D, has a long, marble counter with a gleaming soda fountain. Cool inside, it's a relief from the long, hot workday. True got his Coca-Cola, as promised. Sat by the fountain.

In the far corner, out of True's hearing, Harlowe spoke to a sandy-haired fellow named Ira K. Brewer, who worked part-time for Mr. Buzzett as a 'soda jerk.' Brewer was well-liked in the town.

"Collis Hutto is on the 7:44."

"Collis comin' home? I don't know anything about that, Pratt!"

Harlowe *knew that Brewer knew.*

The man in white, uniform cap was related by marriage to Collis. He likely knew where Collis has been the last four years. But he never would say.

"Aww, Pratt, I don't wanna get mixed up with this."

Harlowe looked at him with his piercing eyes. Brewer's effort to evade the subject—and those eyes—by picking up the broom and furiously working the crumbs toward the back room wasn't working.

He sighed. "Pratt, we've been through this before—a dozen times, the same questions!"

"I know it. And I reckon we'll go through it a few more times until I get some answers." Harlowe was very calm when he said this, but he noted the younger man's eyelid twitch, and the way his lip quivered.

"Pratt, you don't know the trouble this'll cause for me. He's my wife's brother!"

Brewer just about cussed in the middle of the drugstore, his face turning beet red now, the knuckles on the broom white as a sheet.

"He's been up in Tallahassee?" Harlowe pressed.

The man cussed under his breath.

"How's that?"

Brewer turned to look at True and stopped himself. "Nothing!"

"I wanna know where he's been. I'm gonna find out." Harlowe talked low, but the look in his eyes was such that Brewer knew he wasn't of a mind to relent.

"I done told ya, I don't know!" Brewer hissed, loudly enough to belie his effort at a whisper.

The long hand on the clock made a loud jolt forward, startling Brewer. He knew that Harlowe knew how nervous he was.

His eyelid twitched as much as the broom, which he set back in motion. Harlowe glanced at the clock. "All right. But I'm gonna find 'im. I'm patient."

Harlowe eased down the counter toward his nephew, perched up on the stool, his legs dangling shy of the floor.

"Good?"

True nodded, happily. The soda jerk followed, running his rag over the counter. He'd calmed down some. He looked over at True. "You holler if you want another'n, now. You want another'n?"

"Nosir. Thankya."

"Yo' daddy still workin' at the sawmill there?"

"Yessir."

"He's a hard-worker, yo' daddy is." True's father, Foster Fulton—known as "Foss"—is formean of the Green Point mill. He stood taller than most, broad-shouldered, and handsome.

A few customers walked in, then, and Ira was busy.

True finished his drink. Harlowe nodded, "goodbye." They walked outside into the still-balmy sunlight.

The boy sat on the seat holding his toy automobile. *I'm glad I done that,* thought Harlowe.

Before they left for the ferry, True asked something. "Can I keep the car at your house?"

"Sure, son."

FIVE

Apalachicola—A Few Minutes Later.

The sun made the "faces" of the stores glow in the golden hues of fading
daylight as they drove up Market Street. Harlowe always slowed down
when they neared W.O. Anderson's Ford dealership, at the corner of
Market and Avenue F. Both looked to see whether the lot had new trades.
Harlowe proceeded up the street to his house at Market and Avenue I.
Pulled in the shell driveway.

This house is True's favorite of all his uncle had built. He'd examine the
details fresh every time. The wrap-around porch with a swing. The dormer
with three windows which look out over Scipio Creek. Inside, the living
room had exposed beams and clean white shiplap walls like a riverboat
saloon. The fireplace had a long, white mantle. Beside it, there was a rack
for fishing poles. The hall was plastered smooth—in an alcove, there, was
a telephone! At the end of the hall Harlowe even had a flush toilet and
gleaming porcelain sink—the house had indoor plumbing!

They put up the tools—in the shed—and washed up in the kitchen.
Harlowe let True run the water in the long sink, and lather with a white
bar of soap.
"I know I gotta carry you home. Only I gotta meet the train. Caint run
over on the ferry and make it back in time."
True nodded.
"Well, what I might could do is phone for your momma and tell her you're
havin' suppah with me. That okay with you, son?"
True nodded. "Yessir."
Harlowe walked down the hall and telephoned the little store in
Eastpoint—the only phone over there. Mr. Tommy said he'd run the
message to Miss Lexie.

Harlowe read some papers a spell. True played with the car and didn't
bother him.
Presently, Harlowe closed the desk and stood. "I sure hope you're hungry,
True. Stew. A piece of pie. Whatever ya want."
True nodded his head. *Sure sounded good!* He knew Harlowe liked to have
his supper at the Riverside Café, down at the waterfront, corner of Water
Street and Avenue G, a short walk from the house. As it turned out, that's
where they were going.

True could already smell the oyster stew and coffee as they passed the
Economy Cash Store and neared the corner. The Café is white and slat-
sided, its name in large letters below the open windows. The Lavontas',
another Greek family, *run the place* and everyone in the busy restaurant
said hello to the Sheriff and his nephew when they walked in.
The windows faced the Apalachicola & Northern depot, which suited the
Sheriff's purposes. He bought something for the boy and himself. Coffee
and cigarettes seemed to be a greater part of Harlowe's nourishment,

however. More than the food he touched. True could see Harlowe didn't
have much of an appetite tonight.

Windows open to the sultry air, his uncle kept sipping that scalding coffee.
Kept puffing smoke. Kept an eye on the depot as True finished his stew
and Mr. Lavontas refilled their cups.

Not a soul moved on the street or the train platform. The colors grayed
with dusk, yet the bugs remained loud, the heat and humidity still going
like a pressure cooker.

Harlowe could almost feel his watch ticking. The depot was motionless,
only the glow from the window of the railroad agent's office (and Western
Union) evidencing any forthcoming activity.

Harlowe opened that watch. *The train should be passin' Sumatra now. Was
Collis even on it? There was a good chance he wasn't.*

Harlowe heard he was. Heard talk that Collis wanted to come home and
see his sister. *It paid to keep your ears open thataway. He might want to
tell what he knew. I've waited four years. Don't want to miss him if he's
inclined to talk! Might be* all *talk—but I got to try.*

The editor of the newspaper came in for his coffee and sat down with
Harlowe and True for a spell, before finding a place at the counter. One of
the town's doctors, George Weems, also spoke to the Sheriff, as did nearly
everyone who passed their table on the way out, True realized.
"A piece of pie for the boy?" asked Lavontas.
"Whaddya say, True?" asked Harlowe.
The boy nodded happily. A big slice of lemon pie, which costs a nickel, was
set before him. Eating in a restaurant was a huge treat for True—and now,
pie!

Harlowe looked at his watch, although he needn't have, the waning sun
telling him it was near eight o'clock. He paid for the meal and they took
the long way, back. Many of the stores had closed for the evening.
Harlowe checked each doorknob. True realized he did this every night.

They saw the lights of the *Dixie* come on. People buying a ticket for *Little
Ceasar.*

Ahead, a couple more stores closed, as the last customers trickled out.
There wasn't always a set time—sometime after sundown. And Harlowe's
movements weren't hurried. Life moved at the pace of the tides, the flow of
the river, not by the second hand. Apalach didn't have one traffic light. It
is the kind of place where heisting a few cigars and canned goods at
Duggar's Store made the front page of the *Times.* It's a world away from
the postcard destinations further south. Isolated. Tranquil. It was
Paradise.

He noticed how True was observing this "ritual" of his. He lay his hand on the boy's shoulder. "Sure is a pretty evenin', ain't it son?"
True nodded.
They enjoyed walking along beside the tracks, the stars above them so clear and bright.

Entering the house, Harlowe switched on a lamp.
He glanced over his papers again. Shut them away in his desk like before.
"True, I need you to wait here while I go meet the train. You'll stay here and run that new automobile of yours, won't you son?"
True nodded. He'd been holding the toy, looking at it and looking at it.

The hand of the mantle clock clunked forward. *Ten 'til.* He hadn't heard the train whistle, but she was generally late. A few more minutes, he reckoned. "All right, son, I'll be back here, soon, and we'll make the last ferry."

SIX

Apalachicola. Saturday, 8:05 pm.

Harlowe smoked up another Chesterfield but the big man hadn't got off the tardy 7:44. The other passengers had, but Collis Hutto stayed in his seat by the window just staring ahead. Like he was reading the paper or getting up the nerve to face his sister and brother-in-law waiting at their home on 12th Street. *It's possible Collis changed his mind and decided to keep riding—on to Port St. Joe.*

Harlowe put out the cigarette. Crossed the dark street. The little train was like something out of a Saturday Matinee "Western," the old wooden coaches and the steam engine, which sighed and exhaled like a tired animal. Equally quaint was the wooden depot, a small building with two wood stoves. Shadows had embraced the depot and the benches where passengers waited, dusk turning daytime colors to gray, save for the illumination of one electric light at the depot, and the jumpy, yellowish glow of the kerosene lamps emitting from the windows of the passenger car. "Howdy, Pratt!" said the conductor, Mr. Harper, seeing the sheriff approach.
"Evenin'."
"Whatchya doin'?"
"Just wanna talk to this fella. One of your passengers."
"Yeah?"
"Yeah, he's still on the train, theah."
"He sure is. O.K.," said the conductor," snapping his watch shut. "We've got time. He's an orn'ry cuss. He may not wanna talk to ya. Tell 'im if he wants to ride to St. Joe, he'll owe me seventy-five cent."
"Yessir. I'll say that."
Harlowe climbed aboard the train. He opened the door of the coach and walked up the aisle of wooden pews. "Been a long time, Collis," said Harlowe, from mid-way back. The man had broad shoulders and the way he leaned forward Harlowe half-expected Collis would want to "bow up" and fight.

But Collis just kept reading, ignoring the Sheriff. Harlowe continued up the aisle, the man still engrossed in that newspaper. Harlowe could now see that was what he was doing, reading the doubled-up paper with his face close to it like he didn't have his spectacles. *I know damn well he hears me*, thought Harlowe. "All right, Collis, they're fixin' to kick you off. Ol' Harper wants to get going. Come on."

Harlowe thought he saw the man twitch. *It would be just like Collis to play possum and try to sucker-punch a fella. But he's just settin' still.* Harlowe reached over. Shook him by the shoulder—carefully, for the man might take a poke at him if he was woke from a nap. But Collis just slumped across the wooden bench—*dead.*

Harlowe didn't have to be an M.D. to know that. It was obvious! And it hadn't been long. Collis was still warm. *"Damn, son! You never was much count. You sure ain't no use to me now."*

Harlowe tried to set the dead man upright in the bench. When folks talked about 'dead weight' they weren't fooling. The big man must have weighed every bit of two-fifty! The Sheriff got him to where he wouldn't crumple to the floor.

Harlowe looked down at the doubled-over copy of the newspaper. This morning's *Tallahassee Democrat.* It was clutched in Collis' right hand when he died and fell to the floor when Harlowe had tried to rouse him. Harlowe looked at Collis' suit-of-clothes. A very nice wool suit. Silk necktie. Harlowe wondered how the shiftless fella could afford a rig like that! He caught himself reflecting poorly on the dead man. He didn't care to do that. *But, hell, the man* was *'sorry!'*

Harper, the Conductor, came walking up the aisle. The lantern light cast a pallor on the dead man and he could see it too—that and the look on Harlowe's face. "Damn!"
"Yessir. Better phone for Doc Murrow, hear?"
"Yeah, Pratt," the conductor replied, walking out to go use the telephone in the railroad agent's office.
Harlowe didn't need the Doc to tell him *the what.* But he needed Doc to tell him *the how.*
J.S. Murrow lived at the old Raney mansion. It only took a moment for the older gentleman to walk over, toting his medical bag, after he got the call.
"Evenin', Pratt."
"Evenin', sir."
"Why, it's Collis Hutto—Ol' Beadle."
"Yessir," replied Harlowe, stepping back to give Doc room to work in the confining aisle. "No marks on 'im, sos that I could see."
The Doctor bent over the decedent and began the examination. Harlowe turned to Harper. "Where did he get on?"
"River Junction."
"Anybody with him?"
"No, sir, he's by hisself."
"Did anything seem to be the matter with him?"
"Why, he didn't make a sound. He read his paper and I-I never noticed nothin' wrong!"
"My only witness," said Harlowe. *He never would talk about that night— four years ago. He done left town, caught the train to Atlanta, which was as far as I could track him. Now he's dead.* Harlowe slapped his hat against his thigh. "Damn."

"I'll need to get him to my examination room," said Murrow. "Can you fellas get him over to my office?"
"Yessir," Harlowe replied. By that time, Harlowe's Deputy, T.K. Brewer had climbed aboard the train car. So did a couple of his poker buddies—who appeared as if they'd commenced to tie one on a little early tonight.
"Damn, that's Beadle!" one of them slurred.

"I phoned Mr. Sangaree, he's fixin' to meet us here with his hearse," said Brewer.

Harlowe nodded. "Why don't you boys wait outside for now." Harlowe then checked Collis' pockets—before his clothes were removed and kinfolk called and everybody shut their mouths tighter than an oyster. The man had twenty-nine cents' change. Then there was something Harlowe nearly missed as it fell to the floor. A tiny, crumpled bit of paper! He retrieved it from under the seat, and realized it wasn't merely wadded up, but it had been folded many times. When he smoothed it out he could see it was a half-torn bit of stationery with something scrawled upon it. *S...4...4? No, it reads 5...4...4.* That might be an address. Or a telephone number in a town a little larger than Apalach. The paper—good quality—was from a hotel, he reckoned, but the half Collis had was the bottom, minus the name of the establishment. It gave Harlowe very little.

While waiting for the undertaker, Harlowe looked over the scene one more time. The young man's clothes were not just of a fine quality, they were well-cared for. They'd been brushed recently. Collis' hands and nails were cleaner than when Harlowe had seen him last. He'd put on weight. While he hadn't much money on his person in his final hours, he'd been living to a reasonably comfortable standard—somewhere.

Headlights flashed the windows of the coach as V.I. Sangaree drove up Water Street, then backed the hearse to the train coach. Sangaree and his son, Daniel, climbed aboard. The boy blanched, the sight of the big man turning splotchy in the sticky heat naueseating. "E-Evenin', Pratt."

"Evenin'."

"Ready for us?"

Harlowe nodded. Then he had to help Sangaree and his boy roll Collis onto the stretcher.

They wrangled the body through the narrow aisle and down to the hearse. Given the size of young Collis Hutto, it was a chore. Finally, Sangaree slammed the doors, and gave a relieved, phew! He wiped his brow. And Daniel wiped his neck. The corpse was handled with as much grace as hauling in a wild hog. Death seldom cast a comely figure. And a man had scarcely the dignity of a slug-shot pig when he was turning grey and bloating on an undertaker's slab—or in a train car on a hot night.

Harlowe was sweating, to the point of being cold and clammy like a case of heat stroke, and for a different reason than the undertaker. It was dark on Water Street now, the sky inky black over the River, the rustling sawgrass. Harper approached the sheriff quietly. "Collis had one bag with him, Pratt." Harlowe followed him and they looked in the valise. It contained nothing but the usual items a man would travel with. Harlowe shut it. "All right, his kinfolk can come get it."

***

Doc Murrow lived in the old Raney Mansion, two-blocks away, on Market Street. His office was in the side-addition which faced Avenue F. It was to this office Collis' body was taken.

Harlowe smoked outside of the well-lit room while the Doctor examined Collis. It didn't take long. The doctor stepped out into the hall of the old house, which was built by a cotton-broker before the "Late Unpleasantness" which befell the South. The hall was aglow with the yellowish light of incandescent bulbs that cast shadows from the elegant bannister. Harlowe wondered if his heart was beating as loudly as the clock behind him. Murrow retrieved a cigarette. Harlowe struck a match for him. Murrow took a puff, like it was medicine, before he spoke. He knew Harlowe had been trying to get information from Collis for the last four years, how important it was to the Sheriff, and to the whole county, perhaps. Finally, he looked Harlowe squarely in the eye. "Heart attack. Nothing could have been done." The older fellow looked at the clock's face, opposite. "I'd say he died a little more than an hour ago. I am sorry, Pratt."

Harlowe nodded. He was surprised, then, when Dr. Murrow took him aside, in the space between the staircase and the doorway of the kitchen, just out of earshot of the others. He spoke in an undertone, the greatest look of concern on his face. "There is one thing I thought you ought to know. I am not certain what it will mean to you, and for your inquiries."

"Yes, sir?"

"I saw bruises, Pratt. On his belly. One or two days old. He's been in an altercation, I believe."

"Well, Ol' Beadle got crossways with somebody. He could talk his way out of a lot ot things, but not this time."

"Do you know whom?" asked Murrow.

SEVEN

Apalachicola, Saturday. 9:30 p.m.

Small-county sheriffing kept you busy with lost cows. Dear ladies pouring coffee in dainty china cups. The unwelcome task of serving papers. Men stopping you at the barbershop or the bench in front of the A&P to tell stories or complain. Days passing with the mundane. The monotony. The heat. The yellow flies upriver.

Sleepy—nothing to do—until there was.

Bad things had the habit of breaking loose like a train jumping its tracks. No warning. No easing into it. *You just had to face it—mostly alone.* He could fit his entire department in one automobile! T.K. Brewer and D.C. Twiggs are his deputies. C.A. Seago, the jailor. He had no salary. His men had no uniforms. The county didn't even provide a badge!

There's no time to moan. Harlowe needed information—and quickly. He looked at his watch. It ticked mercilessly fast upon these slow hours.

Uptown was dark, save for the bulb glowing at the closed Standard Oil station at Market and Avenue E. He returned to the depot, catching the agent before he closed up. A quick scrawl on the A.N. Telegram form and he got off a message to the Police Chief up in River Junction.

Harlowe found Ira at the pool hall on Avenue D. "I told ya, Pratt, I don't know anything!" Flashing his annoyance, Ira sunk the 4 ball in the middle pocket with a hard tap of his cue.
He avoided Harlowe's steely blue eyes. Lined up another shot hoping the lawman would go away.
"What did he tell you?"
"Pratt, that was four years ago. Ask him!"
"Reckon I lost that opportunity 'bout an hour ago."
"Huh? Whadya mean?"
"He's dead."
Ira nearly dropped his cue stick. "What am I gonna tell Betty Sue? It's her brother and all."
"I know it. Would it be...easier if I broke it to her?"
"Yessir, it would." Ira swallowed. "Thankya." The fellow started to add something, but stopped.
"You got somethin' you'd like to tell me?"
"No. Well, I thought—." Ira stopped himself. Clutched the pool table tighter.
"How's that?"
"All I's gonna say was, Collis—."
"Yes?"

Ira turned away, red-faced, then shot Harlowe a look. "How'd you know he's comin' anyhow!" he snapped.

Harlowe offered to drive Ira home. He turned down Avenue E, Ira talking nervously, as if he had to fill the silence. Going on about the game he'd won while ago. The beer he was missing out on, now.

Harlowe wasn't much on small talk. He looked over at Ira. "Did Collis mention anything about a package?"

"That's what I was doin'—takin' on a package!" Ira slapped his knee. Bellowed out a laugh.

Harlowe gave a grin. "Well, I prob'ly saved you from another fight with Miss Betty when I interrupted ya."

"Yeah, well," Ira slurred. "Ida taken muh chances. Ya gotta spoil muh fun. Only fun I have, ya know that?"

"Did he mention mailing something out, after he'd left Atlanta, when he was passing through River Junction maybe?"

Ira flicked his cigarette out the open window—as Harlowe turned up 12th Street. Ira answered low. "I dunno."

"He mention mailing something down here, to Apalach, maybe?" Ira looked out over the dark street, distant and sullen. "Nosir. He didn't. Damn, Pratt, you are stubborn as hell!"

"Yes, I am."

Harlowe pulled to a stop in front of the Brewer's little house.

He knocked. Mrs. Brewer looked to him. Then, her drunken husband. Then, back. She listened. Harlowe broke the news to the young woman as gently as he could. "Beadle? No!" she cried.

She teared up. Ira wasn't much comfort and Harlowe felt bad for her. She had her hands full. Three little ones. A husband who still had some growing up to do himself. After a few moments, she quieted. She looked at him. "Would you like some coffee, Sheriff?"

"Please don't trouble yourself, ma'am. I appreciate it."

He sat with her. Answered her questions. She was more receptive to talking than her husband. Harlowe didn't press her, it seemed like she wanted to talk about her brother. All she knew. It wasn't much as would help Harlowe. He knew it might help her, so he listened.

He had to ask if Collis mentioned any trouble with any persons. Harlowe was sure the answer would be no, but had to ask. She said no, he hadn't. Harlowe had no reason to doubt Mrs. Brewer's veracity. Politeness required he accept coffee on her second offer, even in the midst of mourning and the neighbors arriving to console the family. He thanked her as she poured. After he'd had a cup, he said good-bye. Walked out on the porch. The air had cooled, just a tad. There he found Mr. Brewer, who wanted to talk baseball—and offered his cigarettes. Ordinarily that would suit Harlowe right well, but he had to make that last boat.

EIGHT

Apalachicola, Saturday. 11:10 p.m.

True was asleep. Harlowe picked him up. Toted him out to the truck.
Two hoots from the whistle.

They reached the ramp at the end of Avenue E just as the *Save Time*
finished loading. Wing hollered, "Howdy, Pratt!" Harlowe eased the truck
aboard, behind two Model T's and two larger automobiles from Tallahassee
and points north.

The deckhand dropped the lines. Wing nudged the throttle and the ferry
pulled out—a few minutes late, but schedules aren't so unyielding here.
Harlowe stood at the rail, looking out over the shimmering, inky expanse,
out at the darker ribbon of marshlands, the encircling stars, which were
still brighter away from town.

The boy slept while Harlowe smoked and mulled. True woke when the boy
who sold concessions, came by making his rounds, like at a ballgame.
"Cold drinks! Peanuts!"

A tourist couple in a Ford took him up on the cold drinks. But many of the
locals, couldn't afford the concessions—including Harlowe. But he and the
boy both enjoyed the ride, and the way the Bay looked different at night.

True was thinking how some boys rode the ferry alone, but Harlowe always
carried him over. He liked his uncle being around. He thought Harlowe
might not do that, always, and it was nice.

Harlowe was thinking, maybe he worried too much about the boy.
Everybody else would let their youngun's ride alone. Or go anywhere else
in the county. That's how it's always been. No one worried about it. No
one could conceive of a reason to. But as he looked over the rail, out into
the darkness, he couldn't help think there was a reason. *There's a man out
theah— who kills boys.*
While things like that just didn't happen in Florida, *it had happened.* And
Harlowe had no idea where this man was—not in all this country that
stretched as far as he could see, or a million other places that were merely
a train-ride or, now, an automobile-ride away.

I don't know if I can solve it.

The dark water rolling beneath them, they inched toward the dark
silhouette of pines and the bluff-shoreline—Eastpoint.

*These last four years have not been too kindly. I had nothing before. Now
I've got even less.*

He couldn't help think of that night. When the telephone rang. He could still feel it, what he felt when he walked down the hall to answer it and heard True's voice on the other end! Little True using a phone! Birch had let him go to the store. *Don't stop for no one!*

The feeling over the lines was like electricity in the air before a peel of lighting.
I just had to go. Claudie tried to talk me out of it. "You aren't the sheriff anymore, Pratt!"
"Why, that was True! The boy has never used a phone before, and he's phoned me now."
"It's not your problem!"
"Those people trust me," I said. "I just gotta go."
"No, Pratt!"

The trip was rough, the ferry nearly swamped, but Wing got us across. I got over theah as quickly as I could. Unfortunately, more than an hour had passed. The few words Birch said were full to the brim. "Pratt, our boy's missing!"

Harlowe waved to Wing as he rolled off the ferry into Eastpoint.
He drove to the start of Old Ferry Road and stopped.
The main road wasn't paved, then. It was just a little dirt road from the ferry, through Eastpoint. The hot blacktop was laid over the events of that night. Maybe they had to be covered with something—like a bandage.

He took True home. Saw that he got in.

NINE

Apalachicola, Sunday.

Morning dawned slowly, silently like the opening of a rose. That moment just before an Apalachicola sunrise deserved to have its own name but didn't. It was like the opening credits for the sun. Harlowe couldn't imagine it would be more peacful or beautiful anywhere else on earth.

Looking out over Scipio Creek, a tinge of pink on the great canvas of sky, the *Venezellos'* mast and boom silhouttted in the gentlest rays of light which made it to his eyes. The water was still and quiet. The open country in front of him stretched out as far as the eye could see. All was silent save for a few lingering crickets.

He'd walked down to watch the sun come up—enjoyed his coffee as it rose above the river. The color and silken flowering of light was worth the insomnia.

It promised to be a nice, lazy day. Bells would ring and families would attend services in the several churches in town. Afternoons would be whiled away sitting on porches, under the live oaks that shaded the pretty avenues that had been laid out in a grid over the city a century earlier. Later on, folks would be at the ballgame—Apalachicola was playing Moultrie. Women would wear dresses. Men would wear boater hats.

Demo George had a new trawler on the blocks. She'll be a lovely boat when he finishes her. But he wasn't working on her today.

A big laugh and a smile. "Moanin,' Mr. Pratt!" Cleve Crumley was the town's taxi driver. He owned a yellow Buick car. Every morning, the colored man sat by his taxi, reading the paper, laughing hearily at something that amused him, waiting for the train to pull in.
"Howdy, Cleve."

Harlowe looked in the box as soon as he got up. If there was any risk he'd forget what he had to do, that skull brought him right back. Like swinging into a swimming hole and coming nose-to-nose with a cottonmouth.

Dr. Murrow opened the discussion in his parlor. Present were the undertaker, the decedent's brother-in-law, and Harlowe. "Collis was obese, yes," stated Murrow.
"He got good'n fat since I saw him last," admitted Sangaree.
"He was winded just walking to the store, is what my wife said."
"Oh?" asked Murrow.
"Do you really need me for all this?" Ira protested.
"You may be the only one who can shed some light on his recent health, Ira," replied Murrow.
"All right. Yessir. Any of you fellas got a cigarette?"

Murrow opened a drawer. Retrieving a pack. "Had your wife seen her brother recently?"

Ira tapped out a smoke. "No, that was the last time she saw 'im."

"And when was this?" asked the Doctor.

"Well." The younger fellow finished lighting up. Took a long drag on his cigarette. "Right before Christmas. When she went to see her aunt up in Albany."

"Did she comment on his health at that time?"

"Nosir. All I know is she mentioned that part about how he was winded."

"I see."

"I really need to git home," Ira interjected, jabbing out his cigarette. "What it boils down to is what, heart trouble? That what he died of?"

"Ira?" Harlowe asked.

The soda jerk smirked. "Hell. It's just surprisin's all."

"How do you mean?" asked Murrow.

"I always thought he took after Josiah Brewer's side of the family—big strong people. You know—good health."

"Well, I'd tend to agree with that. As a young man he was never sick a day. He was in fine condition," Murrow recalled.

Harlowe turned to the doctor. "But, now, more recently, after you've had a chance to examine 'im?"

"Why, he was in *very poor* health I would say."

"And it was his heart, sir?" asked Harlowe.

"In my opinion, yes," Murrow replied.

The doctor was sure of the findings.

"All right then, I got to go," said Ira, getting up. "Thankya for the cigarette, Doc." He was already at the door.

They listened to Brewer descend the steps and turn down the sidewalk. Sangaree shook his head. "Pratt, I'm not sure when I have heard someone more evasive in all my years. That Ira Brewer!"

"Yessir. I appreciate your help, V.G.," Harlowe stated, shaking his hand.

After the meeting adjourned, Murrow had a further discussion with the Sheriff.

"Pratt, I've been a doctor many years. However, on this, the more I think on it—I just don't know."

"Yessir?"

Murrow wiped the lenses of his spectacles. "Pratt, I'm no pathologist. I'm a country doctor. Mostly I treat cuts. Remove fish-hooks. Set bones. Deliver babies." The old Doc gave a grin and a nudge to the elbow. "Every now and then I get a real exciting case like an ingrown toe-nail."

"Ha!"

"Nosir, on this matter you need an expert. It is my opinion that Doctor Elston—up at the state hospital—ought to be consulted. He is an expert on these cases, having served in the medical unit these last several years at the asylum. Do you know him?"

"I know *of* him."

"I believe he will be able to render an opinion as would help. Of course, he's quite familiar with all manner of diseases, pathologies, and injuries among the asylum patients. Not only that, he has extensive experience dealing with fractures, car accidents, and so forth."

"I understand." Harlowe was aware that injured motorists were often brought to the asylum's "Receiving Hospital" when there were wrecks along the state highway. There wasn't another hospital in the Apalachicola River Valley.

"Consequently, Dr. Elston has treated a number of accident cases. I attended an autopsy where he presided, and I was quite impressed with him."

Harlowe nodded.

"If the idea seems favorable, I could telephone him and ask him to come—quietly, and in the strictest confidence."

"Yessir. Please."

Murrow reached for the candlestick telephone on his desk. "Good Mornin' Miss Hilda. I need to place a call, person-to-person, to Dr. Elston at the asylum for the *in*sane. This is a matter of the strictest confidence. Yes, I'll wait."

In ten minutes the long-distance call was connected. Harlowe could hear the other end of the conversation through Murrow's earpiece.

"Yes, this is Elston talking, who's this? Oh, Dr. Murrow. Whaddya—I mean, how do you do? Come down there, all that damn way? I haven't time for—oh, you say it's a pathology matter? Very well. I'll be on the next train."

***

"He's comin'—on the 7:44."

Harlowe and Murrow waited on the platform. The summer sun seemed unwilling to retire, its rays yet rubbing their faces. Murrow checked his watch. Presently, the younger physician stepped down, shook hands, and gave them an earful. The heat and uncomfortable ride really had his dander up!

Elston was in his early forties. Pencil mustache. Neatly dressed. He looked familiar, though Harlowe couldn't recall when they'd met. They took the taxi to the Raney House. Sangaree was there. So was Deputy Brewer and the coroner, Evans. The latter was a lawyer, not a doctor at all. When Murrow asked for Dr. Elston to come for a second opinion, Evans was informed, but declined to call a jury for a formal inquest. Still, Evans didn't pass up an opportunity to come around and politick. He gave the body a perfunctory look and proceeded to glad-hand the room, which seemed to nettle Elston a great deal. He'd already put on his smock and head mirror. Wanted to 'get on with it!' When he pulled his surgical tools from the case, the more squeamish in the room realized Elston intended an *autopsy*, not just a discussion!

"Name?"

"Hutto," stated Harlowe. The way the country sheriff said it, sounded like *Hut*-toe to Elston.

The doctor looked at the bruising to the man's abdomen but said nothing of it. Elston made his first incision. "The man certainly was obese."

The county coroner had had enough by this time and retired to the porch, Deputy Brewer right behind him.

Elston proceeded. "I saw you once, Sheriff—car accident."

"Oh, yes...I remember that," replied Harlowe.

Elston had been in the Great War. When someone mentioned that Harlowe had been among the men from Apalachicola that volunteered, he became much more loquacious. He talked while working over the man's chest. Only Murrow and Harlowe remained in the room by this time. But, the doctors' discussion of the Parisian nightlife faded to the background when Elston held a heart in his hands.

"Say," remarked Elston. "*This* is interesting."

The house was silent, now, in anticipation. Suspecting some foul play, or perhaps merely some gossip to be gleaned, Deputy Brewer leaned in the doorway.

"Yessir, there you have it!" stated the young physician.

"What is it, Doctor?" asked Murrow.

Harlowe's own heart beat faster. He sucked in a breath.

"Myocarditis. Aggravated by excessive drinking. No doubt about it— definite signs of a diseased heart!"

Harlowe exhaled. *Sure am glad it wasn't somethin' else!* he thought, the case enough of a dime novel, already.

"The bruising, sheriff?"

"Yessir?"

"Three-days-old in my estimation. That business certainly didn't kill him. But—someone worked him over."

"Yessir."

"That is my medical opinion. What that means as a matter of law is up to you."

The Doctor commenced his stitching.

The sewing done, Elston's business was finished. Harlowe knew *his* was not. He felt like he was in a riptide. Swim until you're exhausted and find yourself further out to sea. He stepped into the hall, gave Herring's note a glance. On it was an address—Collis's last. *"C/o Acme pool room, Atlanta."* Now, there was no return address on the package, double-bound with twine, within which was the skull. Had Collis something to do with it? Harlowe could only wonder.

Elston finished washing up and answered all the questions posed to him by Murrow and the others, the man having impressed everyone with his knowledge. As the smalltalk began to bore him, he followed Harlowe to the porch. It was cooler away from that examining room. The final stripe of sunlight fading out, the temperature was, at last, a tad more hospitable.

"An old Devil Dog, eh? I patched up a few of you fellas. You don't seem as relieved as the others here. Is it the bruising?" Elston answered his own postulation, "Probably nothing."

Harlowe looked Elston in the eye. "There's one other matter that...weighs on my mind."

"Oh?" The Doctor paused with great interest. He appreciated talking to a man not given to speak in exaggerated terms.

Harlowe spoke quietly. With weight. "Yessir, I wonder if you wouldn't mind takin' a look at it—over at my office."

The two men left the crowd lingering on the porch.

They walked to Harlowe's truck. They passed a few blocks of houses, a cemetery, and Elston saw Victorian gables and chimneys poke above the trees. The old, red-brick courthouse stood in the town's deadcenter.

Behind it, at the back corner of Avenue I and 12th was a tiny jailhouse built of the same bricks. A wooden fence was attached, presumably to contain any prisoners while they used the outhouse.

Harlowe parked. They entered the back door of the courthouse. Harlowe turned on the light. Led Elston up the narrow staircase to a hall lined with dark panelling and volumes of the Southern Reporter. A sign read, "Sheriff's Office." The latter was a single room behind the courtroom and judge's chambers.

Harlowe opened the window to let in some air. It overlooked the town, the lights of Sheip's sawmill like little eyes in the distance.

Harlowe switched on the desk lamp. Its yellow light made the room seem hotter, as if illuminating the mugginess. He unlocked a wooden box. "Yes, I see." Elston leaned over it, looking down at the small, bare cranium inside, fanning himself with his hat. "No signs of any abnormality. No injury. It is certainly a child's skull. You see the sutures? That's what these are called, here. I believe the skull is that of a male. Yes, I am certain of it."

Harlowe nodded. *That was important.*

"Something else," said Elston.

"Yessir?"

"I was just thinking it may give you a little more. I don't know."

"Yeah, Doc?"

"Sheriff, it's possible to identify an individual by his dental characteristics, work done on the teeth and so forth. Now, I see no signs this little fellow had any dental work. He hasn't any missing teeth. Has an adult tooth coming in, here—see? Nothing unusual about that. Not uncommon for a kid of, oh, eight or nine years. Now, a dentist who had examined the boy could tell you—well, had the Birch boy seen a dentist?"

"No, sir, the Birches caint afford one."

"I see. Well, that makes it a good deal more difficult, doesn't it?"

"Yessir."

"I can't imagine what you're up against in something like this," Elston remarked, noting the paucity of equipment in the room.

"Well, I surely thankya, Doc. What you've done is a mighty big help to us."

"Don't mention it." Elston wiped the sweat from his neck with a handkerchief. "Damn this heat."

"Yessir. It gets hot in this buildin'. We can go back outdoors now. It's cooler."

They left the way they'd come in. Harlowe fished out a Chesterfield.

"Smoke?"

"Fine."

"Light?"

"Sure." The doctor took a puff. Cast a glance up the empty street. "So, what in Heaven's name am I to do around this town until my train leaves in the morning?"

"Well, sir, we gen'rally go to bed right about now."

TEN

Sunrise. The workday beckoned. Harlowe tucked his shirt, put his hat on, to meet it.

Shrimpboats motoring out. The whistle blowing at Sheip's sawmill, the men walking from across town. The scent of fresh cinnamon rolls in the oven at Clark's Bakery, on Commerce Street. Mrs. Jenkins' biscuits and bacon, drifting likewise from her kitchen at the Fuller Hotel. The mule-drawn ice wagon jingling away from the plant, off to deliver to folk on "the Hill."

Harlowe's elderly neighbor, Hattie Slocumb, humming a hymn while she watered the puffy hydrangeas which ringed her porch.
He waved to her. "Good mornin', Miss Hattie."
"Mornin' Sheriff!"

A gentle breeze most welcome for mid-July rustled in the oak leaves. The sun was warm under a pale blue sky, not yet the blazing fire it would be in another hour.

Harlowe received a reply letter from River Junction—signed by R.W. Millirons, the Police Chief up there. That was last night. Mr. Harper brought it to Harlowe, special, for it was Sunday—and, of course, they'd met at the Riverside for coffee. Harlowe drafted a reply: stated that he was coming but asked the Chief to keep it quiet. This letter he'd already dropped in the mail bin at the depot. It would arrive in River Junction this afternoon.

Harlowe sat in his office. He read through notebook pages browned by the humidity of the preceding four years, stained by sweat, rain, cigarette smoke as he carried them countless places. While the little books were filled with writing, he was no closer to finding out what happened to eight-year-old Gibby Birch than the first night he didn't come home for supper.

Harlowe *meditated* on the facts. *This fella drove an automobile. Had hands and feet. But I have no face to look for!*

Ol' 150 was backing in to town, her whistle and bell a comforting sound, like the voice of a friend. He drove down to Water Street to meet her.

Three passengers got off. The young couple had ridden in from St. Joe to visit their kinfolk and were collecting their parcels. The older fella—a businessman—was arranging a ride with Cleve Crumley and his taxi, to a room at the Gibson. Harlowe got out of the truck. He walked around the engine, which panted and sighed, like she was catching her breath. The man gave her tender a splash of water. She'd be pulling out at 10:20 a.m., more or less. Probably a little late, Harlowe thought, snapping his watch shut.

He found the engineer and the conductor arguing. Layne squirted oil at a connecting rod. "I tell ya she ain't slowin' down! I've been runnin' her for fifteen years and she's runnin' like she always has—well, howdy, Pratt!"
"Howdy, boys."
"I've been tryin' to tell Layne, heah, that we're getting' later and later every day," Harper complained. "This old kettle's due for an overall, but I caint convince Layne. Er, maybe it's him that needs an overall!"
Harlowe grinned at that.
"Say, you gonna ride with us, Pratt? Ain't got to talk to ya much lately," said Harper.
"Or you fixin' to go to Eastpoint?" asked Layne.
"Reckon I will take the ferry over this mornin'. Well, so long boys."
Harlowe walked back along the train. He glanced over at the folk waiting to board her.

In the waiting room, the train bulletin catalogued the old familiar stops— there on the blackboard. As ever, the times were scratched through, fifteen minutes added on all the way up the line! And, another ten minutes had been added to the "10:20!" Elston paced the platform, fit-to-be-tied!
He jabbed his finger toward the timetable. "Damnit! How can a railroad be this far behind schedule and stay in business?"
Harlowe grinned. "Well, they've always run a little slow."
"Hmmph! I'll be happy to get home, I can tell you that!"
"Well, goodbye, Doc, I sure do thankya for comin'," said Harlowe.
"Don't mention it."
"Goodbye! Looks like I've a bit of a wait—yet!"
"They'll have to load the freight. Enough time for a cup o' coffee, prob'ly."
"I've had mine at Murrow's house. So long, Sheriff."
"Goodbye."

Harlowe walked to the Courthouse. Opened the next notebook. Found where he'd talked to the boys who used to work with Collis. Those boys, and Collis, had worked for Joe Taranto in '27—but, in Collis' case, not the whole year. *He was fired!* He was a shucker and packed shrimp in barrels to ship on the train to New York. And that was the only job he held for any length of time. Harlowe remembered what people said then: *'Lazy as the day is long.' 'Just stopped showin' up!' 'The boy went 'round town tellin' people he was goin' into bidness for hisself—guidefishin' for tourists.' 'Hell, he weren't no good at it and no one used him!* He got to where people said he, *'wouldn't hit a lick at a snake.'* That's pretty low. Almost as bad as what Mrs. Ruge said, that Collis was *'sorry.'* Harlowe knew he got that reputation the last several months he was around.

Harlowe turned the page: *'Told sister he'd been working on the boats like always.'*

Yeah, he done lied to his sister, Harlowe recalled. *But what* was *he doing?*
How was he eatin'?
Harlowe read the next entry: *'talk around town that he had him a client.'*
Well, that would explain where the money come from.
In a small town, rumors bob up like mullet. But no one knew who he was,
this client.
He might be the murderer! Or a witness that knew somethin' as would
identify the killer.
Collis was the 'spoke' in the wheel connectin' all of it and now I have nothin.'
The closest I can get to what Collis knew would be Ira—who knew him
better than anyone.

The telephone jingled—papers to serve. Harlowe hung up—and sighed.
The routine business of sheriffing. It kept him from Gibby's case. But he'd
always come back to Gibby. There wasn't a day that went by that he didn't
work on it. Think on it.

He drove to Mayor Popham's oysterhouse with the papers. Ugly,
"somebody vs. another," "pay-up" mumbo-jumbo was typed within the
folded documents. It was sad business. The place might close because of
it. Harlowe went in and handed it to the overseer and brought the "return"
back to the jailhouse.

The jailor, Chatham A. "C.A." Seago, was inside, holding a knife. Cigar at
the corner of his mouth, he was slicing bread for a sandwich. He was
short, but massive, an affable bull, with a huge face and neck to match.
Shoulders that could freight two, eighty-pound sacks of flour when he
worked as a stevedore in former days. His forehead was white where his
hat set. The rest of his face, red from being on the water nearly every day.

Harlowe dropped the paper on the desk. "Would ya give that to the Clerk
when he's in?"
Seago kept cutting. "Yeah, boss."
Harlowe grinned. "All right."

He got back in his truck. Drove down Market Street to Buzzett's. Nosing
the truck to the curb, he saw Ira Brewer through the window. Harlowe
walked in. The soda jerk kept wiping the counter, absently, eyes helf-
squinted, his movements equally languid. Mr. Buzzett was in the back
room, looking over a prescription for the lady waiting to pick up the
medicine for her little gal. Harlowe spoke to her as he passed. It was dark,
cool, under the high ceilings and the circling fans.
Ira didn't look up. "Can I get you a Coke-Cola? On me."
Harlowe took a stool. "No, sir. Wouldn't mind a coffee, though."
Ira poured it. Harlowe could see he was annoyed, thinking he'd be
questioned again. Buzzett continued on in the back room. The white
smock turned toward some bottles on the shelf. He counted aloud, making
sure he dropped in enough pills.

Ira, nervously, polished the soda fountain. Harlowe didn't ask him
anything. Ira, seemingly unable to help himself, started talking, as he

wiped the counter—again. A fellow could see his face in the marble, mahogany, chrome.

"Yeah, he went to Atlanta. Got 'im a job working for this fella, up there."

"Uh-huh."

"He liked it up there. Big city. Excitement. Gals."

Ira went on. Then he stopped. "Say, I've had enough of this. You pumpin' me for information."

"I haven't asked you a thing, Ira." Harlowe was easy-going, grinning like Harry Carey.

"But y'come in here, starin' at me. Just as bad as leanin' on a fella—and y'know it!"

Harlowe lit a Chesterfield. Slid Ira the pack. "I'm not leanin' on ya. I'm just tryin' to figure out a few things. I generally do—I'm patient."

Brewer got him a smoke for later. His face twisted up in a scowl. "Yeah, yeah," he muttered.

Harlowe's grin faded. He leaned in, that steely look on his face like Mr. Carey got in his lawman pictures. "He ever tell ya why he left town so sudden?"

"We puttin' him in the ground today, Pratt! My wife's buryin' her brother!"

"Just answer my question."

"I told you I can't remember him talking about it!"

"He up and left town—for four years—and told y'all nothin'?"

"That's right. You can ask me a dozen more times and it'll be the same answer, *Sheriff.*" That last word he'd delivered with more frost than the ice cream behind the counter.

"Collis knew somethin'."

"That's his business!"

"Collis caint help me. But you can."

The thwack of the door to the backroom was Brewer's reply.

Harlowe patted Merle Herring's note in his shirt. *All right. The boy was livin' in Atlanta. The package was postmarked River Junction R.P.O. That's somethin' to go on.*

He finished the coffee. Thoughts swirled like the smoke from the ashtray. *We're isolated here. You didn't know how isolated until you left. That long ride on the train, comin' home in 'Nineteen. Woods and wilderness that go on forever. And Apalach is a little dot at the end of all of it, down on the 'elbow' of the Panhandle. Up until a few years ago, it was nearly impossible to get here by automobile. Maybe that's why it's stayed the same— Paradise.*

But things are changin'. Paved roads, bringin' in more tourists, more strangers. Reckon the man I want is among them, comin' and goin' as he pleases? A bridge will change it more—if they ever build one.

He left a dime on the counter. Walked out.

Collis' funeral would soon begin. Seago came. Mrs. Brewer. Ira arrived late, pulling off his apron.

Sangaree held the reins of "Black Satin" and "Midnight," the casket was carefully deposited within the spotless hearse. Stores closed their doors. Churchbells rang. The few cars in town all came to a stop. Sangaree carried the casket to the cemetery. Dotted with live oaks and dignified headstones from the city's earliest days, the cemetery occupied nearly two blocks on Avenue E, forming a lovely, wooded space in the middle of town.

His family must have really scraped up some money! It was a nice funeral, and there was a fine headstone ready to go up. Harlowe heard Collis' sister sold some of her jewelry to put up the cost.

Only immediate family came. Harlowe had wondered who would show. His presence drew a scowl from Ira. *"Official or not?"* wondered the soda jerk, although he didn't say it out loud.

The preacher finished praying, speaking kindnesses over a man who did nothing but raise hell and avoid work if he could—which everyone knew. Now, the answers were lowered into the ground along with him. People knew that too. As the crowd began to break, stream away, Harlowe saw a man who worked at the sawmill. The fellow thrust his hand as he moved along. "Afternoon, Shureff. Hate to see a young man pass."
"Ed, I'm glad to see you, hear?"
"Come by and see us sometime."
"Yessir!"
Harlowe climbed in his truck. He couldn't help think that Gibby's family had no funeral for their boy. *We never found a body. Consequently, they never got to bury their son.*
Well, now, perhaps they could.
It's Gibby's skull—I know it!

A Bonnie Blue sky. Sparkling river, its pace unhurried. Water Street rested in a lull between the train's arrival or the unloading of shrimpboats. The hum of the electric company, the growl of the *Save Time's* engines, filled in the normal cadence of the town.

Harlowe drove up the ramp onto the waiting ferry. Wing walked over to the truck. Sawed his hand. "Hey, Pratt!"
"Howdy!"
Wing nodded toward the out-of-state cars aboard. "Makin' a little money today!"
"Good!"
"Nice day for a drive!"
"Sure is! How's True doin'?"
"Pratt, he's doin' a *jam up* job! Glad I hired 'im."

Harlowe knew he had to leave town awhile. It put True in a bad spot. School was out and Foss Fulton expected the boy to work. So Harlowe had arranged a deal with Wing. At first, Wing thought he might not want to scrape and paint the *Save Time*. "Liable to scrape off the dirt what was holdin' her togethuh!" he'd said. But then he thought, with more tourists coming, he ought to make the old barge look nice, "before I take them Yankees' buck-and-a-quarter!"

As it turned out, the arrangement suited True's daddy. The wage was a tad better than what Harlowe could pay. And, while Harlowe knew his sister would never say so, the Fulton's could sure use the extra cash money.

"Your nephew's a fine boy, Pratt. Look at 'im go!" declared the old captain. "Ya sure I can keep 'im another day or two?"
Harlowe nodded.

The Save Time rolled forward. Harlowe watched the last of the oysterboats—'cat boats' with their mast forward—heading in. Sailing toward Cat Point. Presently, the *Save Time* landed. Harlowe stopped at Eastpoint's only intersection. The new paved highway ran through, East-West. The "Old Ferry Dock Road" and the "two-rut" road down to Cat Point slanted off from it, both unpaved.

He turned down the latter. It would take him to the place those boats had headed for earlier—Cat Point. It sticks out from Eastpoint like a chin, a patch of low-country hemmed with sawgrass and white sand.
Quiet and beautiful. Low and vulnerable. In fact, down there the water appeared higher than land—like it was but a leaf cupped on the surface.

He passed the schoolhouse. Lovely palms lined the road down to the oysterhouse and Tommy's Store, which stood opposite. Egg Brown's truck was parked in front of the store. Harlowe pulled aside of it.
Walked in. "Howdy, Pratt!"
Small talk. Then the conversation turned to Gibby.
"We all loved Gibby," said Brown. "He'd always speak to me. Or wave to me as he come in on the boat."
"I'd see him walkin' down the road after he'd been huntin' the flatwoods," added Tommy. "That boy lived in the woods!"
"And on the water," said Brown.
"That boy had such a sweet smile," said Tommy's wife. "It brightened us considerably, seeing him come marching through that door! It surely did! On a hot day, their work ending, all the oystermen and ladies loved to see him come a-runnin', carryin' a fish!"
"He meant a lot to us all," said Brown.
"It was like a part of Eastpoint ripped away. It hurt this whole place," said Tommy.
"Yes, it did," Brown agreed.

Harlowe turned down a more primitive path which cut clear across the 'Point. Along it, three houses clustered nearest the store. These persisted like the people who lived in them. Barely higher than the sawgrass, they looked as if one storm could carry them away like a stack of pine needles.

Three more houses, similar to these, sat further down the trail. He headed for the last, at water's edge. Its windows overlooked the Bay at its greatest breadth, its prettiest. It had a low, tin roof. Was constructed of wood salvaged from a steamboat. Nonetheless, it had been freshly white-washed. The yard was clean, with flowers circumscribing the porch—many hours had he spent on *that* porch, with the Birches. Aubrey Birch's oysterboat was tied to the little two-plank dock around back, a palm leaning out toward it.

The Birches had little cash money. They traded for what they needed. Hard times were a constant, as relentless as the cold in early February or the looming tab at the general store.

He didn't see Mr. Birch, but Mrs. Birch was pumping water from the well. She dropped the handle when she saw Harlowe.

"Why, Shureff Pratt, this is a surprise! I was just fixin' to put on a pot of coffee!"
"Howdy, Miss Birch."

Lillian Birch was tall, spare. Her hands were tanned like leather. Etched rough from work. Around her eyes were the beginnings of lines from sun-squinting, like hairline cracks in porcelain. Still, Lillian Birch was a handsome woman, with strawberry blonde hair and youthful freckles below her eyes. Her face was almond-shaped with intelligent eyes, brows that formed question marks when she was thinking. Those eyes were quick to sparkle when she laughed, but Harlowe knew they'd shed a lot of tears the last four years.
"Aubrey's around back? Aubrey!"
Aubrey was working red-hot iron into baskets for oyster tongs. He set down his hammer. "Yes, momma?"
"Come over here, Aubrey! Mr. Pratt's here!"
The oysterman walked around. A head shorter than Harlowe, he had wiry arms and muscled shoulders, as if he were assembled for tonging oysters. Working on the water every day of his life had tanned his skin like red patent leather. A shock of coarse sandy hair, matching Gibby's, topped his round head—which resembled his son's, likewise. Aubrey was a good provider, with a quick, ready mind and hands that could build an oysterboat or just about anything. They ate more salt pork than chicken, but he cared for his family.

Harlowe heard Aubrey hammering iron over that fire when he pulled up. The tongs, when finished, resembled two large rakes, that by means of their twelve-foot wooden handles, worked like scissors to snatch the oysters from the bottom of the Bay. Birch made his own. Made them for some of the other oystermen.

He bounded up, sawed Harlowe's hand. Lillian got the coffee percolating and they sat, drinking it on the porch where it was cooler. After the small talk, Lillian Birch spoke about her son. It was an open wound that hadn't healed, Harlowe knew. Gibby was their only child.
She told stories about Gibby—how helpful he was, how funny he was.

"He was a typical boy! Always wantin' to be outdoors!" Like most boys in Franklin County, Gibby was throwing a castnet and fishing with a sapling pole ever since he could walk.

Harlowe listened. Aubrey just looked off to toward the Bay.

Mrs. Birch finished her story. "Everyone loved Gibby!"

"Yes, ma'am."

"More coffee, Pratt?"

"Thankya."

"I'm glad you enjoyin' it."

"I ain't given up. I promise you."

"I know that."

She was quiet a moment, tears welling in the corners of her eyes.

Finally, she looked back. "Gibby was so excited to take the skiff out. I told 'im I was fixin' fried chicken. And he told me he's gonna bring a redfish home—we'll have him for supper too!" Mrs. Birch laughed at that.

"He was always home for suppah," said Birch.

"He wouldn't have missed my fried chicken! That really was a treat. We so seldom had that."

Harlowe nodded.

"But, he didn't come in," she said. Restating the obvious made it no less painful.

"It's funny. He was so eager to get out on the water he was out that door like a shot. Then he come a-runnin' back and give me a big ol' hug. I'm glad he done that!" she added.

Aubrey added, "I told 'im he could take the ol' skiff. I was smithin' a set o' tongs. Maybe if I hadna—."

"You caint think that way," said Harlowe.

"Storm come on so sudden. Even so, he wouldna stayed out. He woulda come in the first dark cloud," Aubrey reckoned.

"Yep."

"Tried to tell Shureff Pender that—that boy knew the Bay well as I do," Aubrey continued.

This was one time Harlowe wished he had the command of words of somebody like Willie Popham. This seemed like something for a preacher or Doc Murrow, but it fell on him to say. A country sheriff had to be so many things. He just couldn't find the words.

"Mr. Pratt, is there somethin' else you wanna say?" asked Mrs. Birch.

"Well, Miss Birch. I received a package. It's the reason why I came. It had—what was sent to me was a...skullbone--."

"*What?*"

"The skullbone—I reckon it could be Gibby's--."

Lillian screamed. "Y'mean, someone sent it to you—my child's head?"

Aubrey took her in his arms. She sobbed into his shoulder, her body moving spastically, as if she was receiving jolts of electrical current. *"Why, Aubrey? Why? What kind of man?!"*

"Not knowin.' That's what's so dang hard," said Aubrey, holding his wife's head.

Lillian wiped her eyes. "I've cried jugs o' tears. I reckon I'll cry many more." She touched Pratt's shoulder.

45

Aubrey asked, "Y'pray with us?" They took hold of him before he could answer. Aubrey closed his eyes. "If it is our boy, he'p Mr. Pratt to find the one 'at done it. If it ain't, let this child's mother and deddy know what happened to their youngun." Aubrey fought back tears of his own. "The voice of this child's blood crieth from the ground! We ask this in Jesus' name!"
"Amen."

"Why? What kind of man?" those words kept Harlowe awake. He didn't know the answers. The best he could think, the man killed Gibby for the sake of it. Some kind of thrill-seeking like those boys in *Rope.*

That night, Harlowe pulled to the side of Avenue E. At 17th Street is a pretty two-story with a picket fence, porch stretching across the front, lights burning brightly in the windows. It's G.E. Pender's house.

Harlowe thought back to the day he set foot on *this* porch.

The smell of hot apple pie wafted out of the kitchen. Pender cranking that ice cream machine.
"Shureff, I believe theah's more to this. In Tallahassee--."
"Pratt, I'll look into it."
By a twist of fate Garland Ellery Pender had beaten Harlowe in the '24 election. It put Harlowe in the position of coming to his porch, hat-in-hand. Pender barely looked up from cranking. "Can ya hand me that sugah, Pratt?" His kids played happily in the yard, one tot bounding up the steps into the house, looking back and smiling at her daddy.
"Can this wait, Pratt?" Cranking—Cranking—On he twirled that handle.

Harlowe went home. Felt for the switch beside the back door and cut the lights on. They glared hot against the kitchen's white shiplap walls. The sounds of a hot night washed over him. Crickets. Refrigerator humming. He poured cool milk, listening to the train as she left the station.

ELEVEN

Apalachicola, Tuesday 6:30 a.m.

Harlowe got up. Walked down to inspect the progess of Demo George's new trawler. She looked like she was growing from the blocks, from the grass and sand along Scipio Creek.

He met the early ferry. This he enjoyed—for the quiet, the way the Bay looked, the coolness. Wing let go of the lines and they slipped away from Water Street.

Harlowe got out of the truck. Watched the town shrink, slowly, behind them. After they landed in Eastpoint, True appeared, the boy with scraper in hand, ready to work!
"Howdy, son!"
"H'dy, Uncle Pratt!"
Harlowe was pleased to see his nephew eager to work—even the second day. He *was* such a fine boy! Harlowe was glad other people saw that, not just his uncle.

Harlowe said goodbye to True and Wing. "I'll keep an eye on the boy and see he gets home when the work's done," said the latter.
"I appreciate it."
"Yessir!"

Harlowe eased the Model T up the ramp, following the tourists. He did a double-take, seeing a boy throwing a castnet on the shore. *Gibby?* He blinked. *No—True's brother.*
Harlowe waved to him.

He followed the tourists on the blacktop highway. The latter had been built to carry the tourists though Eastpoint and over the long-contemplated, long-awaited bridge.

Moments later he reached Green Point and the turnoff for the Sumatra Road. The sand-road hadn't been graded in awhile. His wheels bounced over the ruts. It was a lonesome, dark path through the pines—up through Tate's Hell, one of the most mysterious woods in the South—and on to the town its name referred to.

Tate's Hell loomed, always in sight, just beyond the land Eastpoint families had cleared and planted, the piney flatwoods where they tapped and cut timber. It's many arms—of vines and branches—grasped at and pushed back at the little settlement. Children were warned not to go too far into those woods. They knew the legend of Cebe Tate who got lost searching for his cattle, and for whom the forest was named. Gibby's disappearance was a more recent, "object lesson." Rumors circulated in such a little place. Some thought Gibby may have gotten lost in Tate's Hell. Some thought a

Monster took him and might come back. Man or boy, tempted to enter those confines, often felt he had a dozen eyes watching him.

As peaceful as it was now, Harlowe felt those eyes, that feeling that a cottomouth was near, somewhere in that jungle which nearly strangled the road.

He passed Whiskey George Creek. Now, open flatwood prevailed. Widely spaced pines and a floor of saw palmettos. You could see far into the woods. The dew and gentle light made the place looks so peaceful, so pretty. *But It'll lull you in like a pitcher plant would a fly,* Harlowe knew.

What he looked at through the windshield would be unchanging for many miles. The MotoMeter in front of him. An arrow-straight cut through a million near-identical trees. Lots of time to think. His mind's already busy, the truck bouncing over the sand ruts, jarring his body, the first 'page' of thoughts turning to the next. Rattling along just fast enough to get a breeze going.

He thought about the tranquility his people knew in Apalachicola, and the danger—"out there." It could come down the tracks or, more-and-more, down these highways. It might come from River Junction. Or Tallahassee. Or beyond. Even on this poor little road, which ran from the coast to US-90, near River Junction and the state line, trouble was just two or three hours away.

The State insane asylum lay at the end of this road. It wasn't lost on Harlowe that danger could come down from there. It bothered him every day since Gibby disappeared. There were inmates of the asylum he knew were very dangerous men.

TWELVE

They were being watched. While the kids played ball, he stood there behind a tree, looking at them. It was a dead pine, "cat-faced" by the terpentine tappers, an odd totem whose warning went unheeded.

Home plate was four pinecones, like the other three bases. The little pitcher, Lonnie Williams, wound up like Grover Cleveland Alexander. Lonnie's brother, Denny, swung at that ball with all his might. When he heard that solid "Crack!" he knew it was a homer. The ball rolled into the woods and he ran the bases in triumph.

None of the boys saw the figure in the shadow behind that tree.

The boys were playing in the road in front of Lonnie's home, a watermelon farm with orange trees and a sun-grayed house set further back. The boys played baseball here more times than they could count. But, tangled woods like a wall, stood yonder, marking the boundary of Tate's Hell, which commenced at edge of the Williams place and ran clear to the Carrabelle River. It was a place of many eyes, and in this instance, there was the malignancy in the human eyes feasting on the little ballgame. Right there at the edge of *Hell.*

And, then, the little boys came to *him!* They ran into that dark treeline looking for the ball. It was the only real baseball they had and they didn't want to lose it! Denny nearly crashed headlong into the cat-faced pine! The fellow behind it sucked in his gut and turned his body sideways to avoid being seen. His heart was pounding. The little-darked-haired boy was close enough he could grab him in one swoop! *He nearly fell in my lap and--.*
"I see it, Charlie!" interrupted Denny. The boy reached down through the twigs, trying to avoid the sharp greenbrier creeping along the ground. "Come on, Denny!"
"Almost got it!" he said, slipping his small wrist through the gap.
Gosh, it's spooky here, thought the boy. The humidity from Tate's Hell burning off in a hazy mist, the sunlight filtered down through the branches, pine quills, and leaves, like fingers of light. Denny had the slithery feeling that a cottonmouth might be nearby. Denny shook it off. He wasn't no sissy! There! He got ahold of the ball. Hollered back to his pals: "Got it!" The fellow was barely armslength from Denny, but the boy didn't see him! Carefree, Denny made a dash for their makeshift diamond, happily tossing the ball in midstride, to the third baseman, his cousin, Butterbean.

The little pitcher wound up again. This time it was Charlie's turn to swing the one bat they had.

The fellow continued to peep at them. *The boy was so close. I could have touched his head when he leaned down 'n got the ball!*
I coulda had him in the car by now and—well, that wouldn't do. Why, I'd be caught for sure if I take chances like that. The other kids woulda told someone! What the hell's the matter with me?

The thought of getting caught, the adrenaline, the rush of elation that came and went like a gust of wind, the feeling of his stomach dropping, it was all too much. He crept a few paces into the woods, until the sound of the children's playing faded, and vomited.

He slipped past the last house in the settlement, down to his Ford, the fishing pole poking out the back of the black Model T. It was identical to a million others in the South.

His heart still pounding, louder than the sounds of the bugs and crows, he pulled his hat low. Mashed the starter. With shaking hands on the wheel he snaked his way out a trail once used by terpentine tappers, out to the Coastal Highway. As fast as the little Ford would move, he left the pines and scattered rooftops of Eastpoint in the rear-view-mirror. For now.

He reached the turnoff at Green Point. He spun the wheel over, taking the desolate road North. Now, he could breathe.

THIRTEEN

River Junction, Later that day

"I wish I could he'p you, Pratt. I surely do. I just don't know anythin' else to tell ya."
The hundred-degree heat that soaked through the city jail had stifled activity of any kind on the part of the man behind the desk. R.W. Millirons, River Junction's police chief. He drawled the words out as slowly, languidly as the river flowing by, like it was an effort to push out every syllable. He looked through eyelids squinted shut like sweaty venetian blinds. He was a tad pudgy, nevertheless he dressed well. Blue-striped shirt. Bow tie. Suspenders. White straw Stetson fedora. He was around thirty-five, Harlowe reckoned. Slowly, Millirons daubed his forehead with his handkerchief. Tipped forward in his chair. He raised his cigarette to his lips. Even that movement was unenthusiastic.
Harlowe read the letter back to him.

"That's it. Right there. You know everything I do on the subject."
Harlowe nodded. "The Hutto boy had a room at the Shepard, then?"
"Yes. Spent two nights over there. Paid in advance." Millirons' eyes looked more bored, uninterested, with each tick of the regulator on the wall behind him.
"Go on."
"I talked to the man at the *hoe-tell*. Ain' much to it. The boy checked out an' got on the train that carried him down to y'all. Like I said, ain' much to tell ya."
"Just a man passin' through, eh?"
"Why, sure! I hate it that you drove all this way...for nothin' really." The Chief wiped with the rag again—the last time had done him little good.
"My goodness. It sure is hot today," he muttered, turning to look out the window, shaking his head at the impossibly loud buzzing of the cicadas.
"Is there anything else you can tell me? Anything at all?"
"No, sir. I'm sorry you drove all this way for nothin', Pratt."
Harlowe nodded.
"I don't think there's nobody else that could h'ep ya. I asked around. I done what I could," he drawled.
"Did he make it up to Chattahoochee?"
"I don't believe he did. I talked to one or two people at the store up there. Wanted to do more, but I just aint had time, Pratt."
"Yeah."
"I am sorry about that boy, Pratt. Gibby, I mean. He was a good young fella." Millirons met the Birch boy when the latter stowed away on a riverboat a few months before he went missing.
"I appreciate that."
The man eased to a standing position. "I got to git home for dinner. Preacher comin' over and Nona won't like it if I ain't around when he gits there." Millirons held out his hand. "I'm sorry I can't he'p you more."
"I reckon I'll ask around some more."

"All right. Good to see you, now. Let me know when you got more time, we go huntin'." Millirons opened the door, the cue that the meeting was concluded.

"Goodbye, Pratt."

Harlowe nodded. He walked to his truck, which he'd left next door at the wood-framed garage (a hand-crank gas pump stood in front and the man there had finished filling the truck and topping off the radiator). Harlowe paid two bucks for the gasoline; presently, Millirons, at the wheel of his open Buick, emerged from the garage, giving the horn a tap as he motored away.

Harlowe drove down Chattahoochee Street. His tires rumbling over four sets of tracks, he passed the depot and swung over to the Hotel Shepard, parking in front.

He looked over at the travelers standing on the platform, waiting on their train. The mid-day heat was oppressive, but it did not lessen the activity of trains coming and going, people rushing to make their connection, the taxi leaving with a fare. River Junction was a busy place, where four railroad lines met, carrying tourists and businessmen to and from the "postcard destinations" of Florida, and all kinds of freight moving in like manner. The wooden, two-story depot was the largest building in River Junction— followed by the Shepard.

Ornate lamps with green glass shades glowed brightly in the lobby, the drapes restraining some of the intensity of the sun outside.

Harlowe approached the desk clerk, showing him Collis' photograph (which his sister had provided).

"Oh, yes! I remember him. No, he didn't say anything about Apalachicola, why he was going there, no sir."

"Nothing about who he'd been a-workin' for?"

"No, sir."

"May I see his room?"

"Certainly. It's room twenty. It's unlocked. Look as long as you like."

Harlowe went up the staircase, the wood creaking under his boots. Reaching the top, he turned down the hallway, a narrow, low-ceilinged passage lined with doors, and blood-colored carpet. He passed the bathroom for that floor. He looked in. It was spotless and typical of the facilities available in a small town, a claw-foot tub, sink, and a commode, the fresh but heavy smell of soap and linen.

The numbers on the doors grew larger until, at the end of the hall, where the shadow had fallen over a little niche with two doors, he found Room 20. The hotel had nothing anywhere close to that *5-4-4* number.

He opened the door. Stepped inside. His eyes surveyed the room. For a good, three-dollar room it was typical in size and furnishings. Three bucks was a good sum—there was a time when Collis would have slept on the bench at the depot.

A brass bed. A couple chairs. The walls were papered in a dark pattern. The sound of a train puffing carried in from the street outside. He looked over at the sink in the corner opposite the door, the fresh bar of soap and towels on the rack. There was no toilet in the room in small hotels like this. He cut on the lamp, pulling the chain on the hurricane fixture beside the bed. He opened the drawers on the night table, one-by-one. He looked in the chiffarobe. He found the drawers and hanging space clean, like the rest of the room. The latter was devoid of any signs or scents of its former occupant; it smelled clean with a feint scent of tobacco and soap.

Harlowe examined the stationery on the table. He ran his thumb over it. It was a good quality paper and felt similar to the "5-4-4" scrap that Collis had kept. Harlowe reckoned it was identical. He held up the paper to the window light to see if he could find the impression of other writing. What was there was not decipherable and he couldn't see even the ghost of "5-4-4."

It was stuffy in the room. He opened the window. Tepid as the breeze was, it offered relief and he lingered at the opening. He looked out upon the street, the brickwork of the bank and Boykin's General Store, the varied rooftops of River Junction's business district. A locomotive puffed away from the depot, drowning out all other sounds.

A man could watch the comings and goings of the town, from this room: The taxi, laden with a trunk and a young married couple groaned as it climbed the hill. The express delivery wagon clattered back down to the depot. Collis could see who came and went: by train, by automobile. *What did Collis see? Who was he waiting on? Who was associated with that "5-4-4?" Who was after you, son?*

He stood before the sink. The mirror reflected the bed and the wallpaper, but no face, friend or foe. He looked back to the bed, the chiffarobe. Collis stayed here three days. Whatever he was thinking, whomever he saw, he took it with him, he left no traces in the hotel room. *He was here and he was gone.*

Harlowe descended to the lobby, walking up to the desk clerk. "I wonder if I could ask you somethin'."
"Yessir?"
"When the young fella got here. Would you know if he came directly from the station?"
"Yessir. He got off the train from Climax. He come around not more than five minutes from the train pulling in. I remember that. He checked in. Stood right where you're standing. Then he must have gone up to his room. I had to tend to something and he'd gone upstairs, I'm assuming. I didn't see him for the rest of the evening."
"Yessir."
"Is there anything else I could tell you?"
"Did he get any visitors? Telephone calls?"
"No, sir."
"Anything else you remember."
"No, sir. I don't think so."
"Much obliged." Harlowe put his fingers to his hat, in goodbye, and walked away.

He walked the busy little area along Railroad Avenue. He talked to the fellas at the harness shop, where a farmer had brought his mule team for a fitting. "Nosir, I haven't seen him. Sorry, I caint he'p ya," said the owner. Harlowe turned to the farmer, showing him the photo. The farmer politely smiled and shook his head. Next, he talked to the man at Scarborough & Co. General Store, the biggest in town, a two-story wooden affair with a gasoline pump in front. Canned goods were stacked in the windows, heaps of 89 cent overalls and sacks of Dixie flour inside. He approached the clerk behind the counter. Showed the photo. The man shook his head. "Sorry, mister." Harlowe had the same result at the grocery store at the corner of Railroad and Chattahoochee. And the little barber & billiards room beside it.

Harlowe wore out leather from one end of Railroad Avenue to the other, down the line of little brick storefronts, finding the people were all happy to help him. But they simply *couldn't* help where young Collis Hutto was concerned. At each one they'd look at the picture. Hand it back, politely. The gal working at the bank offered him a ladel of water. He drank it, looking out at the street devoid of shade trees. Marveled at the storekeepers that kept on here, where flood season was known to bring the Apalachicola waist-deep over this section.

He drove down past the grist mill, to the houses down Chattahoochee Street, below. It was steamy in the low-lying outskirts of town, the echoes of a whistle wailing, engine puffing, swirling about him. He felt like he was trapped in the cab of a locomotive, baking in the heat from the firebox.

He saw no "544" address anywhere. He returned to "Downtown" River Junction. Stopped at the drugstore which had a sign in the window advertising coffee. *It's so hot it might cool me off!*
The man behind the counter wore a bow tie and apron. He was short, but stocky, with one cauliflower ear. Perhaps he boxed in the army. He was about the right age. You got to know a certain look of a fellow veteran. He poured black coffee into a china cup on the counter. "I don't know of any house numbers that high. No, sir," replied the fellow. Without comment he retrieved, from under the counter, the St. Joseph Telephone directory for River Junction-Chattahoochee. "Care to check the directory, sir?"

Harlowe thanked him. Opened it. Perused the listings. The man began to answer the question right about the time Harlowe saw there was only one or two "544" addresses in the city on the high bluff. "No, sir, you won't find many in Chattahoochee either," the fellow declared.
Harlowe looked up.
"Reckon it's a telephone number?" offered the man. "It could be, but not 'round here. As ya can see, the telephone numbers ain't got more'n two-digits. Not like no big city." Indeed, like other towns along the A.N. R. R., River Junction had two digits only—if they used numbers at all. Like in Apalach, you'd tell the operator, "Doctor Murrow, please," and she'd connect the call, and that's how it was. Of course, Tallahassee had three digits.

The man refilled Harlowe's cup. "They owe some money, the folks you lookin' for?"

"No. Just lookin' for some information." Harlowe sipped the coffee. *Maybe, it* had *cooled me off some.*

The fellow turned to wipe the counter and prepare a sandwich for the other customer that had come in. Harlowe had another coffee and mulled, silently, while the other men spoke of local events, people, the *Phillies* and the *Cubs*. The conversation came 'round to the late war. The man *had* served in the army.

"Finished with the directory?"

Harlowe nodded. "I sure appreciate it." He put down a dime for the coffee. Said goodbye to the ex-soldier.

Harlowe saw the taxis had returned to the depot, their drivers waiting on the next train, which was pulling in now. He walked over to the first—an old Overland parked by the platform—and showed Collis' photograph to the man behind the wheel. "I wonder if you've seen this fella?"

The driver shook his head. "Sorry mister."

The other taxi had pulled away before Harlowe could address its driver. Harlowe looked at the timetable on the wall outside. *Well, one thing's sure—those boys will be back.*

He'd show that photo to half the town if he had to.

FOURTEEN

River Junction, Later that day.

Puffing engines. Jostling freight cars. Clanging warning bells. The switch engines and their crews toiled endlessly in the July heat—which broke the 'century' mark!

Mercifully, the platform provided shade for the arriving passengers. Harlowe, joining the throng in their good suits and dresses, entered the "Union" station, so named because it was used by all four lines. The waiting room was hot despite large open windows. Harlowe made his way across the large space, through the crowd. It was abuzz with folks consulting the timetable. Contemplating where they might have a meal before their connecting train arrived. A big clock stood in the middle. He passed it. Stepped up to the ticket counter.

"Can I help you, sir? Oh, hello, Mr. Harlowe!"

"Howdy, Mr. Tierney." Harlowe asked the ticket man about Collis. Showed his photograph. "Have you seen this fella?"

"Oh, yes. He came in on the 3:05 from Climax. Wednesday afternoon, last."

"I wonder if he mentioned anything about the business he was on?"

"No, as a matter of fact he didn't. He seemed a little sullen."

"Sullen, you say?"

"Yeah, real quiet, y'know."

"Like somethin' was botherin' him?"

"Yeah, he acted strangely. I don't know how to describe it—."

"Yessir?"

"It's hard to say how this fella was actin'."

"Well, how did it strike ya?"

"I tell ya. He acted like this was the end of the line. When he left, he walked off a-ways and just kept a-lookin' back at me, almost sad-like. As if he needed help. And I waved for him to come back to my window but he got this sort of contented look and waved 'goodbye.' Walked off. You see some things in a rail station, but that was the damnedest thing I've seen in a while."

"Yessir?"

"I hate to say this—."

"Go on." Harlowe, at last, was gleaning something of Collis' mindset those last few days.

The man lowered his voice. "I smelled the liquor on 'im. But he didn't seem drunk. More 'hungover' is how I'd describe it."

Harlowe thanked him. Walked outside. Watched the 'turnaround' of the big Atlantic Coast Line train, the passengers board, the long string of coaches leaving.

It wasn't long before he heard another whistle, a familiar one, the A.N.R.R.'s 4:10. He listened to her little engine puffing her way up from the Georgia woodlands, and squeak to a halt upon the crossing of Chattahoochee Street yonder.

This *crossroads* again. There were four passenger trains a day running here—and that was only counting the little "A.N.R.R." If there were witnesses that could help him, they were more than likely gone. They could be anywhere. If you had the fare, these tracks ran to New York. Or Los Angeles.

The last few puffs of steam. Engine No. 301 ground to a halt, her open valves releasing a humid spray over the platform, a structure far longer than needed by the one-coach train. Harlowe walked down to the mail car (the Railroad Post Office).

He looked in the door. "Howdy!"

"Hey, Pratt!" exclaimed the Postmaster, a thin, white-haired fellow.

The man, like the rest of the train crew alternated with Layne, Harper, and the men on sister engine, Ol' 150.

The younger postman, looked up from his work. "How-do, Mr. Harlowe!" They all knew the Sheriff.

"Long way from Apalach ain't ya?" added the Postmaster.

"Yeah, I reckon. I'm lookin' for a little information." Harlowe put his foot up on the step and leaned on his crossed arms, as was his manner.

"Sure thing, Pratt."

Harlowe pulled the packaging from his coat. "I showed this to Ellis the other day, at the depot *down theah.*"

"Yessir?"

"Hadn't had a chance to ask you. Wonder if ya'd take a look at this."

Harlowe handed it to him, the paper packaging from the skull, stamped with "River Jct. & Apalachicola R.P.O."

"Yessir, that's ours. Mailed Friday, eh?"

"Yessir. Did you see the man that mailed it?"

"No, but Silas may have. Hey, Silas, can you take a look at this for Mr. Harlowe?"

"Sure. Be glad to," said the young fella, the postman with a thin face and right-friendly smile. He came over to the door. Examined the markings. "I didn't get a look at 'im, Mister Harlowe. It it was pretty busy at thetime."

"You didn't talk to him, then?"

"No, sir, we had a lot of folks mailin' that day, seems like."

"Did he say anything about what it was?"

"Well, sir. There was something."

"Go on."

"Well, when I went to weigh it, I ask him also, 'was it fragile,' 'will it break?' like I always do."

"Yeah?"

"That's when he said somethin' odd, like 'it'll break a lot of things.' Uh, 'it's broke *me,*' or somethin' like that," explained the postman.

"He said it like that?"

"He said it just that way, yessir. Kinda 'matter-of-fact.' I believe I said somethin' like, 'whachya got in there?' just not knowin' what to say. But he looked off—like he was lookin' a mile away."

The Postmaster looked at the torn packaging again.

"Anything else y'all can tell me, I sure would appreciate it," said Harlowe.

"I don't think we can tell you much. Just regular two-cent stamps like every post office in the country has. Nothin' we could tell you about your man you don't know already," said the white-haired fellow.

"Either of you know Collis Hutto?"

"Know of him, but I never met him," said the postman.

"Same here, Pratt," declared the Postmaster. "I's sorry to hear what happened. His sister is a fine woman. Musta been a terrible shock."

"Yessir. She's takin' it well. But that was her only brother."

"I gotta get this mail in the sack and out the door," said the postman. "I wish I had paid more attention that day, Mr. Harlowe."

"That's all right, son."

"Y'wanna ask me anything else?"

"One other thing. Did that fella come alone when he mailed this thing?"

The postman dragged the sack out the door. "Yessir, I'm sure of that."

The Postmaster looked Harlowe in the eye. "The boy was mixed up in something, then?"

"Maybe."

"Ya reckon Collis got hisseff crossways with the wrong sort?"

"Could be."

"If I know you, you'll get to the bottom of it."

"Thanks, Van."

"Sorry we weren't more he'p to ya. I'll be seein' ya."

"All right. So long."

Harlowe walked away. Toward the engine.

He saw the heat waves radiating from her. Felt the fevered temperature. Behind them another engine pulled away, the pressure of the steam starting the heavy freight cars for cities distant.

"Hey, Pratt!" called the engineer, Hiram.

"Howdy!" Harlowe reached up to shake his hand. "Granby around?"

"I'm right here, Pratt," replied the conductor (he was the fellow that alternated with Harper).

Harlowe showed the men the photograph of Collis.

The engineer recognized him. "Sure, I know 'Beadle.' It really is a shame." Granby also knew and expressed similar sentiment. Being a small line that ran the length of the Apalachicola Valley, word about Collis had gotten around.

"Did you see him on the train from Georgia, this past Wednesday?" asked Harlowe.

"No. Didn't know he was ridin' with us that night. Gen'rally, he woulda said somethin' to me," said the engineer.

"But not this time."

"Nope."

"Anything else that may have seemed odd that night?"

"No, sir."

"No, Pratt. Caint think of a damn thing. Pulled outta Climax like we always do, made our stops. Nothin' unusual," stated the conductor.

"Collis alone?"

"Yessir. He was. B'lieve he read the paper, didn't have to holler for him to git back on the train any of the stops. He just kept to hisseff."

"I appreciate it," Harlowe replied, tucking the photo away. "So long."

"All right, boss!"

"See ya, Pratt!"

He crossed Railroad Avenue to the post office. It occupied about a third of Scarborough's bottom floor.

The Postmaster, Dudley Morgan, was a friend:

The clerk at the counter called him. "Mr. Morgan?"

The older man turned around. "Oh, hiya, Pratt! I got your telegram! I wired you an answer this morning."

"Well, I appreciate that. It must have been on its way while I was on the road."

"I didn't realize you were in town. I'm afraid I can't tell you anything. Well, not much as would help you."

"Yessir." Harlowe handed him the packaging.

The man looked at it. "He had a parcel you say?"

"Yessir."

"No, I don't recall anyone coming by to buy stamps or for any other purpose."

"Have you seen this man?" Harlowe asked, handing him the photo. The Postmaster and the clerk both looked.

"No, sir." The Postmaster handed it, and the torn piece of packaging, back across the counter. "I just wish I could tell you more.

"It's all right."

"Is this some sort of mystery—like detective business?" asked the man. "You trying to find someone?"

"Could be."

"Hmmm. That looks like a woman's handwriting. I'm sure you noticed that."

Harlowe nodded. Collis couldn't write, according to his sister.

Consequently, whomever wrote it was someone he'd like to talk to. Just one more thing he *didn't* know.

"Well so long."

The men said goodbye. "If there's anything we can do for you up here, you just let me know!" declared the Postmaster.

"Well, I sure appreciate it," Harlowe replied.

FIFTEEN

Near Chattahoochee—Later that day.

The onyx waters of Mosquito Creek divided the twin cities. Harlowe crossed the little wooden bridge, leaving River Junction in the rear-view mirror. His truck groaned up the steep hill—up to Chattahoochee.

The latter was built up on a high ridge overlooking the Apalachicola River, which twisted and turned for a hundred miles before it reached the Bay—and home.

Chattahoochee is a likeable, friendly place, much like his own hometown—an "Anywhere, U.S.A."
Washington Street is the main road through town. Along it, the sidewalks were shaded by tin awnings. Fords and Whippets were parked, nose first to the curb. The diner had a Coca-Cola sign on the roof. It wasn't too busy today, Harlowe noted. Satuday was when the farmers come to town and businesses stayed open late. But a young couple paused in front of the hardware store, gazing at a new Speed Queen in the window. New automobiles were available at the Ford agency on the corner.

Harlowe pulled over, across from the movie house. A picture called "Manslaughter" was playing. He lit a Chesterfield. Watched the cars streaming up from the Victory Bridge. US-90 ("The Old Spanish Trail") ran up from the bridge, continuing via Washington Street. Tourism was at least one thing alive and kicking after the "Crash." The government encouraged folk to travel, to come through these little towns, like these people were doing now—keeping the filling stations and diner busy. Harlowe noted the tags on the cars as they came up the hill. Missouri. Alabama. Indiana. A man could drive from St. Augustine to San Diego—clear across the country—on this "Old Spanish Trail." Images of explorers and adventure festooned maps and signs along the way.

He'd reached the other end of *that road*—the one through the woods which threatened to bring danger to his *Paradise*. He had the lingering feeling the man who took Gibby came from outside--on these roads. He had to look for the shadows of men *who could come from anywhere*.

He listened to the whistle from the switch engine toiling at the railyard. It wasn't just the highways that criss-crossed this place. This was a hub with many spokes, people coming from the North, South, East, West—and moving fast.

This was a great part of the problem Harlowe faced. The days were gone where a man could flee no faster than a steamboat or his horse could carry him. A man could leave Harlowe's section and, by these highways and railroads, be in another state before anyone realized he'd came and went. In the last four years, that ability had only hastened. The distance, the difficulty in getting to Apalach no longer protected the town.

The state line was a half-a-mile from where he had parked. It had certainly occurred to him that whomever took Gibby, someone he hadn't even thought of, may have slipped across the Georgia line and was gone forever. That thought woke him up with a chill many-a-night.

So did the patients at the asylum, yonder. He started the truck, and eased into the flow of Model T's, Whippets, Chevrolets. He found himself looking into the grounds of the asylum, with its great oaks, the grand, Greek-revival architecture. Some of the buildings had been whitewashed, making them oddly bright in the July sun, spectral even, holding a foreboding quality even in the afternoon. He couldn't help think of the men behind smudged windows and gaps in the fences—just a baseball's throw from the highway and downtown, the dangerous inmates there. Traveling by automobile, they'd be right in his lap before word came of their flight, with as little warning as a hurricane. He'd checked them over, in '27. He walked in and found the superintendent of the hospital in his office. They'd looked at the records and no furloughs of violently insane men were made at the time of Gibby's death. He'd walked down that aisle and looked at the row of poor tormented faces. The men held in those wards and fences, still concerned him.

He didn't know if the man he wanted had come through this busy place, but Collis had, and that was enough to bring him here.

Collis was here three days. Maybe we can find out why.

River Junction and Chattahoochee shared the same police department and governance. What separation there was owed to the great difference of elevation and the presence of the busy railyard and depot in one. He'd walked River Junction, where the business section, the depot, industry of various sorts, and mercantile homes were found. His attention now turned to Chattahoochee-proper, a mostly residential section with lovely homes and tree-lined streets. However, Main Street was a bit different than most little towns. It ran through an insane asylum.

Harlowe turned down Holly Drive, into the hospital grounds. The sun glinted off the guard fence of the criminal unit. Behind it, the most dangerous men were kept, in housing made of gray stone, stained from the humidity, like tears streaming from the openings. A man shrieked something unintelligible from somewhere within that building. Ahead loomed the castle-like "shot tower" of the old arsenal. He passed beneath it, toward the superintendent's quarters with its oddly cheerful gingerbread porch.

At the end of the street, Holly dead-ended into Main. There stood the Receiving Hospital and Administration building. He parked. Looked toward its portico which had columns like Arlington House.
He crossed the lawn. Opened the door to a long, quiet hall. A receptionist, a nurse in hat and white dress, was seated behind a wooden desk at the far end. She didn't look up from the chart in front of her. He walked down

the hall, its bare walls painted a feint green intended to induce calm. The woman looked up as he neared. "May I help you?"

Harlowe removed his hat. Took one last step up to her station. She was in her late thirties, with brown hair restrained beneath her hat. Her voice was friendly, but her eyes seemed to hide a tiredness, probably from years of working here—or from the wilting heat, Harlowe thought. "Afternoon, ma'am." Harlowe told her who he was, what he'd come for.

"Oh, yes. Mr. Neal said to expect you. I have the records here. And he— that was how Mr. Neal put it--."

"Yes'm?"

"He said 'you might have saved the price of your wire, as there were no furloughs given at the time you specified.'"

She handed Harlowe the cursive-written pages.

"No, ma'am, I see there weren't none."

"In particular, the men you mentioned—were all accounted for."

"Thankya, ma'am." *Well, that answered that,* thought Harlowe. "Oh, there is one other thing."

"Yes?"

"I thought I might say hello to Dr. Elston, since I'm here."

"Of course. His office is down the hall. Yes, that way. Right down there."

"Thankya."

Elston was just coming out of surgery, when he ran into the Apalachicolan. Despite his reputation for gruffness, Elston was right friendly! "Come back to my office, Pratt!"

They walked down the hall. There was another nurse behind a desk. "Oh, this is Mrs. Prentice," said Elston.

"Good afternoon," said the nurse.

"Afternoon, ma'am."

"Come in. Sit down. There's a belt of booze in the drawer if you want it." Harlowe declined.

"Have you gotten any further on the matter of the child's disappearance?" asked Elston, facing the mirror while he tied his necktie and put on his coat (the Doc dressed right handsomely).

"I haven't got much fu'ther, nosir. That's the reason I'm here."

Elston settled in behind his desk. He lit a Camel. The electric lights reflected from the tinge of silver in his hair, which was not unexpected for a man, who like Harlowe, had entered his early forties. Elston made small talk, cheerfully. He liked talking and Harlowe let him do most of it. Then the Sheriff showed him the packaging.

"The skull. I cannot get over the way he mailed it like you'd mail a—a book or a tin of cookies!" Elston let loose a string of profanities on who would do such a thing! "Well, you've summarized the records to me, I don't think it came from anyone here. If they say everyone was accounted for."

Harlowe nodded. "That's what they said."

***

He drove all over Chattahoochee. He found *the* 544 residence from the directory: 544 Chattahoochee Street was a fine two-story, amongst similar homes on the street, which became a quiet, oak-lined avenue in this part of the "two cities." Harlowe knocked. He was ushered in for coffee in the parlor, but the nice lady didn't know Collis! Her husband returned from work, and it was determined he had no idea who the deceased was or why he'd made his final journey. Harlowe thanked them. Got back in his truck. He drove around and confirmed there were no other 544 addresses. *There's the Chief's Buick parked at his house on Flowerwood.* The signs of the family at supper were noted.

Harlowe crossed US-90, pulling into the diner's dusty parking lot. He walked through the gaggle of automobiles that crowded there—a mix of local and out-of-state tags on them. It was a menagerie of faces and hats in the café as well. The loud murmur of conversations and the clang of silverware.

He found an empty stool. He barely glanced at the menu before the man behind the counter approached. He was round-faced, forehead damp with sweat. "We got the best hamburger in town. Best beefsteak. Any kinda pie you wohnt! Coffee-to-start-with?"
Harlowe nodded. The man set down a mug. Splashed it full of coffee. "Have you a look for a minute! We have our specials, on the sign theah. All our pies are on display down at the end o' the counter."
"I appreciate it."
The man stepped away to take orders from other customers, while the waitress took care of the booths. It wasn't but a minute before the man returned. "You new around here? Earl Fenton's my name."
Harlowe told him his. Shook his hand.
"Y'all stay pretty busy," Harlowe remarked.
"Everyone comes in hea! You settle on somethin'?"
"Yessir. Hamburger. Hash-browned taters."
"You got it."
At that, the old man on the stool beside him gave him a nudge with his elbow. "Hey—I hear you're askng about a fella. Ain't ya gonna show *me?*"
Harlowe looked over at him. It was little surprise word would get around a small town. "Sure. Have a look," said he, certain it would do no good.
"No, I ain't seen him," declared the old man. "He done somethin'?"
"Well, he ain't done nothin.' Just lookin' for some information. Thanks, anyway."
"Lou told me who you was!"
"Yessir?"
"Lou, down at the hotel!"
"Oh, yes—yessir."
"Ainchya gonna show Earl?" The old fella nodded to the gentleman behind the counter.
Harlowe nodded. When the man in the apron came back with the food, he broached the subject as advised by the hoary-haired gentleman.
"I wonder if I could ask you somethin'."
"Yessir?"
Harlowe slid the photo across the counter. "I wonder if you've seen this fella?"
"No. Don't believe I have."
Harlowe began to put it away.

"Wait a minute. May I see that again, sir?"

Harlowe slid it back.

"Oh, yes. Sure, he was the one! From last Thursdee, I mean!"

"He was here?"

"Yessir—more coffee?"

"Yeah. You say he was here Thursdee?"

"Oh, sure. 'Scuse me a minute." The man left to flip the hash.

When he returned Harlowe asked, "Did Chief Millirons talk to ya?"

"Sure. He's here most days."

"You told the Chief about this fella, then?"

"Nosir, he ain't asked me. 'Scuse me."

Millirons hadn't checked at all. Why would he say he had?

The man came back to refill the line of cups along his counter. Harlowe's, too. "I can understand why someone would come askin' though. The fella kinda stands out, you know."

"Yessir?"

"Like I said, *everyone* comes here. We stay busy. But folks just come in and eat. Have coffee and get back on the road. Or go back to work, if they're local."

"Go on."

"But they don't raise a *ruckus,* gen'rally. This fella—he raised *hell* with a man! And vice versa! Cussin' up a storm, right out front, theah! Y'just don't hear people talk that way, 'round heah."

"What was it about?"

"I really couldn't make no sense of it."

"Did you recognize this other fella?"

"Nosir—stranger."

"They commenced to have words—right out here?"

"Yessir. So, I ask 'em to leave—both of 'em. The fella in the picture apologized. Said he wanted to have his food."

"All right."

"But this other man said, 'no!' He told the young fella to get in the car. He did! Left most of his food, too!"

"What can you tell me about this other fella?"

"Not much. Excuse me while I take this order? Gotta help Jeannie when we're this busy!"

The man took the order. Poured coffee for the couple that had just come in off the highway. They dressed nicely, like they were traveling, Harlowe thought. Harlowe drew a question mark with his pencil and waited for Fenton to return. He looked down the counter, the hats, faces. The man worked his way back. Leaned an elbow on the counter. "Where was I, now? Oh, you'd asked me what he looked like—the other fella?"

Harlowe nodded.

"Well, he was kinda stocky. Not real tall, now. He had light, sandy hair. He seemed young to me. Oh, I reckon he was 'bout twenty-five."

"You remember anything about the way he dressed?"

"He had a grey hat. Nice Stetson—new!"

The echo of a train whistle rose over the murmur and clink of the diner, for an instant.

The waitress, Jeannie, set plates of hash and eggs before the couple. "How much farther to Tallahassee?" asked the man. He spoke like a Yankee.

"Oh, 'bout an hour-and-a-half," replied Jeannie, filling his coffee cup.

"We're on our way to Miami," said the man.

"First time?" asked Jeannie.

"Yeah," replied the woman. "We stopped to see my husband's relations along the way—in Mobile. Decided to take the Spanish Trail the rest of the way!"

"How exciting! I've never been to *Miamuh*," said Jeannie.

"Get people from all over," Mr. Fenton interjected. "Coffee good?"

Harlowe nodded.

The door jingled. A truck driver walked in, down to a booth just vacated by a salesman.

"'Scuse me, Mr. Harlowe," said Fenton. He set a mug for the driver. Though it seemed like his eyes were closed, he didn't spill a drop. "Hey, Smitty."

"Evenin', Mr. Fenton."

"Hash, eggs over easy, coffee?"

"Yessir."

"You got it!"

Fenton poured the last of the pot for Harlowe. "So, where was I? Oh, I remember—I had to tell them boys to go!"

Harlowe nodded.

"So, they get in the car and tear outta here lickety-split, headin' to the filling station where they pull in."

"The one down yonder?"

"Yessir, down the road, theah. And, then, the young fella got out and kept talkin' to the man in the car. They kept on a-hollerin', the two of 'em, theah. 'Could hear 'em from where I was, at the door, all the way down the road! Broad daylight! I thought the police chief might come but he didn't. The boy—one you showed me—got in the car, 'ventually."

"Eventually?"

"Yessir, the boy give the other fella *a time!* Didn't look like he wanted to get in *a-tall!*"

"Uh-huh."

"But the other fella musta persuaded him. He got in n' they lit out like grease-through-a-tin horn—well as near to it as a Ford will do."

"Model T?"

"Yessir, a Model T—afraid I ain't helped ya much with that! Excuse me again."

In a moment Fenton returned. "You said the second man had a gray hat--."

"Yes, the other—uh-huh."

"Can you remember anything else about 'im?"

"Not too good, sir. Just a hat and a young face. Caint tell you more than that."

"Can you tell me anything more about the way he dressed, Mr. Fenton?"

"Shirts and ties. Both of 'em. No coats! Just their shirts! Striped shirts with the arm band, heah."

"How tall was the second man?"

"A tad shorter'n you."

"Reckon the waitress got a look at the other fella?"

"You can ask her! Oh, Jeannie?"

The woman hustled over with a coffee pot.

"Jeannie, this is Mr. Harlowe. He wants to talk to ya."

"Surely."

Harlowe asked her about the man.

"Sure, I remember 'im. I heard 'im hollerin' at the heavy-set fella!"

"Can you tell me what he looked like?"

"I only saw part of his face—had his hat low, y'see. He had nice sandy hair! Had a, uh, square jaw. Thin mustache. *Broad* shoulders. Strong-lookin.' Not so bad to look at it, when you come right down to it!"

"How old was this fella?"

"Oh, twenty-seven. Twenty-eight, I guess. No more than that."

"Could you tell me how tall he was?"

"Oh, six foot!"

"Could ya make out what they was sayin'?"

"No, sir."

"I couldn't make heads not tails of it. Just hollerin,' cussin's all. I closed the door on account we had ladies here, but they just kep' on."

Harlowe held up the photo. "And the stocky fella insisted Collis leave with 'em?"

"Yessir. I caint emphasize that enough. The boy didn't look like he wanted to go!"

"Which direction did they leave?"

"Thisaway—towards Tallahassee! Excuse me while I tend to these folks!"

"All right. I appreciate it."

A hat and pocketbook went by in a hurry. "Goodbye! Goodbye!" said the tourist woman. "Thank you!"

"We wanna make Tallahassee before it gets too late," declared the husband.

"Yes, suh! Y'all be careful. Them roads' is dark out theah!"

Harlowe paid his tab. Walked back through the jumble of hoods and fenders to his truck.

It was near dark. The lights glowed at the filling station down the street in the "Y" in the road, where US-90 meets Flowerwood Drive. The attendant began pumping gasoline for the couple from the diner. A dusty Model T pulled off the highway, to wait its turn.

Harlowe eased in behind it. The busy attendant shot him a glance. "Be with ya, shortly, hea!" He finished with the tourists, then commenced to pumping gas for the man in the well-travelled Flivver.

Presently, it was Harlowe's turn. He eased alongside the pump. The man rubbed the truck's windshield with his rag. "What can I do for ya, Mister?"

"Oh, dollar's worth of gas is all."

"You got it!"

He started cranking the hand-operated pump. Click. Click. Click.

"Yessir, it's constant! An' busier since they paved the road through town, seems like!"

"Say, there's somethin' I'd like to ask you, if ya don't mind."

"Sure, mister."

Harlowe showed him the photo.

"No, I ain't seen 'im."

Harlowe handed the man the money for the gas. He described the Ford. The men.

"Two men, young fellers?"

"That's right."

"Thursdee, ya say?"

Harlowe nodded.

"Oh, yes, I seen them boys. Two of 'em in the Ford *see*-dan."

"Could you describe the men?"

"They's white fellers, o'course. They had new hats. Ties and shirts. They dressed well. Pulled in for gas when it was purty busy. I really didn't pay too much attention, but--."

"Yessir?"

"Well, they didn't seem quite right. Didn't *look* right."

"How's that?"

"I dunno. I seen the one feller twice! I oughtta mention that."

"Yessir?"

"The tall, big one come along by hisself. Ask me about the Shepard *Hoe-tell*, where it was. But like I say—well, jus' the way he was talkin', maybe."

"Yessir?"

"Well, the way he talked. *Smart,* you know? Talked *smart* like in 'em gangster pictures."

"Go on."

"Well, I watched which way he went, thought he might be up to no good. He proceeded to the diner, looked like he was fixin' to go on in, so I didn't pay no more attention to 'im."

"All right."

"Then he come back with the other feller—the tubby one."

"Back here?"

"Uh-huh, yessir. An' they got to arguin' amongst theyselves! I told my wife, somethin' didn't seem right ' bout them boys!"

"Yessir?"

"Jus' the way the one feller—the tall, big one kinda had a *sneer* on his face. The other one, the tubby one, act like a whipped dog."

"Yeah?"

"Yessir, like he was *caught!*"

"What about the car?"

"It was black—Model T. I know that don't do ya no good. I'm sorry I caint tell ya more about it."

"Did you see the tag?"

"Nosir. Didn't pay it no mind. Wish I had, now."

"Any dents, broken lights, somethin' that stands out?"

"Nosir. Looked jus' the way Ol' Mr. Ford made it."

"Do you remember if these fellas came back?"

"I dunno. I had to leave momentarily for a tow. Finished with the last customer, put a sign up, closed, went down Bolivar Street. Mr. Tomkin's Ford broke down on 'im!"

"Yessir."

"I hope I he'ped you, Mister Harlowe. I jus' didn't pay too much attention at the time!"

"That's all right. I appreciate it."

By that time, the taxi driver—the other one—stopped in for gasoline.

"Have you talked to Fred?" asked the attendant.

"No."

"Lemme introduce ya."

"Hey, Fred, this here's Pratt Harlowe. He'd like to talk to ya!"

The driver reached out his hand. "Glad to know ya."

"Howdy," replied Harlowe, putting his foot up on the running board of the taxi.

"I've heard o' you."

Harlowe nodded. Pulled out the photograph. "You see this man?"

"Is he in trouble with the law?"

"Not with me."

"Okay. Yessir, I seen him. I carried 'im up here in my car."

"When was that?"

"It was...last week sometime."

"Where?"

"It weren't no place, exactly. The young feller wanted to be put out at the corner—by the picture show." The driver pointed to the glowing sign three blocks nearer the river.

"He got in at the depot down theah, 'n I run him up here."

Harlowe asked about the two strangers in the Model T.

"No, sir, I caint hep' ya there. I ain't seen no one like 'at. Not sos I paid attention. Lotta cars come through here though."

The attendant left, then, to help a man, come in off the highway with a boiling radiator. "You from around here?" asked Harlowe.

"Nosir," replied the taxi driver. "My wife is. I'm from Grand Ridge. Across the river, theah."

"Sure, I know Grand Ridge. Can I ask you somethin'?"

"Sure, Mister."

"What do ya think of the po-lease 'round here?"

"Ha! They ain't much."

Harlowe grinned.

"Ain't much a secret 'round here—Millirons covers for them moonshiners. They can commit murder right out here on U.S. Nine'y and he'd set in his office twidlin' his thumbs! Hell, everyone knows it! I ain't got no use for him."

"Is that right?"

"I ain't gonna lie. He's run me in before. Wrote me a ticket for speedin.' In this cab—can you imagine?"

"Nosir, I caint."

"He sure did! Carried me to the jailhouse and fined me!"

Harlowe shook his head. "Now, the young fella got out by the picture show, then?"

"Yessir. But he didn't go in."

"See which way he walked?"

"Thataway. He done sashayed around the corner. I could see in the mirror, when I turned."

"All right."

"You can ask the man theah. I'll betchya my next fare he didn't buy no ticket."

"Ask the man at the movie house?"

"Yeah, that's him, now, walking this way."

The fellow wore a gray hat. Appeared to be in his forties. He came over to chat with the taxi driver and the attendant, as he often did while a movie was playing.

Harlowe showed him the photograph. "I am positive! I'm at the theatre every minute we're open. And he didn't come in that entire afternoon. I'd swear to it!"

Harlowe thanked the men. Got back in his truck.

They wished him luck. Waved goodbye.

Harlowe turned down Main, into the grounds of the hospital—taking the route Collis would have walked. The moonlight filtered through the branches, flickering as he rolled along. Ahead, the "faces" of the buildings glowed, apparition-like under oaks and Spanish moss.

He followed Main around to the Receiving Hospital. He reckoned some of what the taxi driver told him could explain why Millirons was so complacent. Moonshine, for instance. Collis had been a moonshiner. A competitor to these local boys. Maybe that tied in.

Collis walked in here. But, why?

A few dots of light glowed, down Main, against the black backdrop. Like burning little eyes, these lights weren't just guiding the way to a barbershop or movie house; the feeling was institutional, prison-like. The guard fence, yonder, shimmered in their glare.

Harlowe pulled to the curb. A train wailed in the distance, long and sad like you hear on a sleepless night. Then, suddenly, a terrible scream—from a man—from some window on the grounds.

He got out. Walked up the silent steps. He looked up at the columns and the white walls, which glowed against the dark sky and the shadows of trees. A single light hung over the entrance, like a solitary torch burning before a crypt. That scream hung in the air like a peel of thunder, magnifying the disquieting feeling in his stomach. Unsure what would come next, he reached for the door.

SIXTEEN

Chattahoochee—Tuesday Evening.

The hall felt yellow and sultry. Orbs of white milk glass hung from the ceiling, emitting a hot, sallow-light from their incandescent bulbs. The interval of those lights cast irregular shadows. Falling from the corrdior signs. Darkening the sunken features of the old man left, forgotten, in a chair.

Harlowe's boots echoed on a floor recently doused with ammonia, the smell of which permeated his nostrils. He walked the long corridor, down to the receptionist desk and the replacement nurse, slightly older but similar in features, seated behind it. Beyond, was a locked door of heavy oak. And, at that instant, it swung ajar. Two orderlies in white had a fellow in their grip. His eyes were blank as a store mannequin. He didn't even see Harlowe. Just kept repeating, "Yes—Yes—Yes." The orderlies proceeded by, marching like "machine men," only the sweat beading on their foreheads revealing they were flesh.
"Good evening, sir," said the nurse.
"Evenin.' I wonder if you could help me."
"I'll surely try."
Harlowe removed the picture from his coat. "Have you seen this fella?"
"Why, yes, he was here!"
"When?"
"Oh, last Thursday, I believe it was."
"Yes, ma'am?"
"He came here and spoke to me. Seemed like a nice young fella. He wanted to visit with a patient of ours."
Harlowe nodded.
"He wanted to see Mr. Whittle."
Mr. Whittle?
"Yes, sir. E.F. Whittle."
Harlowe didn't recognize the name. "Did he say why he wanted to see Mr. Whittle?"
"No. He didn't say. Not that I recall. But then given what happened, I- well—"
"Yes, ma'am?"
"Perhaps I shouldn't say this. I certainly don't wish to cause any trouble."
"Yes'm?"
"Well, the young fella was speaking to me and asked for Mr. Whittle and all of a sudden Mr. Kern—he's one of our orderlies—came out and the two of them had a *dreadful* argument."
Harlowe nodded.
"Practically shouting at one another! I think they may have known each other—It seems like Mr. Kern knew the fella. Called him a certain name— Weevil, or something."
"Beadle?"

"That may have been it, yes. Yes, I think it was! Anyway, the young man *insisted* he was going to see the patient. But Mr. Kern said it was impossible and that the young man ought to leave."

"Did the young fella say why he wanted to see the patient? It's very important, ma'am. Even the slightest thing."

"Hmmn. No, sir. I don't think so."

"Did he say anything to suggest why it was so important to him?"

"No, he didn't. And that's what made the entire affair seem so peculiar. I haven't the slightest idea why he wished to see Mr. Whittle—who is a dementia patient. Nor did I have any idea why Mr. Kern should react so strenuously, when normally he is so good-natured."

"I wanna ask you somethin'—about Mr. Whittle?"

"Surely."

"Mr. Whittle is being treated by a physician, is that right?"

"Yes, sir."

"Might he be available to speak with me this evenin'?"

"Well, he lives on the grounds. So, it's possible. Would you like me to telephone him?"

"Yes, ma'am. I'd surely appreciate it."

The woman phoned the doctor at his quarters. "He'll be here shortly."

"Thank you, ma'am."

"All this excitement where Mr. Whittle is concerned. You know he hasn't had a visitor since he was admitted."

Harlowe shook his head.

"Poor Mr. Whittle. Such a nice old man! He's often lucid, you know?"

Dr. Fordice arrived in the hall, presently. He led Harlowe to an office, down a side hall lined with closed doors. The man was round-bellied, dark with silver waves over his ears. *Probably in his early forties,* Harlowe reckoned.

"Sit down, please," said the Doctor, snapping the light switch. Harlowe accepted the seat. After the doctor offered a cigarette, the lawman explained his purpose, and that he might need to speak with the ward, Mr. Whittle.

"Oh, I'm sorry. I fear that is out of the queston," replied Fordice.

"Yessir?"

"You see Whittle was moved to isolation. He cannot receive visitors."

"He was moved to isolation—why's that?"

"Why, he had a terrible episode. He tried to harm himself, of course."

The doctor seemed a little standoffish. He puffed at his cigarette. He was terse, perhaps haughty. Harlowe wondered if he was judging rightly. Harlowe asked of the man's condition and Fordice seemed more willing to elucidate on the subject.

"So he definitely has dementia. And perhaps a disease of the mind we don't yet understand. And, I must tell you, there is evidence of *paranoia*—in his past behavior."

"And he's in an isolation ward now?"

"Sadly, yes. All the man's things are taken away and he is moved out of his regular ward and put in isolation."

"That's normal in this type case?"

"Oh, yes. That is standard procedure. Remove anything that could be harmful to him. He's placed under observation." Fordice seemed forthcoming, after all.

"Who else has been in to see Mr. Whittle?"

The doctor opened a file. "No one. He hasn't any family. His wife is deceased."

Harlowe walked with Fordice, back to the nurse's station. The Doctor asked of the old man's things. "Sheriff Harlowe would like to see them."

"I can show you. This way," she replied, leading the men down a side hall to a locked door. "He liked to paint pictures," the nurse explained. While she unbolted the door.

"Oh, the paintings. All these were taken from the patient. They will be returned when he goes back to his room," Fordice stated.

"Yessir," replied Harlowe.

The nurse opened the heavy door. "I'd like to show you the paintings," said Fordice. "Really quite good. And we encourage patients to sketch and keep their minds and bodies occupied in restorative pursuits."

"He's a sweet, harmless old man, really," said the nurse. She turned on the light, revealing orange crates with various names affixed—the contents of some of the patients, a bowler hat from life on the outside, a baseball glove, a clock. Whether the items were confiscated or kept for safekeeping for a prospective date-of-discharge was not obvious.

Dr. Fordice agreed with the nurse. "Sometimes he gets riled up. This last time was worse. I had to order him restrained."

"He's how old now?" asked Harlowe.

"Seventy-six. He's getting good treatment, a regimine of fresh air and sunlight."

The nurse looked for the crate with Whittle's things. "Oh, here it is!" Harlowe helped her with it.

"That's funny, they aren't here," noted the doctor. "Nurse, have you any idea what may have happened to them?"

"Why, no doctor. I can't understand it. They were here when you had me move his things."

"I don't know what could have happened."

"Was there anything unsual about the paintings?" asked Harlowe.

"I don't think so. The ones I saw were lovely farm scenes. Reminded me of the places we had back home in Madison."

"What happened in the episode the old man had?"

"I had a report he'd been violent," Fordice stated. "I understand he tried to strike an orderly."

"It was bad enough the old man had to go to to isolation?"

"Why, we had no choice! *I* had no choice, once I had the report!"

"Have you, yourself, ever seen him act belligerently?"

"Well, no," admitted Fordice. "Now, look here, if you're accus—"

"I ain't accusin', Doctor—I'm just askin.'"

Fordice escorted Harlowe back to the main hall.

The heavy door slammed behind them as loudly a gavel dropping in that marble corridor.

Fordice paused to light a cigarette. "Mr. Harlowe, it is late. You may see the patient in the morning and obtain any answers to your questions which you should desire."

"Thankya, doctor."

"Of course."

Harlowe turned to the nurse. "Evenin,' ma'am."

"Good night, sheriff."

The old man was still in the chair.

Harlowe walked down the steps. He breathed—the air, the vast, violet sky markedly less oppressive than the atmosphere he'd just departed.

Yet he had the feeling of eyes on his back. He turned to see the glint of a face in the window. It was a big man, dressed in white; the fellow sucked in his gut and tried to fold close to the wall. Harlowe walked over to the open window. Said, "Evenin'! Hey, there!"

The man slinked along the wall, away from Harlowe. "Wait a minute. You wouldn't happen to be Kern would ya?"

A brusque voice replied from the darkness. "What about it? Who are you?"

"Pratt Harlowe. Now, how ya know Collis Hutto? What was Whittle to him?"

The man closed the window.

Harlowe looked in at him. "I'll be back, heah?"

He walked to his truck. Sky, black as ink ringed the asylum, the high ridges dropping off sharply at the edge of the city, as if it were an island in the middle of a dark sea. It was no mystery why this place was chosen for a fortress in his grandfather's day. He gazed out into the treetops and valleys beyond the steep dropoff, behind the wards.

Harlowe found a payphone. Waited for the operator to connect him, long distance, to Collis' sister. She was alone. "Did Collis ever mention a Jack Kern?"

"No, sir."

"A Mr. Whittle?"

"No, Sheriff."

Down at the bottom of Chattahoochee Street the coach windows glowed hot while passengers boarded. The *Florida Limited* moved. Faster and faster— red lantern darting into the night. The hostling of freight cars continued. Below the depot, in a shadow, Harlowe folded himself into the cab of his truck—dozed.

SEVENTEEN

Chattahoochee, Wednesday

Harlowe walked into the Receiving Hospital.

Down that corridor.

The younger nurse was back. "Oh, yes, Dr. Fordice is expecting you. He'll be here shortly."

A quarter-hour passed. Harlowe struck up a conversation with the nurse. "By chance were you working at the hospital when Mr. Whittlle was first committed?"

"Yes, I was."

"I hear he's a very nice old fella."

"Oh, yes. And he was quite lucid when he arrived."

Harlowe nodded.

The door clicked open. Fordice appeared with an orderly. They escorted Harlowe down Main, leading him on a path behind the old "shot tower," and other pre-War (that is, antedating 1861) structues, to the ward which faced Maple Street. The cicadas were already raucous, the sun hot, although it wasn't yet a quarter til nine.

The orderly's keys jingled down the path. "Gonna be a hot one," said he, his predictions as languid as they were superfluous. As they reached the front of the ward, Harlowe noticed the faces behind the chicken wire. These unfortunates were housed in terraces. That is to say, they resided on porches turned into cages and stacked three stories. Like chickens in a coop.

They entered the building, which despite the shade offered by its anteroom, was as hot as an outhouse and scarcely more tolerable in atmosphere. They turned down a hall, narrow and low-ceilinged. The jangling keys were used to enter a dim cell with a number on the door. Therein, was Whittle, soaked with sweat and convulsing in the corner.

"Malaria," advised Fordice.

"He's quieted some," growled the orderly with the key ring.

Whittle was a slight man, hair dark for his age, his mouth shapeless as he'd lost most of his teeth.

Another orderly appeared, then. He was portly with sweat stains on his shirt. He passed Harlowe, his movements languorous, a smirk slanting across his face as he retrieved the patient's untouched tray of food.

Harlowe went over to the mat the old man rested on. He crouched to Whittle's side. "Mr. Whittle?"

"He won't answer ya," interrupted the second orderly.

"This is Kern," advised the Doctor, with a nod in the orderly's direction. The latter leaned against the doorframe, squinting out from behind his bangs, that sneer seemingly ever-present on his face.

Harlowe looked at Kern, that face, porcine and sweaty, its mouth at once impudent and lazy. "We met last night," replied the Apalachicolan.

Harlowe spoke to Whittle. Called his name. But the old man only breathed, laboriously. He appeared unconscious. Like a machine whose power had been cut. He was soaked with sweat from malarial fever, it seemed.

It was unbearably hot. *Even those porches had to be better than this,* Harlowe thought.

Harlowe rose. Turned to Fordice.

"Doctor, how long will Mr. Whittle remain *heah?*"

The Doctor felt the old man's chest to evaluate his breathing. "Until a staffing should be conducted. We have our policy, sir."

Harlowe turned to the big orderly. Held up the picture. "Do you know this fella, 'Beadle'?"

The orderly smirked. "No."

"You're lyin'. What went on heah, with you and Beadle Hutto—the old man?"

The orderly turned his wide back, his slow steps like an expletive-laden reproach, acted out in sheer disregard for Harlowe.

Harlowe walked out. Looked back and shook his head. "Poor old fella."

The orderly banged the door shut, rattled his keys. The sound sent a chill up Harlowe's spine.

They left, Fordice and Harlowe walking, alone, out into the blinding sun. On Main Street. "That fella knows more than he lets on," Harlowe declared.

Fordice sighed. "I agree. I don't know what it could be. If I'd known I would have let the visitor—what did you say his name was?"

"Hutto."

"Yes. I would have let him see the patient, had I known. Whittle is mostly harmless. Truly so. In fact, I think he's—."

"Yessir?"

"Well, he—he. He'd just had an *episode.*"

Harlowe wondered what the Doctor was holding back. "Who reported that episode?" They'd reached the front walk to the Receiving Hospital by now.

"Why, the orderly. Kern."

Harlowe looked over at the doctor.

Another sigh. "I shall speak to him about it, of course. But the fact remains the man grew quite violent and came near to injuring Kern, and another orderly besides!"

"Yessir. I understand." Harlowe looked at Fordice with penetrating eyes. "Doctor, do you think this man should have been committed heah?"

Fordice opened the door. He stepped back to the corner in the hall. He leaned in close to Harlowe, as if to take him into confidence. But something held him back. He glanced toward the nurse. Lowered his voice. "That is not for me to say. I think if he had family to care for him, he might remain at home, under supervision. But I understand he hasn't any."

"He was committed after a petition?"

"Yes."

"And that petition referred to the *paranoia?*"

"Yes, it did."

"Have you seen signs of it—paranoia?"

"No. But he was committed. It was done by the court--."

"Some of the staff said he was lucid when he arrived--."

"Just what are you driving at, Mr Harlowe?!"

"Well, seein' how he was lucid, people commentin' that he was, I'm jus' wonderin' why his case wasn't reviewed, is all."

"That-that's not my function, here. He was committed—it was reviewed by Mr. Raines!"

"Yessir, I understand that." Owens Cecil Raines was the prosecuting attorney for the Second Circuit of Florida.

"My authority doesn't extend to such decisions. That's not within the duties of the staff physician!"

"Yessir."

"Now, would you care to speak to the other staff, Mr. Harlowe?"

"Yessir."

"If you wouldn't mind waiting in my office, I'll send for them."

"That'd be fine."

Quietly, the Doctor had the other orderly summoned. Like Kern, he'd say little and Harlowe suspected he knew more than he was letting on, but *what* he didn't know.

A Nurse Dearden was summoned next. She expressed that Kern was acting strangely lately and pleaded that what she said should be kept in confidence and not revealed to the orderly, of whom she seemed afraid. Harlowe assured her it would remain confidential.

Fordice removed his spectacles, both embarrassed for the goings-on under his nose, exasperated that it might land him in the superintendent's office. Harlowe could see that the Doctor wanted to clear it up—but quietly. "Why was old man committed? May I see the paper?"

"Why? What do you want out of this? He's been committed, by a Court! What would you have me do--."

"Isn't there anywhere he can go, old soldiers home, maybe?"

"Why, it isn't so easy as that! He's indigent, he was never a soldier! There's no one to care for him!"

"I'd still like to see that paper."

"Come with me please!" They started down the hall for the nurse's station. But before they reached the front hall, Superindent Neal, himself, interjected.

Neal, in a blue pinstripe suit, seemed annoyed, like he'd just received an 'earful' from someone. He jabbed his finger. "I don't know what right you have to conduct an inquiry at this hospital, Mr. Harlowe, but the patients' privacy must be considered! I hear you've been accusing staff of malfeasance and questioning the treatment of the men here! This institution is entitled to the good order of its functioning and I'll not have it disturbed!"

"I don't wish to disturb it, sir. Jus' wanna know--."

"I've heard what you're implying. We have followed all the proper procedures, sir!"

"Sir, I believe we can clear this up if I can see--."

"Good day, Sheriff!"

That was Harlowe's 'prompt' to leave. In case he missed it, Kern opened the doors, and the man with the keys loomed like a guard dog.

Harlowe looked the superintendent in the eye—a man he'd known for several years, and up to this point their interactions were marked by cordiality. "I'll find out what I wanna know—I'm patient."

"Good day, Sheriff Harlowe!" came the perturbed reply.

The doors slammed. A train wailed, down yonder.

EIGHTEEN

Chattahoochee, a few minutes later.

Harlowe climbed into his truck. To his surprise, there was something on the seat—a leather pouch. He opened it. Inside were folded, dog-eared papers. Whittle's paintings!
A dozen of them.
Carefully, he unfolded them. Some, were bright-colored renderings of the hospital buildings. In others, Whittle had recreated vibrant farms—in country that might have been a number of places in North Florida or Georgia.

The last one struck him like a blow to the chest. Whittle had drawn a young boy with a sapling pole sailing a little skiff—just like the one Gibby was fishing on! An oddly tall hat, brim shading the eyes—like Gibby's! The boy was painted in bright colors, yet on his face, was a look of terror. Blue clouds swirled about in an impending storm. He'd painted blue waves. *Angry waves, like to swamp the boat*, Harlowe thought.

Whittle set the scene as if he were there when Gibby went missing!

The boy in the painting was looking at someone—a slender, gray figure ashore!
The latter had no face—Whittle hadn't made him one. He'd left rough gray brushstrokes, just a blur where his features should be. Like he hadn't finished, hadn't got to it, the face, where the identity of a man lay. It was all the more menacing, this man faceless as he was, standing there, *watching*. A malevolency poured from the paper, as chilling as someone standing, hooded in the darkness.

Why was the old man sent here? There seemed no reason. Until you considered what was in the paintings. Someone wanted to keep the old man from ever telling what he knew.
But whom?
Wait a minute, there's something else in here. Harlowe felt another paper inside. He unfolded it. The scrawl was barely decipherable. But he soon realized who it was from—Elston. He'd written thus:

> *Might be of use to you. Keep me out of it!*
> *Diner -- 10 o'clock. If you want more.*

Harlowe parked near the back of the lot. The place was busy. He said hello to Earl and Jeannie and proceeded to the back corner booth, where the doctor leaned over a cup of coffee, his hat low on his face.
Harlowe folded himself into the booth, opposite, finding a cup waiting on him. "He made his own colors," Elston began. "All the patients have is charcoal. Or pencils. But he mixed the paints. The old boy is a pretty good artist. No mistaking what that is."
"No, sir. Where--."

"Nurse found them. They'd been secreted in the record room."

"Oh?"

"You'll never find out who did it."

"No. I reckon not."

"Whittle came from Tallahassee. Retired from the G.F.& A. Never any violence. Nor any ill treatment of children indicated."

"Go on."

"Kern is from Tallahassee, originally. He has a good record here. But I heard it said he acted strangely where this patient was concerned."

"Have you any idea why? Or what the connection was?"

"I haven't the slightest idea. One other thing."

"Yeah, Doc?"

"Have some eggs and hash. I'm going to. It's better than the hospital food."

"All right, Doc. Believe I will."

Jeannie brought them plates of food—and it *was* good.

Elston flopped his napkin on the table when he'd finished. "Did you find out *anything* on this trip?"

"Well, I came with a head full o' questions. I'm leavin' with a head full."

Elston lit a cigarette. "Why did Collis stick around here for three days? Who was the old man to him? Who was that fella in the Ford?"

"Yessir, that's about it."

Harlowe said goodbye. Drove into the summer rain. The sign read, "Tallahassee 44 miles."

NINETEEN

Near Tallahassee

He followed US-90, a concrete lane just wide enough for two Fords, which ran through Havana, down through dairy farms to the Capital City.

Heifers grazed by the city limits sign and farmland persisted for a fair piece—though the state capitol was less than two miles distant.

Downtown, he turned onto College Avenue. Pulled to the curb. Walked to Burdines Drug Store at the corner of Adams and College. The place seemed dead, even for a Wednesday morning. The man at the fountain seemed glad to see him. "Good Morning, sir!" Surely, this visitor would spend a nickel on *something!*

But Harlowe only glanced at the *Democrat*. One headline was a man arrested for moonshining—Tallahassee doing its part to uphold Prohibition. The other announced "Local Sheriff to be Guest Speaker" at one of the churches downtown. Harlowe proceeded to the phonebooth, closing the door and taking the earpiece off the hook.
"Information, please. Yes, ma'am, I'd like the listing for 'five-four-four.'"
A brief pause and the operator intoned:
"W.N. Ledbetter. 403 South Bronough Street. Will that be all, sir?"
"Thank you, ma'am."
I'll be damned. The High Sheriff of Leon County.

He walked outside. Around him were small storefronts, one or two stories high. A church steeple poked up above the oaks. And the capitol dome, the city's tallest structure, loomed down the street. Men in suits walked to their offices. Tourist cars drove South—on the Dixie Highway.
"Who could hurt a child?"
"Who coulda done that?"
It could be anyone.

Harlowe drove a block East, to Monroe Street. It was wide and devoid of cars. *Hard times.* He pulled up in front of the courthouse. The building had been renovated in the Twenties, leaving an austere facade devoid of columns or expected Southern courthouse vocabulary. Harlowe entered. Started down the hall. The sign at the end read, "Sheriff's Office."

Visiting another sheriff's county, the courtesy of a visit was expected. He opened the door. Asked to see Bill Ledbetter. "He isn't in, sir."

Harlowe drove to Ledbetter's home. He found it three blocks away. A big two-story with attic. The Capitol dome capped the backyard, rising over spotless laundry on the line, and the tidy garage. Mrs. Ledbetter's roses added splashes of color down one side. Harlowe parked in front. Walked up and knocked.

"Why, Pratt Harlowe. How in the world are you?! Come on in! Look who's here, Ava!"

Ledbetter ushered the visitor inside. The local sheriff was in his late thirties. Popular. A good-natured, back-slapper of a man. Tall and square-jawed with a full head of dark hair, he was reckoned to be quite handsome by ladies. Mrs. Ledbetter was two years her husband's junior, auburn-haired and demure. The lady of the house took Harlowe's hat and the guest was made to feel like the long-lost brother returned home. "If we knew you was coming, I would have baked a pie! You will stay for dinner, won't you? Oh, we'd love to have you!"

"That's mighty nice, but I don't want you to go to any trouble," replied Harlowe.

"Nonsense! Oh, I'll get you some coffee," added Mrs. Ledbetter. The latter was brought to him with no chance to decline such miminmal hospitality. They'd brought him into the parlor, the drapes making the day's blistering sun a bit more civilized, the soft hues of the paper, the good upholstery and upright piano all a testament to Mrs. Ledbetter's taste and love for her home. Her pride in the framed photos of the children was equally evident. The Ledbetters provided the warmest small talk for a quarter hour.

The lady of the house was a fine woman, and Harlowe didn't mind visiting with her. As he looked over the china cup, he couldn't help but think the man of the house was spreading it on a little thick, with this talk of mullet and all the things a "coastal hick" was supposed to be interested in.

Some people up here look down their noses at folk who make their living on the water, Harlowe comprehended. *Well, give 'em what they expect! Let 'em think you're dumb!*

"Oh, yeeeah-ess!" he declared, talking like a field hand. "If I didn't have to serve them papers 'n things, I'd spend *all* my time frog gigg...*in'* and fiiiish...*in'* Indian Creek! *Yes, suh!*" The slap to his knee, and clumsy wiping of his mouth he threw in for added effect.

Ledbetter ate it up. "You and me *both,* Pratt!"

"Y'all have a gen'ral store up here, Bill? I'm plumb outta chaw tobac-key."

"Oh, I'd try Gramling's on South Adams, there. They got your feed, groceries, canned tobaccos, anything you like."

"You mean to say they got all that in one store?! Oh, my goodness!"

"More coffee, Mr. Harlowe?"

"Thankya, I b'lieve I will."

Mrs. Ledbetter poured it from her nice service. "Now, I believe you have some business you'd like to talk to my husband about. So, I'll leave you men to it."

Harlowe half-rose from his chair, putting his hand to his heart. "Thank *you,* Miss Ledbetter! They *is* a little piece o' sheriffin' bidness I've been *strugglin'* with! It's jus' givin' me *fits!*"

The woman drew the doors closed between the men and her kitchen. The conversation proceeded with the addition of tobaccos, Ledbetter lighting a cigar.

"Givin' you fits? Maybe I can help."

"I *sho' do* apppreciate that. Like I say, it's givin' me a...*time.*"

"What is it, Pratt?"

"Well...it's poor Ira Brewer's wife. Y'see, her brother passed. Collis Hutto? And there's some matters that need clearin' up. I hate to bother you--."

"Not a' tall, Pratt. Go ahead."

"Well, Ol' Collis come through River Junction last week n' left some bidness—some difficulty with a bill, I understand. I wonder if ya he'ped him when he come this way?"

"Oh, well, I didn't know he was in town, Pratt."

"You didn't?! I thought *sure* he mighta come to you...over this, uh, this difficulty!"

"No, Pratt, I never saw him."

The man was so confident in his lies Harlowe nearly believed him. But it was the small pulse of the artery at his collar that gave him away. He was smooth, but when he thumbed his collar, tight from the necktie, Harlowe could see his heart was beating fast.

"I'm onto somethin'," thought Harlowe. "Ya mind if I ask around? See if I can figure out this thing? It's jus' that his sister could use the money. I prob'ly won't get nowheres with it, but I got to try!"

"Not at all, Pratt! And if I can he'p you, why you just holler!"

"Well...I sho' do 'preciate that now! I *sho' do!*"

"Don't mention it! You're a friend and I wanna help any way I can! Pratt, I'd really like to see more of ya! I'd like you to come to our Elk's Club suppah sometime. I--." The High Sheriff was interrupted by the telephone jingling in the hall. He asked to be excused, closing the doors behind him.

Harlowe glanced around the parlor. A lovely room—Fireplace—Fine lamps. The home was more-than-comfortable. Yet, it wasn't of such size that Ledbetter's voice didn't carry through those doors. Harlowe got the gist of the call: president of a local bank and some social function. Ledbetter was plugged into things like the wires at the telephone exchange. He was hooked into a tangle of interests that could buy and sell Franklin County a dozen times over.

"Yore my friend, Pratt," Ledbetter reminded him. "Why, there oughta be a way we can work together. Why don't I have the boy come in and talk?"

"That'll be fine, Bill." It was Whittle's nephew.

Mrs. Ledbetter served her fried chicken on her good china. And Harlowe wasn't embellishing when he said it was the best he'd had in as long as he could remember. How she found time to whip up a cake, Harlowe didn't know, but there it was!

"Oh, and Mrs. Ledbetter, I *thaaank* you very kindly for the coffee and that *chocolate cake! Best...I've...had in a coon's age!*" he drawled.

"I'm glad you enjoyed it, Sheriff."

He said goodbye to Mrs. Ledbetter. The "High Sheriff" pumped his hand and clapped him on the shoulder.

Harlowe started the truck. Sighed in relief. 'Courtesy' had taken the better part of two hours!

Next day, Harlowe waited in Ledbetter's office and Whittle's nephew didn't show. "I don't understand it!" said Ledbetter. "He told me he was comin' in!"

"I think he may have left town," thought Mealer.

Harlowe told Seago about it. "We give him the courtesy of lettin' 'im know we're in his county, and he does somethin' like that. I won't be goin' back."

The following morning, Harlowe was waiting when the lights came on at the Tallahassee courthouse. The Assistant Clerk of Court let him look at the record books.
He asked to see the pleadings for Whittle's commitment. There were none. Not one scrap of paper!
"You sure?"
Harlowe turned to look back at the man, there. He looked as uncomfortable as a tree frog stuck to a windshield. Harlowe jotted down the name of the lawyer who handled the sale of Whittle's home.

He found the lawyer's office—204 East Pensacola.
"I have some questions," said Harlowe.
The man shuffled some papers. "I can't talk to you. Attorney-client privilege!"
"If Whittle asked you to sell the house, he'd have some money comin', wouldn't he?"
"Now, see here! That was a private transaction! I want you to leave this office!"
The glazed door slammed behind him.
More than anything that fella seems scared! thought Harlowe.

He stopped at Maxwell Drug Store. The phone book gave him the name of Whittle's nephew. His only relative. Harlowe found he hadn't left town—he was sweeping out his store!
"I honestly don't know what happened. I didn't have much communication with my uncle. But he was always a keen-minded old fellow. I can't imagine he'd let that house go without a fair settlement!"
Harlowe believed him.
"You been to see him?" asked the younger man.
"Yessir."
"I'm afraid *I* haven't." The man looked away, sadly.

The rain poured out over the headstone—Mrs. Whittle's. The oaks at the Park Avenue cemetery stood silent watch, black and shrouded with silver, glistening moss which hung from branches twenty feet in the air.

In the same plot, were marble slabs for the rest of Whittle's kinfolk. Old Man Whittle had no one who could speak for him, not among these stones.

But, what about his friends and neighbors? Harlowe found the city library, a narrow, ornate building five blocks away, on Park Avenue. They had a 1927 City Directory on the shelf. Harlowe flipped to the address. *Whittle, E.F., 415 East Call.*

Harlowe drove two blocks to the large, wood-sided Victorian. Pulled to the curb in front and rang the bell. A housewife, holding an infant, answered. She appeared to be in her late twenties. She'd been cleaning. She wore a scarf over her hair, which was midnight black. Her face was quite fair.

Harlowe cupped his hat. "'Afternoon, ma'am. My, isn't she a pretty thing!"

"Good Afternoon—thank you! Say, if you're selling something, Mister, I already bought from the Fuller man."

"Oh, no, ma'am, I'm not selling anything. I'm Pratt Harlowe—from Franklin County. I'm the sheriff *down theah* and—."

"Where again?"

"Franklin County, ma'am."

She raised an eyebrow. Didn't get too many visits from an out-of-county lawman, and an Apalachicolan at that!

"Reason I'm here is on account of Mr. Whittle."

"Oh, that poor man! I'm forgetting my manners. Won't you come in, Mr. Harlowe? I'm Mrs. Davis." She extended her free hand.

He took it. "Glad to know ya."

"The parlor's through here. Oh, may I take your hat?"

"Thankya." He looked around. The house was freshly painted. It spoke nothing to him where Whittle was concerned.

"Please sit down."

She placed the infant in a bassinet. She sat on the piano bench.

He settled, then, on a red, stuffed chair.

She explained how she and her husband came to know of Mr. Whittle, rocking the baby as she spoke. "We bought this house at auction, you see." She lowered her voice, adding, *"After he was committed."*

Harlowe nodded. The kind woman nearly shivered at the thought of the man—any man—going to the asylum.

"We never met him. But we heard things."

"Yes, ma'am?"

"Oh, just that he was a nice man. Things like that. Mr. Harlowe, would you care for some coffee? It's no trouble. I've a pot on the stove."

"I'd like that. Thankya."

She returned, carrying two cups.

Harlowe took a sip. "Would you remember who it was that mentioned him—anyone in particular that knew him well?"

"Gee, I don't know, sir. Not really. There's the fella at the market, people like that. I mean, the other neighbors, the Searcys' and the Douglass's were living here then. They might be able to tell you something."

"Yes, ma'am."

"Mrs. Sadler has been here for years. She could probably give you details the rest of the girls around here couldn't. You're after definite information, I imagine. Not just the usual neighborhood gossip!"

"Yes, ma'am. That's what I'm lookin' for."

"I thought so. Must be important!" She stirred her coffee. She cast a look at him, hoping he'd tell her more.

"Well, I'd settle for gossip, if that's all I can get."

The woman laughed. "I understand. Say, I just finished a pie. Would you care for a slice?"

"Thankya, ma'am, but I don't want to put you out."

"Oh, don't be silly. I hope you like coconut pie—do you?"

"My favorite."

She smiled. "Comin' right up, sir!" she said, marching off to get it.

He hoped everyone might be so helpful. That thought was interrupted when she reappeared with the pie. He took a bite. "Boy, that is good! Say, you mentioned something while ago, about the market—."

"Yes, the A&P! I do my marketing there. The owner knew the old man. I'm sure of that."

"Did Mr. Whittle leave anything here?"

"No. I don't think so. Anything in particular?"

"No, just wondering."

"I understand he and his wife had lodgers. It's a large house as you can see. We repainted and did some sprucing up. But nothing was left here."

Harlowe nodded.

"Can I get you another cup of coffee?"

"Oh, no, ma'am. I've got to get going. I sure do appreciate it. Best pie I've had in ages!"

"I'm glad you like it. Oh, Mr. Harlowe?"

He finished the last bite. "Yes, ma'am?"

"I don't know about—well, I've only read books and things. But are you on a case—is it something like that?"

He told her about Gibby. In a way he was reminding himself where it all started—despite detours through River Junction, Whittle, everything else. "Oh, how sad. And how interesting. How wonderful, you showing such concern for that lost boy! Now, how long have you been a lawman?"

"Oh, on and off, twenty years."

"The stories you could tell, I'm sure!"

She told him things about herself, then, about her husband who was an insurance man, thirty years old, and was doing well, despite the 'Crash. They were lucky.

"Mrs. Davis you have been most kind. I hate to say goodbye, but I must."

She took up the infant. Saw him to the door. "Goodbye. Say, goodbye, Dottie!" she told the baby, waving her little hand for her. They waved from the porch as he walked down the sidewalk to the house next door, the latter similar but not as brightly-painted as the former Whittle home.

He knocked. Presently, a middle-aged woman answered. She was friendly, but as soon as the conversation turned to Whittle she grew sullen. The same was true of the neighbors on the other side, and around on Gadsden Street. He rang the door of the Cory residence. No one was home.

Mrs. Sadler was more talkative. More insistent he come in for coffee.
"Trouble started when his wife died," she advised.

"Trouble, ma'am?"

"Yes—the poor man alone in that house, no one to look after him!"

"I see."

"What did y'think I meant?"

"I don't know. Trouble with his health. His business."

"No-no!"

"Did the old man have any enemies, Mrs. Sadler?"

"Huh?"

"Did he get himself crossways with someone?"

"I don't want to spread gossip. I deal strictly with facts! *Crossways* you say?"

"Yes'm."

"Well, I dunno."

"Someone important, maybe?" Harlowe pressed.

Maybe he pressed too far. The woman looked afar off, like her eyes were focused down the hall and out the door. "I wouldn't know," she replied. That was as far as she'd go. She changed the subject to her sciatica, all the curses of middle age. "You really need to watch what you eat—you too, a man your age!" she warned. While she was talking, he caught a glimpse of himself in the mirror over the fireplace. *I am middle-aged, myself, when you come right down to it.*

She popped up from the divan. "Now, you'll have to excuse me. I must check on my upside-down cake! Remember what I said, now!"

He donned his hat, chuckled to himself as the screen door banged shut.

The A&P at 318 South Monroe was austere. Lights dim. Shelves bare, save for the canned goods. Worried housewives counted their pennies for canned chilli and canned coffee, and marched out. Harlowe waited his turn. The clerk's mouth closed up tighter than an oyster when Harlowe called the old man's name.

He tried some of the other stores. And the Leon Milk Company. The milkman for Whittle's neighborhood was even more reticent.

Harlowe turned back to Collis and his "pal." He spoke to the man at the Standard Oil station—424 E. Tennessee. He was friendly. Then Harlowe showed the photo and his color drained. "Nope, ain't seen him."

The look in his eyes. He knows something. Something's off, Harlowe reckoned. *Like they'd all been talked to!*

Harlowe—on a tip from Whittle's nephew—found the Doctor who treated Whittle's late wife. He walked up to the yellow-brick building at College and Monroe. Looked at the directory. *Third floor.* He climbed the stairs to find a fidgety little man. Dr. Harvey.

The conversation was abrupt.

"I never saw Mr. Whittle! I don't know anything about him! Good day!"

The frosted door banged shut.

He's lyin'.

He drove down Gaines—the quiet residential lane ran to the depot, the industrial area. Near the depot Harlowe found the place formerly rented by Mr. Kern, the last structure in a line of depressing shacks. A barefoot child stood on the porch, next door, watching him. "Got anything to eat, Mister?"

"Where's your momma?"

"I dunno. I'm hungry."

A freight train puffed and rattled by, mere yards from the back door. Harlowe looked around at rotting wood and filth. He'd grown up with very little. Saw war-time depredations. But, this was a *grinding poverty*. White and colored alike had the rug pulled out from under them by distant forces none of them could see, feel, nor fight back—the hurricane down in Miami, the stock market up in New York.

He had a can of peaches. He gave it to her.

A baseball's throw, yonder, was the warehouse district. Down at the S.A.L. repair shop on Gaines, he found two old-timers who'd worked on the old G., F., & A. line, sitting around the coffee pot on the wood stove. Spitting tobacco. They wore overalls, slouch hats, gray stubble on their cheeks. "Yessir, Whittle was a brakeman fur many years. He was a good ol' man and, pardon the expression, he was 'railroaded!'" said one.

"Yeah, he was," said the other.

When Harlowe asked how they meant by that, they said the old timer was nothing more than a little forgetful. "Like anyone would be who's seventy-five years old!" said the first man.

"Never shoulda-been sent off," the other agreed. "No sooner as he retired, his wife dies on 'im. Then," said the old man, pausing to spit tobacco juice, "they done 'im like 'at. The judge 'n them!"

Harlowe showed the men a newspaper clipping about Gibby.

"Nosir, he never mentioned that."

"E.F. always got on well with children, with my grandchildren in particular. He was like another pawpaw to them younguns! A gentle ol' soul."

Both men agreed Whittle never mentioned Collis, or Gibby. Whittle knew no one in Eastpoint, so far as they knew. Of course, "He rode 'clown' on the Carrabelle run, every day, for years!"

"Would you know about some paintings he left?"

"Paintins?!"

"Yessir. Pictures he painted."

"Didn't know he done that," said one.

"Well-I'll-be-darned!" declared the other.

Back "uptown" Harlowe walked the sidewalks. Hotels and lunchrooms. He asked of Collis, the stocky man. People looked and shook their heads.

The Hotel Floridan overlooked Monroe and Tennessee Streets. It had 110 rooms, each with its own bathroom. Rumor was, more State business was done in the smoking room, here, than at the Capitol!

Harlowe wiped his brow. Entered the lobby.

The friendly clerk offered him a Coca-Cola and practically wouldn't let him leave. The man had all the staff come look at the photo.

Walking out, Harlowe noticed Ledbetter's Ford parked at the curb, yonder. Harlowe joined the shoppers' slow stream on the hot sidewalk. Making sure he wasn't observed, he slipped around the next block. Entering the hotel through the backdoor, he eased down the hall. Peered around the corner. There was Ledbetter—the High Sheriff slapped the clerk on the back and laughed.

I see what he wants me to see.

After Ledbetter drove away, Harlowe crossed the street. Walked down to the Standard Oil station—103 N. Monroe. The attendant, wrapping his hands with a rag, spun the radiator cap off the boiling-over Essex, steam and spray spouting like Old Faithful. Harlowe showed him the picture.
"Gotta wait, anyhow, sure I'll look. Uh, nosir. Don't recognize him."
Harlowe gave him the description of the stocky young man.
"I caint think who that would be! Why, it could be several fellas 'round here. New Stetson hat—you see plenty of 'em! You like a Coke-Cola, Mister? Gonna be here awhile, 'til this thing cools off some. I'm gonna have one."
"No, thanks. I appreciate it."
"Don't mention it." The man pulled a bottle from the cooler. "Y'wanna ask me somethin' else?"
"You see a lot of people come through here."
"Yep."
"You seen any strangers in town, anyone hangin' around?"
"Tourists or suspicious-like?"
"Suspicious-like."
"Nosir. I ain't seen anyone that didn't act right. Just the usual—folks that come in off the highway, locals like the judge, here." The man finished the cold drink. "Ah! Sure was good! Oh, here comes the judge, I better git this done!"
"Well, I appreciate it."
"Yessir!"
"So long."
Harlowe checked every filling station in town, anyone who might have seen the man who'd driven Collis to town—or heard *something.*

He talked to an acquaintance at city hall on Adams Street—a policeman. He worked for the city, not Ledbetter. Harlowe handed him the photo. "I wonder if you mighta heard of some trouble. Some boys may have worked him over."
The policeman shook his head. "No, Pratt. Sorry!"

The Whittle's lodgers had left town. Harlowe baked like bread on the sidewalk, finding that out. Not a soul in town remembered seeing Collis or the other man.

Half-a-mile from the Capitol, the pavement stopped and he motored down dirt plantation roads little changed from the time before Secession. He got his boots dusty talking to housewives and farmers.

He took Monroe, north, past the beauty shops and Elks Lodge. The road quickly turned residential. Big oaks and stately homes lined it. Spanish moss—Verandas—Old families. That gentility was belied by how this town really functioned.
Harlowe looked. And thought.
There's a "town behind the town." It has the ugliness you'd see in a big city with 'machine' bosses—maybe better hidden. Ledbetter's got some fooled.

Some scared. He's plugged in like a switchboard. He's got out the word I'm in town. He's blockin' me.

Harlowe passed the Y in the road, where the Thomasville Highway commenced. He stayed on Monroe, reaching open country near Lake Ella, rolling green pasture dotted with black and white dairy cows. The area's rural, though it's mere miles from downtown.

A man named Chandler built a Motor Court at the lake, with Spanish-style cabins with red roofs, befitting "The Spanish Trail" route to *Havana* and points West. Chandler was building more cabins, now. He'd opened a filling station—the first one motorists would come to, as they arrived on newly-paved US-90. *Collis would have passed it.* Harlowe pulled in to the pumps.

Harlowe sat there for a moment, imagining Collis and that car ride. Had he looked out the window as he was taken past here? Did they stop to fill up? Had the stocky fella already worked him over?
The attendant walked over. Daubed the windshield. "What'll-it-be, Mister? Fill 'er up?"
"I could use a little oil."
"Comin' right up."
"Say, have ya seen this fella? Maybe ridin' with a stocky fella in a Ford?"
The attendant spared only a terse glance. "Nosir. I ain't."
The fellow funnelled in a quart of oil. Shut the hood. Harlowe paid up. Asked, again, about the man with the new hat. "Maybe spendin' a little money. Maybe more than usual." Harlowe described him, the car.
The attendant turned away. Commenced sweeping the doorway of the station. "I wouldn't know. Now, you best go! My bossman don't like me jibber-jabbin.'"

***

"Well, I probably shouldn't be tellin' you this," said the man at Brown's Menswear. "But, I heard the old man really got into it with one of his neighbors. People were talkin" about it."
"Go on," said Harlowe.
"Well, they got to hollerin.' Really goin' at it, Whittle and him."
"Yessir?"
"Somethin' that the boy—the neighbor's son—had done."
"Have you any idea what it was about?"
"No, sir. I don't"
"Do you know whom?"
"No, I don't."
"Have you sold many gray fedoras lately—Stetson brand?"
The man smiled. "All the time. Would you be interested in one?"

Harlowe walked out into the throng, the oppressive heat.
There, from a store came a man in a new stetson fedora.
Stocky. *Could that be him?*
He turned in front of Harlowe. Smiled beneath a handle-bar mustache. "I beg your pardon."
Harlowe shook his head. Grinned.

89

Harlowe asked around but couldn't confirm the story about the argument.

He phoned Elston from the drugstore. "I don't have much change, Doc, so I gotta keep this short."
"Okay."
Harlowe filled him in on everything he'd learned about Whittle.
"I dunno if he's a victim in all this or the killer."
"It is *damned peculiar*, Pratt. As infuriatingly baffling as Agatha Christie's 'missing' eleven days!"

TWENTY

Tallahassee. Later that day.

Drought. It ruined Apalachicola's oysters. Here, it brought a brilliantly limitless pale blue sky without the prayer of a cloud, and furnace-like heat. Landlocked, breezeless, the Capital City was so hot Harlowe's ears rang— from the temperature and the cicadas, both.

He wore out leather on the sidewalks that were hot enough to fry. Harlowe dug into Mr. Kern's life. Tracked down kinfolk and old classmates. He found nothing, couldn't determine a link to Collis whatever. He left Van Brunt & Yon Harware and crossed off the last lead he had for the orderly. He put away his notebook, started back to his truck.

He saw something out of the corner of his eye. That fellow in a light suit standing there, across Adams Street, behind the car.
Harlowe kept walking, slowly. The man had stopped in the shade of an awning. *That fella might be waiting for his girl at the beauty shop—or he might be tailin' me,* Harlowe knew.
Harlowe turned the corner onto College Avenue. He couldn't tell if the fellow was following. Harlowe paused to light a cigarette, glancing in the sidemount mirror of a parked automobile.
He's back there, all right. Harlowe could see the face now. One of Ledbetter's men—Mealer.

At Maxwell's, Harlowe turned the corner. Down Monroe. The man turned, too. *I can hear the scrape of his shoes. I feel him back there,* Harlowe thought.
Every footstep, getting closer.
Quickly, Harlowe ducked into McCrory's 5 & 10. Up the aisle. He lost himself among the shoppers and cosmetics. Becoming just another hat. He eased out the back door—out to Jefferson Street.
The fellow walked up the aisle. Looked at a face or two. Walked out.
Harlowe looked around the corner. Watched the deputy leave. The man wiped his neck. Got back his car. Harlowe grinned. *Ninety-five degrees in the shade and the boy's had enough!*

Free of his tail, Harlowe talked to the mechanics at the automobile dealerships on Monroe, the old man on the bench at the courthouse.

It was getting dark. Harlowe passed the big church on Monroe. Shaking hands on the steps, was a tall man in a charcoal suit. Harlowe recognized him—the State's Attorney, O.C.
Raines.

Harlowe drove down to 403 South Bronough. The lights glowed from the dining room windows as the High Sheriff finished supper with his family. As menfolk up and down the street settled in with their paper and tobacco, Ledbetter combed his hair, buttoned a starched shirt, subsequently emerging for activities a mite less sedate than that of the neighboring husbands. He climbed into his sporty Model A. Backed down the driveway. The car chortled, happily, as Ledbetter pulled away, a carefree jaunt in mind.

Harlowe trailed, several car-lengths back. The newer Ford's taillamp darted across Monroe like a red firefly. Landed behind the courthouse.

Ledbetter seated himself behind his desk, a throne with a telephone, inbox and outbox. It was dark in his office. He sat. Finally, switched on the desk lamp.

Harlowe slipped down the hall, soft-stepping along the wall, staying in the shadow until the voices grew distinct—Ledbetter and his brother-in-law. Harlowe listened beside the lettered-glass door.
"Don't lose sight of Harlowe. I need to know when he's nosin' around."
"What about that other thing?" asked Mealer.
"Ya worried? Driscoll will come through. He's a careful man, I'm tellin' ya."
Who's Driscoll? Thought Harlowe.

Harlowe looked at the frosted glass. L-E-D-B-E-T-T-E-R. He'd been sheriff since '23, appointed by the Governor after Bob Jones was snared in the convict lease scandal. Before that, Ledbetter had been a part-time deputy—when his father-in-law was sheriff. Ledbetter started with two deputies. He rode his horse to Miccosukee to serve papers, and spend the night up there. In the morning, he'd ride to Chaires and on down to Woodville—"riding circuit" in this manner took him three days. It was little different from how things were done before the War Between the States. It was plain to see Ledbetter had done all right for himself in recent years. New car—Big house—More men.

Harlowe slipped outside.
Through the back door, a man entered whom Harlowe didn't recognize. Harlowe listened through the open window. "Whaddya say, Durfee?" *Another one of his deputies.* Ledbetter had four. On top of that, he just hired a "Chief Deputy," who politicked for the High Sheriff, mostly.

Harlowe thought about the man who picked up Collis in Chattahoochee— the description didn't match any of Ledbetter's men.

Harlowe tailed Ledbetter home. Watched him stumble in, the family man returning to his fireside bright.

Harlowe walked into the lobby of the Cherokee Hotel. Flipped through their telephone book.
Driscoll, O.M., Chaires Apartments, 209 S. Calhoun.

Harlowe found the apartment house. He entered the foyer. "Driscoll" was written on the mailbox for Apartment 9.

Harlowe climbed the stairs. One flight. Proceeded down the hall. It was narrow, dim. A ball-bat and glove stood in the corner. He knocked at Driscoll's door. He heard no movements inside. But, across the hall, the door cracked open—someone peeking out. The door cracked a little more and Harlowe could see a white-haired man.

"Lookin' for Driscoll. He around?" asked Harlowe.

"He ain't in," answered the fellow.

"Know what he does for a livin'?"

"Work? Bah! He likes the pool halls!"

"Is that right?"

"Yeah, that's where you'll find him. Ya want I should tell him you was here?"

"No, I'll tell 'im."

The night air was sultry. The sidewalks still radiating heat, long after sundown.

Tallahassee's night life beckoned with hot, naked lightbulbs casting a glare on dark streets and the clang of "tack pianos" drifting down the slanted cement where Jefferson Street and Park Avenue plunged down to unilluminated residences, West. There were four of these little "places of amusement," pool halls and ten pin alleys, in a two-square block area just a baseball's throw from the courthouse.

He crossed the pitch-black street and walked into the first one, the low-ceilinged hotbox confining and smoky. 'Rough customers' cut an eye at him, but the sounds of boisterous laughter, the break of a cue ball went undiminished. Driscoll wasn't there. Quietly, he showed the photo of Collis, asked men if they'd seen him. None had.

He left, the piano notes from the first joint faded, the clanging from the next one competing, then taking its place. He went in. Driscoll wasn't there. He showed the photo. Folks shook their heads and returned it. The men—in workshirts and ties, railroad men, the boys who worked at the crate factory, other fellas on the bum after losing a job—*wanted* to help him, if they could. But, they hadn't seen Collis.

Then, others, knew more but wouldn't talk. He could see it in their adverted eyes. They closed up like oysters as soon as he showed the photo.

Harlowe didn't see any of Ledbetter's men. But there were plenty of others who would inform on Harlowe for asking questions. For instance, the men serving Coca-Colas (or something stronger from under the counter). Ledbetter had people loyal to him—or scared of him.

Harlowe left, certain the telephone call being placed right now would be to the Chief Deputy.

The last pool hall was on Monroe Street, itself. A floodlight reflected off a Coca-Cola sign on the roof, casting a knife-like shadow down the sidewalk. The building wasn't much bigger than a smokehouse, made of dark, baked brick, hot to the touch as Harlowe walked up to the open doors. He looked in on the crowd, music and cigarette smoke drifting out with the heat. Cigarette smoke swirled about faces and hats. One of those new "juke boxes" hummed in the corner.

Men swigged bottles of Coca-Cola to cool off while they waited for their shot. The music kept it lively. Popular numbers. Hillbilly tunes. Laughter interspersed with the clack of the cue ball. A bottle would occasionally emerge from a back pocket, to be "turned up" by a man with his back to the crowd. "Officially" Prohibition was the law—and Tallahassee had it even before the Volstead Act—but the "practice" was a little different. Near the juke box, Harlowe saw a new Stetson—broad shoulders—pencil mustache. The fellow knocked back a "tonic"—it was Driscoll.

Harlowe ordered a bottle of Coke. Sat in the shadow. Driscoll didn't see him, his attention occupied by the body underneath a low-neckline dress and dark, "bobbed" hair.

Harlowe made out most of what was said (reading Driscoll's lips). *"We oughta go ridin' one night. I got a friend that just bought an old plantation. We could go out there..."* Something about, *"Moonlight...your hair...free tomorrow night."*
The woman was more boisterous. Her voice carried. Harlowe could hear her outright. "Gee that's swell!"
She laughed at Driscoll's jokes like she's getting paid by the hour.

Ten minutes passed. Driscoll continued cutting up with the gal and her friends, who had come in after Harlowe. They were having a big time!

None of that helped him. *What were Driscoll's dealings with Ledbetter? Did that 5-4-4 number in Collis' pocket tie in?*

Harlowe looked out front. He saw another puff of smoke from that parked Chevrolet. The fellow had been sitting there for five minutes. Harlowe recognized him—the Deputy from the courthouse. A little hall led to the toilet. Harlowe slipped out that way, into the alley.

Harlowe continued watching from his truck. Saw Driscoll leave the pool room, climbing into a Model T. He spoke in hushed tones Harlowe couldn't hear. Then the driver started the car.
Here we go.
They drove down South Monroe, along the recently paved section below the tracks.

At the bottom of the hill burned a solitary bulb. The Model T stopped there. The men shrieked something like a rebel yell and went inside. Harlowe listened, watched. The joint's a "blind tiger," an illegal tavern outside the city limits.

They'd get good and loaded. I've seen all I'm gonna see tonight, Harlowe knew.

He headed for Chandler's Motor Courts. Parked beside his cabin. It had cooled some, the two-lane highway and dairy were quiet, the nightsky big and black.

Then, headlights shined in the distance, as a car approached from town. It slowed as if to turn into the Courts.

Harlowe went inside. He looked out the gap of the curtains. He thought the two, dim bulbs shining was a Model T. The automobile rattled to a dead stop, turning so the lights fell on the windows of his cabin.

Harlowe's hand went to the Browning in his coat.
At that instant, the driver—whomever he was—put the car in gear and wheeled about, back toward Tallahassee. Harlowe watched the taillight shrink to a dot and disappear.

He wasn't hungry for all the coffee and pie he'd been plied with earlier. He turned in, his automatic in reach. The windows of the cabin were open, the curtains limp, no breeze to rouse them against the damp heaviness of the air. The night was hot, loud, and long. Finally, the crickets and mockingbirds drowned out his thoughts. He slept.

TWENTY-ONE

Tallahassee, Thursday.

Harlowe pulled to the curb on Monroe. His "T" blended in with the farm trucks. He looked yonder, watching Bill Ledbetter climb down from his Sport Coupe.

Harlowe got out, following the Sheriff on the sidewalk. Ledbetter turned to look over his shoulder as a horse-drawn milk wagon clattered past. Harlowe folded tight against the bricks. But he needn't have. Ledbetter's eyes were drawn to the gal who walked out of the dress shop.
The High Sheriff did some window shopping. Some flirting. Then, went home for dinner. Had chicken. Harlowe waited. Ate nothing. Number "544" was the best lead Harlowe had, and he was going to follow it...*and the man it corresponded to*, until something broke.

Ledbetter got in his car. He proceeded north on Monroe. *Where are you, going?* thought Harlowe, tapping his wheel. Up a block. Then another. Harlowe hung back in the light traffic, hoping to stay out of Ledbetter's rear-view mirror.

Ledbetter turned down a side street, then onto Calhoun. He slowed when he neared the apartment building—Driscoll's.
His movement—tossing his cigarette down—seemed to say he was distressed.
Suddenly, the sheriff put his car in gear and roared away.

Ledbetter stopped at the courthouse, but left soon after, crossing Park to the Standard Oil station for a fill-up. He was backslapping and politicking like his old self.

Ledbetter made the rounds of the downtown automobile showrooms, Harlowe in the background blending in like the sidewalk. The man from Apalach had evaded the tails all day. Dressed in workshirt and boots, dark necktie, grey coat, his fedora low on his face, Harlowe looked like just another farmer or tradesman "come to town." He blended in with anyone else looking in the showroom windows, longingly, at a new Chevrolet—invisible, struggling, forgotten men.

Harlowe bought a paper from the boy on the sidewalk. Put his foot up on the running board of a car, waiting for Ledbetter. When he emerged, Harlowe moved down the street, like anyone browsing the store windows.

People walked the sidewalks. Did their trading. Lucky children received a stick of penny candy at the 5&10 store! Life went on with no thought to a boy missing four years—from a place seldom visited.

Beneath the awning of the furniture store Harlowe folded his paper.

After visiting with folk all along this side of the street, Ledbetter crossed to the other. Inside the Palace Barber Shop he had a right good time politicking while he got a haircut.

Afterwords, he strolled ebulliently down the sidewalk to Maxwell Drug. He entered the phonebooth in the store. From the look on his face, the call seemed too personal to be sheriffing business. The grin faded. He got red-faced and slammed down the earpiece!

He didn't notice Harlowe when he left. Ledbetter stopped to flirt with a gal. Strutted in to the Schwob Co. store at 118 ½ South Monroe.

Harlowe watched through the window. *Ledbetter got 'im a new shirt.*

Harlowe found a shop on College Avenue. Rented a camera. The man showed him how to use it. While Harlowe didn't say so, *he only wanted to take one picture.*

TWENTY-TWO

Later that day.

The man at the shop had the photograph developed in two hours.
Harlowe rushed it to Mr. Fenton, in Chattahoochee.
The man slapped the counter. "Yessir, that's him! That's him!"
He'd identified Driscoll—he was the man who picked up Collis!

Harlowe found Driscoll shooting pool at the joint on Monroe.
He showed him the photo of Collis. "You were seen with this fella."
"Never saw him before."
"Half-the-town saw you two fussin' at eachother."
The man looked away. Lined up his next shot. "I tell ya I don't know 'im."
"You deny bein' in Chattahoochee last Thursdee?"
Driscoll sunk the thirteen in the corner pocket. "I don't have to deny
nothin'. I ain't gotta talk to ya. You ain't the law—not around here."
"Collis was askin' y'all for money, that it?"
The husky fellow would say nothing.

Harlowe waited behind the courthouse.
Finally, Ledbetter emerged from the back door. Climbed in his car.
Here we go.
Harlowe "gave him some line"—let him go on. Then, the taillight fading to
a red firefly, Harlowe eased the truck from the curb.
As long as he could see the taillight, he wouldn't lose him.
They proceeded to the old tourist camp, on the southside.
Vagrants looked up from their cookfire as the headlights approached. The
fire, the light from piles of burning trash outlined makeshift tents pitched
by hobos there.
Ledbetter doubled back. Turned onto Gaines. Then Boulevard. Made a
fast right onto All Saints. By a clump of trees, he pulled over. Cut his
lights.

He's seen my lights, Harlowe knew. Harlowe had to think fast. He turned
down St. Francis, cut his lights. Halted before a small frame-house.
It worked. A moment passed, and through the yards of the little wooden
houses, shanties, Ledbetter's lights flashed on, the Model A moving again.

Ledbetter pulled over in front of a warehouse on Gaines. Tracks and
spurlines crisscrossed the area through a patchwork of commercial
buildings, yellow and red brick glinting in the floodlights of an adjacent
wholesaler. Otherwise, it was dark as Hell.

Harlowe walked along the spurline tracks, quietly, inching up an alley to
the corner of the building where he could see the dark outline—Ledbetter's
automobile.
Was he waiting on someone?

The night air was heavy, loud. *Was that someone approaching?*

He tried to distinguish any human movement over and above the insects. *No one's there.*

Suddenly, headlights flashed up yonder! On Gaines. Moving quickly! Harlowe stayed behind the brick, watching. It passed the corner, slowing down. *It's a Model T.* As it passed Ledbetter's car, two men leaned out, gave a 'hoop and a holler,' but sped away, turning down Gay.

The street was dark again. Harlowe couldn't see what Ledbetter was doing. *He's just sittin' theah in the dark. It doesn't even look like he's smokin.'*

Presently, the lights of another car flashed from behind the edge of the brick. Harlowe ducked back, watching the car pull in behind Ledbetter's. The older car was a battered "T."
A husky figure stepped down from it. Walked up to Ledbetter's car. Got in.

Harlowe couldn't see his face.
He heard them arguing. "You stay away from her, understand!" Ledbetter roared.
The other man said something back. "Lay off! She's my girl!"
In the slivver of light that fell over Ledbetter's car, Harlowe could see who the other man was—Driscoll.
They nearly came to blows. Finally, they slammed doors. Roared away in their automobiles, in separate directions.

Harlowe ran to his truck. Pulled around on Gaines. The Model T's taillight faded down the street like a tiny firefly. Harlowe followed. He saw the road dead-ended into cow pasture. The other car turned down a dirt road—the Lake Bradford Road. Ahead, the "firefly" darted beneath Cory Concrete Company's big gray silos, which loomed over the road and the tangle of spurlines that covered the area like Mexican clover.

Harlowe passed the silos. He'd closed on Driscoll's car now. They passed the Elberta Crate Factory. Silent at this hour, the smell of cut pine drifted from the yard; the dark smokestack poking up above the innumerable boxes stacked for shipping on the adjacent track. *Is he headin' down to the lake?* wondered Harlowe.

The old Ford pulled off into the woods opposite the factory. Harlowe pulled over. Approached afoot. It was pitch-dark. He couldn't see more than two paces in front of him. Quietly, he threaded his way through the woods, until he could smell the man's cigarette, see his car in the moonlight.

The crickets drowned out the sound of human movement. But the hair stood on Harlowe's neck. He had the feeling like snakes were around. That someone was lurking behind the trees. He got behind a pine.
At that, a man emerged from his hiding place. He passed through the slivver of moonlight which streamed through the branches. His skin reflected back like dark laquer—he was colored. He passed within two yards of Harlowe, making for Driscoll's automobile.

He climbed in. Driscoll handed him something, Harlowe saw, the moonlight bathing the faces in the automobile. *It has to do with moonshine.* The colored man palmed the item. High-tailed it out of there, cranking an automobile down the street. The white man did likewise, putting the car in gear and tearing away.

Harlowe ran to his truck. Mashed the starter. Suddenly, someone emerged from the darkness and snatched the door open. He tried to get ahold of Harlowe's sleeve!
Harlowe slugged him. Got the truck in gear and rolling.
The man swung back! He grabbed the steering wheel, trying to hold on, the truck gathering speed.
Harlowe had never seen this man before! He dressed like a hobo, wearing a rumpled slouch hat. He let loose a current of expletives, trying to stop the truck. Harlowe, overcoming the man's grip, spun the wheel and yanked the throttle back, swerving around the corner. That sent the fellow tumbling off the running board, his profanities fading in the mirror!

Harlowe steered down the unfamiliar street. Found Gaines. Tried to see if he could spot the negro's car.
Lost him.

***

Harlowe looked in the window of the Palace Barber Shop. Then the Busy Bee Café next door. *There he is.*
Harlowe tilted his hat low. Went in. Sat at the counter and ordered a coffee.
Driscoll sat in back, his Stetson on the table. *He's alone.*

Harlowe's eyes scanned the crowded lunchroom. Seated at a table in the middle was Bill Ledbetter. Eating with three other men—who laughed when he did.

When Driscoll got up to pay his check, Harlowe noticed he didn't speak to Ledbetter, nor did the High Sheriff acknowledge the other fellow. Not so much as a nod.
Harlowe heard the waitress making change, for Driscoll. "Bye, Obie."
"Bye, Honey."
The younger fellow left. Then, Ledbetter, going another direction.
Deputy Mealer got out of his car at the curb, down the hill. *Did he recognize me?* Harlowe wondered.
Harlowe glanced back in the reflection of a car window. *He's comin' this way.*
Harlowe ducked into Burdine's. Slipped behind one of the display aisles. He watched the front windows, the large plate glass afforded a good view of everything that passed. The deputy continued on his way—crossed Adams, entered the "Tallahassee Cafe."

The store was quiet. It was dim inside. The hanging lights weren't illuminated. The owner had the doors open to save electricity. Harlowe slipped out the back. Slipped back to his truck.

***

Men marching home from the Crate factory, down the side of the road with lunchboxes. Harlowe saw the colored man among them.

***

Harlowe watched Driscoll park his automobile near the *Daffin Theatre*—College Avenue. Harlowe in the darkness, looked up at the lights of the theatre up the hill. *City Lights* was just finishing. The movie would let out soon—*here comes the crowd, now.*
Driscoll ran into the dark alley behind the theatre. Harlowe followed. He saw a young woman exit the stage entrance.
Driscoll confronted the ticket girl. "You're gonna stop seein' him, ya hear me!"
"Obie, please! Someone will hear you!"
Driscoll grabbed her, violently. *"I'll tell him!"*
"Tell 'im! See what good that'll do! He owes me big, see!"
The woman broke free. Running back inside.

The throng of people dissipated into the night air. Driscoll sat in his automobile—drinking.

TWENTY-THREE

Tallahassee, Friday.

A neighbor woman was the best source. Driscoll always paid his rent on time. Dressed smartly! Didn't work 'nowhere's in particular!'
Harlowe talked to the storeowners where he spent his money.
Brown's Clothing Co. and New Way laundry were paid up.

Sounds like 'shine, Harlowe suspected.
Harlowe found Driscoll at the pool hall.
"You sure don't work no regular job. No one seems to know what you do for a living, but you seem to be making good money."
"Yeah, I guess I'm just smart. Maybe you oughta be smart--"
"Runnin' moonshine?"
"Moonshine? Why, that's crazy."
"What does Ledbetter owe you for?"
The man's fingers went white as he clenched the cuestick.
"Nothin'."
"You gonna cover for 'im, after he's done you the way he has—stealin' your girl?"
"It's not—look, are ya lookin' to get your ears boxed? Why don't you go back to your cowboy county? I'm through talkin' to ya."

Harlowe followed him. Down unlit sidestreets. Along the tracks. By the warehouses. The man turned up a bottle and stuffed it back in his coat.
He stepped into a shadow, cutting through a dirt-floored alley. He looked into a colored pool hall at the bottom of the hill.
He kept going, stumbling down the hill, in the loose dirt.

It's darker than ten-feet-down in the street, Harlowe thought.

Someone might be lurking at the next corner, in one of the black alleys that randomly sliced the warehouse district. Anyone could be hiding in the shadows, the inky abyss that swallowed everything not an armslength in front you. Harlowe knew he could find himself cornered like a rat. He crossed these voids carefully. Even the next one, the unnaturally bright light shining on a Pabst tonic ad painted on the bricks was no comfort, the nooks and crannies, there, a perfect place to hide.

He stepped back into the pitch-darkness. The yellow dot in the distance.
The rumble, as the train grew closer, outlining shanties and clotheslines.
In the flickering light, Harlowe saw Driscoll look back.
Then, saw the latter's shoulders, hat slip into a warehouse.
The train shook it the next instant, while Harlowe dashed to the window.
Saw another man step out of the shadows.
Sackett.
Driscoll handed over an envelope. The two men scattered, back into the darkness.

***

Saturday was when the farmers came to town. Model T's. Mule-drawn wagons. More traffic than you'd see in Apalach when the ballteam played Carrabelle!

Driscoll walked over to the Courthouse.
Harlowe watched from the shadow of an oak in front, behind his newspaper.
The man lit a cigarette, but didn't go in.

A boy approached. "Say, mister, can you tell me where there's a telephone? My mother needs it."
"I believe they have one in the grocery store, theah."
"Thanks, mister."

Harlowe found nothing that tied in with Collis, Whittle, Gibby.
He was hot, his feet hurt from walking the sidewalks.

Harlowe entered the "Tallahassse Café" on Adams. Sat down beside Driscoll at the counter. "Howdy."
He slid the photo of Collis toward the younger man. "You were with him in Chattahoochee. You brought him over heah."
"Never saw him before."
"You're into moonshinin'. Everyone knows it."
"You're crazy."
"I know Collis was getting paid—quite a bit of money."
"Maybe you should get wise to yourself! Before ya get into trouble."
"I'm gonna find out what you owe Ledbetter. I'm patient."
The man flicked his cigarette to the floor and walked out.

Harlowe sat there. Had a cup of coffee.
Moonshine might explain why Collis got cross-ways with these Tallahassee boys, Harlowe reckoned. *But it hardly seemed to tie in to Gibby. The rum-runners, who were landing their crates near Eastpoint at that time, would be a more likely connection. Maybe Gibby saw something he shouldn't have? I can't tie Ledbetter to rumrunners. He was thick-as-thieves with local moonshiners, yes, but not the out-of-town importers bringing in the stuff from Cuba.*

Ledbetter's car sat in front of the Elks Club. Harlowe crossed Monroe— straight for it. Ledbetter politicking from behind the wheel. Harlowe put his foot up on the running board. "Howdy, Bill!"
"Why, Pratt, I did't know you was in town!"
"Yeah, still lookin' into this thing—Collis' sister told me he left her a note...sayin' he tried to reach ya! Did ya know that?"
"Why, no."
"I *sho'* wish he'd gotten hold to ya—this whole thing coulda been resolved!"
Harlowe watched Ledbetter's face. Ledbetter kept his composure, his lip trembling just the slightest bit, his face showing a tinge of red, then blanching.

He recovered quickly. "Pratt, I wish he had, too. I'm sorry you've come all this way and couldn't find no way of helpin' his sister. You lemme know if there's somethin' I can do, hear?"

"I sho' will."

"You a good man, Pratt!"

Funny thing was, Ledbetter didn't know Collis couldn't write. Not one jot. While the High Sheriff had the reputation for a poker face, it seemed that his cards showed just this once.

TWENTY-FOUR

Eastpoint—later that day.

He was back at that intersection. He couldn't help but think of the tire tracks he'd found, right here, the night Gibby went missing.

They led East.

He'd seen them when he first reached the settlement—barely, in the feeble glare of his flashlight. He returned to them after he visited the Birch home. He squatted there in the rain, looking at them. He could still feel the dread he'd felt. Watching the rain wash away all the clues you had. Or ever would have. Like a sucker punch to the belly—no, the feeling in his stomach was worse, like dropping on a large wave in the Gulf, that first big wave you met when a hurricane struck.

The tire tracks—even now—were the only clue he had to the identity of the man.

They run down to Cat Point and come back, headin' East—I thought. The damn rain washed them away before I could get a good look.

He slipped in here. Grabbed Gibby. Then he was gone like a summer squall. I believe he got away up the Sumatra Road.

Harlowe waved to the folks looking out from their doorstoops. He'd stopped in the road, after all. These little houses and hardworking people. Life was harder here—no electricity, nor running water. The roads—except for the new highway—weren't paved like the streets in Apalach. No one had an automobile, here, in '27. Only Egg Brown had got one, since.

There's no way to compare tire tracks but by sight! However, Harlowe had some clues—molded into the tires were the words, "Non Skid." Harlowe saw those letters pressed into the dirt before the raindrops washed them out. Harlowe knew the kind of car they belonged to.

Few cars came through Eastpoint. People would stop and watch it if one came by. Like folks were doing now! If folks heard a car in the middle of the night they got up to see where it was coming! Except that night. It was raining so hard, people hunkered down in their homes. No one saw it!

Even if someone had seen it, it wouldn't have done any good. The tracks were from a Ford. You might as well say you saw a pine tree or a mockingbird! There was a Ford agency in every town in the Southland! A million Model T's were owned below the Mason and Dixon! Nearly all were black!

The tires could fit a truck—Harlowe's had them. Luck was on this fellow's side—rain, darkness, anonymity all doing his bidding.

He'd thought of bootleggers. They had a lot of luck on their side. And no easier to track down than a Model T. Their boats, carrying crates of Carribbean rum, used to slip right in here. They'd come in at Magnolia Bluff or they'd land on the old McCannon place, where it was desolate. Get the crates ashore. Then load a truck and slip away up the Sumatra Road.

Since then, the road to Carrabelle was paved, the Tillie Miller bridge built, and bootleggers landed their booze in the woods near the Crooked River lighthouse. They'd truck liquor directly to a thirsty Capital City, the folks at the State Road Department having made it much more convenient! Harlowe made his presence known a little more in that wild section, and he had some inkling they'd started using a more remote location near Alligator Point, but he didn't kid himself that they'd stopped coming.

The night Gibby disappeared, only a bad, sand-road ran between Eastpoint and the Carrabelle River. Harlowe was sure no one made it very far on it in such weather. He'd followed the tracks. He'd passed the Sumatra Road and headed for McCannon's place on that rough set of ruts, spray whipping up from the Sound.
He'd reached Green Point where Zeb McCannon lived and had his terpentine still and sawmill. From the McCannon homestead on through the old man's land, you could take a Model T as far as the Carrabelle River. It required running on the beach, some. There wasn't a house for miles, out that way.

The tracks stopped—before the lights of the old man's house came into view. It became apparent to Harlowe the Ford hadn't travelled far into McCannon land, and he turned around. There was no bridge to Carrabelle, then. The driver, whomever he was, drove north, up the Sumatra Road!

Harlowe saw no indication that a boat had landed, nor a heavy-laden car had been through. The whole "rum-runner" idea never seemed too plausible. While Harlowe was coming back he stopped to talk to McCannon and his boys who were searching their land. They hadn't seen a trace of an automobile.

Harlowe made it back to Eastpoint in the storm, the rain blowing sideways now. All the Eastpoint menfolk (except Foster Fulton) were searching the pine flatlands for Gibby, beating through the saw palmetto, toting lanterns, hollering into the darkness. They walked the shoreline at Magnolia Bluff. Picked around at the edge of Tate's Hell. Harlowe found some of them, soaked like dogs! All these men were looking in the wrong area. Sheriff Pender needed to send the men and horses North! Someone needed to motor up the Sumatra Road and see if there were more tracks—any sign of the little Ford!

"I'd like to ride up yonder. Look for the Ford. Anything suspicious," he'd suggested. This was taken under advisement by Pender. He was the Sheriff. As dawn broke, Pender asked Harlowe to take the boat around.

Search for Gibby in the water. Harlowe did. Then, Pender asked Harlowe to help canvass the houses.

They walked, together, around Eastpoint. *Any strangers around? No.* Pender seemed to welcome his help.

Harlowe asked, again, about going North. Pender said, no, he'd phone for the sheriff in Liberty County. He said he'd send a man North. He heard Pender call for a dog—from Estiffanulga.

Harlowe told Pender everything he did from the time he arrived in Eastpoint. Asked Pender's permission for everything he did. He didn't want to step on Pender's toes. Harlowe trusted him. Later, Harlowe learned there was no further search. Mr. Twiggs said they didn't do it. And Sheriff Chestang told Harlowe no one called him. Harlowe was mad, now, he didn't go up the road, Pender be damned!

If someone camped up North, any signs of them were lost! Any other time he offered information to Pender, the latter looked at Harlowe as if he was dog-tired and Harlowe was asking him to run a mile! "I'll look into it, Pratt," was his response, spoken with all the energy of ditchwater. He couldn't be bothered.

Aubrey Birch and True stayed out all night. Before Birch lay down to get some rest, Pender asked to use his boat. The storm had passed, leaving a choppy bay, a stiff breeze, a sky too blue and pretty for what had happened the night before. In the breaking dawn, they sailed around Cat Point, toward the ferry landing. That's when Harlowe saw it. Gibby's capsized skiff! But there was no Gibby, not even his hat, nor fishing pole, and not the first suggestion of a clue floating in the water.

Harlowe turned down the road to Cat Point.
Then down to the Birches.
More memories deluged him. That porch was where they'd gathered four years ago. Eastpoint residents descended upon this place as if they sensed in the air that something wasn't right. Neither the porch, nor the front room could hold everyone. And there Harlowe came. Aubrey was beside himself. Fixing to go back out. *"I-I searched the shoreline—with True! Ain't seen hide nor hair o' the boy!"* Harlowe looked in and saw Lillian, Gibby's mother. So small and fragile in that rocking chair, like a baby wearing her papa's coat, she looked much younger than her years, barely older than a child, herself. She rocked, eyes closed, silently praying. She didn't cry. Perhaps she was too shocked to speak. The older women cried out prayers. Shouted hymns. Held Lillian's arms. The wind interrupted with shrieks, shaking that little house. The rain blew sideways across that porch when Harlowe, himself, left to search.

He recalled the looks on their faces when he got back, soaked to his skin. Mr. and Mrs. Birch asked him if he'd found Gibby. He just shook his head. He hadn't found him. The Birches shivered close together on that porch, silent and still, like pale scarecrows in the wind that tugged at their clothing at that inhospitable hour of the morning. It made Harlowe shiver to think of how they looked.

They had questions for him. He didn't have answers.

He had to tell them it looked like someone had taken Gibby. They were bewildered—that was as far out of their comprehension as the River drying up.

"Who could hurt a child?"

"Who coulda done that?"

They searched his eyes.

"Was our son...murdered?"

"Was he?"

Harlowe didn't know. Didn't know what to tell them.

"Pratt, tell me the truth!" pleaded the child's mother.

Harlowe couldn't answer. He removed his hat and stood at 'attention' in front of Mrs. Birch—what you did in the Marines if you didn't know what else to do.

He was ashamed he hadn't sufficient words, ashamed he was dripping water all over the floor of her tiny, but spotless, house.

He tried to be honest with them that morning. And since.

Right now, all those anguished conversations flashed across his mind.

"You ain't never lied to us," Aubrey said once.

"We trust you."

"They're fine people and I hate that—."

His thoughts were interrupted by the door-squeaking. And Lillian Birch coming out.

"Howdy Sheriff! I'm so glad to see ya! Got the coffee on!" she declared, cheerfully. "I heard you comin'! Aubrey's 'round back."

He tipped his hat. "Howdy, Miss Birch! Lookin' forward to a cup of your coffee."

"I sure am glad to see ya!" She smiled. Harlowe could see reflections of Gibby's chin, the dimples which formed when he grinned.

Harlowe started to walk around, but Aubrey was already coming to him.

"Hey, Mister Pratt!"

"Aubrey," Harlowe acknowledged, shaking hands. "We glad you back, Pratt!"

"How'd you do today?"

"Oysters are bad this year. What I sold today was hardly worth gittin' up for. This drought's killin' us! C'mon, lemme showya sump'n!" Birch led him back to the open lean-to, where he was smithing a basket for the oyster tongs he was making. Showed him the work and made conversation the way men do.

"Boy, I'll talk your ear off, if ya let me! I b'lieve the coffee's ready by now. Come on in the house!" said Aubrey.

Harlowe followed, removing his hat before crossing their threshhold.

Mrs. Birch ushered him over to the best chair in the front room—one of two, a combined parlor, kitchen, and dining room. "Coffee is hot—and strong!"

"Sounds good!" said Harlowe.

Lillian touched her husband's arm. She knew he was tired.

"I come in off the water. Repaired a hole in the boat. An' commenced to workin' on them tongs I done showed ya."

Harlowe nodded. "I hear the preacher's prayin' for rain."

Mrs. Birch gave a grin. "I sure hope that preacher's livin' right!"

They all laughed at that.

"You look tired, Pratt," said Mr. Birch, handing him a steaming, tin cup. Harlowe received it, gladly. *I must 'look a sight'—worse than the bum who'd tried to rob me!*

The couple pulled up chairs to face him, eager to hear his report. Harlowe knew they'd appreciate a visit. They were anxious to hear what he'd learned. As usual, he felt he lacked the words, felt no shortage of shame he didn't have the answers they hoped for.

He began with a description of Kern. "No, sir, I aint seen no one like that," the couple agreed.

Same with Driscoll.

The description of Whittle elicited an identical response.

"Whittle *could* have slipped over to Eastpoint. But that's unlikely. I don't think he had anything to do with it. He is a..."

"Yes, Pratt?" asked Mrs. Birch.

"In a way, he's a *victim* of all this—whatever went *own*." Harlowe explained how the man was committed to Chattahoochee.

"That's a shame," said Aubrey.

"I believe I told you I checked on any strangers in Carrabelle."

Birch nodded.

In fact, Harlowe looked into *everyone* who'd come into the county in the days before Gibby disappeared. In Carrabelle, he talked to everyone at the depot and the hotel there. He talked to Wing and the Captain of the other ferry, the *Short Cut*. He questioned men on the commercial vessels and cabin-cruisers. Even passengers who'd come in on the *SS Tarpon*, which ran to Mobile.

Any strangers come through town? Had they seen a man in a Ford who didn't act right? Been to Eastpoint? He'd talked to damn near everyone in the county—from the Ochlockonee to the Gulf line!

Harlowe knew Collis had guidefished for *someone* at Cat Point the day Gibby took missing. Someone had to have seen the man! If he found the client he might have him a witness! One who had to have seen the little skiff Gibby was on and what happened to it. He let Pender know everything he did—Pender would thank him. And left it at that.

"Well, I checked again," Harlowe continued. "No one in Carrabelle remembers Whittle. He'd never leave the train." _So, even now, no one was unaccounted for among the hotel guests and men who'd come through on the G.F.& A. line.

These conversations always turned to Gibby, himself. "He loved bein' on the water," said Mrs. Birch. Their eyes went to the window. You couldn't help but think of Gibby when you looked out there. The Bay at its widest. The gentle rustle of the sawgrass in the breeze. The unspoiled marshland

and creeks and glassy, clear, silvery water that cradled Eastpoint. Harlowe told them how he'd seen Gibby on the bank of Indian Creek, fishing, many a time, the sawgrass taller than he was. "You couldn't hardly keep him away from that creek!" said Mr. Birch.

"We 'preciate all you doin', Mr. Pratt. We know you'll find our boy—or find out what happened to 'im," said Gibby's momma. She meant the words just as she'd said them; but Harlowe couldn't help feel a punch in the belly from the meaning of each of them, from the fact that he *hadn't* done his job and *couldn't* even fathom when he'd get it done.

"You're stayin' for suppah. Don't try to make an excuse, now!" the woman insisted.

***

Harlowe watched the dark shoreline fade away—from the rail of the *Save Time*.

The opposite way beckoned the lights of Apalachicola. The city of lovely old homes and trees and picket fences grew from small glowing orbs to definable buildings on her shore.

A place where there's little crime and people looked out for one another—which made sheriffin' pretty easy. Yet, there's that road.

He thought certain the fellow had come from someplace North. Someone had to have seen him!

He'd talked to folk in all the little settlements on the way back. Talked to the other passengers on that last train Collis rode. He even talked to the agent at the Sumatra station, smallest on the line. The folks just thought Collis was asleep. He didn't appear to be "out-of-sorts."

He'd talked to Mr. Harper again.

"Any strangers ride that day?" he'd asked the conductor.

"No, sir we had nine passengers down. Five up. I knew every damn one of 'em."

"Just like that night?"

"Just like that night, yes. No strangers."

He carried with him so many details of that last day of Collis' life it made his head spin. He even knew what Collis had for his last meal in River Junction. Fifteen cent bowl of soup and coffee at the diner!

For all that, he had *nothing*. He was playing catch-up in everything he did. The killer had a four-year headstart.

Harlowe pulled in to his driveway. Cut the kitchen light on. He leaned the coach gun in the corner. Hung his hat. *Now, where's that cigarette tin?*

He found one in the pantry—empty.

He sighed. *The stores are closed until morning, and—.*

He heard a noise—like a footstep. He eased down the dark hall. That's Claudie's robe hanging from the door. The bathroom he'd kept as she'd left

it, even the pink things she'd picked. *No one's in theah. The window's latched.*
He looked in the shadow. In the bedroom.
Is that her perfume? No, I'm imaginin' things. I'm plumb tired, is all.
He sat on the bed. Then, down the hall, he saw her! Standing there as plainly as that night in '29 when she left the second and final time. *"The boy is dead. You've stopped living! I want to live!"*

Maybe she's right.

***

Harlowe walked up to the Seagos' house. Looked in the screendoor. "Howdy!"
"Come on in, Pratt!" said the jailor.
The man of the house sopped his plate with a biscuit. "Mornin', Pratt!" said Mrs. Seago.
"I took messages while you was away, boss. Got 'em heah."
"Have you eaten, Pratt? I can set a place for you," said Mrs. Seago.
"I sure appreciate that, but I don't mean to put you to all that trouble. I just thought since I was--." He started to mention if any mail came, but Binn anticipated that.
"Over there," said Seago, nodding toward the china cabinet, and grabbing another biscuit.
"It's no trouble, Pratt. We'd be pleased to have ye!" said Mrs. Seago.
Harlowe looked though the letters. *Any reports of missing persons? Yes, one from Attapulgus and one from Blountstown. Neither were children.*

***

Harlowe led in the prisoner, the fellow cussing and hollering.
W. A. Harlowe, is known by "Dubya A." Or, mostly, by *Jeter.*
He's Pratt's brother.
Jeter wasn't the only one to voice complaint. "Now, I have to sleep at the jail! We have a prisoner!" Seago cried.
Jeter worked on the snapper boats at one time. Of late, he occupied himself with one thing only—getting drunk. Skinny as a fence rail, his hands shook like a nervous bride.

Jeter fell to his knees on the dirt floor of the cell, adjacent the bucket that served as the "facilities." He looked about him, the dank, brick walls embedded with the smell of sweat or worse. "Y'lock me up in here, s'filthy place! I'm your brother, dammit!"
Pratt looked at him. "You expectin' a *fine hoe*-tell room? Don't like it, don't break the law."
"Yeah—it sure ain't the *Dixie Sherman!* Y'could at least give a feller a bed!" slurred Jeter.

***

111

Harlowe carried Lexie's pies over on the *Save Time.* They brought her a little cash money.
Harlowe and the boy looked out from the rail.
"Ya like working for Cap'n Wing?"
True nodded.
"I'm glad to hear that son."

They waved to Wing.
The sounds of Sunday morning in Apalach met True's ears. Churchbells. Lovely notes drifting from different directions all at once. People walked to services in their best clothes—neckties, dresses, hats. They talked with neighbors under the oaks at Gorrie Square, at the old Episcopal church. Uptown was tranquil. Streets uncrowded. It was the one day Sheip's whistles were silent.

Sunday afternoons were tranquil; folks relaxed on porches to stay cool, at home with their families. As the sun began to wax, and a peaceful and quiet evening approached, many would get ready to go to evening services.

Others would see the cooler hours come at the ballgame. In fact, half the town turned out to fill the stands at the town's little ballfield.

Harlowe paid True a dime to mow the lawn. Then they took a drive. Dilvered the pies. Enjoyed the tranquility. The stores which lined Market Street were closed Sunday: Gorrie Furniture, the A&P, Buzzett's, and Montgomery's. The city's little brick and wooden stores gave them a sense of pride. A man could buy everything he needed right here. All neighbor-owned.

A little boy in a straw hat, carrying a cane pole and a couple nice "red drum," walked along the awning-covered sidewalk, past Sangaree's barbershop, heading home from an afternoon of fishing. He waved.
"Howdy, Sheriff! Howdy, True!"
They gave a friendly wave back. It was images like that, which carried Harlowe through that time he was far away, at war. They spelled "home" in Harlowe's mind.

Harlowe bought True a meal at the *Riverside.*

They picked up Seago and headed to the ballfield. The line of automobiles started on 12th Street, behind the grandstand, and stretched around Avenue D. Harlowe parked at the end. Houses with porches and sycamores surrounded the field.

They heard the crack of a bat. They smelled the hot dogs. Harlowe thought if he looked under the seats of these automobiles, he'd find the keys to every one. And no one would bother them. No one locked their doors at home, neither. There was an innocence in this place, that he didn't want to lose. The anger rose within him when he thought how someone might steal that from the people here. It made him even madder that maybe he was to blame for letting it happen on his watch.

He pushed that aside. He wanted True to enjoy this, to be a young'un for a few hours. They got their hot dogs from the boy selling concessions in the little booth there. Found room in the stands.

There wasn't a long face in the crowd! Harlowe looked up to see the children smiling and carefree in the top seats of the grandstand. Everyone was on their feet when Apalach hit a home run.
True smiled more than he had in ages. But, when the final score was chalked on the board, it was "them Tallahassee boys" that won.

TWENTY-FIVE

Apalachicola Bay—Monday

Harlowe told True he'd been to River Junction.
"What it was about—was Giib-beh," Harlowe drawled.
"Oh." True realized, for the first time, that the thing that bothered his uncle, was *Gibby's case.*
"Well, that's what I've been a-workin' on. Ain't got much to show for it."
"Is he...dead, Uncle Pratt?"
Harlowe crossed his arm as was his mannerism. Almost looked like he was in pain, but he wasn't. "I'm afaid so, son."
Harlowe explained that Gibby had passed—but hadn't drowned. "I reckon you're old enough to know now—practic'ly bein' my deputy."

True never knew what happened to Gibby. It pleased him that his uncle trusted him. *Told me the truth. Treated me like—well, like a pal.*

They drove to the jobsite. Harlowe had True painting the last bit of trim, the alcove for the telephone in the hall, while Harlowe put on the shutters. True was concentrating hard. "Say, you did a jam up job on that little piece! I won't have to touch that up one whit."
Harlowe's mind wasn't on the work. They hung the light fixtures, True handing them up to Harlowe on the ladder, Harlowe moving like a machine, no feeling.
He had some money due on this house, but when that would arrive was uncertain. Folks weren't always in as much a hurry to pay as they are to have you finish a job!
"Thankya!"
"Lessee if we can finish this mornin'. 'N you and me go fishin'—whaddya think?"
A nod. "Yessir!"

Outside, True picked up around the house. True wiped the sweat away and looked back at it. *She was all done!* Harlowe had described it to him, before they'd started, and now the house looked like something from a magazine. *Just the way he'd said!*

Presently, Harlowe told him he had to go. "Son, go on an' sweep up. I'll be back shortly, hear?"
Harlowe drove away. True worked alone, cleaning, so the house would be ready for the folks to move in.
He swept the dust. Wiped windows. Looked at everything proudly. He was sure the owner would like their new house! Its fireplace, polished floor, and all the care that went into its construction!

Then, True heard something. A strange car! He went to the window to look. To his surprise, the car stopped in front—that yellow roadster!
The lady saw him. "Hello, young man!"
The husband got out. "Is it allright if we come in?"

"We'd like to look at the house one more time!"

They were nearly to the door.

True stood at the threshold, looking up like a finch in a cage. "S-Sure," True replied. Remembering his manners, he palmed his hat. "Yes, ma'am."

"What was your name, sonny?"

"True, ma'am."

"Oh, my it looks so lovely!" she exclaimed, grabbing True on the shoulder as she entered. "Ready to move in!"

The man made a b-line for the row of windows in the living room. "Gee, that view is swell!"

"It sure is." The lady turned back to True. Looked him up and down, noticing the paint smudge on his face. "You're doing this...all by *yourself?*"

"I-I'm just helpin' Uncle Pratt git it ready."

"Cleaning n' painting and all?!" asked the man, putting his arm around the boy.

"Yes'm. I mean, yessir. I he'p 'im. Anythin' what needs done."

At that, a figure appeared at the door, silently.

"Howdy!"

"Oh, hello, Mr. Harlowe!" said the tourist man.

"We're leaving for home now, but we couldn't resist one more look," said the woman. "We stayed far too long, but we so enjoyed your little town!"

"I'm glad to hear that. Y'all drive safe, now."

"Thank you. Goodbye, *True!*" said the woman.

True waved goodbye. Watched the pretty car until he could see it no longer.

***

Harlowe unfurled the sail on his boat. They headed for the flats.

"You can use my new rod 'n reel," he told the boy.

"Really?"

"Sure."

True baited the hook. He hadn't used a storebought pole before, so Harlowe showed him how to cast with it.

Harlowe cast with the other rod. And got nothing. He tried the other side of the boat. No bites. But, it wasn't long before True felt a strong tug.

Harlowe grinned. "Ya got the luck, son!"

True braced himself to hold on. "Give 'im some line. That's it. All right, pull on 'im! You got 'im, son!"

True pulled and pulled. And soon had a big red' flopping in the bottom of the boat!

Harlowe kept looking at the shore, True thought. *But he hasn't said anything.*

They put in. Tied up along the bank of Scipio Creek. A shrimpboat was in. They watched the seagulls in the air, over the dock, the birds happily swooping and trying to make a grab. Their squawks sounded like laughing. "I have a few things to check on and I'll run you home, son."

True nodded.

They got in the truck. Harlowe drove out Avenue E, the main road through town, an avenue of generous porches, oaks, and picket fences. It led to Chapman High School, of which the town was right proud—Harlowe parked at a vacant lot a baseball's throw from the school.

A client wanted to build—if Harlowe could come in under $2500. Harlowe scrawled some figures. *Maybe.*

They drove to the Fuller Hotel at Avenue D and 4th. Spartan Jenkins owned it.

While Jenkins was colored, only whites stayed at his establishment. Of late, the Gibson had superseded it as the town's finest.

Harlowe's boots clopped on the boards of the porch. Jenkins led him down the papered hall. "I'm thinkin' 'bout converting to apartments. You reckon ya could do the job fur-me?"

Harlowe looked up at the peeling paper. Scratched his cheek. "Maybe."

"Boiler ain't workin'. Roof needs patchin'," said Jenkins.

The old man showed Harlowe where the hot water leaked, upstairs.

"It's worse'n I thought! Can ya start today?"

"Well, I can fix the pipes. I might could get to it today."

"Ya got yo helper, I see!"

"Yes, I have."

True looked down, shyly.

Harlowe drove down Water Street.

Backed the truck up to Marks Brokerage.

The tin-sided establishment, at the mouth of the river, sold everything from lumber to groceries.

The man there tallied up the sale. "Got it loaded for ya, Pratt!"

"Thankya."

Harlowe climbed out on the roof to reach the pipes, which ran up the outside of the wooden hotel.

The busted pipe dribbled water all over him as he worked. Yonder at the Gibson, tourists stopped in a Cadillac.

Harlowe trimmed and fitted and finally had the new pipe in, True handing tools out the window as needed. "I think that'll hold her, son!"

Harlowe phoned Tommy's store. Left a message for Lexie. Took True to the *Riverside* for supper. The screendoors and windows were open, letting in the sounds of the arriving train.

And, a moment later, in come Mr. Harper for his coffee break.

"Buy ya a coffee, sheriff?"

"Thankya, Mr. Harper."

TWENTY-SIX

Apalachicola, Tuesday.

Harlowe walked along the picket fence with True, down to Demo George's trawler—she'd be in the water soon. Scipio Creek was an artists' canvas that somehow let his thoughts percolate like the coffee brewing at the *Riverside. The answers are North. Maybe Tallahassee.*

They walked back to the jailhouse. Found it empty. Seago was probably minding the only phone they had. They crossed the "hanging yard" to the courthouse to find him. Climbed the backstairs. Coming here held fascination for True. He could hardly wait! But this time he didn't get to go in the office. An excited Seago met them at the top of the stairs. "Sheriff, you ain't gonna believe what I'm fixin' to tell-ya!" Seago reached out and mussed True's hair. "Hey, boah!"
"All right, what is it?" asked Harlowe.
"It's 'bout Ol' Beadle! Got a telephone call!"
The jailor had Harlowe's attention with that. "Who from?"
"From a gal. Phoned from Atlan'a!"
"She give her name?"
"Nosir. Didn't say who she was. The operator rang, said, *'Atlanta Calling,'* you know how they do. But she didn't say!"
"What was it she wanted to know?"
"She asked one thing. *'Was he hurt?'"*
"That's what she said?"
"Yeah, Pratt—that's it! I reckon she didn't know!"
"Go on."
"I ask her, *'Maybe you'd like to talk to the Shureff?'"*
Harlowe nodded.
"She hung up when I said that."
"She didn't say anything else?"
"Nosir."
"You remember anything else about her?"
"Uh, whacha mean?"
"How she talked? Did she sound old or young? How she spoke?"
"Well...young. An' I could tell she wadnt from 'round here."
"Yeah?"
"Georgie, I am almost pos'tive! I always thought th' gals talk the purtiest up in Georgie! But, hell, that ain't no real detective work, Pratt. Probably don't he'p ya *none*! I mean, the call *come* from Atlanta—you know how many thousands of gals are up there?"
"Well, it's more than I had a quarter hour ago."
"You reckon he had 'im a galfriend up there?" asked Seago.
"Could be."
Harlowe reached for the candlestick phone on the desk. "St. Joseph Telephone exchange—the Chattahoochee switchboard. Yes'm."

Three girls were on duty at their consoles, there, connecting calls. They connected him with their manager, Mr. Surtee. "Oh, it is nice to hear from you, Sheriff Harlowe! My goodness!"

"Good to talk to you too. Johnny, I wonder if you'd check the records of toll calls placed to the sheriff's office. From this morning." Harlowe filled him in on the circumstances.

"Surely. It'll take awhile to trace the connections, of course," the manager explained. They'd trace it from the bigger exchange in Chattahoochee where the Apalachicola wire routed through—and up the line to Atlanta. "That's all right."

"We'll have to call the telephone company in Atlanta. But we'll get started on that in a jiffy."

"I appreciate it."

Harlowe and True went to look at a vacant lot on Prado Street. It had a few scrub oaks on it. Could be had for fifty dollars. "Maybe the next one we build." Harlowe patted True on the shoulder. "Sure couldn't do it without you, son."

Harlowe could see how the house would look on the lot. Described it to True. True tried to picture it, and could, Harlowe described it so well. Harlowe drove down to the depot, then. He handed a letter to the postman on the train. He'd written a letter to the Attorney General about Old Man Whittle's case.

Men leaned out of Sangaree's barbershop, greeting Harlowe as he walked up the street, checking the locks. "Howdy, Mr. Pratt!"

"Howdy, boys."

"Hello, True, whachya doin', boy!"

Harlowe chatted with the fellas a moment. Then walked on. They saw men leave out of work to go practice with the ballteam.

Up the street, Harlowe treated True to a meal at the *Riverside*—for a job well done on the house.

Mr. Surtee phoned back that evening. "I checked with Southern Bell. The toll call came from a public telephone in Castleberry Hill. Station-to-station. She paid the toll and didn't give her name."

Harlowe thanked him. *A payphone. Damn.*

***

In the morning, Harlowe drove to the State Hospital to see Whittle again. He'd set the appointment with the superintendent.

As he drove up to the ward, he came upon the orderlies. Four of them marching past. Carrying a pine box. The men continued marching toward a truck.

He didn't have to ask who the man was. But he found Elston, who had examined the decedent. The Doctor was confident that Whittle had died of natural causes—old age, complications from malaria.

TWENTY-SEVEN

Apalachicola, Thursday.

The Greek served the best coffee in town. A cup of Joe at the *Riverside,* the warmth and contentment it provided, was the one luxury Harlowe indulged, besides his Chesterfields. He sat there, looking out over the waterfront, thinking.

Someone scared Collis—and lured him back at the same time. Perhaps the clues were in Georgia, where Collis had resided in the four years that followed his departure from Eastpoint. Maybe he'd told someone his troubles, how he'd come into money—apparently to secure his loyalty. The key to this could be to find the woman who telephoned. A man told things to his girl.

If he found the man Collis was scared of, he'd find Gibby's killer.

The whistle hooted at Sheip's. The town's largest employer, it remained. Yet uncertainty hung in the air over the smell of bakery and coffee. The mill was down to cutting cigar boxes, the cypress boom over, the giant trees gone, the big skidder and tugboats silent.

Foss Fulton had made the change well—he'd bossed the cypress crews and their two-man saws and now he was foreman at Green Point, cutting pineboard. He'd always been able to thrive. Harlowe wondered if the rest of the town could dust themselves off so easily if times got worse.

***

Brewer looked out the window. People gathered around the courthouse, talking, as was common in the rural South.
"He's so damned quiet. I never know what he's thinking," said Deputy Brewer.
Seago nodded to the door. Those soft footsteps were given away only by the creaks of the old courthouse. And, presently, Harlowe stood in the doorway.
"Mornin', Pratt!" exclaimed Brewer.
"I'll be gone for a couple days. C.A. will know how to reach me."
"Sure, Pratt!" acknowledged the deputy.

The latter left. Harlowe went through the mail.
He recognized Seago's footsteps up the staircase.
"What's that, C.A.?"
"I run into Foss. He had Little Foss with 'im. Said, 'this's my littlest alligator!' Jus' as proud as he can be. He'd *tickle* that boy! Git him to laughin'! I tell ya its nice to see a deddy like 'at! The way he'd go on—said

the li'l feller'l 'throw a football like 'is old man.' It kinda tickled me! You don't always see that."
"No. You don't."

Harlowe headed "uptown." The churchbells were ringing—it was noon. The packers, on break from the canning factories, smoked cigarettes and laughed.

Harlowe proceeded to the bank at Avenue E and Commerce, where he cashed the check for the house. The owner was pleased with it. Now, Harlwoe had his trainfare.

He wore his good coat and a short, western bow tie. Walked to the depot. The timetable was written in chalk—each entry lined through and updates scrawled above. Harlowe chuckled. It would be a shock if the train *was* on time!
He waited outside where it was cooler.
Presently, the evening train backed in, hissing and catching her breath. "All aboard for...Beverley...Fort Gadsden...Sumatra...Vilas...Telogia...Hosford...Greensboro!" cried Harper. He'd called those names so many times it sounded like he was talking in his sleep.

Harlowe felt the train jolt forward. They rolled, at a walking pace, up Water Street. Passing his house. The outskirts of town. And woods. A puff of air teased at the windows, now, as they clicked along over the river on the iron bridge, gathering speed. The sun settled, behind them, the water reflecting its silvery hues, the tips of the sawgrass glistening, as the train proceeded over the trestles through pretty low country.
Whistle crying, they made the Sumatra Highway crossing. From there, the tracks cut North to parallel the road up through Tate's Hell.

Harlowe stretched out on the hard wooden pew. The CLICK-CLICK-BANG of the cars was just fast enough to generate a breeze. A wiff of "lighter knots" (what the engine burned), mixed with the smell of hot oil, creosote, and the pines, drifted in the open windows. Harper lit the coal-oil lamps, one-by-one down the car, the yellow light slowly reaching back to Harlowe.

The little train made frequent stops. Some weren't on the map. Like "Brickyard," where the train halted in the woods and a married couple hopped down with their box of groceries. Layne didn't even blow the whistle; he let off those folks, and the train strained forward again. For many, the train was the only way to get to town—the main shopping center in the southern Apalachicola River Valley.

They crossed the Liberty line and soon reached Sumatra station. Harper admonished, "Ladies don't forget your packages, umbrellas, and babies, cause the train leaves promptly!"
(It really didn't).
Freight had to be loaded. The train replenished the water and lighter knots exhausted on the run from Apalach.

Harper got the "high sign" from Layne and snapped his watch shut. Made one last check. Repeated his announcement—one call shorter!

The train bumped forward. And proceeded up the lonely track. Harlowe stood on the platform for more air, rolling along that endless sea of pines. Occasionally he'd spot cattle in the saw palmettos, or a farmer tending melons in the field.

Hosford was a short "whistle stop" like the others. "All aboard for Lowry. Millman—Elmira—Sedalia—Juniper—Greensboro—Hardaway—River Junction—and-points-north!" cried Harper. Up through the dark pines, on the persistent grade. Stopping and climbing. Stopping and climbing. Harlowe listened to that whistle howl, the diminuitive engine panting like a horse on a hard run.

"You mind if I ride in the cab a spell?" Harlowe asked, while they waited in Sedalia.
"Hell, you don't even have to ask," replied the "runner." The engineer and fireman, Robert, liked having Harlowe in the cab. Helped pass the time. Harlowe grabbed onto the rails and climbed up. Layne gave the throttle a shove and the fireman rolled dice against the side of the cab.

Harlowe asked of Layne's wife, how she was getting on. But that was as far as the small talk went. Layne knew the sheriff wasn't a talker.

Harlowe felt the heat from the fire. He was sweating. They all were. Harlowe watched Robert open the butterfly doors, feeding more roots to the glowing-hot amber mass at the bottom of the firebox. He fed another lighter knot. Then another. Like feeding some fiery beast. The pressure of steam is what turns that dial, forces those pistons, pulses through the iron plate. The machine shook, breathed, had to be cared for like a living thing, and
Harlowe could see both men enjoyed what they were doing. Layne turned to Harlowe. "Nothin' else I'd wanna do, Pratt. Lookin' out at thsee farms, all this the open country—seein' things mos' people nevuh git to see."

Harper's rote announcement got shorter, the ground higher. *Greensboro! Hardaway!* They enjoyed the clean scent of the pines, up that narrow cut through the woods, up to the high places near Chattahoochee, down again to River Junction.

"That's the Georgie line!" Layne declared. Rolling hills and lonely pines lay before them. Harlowe listened to the two men, enjoying the feeling and the smell of the old train.

Collis sure acted suspiciously. Harlowe's mind went over it. Couldn't help it. Collis' paying his tab at the Nichols Store was the fly in the buttermilk! *"Done paid his bill in full. Which he ain't never done before, not once in his life,"* said the storeclerk. In fact, Collis never had more than a sawbuck at any one time and now he was settling up in cash money! He'd come into this windfall merely weeks after Gibby went missing. The same was true of

Collis' tab at Marks Brokerage. *"He done paid me. Everything. I scarcely woulda believed it,"* the man told Harlowe. Collis' past-due rent was satisfied too. *"The boy paid in cash money—and in full!"*
Within days of clearing his accounts, Collis left town without even saying goodbye to his sister!

They descended a ridge—lovely and dark with pines—as the track descended toward the Flint. But after a few miles, the next ridge appeared. Robert began feeding more lighter knots, the heat more brutal and breezeless as the train labored on the grade—*to Climax station!*

TWENTY-EIGHT

Climax, Georgia—later that evening.

From Climax the railroads ran to nearly any other town you'd want to go to in the State of Georgia.

The Moultrie ballteam waited at the station there—on their way to Apalach.
"Howdy, boys," said Harlowe, as he entered the waiting room.
"How do, Mr. Harlowe?" Most of them knew Harlowe and, good-naturedly told him what they thought the results would be tomorrow afternoon.
Harlowe looked over at the timetable. He'd phoned the A.C.L. agent before he'd left home. *"C.R. Hutto arrived on the 12:32 from Thomasville, by way of a connecting fare from Albany,"* the man had told him.
Harlowe approached the agent's window. Purchased a ticket to Atlanta.
Harlowe showed him Collis' photograph. "Oh, yes. Was it you I spoke to the other day?"
Harlowe nodded.
"I'm sorry, but nothing stands out. He was by himself when I seen him. That's about all I can tell ya."
"Was he totin' anything with 'im?"
"No. No bag."
"He have a package, a bundle?"
"I wanna think he was clutchin' a paper bag."
"Oh?"
"No. It was a thing—about so big—wrapped in newspaper."
"Could you tell what it was?"
"It was just a bundle. About this size!" The man indicated something skull-size.
"Did he say where he was headed, what his business was?"
"No, sir."
"Anything about Eastpoint?"
"Nope. 'Fraid not."
Harlowe thanked the man. Said goodbye to the ballplayers. They had a bit of a wait for their train. Harlowe's was pulling in now!

***

Rolling along through farmland at last relieved of the scorching sun, they neared Thomasville, a lovely town where the A.C.L. had a busy station. Harlowe looked around town while he waited, walking up to Broad Street. Downtown was still, at this hour, and he walked along that avenue of department stores, office buildings, movie houses, alone. He returned to see the man throw the switch for the train to continue up to Moultrie.

2:30 a.m. While the others slept, he looked out the window. Over endless cotton fields. The lonesome whistle mourning over the crops and hills—the suffocating heat, the looming shadow of Boll Weevil. The humid night air, touched with the smell of cotton, puffed in the window. Harlowe was grateful for the breeze. Out there, the stagnant humidity mercilessly beset a section ravaged by drought. The mugginess, with sweat dampening necks and brows, cruelly *teased* the men and women and kids toiling in it, now trying to sleep in it—without yielding a drop of rain. He looked out at the darkness, the occasional outline of a house. Before the sun came up, families would be working those fields, even little children hand-pulling weeds. And they'd be hand-picking what surivived this drought, come September. The Depression had hit hard in the Southland.

***

The train crossed the Flint's iron bridge, and pulled in to the Albany station. The cotton town was the last place Collis was known to have spent some time. *He has kin, here.* Harlowe could smell the change in the land. While further north, it was *lower in elevation*, and remained unkindly hot.

He asked the ticket agent, "Have you seen this fella come through here?" Harlowe held up the photo at the ticket window.
"Yessir. I think so. Been a couple weeks, if I ain't mistaken?"
"That's right."
"I didn't talk to him. I b'lieve Elmer did. Elmer, would you mind?"
The man stepped over. "Yessir?"
Harlowe showed him the photo.
"Why, sure—Beadle Hutto! He's kin to my wife. He wanted to play cards while he waited on the train." The man laughed. "Had a good bit of money."
"Oh?"
"Yessir. Twenty dollars, as a matter of fact!"
Harlowe didn't say anything, he was a little surprised the boy had that much. But given the three-buck room and the other details, he'd apparently gotten used to living it up.
"Expecting to come into some more in a day or two."
"He said that?"
"He did. Talked kinda nervous. Talked a lot. You know how it is."
"Uh-huh. Did he say where this money would come from?"
"No, sir, he didn't."
"Was he alone?"
"Yessir. I seen him settin' in the waiting room for a good spell. I sure didn't watch him the whole time he was here. But he was alone, hat down like he was sleepin.'"

Harlowe napped on the grass, by the river, a block from the station. He slept until the sun came up and the fleeting coolness of the early morning began to recede. He had breakfast. Asked the usual questions in the usual places. But he found no one who interacted with Collis. A few *knew of him,* from his kin. But no one remembered *seeing him* last week. He apparently made a bee-line for the depot and there he sat. *He must have rode the train out of Atlanta, or hitchhiked west.*

Harlowe walked to Collis' aunt's little bungalow on Whitney Avenue, a half-mile from the river. Collis' cousins and other kinfolk, had stopped by. All of them were willing to help.

Aunt Tessa told him, "I was unable to attend to the funeral. I was feelin' poorly. I had what you call heat stroke. I like to died if my son hadn't found me—out here in these flowers. I thought I'd be all right in the shade, theah. As much as I don't like to admit it I'm not a young girl anymore!"

"I'm glad you're better now. You look good!" said Harlowe.

"Well, I'm doin much better."

She asked to see the photo of Collis. "Oh, yes—Beadle! He was such a sweet little boy! I used to keep him. For a brief time after his daddy passed, before his mother wed Mr. Hutto. Oh, he could be mischievous, now! But he was a good boy, then."

"Was Beadle in trouble?" asked one of his cousins.

Harlowe explained the situation.

"Seemed he had somethin' on his mind," the old woman believed. "I didn't pry. We reckoned it was trouble with the law. But *you're* the law, so I reckon you'd know."

"No, ma'am, he was in no trouble with me the last year or so. He was—."

"You can say it, Sheriff, we know he could be orn'ry! We still claimed him—but just barely!" They laughed at that.

"Well, he wasn't wanted for anything, far as I know."

"That's good," said Aunt Tessa. "I'd like to help you, Sheriff. I hear from my niece that you good people. But none of us know much. Beadle was kin to us, but he he wrote so seldom. He wrote his sister more, I'm assumin.' He didn't stop by the last time he was here. I heard from Elmer, down at the depot, he came through this way."

Harlowe nodded. "Would you happen to know where he was stayin' in Atlanta?"

"No, sir, I don't know where he was livin' in Atlanta."

"Yes, ma'am."

She thought about it some and recalled something. "Oh, that's not true, now. He lived in one place by a cotton mill. I suggested he try to find work theah. But Beadle was funny. He was interested in the pool halls, not work." The woman grinned a little, then shook her head. "He was such a carefree boy, comin' up. You couldn't git mad at 'im, he was such a joy then. But the boy would not hold a job!"

Harlowe nodded.

"None of us ever met his wife. I do have a lettuh she mailed. Sarah, could you bring that lettuh—in the top drawer of my *bue-row?*"

Didn't realize Collis was married, thought Harlowe.

The girl brought the envelope, sure enough.

"Yes, right theah!" said the old woman. "Decatur Street, as you can see. He moved theah—later *own,"* Aunt Tessa explained.

Harlowe had coffee with them—and they obliged him to stay for dinner. Hearing he had a long wait until the next tain come through, Tessa told him, "You're welcome to wait with us."

"I appreciate it," said Harlowe.

He visited with them a spell, listening to her sons talk about how low cotton had fallen, the hardships the young parents were bearing up under,

125

the weddings of cousins and friends. Presently, he thanked Aunt Tessa for the hospitality and returned to the station. He still had a bit of a wait. He sat along the riverbank until he heard the whistle blow.

He fell asleep soon after the train began rolling. But his nap didn't last long. He was restless. Gazed at the faces of people in the fields, in little towns.

The same bug had hit this area, sending cotton through the floor and bringing the hurt, emptiness to the eyes of the people he passed. It couldn't have been much worse when Sherman marched through this section, Harlowe reckoned. Finally, Atlanta's palatial Terminal Station loomed down the tracks.

TWENTY-NINE

Atlanta, Friday.

"He was a nice feller," said the man, just before he sank the eleven ball in the corner pocket. His pool player's name was Emory. He'd just told Harlowe he recognized Collis!

"Yeah, Beadle was right friendly," said the other fellow, Tom, who'd just lost a penny.

"He come here often?"

"Shoot, couldn't hardly keep him away from here! He's a good pool playuh, now! Took me and Tom, here, many times." The long roll of a cue ball at the next table made both men turn to look. "Ol' Jimmy's fixin' to do without lunch tomorruh."

"We all work at the mill," explained Emory. The pool hall was in the shadow of that cotton mill, in a part of Atlanta that had come to be known as "Cabbagetown" (Harlowe heard a truck overturned, spilling a load of cabbages—and the name stuck).

"When was the last time you saw Beadle?"

"Couple weeks ago," replied Emory.

"Did he mention goin' back to Florida?"

"Nosir," both men agreed.

"Did he ever talk about his business, how he made his money?"

"He mentioned goin' to Tallahassee, now," said Tom.

"A few times," added Emory.

"Did he say the reason for those trips?"

Emory took another shot and missed. "No, nothing about the business he was on, nosir."

"He'd have a little money when he come back. That's all I know," said Tom.

"Did it seem like something was botherin' him?"

"Ya mean *ailin'* him? Don't recall he *evuh* took sick—that whachya mean?"

"That—or somethin' weighin' on his mind."

"Nosir. Not that I could tell."

"Did Beadle live around here?"

"Yessir. Not more than three blocks from here." The man told Harlowe the address. "He didn't stay there long. He got 'im a bigger place, I understand. But he kept comin' around here."

"Would you know where he moved?"

"Nosir."

"Did he have a gal, would you know?"

"Oh, he had a gal. I never saw her. Did you, Tom?"

"Nah."

They'd been very helpful. But now Tom was getting anxious to resume serious play. "Well, I appreciate it, boys. So long."

"Yessir, goodbye!"

"Good luck!"

With narrow streets, and the entirety constructed to a miser's standard, "Cabbagetown" was a 'mill town,' a city-within-a-city, with everything that came with such places, including the 'company store' with puffed-up

127

prices. Company-owned "shotgun" houses surrounded the mill, inhabited by poor whites who'd moved down from the mountains to find work. Everyone here worked at the mill, even children. A block beyond on Tye Street, Harlowe found the shotgun Collis had rented, near a little independent store, and in eyeshot of the mill's brick smokestacks.

He knocked. A man answered. "Yessir, I jus' got home from work. I rent this place now."

Harlowe showed the photo.

"Sure. Met him once—the fella you're speakin' of. He come back for somethin' he'd left here."

"Yessir."

"Is this boy—Young Collis Hutto I mean—in some kind o' trouble?"

"He passed two weeks ago, on the ride down."

"Oh, I am sorry to hear that. I know nothing about him, really. Not his business or anything. I work at the mill. Don't know what he done for a living."

"You recall what he left behind? What he come back for?"

"It was some bundle he had up in the rafters. I really haven't any idea. I had no idea there was anything up there. It stuck my wife and me as mighty peculiar. But he fetched it and away he went."

The fellow that let the house also ran the little corner store. The Italian man was in an apron, cooking. "Oh, the wife, she was a-pretty. A-Longa red hair!"

"Did they leave a forwarding address?" Harlowe asked him.

"Do they ever?"

***

Harlowe rode the Decatur line's green-and-yellow trolley out to Collis' last known address, which Aunt Tessa had provided. It was hot on the streetcar. People standing shoulder-to-shoulder. It clicked along streets and past houses he didn't recognize. There were few automobiles—more people were walking or taking streetcars home. The feeling of hard times blustered about them. The smell of tobacco and sweat. People pressed together, hats over their eyes, papers rolled up in clenched fists. *All these faces. Might one of these people know Collis? Sitting next to me on the streetcar? Shuffling by in the crowd?*

He located the rooming house. Rapped on the screendoor.

A woman's voice came from inside. "I've nothing for panhandlers!"

"No, ma'am." Harlowe took off his hat. "My name's Pratt Harlowe. I'm from Franklin County. The sheriff theah. I was wonderin' if you could he'p me."

She stepped over to the screendoor—she must have been six-feet-tall and had to bend down to see him. "Well, I can't see how. What's it about?"

"Collis Hutto."

Her hand went to her hip. "What's he done *now?*"

"He passed Saturdee night, two weeks ago."

"Hell, I hadn't heard that. Come on in outta the sun. Hurry, now, don't let the flies in!"

"Yes'm." He wiped his feet and minded the screendoor.

"Have you a seat, theah—not that one! That's where I sit."

Harlowe folded himself into the little chair next to the old upright piano.

"When's the last time you saw him?"

The woman took a chaw from a tin on the table beside her. "Why, he hasn't been here in six months. Owe's me a week's rent. You don't think I kilt that fool do ya? Is that what this is about?"

"No, ma'am. *He* wasn't murdered."

"Well, you look like trouble—y'sure you ain't a bounty hunter?"

"No, ma'am. Sheriff, down in Franklin County."

"I heard ya the first time. But how do I know that?"

He showed her his appointment letter, signed by the county commission.

"Hmmph. Well, if that portly little feller wasn't kilt, who was?"

Harlowe explained about Gibby. She softened some.

"I'm gonna tell ya somethin', son, on account 'o that youngun. Otherwise, I wouldn't care to tell you or nobody else. But that fat boy acted strangely— it was something to do with Tallahassee and a man theah. Don't ask me who, or what, 'cause I don't know."

"Wouldya know if his wife his still around?"

"If I knew that do ya think I'd just give up on the money he owes me? Don't know where that heifer is—now. She never lay her head here too often."

"What did she look like?

The old woman spit. "A hussy. Red-haired an' not too friendly."

Harlowe talked to the neighbors who rented rooms in the house.

The landlady knocked on the door, across from Collis' room. Introduced Harlowe. He showed Collis's photo. "I'm just lookin' for some information—about where he moved to, where his wife might be. I wonder if you might he'p me."

"I'll try," replied the woman. "I didn't know them well. Mr. Hutto was friendly. But I only saw his wife come out at night."

"Would you know where they moved?"

"Nosir, I haven't any *i*-dea."

"Well, much obliged."

Collis' other neighbor was agent-telegrapher for the railroad. "He was an odd one. Nervous," he told Harlowe. "I Thought he was runnin' from something. Trying to stay one step ahead of the sheriff—uh, well you know what I mean."

Harlowe grinned.

"Or maybe just a little touched," added the landlady.

"Never saw his wife," the man stated.

***

Harlowe tried the nearest pool hall. Damned if they didn't know Collis— *well!* He hadn't been around in three weeks.

He climbed on the streetcar. It jangled and shook him, the other people pressed in there with him until they'd reached downtown, the streets brash with Model T horns, growling trucks, clattering delivery wagons at the end of "rush hour." Signs, billboards splashed color over the bricks and pavement. On Peachtree Street there were more people than all of Franklin County!

He hopped down. Walked until he found the Acme Pool Room. It had gone bust. But billiard halls were hardly a dying species. He walked into three more, the taste of sweat and cigarette smoke worse from one-to-the-next. The heat from the sidewalks and streets baked him like a loaf of bread, the clamor of the railyard pounded in his ears.

He walked a city seemingly infinite in breadth when one was afoot. More unfamiliar streets contained still more pool halls. He'd walk toward the blare of hillbillly music and go in. He found plenty of talk. But they'd shake their heads, apologetically, when he showed the photo. He'd walk out, the din fading as he walked along the sidewalk, only to be replaced by the first notes of the joint down the block. He could almost close his eyes and follow the guitar-picking—Jimmie Rodgers or Carter Family—and the boisterous laughter pouring from the open doors of the next dive. Collis was known by sight in the gambling dens and brothels fronting Decatur Street. But giving out information wasn't the reason those places existed.

One last pool hall and he'd quit. The place seemed to lean—as if it, like its patrons, was 'tight.' The door gaped open. He looked in at the sawdust floor. The darkness. Heard two men cussing in the corner.
He was thirsty enough, tired enough to ask for a real drink. The men got quiet when he walked in—and he was sure Coca-Cola wasn't the strongest thing they served. A woman, who was a little tipsy, sat in the corner while a man with sleepy eyes racked 'em up at the one pool table they had in there. The woman smiled a slanted smile at him. He struck up a conversation. "Yeah. I know Missus Hutto. Used to see her 'round."
"Know where I can reach her?"
The woman didn't answer.
"Have you any idea where she is now?"
The woman rambled about something. "What they had there...ya ask me and I tell-ya...ya ask me...I tell-ya they moved."
"Yes, ma'am, I know that, but have you any idea where I might locate her—Mrs. Hutto?"
"Ya'know somethin'—I like talkin' to'ya."
"Yes, ma'am. I believe you can help me—I asked you about Collis Hutto?"
"Yeah. He's nice. He tol' us he went by a nickname—uh, Beadle, ya know—ever since he was a kid. Tol' us he'd fished 'bout ev'ry creek in your F'anklin Coun'y. Other'n that, he didn't say much—not 'bout hisself."
"You knew Mrs. Hutto—you knew her name, her Christian name?"
"Church. Ya, I go t' church sometimes."
"I'm askin' about Mrs. Hutto. Have you any idea where she's gone?"
"Right here in *A'lanta*. Had him a li'l money. He ask me an' I say, move, get some nice fresh air. But she wouldn't go."
"How's that? Do you know where in Atlanta?"

"Uh-uh. Say ya wouldn't have a bottle, would-ya?"

Back downtown on the streetcar. The sidewalks still teeming. The men on the streetcorner discussed what was on their minds and on the frontpage of the paper. "President Hoover said..." "That drought relief bill..." "If he don't help soon, I don't know what we gonna do!"

The setting sun turned the sky a burning orange, brushing the buildings with a furnace-like glow. As far as his eye could see stretched the city which rose like a flower from the ash after the Yankees burned her.
He hopped down at the stop, walked the rest of the way to the phonebooth in Castleberry Hill.
He talked to the storekeepers near there. He hoped to get a description of the woman who made the call. But no one saw her! It was a busy morning and no one paid attention to the anonymous woman in the phonebooth.

It was dark now. His feet burned.

At an hour where all would be *still* back home, lights glowed far above the street in the windows of tall buildings, headlight dots of automobiles streamed past. The all-night drugstore yet served to a crowded counter. At one instant, a man in a top hat passed him, hurrying to a party. A bum with the shakes scraped by on cardboard soles the next, his eyes despairing whether he should grab the cigarette butt the rich man discarded or pass it by. Harlowe took it all in, an invisible observer.
He found a buck-fifty room. Waited his turn for the bathtub. Windows open to the hot, persistent sounds of traffic, finally he found sleep.

THIRTY

It's a ways away. But I've got to go!
The man at Rich's Department Store remembered Collis. Told Harlowe what street he'd lived on. Forrest Avenue, in Riverside—near the Chattahoochee.
He downed a coffee and eggs. Hopped on the streetcar. Then another, which travelled up Bellwood Avenue. Harlowe got off at the end of the line. Walked, asked questions, until he'd found the house, a framed cottage, spotless white with a well-kept lawn, a "For Rent" sign staked near the walkway. Dahlias in boxes washed the porch in color. *Collis must have had his little windfall comin' in when he let this place.*
A lady emerged from nextdoor. "No one's home there, mister!"
Harlowe nodded.
"Landlady lives down yonder! That white house."
"Much obliged."
He knocked on the screendoor. "Yes, we own the house. I'm-I'm Bernice Mosby. My husband normally handles letting the houses, but..." She wore an apron, her hands were dusted with flour. Harlowe recognized her. *The 'tourist lady' he'd met on the* Save Time! *Mrs. Mosby and her husband were in Apalachicola at the same time Collis was travellin' on the train. What are the odds of that?*

Harlowe removed his hat. "Well, I'm not here to let a house, exactly. I don't know if you recall, you met me and my little helper on the ferry—and at the house the other day?"
"Why, yes! Of course! What brings you all this way?"
Her expression? Puzzled, Harlowe thought. "Well, I'm looking for some information. I'm the sheriff in Franklin County and—."
"I didn't know you were sheriff."
"Well...I reckon someone had to be. I was the only one wasn't smart enough to turn it down."
She laughed. "Oh, please come in out of the sun! It's hotter than blue blazes!" She took his hat. Led him to the wicker chairs on the porch. "I'll bring us some lemonade!"
"Thankya."
"Won't be a minute," she said, going back inside.
She returned, presently, with a cool glass.
"I know you're probably tryin' to get a pie in the oven, so I won't take up too much of your time. Reason I'm here, Miss Mosby, is about one of your tenants, Collis Hutto."
"Oh, yes, poor man. He's had a string of bad luck, hasn't he?"
"He passed. Two weeks ago."
"Oh, no! He was a nice fella. He was always on time with his rent-money."
"Why did he leave, ma'am?"
"He said he couldn't afford it, had to find a smaller place. That his money had run out."
"And when did he move out?"

"About two months back."

"Was he travellin' back to Florida, at all, while he was livin' here?"

"Not that I know of."

"Did he ever mention anything in Tallahassee—some business theah?"

"No, sir."

"Anything about that *bad luck*?"

"Well, just about the money troubles, is all."

"Did he have a job he went to regular?"

"He went out during the day. Wore a suit. I thought he may have worked in an office, but he never let on what it was that he did. Neither did his wife. She just spent what he made. Flittered off to Decatur Street every chance she could. That's a whole other story and I hate to bore you with gossip!"

Harlowe grinned. "Mrs. Hutto liked to get out—get out and have her a 'big time', eh?"

"Oh, yes! As long as Mr. Hutto could afford it. They were quiet tenants, otherwise, so I didn't question it. I don't like to be one of 'those' landladies."

"Yes, ma'am. When was the last time you saw Mr. Hutto?"

"Well, he came to pick up some of his things about the time we were leaving to go to Florida."

"Was that on a Tuesdee?"

"Yes, come to think of it, we left the next morning. Motored to Tallahassee. Made Apalachicola that Saturday, of course."

"Did he have business in Florida at that time, would you know?"

"If he had, he didn't mention it."

"Was Collis carrying anything with him, when you saw him?"

"Why, no."

"How did he seem that last time you saw him?"

"Like he'd been drinking. And I told him get his things and move along."

"What were the items?"

"Just some old papers and things. I haven't any idea what they were."

"Did he seem scared?"

"No. Just a tad inebriated—and he had one thing on his mind was getting these papers and things. If you've ever dealt with drunks, you know how they get fixated on one thing." Mrs. Mosby shook her head. "Better to just humor them."

"Yes, ma'am. Did he say where he was going?"

"I believe he mentioned moving to a place downtown. I don't recall where."

"Can you tell me about his wife?"

"You've never seen her?"

"No, ma'am."

"You'd remember if you had. She has lovely red hair, rather tall, and slender, quite striking, actually. But—I hate to say this—a little cheap."

Harlowe nodded. "Evuh say where she was from?"

"No, she didn't. Further south, I thought, just from how she spoke."

"She never mentioned her home, her folks?"

"Gee, I dont know. It's possible she came from Valdosta. Waycross. The way she spoke. She mentioned coming up on a farm—I can't tell you anything specific."

"Yes, ma'am. Is there anything else you can recall, Miss Mosby?"

"You know, Collis had a friend that would come by and see him. I have his name somewhere. I can get it for you. I'll be right back." She left to find it.

She returned with an address book. "It was a Mr. Rowe. I've his address there. Collis wanted us to have it."

"Did he say why?"

"Umm. No, he didn't. It seems a little funny now, doesn't it? Like maybe he knew..."

Harlowe nodded. "Maybe."

"Would you care for some coffee, Mr. Harlowe? It's no trouble to make some."

"Oh, no thankya, ma'am. I have to be goin'."

"How's your son? His name was, Ter—."

"True—my nephew. He's fine—he's a fine boy. Best partner I've evuh had in the buildin' bidness."

"Your town's about the friendliest I ever did see!"

"Well, I appreciate that."

"One last thing, Sheriff..."

"Yes, ma'am?"

"How'd you know it was a pie?"

"I saw the flour. The green from the key-lime."

"Oh!"

He stood. "Evuh in Apalach again come by and see me, hear?"

"Thank you, sheriff. I hope I've helped you some."

"Yes, ma'am, you sure have. I thankya very kindly for the lemonade."

She waved. The door shut. He looked back—she's a nice woman, the kind that made a nice home for a man. It sure was peculiar that they'd be in Apalach on that Saturday! But sometimes you got odd coincidences. And had to live with them. *She's tellin' the truth. I wonder what the papers were? Collis' had none on 'im. Only that damn little scrap!*

***

A filling station near the railyards. "I'll try to talk up—over that racket! I heard 'im say he was fixin' to move back downtown!" declared the attendant. "He liked the night life!"

Harlowe nodded. He could understand it. *Collis was a young fella.*

The man leaned in close, hollering over the metal grinder. "Yeah, my bossman knew 'im too! He'd come in here all the time, lookin' at the car my boss was tryin' to sell! Looks like he's finished now, so you can talk to 'im!"

"I'll do that. Much obliged!"

Harlowe approached the owner, who had just finished the valve grind. Harlowe stated his business. "Yeah, I heard he's dead," said the garage owner. "I could see that coming."

"How's that?"

"Just a minute." He turned to yell at the attendant. "Don't forget the windshield, Dewey! I told ya that! Now, where was I?"

"About Collis."

"Yessir. He gambled, an' drank, kept company with women of loose morals, vices of which I don't approve."

"Is that all?"

"He was going downhill! Out of breath just to walk down to the road to get his mail!"

"He get much mail?"

"That's just a figure of speech. I don't believe he received many letters. Maybe from his sister's all."

"Did he travel much while he lived here?"

"He mentioned catching the train a couple times—to Tallahassee."

"Did he say why?"

"No, sir."

"Did he seem scared to go back."

"I don't think so." The man smirked a little at that.

"Yessir?"

"Well, I don't see him bein' scared or worried none! He never did hold a job, up here, far as I could tell! He sorta floated from place to place. Bummed around. What the hell did he have to be worried about?"

***

Harlowe sought Collis' buddy in one flophouse after another. Each one was worse than the next: The smell of rats. The feeling of creeping things behind the walls, unseen. After walking, it seemed, the whole of Atlanta, he knew he'd struck out.

THIRTY-ONE

Atlanta, Sunday.

The Huttos' next residence wasn't as nice as that clean-swept cottage.

Soot from the train fell on Harlowe's sleeve like flakes of snow, the engine bellowing down the siding which zig-zagged away from a factory, an old, red-brick building like many others he'd wlaked past. The boarding house had white, peeling paint. Out-of-work men hung on the stoop, as languid as the laundry hanging the breadth of the wooden balcony, around back.

He looked up three flights of steep, wooden steps, up to the dark windows of the back-room apartment where the landlady lived. The boards were soft and like to give way under his feet as he climbed, the train's puffing interrupted by the squeal of children as they scurried past—down. In the temporary lull in the train traffic, he heard a woman sobbing through an open second-story window as he proceeded—up.
He reached the top of the stairs. Knocked on the doorframe.
A woman hollered through the screendoor. "Whadya want?! If you're here about that furniture payment, you can—." Another train drowned out the profanities.
"No, ma'am, I ain't from the furniture comp'ny. It's about Collis Hutto."
"He ain't here!" she snarled, giving the door a good slam.
Probably owed her money too, thought Harlowe.
Another woman, a floor below, scrubbed clothes in a bucket. He turned to her. "Hiya, Mister."
"Mornin'!" He showed her the photo.
She held it close to her eyes to see. "Don't know him, nosir. Me and my old man just moved in here. Not a very nice place. But it's all he could do."
"Well, I appreciate it, ma'am."

Harlowe checked other boarding houses. People shook their heads. Handed back the photo.

The smoldering sidewalks sapped his strength. Harlowe was about to quit when it happened. "May I see that again?" she asked.
"Sure."
She studied it.
"Yeah! He lived on the end. Next to Mr. and Mrs. McCurdy."
Harlowe looked down at the other door. "They ain't home, now," the woman explained. She gave the carpet a good thud with the beater, sending poofs of dust into the air. Then swung again.
"Mr. and Mrs. McCurdy are both at work. Bless their hearts, they're elderly but still working. Near sixty-years-old, I imagine." The woman sighed. "I hate to say it. 'Cause the young man passed on now..."
"Yes'm?"
"But *he* didn't work. He liked to drink! And suddenly he left. That was his room, that winduh theah! You can go in—Mrs. Gatchell won't mind."

Harlowe entered the dim hall, the sound of the carpet beater fading. The place had that boarding-house smell (a lingering mixture of cooking grease, mustiness, mothballs, and the effects of negligent housekeeping). The lights weren't working. He felt his way to the room at the end of the hall. Pushed the door open. The place had been swept. But in the corner of the bedroom he found something—a broken toy horse. *Maybe Mrs. Hutto had a child?*

"Who are ya?" the voice demanded.

Harlowe turned around to see a large, tough-looking woman with coal-black hair framing her face as granite-like and stern as those new carvings at Rushmore. He told her who he was.

"Hmmph. I figured you for the law, parole officer, or some such, none of which is good for me," said the landlady. "Come on over here away from these big ears," she whispered. "I run a respectable house."

Quietly, he explained about Collis.

"All I know's he left. Ain't been back. He did pay for the week's rent, I'll give 'im that much."

"Yes, ma'am. Is there anything else you could tell me?"

"This important to ya, then?"

Harlowe explained about Gibby.

"Seein' as how there's a youngun involved, I'm gonna tell ya this here. Now, he bought his cigarettes at the store. One at the corner there. You couldn't have missed it if you had your eyes open. He ain't there today—today's Sundee in case you didn't know it—but the little feller at the store may know somethin'."

"I appreciate it."

"Now you got to go, for someone sees us talkin'. No, no, out the back way! Careful of the rug!"

"Yes'm." Harlowe tipped his hat. Did as he was told.

Harlowe found the man who ran the grocery store, at his home, adjacent. He knew Collis and was friendly with him. The man opened the store and led Harlowe in, showing him around proudly. "I sure am sorry to hear about Collis, though—he was such a nice fella! We played cards—don't tell my wife, now! But he never let on about problems back home. I don't think I can help you there."

"He didn't talk about Tallahassee?"

"No—no, he sure didn't."

Well, that's it, thought Harlowe, turning to leave.

"Oh, wait—say, Mr. Harlowe?"

"Yes?" Harlowe let go of the doorknob.

"I almost forgot about the letter."

"The *lettuh?*"

"I was supposed to mail it in the event of his death—or if he didn't come back for it. I thought it was just the prathings of a man in his *condition.*" He reached below the counter, rustling some papers.

"His condition?"

"I mean drunk, sir! Don't tell my wife, you understand, but sometimes he'd bring a bottle around. A little nip never hurt anyone, I say! But Beadle—well, I don't wanna speak agin' the boy, him bein' gone." The man rustled more papers under the counter. "Here it is!" He held out the large envelope with an odd scrawl across it, and a stain of some kind over half of it.

Harlowe took it. The words read:

"Give too sheraff P. K. Halow."

"I didn't know who to send it to! 'Sheraff Halow,' it said. I just didn't know—."

Harlowe left with it, not looking back.

He struggled to read the writing—apparently, Collis had learned, but not well.

"Dear Mister Sharaff Halow, I desir to see my sister one time before I tell you what I know. Then I will be found dead somewheres. Like the feller who died on the track in Sopchoppy..."

Harlowe thought about that part. *There was that young lawyer who was killed in an Overland car in nineteen-hundred-and-twenty-six.*

He kept reading:

> *"If you holdin this letter, than I am gon. So I will tell you I know near where the body is. I feel real bad about it. After he kilt him the feller didn't hide Gibby too good. He come back an move him. I seen him tote them bones off in a sack. I stood thar and watch him. I went back an got that skull. Dug it up sos I could ask that boy for money. If he paid out I'd chuck it in the Gulf. But it bothered me that chile looking at me. Even under a flour sack I felt him a looking at me. I wrapped the skull and send to you to hep you. It is proof of what I say, that the chile did not run away nor did he git hisseff drownd. I do not lie, Mister Halow. I hear the feller move the bones agin. He is buried deep now. I fear thats as much as I dare do at this time or they'll kill my kinfolk. You are right to look in Eastpoint and Tate's Hell. Keep digging thar like you done. The one who done it...*

The last part of the letter had gotten wet and the ink ran. Harlowe couldn't read it.

THIRTY-TWO

Atlanta, Monday.

Back on the sidewalk, beneath a canopy of signs, Blue Yodel No. 9 drifted out an open doorway. He walked until he found the 'hotel for women' and a friend of Mrs. Hutto. "I ain't seen her. Kinda worried about her," said she.

"She was paid up with me. She cleared out weeks ago," said the landlady at the next place.

"Know where she moved to?"

"Heck, no."

Then the next place: "She ain't been here since June. She lit out in a hurry—left some of her clothes." The woman showed him a basket she'd kept in the corner of her sewing room. Harlowe examined the garments: inexpensive frock, no labels, impossible to trace.

"Her husband stayed with her for a few days, oh, back around the first 'o June. Where did you say he was?" asked the landlady.

"He's dead," said Harlowe.

"Oh. That's a shame. The girl had worries. I know that."

He tried another pool hall. The man said he thought he knew where Mrs. Hutto was staying.

Harlowe caught the streetcar. "I'm headed for Cleveland Avenue," he told the operator. "Can I get theah on this line?"

"Yessir."

Harlowe hopped off when they reached the intersection with said street. He walked to the address—which turned out to be a little apartment over a drugstore. An open doorway led up a run of stairs to a hallway. Four doors faced one another. He could touch two at a time without stretching. It was hot as an oven.

The first door masked a whirring sewing machine. He knocked on the next—where he was told he'd find Mrs. Hutto.

A woman in her early thirties answered, wearing a thin robe over her slip. She squinted at him. Yawned.

"Are you Mrs. Hutto?"

"Huh?"

"Are you Collis Hutto's wife?"

"Huh? I ain't had my smoke yet." She rubbed her forehead. "Just woke up." It was near ten-thirty. Her eyes were still closed like the blinds, yet they ran down him like she was doing arithmetic. With little energy—she could see he wasn't a 'swell.' She appeared hungover. "Come on in, better we don't stay out here in the hall."

The whirring sound had stopped. The woman nodded toward her neighbor's door. "Too many prying eyes and big ears."

"All right." Harlowe couldn't help notice she matched the description. Down to the South Georgia accent.

"This way to the 'parlor.'" She flung the newspaper from the one chair she had. "The maid's off Mondees—have a seat." She plopped down on the ottoman. Fished out the last cigarette from the tin on the coffee table. "Say, ya gotta light?"

He struck a match. "Ummm. Thanks. Wish I was," she declared, as he lit her smoke.

"Ma'am?"

"Collis' wife. Ya asked me. Whadya want with him anyhow?"

Harlowe explained who he was. That he was looking for some information. He thought his wife could help. "But you aren't her? I'm told she has red hair."

She exhaled the smoke through her nostrils. "Lotsa people got red hair."

"Would you know where she is?"

"Why don't you ask Collis? I don't know why you're botherin' me—I don't understand it! And askin' all these questions! I don't know how ya found me, but I don't wanna be bothered, see?" Angrily, she stabbed out her cigarette.

"I don't mean to bother you, why—."

"I'm sorry...didn't mean to blow my top. I'm a little thirsty—this heat, y'know!" He could see her hands jitter. Was certain it wasn't a Coca-Cola from the fountain downstairs that she alluded to.

"Get us a bottle n' we'll talk." Her robe was all-of-a-sudden too big for her at the top. And gravity had acted below, too. "I've got nice legs, donchya think?"

"Why, I don't—ma'am, I—."

"It's okay, Mister. I know ya looked. We both know it. Let's get past bein' polite! Do you like 'em or not?"

"Yes, ma'am—I sure do."

"Now, that's better."

"Ma'am, I don't wanna take up your time. I just have a few questions about Collis."

"Oh, Collis—phuey! Look here, come on and be a nice fella," she said, practically dropping in his lap. "Go down to the drugstore and get us a nice...li'l...bottle. It's medicinal—you know, good for ya! Doctor said so! Y'can take the script I got."

Further questioning yielded little more. The woman wasn't a prostitute, she'd been gainfully employed until recently. But she freely described herself as a 'lush.'

"And that's when I lost my job. They closed the factory. They let all the seamstresses go. It's been two weeks and I haven't found another. You know they don't stop chargin' rent when ya lose your job?"

He grinned. "Uh-uh."

"And the grocer won't run a tab like the one back home. Funny how that works, huh? A bottle of rye's—well, no need to dwell on that."

She told him her life story. Talked and talked. Sidetracked Collis by a mile.

He tried, in vain, to get her back on track. "Did you know him?"

"Yeah, I *know* him. We're friends! You're no fun—y'just wanna keep talkin' about Beadle. Why don't you wanna get to know *me?*"

She started telling Harlowe about music and dancing until Harlowe had to end her stalling.

"Ma'am—Collis is dead."

Her expression told the truth.

"How?" Emotion flashed over her face, but she fought back the tears.

"I sure am sorry."

The woman drew her knees up to rest her chin on them, turning her face away. She said it softly to the wall: "Well, you made it home, Beadle."

She recovered. Began to talk more. Repeating funny stories. So it went for nearly half-an-hour. She'd tell him nothing of significance.

Harlowe pulled out two dollars. Laid it on the table. "For the bottle."

"Say, that's swell, Mister! But you'll have to get it. I'm not dressed to go out in public, see? Just go down there and ask for Archie. Tell him Betty Dahlgren from upstairs wants it."

Harlowe walked into the store. Followed the procedures. The bored-looking man was happy to take his money. Slid a paper bag containing a bottle of "medicine" across the counter.

Harlowe returned, gave a tap on the door and she let him in.

"Gee, that's swell!" Happily, she hugged the package. She nodded to the highball glasses she'd brought out and he did the honors.

He handed her the glass. She clacked it against his. He'd quit drinking, some time ago, but he knew this was one instance he'd have to oblige.

She drank it down like it was a life-saving antidote. To him, the taste was worse than bad moonshine, but that old familiar warmth down your throat, into your belly was there—the kind of comforting fire that was far too easy to turn to. The first one was always the best. The second and third rarely lived up to the hype. But only sober people think that way—on their way to losing their fun-loving friends.

"You can take off your coat. Loosen your tie. Relax," she told him.

He hung his coat. She settled on the arm of the chair. "Butt me."

He fished out a Chesterfield for her.

She put it to her lips. "Thanks."

He struck a match. She took hold of his hand and together they lit it.

"You have nice hands. Strong. You work with 'em, but they're not too rough. Ya got a wife?"

"No, ma'am. Divorced me. Hands weren't the problem. Profession was."

She laughed. "You're funny. Here, you take the chair," she said, returning to the ottoman. "I-I'm sorry to hear that—'bout your wife. My old man up n' left me—so we got somethin' in common. She really left ya 'cause you're the law?"

"Yeah. It was my life. I reckon the trouble was I couldn't stop when I got home. She wanted me to quit and keep store—maybe I coulda tried. Maybe we wouldna split up."

"Hmm. Well, I don't truck with cops much, neither. Though, you're not so bad. You don't come in talkin' to me like I'm trash. You've treated me like a lady, and I don't mind sayin'."

"Well, I appreciate that."

"Can't picture you sellin' canned goods."

They both laughed at that.

Halfway into the bottle, she began to open up about Collis. "Yeah, I loved him. Well, as much as I can love a man."

"What do you know about his wife?"

"She left him lots of times. She had a kid. Left her first old man. Collis tried to be its poppa—if you could imagine Collis playin' daddy. Well, she'd leave Collis with the brat and he'd come around and I'd fix 'im something' to eat. She wasn't much. When Collis'd come into a little money, why, she'd come home and take him for all he had. He'd be flat busted, then she'd run off again. I haven't any idea where she is now."

Harlowe looked out the window at the teeming, hot sidewalk. *Mrs. Hutto's made herself 'lost.' Like a penny tossed into the Gulf.*

He looked back at the woman. "Did he ever mention *Gibby Birch?*"

"No."

"Never mentioned the boy?"

"I said 'no.'"

Harlowe showed her the packaging. "Yes, I addressed that package for him. He can write, now. Just not too good."

Harlowe nodded.

"I taught the boy. He wanted to learn. Really strange about it—insisted on lessons every night."

"Oh?"

"I don't know why, but he wanted to learn. He was a fast-learner. At first, I was surprised. He really wasn't dumb."

"Had you any idea what was in the package?"

"No, and he got sore when I asked. I'm a woman, I wanted to know—of course, I wanted to know."

"Did he let on anything about it, about this business back home?"

She sighed. "Yes. I know a little. Bits here and there. He wanted to help you. He didn't mention you by name. But he wanted to help. He told me he worked for someone big, see? He felt bad about it—that he knew where a body was. He dug it up, or something. I'm not sure."

Harlowe told her the package contained the skull.

She cussed. "Are you joshin' me? What a terrible business, I really need a drink now!" She began to cry. "Why'd you make me think about this?"

She quieted some, with the last contents of the bottle. "I can tell you the last place he lived." She provided an address Harlowe had checked out yesterday.

"We didn't exactly talk much," she continued. "But he would get nervous, lonely maybe, and tell me things. Maybe things he shouldna."

"Like what?"

"What good's it gonna do me?"

"I ain't got much, but would two dollars help ya?" He pulled out what would be, other than trainfare, the last of his cash money.

"You're right. And it would."

The woman, tipsy by now, was talking freely. Leaned her arms on his knees to look up at him. Squinted so as not to see two of him. Smiled because she was drunk and happy so long as she could remain so. "Collis said he never shoulda gone to work for this fella."

"He ever call his name?"

"No. He called 'im 'Bossman'."

"Do you know what Collis did for this man, what kind of work?"

"Dunno what he did. Women are good at findin' out things, you know that?"

Harlowe nodded.

"But women's intuition failed me that time. 'Couldn't dope out a thing! Collis certainly didn't punch no time clock."

"All right."

"He's really tight-lipped about the business. But it was *bad business*, you can be sure o' that! I knew enough not to wanna know too much for my own good—unlike you."

"Yes, ma'am."

"You can stay awhile—hot as it's getting out there." She pressed against his chest, fanning herself with the newspaper.

"That'd be mighty nice, ma'am. But I'm kinda in a hurry. Gotta stay after this thing."

"I understand. I can see you're a determined man. Don't see that much these days. What else y'wanna know?"

"He mention a *lettuh?*"

"Alls I know is he was workin' on it. Over and over. Tryin' to get it right. Never showed it t'me. Where is it now?" At that, the woman put her arm around Harlowe. "Never mind. I don't wanna know."

"One other thing."

"All right."

"What did he have to do with the man at the hospital, Kern?"

"Well, I dunno if I oughta tell ya that." She twisted a strand of hair in her fingers. "How much of this is gonna come back on me?"

"I'll keep your name out of it."

She wobbled a bit, tipsy, but held onto Harlowe's shoulder. She looked away, like she was looking far beyond the shabby yellow walls. "He was scared. He'd say things in his sleep. The fella he worked for in Tallahassee threatened to commit him."

"Go on."

"He threatened to put him in the nut-house! I asked him about it. He seemed like he was really scared of that. And he mentioned a fella— what did you say his names was?"

"Kern."

"Yeah, that's it. He said something about Kern and the docs out there, that they'd do what this 'Bossman' wanted. But I told him, 'bah, horsefeathers, they can't just commit ya for no reason!'"

"Yeah?"

"But he tended to believe it. He'd call him 'Bossman.' 'Bossman' would say, 'take the bottle and the money I gave ya and hesh up!' Oh, he's the 'Big Six' around there, all right! He must be, from the way Collis talked. But he'd never say who he was."

"Never let on who he was or what kind of business he was in?"

"No." She pressed her body against him, her face against his, he could feel her breathe. Her perfume was cheap. Some of yesterday's makeup had streaked her face from when she cried. She closed her eyes. She was soft against him. Vulnerable. Trusting him. Her eyes closed, her neck, her wrists so delicate, he noticed now. She whispered to him, "Are y'sure ya won't stay—Pratt."

***

The heat lingered, the movement of the trolley providing no relief. A little eau de toilette lingered on his shirt. He boarded the train at Spring Street, fading to sleep as they crossed the Flint.

THIRTY-THREE

Eastpoint, Tuesday.

The day started as any for True. He did his chores. Looked out to count the sails of the oysterboats heading for the bar, where the men would 'tong' until the sun got broiling hot.

The boat with the red patch was Aubrey Birch's. True's mind went back to that day.
True looked at Aubrey trying to comfort his wife. He'd never seen Gibby's folks when they weren't smiling and happy. They had a blank, empty look on their faces, like ragdolls that had lost their stitching or button eyes. They seemed so much older than they had the day before.

Harlowe arrived, presently. Egg Brown put his truck on the ferry behind theirs. He carried his eggs to Apalach to sell. Eastpoint's "post office" was in the parlor of the house Brown shared with his sister—when folks needed to get their mail, they just walked right in!

Harlowe took True to the *Riverside* for breakfast. A tourist couple at the counter was asking about the bridge. "Oh, the bridge! Only those pilings, theah," explained Mr. Nichols.
"They drove in two pilin's and quit! Them Tallahassee boys caint decide *what* to do. Won't be surprised if it ain't never built," opined Mr. Porter.

Dr. Murrow waved them over. "Good Mornin', Pratt! Young man—my, you're gonna be a tall fella! Sit down, boys, sit down!" They chatted a moment, before the doctor took up his medical bag, heading out on a housecall.
Nichols set their plates on the table. Varied conversations drifted about the main room of the *Riverside*, one picking up if another lulled. At one table, men discussed the "service"—the young fellow at the table was interested in joining up. His father was skeptical. "Why, all you'll do is march all day! There ain't a war on, son!" He looked over at Harlowe.
"Pratt, you was in the service, wasn't ya? Had yo'self a *fine* adventure?" Harlowe gave a grin. "Well, I was lucky, David. I just drove a truck was all."
"An' that's all this boy'll git to do! Tell 'im—there won't be another war!" Harlowe nodded. Went back to his bacon and eggs, as True listened to all the sounds floating around the place.
Then, Seago walked in. Whispered to Harlowe. "You got a phone call, Sheriff."
Back at the office, he returned the call—to Collis' sister. The young woman seemed desparate. "Could you come to the house?" In a hushed tone, she implored. "I'd rather not say over the telephone. *Please!*"

Harlowe left True at the jail with Seago. Drove over. The woman met him at the door. He removed his hat as he stepped up on her porch. "Howdy, Miss Betty."

"C'mon in, Mister Pratt. Ira's at work and I-I'd rather he not know about this."

Harlowe nodded. Wiped his feet. Followed her inside the small house. The living room and entrance were all-in-one and she directed him to the good chair on the other side of it. She poured coffee and sat opposite, her hands wringing her apron as she struggled to find the right words. "I've fretted *so* about all this!"

"It's all right. Take your time."

"Well, I hate to say it and git someone in trouble. But I-I feel I owe it to— well, it's about someone I think you'll want to check into."

"Go on."

"Well, I was cleaning out some things here and came across this slip of paper." She handed it to Harlowe. It read, *"T.S. Barnhart."*

"I wrote that for Beadle. But, it troubles me now."

"Ma'am?"

"Well, we were pleased he had work, Ira and me. When I run across the paper I remembered this fella come by the house here. And-there was somethin'—well, he just didn't act right." Mrs. Brewer's tears welled. "I'm sorry. I plumb forgot about that—and it mighta helped you—about my brother."

"That's all right."

"He paid Collis. Guidefishin'. At least once. I-I don't know if there were other times. I don't remember."

"This was how long ago?"

"Oh, three or four years, I imagine."

"Anything else?"

"He was a salesman. And—askin' around here this week—other people told me he'd done things—."

"Yes?"

"Things that scared them, Mister Pratt!"

Based on Mrs. Brewer's description, Harlowe recalled the man as well. He'd been around in the 'Twenties. Then he'd just stopped coming. He drove a Ford.

"I appreciate you tellin' me this."

"I feel better now. I hope it'll help you clear up some things."

"Yeah."

"More coffee, Mr. Pratt?"

Back at his office he made some telephone calls about Barhnart. He'd been committed to the State insane asylum. "In nineteen-hundred-and- thirty? Ya'sure? Thankya."

Harlowe rang for Dr. Elston. The latter wasn't in.

He left to pick up True.

They watched Demo George launch his new trawler, the boat gently settling into the water.

145

They drove on down to the Nichols' Store. The lady behind the wooden counter, the old boards painted bright green, took down a grocery order over the telephone. "I'll have it they-uh direc'ly," she said. "Goodbye!"

She retrieved a tin of Chesterfields before Harlowe cleared the threshold— she already knew what he wanted.

"Hello, Mr. Pratt!"

"Howdy, Miss Nichols."

True took in everything. The clean, white shiplap walls which reflected the light from milkglass lamps hanging from the high ceilings. The eclectic mix of merchandise. From meats...to clothes...to the Whirlpool in the window.

True examined the big, black coffee grinder and the meat scale on the counter as the grown-ups talked. Harlowe paid cash money for the cigarettes and other things!

The lady was always nice to True. "My, how tall you've gotten, True! What are you in the fourth grade now?"

"Yes'm," True replied, shyly.

"Those blue eyes! My, the gals are gonna go for you!"

True blushed.

"I remember when you first come in here! You was so bashful ya used to hide below the counter, remember?"

True nodded, even more red. He remembered; he'd come with Harlowe when the latter purchased meat wrapped in paper. His head barely came up to the counter; he'd duck while she said hello and made a fuss.

"Well, it was good seein' ya! Say hello to ya momma fur'me!"

Awkwardly, he said goodbye.

Outside, Harlowe slid to the passenger side. "You can drive, son."

It was exciting and frightening all at once! But Harlowe's advice was simple, encouraging. True got the truck started—and moving down the road! "Keep it between the ditches. You doin' fine, son."

True steered all the way to Prado Street! There, they drove in stakes on the lot. Ran string to mark where the foundation would go.

True looked up as his neighbor, C.P. Williams, clattered up the street on his mule-drawn wagon full of watermelons—his daughter, Marlene, *aside* him. Two kids from Apalach ran along behind, salivating over the melons and hoping Mr. Williams might let them have one!

He didn't. C.P., a fat-faced, sweaty man, grunted something. The tiny girl hopped down, toting a watermelon bigger than she was, struggling to reach the door of that house.

They'd ride the ferry over and go door-to-door, Marlene or one of the other kids delivering melons and returning with the money, while C.P. lounged on the seat with a jar of moonshine at his feet.

"Hey there, Pratt! True!"

"Howdy, C.P.!" replied Harlowe.

"Hey, Mr. Williams," True answered.

Marlene toted another one. Hauled it, smiling, to the next door.

And on they went.

After a while the Apalachicola boys got bored and ambled off to find some other summer diversion—play "kick-the-can" or swim at Ten Foot Hole. They wouldn't be so lucky as to have a melon fall off the wagon!

***

It's a man's house. But it seemed like some things a woman done. Lacy curtains and pink-flowered paper decorated the bedroom. A lady's robe hung in the bathroom. True remembered Aunt Claudie. Harlowe kept her things, everything in its place, as if she still lived there. *Was she comin' back?* True noticed people shook their heads, sometimes. *Like they was feelin' sorry for Uncle Pratt. Somethin' to do with Aunt Claudie.* True reckoned he wasn't old enough to understand all that.

The sun was retiring. True heard the whistle. Sat on the porch swing watching Ol' 150 backing into town. Harlowe watched with him.

They walked down to her. True heard the train's sighing as they neared the depot.

Harlowe stopped to talk to Layne. Then handed the letter, addressed to the Sheriff in Waycross, up to the railroad postman. Harlowe determined Mrs. Hutto had a sister in Waycross.

The sunlight grew ever more muted, True watching the men load barrels of iced-down shrimp and oysters. "The railroad ships all the way to New York," Harlowe told him. "All the way to a place on *Fulton Street.*"

True marveled at that.

Mrs. Slocumb walked up—her little dog was lost. People often stopped Harlowe on the street with one thing or another. She went on for several minutes. Seago had found them by the time she got to the home stretch. "I-I feel better now. You're a good listener. But you don't talk much!" she said, batting his arm.

"Why *don't* you talk much?" wondered Seago, as the old lady walked off. "Seems like I do all the talkin'. Or Doc—one. You the quietest feller I ever did see!"

"Well...I never learned anything listenin' to myself talk."

"Shoot, Ledbetter and Pender sure don't feel thataway. They carry on like they're a fount of knowledge for theyselves!"

Harlowe shook his head. Noticed True looking up at him. "Well...that's a lot of it, True. Struttin' around with a badge like a bandy-rooster ain't what its about. A lot of it's Payin' attention to things. Bein' a good list'ner. Ya caint be afraid to get in the car and go talk to people. I ain't never solved no case settin' around a rest'runt, visitin'."

Seago nudged True in the ribs. "That's the most yo' uncle has ever talked right there, boah!"

"Bah!" Harlowe snapped his watch shut. "I best get you home, son."

Harlowe always thought if he did a good job the people would support him. Some said he should have talked more, not let Pender come in and say all the right things and beat him. The people must have seen Pender was just talk, however, for they returned Harlowe back to the office in '28 and since. That was enough for Harlowe.

THIRTY-FOUR

Eastpoint, Monday.

"Timothy Barnhart?" asked Mr. Tommy.

"Yessir."

"Come to think of it, I saw this fella. He come in the store, here. Yessir."

"Tommy, do you remember when he was here last?"

"Oh, 'bout four years ago. Caint tell ya anything more specific, Pratt."

Mrs. Quick had come in by now.

"I know him, Shureff! He was that drummer!"

Another woman recalled him selling from the back of his automobile. Brooms, mops, and things, for the Fuller Company. "He fished the East Bay, sure. And Indian Creek," added Sonny Brewer.

Harlowe left the store. Motored to Tallahassee. To Call Street. Children ran down the sidewalk chasing a barrel hoop as he pulled up at the house next to Barnhart's. He spoke to Barnhart's neighbor, Mrs. Dorrance. "Mr. Barnhart minds his own business and gets on well with everyone; we see him, but rarely see his wife."

Another neighbor, Harlowe had met when looking into the Whittle matter. "How does he get along with children?" Harlowe asked.

"Oh, fine. Well, what do you mean?" asked the woman. "Like, is he kindly towards them?"

"Ma'am, I know this is unpleasant. But do you think he could ever hurt a child?"

"Oh, my! No, sir, I don't believe so."

"Was there evuha time—that you know of—that he mighta said somethin' out of the way? Or done somethin' around a youngun that they didn't care for?"

"No, sir. He got on fine with mine—my children. Never did he do or say anything out-of-the-way."

The neighbor across the street worked at the Standard Oil station on Monroe. Harlowe found him down in the grease pit, there.

"I thought there was something off about him, yessir."

"How do you mean?"

"Well, Barnhart would *always* talk to younguns. Made a point of it. Or he'd stop mamas and wanna talk to them about their babies."

"Yessir?"

"It made people uncomfortable. Maybe they wouldn't say so, but that's what I saw. Like they'd want to get away from him."

"Yessir?"

"Hard to say exactly. It's like he's *too* friendly. I—well, it's probably nothing. He was nice—but maybe *too* nice. Like a cat that won't leave ya alone."

"Uh-huh."

"I understand he'd offer to 'ride 'em in his automobile—the younguns."

"Oh?"

"Yessir! He'd carry them to the ice cream parlor. Some of the boys on Call Street." The man had finished the grease-job on the sedan. Climbed up. "'Scuse-me while I clean up."

Harlowe nodded.

While he scrubbed his hands, he continued. "Sos, it went like this. All the younguns where I live are goin'—we live at Gadsden and Call—up the street from Barnhart."

"Yessir."

"My younguns wanna go."

"Yessir?"

"I told them kids, 'no!' Just what I was tryin' to say while ago. I jus' didn't keer for him—the way he was actin.' *Too* nice."

"Barnhart was a salesman then?"

"I understand he was with the Fuller Comp'ny. I hear he got fired—anyhow, I ain't seen 'im."

"All right."

"You know I ain't from here."

"No, sir."

"Me and my wife moved here from Mississippi. Reckon I didn't know no better!"

Harlowe grinned.

"I mean, I told a deputy-sheriff about it. And I tell ya, I wish I hadna!"

"Go on."

"That feller told me, 'it ain't a good idea to *cause trouble.'*"

Harlowe nodded. "One other thing. Did Barnhart mention drivin' down to the coast?"

"He mentioned fishin' a lot. He'd talk about—oh, that place down there somewhere. What's the name of that little fishin' village?" The man snapped his fingers. "Eastpoint!"

"Is that right?"

"Yessir. 'Said he found some creek down there—some local kids showed it to him."

"Was that Indian Creek?"

"Why, yes! As a matter-of-fact, he offered to take my boys there."

"Oh? When was that?"

"Last year, I b'lieve. Nothin' wrong is there? Like I say, I didn't keer for him, but *was there* somethin' wrong?"

"I'm gonna talk to the fella. Maybe we can straighten it out."

"I hope I hep'd ya."

"I sure do appreciate it. So long."

Harlowe found out Barnhart was now working at the Daffin Theatre. Harlowe went to see the owner in his upstairs office.

"I've had no complaints about him. He's doing a fine job here," said the man.

Barnhart wasn't at work yet, so Harlowe talked to the other staff. "Mr. Barnhart's a little odd but he's O.K.," said the usher. "He gets along with everyone."

The ticket girl laughed. "Ol' Mr. Tim? He's harmless—funny old coot!"

Harlowe walked over to Maxwell Drug and used the payphone, placing a call to the District Manager at the Fuller Company Branch Office in Jacksonville. "Yeah, I had to let him go, Mr. Harlowe."

"Yessir. Might I ask why?"

"He wasn't a good salesman. Awful, really!"

"Had he done something out of the way?"

"No. I don't recall any complaints about him—he just didn't work out! Couldn't sell water in a desert!"

"I have to ask this. I'm 'fraid it's a difficult thing to say."

"Go ahead!"

"Did he behave oddly around children—mistreat them in any way?"

"No problem like that—I'd tell you if he had. No reason not to," insisted the manager. "He was a little peculiar, maybe. Hard to get to know. Just not a salesman! Say, you lookin' for a job—I've an opening?"

"Well, I appreciate it. But, no, sir. Thankya for the information."

"Gee, that's too bad. So long!"

"Deposit twenty-cents for five minutes please," said the operator.

Harlowe dropped in more coins.

"Elston-speaking!"

"Hello, Doc. This's Harlowe."

"What's up?"

"Doc, with all the education you've had, wouldya answer somethin' for me?"

"I'll try—what is it?" came the Doctor's terse reply.

"Well, it's about a man who would...*fancy* a child. I reckon that's how to say it."

"No one knows, precisely, Pratt. But I'd say *fancy* describes it. Such a man's *attracted* the way a normal man would be for a grown woman, exclusively. Only for him it's a child. He may be married, may have some normal occupation. But he has this inclination which he acts upon. Not much is known about the type. There are few books on the subject. Maybe someday there will be more. Damnit, it's not like a heart condition! I wish it was, Pratt!" The Doctor cussed at the thought of such a man, loose—and as inscrutable as a droplet of Spanish flu.

Harlowe described Barnhart's behavior.

"Is it an inordinate interest in children? How do you separate a kindness, a fondness from clues a man has violent or perverse tendencies? It's a question of degree—like anything else. Like the line between a healthy love—or obsession!

"Did you treat this Barnhart?" asked Harlowe.

"Yes. And I saw no indication he had any such proclivities toward children."

"Did he know Whittle?

"He was in here with Whittle. Their relationship, from what I gather, was no more than that."

"Yessir."

"He has a history of disturbed behavior. He can be violent if his ideas are challenged. He is connected, Pratt. His family owned a plantation, years ago. Still living off their name. It would seem you're on the right track."

Harlowe drove to Barnhart's residence—the Mae Apartments at 115 North Calhoun. The place was near Call—a block from Whittle's old house. Mrs. Barnhart was in front, washing a Whippet automobile.

Harlowe tipped his hat. "Howdy, ma'am. I'm lookin' for Mr. and Miss Barnhart."

"I'm Mrs. Barnhart."

"Glad to know you, ma'am. Sure is a pretty car."

"Thankya."

"How long y'all had it?"

"Oh—four years. We owned a Ford, before that."

"Traded her in, eh?"

"Yes, we did. And my husband got this one."

"About four years, you said?"

"Uh-huh, about four years ago. Why, is it important?"

Barnhart came out. The fellow was tall and heavy-set, with a gut, a lumbering, sauntering gait. He had the kind of face that blended into the background like beige wallpaper. While his face was near expressionless, he seemed on edge. His veins pulsed. He clenched his fists. "What's this about?" he demanded.

"My name's Pratt Harlowe. From Franklin County."

"Yeah?"

"I'm the sheriff down theah."

The man went white.

"You've been to our county, some."

"I've been there, sure. Why?"

"Were you there in the Fall of nineteen-hunnerd-and-twenty-seven?"

"In the Fall, that year, sure. Why, is there something wrong?"

"Just lookin' for some information. Were you in Eastpoint at that time?"

"More-than-likely. I like to fish down there."

"Did you hire Collis Hutto to guidefish for ya?"

"A couple times. Back in twenty-six. Twenty-seven."

"Have you talked to him since?"

"No, I've had no contact with him. Unfortunate what happened."

"What do you know about that?"

"Just what I read in the newspaper when I traveled to the coast."

"A few weeks back?"

"Yes."

"Did you know E.F. Whittle?"

"Never met him."

"When did you sell the Ford?"

"About the same time. Why?"

"There's nothin' wrong, sir. Just lookin' to clear up a few things.'"

"You can ask the man where I traded it. He'll give you the date. This is about that little boy, isn't it?" Barnhart grinned, oddly.

"What do you know about that?"

"Only what I saw in the newspaper when it happened."

"Did you see that boy—when you were fishin' down theah?"

The man slowly looked away. "No."

Harlowe drove to the Willys-Overland agency a block West—209 East Call. The salesman produced the record of sale—Barnhart traded his Ford the third of October 1927. *Two weeks after Gibby took missing.*

Harlowe watched Barnhart enter the Daffin Theatre to start his shift as a projectionist. Harlowe steadied the rented camera on the door of the truck. Using photography was novel for a country sheriff—but he saw no other way.

After the photograph was developed, he showed it to some of the boys in Carrabelle. They remembered Barnhart—from around the time Gibby went missing. The Birches did not recognize him, however. *"Never saw him before, Mr. Pratt."*

***

"Sold the car two weeks later!" exclaimed Seago.
"Yep."
"And what about them little boys in Carrabelle?"
"Well, he asked those younguns—who were fishin' down theah—if they'd show him a good fishin' spot. Tried to get one in the boat with 'im."
"Ordinar'ly, I'd never question that. Someone bein' friendly. But with the man you lookin' at...All the things you mentioned jus' now—*shoot! He done it!"* concluded Seago.
"Could be. But if we arrested all the odd characters we'd have to build us a new jail."
"You right about that!"
"Bein' odd doesn't mean he done it. But I reckon *I am* gonna have to go back to Tallahassee."

Harlowe backed the truck in at Marks Brokerage.
"Howdy, Pratt! We'll have ya loaded up in a jiffy!"
Presently, the men loaded the iron pipe and 2 x 4's, and they headed for the jobsite.

Harlowe and True framed wallstuds and sweated. Harlowe moved robotically, cutting boards, hammering nails, his mind elsewhere.

A letter waited at the house. The Waycross Sheriff informed him that Mrs. Collis Hutto—formerly Myrtle Campbell—had moved to Kansas. Sheriff Gordon enclosed the address he'd obtained from the sister. Harlowe promptly penned a correspondence to Mrs. Hutto, and not long after received his envelope back—the Topeka postmaster stamping it, "Return to Sender."

THIRTY-FIVE

Apalachicola.

The house on "The Prado" took shape in the long, hot August evenings. Harlowe motored to Tallahassee most mornings, picked up True on his way back, and they'd work until it became difficult to see in the fading daylight.

Today, True noticed fishing rods out the back of the truck. Harlowe was taking him fishing when they got through!
Harlowe was the first to take him fishing, True remembered. Harlowe took time to teach him things his old man hadn't patience for. Casting a line. Catching a ball. Foss never wanted to "fool with" the boy.
I caught my first catfish with Uncle Pratt. Now, he's he'pin' me learn to fish with that new rod n' reel!
True felt a pull!
"Uncle, Pratt! Look, here!"
"Give 'im plenty of line, son!"

That night, Harlowe cooked the fish. In the kitchen, he poured some cool milk for True. The white light was hot against the blackness outside. True listened to the fish frying and the train leaving the depot. He was happy he didn't have to go home tonight.

***

Harlowe walked in the lobby of the Daffin. He heard the organ—the children's matinee playing.
Barnhart was lurking by the staircase. He spoke to some boys, then turned about, heading upstairs.
Harlowe followed him up to the projection booth.
"Oh, Mr. Harlowe. May I help you?"
"I'd like to talk to you about some of your trips to Eastpoint."
"Like I told you I liked to fish down in Eastpoint. What's all this about? You still trying to find the one who kidnapped the boy?"
"Just lookin' for a little information, Mr. Barnhart. You used the word, 'kidnapped,' just now...what makes you say that?"
"I just assumed that, of course."
"You say you like to fish down theah—anywhere in particular? Indian Creek, maybe?"
"I suppose so. Why?"
"So you have fished Indian Creek some?"
"Yes."
"Back in nineteen-and-twenty-seven?"
"Sure."
Harlowe pulled out the photo of Gibby. "Have you seen this boy?"
Barnhart looked. "Probably seen him around."
"Down at Cat Point, maybe?"
"Coulda seen him there. I've been there."
"Did ya talk to him?"

"I always speak to children. I speak to everybody. I mighta showed him a lure or something."

"When?"

"Three or four years—I know that's the time you're interested in, so I'll just be out with it."

"You talk to 'im just that one time?"

"I suppose so. I know why you're asking—you think I did something to him?"

Harlowe held up the photo. "*Do* you know what happened to him, Mr. Barnhart?"

The man got an odd smile. "No."

"Can you account for where you were the third week of September, nineteen-hundred-and-twenty-seven?"

"Why, I don't know. Third week, you said? Could you narrow it down?"

"Monday the 19th."

"I was selling. Door-to-door. On the road. Here. Between River Junction—and your Franklin County."

"You sure about that, Mr. Barnhart?" *One thing about this fella, he's a middling in appearance, harmless-looking. It makes it all the more frightening. He could slip into a place, no one would notice 'im. He has a way about him, even when he wanted to be impudent, of coming across like milquetoast. Is he a broken piece of machinery, wound up and ready to snap, taking out his rage on a trusting child? Look at the way he clenches his hands togethuh. I wish I knew more about what a child-killer thinks, what makes him 'work' thataway!*

"Monday, sure. I was on the road—most of the day."

"You remember where?"

"I was a drummer. You go from town-to-town."

"Can you narrow it down—what towns were you in?"

"Why, Chattahoochee...Tallahassee...Mighta made it to your Eastpoint, I suppose."

"You have salesbooks, haven't you? Who did you sell to?"

"You'll have to excuse me, Sheriff, I have to get into the booth. We've another picture starting!"

Harlowe commenced interviewing housewives in Barnhart's old territory for the Fuller Company. He went down the list, every house, and all of them liked Barnhart. No complaints. Some thought Barnhart had been by in September of '27, but couldn't recall the date.

***

The telephone was jingling when Harlowe got home.

"Hello Mr. Harlowe. I think I can help you." It was Barnhart!

"Yeah?"

"I've got my sales books, here. You come over and we'll clear this up."

Harlowe reached Tallahassee by 1:30 a.m.

Barnhart waved Harlowe inside. The house was dark and Harlowe stayed on the porch.

155

"Cut the light on," said he.

"Sure." The projectionist switched on a lamp, casting a cone of light onto the porch, and down the short, narrow hall which led into the house.

"Anyone here?" asked Harlowe, stepping inside.

"My wife."

The man had a book open on the sofa couch. "There's my salesbook. See?"

Harlowe looked at it. The man had made a sale the 19th September, in River Junction, in the morning. He didn't make another sale until September 30th.

"It doesn't account for where you were that week, Mr. Barnhart."

"No, it doesn't." It was the opposite of an alibi—yet Barnhart seemed almost gleeful in its ambiguity.

Suddenly, there was a crashing noise in the bedroom.

"Is that your wife?"

"Come on out!" Barnhart shrieked.

"Easy," said Harlowe, trying to calm him. The fellow had been cool as a cucumber, and went to shouting in a way that made the hair on Harlowe's neck stand on end—without warning. Harlowe recalled what Elston said about the man.

A timid figure emerged. The woman was in her early thirties. She wasn't homely so much as her face was featureless, expressionless—like a porceilain doll.

Harlowe removed his hat. Barnhart started fussing at his wife—something about not ironing his shirts. While the fellow was occupied, Harlowe glanced down the hall. In the back bedroom, he saw something! A teddy bear and toys. "Have you any children, Mr. Barnhart?"

"No."

"What about the teddy bear and things?"

"Those-those are for my sister's kids."

Barnhart continued to berate his wife. She tried to heat the iron. Dampened a cloth to steam the shirts.

Harlowe sat astraddle a chair, watching them. He patted his pack of Chesterfields. "Smoke?"

"I don't want one, no."

Barnhart wanted to show him some movie posters he'd saved. The violent-type pictures. The wife's arms moved like the connecting rods of a steam engine, as she ironed.

Harlowe turned to Mrs. Barnhart, asking about the Ford.

"Why did you get rid of it?"

She looked to her husband. "I-I dunno."

"It was worn out," said Barnhart.

"I checked with the dealership. That Ford was only two years old."

"I don't see what difference it makes! How can that matter?!" exclaimed Mrs. Barnhart. "Has my husband done something? You ask all these questions, try to trip up my husband. Why does it matter, just because he sold the car!"

"Take it easy. I didn't say it did."

"I-I'm sorry," she said.

"Have you any other questions?" asked Barnhart.

"No. I appreciate you seein' me."

"I'd like to show you something if you've a moment."

"All right."

The man moved toward the closet. "Just a minute," interjected Harlowe. He, carefully, opened the door, first, to check.

Barnhart spoke in a devilish whisper, his eyes wild. "It's my new reel. For when I fish your Indian Creek...again."

Harlowe met the man's stare, his penetrating blue eyes as unflinching as Barnhart's were crazed. "Then, I'll see ya around."

Harlowe held that stare, slipping out the screendoor behind him.

***

Harlowe sat in his truck, waiting for Barnhart to come out.

He could hear the couple *fussin'* from down the street, the windows open.

Presently, Barnhart left with a doorslam, shuffling down the street. He turned the corner, creeping along in the dark, looking toward houses.

Harlowe followed, trying to determine what he was up to.

Barnhart lumbered to a place behind a tree. He stood there—in complete darkness—for several moments.

A man turned down his driveway, and Barnhart slid around the tree to avoid the light falling on him.

Is Barnhart fixin' to jump out and scare the man half to death? Harlowe wondered.

But Barnhart took off, back the way he'd come.

Harlowe continued to tail Barnhart. He found the projectionist took his walks every night. Saturday, he worked the kid's matinee.

***

Sunday, Barnhart opened up his shed, fiddling with something in the dark corner. He came out with it—a fishing pole—which he put in the back seat of his automobile.

Harlowe followed him out of town—down to Indian Creek, where Barnhart fished, alone, most of the day. Then, took a nap on a blanket beside his car.

Barnhart awakened. He left the bright spot in the moonlight, receding into the shadow of the woods, walking along a hogtrail—toward the Fulton place.

Barnhart hid behind a tree, while Foss sat on the doorstoop, drinking. Barnhart crept around, from tree to tree, like he enjoyed the risk of getting caught.

Presently, the man slipped back to his car. And slept.

***

True knew Harlowe always had the case on his mind. When he stirred paint cans, when he sawed baseboards, anything. His uncle *meditated* on little details. He was thinking about it, *now*, as they finished painting.

True's arms ached from reaching over his head to paint the trim pieces, but he felt good coming home. He felt proud to have put cabinets up, painted them, and made the bedroom pink just the way the customer wanted. He felt good when Harlowe told him he'd done a jam up job! He climbed down from the truck. Waved goodbye.

Foss was just getting home, too. He'd finished the workday at McCannon's sawmill at Green Point. He arms, neck wore a coating of sawdust, which stuck to his sweat. He took the first turn at the water pump outside, shot a disgusted glance at True. "What the hell has that uncle 'o yours got you doin'—pink paint all over ya?"
Lexie gave Foss a smooch. Handed him a towel as he come in. "We're havin' your favorite for suppah, Foss!"
Foss settled into his chair at the head of the table. His trim mustache flattened to a frown. "I have it right here, Foss," said Lexie, hurrying with the bowl. "Some good stew! 'Cause Deddy works so hard!" she told the children.
Foss gave a nod, seeing the steam rise from the bowl—supper had better be bubbling hot when served.
True, about to fall asleep he was so tired, lifted his arms and quietly finished what was set in front of him.
"More stew, Foss?" asked Mother, ladle in hand.

THIRTY-SIX

Eastpoint

September meant a return to school. True had "butterflies" the first day, like always. But he got busy with his chores, chopping stove-wood, before it was time to walk to the schoolhouse.

As he swung the ax, he couldn't help thinking of *that* first day of school. *He saw Gibby running up the road to meet him—all the way to the house. At that time, Wing's ferries still landed by True's house and it was just called the "Ferry Dock Road." And Elmer Smith's bar, across the road, hadn't burned yet.*

Gibby looked as happy as a hounddog with two tails! As usual, he saw a new adventure in it all. New opportunities to play baseball or fish and that was what Gibby talked about—that and a dozen more, fun things he wanted to do, as they walked side-by-side down the road to Cat Point. Mr. Brown— who everyone called Egg Brown because he made his living from selling eggs—came out to say hello and chatted with Gibby. Everyone loved Gibby—but Brown had been the boy's teacher, last year. The kind gentleman wished them well and they continued. They passed Brown's last fencepost and True knew it was inevitable.

He heard the other children playing, the crack of a chert rock on a mill scrap. A floor of pine straw amidst the tall trees was their playground. Butterbean Williams saw True's face. "What happened to you—tangle with a bear?"

"Hey, leave him be or I'll clobber ya," Gibby told him.

"Okay, Gibby. Damn, I didn't mean nothin' by it!"

"Jus' lay off 'im today, a'ight?"

"You fellas wanna play ball?" taunted another Williams cousin.

"Hell, yes!" replied Gibby. "True, y'gonna play?"

True shook his head.

Gibby was first to bat. He went through an elaborate ritual over home plate. Gyrating. Lining up.

"He thinks he's gonna hit somethin' with that," teased the Daughtry kid.

"I sure am, boah! You jus' watch!" retorted Gibby, squaring off like he was Ned Porter. Denny Williams let loose. Gibby swung. The bat connected good. He'd clobbered it! It shot speedily into the thick saw palmetto, yonder! That counted as a homer! The husky kid ran the bases (heaps of pinecones) beaming with pride.

True watched as Gibby struck out his cousin Jimmy Muldrow. And he was fixin' to do the same thing to Billy Wendels when the game was called by Miss Hazelwood—a stern figure in long skirt, ringing her handbell. The children scurried to line up at the wooden steps. The older children—True and Gibby attended with a dozen other children from seven to seventeen years of age—saw to it the line was straight. They filed neatly past the teacher, one-by-one taking their places inside the tiny wood-frame building. It was one of the buildings original to the Quaker colony. Inside, it was sheathed in bare wood aged darker than tobacco juice, the floor worn smooth by dozens of little feet that passed through in the thirty years since the school's founding.

Wooden, double-seater desks filled the room. These were made of dry wood as dark as the walls, the hard seat firmly affixed to the floor and normally shared by two students. Each child took his place, seated at them, hands folded in front, ready to pray and say the Pledge of Allegiance, salute the flag, and begin their lessons. Gibby sat two rows ahead of True. They sat toward the back, but Miss Hazelwood had split them up, moving Gibby up a tad closer.

The teacher shot a look at True. "Take off that coat, young man!"

"But Miss—." Gibby interrupted.

She held her hand up to silence him.

"Truitt! Take it off—now!"

"Yes'm."

The sight startled the teacher. "Oh!"

"True got a whoopin'!" whispered Denny, snickering, which led the girls to giggle, until they saw.

"Truitt, you may put it back on. Let's open our readers, children."

The reciting of new words, learning the Declaration by rote, and Mrs. Hazelwood's prompting the youngest students' answers to mathematical problems was uneventful. Gibby slunk low in the seat, hoping to avoid being called upon in the lesson on 'manners.' There were more interesting things beckoning beyond the windowpanes. Fun things.

When it seemed it couldn't get worse, the instruction turned to a book called Little Women! Gibby nearly slid out from his desk when he heard this! This book was for the fifth and sixth grades and he was supposed to keep going in his McGuffey reader while the older children recited this story. If he finished his reader, as the bright second and third grade students had done, it was encouraged that he follow along with the older pupils' reading. Bah! The advertisement for a new Neptune outboard he swiped from the Montg'y Ward catalogue in the outhouse was far more interesting! All he wanted was to get through his grammar and ciphers and endure the girls' taking turns reading Little Women at each other and run home as fast as he could. He'd do his chores. And, at long last, go fishing! But, oh, boy, look at that motor! That feller out on the water!

"Gibby? Gabriel Birch?!" Gibby didn't hear Miss Hazelwood. He looked up with a start when she appeared beside his desk. "Daydreaming again? I can't git you to quit goin' on about fishin' or boats, can I, Gabriel? You've been looking at magazine advertisements again, haven't you?"

Gabriel. He hated when they used his full, Christian name. It reminded him of the feller with the horn. What kind of oysterman has a name like that? he thought. The snickers from the first-grade boys only made it worse. "Yes ma'am," he replied, quietly, his face turning red. He folded the store catalogue pages which were blocking his grammar lesson. The sixth-grade girls resumed their readings, until—"Just a moment, girls," said Hazelwood. "What are you doing, Gabriel?" Miss Hazelwood was fit-to-be-tied!

Gibby tried to hide the worms he dug up and was keeping wet in the little cigar box he had in his lap. But Hazelwood was too fast, advancing down the aisle like a soldier going "over the top." True hung his head. His friend had been caught at it.

"What on earth is that?" demanded Hazelwood. When Gibby showed her, she put her hand on her hip. "Get those out—out of here! You really must take your lessons seriously! Don't you want to be a good student?"

Gibby mumbled something.

"Speak up, Gabriel!"

"Well, ma'am, I don't mean no offense. But I jus' wanna be an oyster man like my deddy!"

"What will you do if something happens and the oysters are all gone? One blight and it's all gone!" She thought that her emphasis was driving home the point that without education all endeavors were subject to great peril! And with the river as low as it was, surely he'd understand! "What would you do then?"

"Shrimp!" he replied, not missing a beat. The class burst out laughing. Even though Gibby meant no disrespect, Mrs. Hazelwood was madder than a hornet! Flippant, was what it was! How could he not see the hazard? And yet, you really couldn't be mad at Gibby. She shook her head. She pointed—directing Gibby to take his bait outside! He began moving, ever so slowly.

True tried to avoid Hazelwood's gaze. Hoped to disappear under the desk. But it didn't work—she'd turned toward him now. "And what about you, Truitt?"

"Ma'am?" he answered, shyly.

"Are you going to join your friend in his efforts to remain uneducated?"

"Umm...I-I dunno."

"He wants to oyster, too!" Gibby exclaimed. "An' he'd shrimp with me if the oysters ain't too big! We'll both work for Demo George!" Gibby wanted to make sure he spoke up for his pal.

Hazelwood looked exasperated. "That's just enough of that!" she replied, wheeling about to face the miscreant boy. "Outside with those things! Hurry!"

Gibby toted his box outside and returned, sauntering back like George Bancroft in Underworld. Hazelwood pointed to the corner. And he slumped, forehead to the wall. Held his McGuffey Second up in front of his face. Tried to hide his yawns—because he was bored enough to 'fall out.' "Now, you're going to try your best to finish this lesson, aren't you?" declared Hazelwood, tapping the end of her ruler on his head.

"Yes'm, Miss Hazelwood."

Gibby knew he'd be cleaning blackboards this afternoon. The schoolteacher could make him do anything and he'd do it—or face worse at home. Aubrey Birch was the fairest, gentlest of men, but you didn't sass the teacher. There was no defense. There was no 'lawyer man' here—not like the ones down at the courthouse that got paid cash money to talk a feller's way out of his punishment.

Boy, if only I could pay someone to git me out of this sos I could go fishin'! Gibby thought. But that was for rich folk. A poor boy don't git out of doin' his time like that. With any luck, I'll git it over with and git out on that dock—and all this here trouble would be behind me!

Gibby admired how True paid attention, how he worked at the books, learnin' to read and write, following the instructions and the recitin' by the older students when it was their turn. Look—True's already makin' them letters better'n I can! I got outta practice over the summer. I didn't write a damn thing, not even my name! *he thought, proudly.*

Gibby just wasn't interested in anything besides fishing. Or hunting, when it was the season. He thought only of his next catch. Saw no need to think too far beyond that. Redfish don't care how you wrote or read! Them Reds sure didn't wanna wait for no feller to set there and write 'em a strand of poetry!

Gibby noticed True was hollow in his cheeks. All he had to eat was a boiled egg and a small tomato in his dinner. Hard times seemed to be getting worse in Eastpoint, but the Fulton family was struggling more than most. Gibby knew about Mr. Fulton and his ways. His momma warned him to steer clear of "Foss." When Miss Hazelwood was distracted, he crept back to the desk. "Here, have this piece o' fish," said Gibby. "I caught this'n myseff. Smoked it real good! Takin' the skiff out after skoo. Ya comin' with me aincha?"

Lexie's voice interrupted True's thoughts. "Don't forget your dinner!"
True picked up the pail he carried his vittles in. Tucked in his shirt-tail. He had no shoes. He'd outgrown and worn them out, so he'd start school without them.
Foss shot a look at him. "After skoo, ya getchya ass over to Old Man McCannon's."
"I don't wanna work at the oysterhouse, I—."
"I don't keer *what* you want! You'll do what I tellya and *like it!*" Foss spat.
"But I told Uncle Pratt—."
"'Bout time you start keerin' 'bout what I say. You git over to the oysterhouse after skoo. There'll *be* no more runnin' off to your uncle!"
True shrunk into the corner.
Lexie handed Foss his big lunchbox, as he fussed about Harlowe and the boy. "He's gettin' too much like your damned brother!"
"Yes, Foss—I."
"I don't like 'im runnin' over there."
"O.K, Foss."
"No wife, no kids of his own, jus' mindin' everyone else's bidness." Foss looked over at True. "It ain't doin' *him* no good."
"All right."
"Maybe Old Man Mccannon will beat that damned bashfulness outta him."
Lexie nodded. "Go on to school, True."

***

The 'pop' sounded like a gunshot. The wheel pulled. Harlowe slid to a stop on the flat tire.
The isolated country south of Sumatra had no settlements. Yet, while he got out the jack, worked to get the tire off, he felt 'eyes on him.'

Harlowe saw no sign of 'company.' But it was hard to tell, these woods gave you a feeling of eyes watching anyhow.

The section harbored a few 'rough customers.' The kind that'd just as soon take a shot at a man as look at him.

He glanced out at the pine flatwoods of Tate's Hell. The floor was blanketed with saw palmetto and stretched to infinity. *A fella hiding way back in theah could see you, but you caint see him and there's nowhere to hide on the road.*

He got the spare on. He'd be glad to see that Tallahassee sign.

***

"Egg" Brown was back to "keeping school" this year. The old man's farmhouse's second-story roof and the church's wooden cross loomed above the scrub pines, both equally foreboding to a young boy. True was almost to the schoolhouse. He reached the turnoff, the path through the pines and saw palmetto which was darker for all the pine boughs above his head.

He made a straight line for the door, past Mr. Brown, and took his place. Gibby's old desk was still empty.

As it was the morning after.

He couldn't look away from the empty desk. Gibby's desk.

It was like how they showed "The End" on the screen in a cowboy picture, only much worse. Gibby was lost. Maybe dead.

All the other children were talking about it when Mrs. Hazelwood shook her handbell. All except True. He couldn't stand to talk about it. He just looked at that desk.

The teacher began the prayer. True looked down, feeling the tears at the corner of his eyes and fighting them back.

"Truitt? Oh, Truitt?" went the far-away voice.

Truitt? Only schoolteachers or Mother and Deddy call me that. Not since Uncle Pratt shortened it.

The teacher saw True's mind was miles away. Mercifully, she called on someone else to lead the Pledge.

They're all talking about Gibby, *True thought. My best friend.*

He couldn't concentrate on anything else. It bothered him, it made him shiver, thinking his pal was lost somewheres-dead somewheres. He had that fuzzy, hazy feeling from being up all night.

He was hungry. It only made him miss his friend more. Gibby often brought him a piece of fish. Gibby was that kind of fella. He knew True was going to bed hungry. He knew True was down to skin and bones, he was about the skinniest kid after workin' all that summer for McCannon.

The class began their ciphering.

"Truitt? Truitt?" the voice repeated.

"Yes'm?"

"Truitt? Oh, you heard me this time," said an annoyed Miss Hazelwood. "Are you paying attention to any of this, boy? What is the answer to the next conundrum?"

"I reckon I don't know, ma'am." If she can see I ain't payin' attention, why does she ask, with a fifty-cent word thrown in? Boy, I'd better not say that! Gibby might, but I caint, *thought True.*

"Were you paying attention?"

"No, ma'am." No use lyin.' Maybe she'll quit. No, she ain't gonna quit, *he saw, the teacher's hands going to her hips.*

"Listen, Truitt Fulton, what happened was terrible. And the men are still looking, you can be sure of that. But we cannot neglect our arithmetic. You'll have to stay after school today."

"Yes'm."

Today. The drone of reading, the clack of numbers on the blackboard. True counted the hours dreading a return to Graham McCannon's oysterhouse. He forgot all about being nervous around the other kids or being asked to recite something. Now it was just McCannon! By the time the day was over, True was glad Mr. Brown hadn't called on him and no one asked him any questions. He wasn't sure he could speak without his voice breaking.

He left the schoolhouse quickly, alone down the path in the pines. He could see the roof-peak of the oysterhouse from there. His heart beat faster with every step toward it.

The oysterhouse floated on its wooden pilings. Its gabled roofs pointed upwards. Going 'everywhich-way.' It had seen a coat of white paint at some point—before True was born. Sunbaked and as salty as an old gull, it was a fascinating run of gray-weathered docks and walkways and places for a boy like Gibby to hide and play and fish. It brought more of those first-day-of-school butterflies to True.

The general store across the road. "Dry goods, sundries, & notions, Tom Estes, propr.," read the sign. Mr. Tommy had the only store in Eastpoint. White paint peeled from clapboard. Smoke puffed from the woodstove.

True swallowed. Proceeded down the walkway. His soles burned on the wooden planking as if he was marching toward the door to Hades. Gibby fished off of the dock, yonder. True could see him just as clear.

He removed his hat. He stepped over the threshhold, heart pounding. Further inside, was a door which said "OFFICE." It seemed large enough for a giant. And, indeed, Mr. McCannon was as big as a tree. He was the kind the fellas at school told stories about—in lieu of ghosts and Sherman. Grown men told their stories too, like the time McCannon threatened to buggy-whip a fella who wouldn't refund him the purchase of a horse. True worked for him that one summer. He knew firsthand how hard a man McCannon was.

True pushed the door, which gave a groan on its hinges. A booming voice made him jump back like a skittish pup. "Come on in here, boah!" True couldn't see him. His eyes hadn't adjusted to the darkness.

"Over here," said McCannon, more quietly, as True entered the shadow. McCannon actually smiled. "I hear you a hard worker?"

"Y-yessir."

"Then we'll git along fine. Y'can start on that mess 'o shells theah."

"Yessir," said True. It seemed the old gentleman didn't remember him—but True wasn't going to press the issue one way or the other. But then the old man caught him by the elbow!

"Boah, it's too bad your buddy ain't with ye! He was a real good worker."

***

Heat clung to the low ceiling. The cookstove baked both biscuits and boys. True finished adding stovewood. Paused to wipe his brow. Lexie looked up from her stirring. "Set the table, True. Deddy'll be home soon."

True automatically set the first plate at Foss's place.

Foss barged in and barked, "let's eat."

Lexie ladled his portion of stew on the china plate—the best portion—and served him first. Then she brought over the pot of peas for him.

THIRTY-SEVEN

Tallahassee

Without True's help, the Prado house didn't proceed very rapidly.
Harlowe drove to Tallahassee—leaving plaster and tile undone.
Harlowe saw Mrs. Sadler. "Anything unusual about Mr. Barnhart, you say?"
"Yes, ma'am."
"What do you mean? Why do you want to know?"
He explained it was to do with children.
"I don't know why you're concerned with him—he's a *nothing.* What baffles me is the Eubanks family."
"Ma'am?"
"The boy, the entire family, just up and left town—two years ago. Now there's a mystery for you if I ever saw one."
"Their name was Eubanks?"
"*Ye-ess.* The boy was eight. They lived on Meridian, there." She fetched her city directory from 1929 and showed him the address. "Something happened to that boy, they left all of a sudden!"
"Oh?"
"Yes, sir. You'd have to ask them, what. Y'know you really need to take care of yourself—all this tension isn't good for a man your age! I imagine you're a coffee drinker!"
He scrawled the name in his notebook. "Yes'm—thankya!"
Harlowe walked to the small bungalow. Then, Harlowe walked back along College Avenue, to Barnhart's apartment.
"I'll be darned." Door-stoop to door-stoop, walking down College, stretched shorter than the *Florida Limited!* Harlowe walked it. *Barnhart could see the boy's rooftop from his second-floor windows!*
Whittle's old house was of equal distance—the three points forming a triangle!

Harlowe talked to people about the Eubanks'. Until Deputy Mealer flagged him down. "The Chief Deputy wants to talk to ya."

Harlowe noticed the desks when he walked in. He counted three telephones—including one on Chief Deputy Royce Sackett's desk. A young woman, the secretary, was busy watering geraniums by the sheriff's windows.
A quarter-hour passed before Sackett came in. Stubbed out his cigarette and waved Harlowe over. He looked aggravated.
"Have a chair, Pratt."
"All right. What did ya wanna see me about?"
"Just a friendly visit." He offered Harlowe a cigarette. Harlowe declined.
"I dont know what goes on in other counties, but things like that don't happen here, Pratt. Kids might run away, they turn up again. Some people like the Eubanks move away. We have that from time-to-time, like you would anywhere. Mostly, people wanna stay. This's a good place to live—it's my job to keep it thataway."

"Uh-huh."

"Pratt, we just don't won't to alarm people, needlessly, with trouble from out-of-town. Things that don't concern us."

"May I see the cards on the missing children reports?"

"They ain't none." Sackett looked to the girl, who was by now making a pot of coffee.

She opened a cabinet, looked inside and shook her head.

Sackett stood. "Y'see, things like that don't happen here, Pratt." He walked Harlowe to the door. "It sure is good to see ya!" He sawed Harlowe's hand. "If I can he'p ya, just holler."

Harlowe said goodbye. The door with Ledbetter's name on it clicked shut.

In the hours that followed, the lady at the A&P told him, "Heard the Eubanks' moved someplace up in Alabama."

He walked. Knocked on doors. For nothing.

***

It was like he was missing a brother, an arm, a whole side of him. That's what Gibby was like.

True saw them playing ball. *The Williams boys and them.*

When they were little, Gibby would speak up for True. He'd drag him along fishing. Make sure he wasn't left out. *"Y'all, True's gonna play—he's your pitcher, now!"*

But Gibby wasn't here. True went on mending the fence—glancing at the ballgame between nails.

Lexie approached. Whispered, "Deddy expects you to get your chores done before you leave—Deddy works hard."

True nodded. Finished it up and ran down to the oysterhouse. He entered and commenced scraping the gray worktables, hauling the shells outside, to the mound aside the building. It was like a mountain to a kid. He raked a mess of shells clear of the vents outside, too.

He ran to school. Got there just in time. Forced himself to pay attention. He did what was expected of him. *You get in trouble if they catch you daydreamin'.*

School dismissed. Then back to his job. This time, cleaning the oysters with water after they were shucked by the adults.

McCannon was pleased with how the boy worked. He "graduated" True to shucking. He was given an apron like the others. McCannon warned him, "no dawdlin'. Work fast, boah!"

True found it was no 'promotion.' The building was like an oven. His hands were worked numb. Sweat stung his eyes. He stopped to wipe his brow and McCannon came out, hollering, "git back to work!"

There was scarcely a boy in the county who couldn't open an oyster. But True watched the shuckers working alongside him—how they did it so quickly amazed him.

"That's it, ya pry 'im open and drop 'im in da bucket," said the old colored man to his right. His name was Bingham—and he was the fastest. A heap of empty shells covered the table in front of him. He dropped those oysters one-after-the-other into the pail, working that button knife as if he were a machine. The shuckers all stood at their tables, prying, sweating. Bingham was the most talkative.

"Don't worry 'bout da bossman! He holla at ever'body! Ya jus' keep on like you is. It might help ya to hum a little song. Keep a rhythm, like 'is." He showed him, by singing a song as he pried open an oyster, and dropped him in the bucket, with movements as smooth as a man dancing with his girl.

True turned around when he heard his name. "Uncle Pratt!"

"Hiya, son. How you likin' it?"

"I like it all right."

"Good! Hello there, Bingham."

"Moanin,' Mistuh Pratt!"

McCannon even came out and was friendly. But Harlowe couldn't stay long. He patted True on the shoulder. "Just wanted to look in on ya." With that Harlowe walked out into the blazing sunlight. True listened to the truck drive away.

"Yo uncle a good man," said Bingham. "He always leave a man his dignity. I don't expec' you know what dat means, now."

True shook his head.

"You will someday. You jus' listen to yo' uncle and watch how he do."

True nodded.

Harlowe looked back at the oysterhouse. Lexie had told him he ought not come by the house anymore. Foss wouldn't like it.

***

"He used to ask me to look in on his house while he was away. Mr. Barnhart was away often—several days at a time," said Mr. Farris. The latter was barnhart's neighbor, letting a room behind him, on Gadsden Street.

Farris had just returned home from work. He was feeding his pet mice, in a cage.

"Have you any idea where Mr. Barnhart went on these trips?"

"I wasn't prying, of course. But I understand he went fishing quite a lot. Fall of twenty-seven, into early twenty-eight. As I say, I'd look in on the Barnharts' apartment, tend to their cat."

"Did his wife go with him?"

"I didn't say that. She went to her mother's while he was gone."

"Was he gone any, during the month of September of nineteen-hunnerd-and-twenty-seven?"

"I can check my diary. I'd be happy to."

"Would you do that? It's pretty important."

The man retrieved the book. He noted watching the house September 18.

"And so you were friends--."

"I'm an acquaintance, not a friend. Note that correctly."

"Yessir. I wonder if he mentioned meeting any children down theah, anything you can recall?"

"I don't recall him saying anything of the kind."

"When's the last time you spoke to him?"

"I try to limit my interaction. We're neighbors. I speak to him is all."

Farris was another "Joe Average." He could be anyone's uncle or fellow down the street. He was a butcher at the A&P at 308 South Monroe.

Harlowe walked back to his truck. Before he could climb in, a car pulled, slowly, around the corner—Ledbetter's. "Why, Pratt! This's a surprise! Good to see ya!" He thrust his hand out the window.

Harlowe shook it. "Howdy, Sheriff."

"What brings you this way?"

"Oh, still lookin' into this matter for the Hutto fam'ly."

"Well, I'm late for a meetin' at the Elks Club. If you need anythin'—anythin' at all, just call me!"

"I'll do that."

"And stop by the house 'fore you leave. Mrs. Ledbetter'd *love* to see ya."

***

Harlowe finished roofing the Prado house.

He found Farris at work, no one else at the butcher shop as it neared closing time.

Farris was slicing beef behind the counter.

"Uh-huh. How does Barnhart get along with children?"

"Fine, I suppose. I've never heard him *mention* children. He and his wife have none."

"And you watched his house while he was fishin', September, nineteen-and-twenty-seven?"

"Yes. But I must tell you something—Barnhart's no fisherman. Sorta likes to wander around, he'll say 'this spot is no good, let's try over here. No, this is no good, let's go.' Doesn't stick with anything. Consequently, I don't go with him too often."

"You've gone with him, then. Fishing down theah?"

"Yes. Twice."

"Fishing—he doesn't do it right. I go to a good spot and stay put. That's the right way to do it."

"I see."

"You agree, of course."

"Yessir. Where did you go, when you fished with him?"

"Cat Point, I believe it was."

"When?"

169

"Oh, I imagine it around the time you keep mentioning. Barnhart went all the time. He wasn't much of a salesman—a man like that spends too much time on recreating."

"You drove down with him, then, September of that year?"

"Yes. Late that month. You know, Whiskey George Creek is another fine spot—up the road, there. A place you can go and spend the day!"

"You've fished Whiskey George, then?"

"By myself—I want to make that clear. I'm no friend of Barnhart's."

"You two have a falling out?"

"Not exactly that. I just don't care to associate too closely with a man that..."

"Yessir?"

"Let me just say, I haven't gone with him in four years. Note that."

"Uh-huh. Did Mr. Barnhart do somethin' you didn't like?"

"Mr. Barnhart is Mr. Barnhart. It's nothing to do with me."

"Yessir. When's the last time you were in Cat Point?"

"Not since the time you keep referencing."

"Well, there's somethin' about that September I been wondering about?"

"Yes, what is that?"

"Do you know why Barnhart sold his car right after that?"

"Did he sell his car right after? Now let me see...Yes, I do recall him 'showing off' the one he has now. Why?" asked Farris, sympathetically. "Say would you like some of this liverwurst—it's a fine meat!"

"No, thankya. Do you know why he sold that car—the one he took to Eastpoint, that September?"

The man picked up his knife. "Mr. Harlowe...that was *my* Ford. We made that trip in *my* car."

"Oh."

Farris drew the knife back to slice through the beef. "So...those could have been my tracks," he breathed.

They were alone in the store, the street dark through the open doors.

A passing freight shrieked. "Where is your car, now?" asked Harlowe, backing toward the end of the counter.

"I don't drive to work. I can walk. As you know."

"Yessir."

Harlowe held out Gibby's photo. "You know this boy?"

Farris looked at it. Made another cut of the meat. "No. Anything else you would like to know?" he asked, holding the knife.

"No, Mr. Farris. You've been helpful."

Harlowe walked behind Farris' house. The Ford had those same tires. 'Non Skid.'

Harlowe opened the back door. Looked in the seat. There was a folding fishing rod.

He walked to the Eubanks' old house. You could see Mr. Farris' place from the front porch!

Had the boy walked right past here, on his way to school?

***

Barnhart invited Harlowe to come up into the projection booth. The afternoon movie was playing. Barnhart looked out at the audience, through the little window in the booth.

He gestured for Harlowe to look. *There's a man on the bum after losing his job. A lonely girl. An old man who was needed nowhere else. Two children who'd paid their fifteen cents after school let out.*

"Fun to watch, isn't it?" asked Barnhart, leaning in to be heard over the click of the projector and the din of the western shoot-'em-up unfolding onscreen.

"The movie?"

"The people. That's what you were doing, correct?"

Harlowe nodded.

"Me too." Barnhart's face was spectre-like in the flickering light.

"Talkies have ruined pictures—but I still enjoy this." He touched Harlowe's arm. "I think the children are the most interesting. Don't you think?"

Harlowe lit a Chesterfield. "Maybe. Why don't ya tell me about it."

"*Sooo*...innocent aren't they?" Barnhart breathed. "Everything is new to them, the excitement! For instance...it must have been something for the boy, there. *So dark. Lonesome. Someone creeeeeeping up and grabbing him!* Oh, it was more than frightening! He probably felt terror for the first time!"

"Ya mean Gibby?"

"Oh, *yesss*. Yesss."

"How do you know Gibby?"

"I've followed the case. In the paper—back when it happened."

"Uh-huh."

"May I ask you something I've often wondered?"

Harlowe nodded.

"Do you really think he acted *alone?*"

"How do you mean?"

"I mean, wouldn't the, uh, Bobby Franks case be an...*example?*" the way he said the word sounded eerie as a crypt. "I should think he'd have a partner, don't you?"

"Why?"

"How would he handle the boy, and drive at the same time?"

"It's a fair point, Mr. Barnhart."

"Would one man be able to get the boy into his automobile? Is that possible, Mr. Harlowe?" The man looked ghoulish in the light. He acted like he was enjoying this. Like he was on stage, or on that screen himself.

"I didn't know the paper reported on it," said Harlowe, stubbing out the cigarette.

"It must have."

Harlowe held up the photo of Gibby. "His mother and daddy want to know where he is. Would you know somethin' that would help us find 'im?"

"No, not *I.*"

"What do you mean by that, Mr. Barnhart?"

"Oh, excuse me." The "The End" flashed on the screen. Barnhart sprang forward to stop the projector, the booth going quiet as a tomb.

The Daffin closed for the night. Harlowe watched Barnhart leave from the back door. Walk home.

171

In the days that followed, Harlowe sat in his truck, watching.
The gray light of twilight. Did his eyes see movement—or merely vague particles floating in his tired eyes.
Was that the door opening?
Yes. And Barnhart slippin' out. He lurked behind a magnolia. Then, proceeded up College, stopping at Farris' house. He walked up to the porch—stopped—ran into the darkness.

Harlowe could establish no connection—either as to Barnhart or as to Farris—to Whittle, Kern, or the Eubanks.'

***

Driscoll got out of his car. Walked into the Barnes Apartments—703 N. Monroe.
Harlowe slid across the seat, getting out at the curb. He entered the little foyer of the building. He scrolled the names written, there, on the mailboxes on the wall.
'Capps'—one of Ledbetter's men.
Driscoll left, quietly, though a little red-faced.
Harlowe stayed. He'd see who else came out.
Presently, emerged a man in a boater hat. Harlowe recognized him—Deputy Capps.
He got into a new Ford, making the rounds at various places around town. Harlowe followed. While the deputy was careful, he wasn't careful enough about the tail. At a quarter-til-five, Harlowe watched him carry a valise into the backway of the sheriff's office. *I believe they have a word for what he is*—bagman.

THIRTY-EIGHT

Tallahassee, Saturday.

Little kids, excited to see a shoot-em-up picture, hurried to the movie house. They walked alone—they were eight-years-old, after all.
Harlowe shivered. Barnhart was on one corner and Farris lurked in his little window on the other! Harlowe saw him look out at the passing kids.

Farris' neighbor said, "He's a decent fellow. Always kind."
Harlowe tipped his hat. "Well, I 'preciate ya talkin' to me."
On to the next.
A woman on South Gadsden ironed a workshirt, her movements in sync with the rhythm of the Maytag sloshing away on the porch beside her.
"Y'know if you were a *real* detective you'd learn something."
"Yes, ma'am?"
"Sure! It's staring you in the face and y'can't see it! Farris wasn't the only odd one 'round heah."
"Ma'am?"
"Line Colbert."
"I don't believe I've heard the name."
"Well, I can't help that. What you're asking about—men in the neighborhood, you ought to be looking at *him.*"
Harlowe found that the man was sent to the state prison in '28. Harlowe walked into the Clerk of Court and checked the old dockets.
"Carnal abuse of female under 10." Hell.

No one wanted wanted to talk about it. Harlowe found out the reason:
Colbert's Daddy worked for the state chemist at the capitol. Boys, coming home from the grammar school, passed by, toting their books.

Harlowe motored to Chattahoochee. Patients were sitting in chairs in the hall, motionless, staring blankly. "Right this way, Mr. Harlowe," the nurse directed.
Elston listened with interest. "Say, you mind if I bring in a colleague?"
"No, sir, I don't."
Elston reached for the telephone. "I trust this fella. Dr. Cotillard? Could you come to my office? Yeah."
Presently, the young psychiatrist appeared and Elston asked Harlowe to re-state the pertinent facts.
The young Doctor nodded, enthusiastically. "Striking a rural area such as Eastpoint. And what you are facing, with modern automobile travel meaning this man may have come from anywhere—I'm afraid my field is only beginning to consider the mind of such a man." Cotillard had a slight French accent—was in his late thirties, Harlowe thought.
"Doctor, in your opinion would he go on and lead a normal life, would he just fade away?"

"Yes, he might stay out of trouble. He could control his impulses—for a time. No one can be sure. He's not quite a ticking time-bomb. But there's a danger, none-the-less. I wish I knew more to tell you, Mr. Harlowe."

Harlowe mentioned what he'd encountered in Tallahassee.
"Oh, yes," Cotillard declared. "Very often people don't do anything about it, they can't do anything about the fellow down the block, it's just unspoken, something children are quietly warned about. They live with it. *"Be careful around that fellow,"* they'll say."

They can get in a car and be in my county in less than two hours.
Who else is out there I don't know about?

Records at the city hall revealed something to Harlowe. Colbert had an alibi the night Gibby went missing! He was in the city jail.

By now, the district manager of the A&P Company had responded to the telegram—about whether Farris was at work the evening Gibby went missing.
Harlowe heard stories about Farris. How he'd invite the children over to his home. But his neighbors said he'd let them run his toy train, was a kindly sort and gave the children something to do in these bleak times.
"He lives alone." Harlowe heard that more times than he could count!
Living alone *is* unusual. A man who wasn't married by twenty-five *is* unusual. And Farris, thirty-one, had never wed. *Ought that fact condemn him, the fact that he lives alone? Hell, so do I.*

Harlowe read the telegram. *"Mr. Farris was working the evening of the 19th September."*
Harlowe walked out of the Western Union office.
It was dark now. He crossed Monroe. Passed McDaniel's barbershop at 117 East Park. Doors open. Line of farmers waiting. They'd be open until midnight.

Nearing his truck, he heard someone call his name—a car pulling alongside—Sackett's. "Evenin'! Nice night, ain't it?" The small talk, Harlowe was certain, was a prelude to what Sackett really wanted. "Well, Pratt. Jus' wanted to say, we glad to have ye—always! But we do things a certain way 'roun here. You need to get up with someone, why, all you gotta do is ask. I'd be delighted to help ya any way I can, if ya tell me who you lookin' for."
Harlowe nodded.
Sackett looked straight ahead, fingers tapping the wheel. "We don't have these problems heah. Not like Chicaguh or some o' them cities. This's a good place to live—we gonna keep it thataway."
Harlowe nodded.
"Why, if any of us thought someone was doin' something to hurt one of our younguns, y'think we'd stand for it? No, sir, not for one minute—w'ed tar n' feather 'im ourselves!"
"Well, somethin' happened to one of our younguns. Maybe it wasn't someone who lives heah. But someone heah knows somethin.'"

"I like you, Pratt. I say this as yer friend." He let a matchflame lick his cigarette. "People in this town won't like someone comin' in—and bringin' problems *heah*. Would'n wanna see ya get *burned,* Pratt."
"Well, I appreciate that."
Sackett tossed the match. "This ain't your county, son."

***

The last week of October, the fair was in town. Harlowe followed Barnhart there, the latter walking around, watching people try to shoot their way to a prize.

Harlowe followed him down the midway. Past "The Vampire Lucelle" up on her stage. Past the "Midget Village." Barnhart paused at the dancin' chicken booth—but moved on. He stopped to watch the action at another shooting gallery. The bang of the guns competed with the carnival music and barkers!

An organ grinder with a monkey on his shoulder, came down the midway. Children gathered around the jovial man. They watched him delightfully; he smiled and laughed with them, playing his music, dancing as he cranked the music machine.

He moved in their midst. Up and down. Up and down. Laughing. Laughing. The kids leaning in close. The monkey dancing, taking a peanut from the children and chattering. The man laughing. Dancing in their midst!

The little boys followed him almost trance-like. The man, cranking and cranking, dancing and dancing, the kids swept along with him. It give Harlowe a chill, just how vulnerable children truly are, how defenseless they are in a country on wheels! These fair workers would be long gone by the end of the week.

That wasn't all. Ledbetter had spoken. And, while he was too *hospitable* to convey a discordant message, himself, he'd very thoughtfully sent two of his men. Their automobiles sat at the entrance to the fairgrounds. Skinny hounds in hats, their paws resting on the steering wheels. *Watching me,* Harlowe realized.
Barnhart was into some weird things. Did that mean he was guilty?

The deputy followed Harlowe to the county line, only. The mirror was clear, but his thoughts were crowded the rest of the way.

He moved over for an oncoming car—the road skinny and hard to see. *One car, like that one, could pass without notice very easily. How many thousands cross the highways of the state, calling little attention to themselves?*
Later, at the *Riverside*, the men listened to Sharkey defeat the Italian, Carnera, in the fifteenth round.

***

Harlowe located Mrs. Eubanks working at a sewing factory in Dothan.
"Nothing was wrong a'tall. I had to move. Only place I could get work!"
Harlowe thanked her.
Walked out into the heavy night air, a train whistle out yonder.
He'd struck out.

THIRTY-NINE

Apalachicola, October.

Seago was waiting when he got home. "I don't think any of them had anything to do with it," Harlowe told him.

"With all 'o that?"

"Well, just cause he's odd doesn't make 'im a killer."

"That's enough about all that—don't even take yo hat off!"

"Why?"

"Come on! You havin' suppah with us! Penelope will have it near ready, I expect."

"You sure it ain't no trouble, now?"

"Nah!" Seago flung open the passenger's door. Drove them down to the Seago residence on Avenue I—across from the jail.

Seago got the screendoor. "Come on and get inside 'fore the flies. Come on in hea! Baby—look who's back!"

"Why, good evenin' Pratt! I made fried chicken!"

Harlowe took his hat off. Wiped his feet. "Well, I sure appreciate it. 'Preciate y'all havin' me."

The lady of the house took his hat. A whole heap of food was already on the table.

"Go on'n fix-ya-a-plate!" said Seago.

Miss Seago sets a fine table. Mighty fine. This is...like family. It touched Harlowe. "Y'all are very kind to go to all this."

"Nonsense, it's no trouble!" said the woman.

"Getchyou enough! Then we fixin' to say Grace!" declared Seago. The couple, whose children were grown, held hands. They took Harlowe's hands and gave thanks for the food and having Pratt with them.

"A'ight! Git after it!" said the big man, tearing into the leg.

Between mouthfuls, Seago began a new story about his last hog hunt. Some of Harlowe's weariness was forgotten.

***

"Ooh—it's hot as the dickens!" cried Seago. "How much longer we gonna be out here anyhow?"

Harlowe poked the soft ground with a long stick, feeling for anything buried there.

"Where you learn that?" asked Seago. "Why caint Brewer and Twiggs hep' ya on this. Shoot, they younger'n-me!"

"They're lazy as the day is long. You'll complain the whole time, but you'll work."

Seago cussed. "Y'really think we'll find somethin'?"

Harlowe nodded. "I'm sure of it."

They continued checking the wilderness up along the Sumatra Road.

Then, Harlowe wanted to dig up Elmer Smith's saloon! Seago couldn't believe it!

Only the chimney remained, but it had flourished during Pender's time, an old log house that had been turned into a tavern. Folks, from Eastpoint and Apalach, both, went there to dance and fight. Some folks said the local wives got together and "rid" the settlement of this "nuisance." In late '29.

Harlowe poked in the ashes.

"What if Foss' dogs git to yappin'?" Seago wondered.

"I don't keer," replied Harlowe.

The men patrons all searched for Gibby. Later on, these fellas and the two gals there that night, told Harlowe no one saw anything. It was just bad luck. The storm came. People hunkered down. They didn't see anything on the road.

Harlowe turned a shovel where the old back doorstoop had been.

"Look yonder, that's C.P. Williams standin' there, Pratt. Musta heard yo' truck."

"Yeah."

"Half Eastpoint is probably wonderin' what the hell we doin.'"

"That's all right."

"Oh, I see! You a sly ol' coondog—I shoulda known. Now, we checked all o' this heah. Can we go now? There' ain't nothin' here, 'n these damn skeeters 'bout to carry me off, son!"

"All right. We can break off for tonight."

***

"Listen at this. 'Judge Crater Mystery Baffles.' Up in New York," said Seago, holding up the paper. "Still missin.' They may never solve it! So many places a man can fall, or get put. All along that Long Island there."

"No trace, eh?" asked Harlowe.

"Well, it says here that—."

The jingling telephone interrputed.

It was County Commissioner Corbin Huff.

"Pratt! I'd like to know something of this business in Tallahassee," he demanded.

Harlowe explained it was about Gibby.

"Pratt, I'm getting' calls about this. You need to think about what you're doing. We are tryin' hard to get that bridge. This damn *antagonizing* people in Tallahassee ain't no way to go about it! Think it over."

CLICK.

"What now?" wondered Seago.

"Your case in New York, theah—all the place those lawmen have to look at."

"Yeah?"

"When you're fishin' do you go down lookin' for the fish or do ya bring 'em to you?"

"Why, ya use bait."

"All right."

Harlowe visited with Mrs. Birch nearly a quarter hour. She agreed to his plan.

It was like baiting a line with a crab. Harlowe paid for an obituary in the Tallahassee paper. The *Times*, didn't charge. It said there'd be a funeral—Gibby's.

FORTY

Eastpoint, October, 1931

Normally, in the South the deceased would be laid on the kitchen table for the 'Sitting Up.' Or the casket, if they had one yet, would be placed in the room and open. In this instance it was closed, resting on Mrs. Birch's kitchen table, there in the middle of the mourners—little tots to old men.

Death was not unfamiliar to the people here. It had come often in the thirty years since Eastpoint was settled—bouts of scarlet fever, influenza, drownings. Death was faced at home. Neighbors came together for the family of the deceased. Folks took care of everything without outside help, tending to their own, as there was no funeral parlor, nor doctor in Eastpoint. And the women would put Mrs. Birch's house in order after the funeral.

Folks adjusted to the unusual case. The death was not recent, as everyone knew. They did without the 'Sitting Up,' but they made up for it with more food. Neighbors were still arriving with their arms laden with dishes. Already, there was enough to feed a company of soldiers. In the Southland, food is often the first consideration of neighbors when trouble arises. It's what Southern people do, and the people there, while poor, had assembled a feast worthy of a Governor's passing, Gibby's coffin in the middle of it all.

It was fitting to honor Gibby. All the settlement could do so, now that they knew he was gone. The obituary made it official that his body had been found. It was fitting to allow the Birches their mourning. To honor them.

Gibby's coffin was small. Child-size. *"That's all he got to grow,"* someone said.
"You say Mr. Sangaree just give it to us—for our Gibby?" asked Mrs. Birch. Harlowe nodded.
"We caint afford much," said Mrs. Birch. "It's so wonderful they've done this." Ordinarily, people in Eastpoint had a home-built casket of rough pine. The store-bought coffin was far beyond what they could have purchased for the boy.
"People really were fond of him," said Aubrey.
"Yes, they were," said Harlowe.

"We never got to mourn really."

"Yessir."
They heard jingling. It was the hearse—not the motorcar—but the old one drawn by "Black Satin" and "Midnight."
"Mornin', Sheriff. Mornin' Miss Lillian, Aubrey. I'm back!" Sangaree hollered.
As he whoaed the horses, he reached down from the carriage to hand Harlowe a note. "This is for you," said the undertaker. "I thought this thing would roll right off the ferry—but we here!"

Harlowe opened the note. "Some of the men and women in Apalach got togethuh and ordered this headstone," he explained.

"Headstone?" asked Mrs. Birch. She went around. Looked inside the hearse. Indeed, there was a marble stone, with GIBBY BIRCH on it.

"Oh, it's a fine monument. Mighty fine," said she. "I don't rightly know what to say! That's a nice thing they done!"

Presently, they all gathered at the black-pine church, built long ago by the Quakers, across from Egg Brown's place.

St. George's Sound a vibrant blue backdrop, and the singing drifted over the whole settlement. McCannon closed the mill for two hours and nearly everyone in Eastpoint attended. Not a sound of any other activity other than the funeral could be heard. Men and women, boys and gals, came down from High Point and Beverly. Another carload came over from Apalach on the *Short Cut*.

There was Lexie and the children, Harlowe noticed, from his place at the door of the church. There was so many that some gathered outside, Harlowe among them. He watched, wondering who would come. A stranger? A face known to him?

The Reverend Giles preached, leaving not a dry eye in the church. Then the men carried the coffin out to the hearse, now covered in a fine arrangement from Apalach's florist, the flower's donated by Market Street businessmen. Sangaree started the coffin for the graveyard, the horses jingling up the dirt road. They turned onto the coastal highway. Horses clopping on the pavement. The masts of oysterboats tied along the shoreline waved gently at the procession.

Sangaree drove the hearse into the woods, then. Gibby's neighbors had dug the hole at the edge of Tate's Hell, in the shade of the pines. The men stood up that headstone. No one else had such a stone in Eastpoint— which had never seen anything like today's funeral.

Seago leaned close. "This mean we can quit diggin'?" wondered Seago "If it works," Harlowe replied.

The crowd reassembled. The preacher took his place at the feet of the coffin. The words of "Farther Along" drifted over the wooden markers and crosses as the people, singing, reverently lined up to face the minister in black.

Giles preached again, admonishing the people that, "today is the day of Salvation."

Harlowe stood beside True, his sister and the little ones. Harlowe watched the faces. The late arrivals. He had his men, Brewer and Twiggs, watching the ferries and who came on the train, who motored to Eastpoint. Harlowe examined each face as Giles talked.

To everyone's surprise, behind them appeared a carriage—Mrs. Ruge's old black brougham. Her man pulled alongside the hearse. She stepped down, a dignified form of black lace and taffeta; the crowd parted, allowing her to take her place at the front of the mourners.

Bingham was crying. "Mistuh Gibby! Oh, Mistuh Gibby!"
Lexie quietly sobbed and patted Florie and Little Foss and kissed their cheeks. "It's terrible!" she whispered, as Giles reminded them, "No man knows the day nor the hour!"

True wondered, *If I had gone with Gibby that day. Maybe he wouldna been lost. Did the man know he'd be alone? Gibby wouldna left me...*

The Birches stood like statues, through it all.

Harlowe noted mourners from Carrabelle. The old man from St. Teresa had come. There was Pender, in a charcoal suit, standing aside McCannon.
At that, Seago nudged Harlowe's elbow. "Look here."
Harlowe saw him. Foss Fulton—the fellow joined Lexie and the children. Suit and tie on. The men around him shook his hand.

At that, Giles closed the prayers that would be said this day.
"He leadeth me, Oh blessed thought!" cried he, announcing the next hymn. And then the assembled people sang the words, as he fed them, verse by verse.
"Sometimes mid scenes of deepest gloom..."
"Sometimes where Eden's bowers bloom..."
The place faded to dead silence after the last verse drifted in the breeze.
"...For by His hand He leadeth me!"

Bingham and the other black shuckers and sawmill workers there, standing at the edge of the cemetery, then raised a lamentation for Gibby that carried all the way to the Sound. Everyone in the county was thinking of the likeable young man!
Harlowe thought the killer might as well. He kept watching for the appearance of anyone in the distance, or skulking about in the woods of Tate's Hell.
Why? I don't know. Was he proud of what he'd done, proud of gettin' by with it? Was he sorry for it, come to mourn what he'd done?

Harlowe looked around at all the good, regular folks there. *Who, among all them derived some pleasure from this?*

The somber-faced oystermen, thin, wiry men in dark suits and stiff collars, lowered the empty casket into the ground.

Harlowe looked around one more time. His plan failed. No one took the bait.
Twiggs whispered to him. "No tags from Leon County, boss."
"All right. Thanks, C.W."

People began filing away after the last verse of the colored folks' song, Pender and Judge Evans shaking hands with the menfolk and comforting the Birches.

Pender clapped Birch on the back. Spoke kindly to the oysterman and his wife. Said everyone that knew Gibby remarked how they'd miss him, and what an interest in the fishing and oystering of their section he had taken, and indeed the great pride he had in this county. Harlowe got most of it. Reading Pender's lips.

Harlowe looked around at the people trailing past the Birches, shaking their hands. Tried to read the faces.

The preacher shook Aubrey's hand.
"Yessir, thankya for all you done," said Birch.
"Preacher, that was a fine sermon. Fit for the Guv'ner," said Seago.
Egg Brown patted True on the back. Spoke something to him. Dirt was thrown in on the coffin, a spadeful, then another.
True ran and got something, Harlowe noticed. A sapling pole—True's own. The boy reached down into the hole where they lay the casket and left the fishing pole atop the lid.
You never did git that Ol' Red, True thought.
True looked down into the hole in the dirt. "I promise ya, I'll get the one who done this. I'll help Uncle Pratt. When I git to be a *puhlease man* I'll find out!" he said aloud.
Harlowe had walked up, by now. True looked at him. Harlowe nodded.

The men shoveled in Tate's Hell dirt, closing the wound in the ground. True could see the casket no more.

The last of the cars pulled away.
Harlowe walked his nephew away as the last shovel of dirt was turned.

Bright lights of glowing windows against the dark street. Harlowe opened the screendoor. Walked into the *Riverside.*
The talk was of the Cardinals—they'd won the series, the papers said. Nichols, in white apron, poured coffee.

***

Seago showed Harlowe the newspapers. The *Times* run a story on the funeral. The Tallahassee paper not one line.
"They never mention Gibby's case," said Seago. "Like it never happened."
"Always was thataway," said Harlowe.
Seago cussed when Harlowe handed him a spade.
Brewer was even less thrilled.
"I believe the body's buried in this county," Harlowe told them.
"How can y'be sure? Could be he's livin' in another state or buried a hundred-fifty miles from here, hell" said Brewer.
"I could be wrong. But I think he's close. Let's go," said Harlowe, starting the car.

They'd finish out a hot October, November, digging. It got folks talking, even in Tallahassee.

But nothing new came of it.

Part II

FORTY-ONE

The boy was about seven. He smiled at Harlowe. "Mornin', sir!"
Harlowe patted him on the shoulder, turned to the superintendent, as they
walked away. "Incorrigibility," said the latter, sadly.
Harlowe looked at the other boys, playing baseball. The birds singing in
the pines interspersed with their cheers, the crack of the bat. "They're sent
to us for many reasons, Pratt. Crimes, certainly. Or 'incorrigibility.'
Running away. Or they've nowhere else to go."
Harlowe nodded. He'd seen the same thing on the other occasions he'd
visited the Industrial School for Boys. Some, who'd committed serious
offenses, were as large as men. Some, barely old enough to attend school,
were sent here by parents who deemed it a fit lesson for disciplinary
infractions. Others had run from a bad home. All these ended up here,
this little campus set on a hillside dotted with tall pines, clean, red-brick
dormatories and a water tower. It might have been a small college, or a
prison—the main distinction being the lack of physical bars, perhaps.

None of these boys is Gibby. Harlowe looked at the photo in his palm.
Looked at the faces. Watched them play baseball.

Harlowe walked to his truck. The superintendent seemed as though he
wanted to do right by these young men. He stopped, noting the wooden
crosses in the field, yonder, the January wind tugging at his coat.

He followed US-90 through Marianna. Through many miles of scattered
farms,
looking past the MotoMeter, at lonely road. Crossing the Victory Bridge
over the Apalachicola, he proceeded to Tallahassee. He had the lingering
feeling the man was there. Waiting. He checked the arraignment docket at
the courthouse. He needed another Line Colbert! But it wouldn't be that
easy.

Back at the office, Harlowe read through his notebooks. Meditated on the
faded words.
"A'ight, bossman, I'm fixin' to go eat. Good night."
Seago shuffled, leisurely across the road, his beckoning porchlight.
A moment later, he heard footsteps on the stairs. "Cigarettes an' coffee
ain't a meal," said Mrs. Seago.
"C'mon, we have enough!" said the jailor.

***

The door jingled. True welcomed the warmth of the pot-bellied stove.
Smelled the unusual, but wonderful blending of tobacco, spices, and
chicory coffee that met his nostrils as soon as he wiped his feet.
Thomas Crock run the little store. The short, ash-blond fellow looked up
from his figuring. "Oh, hiya, True! Ya brung me some stovewood, I see."

True nodded. "Momma sent me to trade for a can of beans."

"I see. Y'can put it down over theah. That oughtta be worth, oh, two cans."

True looked about. The colorful candy in barrels, around him. The coffee grinder, over by the telephone. The cans of lard stacked to the ceiling. Sacks of flour crowded along the aisle. Tins of food that looked so good. Tommy watched the thin child. "Need anything else?" he asked.

True hadn't money for anything else. He shook his head.

The sun sank to the treetops, but Foss hadn't come home. Shadows fell through the windows; Lexie scrubbed the floor of Foss' room in that dusk light. The last can of beans bubbled on the stove—Foss' supper.

True looked in on his siblings. They played on the floor of the bedroom that Mother, he and the younger children shared.

True got his fishing pole. Put on his coat. *If I don't bring home a fish for supper, there won't be none—not for Little Foss, Florie, Mother or me. It's Saturday night and Deddy drew his pay.* True walked down to the out-of-use ferry dock. Cast his line. Watched the sun drop behind Apalach, painting brilliant strokes of gold on the Bay.

When True walked back he saw something—Harlowe's truck! He almost forgot about the sheepshead he'd caught!

Lexie met him at the screendoor. Took the fish. "Don't tell Uncle Pratt," she whispered. "Deddy won't like it—he'll be home soon."

Inside, the walls were the color of tobacco juice, like the schoolhouse. It was tidy as a barracks, Harlowe noticed. Foss had the best room. The big bed. The young'uns weren't allowed in there. When Lexie went in to straighten it, Harlowe saw she got funny about him even coming near the door! Lexie locked it after she'd finished. It didn't seem *normal.*

"Howdy, True!"

True smiled, his head down, shyly. "Hey, Uncle Pratt."

Harlowe ate a tiny supper with them. Foss never did come in. Lexie offered a dozen reasons why.

After supper, Harlowe took the kids down to the old ferry landing. They looked up at the stars. Out at the lights of Apalach.

Harlowe enjoyed this.

But it had another purpose. Harlowe was thinking.

I found Gibby's skiff not a quarter-mile from where we're standing.

Was Gibby making for the ferry dock? And home? He would've come right by True's house.

Harlowe drifted off on the ancient sofa, his hat over his eyes, True saw. True got his straw hat. Did likewise.

He'd wanted to be a *'police man'* like Uncle Pratt as long as he could remember! He didn't tell anyone that—he'd fall asleep thinking about riding in a big automobile to stop some holdup or another.

He didn't tell anyone about his pretend game, either. He'd make believe he could turn himself invisible. He'd hold real still and pretend. *You're okay if no one can see you!*

The morning air was cool on True's cheeks. He breathed the sweet smell of woodstoves hanging over the settlement. The Bay was the choppy, deep blue an artist might choose for it. The oysterboat sails resembled white brushstrokes—or even, egret wings—the boats getting closer, turning about.

The last boat was Birch's. The small figure worked his tongs. He was a constant, as present as the tides. True turned away. Walking quickly. Past the Williams' place, the womenfolk picking satsumas from their trees. His books under his arm, hurrying to his job with McCannon to earn a few pennies before school.

Mother Williams hollered, Howdy! True waved but didn't speak to the woman. Marlene, stood beside her—the little gal tiny as wheatstraw. Her light blond hair resembled straw bleached in the sun. Her "dress" was her Daddy's old shirt, which hung down to her ankles. She smiled and waved back.

True was getting faster. McCannon watched him shucking. He asked True, "where's your buddy?"
True didn't know what to say. Bingham spoke up, "He cain't come today, sah." After the Old Man had left, Bingham explained. "The bossman has his forgetful spells. He don' mean no harm.'" After a moment he added, "I know you think about him."
True nodded.
"Yazzah! Poor Mistuh Gibby! They poor boy! He say he go catch a big fish that day!"
Bingham paused to give some water to the kitten that hung around the oysterhouse. "Look at this li'l kitt'n. She the runt of the littuh. Got lef' behind. Ain' she cute?"
True petted her, who barely filled Bingham's giant hand.
"You fittin' to have a birthday arencha?"
True nodded.
"Soon you be a *ma-inn!* I'm an old *ma-inn.* I seen a lot o' change. I sho' have. One day you look back and say, my goodness how'd I git to be dis old! It happen faster than you can open one o' dem oysters!"

The road ran through the middle of Georgia cotton country, white bolls shimmering in the fields tonight. Thomasville was 'a ways' away. No one for miles around—not one soul.
Woulda been mighty easy for the man to slip away like this—crossin' an entire section unnoticed!

He was "hunting" information, on the road with Gibby's photograph over his heart. Checking arrest cards. Lost child reports. From Panama City to Savannah.

Those police chiefs and sheriffs let him look through their file cabinets—
one paper at a time. They were intrigued—or felt sorry for him.

Blue eyes. Light brown hair. Eight years old. I repeated it a million times!
But, no one had seen a boy close to Gibby's description who hadn't been
accounted for.
Arrests for kidnapping. Reports of run-aways. Reports of lost boys getting
in a car with strangers. Anyone who may have *fed* a boy matching Gibby's
description. Or seen a boy in the company of some stranger passing
through. He looked at everything. He knocked on farmhouse doors across
the South. Some kids run off with friends. Some, he could find nothing
on. A report was made, but families moved in search of work.
*There's no telling how many missing children there are! There's no
information on them, if anything's written at all! Mommas and Daddy's
could only wait, quietly, for word that never came.*

In his mind he saw their faces.

*You wouldn't think just standing and flipping through arrest books and court
dockets could be so exhausting! I can hardly focus my eyes on the road.*
The oncoming headlights, approaching Chattahoochee, nearly blinded him!

What Harlowe was doing he learned from experience. In rural Florida,
there's no schooling for lawmen. No texts on how you catch a child-killer.
No state police to help.

He learned by necessity, in a small county, of being the one who had to do
it if it was to get done.
Years of it had honed his instincts. Working robberies and thefts as a
special agent for the railroads trained him to think about proof, how men
move and act, the way a good hunter knows how deer, or what a fish will
do. He was patient, stubborn—a rural lawman on a difficult case had to be
both.

He rolled off the ferry. Mr. Fortunas was changing the poster at the *Dixie*.
The Beast of the City played tonight.
The smell of coffee cooking at the *Riverside* drew him there. His hat tipped
back on his head, he leaned over his cup in the fuzzy state where he
needed to sleep but couldn't, running on some unforeseen reserve of
energy that kept him up.
He'd travelled all over Creation—for nothing.
Tourists came in for breakfast. Then Mr. Porter. He tipped his hat to the
tourist couple. "How y'all?"

FORTY-TWO

March, 1932

A well-dressed woman stepped off the 3:45 train. Avoiding the other passengers, she retrieved her bag. Asked the agent to hold it for her. Then she walked down Commerce Street, alone. Turned the corner at Avenue E. Proceeded to Montgomery's Department Store—to buy thread.

She was about thirty. Tall and slim. Wore a form-fitting blue suit and hat veil. Matching heels. She turned heads and evoked curiosity. Who was she? No one knew! She was pleasant—if armslength! That got people talking all-the-more! Shopkeepers. Customers. But when the woman asked about, *"the Birch boy...if he's been found?"* the salesclerk phoned the Sheriff.

Harlowe saw her looking in the store windows. She purchased a single white rose from the florist. Crossed Market. Heels clicking along the windows of the funeral parlor, ignoring the onlookers at the Standard Oil station.

She glided up Avenue E like a sailboat in the mist. Stopped at the gates of the cemetery. Looked in. Then entered.

Who is she?
Harlowe got out of his truck. Crossed the street. The afternoon was pleasant for a walk, certainly. The sun streamed through the cemetery's lovely oaks, the branches shrouded in Spanish-moss. The water droplets from the earlier rainshower sparkled on the roses growing among the markers. Birds chirped, above. The woman strolled slowly amid the headstones.

Harlowe walked along the fence. The trees with their long branches and moss, and quite the number of headstones in between the woman and he, masked his presence. Moreover, she seemed unconscious of anyone else, her movements relaxed, casual—like one meandering through the Louvre.

The place is like a peaceful park in the middle of town. The stranger continued her stroll through it, looking at one stone or another, Harlowe following at a distance. She turned her head to look at the the men planting baby palms down the side of Avenue E. Continued browsing among the ancient markers, taking them in one-by-one. The sun, gently diffused by the leaves and branches, created rays of light which illuminated certain of the monuments, which she studied, curiously.

He moved closer. He could see her hair now; although covered by her hat, it was plainly on the red side of strawberry blonde. She kept moving, from one monument to the next.
Presently, she stopped—at a very plan headstone. Upon which, she placed the rose.

The grave was one familiar to Harlowe—Collis Hutto's.

She was deep in contemplation, before the stone, her gloved hand resting upon it.
Gently, he spoke to her. "Miss?"
Startled, she turned about. "Oh, I didn't hear anyone—didn't hear you approach."
"I'm Pratt Harlowe."
She seemed to know his name.
"You're wondering who I am."
"Yes, ma'am."
"I am his wife. Was his wife. I imagine that tells you everything—and nothing."
"It's a start."
She looked at him, then; as curiously as she'd examined the monuments of soldiers, yellow fever victims.
"I've been looking for you for some time, Mrs. Hutto."
She nodded, knowingly. "What is your first name, Mr. Harlowe?"
"Pratt."
"Pratt. I don't believe I've met anyone with that name. May I call you that? And will you call me Myrtle?"
"All right."
"I feel as though we have my husband in common. We ought to be on a first-name basis."
"I'm sorry for your loss, Myrtle."
"Thank you. We weren't married long, of course. But he loved me—in his own way. And I miss that—in *my* own way."
Harlowe nodded.
"He never wanted me to meet his family."
"Why?"
"Well, Pratt, I worked in speakeasies. Dance halls. And—well, I'm sure I don't have to spell it out."
"No, ma'am. I understand."
"Collis was good to me. If he came into a little money, why, he tried to make me happy. No one ever did that for me. He'd drink too much; he wasn't himself, then, and I'd leave for awhile. It wasn't because I was stepping out on him. I liked to go out—I won't deny that. But I didn't two-time him."
"Yes, ma'am."
"Did he leave any bills? I'd like to pay up and move along."
"No, ma'am, thankya, but he took care of all that. Quite a sum."
"I never asked him about his business, Pratt. I figured it was a man's business. I didn't question him."
Harlowe nodded. "That's what I've been meanin' to ask ya. Who he did bidness with."
"In Atlanta he always hung out with bootleggers. He tried to act big. But they were wise to him. And they put him back in the pool halls—hustlin' for nickles. That's all he was, Pratt."
"What about in Tallahassee?"
"He wouldn't tell me what happened."
"Any ideas?"

She shivered—though the breeze was warm.

"I don't wanna know. It's dangerous to know things."

"Who scared him?"

"You know he was scared? Then you know *I'm* scared. I-I don't know who it was in Tallahassee. One of the powerful men. The fear was why Collis moved us so much. But then he needed money and he'd start all over. He said Collis asked for too much—that he was 'blackmailing' him. I think that was the word Collis used. But he wasn't! He needed the money for us to live on! He threatened Collis, if he kept asking!"

"Haven't you any idea who he was—even the smallest thing about 'im may help?"

"I don't know anything. Just--."

She's trembling. "Yes?"

"Just someone who can get people to do things, whatever he wants. You figure it out!"

"I don't have much to go on, ma'am. Anything else you can tell me?"

She shook her head.

"Was he a bootlegger, the big fella?"

"I don't know."

"He sure has everyone runnin' scared. Seems like someone needs to do somethin' about 'im. Don't ya think?"

She opened her pocketbook. Looking down for a moment. Then removed a photograph, thrusting it into his hand.

There were five people in the snapshot. Gibby, smiling from ear-to-ear and *hugging* a giant redfish. Beside him stood Collis!

Then, a boy about thirteen. Then another who's face was blurred. Finally, in the background, stood a man well-known to the Apalachicolan—*Foss Fulton.*

"I'll be damned," Harlowe breathed.

"Perhaps, it will be of some use—I don't know," she said, almost inaudibly.

Harlowe looked deeply into the photo in his hands. "Well, I do appreciate it."

"I wish you the best of luck, Pratt."

"Can I help you?"

"No. I have my train ticket. I had just enough to buy that ticket."

"Where are you going?"

"I'm leaving the state. Doesn't matter beyond that."

"Can I drop you somewhere? It's a bit of a wait for the train."

"Thank you, but I'll mange. Did Collis leave any personal effects—clothes and things?"

"His sister claimed them."

She nodded.

"I can ask her--."

"It's all right. I really must go. Is there someplace where I might have a cup of coffee and sit until my train arrives? I'd like to rest and be alone."

"Creekmore's, by the bank, theah. Y'sure I caint walk you?"

"Thank you, but I'll be all right."

"Good luck, ma'am. So long."

"Thank you, Pratt." She startled when the whistle blew at the sawmill, sounding the end of the workday. She walked away.

Later, he saw her sitting at the counter in the drugstore. Harlowe cussed. *Could it be someone right here in Paradise? True's Daddy!*

As he walked back to his truck, someone called his name. "Hello, Pratt!"

Doc Murrow! The latter was sitting on his porch. Harlowe walked over. "It's a fine evenin', Pratt!"

"Yes, sir!"

"Y'see the paper, Pratt? Banks collapsing. Men out of work."

Harlowe sighed. "Yeah."

The doctor looked over his picket fence. Nodded toward W.O. Anderson's showroom. "Hasn't sold a car in two weeks! Not a soul on Market Street. No one has any money. Even Weems takes his payment in trade!"

"Yeah!"

Doc turned to the case. "What it has done to the Birches, I cannot—." The telephone interrupted, and Murrow excused himself to answer it. "You have a good evenin', sir!"

"Same to you, sir!"

Later, Harlowe watched Mrs. Hutto's train leave. She looked at him but, as the engine puffed, turned away. The red light faded to a dot.
Seago stampeded up the street, in a state! "J'hear?! Lindberg's baby— kidnapped!"

***

Harlowe found Cleve Crumley polishing his taxi.
"Ha'doo, Shur'ff."
"Howdy, Cleve! Busy mornin'?"
"I had me a couple customers, yazzah!"
"Where'd you carry the red-headed woman, yesterdee?"
"Ha! How'd you know about dat?" asked the colored man.
Harlowe grinned.
"Oh!" Crumley realized long ago Harlowe didn't miss much as went on in the county.
"I carried huh to Mistuh Ira Brewer's house, *shur'ff.*"
"All right."
Crumley ran his rag over the windshield of the big Buick. "Miss Brewer answer the *doe* and she goes in—dat's all I knows."
"All right, Cleve. I appreciate it."
"Yazzah—have a good day, *Shur'ff!*"
"You take care, now."

Harlowe knocked on Mrs. Brewer's screendoor.

She looked out and smiled. "Hey, Mr. Pratt!"

"Howdy!"

"Coffee's on. Come on in!"

He took his hat off. She poured him a cup at her table which was covered with sewing things. Nineteen years old. She was a little bony, but cute, with her dark eyes, hair. "Nice to have someone to talk to—kids are in skoo. Ira sure ain't much for conversation."

Harlowe grinned. Talked to her about goings on in the county, her people. Then turned toward the matter at hand. "Why did Myrtle Hutto come see Ira?"

"It was somethin' to do with a man in Tallahassee."

"Okay."

"I heard her say she wanted to get to the 'bossman.' She wanted money—that was what I got out of it."

"Yes, ma'am."

"Funny thing is, Ira got real quiet about it. After she left, he didn't say two words to me. Left outta here, didn't say where he was goin'!"

"O.K."

"Say, which one d'ya think? I'm makin' a shirt for Ira—not that he deserves it."

"Well, the blue one."

"Thankya, Shureff!"

Harlowe walked into Buzzett's. Ira looked at him crossways. "Coffee?"

Harlowe dropped his hat on the counter. "Sure."

"I wanna know about the fella in Tallahassee—'Bossman.'"

"That I know nothin' about." Harlowe could see in his eyes he knew more. The fellow went to wiping down the counter, with a fury.

"You scared?"

Ira shot him the angriest look. "He's had people keeled, Pratt! I ain't takin' no chance!" he said, through grit teeth.

Harlowe set the picture of Gibby on the counter.

"That don't change nothin,' Pratt. That's a nickel for the coffee, now!"

Harlowe shook his head. Left.

Was about to climb in his truck when T.K. pulled around the corner.

The younger fellow could see his boss was bothered about something. "What is it, Boss."

"That cousin of yours. Will you mind things this afternoon?"

"Yessir."

"Thanks, T.K."

Harlowe drove up to Liberty County. Talked to men who knew Foss in the old days in the cypress camps.

What he learned surprised him. "You sure of that?"

"Yessir, I let Foss borry my car. Whenever he ask me!"

"Back in nineteen-hunnerd-and-twenty-seven?"

"Why, sure!"

Harlowe talked to other folk upriver. To men who run cattle near Sumatra where Foss was known to hunt—without permission—from time to time. No one had any information beyond rumor. They might have seen a trespasser in the woods, sure. But, nothing specific. *"Maybe the same feller."*

"I like to take a shot at him. But I caint say for sure it was Foss!"

Harlowe showed the photo to Mr. and Mrs. Birch.

Aubrey's jaw dropped.

"Why, I declare!" Lillian stared at it in astonishment. But smiled at the sight of her son in the photo. "Look at him hug that fish! Oh, so precious!"

"That fish is bigger'n he was!" said Aubrey.

"You know, Pratt, I only had one *foe-toe* of Gibby. The one you made a print of." She retrieved her copy from the bureau. Laid it beside Pratt's. "He'd grown taller, ya notice that?"

"Yes'm?"

"Why, I do believe--."

"Ma'am?"

"This was made right before he took missin'!"

"What about this other young fella?"

"He looks so familiar," said Mrs. Birch.

"Looks to be about thirteen," Aubrey reckoned.

"I don't know that other fella a' tall. Caint make out much. His face is blurry and turned away," said Mrs. Birch.

"Mr. Pratt, one thing, though?"

"Yessir?"

"The boy ain't got no car—Foss, I mean."

"He used to borrow his bossman's Ford. The man up in Liberty County."

Though Aubrey rarely cussed, he did so now. "I just caint believe it! I always thought him a friend. Ain't you surprised, Lillie?"

"Ye-ess! I am fit-to-be tied!"

"What do you think, Miss Birch?" asked Harlowe.

"He's *mean*. I used to think he was a fine person, too. But to hear what goes on when he's drinkin'! I tell ya I'd like him to come this way, right now. Ya let me borry your gun, Pratt, you don't have to bother the judge!"

"You'd arrest him, wouldn'chya Pratt? I mean it don't matter who--."

"He has an alibi, Aubrey."

"Who?"

"My sister."

Harlowe noticed some old newspapers. Aubrey explained, "You know, Pratt I read them papers, look for somethin' in 'em. Like maybe someone would find our boy and place an ad. Doc Murrow sends 'em to me. I've done that since he come up missin.'"

Lillian kept looking at the photo.

"I've only got one *pitcher* of 'im."

"You can have it. When we—."

She smiled. "I'd like to have it."

***

Two of the five I caint ask.

Monday, he found Foss at the mill. Harlowe listened to the scream of the sawblade. The puffing of the steam engine running it. The smell of cut pine hung in the air, waiting for Foss to finish his shift.

Foss gave a grin. "What brings ya out this way, Brother?"

Harlowe had to holler over the saw. "Had some bidness with C. C. Land."

"Is he gonna fix up the old McCannon house? 'Bout time."

"He's thinkin' on it. I wanted to talk to you, also. I'll run you up to the house," said Harlowe, nodding to the truck.

Foss climbed in.

They drove along the coastal road, toward Eastpoint.

Harlowe stopped at the crossroads.

"I'd like to show you something." Harlowe held out the photograph.

"This is Gibby Birch. In the photogragh *theah.*"

"Why, sure it is."

"And this other boy? You know *him.*" Harlowe was running a bit of a poker game, there.

Foss' mustache twitched. "No," he lied.

"This big fella—who's he?"

"Never saw him before, Pratt!"

Foss got out. "I'll be seein' ya—Brother!"

Foss had a lot of friends in the county. Men, white and colored, called him "Captain." He was a big man around Eastpoint—the foreman of a sawmill.

Harlowe showed the photo around, all day Tuesday. People thought he knew everyone in the county. This was one time he wished it were so.
He sat down to supper with the Seagos.
"No luck," said Harlowe.
"May I see it, Pratt?" asked Mrs. Seago.
Harlowe pulled the photo from his coat.
"Why, that's Charlie Orr's boy! Dakie! He moved away for several years. Oh, he looks like his daddy!"
"Oh, yeah, you right," agreed the jailor.
"That family is back in town now, over in Carrabelle," said the woman.
"The boy and his daddy lived in Eastpoint, left a couple years ago," thought Seago.
"Yes! Well, it was after—Hmmm—it was after Gibby took missing," said Mrs. Seago. These kinds of discussions fascinated her.
Then Harlowe remembered. "The fella that worked as a tapper for McCannon. His son. He'd be about fourteen now."
"Yes!" agreed Mrs. Seago. "Dakie Orr."

FORTY-THREE

Eastpoint, Saturday.

Harlowe crossed early, to see his sister. Foss was still sleeping—he'd had a big time last night. Harlowe observed the way True got Foss Jr. and Florie dressed. How he started their breakfast. Lexie was busy ironing Foss's shirt. When True asked if the eggs looked fine, she replied sharply, "Caint you see I'm pressin'? Deddy has to have this for work today, True!"
"Yes'm." They walked on eggshells and Foss wasn't even up yet.

True said goodbye, leaving his siblings to play. The scent of orange blossoms drifted sweetly along the "Old Ferry Dock Road" as he passed by the Williams' place, running to his job.

Harlowe could smell bacon—Lexie was busy fixing Foss' breakfast. He'd emerged from his room. Harlowe joined him at the table, and Foss was right cordial, telling stories about the old days in the camps.
Finally, Harlowe looked right at him. "I'm gonna find out—I'm patient."
"The hell you say."
Foss slammed his coffee mug on the table. He put on his pressed shirt and set out for the Green Point sawmill, running out to ride the mule-drawn wagon with the boys.

After he'd gone Harlowe talked to Lexie for a spell. Twelve years younger than he, she wore a cheap print dress, her stylish bobbed hair still hinted at the dances and dreams and popularity she'd had as a young girl in Apalach. "True seems to really look after the younguns. A lot of the raisin.'"
"I have so much to do, Pratt. Foss—True—he's older and he helps out. He-He's old enough to do that for me!"
"Don't you think that's a lot for him? He's only a boy—."
"Pratt, leave it alone! Let's talk about something else. You've been gone a lot—it's a woman, I hope."
"No. Jus' workin.'"
"That poor Gibby—How's Lillian?"
"Hurtin.' Lexie, I need to ask you somethin.'"
"Oh?"
"You said that Foss was home by five o'clock that evenin' and didn't go out."
"That's right. Come in around suppah time."
"Are you sure he didn't leave a'tall, not even for a quarter-hour?"
Her face reddened. "I done told ya that!"
"Take it easy."
"*I'll* take it easy! I think you'd better go!"

***

The Tillie Miller bridge is stuck again.
Harlowe laughed. Helped crank it open. Proceeded across, into Carrabelle. A fishing town, a mill town, with one hotel, a drug store, and a filling

station, Carrabelle is a tad smaller than Apalach. And a world unto itself sometimes. The papers at the drugstore hollered about Lindberg's baby. The "rumor mill" whispered that the sawmill was closing, casting a pall over the town that was tangible. It was especially quiet, even for a Sunday.

Harlowe stopped at the little house the company provided to the sawyer of the mill. The boy's daddy answered the door. The man eyed the Sheriff, guardedly.

"You can come on in. I ain't broke no law have I?"

"No, sir." Harlowe stepped into a dark little room, heavy with the smell of stale cigarettes.

"You ain't arrestin' me?"

"No."

"You want some rollin' tobacco? It's all I got."

"No, thanks." Harlowe explained it was about the man's son. Showed him the photograph.

"Then he ain't in no trouble? I told that boy--."

"He isn't in trouble with me."

"O.K." The man collapsed onto a dirty divan—the only stick of furniture remaining. "There ain't no more chairs, sir. I 'pologize. My old lady run off Tuesday. Y'may have heard."

"No, sir."

"Here, you can sit here, Sheriff."

"It's all right, Mr. Orr. I can stand."

"About what ya asked me--."

"Yessir?"

"Sure, you can talk to him, Sheriff. But he ain't here. He's huntin'. Took the squirrel gun an' walked yonder."

"I appreciate it, Mr. Orr."

The man just looked down. He looked like a pile of rags on the divan. "I dunno what I'm gonna do, Sheriff. Does it git any easier?" Tears fiowed down the man's cheeks.

"Yessir. You gonna be all right. If I can do anything for ya—holler!"

Harlowe found the boy on the bluff.

Waved. "Howdy! You bagged a fair number, ain't ya?" As he approached, Harlowe noticed the bag on Dakie's belt.

"Yessir—seven!"

Harlowe showed the photo. Dakie had grown some, but the resemblance was clear. "Yeah, that's me!"

"You remember when this photo was taken?"

"Sir?"

"When they had y'all stop and take this picture, do you remember that?"

"Yessir, I was there when Gibby caught that fish on his boat. These fellers flagged him down, an' he come in at Magnolia Bluff. Kinda showin' it off, y'know?"

"Sure."

"Hell, ida showed it off. It was a big'n!"

"And the man standin' behind y'all. This fella, here, with his face blurry?"

199

"Huh?"

"In the picture, theah, the one you caint see his face—."

"Sir? Oh, the big boah?"

"That's right. Y'know him?"

"No, shureff."

"You said he was big?"

"Yeah. Tall. Husky."

"About how tall?"

"A little taller than you, I reckon. Husky boy."

"How old?"

"I dunno."

"'Bout your own age? Older?"

"Older. Eighteen—Twenty—Thirty. Hell, I dunno."

"That's a pretty good spread."

"I didn't really pay that much attention, Mr. Pratt."

"Was his hair light?"

"Yessir. I do remember that. Like—you know Stella Davis? His hair was light like hers."

"All right. You remember who all was there? I want you to try to think back now."

"Hell, I'll try! There was the rich feller. Friendly feller."

"Rich?"

"That's just what someone said. I don't know who he was."

"There was a couple kids from somewheres—Tallahassee, I reckon."

"Go on."

"Them boys ain't in the *pitcher* now."

"Can you tell me about those other boys?"

"Oh, they's jus' some kids—'bout sixteen, I reckon."

"Local boys?"

"Nah. They ain't from here."

"All right. But this rich, friendly fella?"

"Well, he was there. He wanted to take that *pichure*. He was nice to Gibby. Gibby left with him."

"You saw that?"

"Yeah. Wanted to see Gibby's boat. Walked down there to it. Said he wanted to see 'im catch another fish."

"Can you describe that fella?"

"Whachya-mean?"

"What he looked like. Was he white or colored? Tall or short? Skinny or heavy-set?" Harlowe drawled.

"Oh, he weren't a nigger or nothin'. He's white!"

"Well, what else can you tell me?"

"Hell, I dunno. Maybe heavier'n you."

"How old was he?"
"I dunno."

"Your age. Your daddy's age?"

"I dunno—just old, I reckon he was at least forty."

Harlowe grinned. "Easy son."

"Sorry, Mr. Pratt."

"What color was his hair?"

"Ahh, I dunno. Brown. Sandy. It wuddint too dark."
"How was he dressed?"

"Nice clothes. White shirt. Good hat. Looked storebought! Like they was sayin', the ol' boy had money."

"Who said that?"
"These kids. Well, this one kid."
"Can you describe *him*—anything a'tall?"
"No, sir, I ain't get a look at him. He was big. Maybe, oh, about seventeen. Maybe younger. I dunno."
"You go to Magnolia Bluff any since?"

"Yessir—sometimes. Visitin' my cousin, like I was that day."

"Ever see this fella again, or those young men?"
"No, sir."
"Anyone else there that you remember?"
"I ain't fixin' to git him in trouble now, am I?"
"No, son."
"Well, Mr. Ira was there. They had 'em a little party. Moonshine."
"Did you see Gibby any more after that?"
"Uh, nah, I think he got back out on the water. I ain't sure. We started passin' a bottle around, if y'know what I mean."
"How well did Foss know these people?"
"They's as thick as thieves, Mr. Pratt."

FORTY-FOUR

Eastpoint, Monday

True saw his reflection in the water. The red print of big fingers on his cheek. He slunk into his desk, hoping Mr. Brown wouldn't see him or call on him. That he'd be invisible.

He made it through without having to talk much.
At the oysterhouse, it was another day like the one before—and the one before that. He moved like a machine. There was comfort in being so. *Be quiet—git your work done.*

After work, True gathered stove-wood. Proceeded to Mr. Tommy's store like Lexie told him.
"Howdy, Mr. Tommy." True maneauvered his armful of firewood up the constricted aisle to the counter. "Got s'more outside."
"Good!" Tommy struck a match and lit the the coal-oil lamp, for it was getting dark. He nodded to the woodbin. "Why, that ougtta be worth a couple cans."

True looked around at the candy and things. By that time, Tommy had the canned beans in a sack for him.
"Thankya, Mr. Tommy!"
"So long, True! See ya in a few days."
"Yessir—thanks!"

When he got home, he chopped stove-wood to keep the house warm for the night. Walked down to Magnolia Bluff with his cane pole. An egret watched him, silently looking back at him. Then, she took off, flapping her wings, resembling an angel ascending to the sky. It grew very quiet before the first crackle of thunder, the clouds rolling, darkening fast. True stayed until the bottom fell out. Caught a sheepshead was all, but the children were glad to have it, and the beans. Dark and rain dripping, they had their supper. Lexie watched the door, fretted. Foss hadn't come home.

When the rain quit, True returned to the shore. Looked to the lights of Apalach. Behind him, his house was dark. No money for kerosene.
"Is Deddy home yet?" asked Florie.

***

Harlowe stopped by in the morning. "What brings you by?" asked Lexie.
Foss burst from his bedroom before Harlowe could answer. "Hey, Brother!"
Foss sawed his hand. Gave Lexie a squeeze. Harlowe watched Lexie set a plate before the big man, who shoveled in a giant mouthful. Foss's grin faded and he spat, "These eggs are *cold!*"
"I'm sorry! I'll fix you some more—I'm sorry!"
Harlowe noticed how Foss looked right past True, like he's glass. How he walked past him like he's invisible.

Foss left for work. True pumped water so his siblings could wash, made sure Little Foss and Florie combed their hair. Meantime, Lexie scrubbed the floor, made Foss' bed, and started his favorite pie.

True looked more like a twenty-five-year-old man than an eleven-year-old boy. His face was like a carving, just set one way. There was something in novels called a 'robot.' True seemed to perform as such, so as not to upset his parents, Harlowe thought.

Before True left for school, Harlowe asked him, "Your daddy ever mention it—Gibby's bein' missin'?"
True shook his head.

***

Harlowe walked the route Gibby might have taken, Mrs. Birch with him. "My sister's light woulda been the first one he saw."
"He woulda headed right for it, Pratt."

***

Sheip's glowed less brightly, the Depression hanging over the county a little heavier. Harlowe got home to find the deal for the Prado house falling through. The man lost his job with the railroad—which teetered on bankruptcy. He and his wife looked terrified.

Harlowe broke the other news to his men. Seago nearly fell out! "That's True's *deddy,* Pratt!"
"Someone right here in the county—naw!" Brewer cried.
"Naw, he didn't do it!" Seago declared.
Harlowe set the photo on the desk.
"One of most well-liked men in the county!" added Brewer.
"Sure, Foss is a likeable feller!" Seago thought. "Everyone likes him!"
"He's a good talker!" said Brewer.
"Oooh, he can tell a good story!"
"Very outgoin', and friendly! Ain't no way he could be a murderer," insisted Brewer. "He's a hard-workin' fella."
Harlowe looked over at his deputy. "Uh-huh."
"Don't bother nobody. Likes his whiskey and carryin' on—you know, set the woods on fire Saturday night?"
"He's a sport, now!" agreed Seago. "Oh, I reckon he's poached a buck deer in his time. But— like you say—he ain't never hurt nobody—no way he done it!"
Harlowe nodded.
"What about this? Somethin' that clears it up, for sure!" thought Brewer.
"Yeah?" replied Harlowe.
"Why, it's easy! Foss ain't never had no car!"
"You're right."
"I don't see how you get around that!" added Brewer. "The tracks."

203

Harlowe nodded. Went back to staring out the window with his coffee—
while the two men heaped superlatives about Foss.

***

Harlowe drove out to Green Point. The older McCannon brother, Graham,
had run it since Zeb's passing in early '28. The McCannons were one of
the richest families in the county. They favored Foss. Ane while the
family's fortunes were on the descent, Graham still had a lot of pull. Zeb
had been the one with real ambition. After Zeb died, a fellow named C. C.
Land had leased much of his terpentine holdings. There was talk Graham
would soon sell outright.

Harlowe listened to Foss talkin' to his men. He could hear bits and pieces,
but he got the gist.
"I ain't got no sympathy for 'em!"
"No?"
"No...not for these fellas that caint make no livin' with all the cypress gone.
Cryin' over the ol' days! I left the camps and come here. Never saw me
bellyachin'!" Foss growled.
"I know that, Foss. But some folk *have* had a rough time!" protested Mr.
Mashburn.
"You mean Nate and them? They as bad as them niggers!"
"But, Pratt--."
"Bah. Always got some scuse why they caint work!"
"Well, now, Foss, if you was let go--."
"Never been fired in my life! I'm smart enough to quit when the goins'
good!"

People did *struggle as the cypress boom ended*, Harlowe knew. *It was a
way of life, hand-cutting the ancient giants. It came to a jarring halt.*

*Circumstances tell the truth more than Foss' words. He left the cypress
company for the job at Green Point August of twenty-seven. He didn't let on
it bothered him, but folks say he began to drink more than ever.*
The steam engine hissed—chugged—shook the building. The scream of the
saw echoed over the St. George Sound.
*Foss had cut cypress since he was a boy. Foss made less money at the mill.
Yessir, it bothered him.*

The money he made, Foss drank up as fast as it come in. And Lexie
ginned up the excuses. Foss insisted True work every day. Yet Foss
demeaned whatever the boy did, like it was a competition between them.
*Almost like he resents True as a rival. Ain't normal. The man I'm huntin'
ain't normal.*

***

True woke up to the scrape of Mother stirring biscuit batter. The chugging
of a gasoline engine as an oystermen ran his boat to the flats. His father
hollering.
Lexie bore the brunt. Then Foss's ire turned toward him.

"Why ain't that boy up?!"

True listened to Foss's heavy boots stomp across the floor. Foss threw the door open to the room Lexie shared with the children. "You tired?"

"Nosir," True answered, hurriedly pulling on his trousers.

Foss vented his anger back at Lexie. "I work like a nigger, from sunup to after sundown, to put a roof over his head and he thinks he can lay there like Bonnie Prince Charlie!"

True got his shirt on. Helped his two siblings into their clothes. Then, Foss grabbed him! "Look here, them niggers that work for McCannon always have some bellyache, where they caint work. He don't put up with it from the darkies. He ain't gonna put up with that from you. He'll bounce you outta there like a ball, y'hear me?"

"Yessir."

Lexie ladled some grits for True, which he had to eat before his daddy left to work. True did so, then started his chores outdoors.

He looked up at the sound of another oysterboat. Motors were starting to replace sails—adding new sounds to the Bay.

Foss looked over at him. "Y'better git on to work."

***

After work, Foss and his buddies went hunting. The old Vrooman place. The latter had been bisected by the new highway. Foss shot a good-sized turkey in the pine flatwoods there, Harlowe saw.

For Foss, hunting consisted more in drinking than actually bringing home something. And he, rather than his shotgun, was on a hair trigger. It seemed everyone had to tiptoe around to avoid 'setting him off.'

He'd gotten worse the last couple years. Harlowe watched him take a swing at Mr. Quick. The Sheriff slipped back the way he'd come—leaving the party to finish their jug.

Foss has been known to run a still from time-to-time. But Harlowe hadn't seen any indication he was running one the last two-or-three years.

FORTY-FIVE

Apalachicola, April, 1932

Harlowe walked along the picket fence, toward the River. Plumbago winked through the slats. Birds singing in the magnolias. A clean-smelling morning breeze blew.

Then Seago drove up, hollering, "There's a man by the schoolhouse in Eastpoint!"
"O.K.!" Harlowe rushed to catch the ferry. Hope he'd get there in time to do some good!

Brewer met him when she landed.
"Boss, the Daughtry boy had to stay after skoo to clean the blackboard. Egg Brown seen 'im."
Harlowe retreived his coach gun from under the seat. "What did Egg say?"
"He was a big fella's all he said."
Harlowe ran to the schoolhouse.
"Hello, Pratt. Theah, in the saw palmettuh's where he'd stood," said Brown.
There was a void between palmettos. A hiding spot.
Through the pines he could see where the children played at recess, but not be seen.
Harlowe saw nothing where the fronds had been disturbed. A hogtrail led out to the new highway. He took it.
Harlowe walked all the way to the road, where Brewer met him.
"You saw something at the Williams' place?"
"Naw, they saw somethin' flagged me down while-ago," said Brewer.
The deputy pulled in to the Williams' farm on "Old Ferry Dock Road."
The little Wiliams' girl, Marlene, was planting watermelon seeds with two little hands.
Harlowe spoke to C.P. Asked him if he could look around.
The man grunted. Nodded.
Harlowe looked for footprints. Saw none. "Runt watched him from the winduh. The other young'uns were at skoo," said Mrs. Williams.
"Ain't no one come through here, Pratt!" scoffed Mr. Williams.
Runt showed Harlowe the spot. "That's where I saw 'im runnin'."
"Did ya know 'im?"
"I dunno."
Harlowe looked over at Brewer. "Couldn't ya track 'im?" asked Harlowe.
"Didn't see no footprints. Some pine straw that was disturbed is all. Over here—see? Don't see where he coulda gone in that mess."
"Where's Foss?"
"No one seen 'im," said Brewer.
"He ain't at the mill?"
"No."
"All right. I want you to talk to Mr. Brown. See if he remembers anything else."
"Yessir."

"I'm gonna folluh these tracks yonder."

"Should I send to the workcamp for a dog, boss?"

"No. Take too long."

Harlowe entered Tate's Hell. Ahead was a blackened pine. It had what seemed to be a burned mouth and ears—it had been catfaced and burned by tappers years earlier. Below it, he noted grass which had been mashed underfoot. *The man stood here a spell.*
He had to work his way in. After about ten yards, the vegetation changed from open flatwoods and saw palmetto to dark jungle, so thick he could not see into it.

It was slow going through a tangle of oaks, shrubs, and vines. It was unseasonably warm, humid, stifling. It was funny how it was so much darker in here—woods that seemed forgotten since prehistoric times.

The trees do strange things in here. Disoriented a fella, disrupted his sense of direction. The sun always seems like it's directly overhead. You could press through the swamp for hours only to find yourself back at the same clearing!

He threaded his way through the sharp Greenbrier vines. They grew thick enough to trap a deer or a man. They could cut you. With their ground mats, they could trip you. This made it impossible to rely on a horse. Even impossible for a man to slip through in places. *Only a fool would try it at night and moving quickly. This fella knows these woods.*

Harlowe made it to a little pool. He worked around it, carefully, along the outer edge as much as he could, for the vines reaching for him.

He listened. Animals could tell you things. He heard none. No birds. Only bugs. He kept moving.

Harlowe patiently found the places where the vines weren't as thick, squeezing between the strands. It was the only way through, yet, he saw no tracks.

He kept going, in the direction, he judged, was the Sumatra Road. Without any distinct features about him, he wasn't certain. The forest dense, visibility no greater than an armslength at times, the leaves and vines solid as a wall.

He found Bear Creek, however. A ghostly light filtered through the treeleaves, white and hazy, the way it streamed through window blinds late in the afternoon. It illuminated a creek-bed bone dry in drought.
Carefully, he moved aside the bank. When the vegetation got too thick, he walked in the nearly dry bed.

It got deeper, suddenly. And the water sucked at his boots.

As he took a step, a branch glinted in a ray of sunlight. Then it slithered to the ground. *It isn't a branch.*

A gator grunted. Then another. Behind him!

Another gator grunt and a splash as the unseen reptile—a big one—moved.

Darkness loomed. And the leaves made it even darker, as the sun waned.

Was that shadow a gator?

That tree a man?

It was oddly silent.

That bent branch of titi, the white flowers hanging down. It's likely he come through here. Harlowe listened carefully. A frog croaked in the little pool. A bird squawked and fluttered from a branch, leaving it rocking. The bugs gave a zinging accompaniment to the suffocating heat as loud as drawing a bow over a fiddle. He heard no sign of any human intruder.

He crept forward, silently, along the creekbank. He'd come about three miles since he'd left the Williams' farm.

What was formerly wet and swampy, had dried up of late, leaving a floor that was soft underfoot, strewn with leaves and pine straw. The forest was so thick he couldn't see more than three yards in any direction; the wall of vines and tree trunks made it nearly impassable.

He reached higher ground after a hard walk, finding absolute silence in the pines. Not so much as a squirrel moved. It was oppressively quiet, jarring even.

No sign of 'im.

He crept along as the woods opened up a little, the area dry as tinder, and littered in red-brown pine straw.

It felt like every tree had eyes behind it, a critter behind it. The flatwoods ran endlessly in all directions. Shadows blackened the farside of those pines, each tree large enough to hide a man. Harlowe's eyes checked every one.

He could be watching me approach for many yards, while I caint see him. *Tate's Hell's perfect for an ambush. Sounds seem to come from one direction, while they're coming from another.*

What's that? Sure sounded like—. Just then, a shadow moved! Behind the big pine! Harlowe raised his shotgun.

Is that his foot? There was little sunlight left and he strained to see.

Hell! He's big—but not human! A panther—six feet long! She looked at him from behind a palmetto frond, her eyes firey and green. She looked him over, then vanished into the shadows.

Harlowe advanced carefully.

Still no tracks.

He found the path the tappers once used. Carefully, he stepped to the treeline. Looked for anyone visible in the moonlight. Listened.

He'd come four miles since he'd left Eastpoint, he reckoned. He followed the road, out, to the Sumatra Highway. He saw a broken branch. Oddly, in the sand he saw no footprints.

The man was using Tate's Hell to come in and out of Eastpoint, unseen! It made the hair on the back of Harlowe's neck stand on end.

***

"Was Foss home when you went by the house?" asked Harlowe.
"No," Seago replied. "T.K. flagged me down after that—and we started lookin' for you."
They drove up the Sumatra Road, a ways, Harlowe wanting a closer look in the daylight.

They looked at the spot along the old logging road where a branch was broken. Harlowe saw no other traces of the man.

"Let's look along the road some."

"Reckon he walked North, crossed the loggin' road, then headed thisaway?"

"Maybe," Harlowe replied.

Harlowe leaned out from the running board of Seago's Ford, looking down at the road as they crawled along.

Seago felt bad for him. There wasn't so much as a cigarette!

"Stop, C.A." Harlowe hopped off before the car ground to a halt. "Look here—see the bootprint, theah," Harlowe pointed out.

"Hmm. He's as big as Foss."

Harlowe nodded. Plain work boot—like a million worn across the South. "I reckon he came out this ol' wagon road. The man has an automobile—I'm sure of it."

The trail into the woods was overgrown; it had been used by mule and oxen teams, years ago. Across the mouth of that road, Harlowe saw tracks from one or more Ford automobiles. Anonymous marks in the sand.

Harlowe questioned the man at the filling station in Hosford. He hadn't seen anyone suspicious.

They headed for home. Bouncing along the dusty road, Harlowe was quiet.

Finally, Seago had to say *something.*

"Foss had time to get down theah, yesterdee, reckon?"

"I don't know—no one knows where he was last night."

***

The doctors poured scotch—very illicit in Gadsden County. Harlowe drank coffee.

"Oh, yes, the Lindbergh case," said Dr. Cotillard. "We still don't know on that one."

"Maybe we know *why*—fifty thousand reasons," said Elston.

"We had no note, no demand for money—the Birches have none. I don't know *why*. What would cause a man to do somethin' like this?" asked Harlowe.

Elston could see it really bothered the sheriff. "Not much is known, Pratt."

"One day there'll be a term for it. Jack the Ripper was considered insane. A maniac. Mr Holmes in Chicago, much the same. It's a bit more complex than insanity, perhaps. You've read of Bobby Franks in Chicago—Leopold and Loeb?" Cotillard asked.

"Yessir."

"They were after some thrill. Some pleasure. Kidnapping and killing a boy--."

"And getting' by with it."

"Yes, Pratt. But they'd appear sane to you and I," said Elston.

"Yeah."

"Would he do it once—and once only?"

"Not much is understood. Someone who offends against a child. I don't think he can stop himself. Don't take it so hard, sheriff, if Chicago detectives and federal inspectors haven't solved the Lindbergh case..."

Harlowe nodded. "I just gotta keep the line in the water and maybe I can bring him up."

Elston muttered an expletive. "I swear, no one I know has the patience you have. Like waiting for a fish all day long!"

Harlowe spent every free moment watching. Who came and went. Who came by the schools. Scouring newspapers in other towns.

He caught nothing.

***

"Today was Gibby's birthday," Lexie mentioned.

True walked up, excited to show Foss the little skiff he'd whittled. "Watch where yer goin'—or I'll make a whitlin' outta you!"

Foss brushed past, out the screendoor.

True looked outside a moment, blankly. Then left to do his chores.
Lexie put up the dishes. Swept. She didn't realize True made the skiff for Gibby. But she knew the date. She'd call upon Lillian later.

***

Mrs. Birch had been crying.
"She's had one of her bad days," Aubrey explained.
Every year on Gibby's birthday the Birches came to town to have coffee with Harlowe.
Then, they'd all have supper with Mr. and Mrs. Seago—the jailor a master of the fry kettle.
Harlowe could smell the cooking from the office windows.
The woman's eyes were as gray as the cotton dress she'd made herself.
She wiped a tear away. Tried to smile.
"I know you worry, too," said Mrs. Birch.
Harlowe nodded. He looked at her hands. She fidgeted, nervously. She did piecework, for extra money. Her hands were indelicate, perhaps, yet they did such beautiful, loving work. Her own clothing would never be as fancy as the work she did for others. Harlowe looked at Aubrey, gaunt, breaking his back to keep the bills paid.
"What is it, Pratt?" he asked.
Harlowe thought. Leaned forward and looked them in the eyes. "Well, the bootleggin' always bothered me. I don't know, but maybe Gibby walked in on those boys...movin' their whiskey... an' they didn't want it repeated."
"I understand," said Mr. Birch. "Ya checked them boys from down south?"
In 1927, bootleggers landed their shipments South of the ferry dock in Eastpoint at Magnolia Bluff. This was once part of the Quaker, Vrooman's East Bay farm. The bluffs are as tall as a man, the area isolated from the houses on the Sound. The shipments came from Cuba.
"I looked at that, checked for any sign—to the Carrabelle River and on the island, *over theah*."

211

"There weren't none?"

"No."

"I seen lights sometimes," said Aubrey. "Reckoned it was fellers landing moonshine or poachin'—one. Ol' Daughtry said he'd get up and look 'when them trucks come by at night.'"

"Yeah. But he didn't know what ws going on," said Harlowe. "Bootleggers put in at Yent's Bayou, also." They landed, there, on McCannon land, despite the old man's guns. Many lonely miles of coastline, with little coves and desolate stretches of beach gave the advantage to the bootlegger.

"What else?" asked Lillian.

"I wonder, sometimes—well, has Sheriff Pender turned a blind eye to this? Or, maybe, he was in on it? He bought him a new Model A Ford. Paid cash money." There were rumors about Pender and the bootleggers. Some said he was paid to keep revenuers away when it was time to unload the boats from Cuba. Maybe he looked the other way if a bootlegger pal accidentally hit Gibby with a car. Maybe Gibby saw something he shouldn't have—and they panicked.

"Yeah, he did!"

"I felt like I had to tell you that, too."

"Sure, Pratt."

"I don't like sayin' it. I don't want to keep anything—I haven't kept anything from y'all."

"We appreciate that," said Mrs. Birch. "You're the only one who has told us anything."

Harlowe nodded.

"I reckon there ain't much for ya to go on, is there?" asked Aubrey.

"No, there ain't. There's one more thing—Pender was in with Foss on his still. The one on the old Vrooman place. I don't know if that's important." The meetings usually ended with Mrs. Birch apologizing, "I done talked your ear off."

And, after they'd gone home, she'd cry.

**

Easter Sunday. Lexie boiled eggs for the little ones to color.

At supper, Foss told a story, an incident out in the cypress camps True had heard before. Lexie was already laughing, the punchline imminent.

"...and that nigger run faster'n a rabbit!" Foss chortled.

He grabbed True—who was looking down. "What's with you?"

"I mentioned Gibby while ago," said Lexie. "But that—"

"I'm tired o' hearing about that boy!" Foss shouted. "He's dead! Let it be!"

And he went on with his story.

True slipped out. Began gathering firewood.

He heard the laughter. Talking. Lexie doing the dishes. The little ones playing.

True thought about Gibby. *Just supposed to forgit it. Teacher and Deddy both said, 'get your work done, boy!' They're still sayin' it!*

True walked down to the old ferry dock. Looked toward the lights. Suddenly, he felt like someone was coming. He turned to see a tall form.

"Hello, son."

Uncle Pratt!

The latter held out something—the little car in its box!

"You can take that home with you son, it's yours."

It cheered the boy like a mess of presents under the tree!

***

"Foss rarely misses suppah. He's home ev'ry night," said Lexie.

"Ev'ry night?"

"Why are you ridin' him, Pratt? You're ruinin' my marriage! Is that what you want?!" She cussed him. Slammed the bedroom door.

Harlowe didn't want to say he knew Foss had been seen riding with Mrs. Danforth, from Carrabelle, in her Ford. More than one "supper time." She and Foss both denied knowing the other. Harlowe finished the coffee and left.

At Cat Point, he looked out at the water. P.T. Daughtry was oystering. The old man was short, lean as a coondog. Leathered skin as dark as a colored man, years spent working in the bright sun. The wiry, fleshy parts worked with the wooden and iron parts like giant human-mechanical scissors. Straining. Sweating.

He waved. But looked away quickly.

Harlowe thought back to that evening. *Mr. Daughtry wouldn't say if he saw Foss that night. He looked at Harlowe, then looked away.*

Along the Sound was a low-roofed cottage, boards grayed and etched by the sun, the wind and salt air. Harlowe knocked. Granny Daughtry answered.

"H'dy, Shureff! How are-ya?"

"Howdy, Miss Daughtry! Just fine!" he answered, taking his hat off.

"Let's git outta the sun—come in in heah!"

She was near seventy. Perhaps older. She had a dignity about her. In the way she invited him in to her clean little kitchen and poured coffee in good cups. Her face and her hands were etched by years in the sun, matching the old boards of her house, her back bent from a lifetime of labor tending melons and oranges. She wore a grey dress, a checky apron. Her gray eyes missed little that happened in Eastpoint.

"I would never say nothin' agin' my neighbors. Y'know that."

"Yes, ma'am."

"But this is differ'nt. I know why you askin'. It ain't for carryin' gossip—knowin' you."

"No, ma'am."

"I've watched you nearly all your life."

"We've known eachother a long time."

"Yes. We have. And I'll he'p you though it pains me to talk about it." She refilled their cups. "Pratt, that boy has got a lot of people fooled. But he has a lot of friends. Y'know that."

Harlowe nodded.

She looked out the window to make sure no one was walking up, then continued. "He takes off for days at a time."

"Yes, ma'am?"

"No sooner'n he gets off work he's leavin.' Off like a shot. Headin' to that pool hall in Carrabelle, over theah. Three nights a week, I reckon. I ain't agin' drinkin'. P.T., he drinks his drams, now. But with Foss, it's whiskey by the jug! He's *got* to have it!"

"All right."

"And—well, he's got his women."

"All right."

"He's *mean!* My Lord, he's mean!"

"Mean?"

"Shoot yes—mean as a cottonmouth! And hateful! For him to do Lexie and them kids like he does? I tell ya, it's a shame!"

"How bad?"

"Pratt, I ain't talkin' about jus' bein' orn'ry."

"No, ma'am."

"Pratt, he's just *cruel!* He ain't let her buy no vittles, hardly. Keeps that gal in a dark house with barely enough food to live! And the way he runs roughshod—well, I don't know if I can describe—."

"You mean beatins'?"

"*Ye-ess!* Like you wouldn't believe! Like ya wouldn't beat a horse! True gits it the worse. But all of 'em. They walk on eggshells, Pratt! He runs that house like he's boss'n a gang of ruffians in the cypress camps!"

Harlowe looked out the window, disgusted.

Mrs. Daughtry shook her head. "To think a deddy would do them kids that way!"

I'm Sheriff but I'm powerless to protect my own sister, her young'uns. In barely a whisper he replied, "Thankya, Miss Daughtry. Thankya for tellin' me."

Mrs. Daughtry often repeated herself. Harlowe listened anyway. "No, we saw no strangers. There was no strangers here that day. Didn't see an automobile all day!"

"Yes'm."

"Gibby loved to take that skiff out to the flats."

"Yes."

"Everyone loved 'im! When he come by the house, here, it would brighten my day! Oh, he was a joy to have around! He'd run all over Eastpoint with 'is fishin' pole."

Harlowe said goodbye. Walked the old Vrooman place. Saw no signs of a still. Yet, Mr. Daughtry looked him up and down when he drove back to the highway.

***

Harlowe knew the house in Carrabelle. He watched Foss emerge from the back door. Bounded over the field into the darkness.

Harlowe knocked as the G. F. & A. train howled.

She opened it, smiling. Then turned white. "Please! I have a husband, Sheriff. A little boy! I caint tell you anything. I would if I knew something!"

"Mrs. Danforth--."

She begged him not to cause her husband, Jim, a railroad fireman, to find out.

"He evuh talk about Gibby?"

Her tears caused her Maybelline to run down her cheeks. She repeated the same thing she'd said a time or two before, "Foss's never mentioned it."

"Never?"

"No, sir! No, sir!" she cried. Harlowe was sure she was telling him the truth.

"Me and Jim are fixin' to move away from here. Makin' a fresh start. Please don't tell 'im! Please don't spoil it!"

Harlowe nodded. Put his hat on. "I won't."

"Thank you! Thank you!"

Harlowe stepped into the shadow, was gone.

***

True looked up from Foss' shadow. "Where's your sister's babydoll?! Did you do something with it?!" Foss howled.

"N-No."

"You better find it!"
"I-I don't know where it is." True looked over at Florie.

"Did you take it? Better answer me, y'little asshole!"
"Maybe it fell behind somethin'," Lexie offered.

"The hell-it-did! He did somethin' with it!" Foss jabbed at True. "You tell me where it is or I'll stomp that car o' yours into the ground! See how you like it when it's somethin' o' yours!"

"I-I didn't take it."
Foss stormed into the children's room. Found the toy in the box True kept it in. He dropped it to the floor and stomped it flat.

True took it in silence. A wheel rolled across the floor, under the couch. That's when True saw it—Florie's doll.

Lexie went on ironing Foss' shirt. Commenced cutting up potatoes for supper.
True toted in the stove-wood. Lexie whispered to him, "Deddy doesn't mean it. He had it hard as a little fella."

True nodded.

"Deddy's a good husband. He's done so much for me."

In bed, True listened to the crickets, Mother, and his siblings sleeping. He wished he was brave enough to slip out. Stowaway on the *Tarpon*. If he had the nerve he'd swing his feet to the floor and go! *Gibby woulda! But I caint move.*

***

No lights shined at Sheip's last night. They'd been out for days, Harlowe realized.
He leaned in the doorway of the jail. "I'm headin' over to Eastpoint. I'll be back, hear?"
"All right, bossman."
He rode the ferry over. One door at a time, he talked to Foss' friends.

"He's the kind of feller ya wohnt as a friend! I ain't got a thing to say agin' him."

Harlowe struck up a conversation with Mother Williams, down the road from the Fulton's. The woman was happy to talk about Foss.

"Oh, I *love* that man! He's such a good neighbor!"

It was the same in every instance. From Eastpoint on up the line.

FORTY-SIX

Apalachicola, May, 1932

Foss strolled into the Chevrolet dealership—Market and Avenue C. He counted out his moonshine money. A nineteen-and-twenty-eight Chevrolet was now his!

He was the talk of the county. His was only the second car in Eastpoint! The talk everywhere was how excited he was to "run that new car!" That "purty 'Shiverlay!'"
He showed it off to Wing, and once he was across, scooped up Lexie, Little Foss, and Florie, and run them over to Tommy's Store.

After he got tired of acting like a husband, he rode the ferry back to Apalach to show the boys at the pool hall.

Harlowe watched him from down the street. A motorist, now, he could range further, faster.
Harlowe followed him to Chattahoochee. Watched him throw a ball with some kids. The water tower loomed over the yard, clothesline. The momma worked like a machine, hanging her washing.
Foss set one child in his car—let her sit behind the wheel.
Foss started the car—with the little gal and two boys in it!
"No-No!" Foss chucked. "All right, kids, ya gotta stay here."
They climbed down. He winked at the woman.
Drove down to the pool hall.

***

Foss was at work. The sawmill whirring. Harlowe found the Chevrolet, parked yonder.
Looked in the back seat.
Shovels!
Harlowe eased the door open.
One was smeared with dried blood. There was light-colored hair on it, too!
Harlowe held the shovel to the sunlight.
The hair was from a deer.

***

Harlowe contemplated over his coffee. "In nineteen-and-twenty-seven, Lexie was expectin.'"
"Florie," replied Seago.
"Yeah. He was gone a lot."
"He was bossin' them camps."
"He was runnin' a still," Harlowe added.
"No secret Pender let the moonshinin' slide for certain people. Foss among 'em. His competitors was the one got raided, seems like," Seago reasoned.

"Yep."

"Ira Brewer was the one who got Foss and Pender started in that bidness. Ya know how everyone likes Ol' Ira. That feller can talk a frog into frying pan! He was the one who talked Pender into it, told 'im how hard a worker Foss was, how much money they could make. The three of 'em got thick as thieves! You didn't know that?"

"I knew Foss and Pender was friends. They come up togethuh, those boys."

"Yeah, Ira was the one got 'em togethuh on the 'shine though. I swear, Pratt, that's prob'ly the only bidness in the county you didn't know about."

"I don't know everything. People think you're the sheriff and you got all the answers, but I don't even know if my own sister's got things she's keepin' from me."

"Yeah?"

"For one, Foss took the train up to River Junction—two days after Gibby was last seen."

"Lexie tell you that?"

"No, she lied about it. I got it from Millirons—arrested 'im for drunk and disorderly."

Seago cussed.

***

Foss pulled the car as far as it would run, up the old tapper's road in Tate's Hell. Foss brought out the five-gallon jugs. Made True load them up. True—struggling to lift them—put them in the floorboards. And back seat.

"I like deliverin' it better than makin' it—more money."

True nodded.

"You'll be comin' from now on. Don't look at me like that. *There'll be* no more lookin' to that damn uncle o' yours!"

True looked out as they passed the Williams' place. Marlene in the field hoeing watermelons. She saw him. And waved.

FORTY-SEVEN

Chattahoochee, May 1932

Saturday morning. Model T's and horse-drawn wagons crowded US-90. Filled the spaces in front of storefronts with tin awnings. Chattahoochee's busy when the farmers come to town—even busier when the *Florida Limited* is in.

Harlowe drove down the hill—to River Junction. The long train blocked Chattahoochee Street while she unloaded her passengers. He waited for the Nichols Dairy truck to pass—walked across to the B&B Café. Found a place by the window where he could see the depot.

The waitress filled his cup.

He asked about Foss.

"Oh, he's a real nice fella! Been in here a couple times. Somethin' wrong?"

"No. Just lookin' for some information."

"Oh."

"Was he with someone when he come in here?"

"No, he was alone. He talked to me some. Real friendly!"

Harlowe nodded.

She patted her hair. "Tell him I said hello! That'll be a nickel for the coffee."

Harlowe found a similar attitude everywhere he went.

"Foss! Nice fella. Tell 'im I said hello, when you see 'im!" said the man at the drugstore.

"Oh, no, no problems a'tall," said the clerk at Scarborough's.

At the filling station, next to the city jail, the attendant advised. "He's a friendly feller!"

"Why, he's a handsome man!" gushed the woman at the grocery store. "Everyone likes him!"

Her husband swept while Harlowe talked. Didn't say anything.

"I don't know his friends. He was in here by himself!" said the woman.

"Well, much obliged, ma'am."

Harlowe walked outside. Started to get in his truck.

The man followed him out. Called after him. "Hey, just a minute."

"Yessir?"

"I think there's somethin' you oughtta know."

"All right."

"I mind my own bidness and run my store—that's it. But what you're hearin' 'round town—I heard you went and talked to some of the other storeowners—Mrs. Evans has already been here spreadin' it."

"Yessir."

"Well, this rosy picture, here, ain't exactly true. Foss comes up here. He gits to playin' cards, wants to git these fellers t'gamblin' with 'im. Throwin' money around. It leads to fightin'. It's trouble—I know Foss has gotten himself in trouble, here."

"Go on."

"There are a few boys 'roun here, ain't got much to do so they throw in with 'im. Caint say I blame 'em. I was young once. Anyhow, my brother runs with them boys. He'll talk to ya. May know somethin' that'd he'p ya."

"I appreciate it. Somethin' else ya wanna say?"

"Well, it's like this here. I think Foss is mixed up in some bad bidness."

"Yessir?"

"I don't know exactly, *what*—and I need to get back inside. You talk to my brother, and he'll tell ya."

Harlowe located the brother. On a small farm, just South of Brown's Dairy, on the riverbluff, Harlowe saw him, hoeing a row of watermelon seedlings.

Harlowe parked. Walked across the field. "Howdy!"

"Yessir? What can I do fur ya? If you from the bank, I'm fixin'--."

"Nosir. I ain't from the bank." Harlowe told him who he was. That it was about Foss.

"Okay—whaddya wanna know?"

"Did Foss mention Gibby Birch at any time?"

"No, sir."

"Did he mention Beadle Hutto?"

"No, sir."

"How was he when he was drinkin'? Did he say anything you found peculiar?"

"No. Nothing out-of-the-way. I seen 'im where he got a little tight, I reckon—feelin' good right along with the rest of the boys. He don't mean no harm."

"All right."

"He'd hunt with us up 'ere sometimes. On my land. Stay with us a few days at a time."

"When's the last time?"

"Oh, 'bout a year ago."

"Any time about four years ago?"

"Sure. Around the fall of nineteen-and-twenty-seven."

"You sure about that date?"

"Yessir."

"I'm fixin' to ask ya somethin' that may sound a little odd."

"Go ahead."

"Could Foss have buried somethin' on your land?"

The man laughed. "What, like treasure or gold? Hell, Foss spent ever' dime he made."

Harlowe grinned. "No. Anything. A box. A bundle."

"No, sir, not on my land he ain't."

"Okay. Anything else ya can remember?"

"There's one other thing."

"Yessir?"

"This may surprise ya, now. A few weeks back, Millirons told Foss to leave town! Sure did! Ain't never heard the Chief run so much as a stray dog oughtta town!"

Harlowe went to find Millirons. But the man at the filling station said he'd gone to Quincy.

Harlowe talked to new faces at Scarborough's. A farmer was loading feed onto his truck. His ears perked when Foss' name was mentioned. He kept looking over at Harlowe. Seemed anxious to get going.

While he was mashing the starter, Harlowe approached, said who he was. "Glad to know ya. I'm the farmhand at Nichols dairy. You a long way from home!"

Harlowe put his foot on the running board. "I reckon so. Do you know a fella named Foss Fulton?"

The fellow shook his head. He seemed nervous, fidgeting with the spark lever. "Well. I best go," he said.

"You sure?"

"Nosir." The man mashed the starter. The truck sputtered. And died.

"I think you do."

"A'ight, say I do." The starter groaned again.

"Would you know if Foss had any trouble, around here?"

The man quit. Hung his head. "I know 'im. He got *me* in a lotta trouble and I don't need no more of it."

"What was it?"

"Foss and me got really drunk one time. I crawled off and found a place to sleep. But he lay in the azaleas, front of one o' the doctors at the hahspittal. Got hisself arrested."

"When was that?"

"Damn near five years."

"Around October, nineteen-hunnered-and-twenty-seven?"

"How'd ya know that?"

"There's somethin' else, ain't there?"

The man nodded. "Yessir. Foss said he'd done something *bad*. Got to carryin' on about it. That's why I had to leave 'im. Layin' face down in them bushes."

"Did he say what he'd done?"

"Nosir. Haven't any *i*-dea."

"How'd you come to know him?"

"Ol' boy used to boss them cypress camps. I worked for 'im at one time. I left the woods. Married a gal from up here. Started workin' for her deddy."

"All right."

"I don't wanna git him in no trouble, now. Don't want 'im comin' after me!"

"Yessir—I understand. You remember anything else he mighta mentioned, places he'd go?"

"Yes, sir—Climax, Georgie! He'd go there from time-to-time. Had him a galfriend up there. Hell, he had 'em up and down the line."

Harlowe knocked on doors at every whistlestop. Talked to every gal Foss had trifled with since '27. But came up empty.

In the moonlight, a field of yellow flowers glistened serenely. The tracks, shiny bars which paralleled the highway, seemed to stretch to *oblivion*. Perhaps, he was there already—he hadn't seen another soul since he'd left Hosford.

The truck began to steam—overheating. He pulled to the side of the road. Near Vilas. He waited for the motor to cool, smoking a cigarette and looking at the flowers in the dark field. They were trumpet pitcher plants. A solid acre of them. He couldn't imagine daffodils being prettier.

He'd seldom seen a painting do justice to Tate's Hell. Beauty and danger intertwined, and from the woods which lay beyond the field, he was certain that eyes were watching. Panther, moccasin, human, perhaps. This place held a number of things there would eat the unwary—even these flowers devoured other creatures for their sustenance.

The "New River," more of a creek really, bordered the field, meandering off into those mysterious woods.

The shadows turned oddly out there in those pines. The crickets chirped— loud enough a man could pop out without knowing.

That shadow moved, he was certain.

Harlowe stepped behind the fender. Cocked his shotgun.

The palmettos rustled, and some animal, unseen, crept on in the night.

Harlowe exhaled. Siphoned water for the radiator—and was glad to get going.

FORTY-EIGHT

Apalach—June, 1932

Ten o'clock. It was already hot—and the kids were making the most of it! Hanging around the ice plant. Watching the men load the wagon, hoping they'd get a piece!

Playing "kick-the-can," yonder, running shirtless like Indians.

Squealing, happily, when the men got done watering the freight train and let them run through the water from the spout!

When the sun reached its zenith, youngsters who had their fifteen cents would flock to the *Dixie's* "Saturday-shootumup-western." Or, go to the ball game, afterwhile.

Whether working or playing, kids spent all summer outdoors!

If I do my job, these young'uns will always be safe, Harlowe thought.
He drove to the ferry. Rode it to Eastpoint.
He saw Foss walking by the schoolhouse, slowly through the field knee high with summergrass and burnweed. Approaching the boys who'd gathered to play baseball. He grinned. Tossed the chert rock back when one of them hit a fly ball.

As Foss neared his house, Harlowe pulled up aside him.
"Hey, Brother! Y'still spyin' on me?"
"You could clear it up whenever ya want, Foss."
"Oh?"
"What was botherin' ya—what ya were carryin' on about—up in River Junction."
Foss grinned from ear-to-ear. "I've got nothin' to tell, Brother."
Foss had shaved. To his delight, people carried on how he resembled that young star, Clark Gable! "Now, Pratt, I haven't done anything. I don't know why you're tryin' to frame me—I'm innocent as a lamb!"
"Who was with you in the picture, Foss?"
"When are ya gonna quit ridin' me? Pretty soon I'm gonna get sore. Ya don't really think I did somethin' to that boy. I could knock your block off for sayin' that."
"Who was the fella in the photo?"
"Ya really think I'm holdin' out? I've told ya what I know—that's on the level! What reason have I to lie?"
"I'm gonna find out. I'm patient."

Harlowe drove to see Miss Hazelwood—*Mrs.* Johnston, now. She'd wed and moved to Carrabelle.
"Gibby acting scared? Never! There was nothing bothering him!"
"Yes, ma'am."

"He was doing well since he come back—since he stowed away on the riverboat." She laughed. "Oh, he had an adventure! But he settled in just fine when he returned. Same Gibby. My gracious, he was a little man! So full of personality. Our own Huck Finn!"

Harlowe grinned at that.

"I thought something was bothering *your nephew*. I had far more concerns about *his* home life."

"Go on."

"We're not supposed to interfere, but it seemed obvious something was happening with Truitt. I more expected something ominous where *he* was concerned. That he'd run away and be lost. Not run from curiosity like all boys do, but *to go!*"

Harlowe nodded.

"These little ones are like angels when they come to us, but they don't always get raised in anything like heaven."

"No, ma'am. I reckon not."

Harlowe thanked her. Cranked the truck. He'd looked at whether Gibby ran away, of course. Everything suggested he was happy at home. There'd been no circus in town to lure a curious youngster!

Harlowe had looked into whether Gibby met someone when he'd run off to River Junction. Harlowe talked to the captain of the steamboat. Found no concerns. It was simply a boyish thing—Gibby's class had just read *Huckleberry Finn!*

***

Harlowe couldn't find where Foss had any connection to Tallahassee. He checked the photographic shops in Tallahassee to see if anyone remembered developing the photo, and for whom. No one did. The cheap paper had no markings that could be traced.

He drove back home.

Sheip's was oddly quiet in the middle of the week, looming over the town like a gallows. Talk was, it may close! Uptown streets were like a ghost town. *Devil Horse* advertised at the *Dixie*, but few could afford a ticket.

***

Harlowe saw True look up at the boys playing ball in the road.

Lexie admonished him in a hushed voice, "Deddy expects to see you workin'. So long as you're not in skool he doesn't wanna see ya sittin' around."

True nodded. Got back to his chores. *Be quiet—git your work done.*

225

Harlowe drove True to the oysterhouse. The boy wouldn't talk about what went on in his home. His expressionless face said plenty.

What ticks in Foss's head? A jealousy, almost—toward his own son!

***

The telephone rang. Deputy Brewer. "Shureff, we broke up the still them colored boys was runnin.' They said Foss was buyin' it from 'em, but ya know ya caint b'lieve a thing they say."

"All right. See ya this evenin.'"

Brewer liked hunting for stills. Breaking them up. He liked the raids Pender used to do. So long as they weren't friends, it was good for everyone, garnering a fine mention in the *Times!* Harlowe didn't care for the practice, but in this instance it served its purpose.

***

Foss came home from work, Saturday. Got ready to leave with his friends. Harlowe heard him warn Lexie about his room. "Keep them kids outta theah!"
He shoved the skeleton key at her. Stomped out to the waiting wagon, his friends and brother, Briley, in high spirits!

Harlowe pulled up aside it. "Howdy."
"Hey, Brother!" Foss grinned.
"Deputy Brewer just broke up the still, Foss. Smashed all the jugs up theah."
Foss gave a sly grin. "That don't involve me, Brother!" Foss leaned in close. "Y'solve that case yet? Maybe y'need to find you a woman—I know a few!"

***

McCannon cut off a piece of chaw. Harlowe looked in and asked him, "ya mind if I borry my nephew?"

"Sure, Pratt—anytime!"

They walked along, leaving the sounds of the oysterhouse, the gulls.

"You like workin' for Mr. McCannon?"

True nodded.

"He's a pretty good ol' boy."

They walked to the Birch's place. Aubrey had his boat running. They hopped on. Aubrey motored around Cat Point. When they reached the flats, he threw the anchor over. They sat on the sides of the boat, looking clear across the Bay.

"True, I'm tryin' to see what Gibby woulda seen. I thought you—knowin' him so well—might could help me."

True nodded.

"He woulda been fishin' right about here," said Birch.

"Yessir." True looked back at the old ferry dock. And his house—the glint of tin roof ashore.

"The men on the *Mary D* saw Gibby—looked like he was headin' in toward the ferry dock. Which woulda have taken him past y'alls house," Harlowe reckoned, pointing out the way he would have come in.

True knew he was one of the last to see Gibby alive. *When he come by the oysterhouse.* It made True's belly tighten like a knot.

"Billy Brewer and them was some 'o the last to see 'im alive...Besides you," Harlowe added.

"Storm was pickin' up, when they seen 'im," said Birch.

True's heart pounded. He racked his brain. *Gibby fished the old ferry dock a lot. The ferry used to come in right by the house. We'd watch Cap'n Wing put in. Watch the automobiles roll off. Gibby used to leave the skiff there, sos he could come by the house. It woulda been the fastest way to get ashore, with the storm comin'.*

Harlowe looked at Birch. "Lexie said Foss was home early. Never left."

"Yeah."

"Was deddy home?" True wondered. *I said Deddy never left. I done told Uncle Pratt. But was that so?*

He'd had it drilled to him so many times. *'Deddy was home'—that's what you say. But, was he? True remembered. No, he* wasn't! "Uncle Pratt?"

"Yeah, son."

True was shaking. "I need to tell ya somethin,' sir."

Harlowe nodded.

True swallowed. "Well, more I think on it, I don't think he was. He told us, 'remember I's here.'"

Harlowe nodded.

"I-I was scared to tell ya—I lied."

"That's all right, son."

True looked up him, as if to ask, *really?*

"You did right to tell me, son."

True, looking out at the ripple of a fish fixin' to jump, exhaled deeply. "Well, I b'lieve I owe him that."

***

Foss left the billiards hall in River Junction.

Emerging from the shadow, Harlowe followed him down Railroad Avenue.

Down to a house by the tracks. A gal opened the door. Pulled him in.

***

No money in the jar. Foss hollered so it shook the house. "You're spending too much money! You're always spendin' money on *these kids!*"

"Foss, I—."

"Dollar-and-a-half in kerosene! Just spend, spend's all ya do! None of ya 'preciate what I got to do for you to have things'!"

"We needed it for the lights, Foss."

"We—aint—got—the—money!" he screamed.

"I didn't think--."

"No—ya thought I'd just work my ass off so ya can keep all'these lamps lit!"

True stayed in his spot on the corner of the bed, making himself invisible, the little ones huddled at his feet.

Harlowe heard it all. Saw Foss drive off. *No matter what, he'll get up the money for gasoline.*

***

Harlowe watched True toting in the stove-wood and a pail of water. Then, saw the boy hurry to work.

Little Foss and the Williams boys were playing ball. They begged Foss to pitch for them. He threw one for Little Foss. Then he noticed Harlowe.

"Hey, Brother!"

Harlowe walked over. "Mornin,' Foss."

Foss pitched the ball again. "Y'solve your murder yet?"

"You ready to confess?"

"No, Brother. 'Scuse me—gotta git to work."

***

Pender came by the office. Offered smalltalk for a quarter-hour.

Harlowe poured more coffee, patiently waiting for him to get to the reason for the visit.

The former sheriff looked out the window, then back across the table. "Foss didn't do it, Pratt."

Harlowe nodded. *Foss could deliver a dozen votes. To Pender, that's no insignificant number.*

***

The sun exposed what was mercifully concealed by shadows three nights earlier. Siding streaked with soot from passing trains. Smudged windows. Walls that trembled like a drunk's hands, as a freight train rolled by. The outskirts of hot, low-lying River Junction.

Through the window, Harlowe saw her working with needle and thread. He rapped at the screendoor. Foss' galfriend got up to answer.

She wore a scarf over her hair. Had large, brown eyes and a pointy chin. She'd only open the door a handbreadth, talking to him through the screen door, peering out with just one eye. "Yes, may I help you?" He told her who he was, and that left eye looked at him 'crossways.'

"You're not in any trouble. I jus' wanna ask ya some questions."

She kept the door cracked. "What's this about?"

"A missin' boy."

"I don't know nothin' about that."

"Did he say anything about Gibby Birch? Anything about Eastpoint?"

"I don't wanna be mixed up in this, no way!"

Harlowe held up the photo. "Ma'am, Gibby was an eight-year-old boy that never come home. Did Foss evuh mention 'im?"

"No, he didn't. Now, I've got to finish this piece-work."

"Yes'm."

"I don't know why you against Foss—he's a good man!"

"I ain't again' him. I'm tryin' to find out about the boy."

"Foss's a good man. He's helped me stay in this place when the bank down the street, there, was about to take it from me."

"Yes, ma'am."

"He never mentioned no kid."

"Did he ever mention problems at home?"

"No, caint say as he did. Didn't seem like he'd put up with none."

"Uh-huh."

"Now I done talked to you enough! Y'best be goin' 'fore people see ya and get to talkin'." I don't need more talk than I already got, Mr. Harlowe." At that, she turned her head and Harlowe could see the shiner.

"You all right?"

"I'm fine. It wasn't Foss—I have other problems 'sides him. Now, please go!"

He tipped his hat. "Yes, ma'am."

***

August.

Pear cobbler and coffee. Harlowe, Seago set their hats on the table.

"It's as bad as evuh, the way he does Lexie and them kids."

Harlowe nodded.

"Y'reckon Foss done somethin' to that boy?" wondered Mrs. Daughtry

"I don't know," Harlowe replied.

The old woman poured more coffee. "I sure feel bad for Lillian. She's a *fine* person."

"Yes, she is," said Seago.

"She's a good woman," Harlowe agreed.

"Sure you don't wanna stay a spell?"

"I'd like that. Next time I'm over here, I'd enjoy visitin' with ya a little longer."

They thanked Mrs. Daughtry for the coffee, cobbler.

"You welcome. Enjoyed havin' you visit with me!"

Seago tipped his hat. "Yes'm. Thankya for havin' us."

"Bye now," said Harlowe.

FORTY-NINE

September, 1932

Raindrops streaked the windows. "Shutup!" Foss screamed.

The little ones had been playing. Now, they were crying.

A portrait of the family crashed to the floor.

Florie pointed at it. "Deddy—the *pitcher!*"

"Shutup! I give ya a place to lay your heads! None of you 'preciate it!"

"Stop it, Foss!" shouted Lexie. "Stop it, y'hear!"

Foss grabbed her by her face, squeezing it in his giant paw. "You better shutup—all of ya! I'll do to you like I done that boy! I'll bury you! And these kids! Your brother'll never find one hair o' your heads!"

Florie was screaming.

True was unable to move he was so scared! His heart pounding, his breaths as shallow as if he stood in an icy rainstorm. His siblings fell in behind him at the threshold of their room.

Foss yanked his belt through the loops. Took it to Lexie. True silently remembered, *You're okay if no one can see you.*

When Foss was through, he grabbed his coat. "I won't be back! And it's your fault!"

"I'm sorry! I'm sorry!" Lexie bleated.

The door squeaked on its hinges. They all turned to look.

A tall figure stood in the shadow. Harlowe! He saw Lexie on her knees, sobbing. Chest heaving. Hair mussed. Finger marks on her face. Welts on her arms. The huddled children. The shattered picture.

"You all right, Lexie?"

"Fine, Pratt—everything's fine!"

She breathed in gasps. The little ones still whimpered, Harlowe saw. "I was headed for the ferry. Thought I'd stop by. Heard the dogs when I pulled up. Figured somethin' was wrong."

"Well, there ain't," Foss retorted. "None o' your bidness what goes on in my house—*Sheriff.*"

"She's my sister. I reckon it is my business."

"Pratt, please!" pleaded Lexie. "I'm all right!"

"That's right. Leave my property. Or I'm gonna stomp your ass into the ground!"

To True, Foss never seemed bigger. The boy felt like a scarecrow ripped by a hurricane! Harlowe looked as spare as one of Lee's boys at Appomattox—despite the shotgun. Foss thought so too. Without warning, he rushed Harlowe like a bull! *He might get the gun!* True thought. But Harlowe slammed the butt end into Foss' head, like a right from Jack Dempsey.

Foss crumpled in agony. Nearly passed out! True was wide-eyed. Lexie clutched the little ones in the doorway behind him. "Don't hurt 'im, Pratt!"

Foss cussed. Started to get up. Balled his fists and lunged at Harlowe—but stopped.

"You just set there!" Harlowe ordered. There was a look on Harlowe's face True had never seen before.

Foss saw it too.

True could hardly believe it. Foss backed down to no one—here he was on the floor like a scared kid!

There was no fear in Harlowe's eyes. That look on his face—stern as a statue of Lee! *I'm gonna remember that look!* True told himself.

Harlowe turned to him. "You all right, son?"

True nodded.

Harlowe patted the little girl on the head. And Little Foss.

Lexie got a cloth for Foss' head, where he was bleeding.

"You gonna settle down, now?" asked Harlowe.

Foss nodded from the floor. Holding his head.

"Don't take him to jail, Pratt! Please!" Lexie begged.

"Git 'im to bed. He can sleep it off."

Lexie continued daubing Foss' head. "I will, Pratt!"

Harlowe turned toward the door; reached for the handle. Suddenly, Foss sprung to his feet! He swung, his fist fearsome as a bear paw! Before True could make a sound, though, Harlowe weaved. A well-timed left connected good. Foss went down—Harlowe knocked him out!

The ratcheting handcuffs reverberated off the bare walls. Then Harlowe drug him out like a buck deer. True heard him say, "I reckon a night in jail will sober you up."

True could hardly believe it!

Harlowe glanced back. "Bye, son."

True thought about that look. *Like he mighta killed Foss if he'd so much as twitched! Boy, he sure set him down! And how deliberate Harlowe acted at the door—Foss' swinging on him didn't surprise him at all!*

True knew Harlowe was a lawman—most of his life Harlowe had been sheriff. But they'd worked so much together, framing and roofing, Harlowe teaching him how to work with tools, at a certain point True just thought of him as a house-builder. He was something far more!

"No, don't take Deddy!" Florie wailed.

"Damn you, Pratt—I hate ya!" Lexie hollered. "Let him go! What am I gonna do without 'im?" she cried.

Harlowe rode back with Foss handcuffed to the doorframe.

Seago helped get him in the cell. They dropped him in the corner like a feedsack.

Harlowe told Seago, what Foss said—about the body.

"He done it!" the big man exclaimed. "For him to mention Gibby like that--."

Harlowe nodded.

"How could he...a man with young'uns hisself...wohnt to hurt a young'un?" Seago thought, the furrows on his big forehead deepening with the question.

"Well...maybe he's drawn to children."

Seago spoke in a painful whisper. *"Why?"*

"I read some books about it, by a French Doctor, named Tardieu, and some others. I don't understand all of it. They say a man who does this is 'psychopathic'—he's ill."

"Hell, I don't know what any o' that means! Doncha reckon Foss jus' got aggravated with Gibby, hurt 'im on accident?"

"Whoever did this, I believe it was intentional."

Seago cussed. "All I know is Foss's pretty muscular-bound. He could handle a li'l feller. He could tote a body with no trouble, put it anywhere he pleases."

"Yep."

"But, somethin's botherin' ya—I can see it."

"Well, it's what *doesn't* fit 'im that...bothers me. Foss is rough. He likes his women. There's nothin' that says he's one to 'fancy' a youngun."

"Why won't he tell-ya the truth?"

"He's orn'ry. The rest...I reckon we'd need the doctors in Chattahoochee to tell us."

"Yeah."

Harlowe noted the calendar on the wall. Today, was one day shy of the anniversary of Gibby's disappearance.

"J'hear, before the rain this morning, Ed caught 'im a three-and-a-half foot bull red?" asked Seago.

"Nah—hadn't heard that. Good for Ed."

Presently, from over in the office, Harlowe heard Foss awaken.

"What the hell you 'rest me for! You caint 'rest me!" You let me go right now! Ya oughta be beggin' me not to hire a lawyer, ya sonofabitch! Treated me worse than a nigger!"

Harlowe stood before Foss' cell. Held the photograph to the bars. "A momma doesn't know about her baby—what happened to 'im. You could tell her. You could help her. You were theah."

He grinned. "Why, sure, Pratt! That's me!"

"You were with these boys. You weren't home, early, the night Gibby went missing. I wanna know what went on."

"Why, you're askin' the wrong person, Pratt!"

"Who's the older man in the background, heah?"

"You got a one-track mind. I've got a knot on my head, you sonofabitch! Open this door and I'll fight you! I'm through talkin'!"

"Where did you put his body?"

Foss cussed him. It went on after midnight. Harlowe kept asking his questions. Both men damp with sweat. The jail like an oven in the sultry temperatures. Foss's head nearly brushed the ceiling and the walls closed in on the man used to the woods. He stomped the floor. Rattled the bars.

"Did you know Whittle?"

"Who?"

"E.F. Whittle."

"No."

"Ya know Kern?"

"No."

"You know this other fella?" Harlowe, again, pointed to the man with a blurred face. Foss knew that Harlowe knew. He physically shook. "What is it?"

"Nothin'!" spat Foss.

"You look nervous as a black at a klan meetin'! What are ya scared of? The fella in the photograph *theah?*"

"I ain't scared of nothin'! You're off your rocker!"

"Ya know 'im. You can call 'is name."

Sweat beaded on Foss's forehead, trickled down his neck. "Please. I don't know nothin'!" Foss cried.

"You lyin'."

"No, I ain't! I don't know what in hell you talkin' about! I don't know!"

"Ya sobered up fast."

"You, yourself, been known to take drams. Bah—you were a *bad drunk*, ever'body knows it!"

"I quit drinkin'."

"Ha! I bet that's why your wife run off—ain't it? Ain't it?!" he bellowed.

Harlowe looked at him. "That might scare your woman. Your younguns. It don't me."

"Look, whaddya want? Money? I'll cut you in what I'm makin'!"

"I wanna know about Gibby. Who was with you when that photo was made?"

"I dunno!"

"You don't know? Did you kill Gibby?"

"Sonofabitch, I swear I didn't!"

"Ya gonna tell me what I wanna know."

"Damn-ya! What can I do? I done told ya the truth. I ain't kilt that boy!"

"Who was Beadle working for?"

"I dunno!"

"What are ya hidin' in that room?"

"You stay off my property!"

It went on until sunrise.

Aubrey was fit-to-be-tied. He'd come to Apalach when he'd heard. On the *Save Time's* first run.

"My wife is on the back porch, cryin.' Caint stop."

Harlowe poured him a cup.

The oysterman whispered, "Tig Vanko says we can take 'im out in his boat—in the hold. Then, I reckon, oh, about thirty miles offshore, I'll toss 'im out." Birch referred to the captain of the shrimpboat, *Greek Girl*.

"Nobody will ever find 'im," agreed Seago.

"Let me handle it," said Harlowe.

"Ya sure he ain't the one 'at done it?"

"I'm tryin' to find that out."

"Judge may turn 'im loose!" said Seago.

"It's Sundee. I ain't heard anything from the judge, have you?"

"No."

"If I can keep him in here I can get him to tell me."

Aubrey had calmed some. "Y'know how I ask 'im if True can come look for Gibby?"

Harlowe nodded.

"Foss kinda growls at me, 'Don't know what good he'd do ya! I ain't goin' out in 'is!' Just nasty as he can be. I never wanted to say that, now. I wanted to believe..."

"I understand."

"Foss is so *well-liked*. Everyone—I jus' don' understand it!"

"Nosir."

"He never did help look, did he?" asked Seago.

"He was out there that next mornin' after he sobered up," Harlowe recalled.

"That's right," Aubrey agreed.

"Whaddya think, Aubrey?" asked Seago.

Aubrey looked at Harlowe, back at Seago. "I done told you how Foss was all wet when I come to the door that night."

"Yeah."

"I didn't think of it then. Thought he'd just come in—got caught in it like the rest of us. But now you say he claimed he was with Lexie—he told her to lie about it?" Aubrey, normally as calm as the creek on Cat Point, grew red. "Foss wuddint at Elmer Smith's, them boys was clear on that."

"Yep," replied Harlowe. "That's what they said."

Aubrey composed himself. But Harlowe could still see in his eyes he wasn't satisfied the court would work justice.

"I want 'im to stand trial. Like we done in Bristol," Harlowe told him. He referred to the Forehand incident. Some, in that day, preferred a lynching. The lawmen, including Harlowe, held firm on a trial.

Aubrey understood. Nodded. "What this is doin' to my wife, I caint describe."

"Just let me handle it, Aubrey."

"Yessir."

"All right."

The telephone clanged. The operator had the party, long-distance. "He's on the line now, Sheriff."
"Yes, ma'am."
"Harlowe, I hope this is important—it's Sundee," growled State's Attorney Raines.

Harlowe laid out the facts.

Raines was gruff, but agreed, "There's enough for a search warrant. Nothin's gonna happen today. I'll speak to Judge Johnson, Monday."

"Would you call a grand jooree?" Harlowe wondered.

"Send me a letter. I'll look at it."

CLICK.

Harlowe penned the letter. Walked it down to the train. Handed it up to the postman.

Harlowe walked back. Foss was hollering to passersby, through the bars. "He mistreated me, boys! Get ahold to my brothers!"

Harlowe walked back to the cells and he hushed.

"You gonna tell me who all you remember bein' around that day. This man, he was from Tallahassee."

"I don't know! I tell ya I don't know! Ask me a hunnerd times and I'll tell ya the same!"

Harlowe crossed his arms. "I'll figure it out. I'm patient."

"I gotta be at the mill! Ya gonna let me out, aincha, Brother? Huh? Ya ain't gonna make me miss work!"

"You told Lexie, them kids—you'd put 'em in the ground like Gibby. How about it?"

"Oh, that—I just said that to scare 'em, that's all! Gonna hold me on that? I've had 'bout enough o' this! C.A., telephone Lexie. My friends'll put up my bail money! C.A.!"

Harlowe walked out. Presently, Mr. Huff walked into the office.

"I just want to put in a good word for Foss. He's a hard worker. I hope this matter can be cleared up."

FIFTY

Harlowe motored back from Tallahassee as quickly as he could make it.

He found Lexie scrubbing clothes on the washboard. "I wanna look in that room, Lexie."

"You have no right!" She turned red and cussed him like a deckhand on a river barge.

He held up the paper. "I have a warrant signed by Judge John B. Johnson."

"Against your own *sister?* You're really *somethin'!"*

Harlowe ignored the comments. Waited for her to unlock the room. Angrily, she flung the door open.

He began with the bureau. Opening drawers. Looking through folded shirts. "Please be careful! He'll know if you messed with those things!"

Harlowe examined the suit-of-clothes hanging in the chiffarobe.

"Pratt, please!"

"I won't hurt it none." He went through the pockets. Hung it back up.

Harlowe lifted the lid of the trunk in the corner. Inside were a stack of papers, folded, bound with twine. Harlowe unbound them. Smoothed them on the bed.

"Pratt—*he's particular about these things!"*

"Letters from the old cypress comp'ny. Popham certificates."

"Leave 'em alone, *please!"*

Harlowe looked out the window. Foss's shed, yonder. Harlowe walked outdoors. Opened the doors. Foss' tools. Axes. Spades. Harlowe examined each one.

Maybe one was used to bury Gibby. No way of knowin.'

The floor was soft dirt. Harlowe got his stick. Poked in the sand.

Lexie carrying on and crying, Harlowe closed the doors. Turned to the burn barrell.

"Oh, you're somethin' else! Y'wanna check my wash-bucket? Maybe I'm hidin' somethin' down in theah!"

239

He poked in the ashes. Saw something. Half-burned—a photogragh! Foss was in it. Whomever was in the other half was gone. On the back was scrawled, *"Whiskey George."*

"What's that?" she spat.

"Nothin' important."

Lexie hissed at him like a panther. "All this, for *what?!* Y'found nothin'!" Ya won't quit until ya ruin my marriage! Claudie left ya because of this foolishness, and ya won't be satisfied til Foss leaves me, is that it?"

Harlowe started the truck.

"You're so all fire sure Foss had somethin' to do with it. That I've lied to ya? That Foss wasn't home all night like I said?"

"He wasn't that evenin', Lexie. He--."

"Why don't ya *tell me* what he done? Since you know so much!"

"All right. Y'all had words. Got to fussin.' Foss went out. Angry. Cussin' you. Later own, he come back soaked to the gills and wild-eyed. Didn't he? He had to think fast—he was scared. Folks were already out lookin' for Gibby."

Lexie didn't answer.

"He told ya to say nothin'. Told ya to lie. That's how it was, wasn't it?"

"No!"

"Everyone was searchin' for Gibby—but him. He knows who all was out theah and won't tell me. He could help but he won't."

"You think your're so smart!"

"No. If I was, ida caught 'im by now—whoever killed Gibby."

"You turn him *aloose!* I need 'im! I love 'im—nothin'll split us up!"

"Lexie, you think he goes to River Junction and Carrabelle to sightsee? He's got his women—whole county knows it."

Lexie slapped him. "I won't ever speak to you again! Get off our land!"

Foss had run a few stills. Had him one on the old Vrooman place at one time. Mighta had one at, Whiskey George Creek. That photo could tie in to that.

Harlowe drove up there, to Whiskey George. It's a clean, broad stream flowing out of Tate's Hell to the East Bay, amidst a lovely, watery, lowcountry. He crossed the wooden bridge that straddled the creek. Pulled to the side of the road.

He walked into the pines a ways. He saw indications that a still had been operated there.

Tommy flagged him down on his way back. County Judge Robert Clary had telephoned.

Harlowe used the phone at the store. "No, Judge, not just that. I suspect 'im of homicide."

The judge cussed. "They—they're asking me about a bond. He has a lawyer now, Pratt."

"Yessir."

"I intended to schedule a hearin' this afternoon. But I believe this must be heard by the circuit judge."

CLICK.

The telephone was ringing when Harlowe reached his office.

"I just read your letter, Harlowe. You haven't enough. If you want *me* to call a grand jury, you're gonna need more that what you got," said Raines. "I've got to have evidence, you understand that?"

"Yessir. Give me time, I'll get more," Harlowe replied. "Would you ask the Court for more time, sir?"

CLICK

Raines turned to his secretary.

"He's listening to those people down there. That family can't accept their boy run off."

"Those *are* his voters, Mr. Raines."

***

The telephone rang again. "Sheriff, I got Tommy's store in Eastpoint. It's your sister," said Miss Hilda.

"Put her on. Thankya."

"Where's Foss? Where's Foss!" she repeated, talking up so as to be heard over the wall phone at the store.

"I got him in the jailhouse."

"Still? He done spent the night over there—ain't that enough?"

"Lexie, I--."

"It ain't that serious noway—merrit people fight! You of all people should—."

"I'm gonna do my job Lexie. I--."

CLICK.

The phone rang again, presently.

It was McCannon.

"You arrested him? Why? I need 'im."

"I got him here and he gonna stay here."

Then, Foss' brothers came to plead.

Harlowe walked down to Scipio Creek. Demo George had laid the keel on a new boat, her ribs poking up like the skeleton of a big fish. *Build something. Do a job and finish it. With the law—are you evuh finished?*

***

Judge Clary strolled down the hall. "Two o'clock, Pratt. Have 'im in the courtroom."

"Yessir."

"Judge Johnson asked me to handle it. Well--."

"Yessir?"

"I don't normally weigh in on these matters, Pratt. But from where I stand you haven't much. Foss is a good worker. And I'm gettin' phone calls. Jus' think about it, n' I'll see ya shortly!"

That again. Because Foss worked hard, because he worked at a mill job, it excused anything else he did. A man could be every kind of sonofabitch but if he worked up a sweat and made money like a mill-horse he had a dozen defenders. Aubrey worked just as hard, he didn't strut about it, he didn't spend a dime unless it was for his wife, and no county commissioner ever called "to put in a word" for him!

Ira Brewer saw Harlowe walking up the street.
Damn.
"Jus' wanna talk to ya."
"What about?"

Harlowe just looked at him.

Ira sighed. "I'll tell ya. I'm tired of carryin' it around. Yeah, I was with the boy. Some people invited 'im to a little party. Moonshine. Women."

"Where?"

"Near Green Point."

"Was Foss there?"

"Yeah."

"Who was Collis workin' for?"

"Some fella."

"You know 'im?"

"No."

"Did you hear Collis call his name?"

"I didn't hear no one call no names."

"Was there anyone else with this fella?"

"One or two."

"You know 'em?"

"Nah."

"Where were they from, these other men?"

"Never seen 'em before."

"They from Tallahassee?"

Ira nodded, timid as a schoolboy.

Harlowe showed him the blurry face. "This one of 'em?"

Ira nodded.

"Can you describe this fella?"

"He wuddint colored."

"I can see that. Can ya tell me anything more about him, his size, color of his hair?"

"Dark-haired, I reckon. Didn't see his face, now—not too good. Had a hat on. That's the truth, Pratt!"

"Foss knew the fellas from Tallahassee?"

"I don't--."

"Did he know those boys?"

Ira nodded.

"Who all was there that day?"

"Don't remember."

"You lyin'."

"No, I aint said nothin.' Nothin' can happen to me for sayin' nothin',"

"Ira, I wanna know who they were."

"I said all I'm gonna say. Now I gotta go to work."

"Did you see Gibby leavin'?"

"I wuddint there, now. When you talkin' about somethin' happenin' to Gibby I wuddint there!"

"Ya see 'im leavin'—was he with someone?"

"Foss was right by Gibby—ask him!"

243

In a third-floor room at Tallahassee's Floridan Hotel, County Commissioner Huff slammed down the telephone and swore.

He turned to Pender. "We are so close on gettin' that bridge—bringin' more visitors to our county! Harlowe will spoil it, now, makin' folks b'lieve there's been a killin'!"

"He's going to embarrass us!" agreed Pender.

Embarassments are expensive, Huff thought. He owned property in Eastpoint. He had plans for a filling station and tourist cabins at Magnolia Bluff, once the bridge was built and Apalachicola was linked, by road, to Tallahassee and Thomasville—and anywhere else tourists and their greenbacks might come from.

A third man attended their meeting—Ledbetter. "Harlowe's a big problem for us. Ruling this a homicide poses many difficulties for us."

***

Uncle Pratt's catching all kinds of hell, True thought. True heard men talking around the oyster house.

Someone mentioned the "Forehand case." *"Harlowe was on that posse that caught the boy." "He don't give up!"* True knew nothing about the incident, but the old men sure seemed impressed!

***

Seago could hear the coroner through the telephone. He was hot!

Harlowe tried to get him to consider the skull and change the official finding on manner of death. "It was an accident, Pratt! You found the boat! That's proof enough! Have you read law or earned a physician's license recently? You're overstepping my authority! You've no right!"

"That skull is proof—."

"This matter's closed!"

CLICK.

Evans once told the Birches, *"y'all need to accept that and not fret over this."*

That always bothered Harlowe.

Evans wasn't a doctor. He wasn't a judge, neither. He was a lawyer and treated with the honorary title. He'd been elected coroner, unopposed, since 1912.

He's also the town drunk.

Huff came out of the hardware store. Shook hands with the other merchants. Seago turned to Harlowe. "They havin' a little meetin.' Huff sure is a good talker!"

"Yeah." Harlowe knew the subject probably touched on who Huff would support for sheriff in November.

They drove to the jail. Looked in on the prisoner.

"You can clear this up right now."

Foss smirked. "Jus' lemme go, Brother."

"Them bootleggers landin' their crates at Magnolia Bluff--." Harlowe paused to light a Chesterfield. "I know you was helpin' 'em."

"Ya cain't prove that. I hunted the Vrooman place—never run no shine! Say what time is it, they oughtta have my bail money by now—my friends."

"I sent a lettuh to the State's Attorney, Foss. Gettin' out, I wouldn't be countin' on. Settin' in front of the grand jury's more likely."

Foss was about to say something. But stopped. He looked out the window at the Auburn sedan. "My lawyer's here. I wanna see what he says."

T.K. offered his advice. "Shureff, I wanna say somethin'. I've heard from people I know up theah. And heah. Since it ain't ruled a homicide by the Coroner. Well, they jus' feel it's been decided and that ought to be the end of it. A lot of people stand to be affected—this whole section. Why cause yourself all that trouble, when it's already decided!"

"Too stubborn for my own good, I reckon," said Harlowe.

A quarter of two. Harlowe led Foss into the courtroom, in irons. Sat him at the Defense table. The esteemed R. Glenister Smalley, appeared on Foss's behalf. Briley Fulton helped raise some money for the big-time lawyer. *But that was nothin'. And a Tallahassee lawyer don't drive down for nothin',* Harlowe knew. Someone else was putting up real money.

Lexie walked in, a small figure in that vast room with its lofty ceiling. "I miss 'im!" she told Pratt.

Aubrey entered, uncomfortably. He'd just come in from oystering. Rode the ferry over. He sat on the hard pew behind the empty prosecutor's table.

Seago leaned in. "Pratt, y'know this lawyer? I hear he's a powerful man up in Tallahassee. Gave the railroad fits, when he sued 'em!"

"Sure is cocky," thought Brewer. "Y'know him, Boss?"

"Sure struts aroun' like a bandy-rooster," Seago added.

Harlowe, reluctant to reflect on anyone, thought about it. Nodded. "Well...he does recommend himself most highly."

No prosecutor attended. Harlowe sat at the big table, alone, save for the ashtray.

The judge walked in. "Afternoon, fellas—how y'all today?"

"Fine, judge!" replied Smalley.

The judge looked over. Smiled. "Foss."

"Howdy, Judge Robert!"

"Judge, this morning I filed for a writ of habeus corpus and we ask for my client's release. He has lived here all his life. He's a hard worker and his job's waitin' on him," Smalley began.

"What would you suggest as a bond, Mr. Smalley?"

"Why, I would ask the court to release him on his own recognizance, Judge!"

"Yeah, I ain't goin' no where, Mr. Robert—Judge Robert," Foss interjected.

The judge looked down at a paper. Muttered, "Sheriff?"

"Your honnuh, he's a murder suspect now. I'm askin' ya to hold him two more days."

"Mr. Raines has said nothing about a grand jury."

Mr. Smalley scoffed. "There won't be one, Judge!"

"Have you charged murder, Pratt?"

"Nosir."

"Has the State's Attorney indicated he's filin' such charges?"

"Nosir."

"And he's not here?"

"No, Judge."

"Then, I cannot consider that."

"Usually, we can hold 'em two or three days," Harlowe declared, surprised. The judge avoided Harlowe's eyes, at that.

"Judge, I object. My client has a right to release!" insisted Smalley.

Clary waved his hand. "Let's cut to the chase, Pratt. Have ya enough to charge him? Have you sworn out a warrant?"

"I'm close to it—mighty close. I've asked the State's Att--."

"What evidence have you?"

Harlowe laid it out. "The State's Attorney has my lettuh. I'll have more, shortly, if only--."

The judge wound his watch. Frowned. "You say Mr. Raines didn't approve a warrant?"

"That's right. Not yet."

"All right." Clary smiled, sympathetically. "It sounds like you're on a fishin' expedition—isn't that right, Pratt? Counsellor?"

"It's worse than that, Judge—he doesn't know what he's got! He thinks he can just sit on my client and squeeze him two or three more days, and like magic, he has his case and gets his name at the top of the page—."

The judge waved his hand. "We can solve that. We gonna deal with *probable cause.* Y'all both know that term. So far, I ain't heard none. And I say to you, Pratt, fish or cut bait."

"If you hold 'im another day and I might have enough—I'm close--."

"I'll lose everything if I set in here, Judge Robert!" Foss objected. At that, McCannon and Huff walked in. Sat behind Foss. The first row of pews.

"My client's employer is here, Judge."

"Yessir, I see! Good Mornin', G.B! Good to see ya."

"Mornin', Judge."

McCannon stepped forward, nearly to the judge's high bench. "Judge, what I wanna say is Foss' job is waitin' on him. Lexie's here and duddint wanna press no charges. Foss's the best foreman I evuh had and I need 'im!"

"May, I approach, Judge? This is a letter from Foss' pastor."

Clary waved Smalley up to the bench. Read the letter. "We're going to set bonds for what he's charged with. You've charged him with batt'ry, Pratt?"

Harlowe looked back at Birch, who was bewildered, disgusted at the Vaudeville show being put on. "Yessir. But all the evidence on Gibby, the statement Foss made about the boy. His daddy is here and you can see. Your honnuh, if--."

"Pratt, wasn't there a findin' of the coroner's jury?"

"Undetermined," stated Smalley.

"Yessir."

"Any change in the findings recently?"

"Nosir. Judge, Mr. and Mrs. Birch--."

"Pratt, I've listened to what you wanted to tell me. And I appreciate Mr. Birch bein' here. We all feel terrible about his boy—bein' missin.'"

Harlowe looked at Aubrey. He was stunned. "Judge, there's one--."

"Pratt, I've listened to what you had to say. You haven't enough to charge him, so then I'm not going to consider that for purposes of this writ."

"Thankya!" exclaimed Foss.

"Don't talk me out of it, now." The judge turned to Harlowe, then. "I do appreciate Aubrey bein' here—Aubrey you and Lillian have my deepest sympathy. If I could do anything to help you, I would—if it were in my power. My hands are tied. What I have to decide here is on the batt'rey charges. I have to give proper weight to what Mr. McCannon says." Clary looked down. "This man has *got* to get to work. He has a job in a time when men are out of work across this country. Lexie, would you come up, please?"

Timidly, she approached.

"Lexie, is there somethin' you'd like to tell me?"

"Judge Robert, he never hit me—I swear it!"

"Very well. You may be seated." The judge cocked his head. "Case's kinda weak, Sheriff."

"What I saw is in my statement, judge, and--."

"I move to dismiss," interrupted the lawyer.

Harlowe looked at him. "He ought to be tried on the batt'ry, judge."

The judge snapped his watch shut. "Y'heard your witness, Pratt. What have we to try? Motion to dismiss is granted."

"Your honor, I--."

"Foss, based on your wife's testimony before this Court, I will dismiss the batt'ry. You're free to go. All yours, G.B."

Seago turned him loose. Unlocked the handcuffs and out he walked.

He pumped hands. Grinned. Turned to look at his brother-in-law. "So long, Pratt! No hard feelings?"

Harlowe stubbed his cigarette. "I'll see ya around."

Lexie got busy readying his homecoming. "I'm fixin' Deddy his favorite stew, you hurry to the store, now, and get what I need!"

True nodded.

Harlowe and his men drove their cars to Whiskey George Creek. Seago. Twiggs. Into the evening they dug, the sun turning the bayou, the creek to molten gold.

"Somethin' was buried in here, I am sure of it," Harlowe declared.

Harlowe noticed where the ground was soft, where the soil had settled— like a giant had set foot there.

Seago nodded. They dug it grave-deep.

Finding only a hole.

"Start fillin' 'er in?" asked Seago.

Harlowe sighed. "Yeah."

They put the dirt back. Sweated.

The train was whining, low, as she crossed the East River trestle, screaming as she approached the Sumatra Road crossing. Harlowe looked out into interminable black wilderness. *Nothin.'*

"Pratt, you done the best you could," Seago told him. "Let's go home."

Harlowe slapped his hat against his leg. "It ain't enough!"

***

The ball players from Albany arrived at the depot, creating a little stir in Apalach!

Harlowe thought he'd talk to his friend a minute, but Doc's Ford wasn't there and Harlowe remembered he was at the ballgame—last of the season.

Harlowe waved to Rhonat Sangaree, at the barbershop. He was closing up early.

Harlowe drove down to the ballfield.

He listened to the crack of a baseball bat, the people cheering. *The people, here, deserve whatever I can do for 'em,* thought Harlowe. *It's my job to keep the trouble away from here.*

I'll keep doing it until they vote me outta office.

He saw the Seagos, Doc. Climbed up to sit with them.

"Y'wanna eat withus afterwhile?" asked Seago.

Harlowe nodded. "Thankya."

"Fly ball!"

FIFTY-ONE

Eastpoint, October, 1932

He hid behind the tree, watching the little girl playing with her ragdoll. Among the dandelions. Standing in the sun's glare, he couldn't be seen by the folk at the farm.

He crept closer. Marlene's back was turned. She didn't see him. He was close enough to stroke her hair, if he wanted to. Her brothers were playing ball, out front. He couldn't get to the boys—that girl would see him and squeal! He could only watch!

He heard a car coming! He retreated into the glare, the trees.

***

Harlowe checked the woods up the Sumatra Road, then swung back toward the Williams' and his sister's place.

***

Lexie wrung her hands. "True, help me look though these drawers! Find us somethin' we can trade for food. We've got to stretch what food we have!"

"Okay."

"Y'need to help me!"

Left unsaid was how Foss was spending his money in the poolhalls.

Lexie heard the truck. Closed the door. "True, doncha go out theah! After he leaves, you git on to school!"

***

Seago found Harlowe working on the Prado house. "Miss Daughtry phoned."

"Oh?"

Seago nodded. "Whaddya gonna do?"

"I aint gonna fool with the boy. I'm fixin' to lock him up."
"A lot of people ain't gonna like that, Pratt!"

Harlowe washed off the paint. Got on the ferry to see Mrs. Daughtry.

251

"He beat her again, Pratt. I done saw the bruises," she told him.

"All right."

"It's a shame. The ugliness. Lexie goin' around tellin' everyone how you done 'im. Sayin' terrible things!"

"It's all right."

"I hear he's taken up with another gal in Carrabelle."

"Thankya for tellin' me."

Harlowe got a different account from Mr. Quick. "He had him a big time! Layin' out all night, raising hell!"

At that Mrs. Quick filled the doorway, giving her husband the side-eye. "Y'think that's how a married man ought to carry on?"

"Well, I--."

"Well, is it?"

"I'm just--."

"Just gossipin' is what it sounds like."

"It ain't gossipin.' I'm jus' tellin' the Sheriff here, what I heard! He wants to know!"

Harlowe laughed.

***

True came by the store to trade for canned goods.

"Howdy, Mr. Tommy."

"Hey, True."

"The usual?"

"Yessir."

The man sacked them up for the boy. "Glad to hear yer daddy's home."

"Yessir. Thankya." The boy's face was blank. *Having his daddy away was hard on him,* thought Tommy.

***

Harlowe looked out over Scipio Creek. The hushed, endless sawgrass. The river flowing peacefully.

Demo George's new trawler sat on blocks. The Greek leaned out her wheelhouse, startling him. "Hello, Pratt!"

"Oh. Howdy!"

"Sorry, Pratt. Y'like to look?"

This sanguinity was interrupted when Judge Clary summoned Harlowe to come see him.

Harlowe found the judge on his veranda. "No secrets in a courthouse, Pratt."
"Yessir?"
"You're thinking about arresting Foss again."
"I haven't decided that."
"Well, don't. It's bad for the county."

Harlowe returned to the office.

Seago looked up as Harlowe tossed his hat on the chair. "You look fit-to-be-tied, Pratt."

"Well. Been up the road—t'see Judge Clary."

"Bah—Judge jus' don't wanna fool with 'im and all the calls he'll git from your sister 'n them."

"Yep."

***

"I have a circuit," said the operator.

"Thankya," replied Harlowe.

A stern, grave voice came on the line. "This is Owen Raines. I read your letter, Harlowe—is that all you have?"

Harlowe laid it out for him at forty-cents-a-minute. "There's a lot more than what's in the lettuh. But that proves it. *Foss's alibi is gone.*"

"You mean around the time the boy was last seen?"

"That's right. *He's got no alibi.* I wanna know, will you call a grand jew-ree?"

"How do you know this boy didn't run away?"

"Nearly all boys will run away from time-to-time. But I knew Gibby and his fam'ly. Nosir, he didn't run away."

"If you think you have something, come see me at my office."

CLICK.

Raines' office is in the second floor of the Lewis Bank Building—its namesake the oldest bank in Florida. They climbed the narrow staircase. Came face-to-face with official lettering on the door. O. C. RAINES STATE ATTORNEY. The glazing muffled a ticking typewriter. Harlowe opened it. Raines' secretary looked up from her Corona, greeted them and, after smalltalk, ushered them back.

The prosecutor stood to his full height. Neatly trimmed silver covered the sides of his head. He wore a dark gray flannel suit with blue tie. Barrister cases crowded with the Southern Reporter lined one wall, giving their distinctive smell.

"Good afternoon, sir," said Harlowe.

"Uh-good-afternoon." Raines motioned for the men to sit. He tapped the desk in front of them with his long, ashen index finger. "I approved the search warrant. But I won't go along with you on this—unless you've more. Has the coroner got back to you?"

"Nosir. He won't amend his findins'."

"Well, there you have it."

"I believe the other--."

"If you have anything else, let's hear it."

"There's what I put in the lettuh, about the alibi. All the things that Foss has declared, if the jew-ree hers that, why--."

"You purport that your *nephew* is a witness in this—do you really want me to call him to testify against his own father?"

"True will tell the truth. He understands he's got to."

Raines reared back in his chair. "Now, I want you to listen. I'm getting calls. You haven't enough to charge *anybody* with homicide!"

"What about Foss' statements about Gibby, what I quoted in the lettuh?"

"They're useless. You've strung together what you *think* happened. And comments he can explain away. You don't have a witness to *anything.*"

"What about Collis' lettuh?"

"No court will admit that—that's hearsay! Let's get back to *what gets admitted into court.* That boy was out on the water and drowned! That's what you got! The coroner's jury found it was an accident, didn't they?"

"Nosir. The *jew-ree* found the manner of death, 'undetermined.'"

Harlowe learned, shortly after the verdict, Pender wasn't at all happy about it. Judge Evans did his best to tell the jury the incident was a *tragic accident.* However, the Eastpoint men *setting on it* went their own way. 'Undetermined,' they said. They so indicated on the verdict form.

"You think that adds anything to what you've got? 'Undetermined' means your own coroner is a witness against you. You don't get to first base!"

"Foss—carryin' on in River Junction—right after Gibby disappeared. That's somethin'."

"It's useless." Raines nodded at the window, almost as if to point out where it was Harlowe was sitting. To remind him those windows looked out at Monroe Street, Tallahassee's main drag. The courthouse, prominent department stores like Sears & Roebuck, several law offices, insurance companies, restaurants, and the State Capitol all lined the red-brick street in a four-block stretch. Any number of local concerns could buy and sell Harlowe a dozen times over. This is a big pond. And Raines is the big fish.

"How's that?"

"You have a *corpus delicti* problem."

Harlowe looked surprised.

Raines looked down his nose. "If you don't understand it, I'll lay it out for you. I *must* have a body or the testimony of two witnesses. *You have no body!* In other words, *you got no case!* You ever read any law?"

"I have 'is skull—you caint live long without that!"

Raines looked at Harlowe like the latter was an imbecile. He jabbed his finger. "No case has been tried, in this State, without a body! You have a skull—*who's skull* have you? A damned redskin? A Civil War deserter? How do you know it's from the Birch boy? *You don't!*"

"Now, how many skulls get put in the mail to a sheriff? Anyhow, Collis Hutto--."

"It's no proof. The storm and the boat are the evidence! I go to court any defense attorney worth his salt tells that jury this was an accident! An alligator dragged the body away or it washed out to sea. And we have a mess on *my* hands. Not yours! I suppose you won't 'get' this unless I repeat it to you. You haven't got enough—*you've no body!*"

"I'll find the body."

"Bah! We're through, here!"

Seago started the car. They drove along in silence. But Seago had to talk! Nervously, he hd to say *something!* "Maybe the State's Attorney's right, Pratt! This's the damnedest, aggravatinest case!"

Finally, Harlowe spoke. "What I have are circumstances. But it isn't as good as a witness. I have Raines's closin' argument, but I lack the evidence to get 'im to make it."

The sheriff, though, said nothing the rest of the way. Seago let him be. *I know he's got a lot circulatin' under that hat o' his.*

FIFTY-TWO

Eastpoint, the next day.

Foss drove onto the ferry. Hollered a greeting at Wing. "Headin' to the poolhall, Cap'n!"

Foss got out of the car and lit up—smoked at the rail as the water churned behind them.

Out from the engine room, emerged two figures. Seago slapped the handcuffs on one wrist. Foss spun, throwing a roundhouse. Harlowe lay him out with the butt of the shotgun.

A dark silhouette approached. Wing slowed and the *Greek Girl,* running no lights, came abreast.

They slung Foss over the rail, down on her deck, and Vanko backed away.

The light from the *Save Time* and the lights of town faded. The flash of the Cape George light grew larger. Brighter.

Foss came to. Heard the diesel. Blinked his eyes and looked back with alarm. As the shoreline shrank. As all traces of land vanished and he knew he was miles out in the Gulf!

Harlowe said nothing. Foss couldn't stop talking. "I-I would tell ya if I knew. I told ya what I know. The fella was from Tallahassee—if I knew more I'd sure tell ya!"

Birch came out of the wheelhouse.

Foss went white. "Ha-hiya, Aubrey! I was jus' tellin' Pratt, here, I told him everythin' I know—honest." He talked and talked but said nothing.

He looked at Pratt—who looked out at the deep water and back. "Why, you're crazy! That war run you crazy!" Foss cried.

"Maybe...I'm only gonna ask ya one more time."

Foss kept alibi-ing.

The cabin door creaked. Foss turned his head. And there stood Mrs. Birch! "Ya tell what happened or I'll throw ya over myself!"

"S-Someone took him—that's all I know!"

"Was he keeled?"

"Yes—yes, ma'am."

"Was there bootleggin' involved?" asked Harlowe.

"I-I dunno."

"I don't care if you were mixed up in that. I wanna know about Giib-beh."

"I told ya what I know!"

"Ya scared to tell me? Ya scared of this fella?"

"I ain't skeered of nothin'! You're crazy!"

"Ya better be skeered of us!" said Lillian.

Foss looked at Harlowe, then out at the hot water, deep and dark, utter terror on his face.

Yet, he remained defiant.

"You wanna die, everyone thinkin' ya killed a child?"

Foss told Harlowe what he could do!

Vanko nodded to Birch. Though Birch was a peaceful man, he grabbed ahold to Foss and they dragged him to the side.

"Y'never had no *body*—that was an empty casket! Now you killin' me for nothin!"

"Just a minute," interrupted Harlowe.

They pulled him back. Harlowe retrieved something from the cabin—a bone!

The faces huddled around, forgetting for a moment what they were about to do, shocked by Harlowe producing a human leg bone!

"We found 'im, Foss. We found 'is bones."

Foss's red face went white. "I had nothin' to do with it—I swear it!" He looked at each of the faces surrounding him, pleadingly, his eyes like saucers. The boat rolled, the seas getting rougher. Foss looked out at the ominous waves. "I told ya all I know!" He looked broken, as limp as a throwaway fish on the deck.

At that instant, Harlowe realized Foss didn't do it. *But he knows somethin'. He knows a lot more.*

Harlowe nodded, understandingly. Lillian watched him, not sure what would happen next! "Tell me what happened, Foss," Harlowe said, like he was talking to a friend.

Foss looked at the water, then back. "The man's from Tallahassee. He'll keel me, Pratt! I'm tellin' ya, he'll have me keeled and nobody'll do a thing about it!"

Harlowe nodded.

"He's keeled other people!"

"All right."

Harlowe's so patient, Lillian thought. *I wanted to jus' shake 'im til he spoke—or knock him in the head and let the fish have 'im!*

"He—I caint, Brother!"

"You can tell me. Nobody'll touch ya."

"You don't know this man!"

Harlowe kept talking to him. But Foss wouldn't call his name.

Harlowe nodded to Vanko. He pointed the *Greek Girl* home.

When the water got shallow, Vanko and Birch lifted Foss to the gunwhale.

"Whaddya doin'?" spat Foss—turning his head, recognizing the St. George coast.

They cut his ropes. Let him fall.

"Pratt, wait! How'll I git back?"

"You can swim!"

Foss's profanities faded in the darkness. They entered the East Pass.

Aubrey nudged Harlowe, "That leg bone...was it--?"

"That was a hog bone, Aubrey."

***

"He didn't do it," Harlowe declared.

That surprised Seago. "You mean that, Boss?"

"Well, there was no sign of a body at Whiskey George. The shed was where he kept moonshine—but no body. Foss likes his women. But I see no indication he was of a *deviant* mind."

"Well, hell!"

"Foss's a mean sum'bitch, but it doesn't prove he did anything to Giibbeh."

***

"More coffee, Pratt?"

"Yessir."

"I hear Foss settled down—for a day or two."

Harlowe shook his head. Left a dime on the counter.

Harlowe fitted Seago's outboard to his boat. He looked over at Demo George, painting the trawler. "She'll be finished soon!" said the Greek, proudly.

Harlowe waved goodbye. Opened the throttle. The little engine puffed and smoked and he steered around to the River.

Two hours passed. Harlowe didn't see another soul. Then, ahead, Tiny Fulton's camp came into view. The latter lived off the land, the river. Some called him a hermit. Others called him crazy.

Tiny's beard was grayer. But the giant of a man was otherwise unchanged. He smiled. Gave a powerful handshake. Offered Harlowe some of the catfish he was frying at the end of his houseboat.

"Was Foss workin' with somebody up in Tallahassee?"

The man spit. "Yeah, Foss was workin' with a feller. Outta town. Bring the bottles from Cuba. Land it near Foss' place. His job was he'pin' them boys."

"Ya know their names?"

"Nosir. That's as much as I could git. Dunno who he was a-workin' fur. Or where, 'xactly."

Harlowe knew Foss was just selling local now. He could find nothing about his old friends in Tallahassee.

***

Harlowe continued watching the Sumatra Road at night. And kept an eye on Foss.
Today, he came by the Fulton house, early, after spending the night, watching.
Lexie gave True a biscuit and coffee for breakfast. Sent him out to do his chores.

"Foss's doing so good, Pratt. Such a hard worker!"

"What about—?"

"Why even bring that up? He—he gets mad some, but so do you! Or anybody! You caint

hold--." Lexie stopped herself.

"Well?"

"The last little while he's been real good!"

After school, True worked hurriedly at the shucking table alongside Ol'
Bingham. Then he had to clear the shells away from the building where
they fell out the vents in a massive pile.

Uncle Briley, Foss' brother, walked in to the shucking room. "Hey, True,
you seen your deddy?" Briley was younger than Foss, a short and cocky
fellow with the thick arms of one who worked the Bay with twelve-foot
tongs since he was twelve years old.

"Nosir."

"That's all right, son, I'll catch up with that sorry sonofa—Oh, nevermind.
I'm here to get that old skinflint to pay me for my oysters!" By this, he
meant McCannon.

True nodded, struggling to move the packing barrels as he was told. "He's
in 'is office."

"All right, boah, be good," said Briley, moseying toward the closed door.

True moved the empty barrels and grinned when he heard Briley and
McCannon's good-natured fussin.'

Then he remembered he had to go home soon and his heart pounded in
dread.

FIFTY-THREE

Apalachicola, October, 1932

Harlowe saw children playing catch by the Chapman School. He saw other kids walking down the sidewalk, before the bell rang. He hoped he could keep them safe.

The A.N.R.R. was heading for receivership and subpoenas and court papers were flying. Harlowe was the one who had to serve them.

He watched Demo launch his new trawler. Then got on the road with the summons.

Later, he found Foss at the mill. Offered him a cigarette.

"Ya ain't gonna grill me?"

"No," said Harlowe.

"Maybe...maybe, I'll come talk to ya, afterwhile."

"That'd be fine."

"Gotta git back to work, Brother. So long!"

But he didn't come in. Two days passed. Then three.

Tommy Crock phoned Harlowe. "The boy done left not more than a minute ago. He's drunk agin.'"

"All right."

Harlowe rode the *Short Cut* over, but Foss had already left with his friends, for Carrabelle, by the time he arrived.

Harlowe visited with his nephews, neice. True seemed quieter, sadder. Like an oyster in his shell.

Lexie had been crying, but she made out everything was fine. She spoke to Harlowe, but didn't invite him in.

The arguments got bad again. Not just fussing. Screaming. Breaking things. Harlowe kept watching Foss, and the woods and roads around Eastpoint, when he could. He feared something bad was going to happen and he couldn't stop it.

***

Harlowe served more papers. The churchbells rang. The phone rang. "Foss is in Apalach. Just rolled off the *Save Time*."

"All right. 'Preciate it."

Harlowe spotted the Chevrolet at the house on 7th Street.

People eating, talking, enjoying time after church—Ira Brewer and his wife, among them.

Seago walked up. "Boss, they need you over in Carrabelle."

"All right. I reckon Foss ain't gonna give it up today."

"Nosir."

That afternoon, when Harlowe rolled off the ferry, all Apalach was abuzz, like electricity in the air from a storm.

Seago flagged him down before he passed the *Dixie* theatre. "Have ya heard?"

"No."

"Well, he come around the corner, theah. Took it too fast! N' rolled that Shiverlay! Everybody's talkin' bout it! Y'know he was ridin' with Alma Papadakis?"

"Oh?"

"Yeah! It like to *keeled* her! Doc Weems's sayin' he might havta send 'er to Panama—to the hahs-spittal!"

"That bad?"

"Yes, sir!"

There was no hospital in Apalach. Panama City was a long, difficult journey by automobile. *It must be real bad!* thought Harlowe. "What about Foss?"

"Sure piled up that car! I reckon that's 'is first and last date with the girl!"

Harlowe nodded.

"Had it in his mind he was gonna drive to Panama—for funsies!"

Other men ran up to Harlowe's truck, chiming in. *"An ol' cypress stump tore through that car, Shureff! You won't believe it!"*

"Ol' Knox thought he done broke his neck. Thought he was dead when he got to 'im! But he was breathin'!"

"That car looks like it was hit by a tornaduh!"

Harlowe rushed to Doc Weems' office. Foss was bandaged like a mummy. Unconscious. Only a stump remained of his right arm.

"Tree took it," said Weems.

"Might he talk?"

"He may recover sufficiently. He may die."

Maybe the one time in his life Foss ever shutup! Yet, I'd give anything for 'im to say somethin.' "How's the Papadakis girl?"

"Pratt, it isn't good. Murrow's tending to her. I've notified Mr. Sangaree to have his hearse ready—one way or another. It'll be a trip to Panama City or to the funeral parlor, I'm afraid, neither of which do I want to have to tell her mother and daddy."

"Yessir."

Harlowe went to look in on the girl. Then, returned to Foss' bedside. Lexie and the children were there now.

Lexie kissed him. Cried over him.

Harlowe talked to True, outside. The boy needed the air.

Harlowe and Seago went to look at the car. Pieces of it littered the grass, the middle of the Y where US-98 goes one way, and C-30 the other.

"He took the turn too fast, rolled it," said Seago.

"Let's go."

In subsequent hours, Foss circled the drain. Lexie fretted. The neighbors hauled heaps of food to the house and True made sure the little ones ate.

Harlowe stood by in case Foss had a lucid moment.

"He's *worrisome* close to dying, such that he needs to get to a hospital, right away," Weems opined.

Harlowe nodded.

"He's in too precarious shape, I dare not move him. Moving him over the roads could kill him."

Weems conferred with Murrow. They decided to put him on a train. Elston was notified. Harlowe saw to it that the patient was gently loaded onto the train. Got Lexie a ticket.

In River Junction an ambulance—from Bell Funeral home—was called to carry Foss to the Receiving Hospital. Immediately, Elston commenced surgery to relieve the swelling on his brain.

Hours passed. They waited. Elston emerged from the operating room, his smock stained with blood. He nodded. Lit a cigarette.

Lexie rushed past to see her husband.

Elston exhaled. "I did the best I could."

"Thanks, Doc," said Harlowe.

***

The nurse came in to check on Foss. The large, muscle-bound body labored to breathe under the oxygen tent.

It was more than Lexie could take.

"Look at ya, Pratt, you the one who's dead! Ya stopped living four years ago. Y'know that?"

Harlowe didn't answer.

"Only reason you ain't blow'd your brains out is that dead boy! Someone done you a favor in killin' 'im!"

Lexie slapped her brother. "Get outta here! I hate you! Hate you, you hear? All this is your doing!"

Harlowe walked out.

"Go on, Pratt," said Elston. "I'll call you."

Down the steps of the hospital. *It's no use.*

Elston telephoned him later that night.

"I'm sorry."

"All right. Thankya, Doc."

Harlowe took out the photo. *Three were gone now.*

***

The Fulton house was lit up. The heavy green couch was crowded with neighbors. More arrived with food.

Inside, neighbors prayed and comforted Lexie and the little ones.

Outside, they gossiped. True heard the talk: *Foss went ridin' with the gal. They was headin' to Panama. To drink and carry on.*

Sparta Jenkins sent food. Seago handed True a plate of it. "Prob'ly the best barbeque between Pensacola and Jacksonville right here!"

Foss' friends came all the way from River Junction. An oddly smiling Foss, dressed in his good suit and red tie, was right there in the middle of them all.

When they carried him to the cemetery, Lexie broke down: "I don't know how I'll go on!" she sobbed. Mrs. Birch comforted her. The other ladies spoke like words to the little ones and True.

"True, you're the man of the house now." Those words echoed around the graveyard, until finally Egg Brown repeated them.

In case it was lost, Lexie squeaked out, between sobs, "you're a man now, have to take care of us!" She clutched the two younger siblings. "I'm dependin' on you now!"

It occurred to True that Lexie had never hugged any of them until she hugged the younguns there.

Lexie quieted as Rev. Giles preached.

True looked up at the casket, on the little rise. The men gently lowered it until it disappearead from view. The preacher prayed and, when he was through, the men had a swig of moonshine. They passed around a jug, and thought the preacher and the women didn't see.

Everyone assumed True was grieved, because he was quiet, just looked down in the hole. "Oh, he's takin' it hard. The poor boy!" They came by and said things to him, to comfort him.

Actually, he was angry. *Foss got hisself killed and left this burden on me!*

Lexie nodded at him, approvingly, thinking True was saying his last goodbyes. That wasn't what True felt. *I wanna hit 'im. Look at 'im layin' there in that box! He's gettin' off easy!*

Presently, the men got their shovels. Began to fill in the hole.

They got to the top. Smoothed it with the spades.

True was invited to go with the menfok, Briley and them, to Magnolia Bluff. The men smoked and passed a jar around; True, despite being told he was a man now, wasn't offered a turn at either. He was obliged to just listen to their *encouraging advice.*

"Hard times will get harder, son."

"Yessir."

Mr. Brown didn't take a drink, but he offered wisdom. "Y'know, your uncle practically raised your mother?"

"Nosir. I didn't know."
"He was on his own at fifteen. It took him a few years, but I remember, finally, when he could afford a house he brought her to Apalach to live with him. He took care of his family when his daddy passed!"

True nodded.

"Your granddaddy Harlowe was a charmer! A gambler! Oh, the stories he could tell! But he wasn't a provider, though he tried. He passed on while your mother was only three-years-old. It was rough on your family," said the teacher.

"Yessir." True noticed he'd missed more turns at that jar.

"Your uncle did a great thing," Brown continued. "But he'll never talk about it. Won't so much as ask Lexie to iron a shirt for him. Though she owes him quite a lot. Well, he just wanted her to have a good life."

I didn't know any of that.

To True's relief, Harlowe had arrived! Patted True on the shoulder. "Couldn't be there while ago. Had a job to do for the Railroad."

Harlowe poured him a coffee in a tin cup. They walked down to Cat Point, looking out at the Bay. "Thought you might like to get away a spell."

True nodded.

The boy was quiet. Harlowe let him be. But, finally True said something. "Everyone boo-hooin over 'im, I wanted to jerk 'im right out of that casket and punch him in the nose!"

Harlowe nodded.

"Am-am I in trouble for sayin' that?"

Harlowe gave a grin. "Not with me."

***

November

These days were shorter, cooler. The smokestacks of the mill, a consant visual presence over the town, were bathed in orange light as the sun retired. The windows glowed at Gorrie furniture, against the grayness of the concrete street. The whistle blew, ending the workday and the muted whir of the saw which was equally unvarying.

"The Papadakis girl's gonna be fine," said Seago.

Harlowe nodded. "I'm glad to hear it."

"Reckon he took the answers with 'im."

"Yeah."

"Folks're callin' it 'Dead Man's Curve'—out where he wrecked."

At that, Brewer came, a-hollering. "Ya won, boss-they done counted the votes and you won!"

There hadn't been time to even think about the election.

FIFTY-FOUR

November, 1932

Bingham dropped an oyster into the bucket. His knife fell to the ground. And, so did he, nearly. True grabbed ahold of him. Kept him from falling. Walked the old man over to a crate where he could sit. "I'm feelin' dizzy, True! Jus' need to set a minute."

"You all right? Can I git you anything?"

"I'll be all right. Jus' havin' a spell."

True ladeled water from the bucket, which helped some in the oppressive heat inside the shucking room.

"You a good friend, Mr. True. Reckon we best git back to it, for' da bossman come out."

True nodded.

Later that day, Bingham handed True a shucking knife he'd made for him. "That's fur you. Enjoy ever' day, True. Y'hear ol' Bingham?"

True nodded.

"Promise me, now!"

"I will. Thankya."

True meant that—but his life was getting harder.

***

Harlowe unfurled his sail. Started his little boat for St. George's Island. He landed at the 'government dock,' then crossed the island afoot. Down to the lighthouse. It stood at the isolated southern tip of the island, called Cape St. George. A lonely compound of windswept houses, yards from the surf, was where the lighthousekeeper, Mr. Buckles, and his family lived. And the Assistant Keeper, adjacent.
Harlowe's coming atttacted Mr. Buckles, who was carrying a jug of oil. "Hello, Pratt!"
The man shook his hand. Was glad to see him. Few people came to the island. "Care to come up with me?"

Harlowe followed him up the staircase to the top, helping him tote jugs of oil—which was a constant chore for Buckles and his girls. The view could only be surpassed by a bird in flight, or an aeroplane. They could see clear to Cat Point, the ferry dock, and the entire Bay. The Gulf's crystal, jade waters were unobstructed for as far as their eyes could see.
"I wish I had seen something that could help you, Pratt."
Harlowe nodded.

"I have racked my brain. I just don't recall seeing anyone on the island around the time of the storm."

"Yessir."

"Popham's men come to check on his cattle. That's about it. The Italians come out here. Y'know they make spaghetti over a fire? Best you'll ever taste!"

Harlowe smiled at that.

"Nice people. Tappers rarely come down this far. Gets lonely for the girls out here." Buckles had a six-year-old daughter, another True's age.

"I imagine it does."

"Wish I could help you. Wish I'd noticed more that day," Buckles lamented, looking out toward Cat Point. "It seemed so typical—until the storm hit and then, of course, when I heard about the boy."

"You remember anyone suspicious that week, or week before that?"

"No, Pratt."

"Have you seen anything suspicious lately?"

"Nosir. Can't say I have. Nor the girls. They would've told me.

"All right."

"Ooh, it gives me a chill thinking of it! The *grey-green* of that water, those *ghostly* white clouds that night."

"But no other boats?"

"None. They'd have been fools to be out in that gale! I watched the last shrimpboats come in, fighting the winds. We had ten-foot swells, that evening, easy!"

Harlowe had talked to the masters and crew of ships from Pensacola to Tampa. He'd talked to the captain of every snapper boat. And the crews of the remaining schooners that plied the Gulf Coast—there were still a fair number around in '27. But, no one was operating off the West Pass that night. Schooners were used for running booze in the Twenties, sometimes landing it on the island to be ferried in on a smaller boat. The schooners are nearly all gone now, hulks left to rot, if any trace is left at all. The old masters he talked to were often as "down" as their ships.

Schooners and smaller sailboats could slip in quietly, evading the lone revenue boat that ranged the Gulf in those days. They had the advantage with many miles of unpopulated coast.

Gibby used to go all over Eastpoint, clear to McCannon's place. Maybe he saw something he wasn't supposed to see, perhaps he run into the bootleggers on the road, while they were landing their crates?

In all his checking, Harlowe turned up nothing.

***

Harlowe watched the *Mary D* coming in, chugging up Scipio Creek. Her crew tied her off behind Demo George's fish-house.

"Howdy!"

"Evenin', Mister Pratt."

Captain Danny was one of the last to see Gibby. He saw to it that the *Mary D* was secured properly. Meantime, a whistle blew, summoning the colored workers to come unload her.

The conversation went back to that day. "No, nothin' unusual. I almost got caught in that storm. But you know that!"

"You came in the East Pass?"

"Yessir, I had to, account o' how rough it was!"

"See any other boats?"

"I've thought about that so many times tryin' to remember, Pratt. But, best I can recall, we seen only one other. The *Frosene,* like I said before. She was strugglin' worse than we was."

Harlowe nodded.

"Y'know, I waved to Gibby? His sail was unfurled an' we all thought he was headin' in—towards the ferry dock. I guess no one saw 'im come ashore?"

"No."

"You found the boat up by the landing, didn't ya?"

"Yep."

"You reckon he made it, or the storm pushed it up 'ere? It always bothered me, Pratt. Never will forgit that day."

"Wind may have pushed it."

"I'll never forgit the howl of the wind over the Bay that night! And them white clouds that come up—like ghosts or somethin'! I thought we'd see a waterspout for sure."

The workers hoisted the heavy bucket from the boat, over to the dock, the men pouring out the shrimp in a tub. The process would be repeated until the hold was empty.

"Looks like y'all did good."

"Yessir, we did."

***

December

Harlowe watched the choppy gray water roll under the *Save Time.*
Winter had settled in.

When he arrived, True was serving the children their breakfast. *He's just like a momma,* Harlowe saw. *Gentle with them, tender.*

Lexie lay in the bed. She was in a 'state' since the funeral. Harlowe said goodbye to the boys. They were off to school.

Harlowe showed the photo of Gibby and the fish all over Tallahassee, hoping someone would recognize the blurred man. A man of means. No one did.

Harlowe showed it in every town between Panama and Atlanta, passing it around until he nearly wore a hole in it.

In '27 Harlowe had talked to the terpentine tappers from Eastpoint up to Beverly. He'd gone upriver in his boat. It was the last days of the cypress boom, the camps breaking up, men out of work. He talked to loggers, anyone in the area.

271

Now, he took his boat North on the borrowed Seahorse, showing the photo to hunters, beekeepers, the tappers working in that section.
Have you seen this fella, with a huntin' party, maybe fishin', alone?
No, sir!
I cain't see 'is face, Cap'n!

He talked to riverpeople who lived in little cabins in the woods, who lived off the water, the land, who never left their section to come to town. *Did they know the husky, fellow?*
No. Why, I caint tell who it is—caint see 'is face!

"*If I just had a face!*" A million times he thought that in the countless hours he spent on his boat or in the woods visiting with people who couldn't be reached by road or automobile.

***

Christmas Eve
It was cold in the house until True got the fire going. The scrub pine in the corner, Florrie and Little Foss finished decorating with homemade things. There were gifts for the little ones beneath it, but Christmas was no joy to True. Lexie only wanted to talk about Foss! The large gift, wrapped in paper, was for a dead man. She sighed, watching Little Foss hang popped corn on the tree. "He looks jus' like his deddy!"

***

Harlowe looked out the window a moment before he left the office. The town looked so peaceful. A silvery light from the full moon shimmered in the tops of the oaks and palms and the scattering of tin roofs that lined the grid pattern of streets between there and the river. A cool rustle from the Gulf reached him. He closed the window and walked home.
"Why not ask a psychiatrist? I'm a medical doctor," replied Elston.
"I trust you," replied Harlowe.
"Hell. Can it wait? We're about to trim the tree."
"Sure, it can wait."
The line was quiet for an instant. Elston could sense somehow the man on the other end wasn't just asking for the information. He seemed lonesome. It was Christmas Eve after all and, so far as Elston knew, the sheriff hadn't any wife, nor children.
"Uh, what is it you wanted to ask me?"
"Thanks, Doc. Do you reckon he'd kill again? How would we know one way or another?"
"I'd say, yes. I think so. Multiple times, maybe, but I don't know, Pratt."
"Yeah."
"I understand his mindset about as well as I understand *cancer.* I wish I could give you some sort of revelation, but I haven't any. I think your instincts are sound. Honest-to-goodness detective work. *That* you know how to do. *That* will see you through. I do believe you'll solve this."

"I'm sure gonna try."

Harlowe wore out his boots and wore out his Ford—trying.

PART III

FIFTY-FIVE

Apalach, April 1933

A little town waking up slow. The peaceful sunrise. The marshland so quiet maybe you could hear Ol' Mr. Sun getting up, gently stretching his arms over the Bay, painting it in yellows and oranges the Good Lord had reserved only for this *Paradise.*

Mrs. Slocomb's rooster crowing.

The whistle at the sawmill piercing the cool air, rising above the snaps of frying bacon.

Harlowe finished his coffee. Got on the road.

In Tallahassee, he talked to Mr. Whittle's old neighbors, even the family that moved away. The argument simmering between Whittle and the other man had to have been felt in that little neighborhood, like the crackle of lightning before a storm. Yet, despite talking to a dozen people, no one recalled it.

Around midnight, Driscoll drove down toward the depot, Harlowe tailing him. Driscoll left his car in the shadow of a warehouse. Harlowe cut his lights and stopped on All Saints. Presently, a truck approached. Harlowe saw its headlights blink on and off. Harlowe slipped down to the corner of a shed, watching the truck back in to a loading dock. Driscoll climbed in the truck while the Negro—the one Harlowe had seen before—loaded boxes. Harlowe reckoned they contained two-pint bottles, but he wasn't getting close enough to look. That was Royce Sackett's Ford parked up Railroad Avenue! And, at that instant, another deputy appeared in front of the warehouse. Two bums, looking to hop a train, saw them, and skedaddled. Not to worry, they'd catch it in the woods, yonder.

But it wasn't so easy for Harlowe. That deputy turned toward the shed Harlowe stood aside of. Harlowe folded flat to the wall. Then, Sackett drove down there! Got out of his car. Stood there talking, but a few paces from Harlowe.
And Driscoll walked over! Lit a cigarette. "This is our best product, for our best customers, boys."
Harlowe wanted to cuss. He dared not breathe.
The colored fellow, done loading, joined the little gathering, "When we get our money, boss?"
"I'll take care of you. Don't worry about that."
"Yazzah."
A train whistle wailed. "Well, I got to go," said Sackett. "See ya around, boys."

275

Harlowe got in his truck. Let it roll backwards, down the hill. Then fired it.

A lot of money flowed from moonshine—to the pockets of Tallahassee politicians.
If it surprised Harlowe that Ledbetter should be so casual about it, he didn't linger on that thought. It didn't get him to a grand jury on Gibby's case.

He got back on the road. Visited every insane asylum from Tuscaloosa to Lexington to Milledgeville. *Had they released a patient in nineteen-hundred-and-twenty-seven who might fit?*
No.
Elston would call from time to time with men he had concerns about. Harlowe checked them all.

***

"It's hotter 'n a June bride! Ain't even nine o'clock!" Seago lamented.
"Dang, that's a mess o' *picthers!*"
Harlowe laid them out, one-by-one for the Orr boy.
Each photo depicted a wealthy Tallahasseean. Several he'd obtained from the newspaper. Some he'd taken himself.
"Take your time, son."
"A'ight." The kid looked. One, then the next, then back again. Seago could hardly control himself, the way the kid sloooo-wly stared at each one was more than the jailor could bear!
Harlowe waited patiently for the boy to look them over.
Orr shook his head.
"You sure, now?"
"Nah, Mr. Pratt, ain't never seen these fellers before!"
The ordeal 'let the air out' of Seago.
Brewer observed some of it. "It's a lot of time, Pratt. You've spent a helluvalotta time on this." He was partly impressed, partly incredulous.
"We gonna find 'im," Harlowe insisted. He turned back to the boy.
"Well, we best get ya to skool."
"Hell, I's gonna play hooky anyhow, Mr. Pratt!"

That afternoon the Birches came to see Harlowe for their son's birthday.

***

Saturday. A boy was fishing with his cane pole. Cast his line out from the bank of the East Bay, amid the sawgrass. Harlowe had to do a double-take he looked so much like Gibby. Harlowe drove to Carrabelle. Fetched the Orr boy, after the latter was done with his chores.
Newly paved, US-319 is a narrow cement lane through lonely country. Through places like Sopchoppy and Crawfordville. The Orr boy smoked, and slept, as they motored north. Two-and-a-half hours. Time to think. Too much and not enough.

Harlowe drove him up and down Tallahassee's residential streets. Stopping at one. Then another.

"That one, comin' down the steps theah."

"The heavy-set feller? Naw, that ain't him."

Harlowe turned onto College Avenue, toward downtown. Orr lit another bummed cigarette. Turned to gawk at the F.S.C.W. gals in a Model T! Harlowe eased the truck to the curb on Gadsden.

Presently, a man pulled into the driveway of the big house. And climbed down from the shiny La Salle. Flung open his garage doors.

"What about this fella?"

"Hell, I dunno! We done looked at...*all-kinda* rich fellers! A whole herd of 'em! I ain't never seen so many people'n my life!"

"Try to remember that rich fella. Close your eyes and try 'n remember."

The kid looked at Harlowe, dubious—but he tried.

"All right. Can ya see 'im in your mind?"

"Hell—not really." The boy opened his eyes again. "Looks like 'im, but I caint say for sure—I jus' caint."

"This man looks like the fella at the creek?"

Orr strained looking at the man as the latter went inside. "Yessir. A whole lot! 'Is hair was like 'at. The ol' boy's tall like 'is. I *b'lieve* it's him."

"All right, son."

"Who *is* that, Shureff?"

"Name's L. B. Cory. Lawrence Boyd Cory."

Harlowe got out of the truck. "Just sit tight."

Harlowe eased around to the alley on Park Avenue, working his way back along the Corys' fence. The corner of their yard touched the old Whittle place, like two pieces of quilt stitched together. An upper window of the Cory house looked down into Whittle's yard.

A figure appeared in that window. Watching. Whomever it was looked out, then ducked back. Harlowe couldn't see the face.

He slipped back to the truck.

"Who *is* this Cory feller?" asked Orr.

Harlowe drove out Gaines Street. Pulled to the side of the road. Yonder were the silos, the masses of gray that were the prominent feature of the warehouse district.

"Ovuh on the silos, theah. See that?"

Orr read the giant letters. "Umm. Ess-Kuh-or-eee. Kuh—con-crete! Damn. Y'mean t' say the ol' boy owns all this here?"

***

"Sure is sim-u-lar," said the jailor.

Mrs. Seago was fixing them breakfast. The photos spread on her kitchen table.

Mrs. Seago turned to look. "His build an' the way he parts his hair. See that?"

"You right," Mr. Seago agreed.

Harlowe had laid out the photograph of Cory (that he'd taken) next to the snapshot with Gibby and the fish.

"But I caint say for sure. The face is just too blurred," said the jailor.
Harlowe nodded.
So much matched, except for the most important part—the face!
Harlowe thanked Mrs. Seago for breakfast. "Have a good day, now."
"You too, Pratt. We so enjoy having you!"

They drove to see Mrs. Birch. Tapped at the screendoor.
"Y'don't have-ta knock, come on in! How y'all?"
They took their hats off. "H'day, Miss Birch," said Seago.
"Miss Birch, have you ever seen this fella? Harlowe handed her Cory's
photo.
"Hmm. No, Shureff. Wouldn't know 'im from Adam's housecat."
"Do you reckon Gibby coulda known 'im—he's a wealthy man who likes to
fish down heah?"
"He never mentioned anythin' like that. I think he woulda. But Gibby was
friendly—he never met a stranger—well, you know that! So, he may've
known 'im."
"Yes, ma'am."
After coffee, they left. Seago looked over at Harlowe, as if to say, *well,
that's that!*
Harlowe handed him the Tallahassee newspaper. Seago read it. "'L.B.—
Lamar—Cory...fishing...Indian Creek...one of my favorite spots'."
Harlowe held up the photo. "Now, we have a face."

***

Harlowe motored to Tallahassee. One pack of cigarettes and countless
thoughts later, Harlowe turned off the road to the concrete plant. He got
out. Looked up at the towers.
Cement from them paved the road he'd come in on.

An old grey locomotive puffed up the spur track. Harlowe waited for it to
pass, then entered the office. It was small, the size of a modest house.
The man's secretary occupied the front part. She wore a long, slender
skirt, had bobbed hair, an indifferent look. She stood; swung open an
unmarked door and announced him.
Lamar—as he preferred to be called—was friendly. Shook hands, warmly.
The office was small, paneled in pine. Harlowe noted the hunting
paintings. Hounds, foxes, and such. "Have a seat, sir! From Franklin
County, eh? One of my favorite places to visit!" Lamar was in his early
forties, and had light-blue eyes and sandy hair. He looked like a man
who'd settled appropriately into middle age, and whom you'd trust to run a
company. He pointed to the photos on the wall, of fish he'd caught on the
coast.
"Oh, I love to fish and hunt—and your county is near *Paradise!* Cigarette?"
Harlowe's eyes scanned the photos. "No, sir."
While Lamar lit one, Harlowe produced the small snapshot from his coat
pocket. Laid it on the desk. "The boy is Gibby Birch. The man,
theah...could be you."

His reply was as matter-of-fact as an order of stone. "It could be me. Yes, I think it is. I seem to recall a boy approaching us."

Harlowe was watching his face. *This fella would be a hell-of-a card-player.* "You recall the boy, then?"

"Oh, yes, the little fella was there. Showed us a red drum he'd caught—he was right proud of it! My friends and I congratulated him, and—I seem to recall someone in our party taking a photograph—then he ran along."

"You didn't see him again?"

"He walked away from there, carrying his fish as happy as a boy can be. I never saw him, afterwards. Our guide may have known him—I don't recall."

"Collis Hutto?"

"Yes."

"Where was this?"

"Why, it was at Indian Creek—just south of it, on the Bluff."

"Closer to the old ferry dock?"

"Yes—Magnolia Bluff—where the 'new' ferry landin' is, I guess."

"Was the boy alone when he left?"

"Yes, I think so."

"Which way was he headed?"

"Well—south."

"And this was September of nineteen-hunnerd-and-twenty-seven?"

"Why, yes—I'm almost positive. Is there"—the man stubbed his cigarette—"anything else you'd like to know?"

Lamar looked Harlowe in the eye, with every answer. He sat behind the desk as relaxed as if he was talking lures or boats. In fact, he turned to those topics, with enthusiasm.

Harlowe returned to his little photo. "Mr. Cory, I'd like to know who else was with y'all that day?"

"I can give you their names, now, if you like."

That poker face. "Yessir. I appreciate it."

The man called several names, which Harlowe took down.

His eyes focused on Lamar's face. *All right, let's see how you do on this one.* "What was the argument with Mr. Whittle concernin'?"

Lamar laughed. "Oh, that?"

"Yessir. Y'all had a disagreement, then?"

"Oh, yes—about the fence!"

"The fence?"

"Sure! I'm afraid I caught the old man at a bad time. I told him about his trees injuring the fence. He fired back about my son and his friends being too loud and it got a little heated! We both cooled off and shook hands the next day. I think Whittle cut one of the sycamores and I replaced a few planks, and that was the end of it."

"Yessir, that was all there was to it, then?"

"That's all it was!"

Harlowe flipped back in his notebook. "I spoke with Mrs. Cory. She didn't know about any disagreement, about the fence or otherwise. Said she never heard of any disagreement—with Old Man Whittle."

"Why, she must have forgotten. Like I said, it was no feud! Whittle and I had a big laugh about it afterwards."

"Yessir."

"What else would you like to know?"

"Did Collis work for you, other than that one time?"

"No, sir. Collis helped put us onto a good fishing spot, Indian Creek, but that was all. Only time I used him."

"You had no other dealings with him?"

"No."

"Mr. Cory, was your son with you at Indian Creek, on that trip?"

"No, he wasn't. Is there anything else, Mr. Harlowe?"

"Nosir. I appreciate ya talkin' to me."

Lamar extended his hand. "Goodbye, Mr. Harlowe. Sorry I couldn't help you more."

Harlowe showed himself out. Looked back at the office, the plant, as the train went by, going the other way. *Well...I have my face. I just caint read it.*

Harlowe waited. If the man's face showed nothing in his office, perhaps his actions would reveal something, subsequently.

Here we go. Lamar walked out. He looked around—like he was making sure he wasn't followed. He got in his La Salle and Harlowe followed to Fain's Drug Store, on Monroe.

"'Afternoon, Lamar!" said the clerk, setting the pie and coffee on the counter.

"That's Lamar Cory. He owns the concrete company, dear!"

"Great angler too!" said another man.

Down the street he walked.

A Negro passed him, delivering flowers. "Good morning sah, how are ya today?"

"Fine, Jimbo!"

Back to his office cool as a cucumber.

Everyone knew him in Tallahassee, Harlowe found. The soda jerk at Fain's was perhaps the most gushing.

"Oh, Lamar is a fine fella. Comes in all the time! Pillar of the community!"

People who worked for him, also: *He's a fine man! Good t' us!*

***

"I agree with ye, but you got bigger problems," declared Seago, sliding the photo back.

Harlowe looked up, as if to say, *"Huh?"*

Seago pointed to the window. "See that car settin' theah?"

Harlowe looked outside. Saw a green Hupmobile coupe. A fellow in a brown hat sitting in it.

"That feller's a private detective. Sent here to catch *you!* Since ya started lookin' at them rich fellers."

Harlowe looked at Seago, as if to ask, *How'd they know?*

"How'd they know? I can tell ya how!" *Meaning Huff.*

Harlowe sighed. "I've nothing to hide."

"That don't matter, son! There he sets. He don't find nothin', he'll take *nothin'* and turn it into *somethin.'* Like yo granny churnin' butter! Huff's agin' ya. Ledbetter's agin' ya. Why doncha lay off for a spell? Hell, go fishin' and take it easy. You've ever' right to! Y'done more than anyone could expect on this thang!"

Harlowe didn't discount Seago's opinion—as "plugged in" as Harlowe was, Seago was wired into his own information, a whole other "switchboard" than Harlowe's.

Harlowe poured coffee. Looked out the window. "What's that fella's name?"

"Hoyt Conway. That ain't your only problem."

"How's that?"

"I hear the guv'ner's peeved. They got his ear, son."

Tallahassee was distant, it's reach generally languid. The governor and other politicians came down only when they needed the votes. But they could make life difficult if they wished to throw their weight around.

"May want to think about it, Pratt."

Seagulls cheered as the Demo George trawler come in. Harlowe watched her motor up Scipio Creek. Listened to the colored packers walking down to meet her as she tied up at the fish house.

Harlowe walked down Avenue D. At the Fuller, Mrs. Jenkins was on the porch, straightening the furniture.

"People say what a fine job you doin'," she told him. "I thought ya oughta know that."

He thanked her. Talked to her about the hotel for a few moments. Squeezed his hat brim. "Have a good evenin'!"

"You too now," said the colored woman.

***

Harlowe talked to the witnesses Lamar Cory named. The bank presidents and men of prominence in the Capital City told him that "Lamar" was with them at the Elks Club in Tallahassee, at seven o'clock, the evening Gibby disappeared. The balance of them stated that the businessman reached Tallahassee by six o'clock that evening, motoring up from the coast.

Harlowe talked it over in the office. "He's a big man. Good reputation. I don't think he did it," said Brewer.

"He has an alibi!" said Seago.

"That alibi is solid, boss," Brewer agreed.

Harlowe nodded.

"This whole thing with Whittle was nothin' but a rabbit trail," thought Seago.

"Maybe. They were happy to talk about their good friend, Lamar. All of 'em. Until I asked them to name everyone else that was with 'em down theah."

"Yeah?" asked Brewer.

"They *couldn't recall.*"

"They *all* said that?"

"Ev'ry one of 'em."

***

Harlowe found nothing suspicious, following Lamar all day.
Midnight, he headed for home. Tired. Sultry air bleeding through the
windows on the deserted street. Suddenly, as he proceeded down Monroe
Street, he saw a familiar car pull across Monroe and disappear behind the
"Blind Tiger."

Carefully, he maneauvered his Ford up a side street, parking on Gadsden.
He eased back, afoot, to watch.

It was Deputy Durfee's Chevrolet. Harlowe saw Durfee standing in the
shadow, watching his car. A fat white fellow and a colored boy were
unloading the jugs from the car, their sweat glistening when their bodies
were touched by a sliver of light from the back door.

Harlowe poked around some of the pool halls, next evening. He found that
Ledbetter's men were delivering to them, too.

***

Harlowe sat on Gadsden Street, watching Lamar's show-place home. His
beautifully-dressed wife straigtened the wicker furniture, brought in the
lemonade.

The rain began. Night fell along with the downpour.
Presently, Harlowe saw two headlights glow. Lamar's big La Salle came
down the driveway, swung out on the street.

Lamar proceeded South on Gadsden. Left on Gaines. He stopped at a
shantyhouse by the tracks. No lights. The yard was a puddle. The door
opened and he disappeared. The rain subsided for a moment, the smell of
rot and cheap perfume drifted in the window.
I don't think he's here to talk about a cement driveway!

Lamar turned onto the Old St. Augustine Road. The antebellum highway
was once the only overland route to the city to the East. It seemed to have
changed little; unpaved, moss hanging from oaks planted to shade the
mule-teams decades ago. Those oaks clung to clay walls which hemmed in
the lane. Some were blackened, grasping for the road with their moss-
shrouded arms like petrified giants.

Harlowe stayed back several carlengths. It was dark, the rain pelting the
truck, the wiper clearing a periscope-like hole to see where the mud ended,
and clay walls and treetrunks began. Soon, he lost sight of the larger car.

Then a red dot glowed. Lamar turned down another dirt road.
Harlowe cut his lights. He halted and watched the La Salle continue,
heading toward some lights, yonder.

Raindrops ran down the windows of Harlowe's truck. Harlowe pulled up his collar and got out. He disappeared into the trees, into that plantation property. He walked until he could see the outline of an antebellum house with a portico across the front—the lodge of what is now a hunting plantation, Harlowe realized.

The isolated old place was pretty active tonight, with a dozen or more automobiles parked around the lodge. There was a fellow watching the driveway. But it was dark, and the rain made it harder to see, despite the lights up there. Harlowe slipped over to the corner of the house. To the window. *Lamar—Ledbetter theah, with 'im. Both of 'em drunk as skunks."*
Driscoll walked into the room. The two men disappeared into the hall. Harlowe, soft-shoe'd to the next window. When he saw Driscoll hand Lamar an envelope, he realized who that deputy had been delivering *for.*

***

Harlowe looked into the office.
"Your brother's over yonder," Seago told him.
Harlowe nodded. They walked down to the jailhouse. Jeter moaned, "Oh, my head hurts! Brewer run me in! I dunnu what the hell fur!"
"I told 'im to."
"I wasn't botherin' nobody!"
"People don't cotton to public drunkenness—even in Carrabelle."
"Hmmph. How long I got to stay in heah?"
"You've spent some time in Tallahassee..."
Jeter squinted at him. "Yeah, I've enjoyed Sheriff Ledbetter's 'hospitality' a time or two."
"You know some o' these moonshiners."
"Sure, I've been in there with 'em. A lot o' them boys. They good boys!"
"Uh-huh."
"Ledbetter, picks 'em up once a year. It's a big show!"
"You know Driscoll?"
Jeter cussed. "Small potatoes—tries to act big. The real ones, boy, back in them days they landed in Eastpoint over theah! Jus' like they owned the place!"
"Bootleggers, huh?"
"Boy, them days!" Jeter turned to Seago. "I done some rum-runnin' over on the Atlantic, y'know?"
"Yeah?" asked Seago.
"You betcha!"
"Now, you know that isn't true," Harlowe interrupted. "Got drunk on rum, maybe."
"Well, I mighta! Bah—*got drunk on rum,* you say! Listen, them boys who came in heah, they were somethin'. You didn't get in their way, that I can tell ya. Anyhow, whachu wanna know all that fur? Whaddya want?"
"Cigarette?"
"Sure. What is it ya want?"
"I wanna know about Lamar."
Jeter cussed. "Don't even bother."

"I'm lettin' ya out."

Jeter looked at Harlowe kind of funny, Seago thought. "What I have to do?" he asked, after he took a puff.

"I want ya to keep your eyes open."

"Huh?"

"Up in Tallahassee."

"Huh? I got to?"

"Either that or ya can stay here. Ya willin' to try it?"

"Work for the law, s'that it?"

Harlowe noted Seago's doubtful look. He nodded and the jailor turned the key. "Get yourself up theah. I'll tell ya what I want ya to do."

The man scratched his ribs. Sauntered out of the cell. "Y'lay off that stuff, now!" Seago advised.

"A'ight Cap'n!"

At that, he scurried off.

***

"It's *simmerin'*, Pratt, I'm tellin' ya! They got the Guv'ner's ear and he's hot!" Seago explained.

Harlowe leaned against the side of the depot, watching train backing in.

"Huff just got the telegram," said Seago. "It's fixin' to git bad."

Harlowe looked at him, as if to ask, *How do you know?*

"I don't have-ta git hit by a train to know I won't like it."

Doc Murrow leaned out of the Riverside. "Mornin', Pratt! C.A.!"

Nichols was already pouring. "How are ya, Pratt!"

"Good, sir!"

The doctor bade them sit down. They swilled coffee, watching the boats come and go. Harlowe Nodded toward the street, grinned. "Maybe we oughta invite Mr. Conway."

The fellow in the gray coupe was parked outside.

***

He talked to more people in the Call Street neighborhood. Still, he found no one aware of the argument Whittle had over the fence.

It gnawed at Harlowe.

So did those "similar crimes." They might be what breaks this thing, he thought. He stayed on the road, looking into cases involving missing boys. He received a letter from the Chief in Columbus on one he felt was promising. He had to give Mr. Conway the slip—he did so, taking the road to Port St. Joe up through Marianna.

But Mr. Huff, lingering in the staircase of the courthouse, heard Harlowe say he'd be gone awhile. He walked back to his hardware store. Picked up the phone. "Long distance— Tallahassee."

He gave Hilda the number. She plugged in to the line that went north.

"Yes, ma'am, I'll wait."

After a few minutes, Hilda rang back.

"I have your party."

"Thank you. Hello? That's right. Yeah, he's still at it. Can't say any more.
I've mailed you a letter. You'll have it in the afternoon mail."

CLICK.

***

Harlowe's telephone was ringing when he walked into the house. "Hello.
Yes, ma'am, I'll hold."
Miss Hilda connected the long-distance party.
"I got me a job at the Elberta Crate Fact'ry—in the boiler room," said Jeter.
For once, he wasn't slurring.
"All right."
"Rented a room." He didn't have to say it was the one Pratt selected,
behind the Texaco on Monroe.
Jeter, as instructed, used the alias, 'Jeb Henry.'
"Jus' wanted ya to know."

CLICK.

FIFTY-SIX

Apalachicola, April, 1933

Harlowe got in late. He was surprised the private dick in the coupe wasn't around. By now, he'd gotten used to him.

Sleep was but a brief interlude. Harlowe woke with the rising sun, golden rays glinting off Scipio Creek, from tin roofs.

He drove to the courthouse. He found Seago and Twiggs sitting, motionless, at the table, the expression on their faces like someone had died.

"Howdy, boys...What is it?"

Seago handed him the paper. The governor's stationery. *"You are hereby removed from office."*

"Damn son, I—I tried to tell ya. I sure am sorry, Pratt!" said Seago.

"What is it I done?" Harlowe asked, the legal mumbo jumbo not registering at the moment.

"Here's what the paper say you done," Seago answered, handing him the morning's *Democrat*.

"'A dozen slot machines found.' Found in my shed. Why, that's—."

"Crazy!" agreed Twiggs.

Harlowe read the rest aloud. *"'State comptroller has jurisdiction over gambling. Hoyt Conway...noted private investigator from Miamuh was retained by the comptroller to look into reports of illegal gambling in Apalachiciola...Harlowe removed from office by the governor for malfeasance.'"*

Seago was incredulous. "Can you believe it?"

"'That he wasn't enforcing gambling laws...was allowing slot machines. Twelve slot machines were discovered on his property and officals claim he was collecting the money for them. Mr. Conway took photographs—.'"

"And he done took a machine, and high-tailed it back to Tallahassee," Seago added.

"They sure put a lot into this," Harlowe surmised. The article noted this was the first time *"police photography"* had been used locally.

"Yeah, they did."

Twiggs swallowed. "You gonna fight it, boss?"

"I knew he was watchin' me—I laughed about it. Didn't think they'd be this—."

"Nasty," said Seago. "Hell, I been in yo' shed—I can testify ya never had no gamblin' parapha'nalia in there!"

"Reckon I oughta fight it?" wondered Harlowe.

"Huff signed a statement agin' ya," said the Seago.

"Guvunuh's appointed Pender," said Twiggs.

"They got it stacked agin' ya," said the jailor.

"Go on."

"Well, I heard this feller, Conway, was brought in by the State Com'troller. Both o' them fellers, gathered at this meetin' up there. The State's Attorney was there. Up at the Guv'ner's mansion."

Harlowe nodded.

"The com'troller was wimperin' like an excited puppy. 'I got a tip!'" Seago cried, in a mawking high falsetto.

"Mr. Raines chimes in. 'He has *foe-toes*.'"

"Then, the Guv'ner phones Mr. Sheip—at his house. Richest man in the county, reckon he has to make that call. Anyhow, he tells Mr. Sheip he's of a mind to do this thing *heah*. An' Sheip ask him, 'Do you *have* to do it?' He tried to defend ya, now."

"He's a good man," Harlowe agreed.

"Yessir. And so they argue an' go back-'n-forth. It was midnight by then. The Guv'ner is pacin' the rug an' fit to be tied! Sheip's still tryin' to talk 'im out of it. It goes on all night! Then—the Guv'ner is tryin' to call Mr. Huff! He's beside hisself because Miss Hilda ain't connectin' the calls."

Harlowe nodded.

"As soon as Miss Hilda comes in to work, he's fussin' at her to wake up Mr. Huff! And Huff proceeded to feed 'im all kinda lies, git him all riled up!" Seago continued in Huff's squeaky voice.

At that, Brewer arrived, listening at the doorway as Seago went on.

"Mr. Huff gave him an earful, son, and by the end of it, the Guv'ner is hollerin', '*I have incontrovertible proof!*' Ooh, he's carryin' on about you, son! '*For him to do this kind of thing down there!*' and so on." Seago deepened his voice when he impersonated the portly governor.

Twiggs was on the edge of his chair by now. "Yeah?"

"'*You have no choice,*' says Huff," Seago again parroting the man's voice.

"How you know all this?" asked Harlowe.

"Miss Hilda at the telephone comp'ny!"

Harlowe laughed.

"I ain't laughin'."

Harlowe couldn't help it. The whole thing was absurd—photography and all.

"That ain't all, Pratt. Y'want I should go on?"

"Sure."

"Your buddy—Ol' Bill Ledbetter."

"Yeah?"

"He was really cute about not bein' at that meetin'. But he was the main one who put a bug in the com'troller's ear. Told him what a sorry, no count, so-and-so you are!"

"That figures."

Twiggs cussed Ledbetter, hearing that.

Doc Murrow entered, interrupting the story. "Good evenin', boys."

"Evenin' Doc."

"They framed you, Pratt. They deposited the machines in your shed."

"Yessir...we figured that. I'm just--."

"It's incredible, Pratt! Disgraceful. Do you want to make a fight of it?"

"You gotta have money for that."

"Yes, lawyers are expensive, Pratt."

"Yep."

"How are you holding up?"

"I'm all right. I just wish they put as much effort into solvin' Giibbeh's case."

"Yes."

"And I'm worried about my men."

FIFTY-SEVEN

June, 1933

Harlowe nailed up a piece of siding. He'd be all right if he could finish this repair job—and start another, Friday. He was still the talk of the county. The Tallahassee paper ran another story—he was tried and officially convicted the minute their typesetter got to work.

Harlowe had True back with him. The boy had a long face. Harlowe realized why. He gave a grin. "It's all right, True. Why, I have more time to relax, now. I can go fishin' ev'ry day!"

"Do you really like fishin' that much, Uncle Pratt?"

"Well...no. But I like spendin' time with you, son!"
True nodded.
"I only became sheriff because I needed somethin' easier than sponge-divin.' I just got lazy and stayed with it too long—that's all!"
"Yessir."

"Don't worry. Let's see if we can get the roof on, then call it a day—all right?"

True nodded—picked up the hammer—and smiled for the first time today.

Raindrops fell. Big as bullets. Harlowe looked over at his nephew. "Y'mind workin' in the rain, son?"

"Nosir—not one bit!"

"Well, I reckon we won't melt. We mend the door, we can break off!"

Harlowe took True to the Riverside. "Evenin', boys," said Harlowe, as they entered.

Huff was sitting with Murrow, Sheip, Seago. Harlowe and True joined them. Made small talk. Huff got more and more red-faced. Finally, said, "I'm sorry about all of this, Pratt! If ya weren't so damned--."

"Stubborn?" answered Harlowe. True saw him grin. *He isn't mad with Huff.*

Nichols bringing their oyster stew spared Huff from blathering. He went on to politicking and a dozen other things. *Huff talked a lot but didn't say much—Harlowe didn't talk a lot, but when he did people listened,* thought True.

Then, Sparta Jenkins appeared at the door. Waved to Harlowe. *"Could ya take a look?"* he whispered.

"Roof's leakin'?"

"No, Mr. Pratt, the tub!" Harlowe motioned for True to finish his meal. Ran with the colored man—to the hotel.

Murrow turned to the commissioner, "you ever hear of a little place called *Château-Thierry?*"

"I b'lieve I have—what about it?"

"It seems those Marines, over theah, got themselves in a little fix. Run out of cartridges behind enemy lines, pinned down like hogs in the brush. Germans thick as fleas shooting at those boys. That 'stubborn' man, who just left here, drove a three-ton Packard loaded with ammunition, under fire, fifteen miles an hour across an open field, bringing cartridges to the boys on the line. Three other trucks got blown to bits making the attempt. When Pratt made it, he asked permission to go back for another load—after a bullet gave him that scar of his, and another took a slice of his shoulder. Some say what he did turned the tide of the battle."

"All right, Doctor. The point remains that he's on the wrong track on this other thing. You boys excuse me." Huff lay his money down and left.

Seago nudged the doctor. "Is that right—'bout the battle?"

"Yes. Don't bother askin' 'im. *'Well...it was more stubbornness than anything,'* he'll say,' and change the subject."

True listened, wide-eyed. *I've never heard that!*

***

They met in a hot, fourth-floor room at the Floridan. "We gonna break him," Ledbetter declared. "He won't *ever* be sheriff again, not after we're through."
Huff stammered, "Y'mean, spread he-he's drinkin' like before?"
"Yeah."
"Good luck finding work with the railroads either," added Raines.
Huff nodded. "I can g-get the word out."
***
Harlowe stopped, watching a Cory Concrete crew pouring cement. The new road would run from Monticello to Thomasville.

On the way back, Harlowe saw one of Cory's trucks at a filling station on US-90, in Tallahassee.

Harlowe talked to the driver, while the attendants pumped gasoline, wiped down the windshields.

"Lamar's got this new state contract. Worth millions of dollars!"

"His comp'nys buildin' roads for the state?"

"Yessir. All over!"

The rich become richer.

"Things have changed, Pratt."

"Well, I thought you wanted to get started on the house?" asked Harlowe. "I've ordered the materials--."

"Gee, I'm sorry. But we gonna have to wait on that, Pratt."

Harlowe nodded. Walked to his truck. No one would hire him to build so much as an outhouse, from Sopchoppy to Panama City! His money was gone. He'd rented his house to an elderly couple. Slept in his truck. None of the railroads had anything for him. His letters were answered, "no." No one needed private detective work—he had to chuckle at the irony that the one job for a private dick had gone to the fellow that framed him! After he'd lost to Pender in the Twenties he was able to scrape by on jobs from the A.N. and Seaboard line, and a few missing persons cases. Not now.

The boredom, too much thinking, got to him the worst. *Well, I've a dime left. Coffee, and a piece of pie!* "No stew tonight—I'm on the bum," he told Mr. Nichols.

Harlowe slipped and fell on the deck. He had to laugh at the contrast between this and his office in the courthouse! *Three months ago, I was the 'High Sheriff' of Franklin County!*

He got back up. Scraped another shovelful of shrimp into the hold of the *Mary D.*

His clothes and body were steeped in the grime, sweat, and diesel oil that was a constant out on a trawler. The hot breeze only teased the hope of relief. The deck rolled beneath his feet like a ponderous bull.

In his younger years, Harlowe worked for the Greeks—sponge diving. He was too old for that, now. But Demo George was kind enough to let him come on with him as a deck hand. *It'll keep me in coffee and cigarettes. Keep my mind occupied. I'm glad to have it!*

So at sunup, Harlowe took in the lines. Jimmy Pappas opened the throttle and they shoved off, leaving Apalach behind them. Seagulls following them in anticipation of breakfast, Pappas handled the wheel, cigarette dangling from his lips. He aimed for the end of St. George Island. Gradually their speed leveled at a tad over seven knots. They went out the West Pass, the water choppy where the Gulf's waves met the Bay. Slapping against the wooden hull, splashing warm droplets against Harlowe's cheek. He checked the nets and the boom. Made sure they were ready. He hand-pumped water from the bilges and performed every grimy task that needed done. When they cleared the Pass, they swung around to follow the coast of Cape St. George, toward the light. After they passed the lighthouse Captain Jimmy throttled back to walking speed. Harlowe played out the net and they commenced their pull. He filled the hold. He cranked down the net again. He shoveled again.

Now, he scooped the last shovelful and cranked the net down for another pull. The diesel knocking, that big trawl-net played out behind them as they motored back along the shore of St. George Island.

Rolling through that hot, jade water, Harlowe watched the coast. A stretch of twisted scrub oaks and pines with no interjection of human life. He looked back at their wake. Not much would escape the net. Slow and steady, the *Mary D* dragged it. It drew everything in—important and not-important. He pondered this, savoring the last swallow of coffee.

Captain Jimmy leaned out of the pilothouse door. "Lookin' like a good haul, Pratt."

That was Harlowe's cue to pull in the net. "O.K.!"
He winched it up, by hand, the big net teeming with the legs and tails and scales of countless living things. There was plenty of time to think while they pulled, but not now. Harlowe loosed the half-hitch knot that tied the net, emptying it over the deck, forming a wiggling, thigh-deep mountainof fish, jellyfish, rays, crabs—and shrimp. Harlowe separated the pile with a rake, picking out the white shrimp that glowed in the bright sun.

Harlowe worked fast. But no one was fast enough for the unwanted fish, the bycatch. The sea gulls and pelicans picked off the lucky ones. The rest flopped around on the deck and slowly suffocated if not for Pappas helping toss some of them back. Harlowe felt sorry for the innocent crabs pulled in by the dragnet.

Harlowe shoveled the shrimp into baskets. When the baskets were full, he swept the bycatch back into the Gulf, tossing in crab and the lot—a reprieve in their 'sentence.' Then he lowered the shrimp baskets into the hold. Since it was very warm out in the Gulf, he had to work quickly—this was the money catch. In the hold, he iced them down for the journey back into town. Then he hand-cranked the empty net to the bottom and the process started all over. Again and again until sunset—until they filled the hold or the ice was gone, whichever came first.

Captain Jimmy, this time, turned to go out further into the Gulf, hoping to catch a little more. They ran out fourteen miles and "pulled" again.

The boat was very seaworthy but she rolled a lot. Harlowe held on and made more coffee. He repaired a place in the net, inhaling the air laced with the smell of shrimp and diesel.

He was pouring sweat and tired. But he kept shoveling what the net dragged up, then down into the belly icing-down the catch for the trip home.

Another pull and the shoveling and icing down was repeated.

In the sultry breezes today, the ice played out first. The sun nudging the horizon, they headed for the East Pass, the 'laughing' gulls swarming astern. Harlowe couldn't help think of Gibby as they rounded Cat Point, and *come across the Bay.*

Men seem smaller, the water bigger—coming in at all of six knots! This boat's a toy compared to what you're up against out in the Gulf! And, theah, our little town. Compared to the Bay, it's tiny!

One man isn't much, tryin' to solve somethin' like this. He had to shove that thought aside as they put in at Water Street. Harlowe jumped off on the dock, tying her off with a bowline knot as fast as a cowboy roping a steer. Demo blew the whistle and the colored people came to "head" and can the catch. It didn't matter what time it was when they made it in, the workers came.

When Harlowe finished unloading and maintaining the machinery, well after dark, he aimed for the lights of the Riverside for his supper. The working-class place felt even more comfortably blue-collar now that he was back on the water. Men who worked on the water and their families, patronized the café mostly. And he'd rejoined them. He'd often joked he became a lawman because that life was too hard. Now, he was right back on the boats. His fedora was rumpled—he was taking on lines and scrapes and whiskers like the "faces" of the trawlers.

Tonight, he'd arrived after the train passengers, who walked over for coffee. There was always a crowd, where familiar sounds mixed together in the little café. The silverware clinking. The comforting pulse of conversations. The new sounds of radio. Ballgames and fights—as they occured! Crackly broadcast from far-away Tampa. The puff of a cooling breeze blowing in the windows. It was as much home to him as any he'd ever had. He enjoyed hearing people talk, the lives being lived, even though he kept to his corner with his cup and cigarettes.

Night after night it's the same. Summer turning into Fall. A little shuteye, then up again. Loading up at the ice plant, while he sweated. Cool off with a hot cup of coffee, while motoring out at dawn. Out on the boats all day, there was no time to do anything else. Pender didn't want him nosing around anyway.

Then, after another long day, Harlowe kneeled on the dock, mending the net. He looked out over Scipio Creek. *One thing I have is time to think. But what good did that do? Could I quit thinking? No—no more than breathing.*

I have work. Food. It's more than many have in the country. I've got to let it alone. Drop the thought of it—out theah!

Harlowe listened to the *Greek Girl* come in. The fishhouse blew the whistle. The black workers came to unload her.

He sat by the window the Riverside. The Greek in the apron wiped the table. "Hello, Pratt. Usual?"

Harlowe nodded.

A traveller sat at the counter. "I'd like the coconut pie and cup o' coffee."

The Greek nodded. Sliced the pie. Put it on a plate.

"No stew, Bill?"

"No, sir," replied the oysterman on the next stool.

A local family came in with their children. The Greek took their order. He didn't need to ask Harlowe if he wanted a refill. Just poured.

Get some sleep. Back at the docks at dawn.

Though he tried to seal himself off from them, the thoughts came back like water rushing in a leaking hull. *I have to do something about Gibby—does anything else matter?*

***

Harlowe climbed the unlit staircase. The old informant hung around the second-story hall of the Carrabelle Hotel. Her source of income was questionable. Her information was not. Tonight, he hoped she'd deal in some of the latter. What she knew about Lamar—who'd stayed at the hotel on some of his fishing trips.
She slammed the door on his arm.
"I wanna talk to ya," said Harlowe. He pushed back. Flashed the tin of cigarettes he'd brought.
She turned up her nose at them. "You ain't the sheriff no more!"
"Hold on, now."
"Pratt, it'll take a whole lot more than that tin there! *Goodbye!*"

Even Jeter stopped talking to him. He freighthopped South in search of more fruitful panhandling.
Harlowe kept asking around about Lamar—people shook their heads, said they were sorry, handed back his photo.

***

Seago tied his apron on. "All right, young'un. Hand me them matches. An' we fixin' to light this off."

True handed him the matchbook from the *Dixie Sherman* lobby.

Happily, Seago lit a fire under the big fryer kettle. "You like to cook," observed True.

"Yeah—I sho' do!"

True recalled Gibby liked to as well. *"Hand me that ol' striper,"* he'd say. *"A' ight, lemme have them matches."*

"We gonna fry up a mess o' fish!" Seago declared. Presently, he had an assembly line going. "Heah, make you a plate! T.K., come get you some of this food, 'fore its gone, son!"

Harlowe made his plate of food. Sat next to True. Seago's back doorstoop.

Seago polished off a third plate. "Son, I'm full as a tick!" he declared, contentedly. "Y'get enough, Pratt? Boah?"

They nodded.

Someone put on a record.

Seago shadow-boxed True in the yard. Harlowe smiled, watching them. His nephew was growing. Harlowe looked over at the people gathered on the other side of the house, dancing—grabbing ahold of some happiness in this Depression.

Back to work in the morning.

"Here, True, have ya some of this. Best coleslaw you ever had, 'im tellin' ya!" Seago declared.

***

Seven months passed since his removal. No one wanted to build. Even the roofing job in Carrabelle the owner was putting off.

Harlowe rolled off the *Save Time*, toward the lights of the *Dixie*. Behind him, folk coming back from the dances in Carrabelle, proceeded. Headlights glowing, people laughing, they headed for home.

Up Avenue E, Pender's pretty two-story house shined. Electric lights aglow, the parlor was bright as an operating room. There, the Sheriff entertained Huff, other notables. A new automobile gleamed under the bulb in the porte-cochère. With the gas stations and the ice company he owned, Pender was right prosperous.

Out of gasoline, Harlowe's truck jerked to a halt by the school. *Well, here's where we'll sleep tonight.*

He listened to the laughter and music. He thought about what Pender had said, in '29. *"I feel terrible about this thing with the Birch boy—but, it is damned inconvenient!"*

"Well, murder's mighty inconvenient," Harlowe had responded.

***

Captain Jimmy tinkered with the *Mary D's* motor. Harlowe stopped to see Ira Brewer's wife.

"Ya know ol' Galen Taylor?" she asked.

Harlowe nodded.

"He was friends with Collis—Ira and his brother, too. He come up with Ira and them."

"O.K. I'll talk to them," said Harlowe.

Harlowe hurried to the docks. Jumped aboard the *Mary D.*

***

Harlowe helped haul the *Venezellos* up for repairs. George let him have the rest of the day once that was done. He drove over to Harbeson City, finding Mr. Taylor at his shanty, near the mill. The man shook his head. "Nosir, I dunno. Sorry I caint hep ya."

Harlowe drove down to Carrabelle. Unfolded the newspaper clipping of Lamar Cory's son, Lamar Jr.

Dakie Orr looked at it. "Damn. Yeah-Yessir that sumbitch was there!"

"He woulda been about fourteen?"

"Yeah-yessir. He was nothin' but a dadburn kid then! Look at 'im now!"

The byline on the photograph indicated Junior was hired as a schoolteacher at the grammar school in Tallahassee.

Harlowe put his last dollar into gasoline. Drove to Tallahassee. He made a bee-line to the high school on Park Avenue—a building with Greek columns up the hill from the cemetery.

The secretary let him look at the school annuals.

He flipped through them. Junior Cory was a husky kid, tall, even as a freshman. Harlowe flipped through 1929 edition twice. Junior wasn't in it. "Oh, yes," said the secretary. "He attended the military school in Montgomery, for almost two years."

"Yes, ma'am?"

"Yes, starting in January nineteen-hundred-and-twenty-eight."

"And he attended there the followin' year?"

"Yes, sir."

Harlowe turned to the annual for the class of 1931. "Junior was back with us and graduated, as you can see."

"Yes, ma'am." *There's Junior his Senior year.*

"Did that help you, Mr. Harlowe?"

He closed the book, nodded. "I thankya very kindly, ma'am."

"Goodbye, Mr. Harlowe."

"Goodbye, ma'am."

Harlowe found Mrs. Birch taking in her washing.

She looked at the photos. "Nosir. I ain't seen this boy."

He talked to her about Jr. Cory, and what Young Dakie Orr said.

"I jus' will never understand how there are people so evil. You know my Gibby never met a stranger. He'd make anyone his friend! Y'reckon, this...boy might have approached 'im. And overcame him?"

"Yes, ma'am. I believe he tried to befriend 'im."

She'd finished with the clothes. He helped her to the porch with the basket. "Now, you come on in the house. I ain't gonna let you leave without some coffee."

"Yes, ma'am."

"Reckon he's gonna do it agin'?" Mrs. Birch wondered.

"I don't know."

She looked out over the water, tears flowing down her cheeks.

Harlowe went to see Sheriff Pender. Harlowe knocked on the door, for it was evening by the time he returned to Apalach. "Pratt—what can I do for you?" he asked, cordially.

"Shureff, I was wonderin' if I could talk to ya, a minute."

"Why, sure. Come in."

He led Harlowe to his parlor. "Have a chair, Pratt." Mrs. Pender's colored girl was busy fixing supper, by the sounds of it. Pender looked at the clock. "My wife will be home in a few minutes—what's this about?"

"Well...it's somethin' new in the matter of—"

"The Birch boah? Thought all o' that had been settled?"

"I have somethin' that I believe...is significant."

Pender listened while Harlowe laid it out. Then, the lights of the Penders' Ford flashed in the windows.

"I'm sorry, Pratt, really I am. Could y'come back someother time? We're about to have supper. And—uh—you're welcome to stay for supper, of course!"

Harlowe stepped off their porch, disgusted. *He caint be* bothered *with it— just like before.*

Harlowe didn't go to the *Riverside* that night. Nor the next.

After the *Mary D* put in, he headed up to Poorhouse Creek, sat on the running board with a jug of rye. He thought about Mrs. Birch. Aubrey said she hadn't stopped crying. Harlowe sipped until he could no longer see clearly the ruins of Bay City mill, yonder.

It was two or three Sundays later, he couldn't be sure. The hot sun woke him, lying in the sawgrass beside the creek.

He crawled to the running board.

Saw himself in the rear-view mirror. On his knees, he poured the jug in the creek.

FIFTY-EIGHT

December, 1933

A magazine ad at Sangaree's barbershop started it. Harlowe wrote to the man and he *'had him a job'—in California!*

The breeze was pleasant, cool. He walked the town his last night. Watched the stores closing. Young couples heading to the moviehouse. He listened to the chugging of the *Beneto* coming in. Went by the old Trinity Church and Gorrie monument.

He ended up by the house on Bay Avenue he'd built with True, enjoying the stars and the flash of the St. George light against a silent, purple sky. He got a lump in his throat, wondering when he'd ever see home again.

Next morning, coat under his arm, he shook True's hand. Said goodbye to Seago, Demo George, and Doc Murrow.

The train started puffing. He stepped aboard. He waved from the back of the car until they could see him no longer.

True listened to the train fade away, his hopes, his world retreating with it.

"Prohibition's over!" the paperboy exclaimed.

Seago bought a paper off him. "Lemme see that. Damn—I can have me a beer, now! I sho' can use one! Look at 'em headed for the pool hall!" he exclaimed.

True realized there was nothing to do but work. On the water. In the woods. As *Deddy* had done and his Uncles Briley and Cullen were doing. *There's no way out!*

True and his siblings were still not allowed to touch Foss' room. It remained a shrine in their midst.

Better days might be "just around the corner." But True couldn't see them.

FIFTY-NINE

January, 1934

Hard work began before sunup, oystering. One day blurred with the next, like falling asleep in the same movie.

Briley worked in undershirt and fedora. Smoking and cussing while he 'tonged.' True's straw hat was soon outgrown. He had to wear a worn, brown hat of his father's.

True would watch Demo George's new shrimpboats. Ruggedly beautiful, they purred along on their diesel motors. He'd think of Gibby. How he liked to watch George's boats going out and dreamed about captaining one.

True missed Harlowe, but, right before his birthday, he got a letter postmarked *Yreka, California.* Harlowe wrote, "I enjoy driving these dumptrucks and log trucks." Harlowe enclosed a photograph. True looked at it for the longest time, his uncle standing beside a truck, cigarette in hand. He seemed happy.

The following week, True heard everyone talking about the big arrest in Tallahassee. Ledbetter caught three members of the Blackie Thompson gang!
C.P. Williams showed True the paper. "The gang was fixing to rob the Capital City bank! Someone tipped 'em off to the Shureff, who staked out the bank with a city police man!"
After a car chase and shooting out the bandit's tire (said the paper) Ledbetter had his man! There he was on the front page of the *Democrat* in his Stetson hat. Ledbetter had everyone taling—from the Capitol clear to Panama!

***

May, 1934
At long last, work on the bridge commenced. Big, out-of-town companies were brought in to do the building. Most of the men they'd need they carried down with them. The papers said it was a *real job!* Way down there on Apalachicola Bay!

Briley and True were lucky to hire on with the crew building the causeway out from Eastpoint. It meant hard work with hand shovels, and Briley lied and said True was sixteen.
"It''ll keep us in beans and biscuits!" Briley told the boy.
The distance seemed impossible, but one dumptruck-load at a time, the earthen bridge stretched more than a half-mile into the Bay!
By August, their part was done. So were their paychecks.

***

September, 1934

The Bay was the last "gap" in the U.S. highway. Now, out in the middle of it, men were driving pilings that would let cars speed right across, day or night!

True and Briley, swinging shovels and machetes, cleared a stretch of the old Vrooman farm on the North side of the highway. Mr. Huff planned a filing station and tourist cabins—anticipating the new customers the bridge would bring through Eastpoint.

All day long, Briley and True listened to the drumbeat of the pile-drivers echoing over the hot water, as they sweated and tipped their shovels. The better-paying jobs out there, or on the dredge boats, eluded them. They were stuck digging in the dirt!

True helped dig the foundations. He looked carefully at every shovelful he turned. Poured over that site for any sign of bones. Half-scared, half-angry. He remembered how Harlowe did it when they first paved the highway! True did the best he could—wishing Harlowe was there!

Mother was still "down" about Foss. Each sunrise, True saw to it his brother buttoned his shirt. He'd set Florie on a chair, wipe the dirt from her face, tie a bow in her apron. She'd gather the eggs. He'd start the biscuits, scramble the eggs. Feed his siblings and carry a plate in to Lexie. He'd get the young'uns off to the schoolhouse and run to meet the work crew on time. The oldest of the Fulton children had stopped going to school regular.

Like a father, True carried in the stovewood to cook, for warmth against the draft.

Took his siblings to castnet for mullet at Magnolia Bluff, just after high tide.

True taught Foss Jr. and Florie. Foss hadn't the patience.

***

January, 1935

As the weather turned 'biting cold,' Briley and True were back to oystering. With ice-numb hands True primed the motor. They'd made Briley's skiff themselves, cutting her down from an old "cat boat," removing the sail, and installing a home-made driveline with Ford motor. They carried tongs made by Aubrey Birch.

True cranked. The engine sputtered to life, settling into a steady chug-chug-chug. Briley drank his coffee and ogled the advertisements in the paper, while True adjusted the carburetor. Briley kept reading while True hauled up the anchor. Then Briley took the helm, opened the throttle, and pulled out ahead of David Quick. The latter hollered, "I'll let you boys git ahead o' me this time. Won't happen agin'!" Briley gave a cocky wave and pointed the boat for Cat Point. True noted the ice on the bow of Quick's boat as they passed him.

301

Both boats cleared Cat Point and headed for the oyster bars—the sandbars out in the middle of the Bay.

True breathed onto his hands to warm them. After about twenty minutes, they reached the bars and True cut the motor, tossed the anchor. It was just now sunrise. Other boats and other men arrived and set to working nearby. They'd holler and say hello and the men would work, "tonging" in pairs, one on each side of the boat.

Behind them, work continued on the Bridge. Piling-by-piling, the elevated concete road advanced across the Bay, until the gap was closed. They went as fast as the concrete men could pour. Big out of town companies, again, did the work—Cory Concrete, for one. Their trucks rumbled through Eastpoint all day. Only the final section remained undone—the steel span over the mouth of the river.

True worked off the port bow, Briley starboard-side aft. It was hard work, for far less money than the bridge crews were getting. They each pulled up twenty, twenty-five, even thirty pounds of oysters, old shells, and mud, along with the odd crab, in the jaws of those tongs.   Sometimes they were pulling from as much as eight or nine feet below the water. They'd lift the tongs up and dump everything on the cull board in the middle of the boat. In the mix, there'd be, hopefully, ten or twenty oysters on a good haul. The boat rocked against its anchor as they did this. Again and again. The tongs dwarfed True but he managed them.

Gradually their work resulted in a pile of oysters in the middle, on the "cull board." Briley likened the sound of the oysters clattering together, as he dropped them onto the cull board, to dice rolling sevens at C.C.C. camp—only better!

The water was smooth as glass, the dew and frost burning off in a brilliant sun as they worked on that beautiful Bay, but True's dream of being a lawman faded. School was becoming a distant memory. Every day, rain or shine, they'd oyster. Each day was long and hard. For True, one blurred to the next.

This was the life of his family. It would be his life, more-than-likely. "Yeah, ya caint beat this, True. We git to work at our own pace, do as we like. Y'know it?" Briley declared.
True nodded. Kept working.

Briley always poked at True a bit, telling him that he could haul up more, faster, but True always matched him every single time, his arms straining to bring up mud and shells—and hopefully a few oysters. Lately good oysters were fewer and further between.

After an hour or two, the pile of oysters was high enough that each new tonging added to the top threatened to tumble overboard, at which point it was time to "cull" them. True grabbed his "cull iron" and set to work, separating the oysters and chopping away mud and bits of shell and rock, tossing back the oysters too small to carry to the oysterhouse. It was hard work, but at the end they'd have oysters that would bring cash money from Zeb McCannon.

Briley, despite his talk, was first to take a break, smoking a cigarette while True culled, putting the big oysters they wanted to keep down in the little hold at the bottom of the boat.

If the younger boy grew tired, Briley would tell him, "cull, while I finish."

Dinner was a few fresh-shucked oysters right on the boat. Every day. True got to where he was sick of the sight of them, though he kept that opinion to himself. Briley opened his oysters with a button knife and eat contendedly, while the boy stared out over the water, thinking.

They'd get back to work after that short break. When they filled the hold in the middle of the boat, they'd head in.

True tied off at the oysterhouse. He began shovelling their oysters into a tub. That, he'd tote inside. Each tub could weigh sixty pounds. And it would have to be filled several times.

Briley, as he did every day, talked across the fence with the gal he liked, who lived near the Birches. True shook his head. Got back to shoveling. One last shovelfull and done! His part was done, the shuckers' would begin.

Today, as True got their money, he ran into C.P. Williams coming out of Mr. Tommy's store. He had Marlene, with him—toting the heavy box of canned goods. Williams hollered, "you doin' all right, boah?"
"Yessir, I'm fine."
Marlene looked over at True and smiled. True just waved and returned to the boat. Marlene was one of Florie's friends and attended school with Florie and Little Foss. Her brother's hand-me-downs hung off her and that straw hat covered a smudged face. *She don't have it easy, in that family,* True thought.

Briley hopped aboard once True got the motor running. They shoved off, taking her back up the Sound, where they beached her in line with the other boats.

"You used to fish off that dock with Gibby, didn't ya?" asked Briley, noticing True look back at Cat Point.
"He was a mighty fine friend."
True thought about that last afternoon. *"A'ight, boah, where's your cane pole!"* hollered Gibby. *The latter was carrying his sapling and wore that tall straw hat which sat over his eyes.*
"I caint go."
Gibby cussed that notion. "Tell 'im ya caint work today, he'll holler but he'll let ya go! Hell, he let me before." Gibby was working for McCannon, too, but not so it interfered with fishing.

303

"Nah, I caint miss work."

"If you too busy t'fish, you too busy!" Gibby declared, parroting his daddy.
The last thing True remembered was Gibby waving goodbye. *"See-ya later, boah!"*

True shut down the motor. He'd thought about that day often.

SIXTY

July, 1935

*You have time to think, heading out to the oyster bar. The drought's worse.
The engine's running rough. You think about things like that.*
Oystering was bad. The river low. It made True remember one of Gibby's
favorite stories—one that Mr. Birch told them—when times were easier.

*"Boys, each drop of water starts out in the Blue Ridge mountains. He's come
five-hundred-miles through Alabama and Georgie! Soakin' up the rows of
cotton, goin' around Atlanta and turnin' the fine industry of Columbus. He's
slowed down from them rapids, proceeded through the South Georgia hills
and fields. He's twisted and turned, driftin' through* mysterious *tupelo and
cypress woods with panthers and moccasins! And, here—joinin' up with his
brothers—he's made us this Bay, with juuust the right mix of fresh 'n
saltwater for oysters to grow big!"*

Gibby at the edge of his seat—the gunwhale. And, afterwards, Gibby went
around repeating it to anyone who'd listen, had it memorized, even the
gestures his Daddy used!

*"Boys, look at my thumb an' fingers. Y'have a main art'ry, see—like my
thumb. And little art'ries—like my fingers. They carry your blood to where
ya need it t'live. The River is like the main art'ry comin' down to yer heart,
only this one carries water to the Bay. Them drops of water I done told ya
about—they're what gives life to the marshland...the fish an' oysters...all
these blessin's we enjoy! The Little St. Marks, Big St. Marks, the East River,
all o' them that branch off from the Apalachicola, are the little art'ries which
feed the marshes over heah—on the East Bay. They like the li'l art'ries that
branch off from yer heart"*

Those small "arteries" made a lovely saltmarsh with passages and
shortcuts Gibby knew better than most anyone. Unspoiled miles of little
tributaries and sawgrass and trees. A half-water, half-land world that
persisted at the mercy of the River—the latter alternating between flood
and drought as it had for centuries. More time than Gibby or True could
comprehend.

There weren't enough of those drops coming down. True heard an old
riverboat captain say the river was so low you could wade it at
Blountstown! The drought was hurting the oysters that should be growing
big under Briley's boat.

True thought about that day. Gibby dropped the anchor. Like True was
doing now.

*Sunrise is like a paintin' that's constantly changin'! We caint afford no
paintin' but we got this right here! Aubrey told them. They'd sat back on the
boat and watched those colors change all around them, while Aubrey*

tonged. Gibby couldn't imagine a life anywhere else. He could feel the 'heart' beating in the ripple of the water, the puff of the gentle breezes.

It wasn't so pleasant today. True and Briley got to work. Each time they pulled up their tongs, they had a pile of old shells—no oysters.
An infernal pounding carried over from the bridge, yonder, the first steel girders being assembled. The criss-crossed bones of that bridge were hammered together over the mouth of the river. The whole thing would spin around to allow boats through, shiny cars to speed across! On their side, Huff finished his "Gorrie Service Station" and tourist court. Hi-Test gasoline pumps. Cabins for tourists to stay in. There was no "trip" somewhere else for True, no tourist court with nice curtains and a radio!

Aubrey started opening an oyster, big as his hand. "The 'spat' is the baby oyster. For him to grow good, he needs salt and fresh water. The Bay has that. It's perfect, boys! Not enough water comin' down, and he gets too salty. People want the big oysters. The sweet oysters. And he grows good when all that fresh water flows downriver! Y'want this one, True?"

Briley looked at their haul. Shook his head. "Damn!"
They'd struggled for every oyster they brought up. They'd commenced as the sun was rising. Stayed out past the time it beat it's hottest. Worked hard. Sweated. Strained. Done everything! But the oysters just weren't growing. "Hardly worth the gasoline to get out here n' back! A'ight, less head in."

They hardly got two tubs. They collected their money from McCannon, and Briley was right, it barely kept them in gasoline—it certainly wasn't enough to live on.

A blond-headed figure stood there as they come out of the office.
"Everything's a-burnin' up. I pray it rains!" said Marlene.
She had her arms full with a paper sack of canned goods. "Y'all will do better tomorruh!" she assured True.
"Yeah—caint get no worse," Briley answered.
"Well, I best git these home. See ya!" said Marlene.
"Yeah, see ya," True replied.

***

Lexie *lay up in the bed.* She'd been there all day. True fried salt pork. Fed the little ones supper.
True made a pallet for them to sleep, at the back screendoor, where it was cooler. His stomach rumbled and growled, drowned out only by the "fiddle" of crickets in the woods which were impossibly loud tonight. *Them bugs's so loud a division of soldiers could walk though here, no one even know it!* thought True. But the snap of a twig in the woods seemed to hush everything else. He looked out. *Was someone out by that tree? Bah—no one's theah!*

Even so, he got the shotgun and set it beside him. Before long his tired
body compelled surrender. He was asleep.

***

Marlene wanted to plant flowers.
Only bare dirt surrounded the house.
"We grow to sell!" barked her father. "Waste of time!"
Mother Williams shoo'd the girl out to play.
She found the boys playing baseball. Cousin Butterbean was struck out.
He cussed Denny for his pitching.
"Cousin Marlene whachyu want?" snapped Butterbean.
"I wanna play baseball!" she hollered back.
Butterbean was fat with a face like a hog. He spat, "Git!"
Denny and Lonny shrugged. And Marlene took up a position as outfielder.
Lonny pitched.
"How many was that?" asked the Quick boy.
"Two, dummy!" said Marlene.
Another strike. And Little Foss was out.
Marlene barged her way in to bat. Hit one across the road.
Butterbean shoved her. "I done tolya, git!"
"You mad cause I can hit better'n you!"
True looked over from the fence—watched for an instant—then hurried to
gather stovewood.

***

The main diversion Briley had for them, was trips to St. George Island in
the skiff. They'd fish. And Briley had him a bottle.

True loved walking on the shore, loved the solitude. Sitting on a dune,
watching the emerald waves roll in, feeling the breeze touch his face.
He sat high, looking out to forever. Water and sky as far as he could
dream.
He'd lie back and look up. It was as if he had an entire world to himself.
How enormous the water and sky were, how narrow the island—like a little
raft in comparison!

They'd fish until sunset. Then Briley would "invite" them to join the
Italians that liked to come over and cook spaghetti over a fire.
They never minded Briley barging in. There were some of the most
gregarious, warm people around. Such a close family. They talked and
laughed and played instruments. Briley was like an adopted member of
this clan. True just listened, fascinated by it.

One day, Briley passed out drunk, early. True walked down the
sandy path that snaked its way through the pines, saw palmetto, and
brush toward the Cape St. George light. There were no roads on St.
George. The path was how the lighthouse keeper moved oil and supplies
over the unpopulated and desolate island. The trail narrowed and True

reached the scrub pines stunted by the wind and salt air. Saw the top of the lighthouse poking up beyond.

All was silent and still. True saw no sign of other human beings. As he walked on, he began to hear the seagulls. The waves breaking.

Now, he could see the lighthouse plainly, and the rooftop of the keeper's house.
A cow grazed yonder. They roamed loose here.
He continued to the surf. Sometimes he'd see the keeper, Mr. Buckles. But today, no one was about.

Suddenly, he heard hoofbeats and turned to look. A girl on a horse! Riding toward him! Then, past him! A flash of black horse. Long black hair just as wild. Horse and rider hurtled down the beach. Disappeared. He picked up shells. Tried to skip them on the water. Wondering who the girl was.
Then she came back! She whoa-ed the horse. The latter panted and snorted. But True thought he was more out of breath, this girl stopping to talk—to *him!*
She inhaled the fresh, salt air. Patted her horse's neck.
True didn't really know what she was saying to him or what he was saying to her, his mind was in a fog, just looking at her. He still couldn't believe she was talking to him.
"Daddy is the lighthouse keeper."
"I know Mr. Buckles."
"Hmmph."
At that, she put her heel to the horse, and they took off like a shot.
She raced up the trail, through the cattle, scattering them.
He realized, then, she was Buckles' daughter, Tennie. She was no longer the little bundle in her mama's arms.

True thought he'd cast a line in the surf. But when he did, they weren't bitting. All he could think about was Tennie and when he might see her again.

SIXTY-ONE

Chico, California—a day later

The bossman sent Harlowe to pick up supplies for the logging camp. He drove the war-surplus Packard. The gears singing, the truck kicking up dust, following the country road into town.

This section is hilly. Reminds me of France, a little...

The bullet whistled past his head. Another splintered the firewall. An explosion. Flames and shrapnel from a shell streamed past like angry fireworks. He swerved to avoid the ditch. Mashed the throttle! Through the flames...

***

Flames feasted on dry boards. The house went up like a candle, smoke filling every nook! Everyone got out—except little Marlene!

Realizing she was still inside, Mother Williams screamed her name! They all did.

No answer.

Then, through the smoke, the little girl came crawling out.

Their neighbors ran with buckets. But, by sunrise, all that remained was ash and charred beams.

Their neighbors toted lumber and tools. Mother Williams praised the Lord—they'd have a home with whitewashed siding and a raised floor, far better than the tar-paper-over-batten and dirt floor shack they'd lost!

While the walls went up, True constructed a new outhouse, the way Harlowe showed him. After he put his finger through the termite-eaten boards of the old one, C.P. Williams said, "well, I been meanin' to git to that." The neighbors said, "now's as good a time as any." And so True measured and cut the boards. Briley helping.

The outhouse done, True helped David Quick shingle the house. The bugs made True's ears ring. He felt like some sort of 'sacrifice' offered up to the beating sun high on that roof. Frying in Seago's kettle would be preferable!

True noticed Mr. Williams reclining against their weather-beaten Overland car, with a mason's jar, lounging about while his neighbors, his wife and girls sweated. Marlene was a hard- worker. Even the youngest girl, Runt, did a man's job!

True was getting hot—and it wasn't just the sun. *Look at 'im layin' under that tree. The lazy 'bout to fall off 'im!*

It aggravated Quick too. He was more vocal. "Look at 'im in the shade, theah!"

True wiped his brow and neck. The more C.P. drank, the more talkative and snarly he got, barking commands at his wife. Paint here! Hammer a nail, there! True gave some thought to flinging his hammer at the fellow— that might shut him up—the hot sun made all the more unbearable by C.P.'s prating.

After a while the girls disappeared, but True could smell their cooking waft past him from the chimney. He was hungry. In a moment he saw the new door swing open below.

Marlene, red-faced from working over the salvaged wood-stove, carried a plate of food to her father. "Bring me a cup of coffee!" he barked. She scampered back to the house to get it. No one offered True, Briley, or Quick a thing. True angrily hammered nails to that roof. *Soon as we git this done the better!*

They were working late to finish and people were saying, "could it be thunder?"

"Rain?"

They'd heard thunder before and not had a drop.

Briley hurried to get the sashes in, in case it did rain!

Marlene painted and worked feverishly. C.P. had lay down from the "hectic" nature of it all.

The little gal looked up at True. But he kept working.

She started talking to him. He wished she wouldn't. *Well, she's 'all right'—she goes to school with Florie.*

Marlene felt a drop. "It's startin' to rain!" she exclaimed.

"I reckon we won't melt," True answered, through a mouth of nails.

Marlene laughed. "That's purty funny. Ya kinda sound like your uncle."

"Yeah."

"Can I do anything fur ya?"

"Nah."

Big drops fell. One here. Another there. Marlene's sisters, Glen and Runt squealed! Ran for the porch!

Briley shook his head. "It's the first rain we've had—best enjoy it, heah?"

***

When Lexie visited the bank in Apalach, True learned that Harlowe had sent her the money to make the mortgage payment. He'd asked her to keep it quiet.

Harlowe sent him a letter, though, and he was glad to have it.

True put it up. Began frying fish for the hungry children who'd gathered at their home.

Look how he cares for the younguns, Marlene noticed, as she walked up. "Hey, True!"

"Hey. Uh-Florie's in the house."

"Okay!"

True seems so gentle, Marlene thought. She looked back at him handing out fried fish. Her brothers were so rough. True's different!

SIXTY-TWO

August, 1935

It was hotter. No rainclouds in sight. They'd scraped up nothing but shell and mud all morning. Briley put his tongs down, sat down on the boat, and wiped the sweat from his eyes and forehead, holding the rag on his face for a long time.

He didn't light up. True could tell he was fretted, not just tired and hot. Briley looked him square in the eye. "We caint go on like 'is, boah." True was fifteen, but Briley spoke to him like a man—True did a man's work and he knew it. "Son, we got to try somethin' else, we fixin' to kill ourselves on this Bay for barely enough to pay the taxes on your mama's house, and mine. We'd starve to death if it weren't for the li'l fish we able to bring home!"
He wiped his face again, sweat continuing to pour down his forehead; his face was beet-red from the futile toiling in the sun. "You willin' to try workin' in the woods?"
True nodded.
"We done tried everything else!" Briley declared.

C. C. Land had taken over running the McCannon sawmill and the terpentine still at Green Point. They went to him, to ask for work as tappers. "I got enough tappers, Briley. I sure am sorry, boys."
"Is there any other work we can do? My nephew and I is--."
"Sorry, boys, I got all I need."

They went north, to High Bluff and Beverly and the camps there. It was the same answer. So they headed upriver in Briley's skiff. *Gibby would be the first to want to go if he was here,* thought True.
There was a freedom in it, leaving civilization behind them, propelled by the little motor into the wild country. The bare skeletons of dead cypress were oddly beautiful along the low country marshes just north of Apalach.

An osprey landed in its nest in a cypress, yonder, its wispy top decapitated by hurricane.

The water made a gentle swish around the bow of the boat; the motor buzzing along, they crossed the unspoiled savannah and woods, reaching the A.N. trestle.

They glided beneath it—and it was like a page turned. A new chapter! One that was inscrutable to True. Most of what he knew was behind him.

As they motored upriver the sun was settling behind the jungle, painting a firey, copper sky and, it seemed, melting into the bronze water. *Which it like to have turned to melted copper too,* thought True. The colors were vibrant. It was beautiful but hot, the dusk scarcely diminishing the heat that had soaked them though the past two hours since they'd left home.

They passed a place called the "Pinhook" where the river made a sharp bend. Foss had worked in the cypress camp there. A few stumps stood like grave markers at the old landing.

Because they were obliged to tarry while True fixed the motor along the way, it was near dark by the time they reached the spot where the smaller artery of the Big St. Marks River branched off from the Apalachicola.

True steered the boat into the grayness, around the bend onto the narrower watercourse. The water was onyx, the trees dark green fading to gray now, on either side. They saw no sign of another soul.

But just then, True saw the glint of tin on the houseboat. And a man standing with a shotgun!

Cousin Tiny!

"Howdy, Cousin' True! Briley!"

The fellow stood six-foot-three with a logger's chest and long beard; he reached out with arms that seemed as stout as oak-branches, helping them tie off to the end of the houseboat. After he sawed at their hands and hugged their necks, they climbed aboard. The houseboat rested beneath the cabbage hammock on the riverbank, the palm trees growing tall and in a straight row, along the edge of the island there. The Big St. Marks with its passageway through the jungle, its creeks, and waterways, and islands, was a lovely world unto itself which stretched down to the Bay. And along the bank, there, like bones sticking up, were the cypress "knees"— the roots that come up for the trees to "breathe". Some of the bigger ones seemed to grasp at the houseboat.

The older man beckoned them in. Lit a kerosene lamp. In the yellow light he looked even more like something that had grown up from the ground here, like a tree, with moss on it, or an old buck with heavy antlers and gray whiskers. The lines on his forehead resembled a map of the rivelets that branched off the Apalachicola. His skin was red from being outdoors every day, leathered like a boar. Tiny spent his days hunting and fishing— hadn't gone to town in years!

He showed the boys where they could stow their gear. He wasted no time letting them relax, and next to none on small-talk. "Ya gotta go fishin' with me, son. You too, Briley. Catch some o' them channel cats."

So they got aboard Tiny's self-made skiff and he carried them back to where the smaller river joined the Apalachicola, where the water was deep. The tops of the cabbage palms glowed at night, and the "cats" swarmed beneath them, in a spot Tiny knew, where a sandbar jutted from Forbes Island on account of the drought.

There, they began to pull them in like they were going out of style! Presently, Tiny yanked the motor 'til she ran, and they headed back to his place.

He tied off. "A'ight. Gon' fix us somethin' to eat, boys." True gathered the wood and the man built a fire on the riverbank and began preparing their camp-fire supper.

Briley was talking up a storm. Never stopped. Tiny would just grin now and then, or cuss in agreement from time-to-time, until he was ready to tell a story—which took precedence. Then he'd go back to tending the cookfire. True just listened to them both. And smelled the frying, for he was hungry.

Then the big man straightened up. "Set down, boys, it'll be ready here soon!"

He set as much catfish as they could eat in front of them. They ate on the porch at one end of the houseboat, the big man reclining, his long legs stretched out on the bench on one side of the porch, Briley and True sitting on the bench, opposite.

"I'll be damned if that isn't one of the best meals I have ever had!" Briley declared.

"Hell, yes. Food tastes better up 'ere, I'm tellin' ya," said Tiny.

Just then, a panther growled in the darkness! True was wide-eyed, listening to her very human-like cries and calls. It made Tiny laugh.

"She won't bother us, fellers. Look here. That's King Cepheus. Stars so clear. Ain't nothin' like it," said Tiny, pointing up to the Heavens.

At that, their cousin was to his feet and already half-way inside when he said, "Good night, boys." He bedded down at the far end. That left them the other end to sleep in—hard bunks with no mattresses, but it was dry inside, the rain moving in now, tapping on the roof and keeping time as it showered the river, lulling them to sleep.

True woke with the sun but Tiny was already grinding coffee. The boy looked around—how things looked in the daylight. Tiny had the only houseboat on that stretch of the river. It was long, flat-roofed, porches on both ends; it had belonged to one of the old logging camps, Tiny said.

It went without saying, they would go fishing with him as soon as Briley woke up.

Briley rose—nosy, he looked around, at the galley in the middle, the room that was like a sitting room, but not the kind a woman would very much approve of, with it's rustic furniture, rods and reels and equipment Tiny kept there. Briley started for the back room, where Tiny slept. But Tiny called him. "Uh—hey, Briley, can you fetch me some firewood? Gonna fry up some breakfast; how's that sound, True?"

True smiled. "Sounds fine."

They ate, and with little warning, Tiny gave the outboard motor a pull and they scrambled to board before he left them. They headed downriver; they passed ancient cabbage hammocks, the trees stately and arrow-straight, not seeing another soul.

They reached a particularly beautiful spot and Cousin Tiny let the boat drift some. He put his arm around True. "Y'see that little gator, boah— right under that limb theah?"

True nodded.

"He's just enjoyin' that shade! Hey Briley!" At that, Tiny tossed him the bottle.

They drifted a ways, on the Big St. Marks, the only sound the little "plop" of the mullet jumping up ahead. Or the slosh of the liquor when the older men had a swig.

"It's all free, boys. I done tried city life. Military life. Didn't like it. Well, that and I got in trouble with the law, some." He nudged True. "Don't tell yer uncle Pratt, now."

Briley laughed at that.

"Not bothered by nobody. 'Can do *whachu wohnt*," Cousin Tiny explained.

"Hell, yeah!" Briley agreed.

"I don't know why nobody'd wanna live in no city when you got this right heah! This's Paradise, heah, this place was made by God n'given to us— y'know it?"

True nodded. It truly was beautiful.

"Gibby...liked it up heah," Tiny added.

"Oh, you knew Gibby?" asked Briley.

Tiny spit into the water. "You boy's like bass fishin'? Sure ya do. Fightin' bass is fun. When y'all come back, why, we'll go to one of my spots no one knows about." True watched his cousin's face as he changed the subject. He didn't know Tiny knew Gibby—but his old pal was the sort that never met a stranger!

They cut over to the little East River, travelling through the marshland and savannah along it, down to the Bay, the Apalachicola delta wide-open and unspoiled as far as True could look. True felt as free as an osprey! But Tiny was careful to turn back when he heard the first hum of another motor. He steered them back up the Big St. Marks. Showed them Chipley Creek—the clear, clean water, meandered through the sawgrass, twisting and turning. It was hard to imagine an artist coming up with something prettier! It origins were a mystery, somewhere hidden in the savannah and the line of cabbage palms yonder.

A white egret fluttered past. "This place's plumb pretty," said Tiny. It was—and a good place to hide.

Tiny baited his line and that's where they fished. They all caught painted bream and trout. The colors were changing so fast toward sunset, the sky a canvass so pretty it made Tiny cuss!

Another night of cat-fishing and Briley said it was "time to git to work. We'll be leavin' in the mornin.'"

Tiny didn't understand why they'd want to work for another man, but he wished them luck!

At dawnlight, they said goodbye and set out to find the work Briley heard was upriver.

They buzzed along on the little motor. "Just a little ways, further. I hope the gasoline holds out," said Briley, pouring in the last of the can.

True nodded.

"I wonder about Tiny," thought Briley.

"Yeah?"

"Y'know. Lives by hisself. Never married. Well, what's he hidin' from? I hear talk that—well, he mighta done somethin' real bad." It *was* odd for a man or woman not to marry—and Tiny was in his *thirties,* no less.

But some people just lived their own way, Harlowe said. *Tiny never bothered nobody.*

They motored along upriver. "This's the prettiest spot on the river!" Briley declared, pointing to the bluff with big oaks, their branches gracefully extending out over the water, and down to embrace it. The leaves were so bright and green, despite the heat, and how low the river looked. "That's Fort Gadsden."

It was nearly another hour until they landed at the terpentine camp, up Owl Creek, where dead cypress, like ancient sentinels guarded the landing. And there were giant stumps, which more-than-likely Foss had cut.

The nearest town was Sumatra. But they found out, quickly, there'd be no forays to town, no pool halls, or anything else that might interest a twenty-five-year-old—or a fifteen-year-old boy.

The sounds of men cussing...the loud calls of the tally count...the chipping of axes greeted their ears as they walked in. A rough overseer spotted them and it wasn't long before they were on the line, cat-facing pines.

It was coarse, arduous work, in the heat, which was not diminished at all for the shade of the pines; it was oven-like and inescapable.

True learned to make a "cat-face," cutting a patch of bark off the tree to get the resin to flow, leaving a scar which resembled a haunting whisker-faced grin. He learned to hammer in the gutter, so the sap flowed into clay "herty" cups. He'd fill cups all day long. He learned ax-chipping to move the cat face up the tree when the old one dried up. Then the scraping to keep it flowing. Keep on filling them cups!

They'd gather their herty cups, pour the resin into barrels and load them onto wagons, their sweat mixing with sticky pine sap, leaving them dirty with no chance of getting clean. The sweat stung True's eyes. The flies ate at him. It was difficult to imagine Hell being more punishing.

Colored tappers worked alongside True and Briley. Black and white were no better than slaves, working the pines there, in that harsh country, with mean men watching over them.

The blacks sang as they worked. The overseers would holler and cuss. True thought one would whip him when he wiped the sweat from his brow, once. Briley said what kept him going was thinking about his gal, and he described things about her which made the younger boy blush.

True had no time to learn about girls. *Keep filling them cups!* True wondered what Gibby would have thought of this. Gibby could work as hard as anyone here. But he wouldn't have liked being cooped up and told he couldn't break off and go fishing when he wanted!

True caught fish for the men. And they liked him for it. Were glad to have it, like Sister and Little Foss. Something other than biscuits!

True didn't think of being a police man, now. Hard to see anything beyond today, here. He just sweated. Missed home—that meant Uncle Pratt. Harlowe's house. Tennie riding her horse.

They found the pay meagre, and what they earned was given in scrip. "Caint send anything home or save a damn red cent! They pay ya in scrip, and everythin' you gotta have they sell ya at their comp'ny store, Indian-givin' that scrip right back from ya! The bill never goes down! Them sumbitches got ya hooked! Why, we caint never get ahead!" Briley cried.

But they couldn't leave those hot, deep piney flatlands, even if they *could* save something! A man tried to make the river and was beaten for it. Escape through the saw palmetto would be brutal, Briley realized, dreaming of a way out despite that bruised-up blond fellow working aside him.

Another white man talked about women. Talked big! And that got Briley going. And talking bigger. An older black man gave his perspective on the fairer sex out there for the choosing in his home near Quincy. "No spendin' money, so caint do nothin' fun in town no way!" he lamented. "No scrip c'n buy yo gal no finery. I gits outta hea in da Spring—I hope you fellas do too!"

"We're stuck," answered Briley. "There ain't nothin' else, anyhow!" he told the boys. "We come here 'cause we played out on that Bay."

True thought to himself, *Uncle Pratt can take it, losing his job, working harder than ever just to get by. I need to do like he would.*

So True never complained. It wasn't missed, because Briley did enough for the both of them. The place, truly, was bleak to a fellow pining for his gal. It had a commissary, an office, and shanties for the workers. True and Briley, however, shared a tent. This shelter seemed like it was left over from the War Between the States, and at the end of their shift, the boys, and two other men, folded into it, covered in resin and dirt, to sleep on rough pallets on the ground.

Once, True woke up in the middle of the night, hearing the sound of the cutters and the tally count. He couldn't go back to sleep after the dream. He slipped away from camp, as far as he dared. It was so dark, somehow even darker and clearer above than that night on the St. Marks. Earlier, it was too hot and he was tired, to eat the salt pork and beans. But now he was hungry and restless. He crept further, to the riverbank for a better view. Looked up. There were millions of stars above and the sight took his breath away.

He thought about Tennie. Recalled some of the things she told him in those brief moments. Slipping back to camp, in the light he had beneath the tent, he scrawled a letter to her. He wrote about the stars. *"I thought of you. Out here, I thought of when we met on the island. I know what you mean about living somewhere where you feel alone. I thought of you and didn't feel alone. I hope you will think of me."* At daybreak, he dropped the letter in the sack for mailing.

A week passed. Then two. Then three. Tennie didn't answer. But True said nothing. It was like a purple hyacintch had come up in the gray sand, then someone snatched it away. It was gone. And so it was *back to it*. Up before daybreak. The hollering. The tally calls. The sound of the axes and scrapers. Sweat, resin, covering tired flesh. The herty cups filling as the lifeblood was squeezed out of *you*. The overseer cussed True like a dog when he nearly dropped a barrell.

The sand, the sap, your clothes—everything gray.

SIXTY-THREE

November, 1935

True lie awake. That day he'd eard men talking, and they'd called Harlowe's name. True realized his uncle had a reputation. They said Harlowe solved every case he had. *Well, except—.*

Briley's tossing and turning interrupted. He was desparate to marry his Cat Point sweetheart and quit this business. He was 'fretted.' "You awake, boah?"

"Yeah."

"I been thinkin.' What I may could do is slip out...git to our boat...git back to Apalach. And I'll save up some money...and send for ya."

True was dubious. "Well...Maybe."

"I'm serious, True! I got to git outta here!"

Briley had the entire wedding planned out, though, in these nightly daydream sessions. "You—you'll be my best man!"

"Yeah—sure."
True thought about getting out too. He contemplated some of the things he'd heard Harlowe say. Things he knew Gibby might have the nerve to do, if he were here!
One night, he laid it out for his uncle.
"Damn, I b'lieve that'll work, boah!"
The next night, when the men beside them were snoring good, they set True's plan in motion. Sneaking out to the edge of camp, they lit the resin-soaked fuse True had come up with.

They hunkered down and waited, watching the flame spiral down the pine. If it worked, it would touch off the four shotgun shells Briley swiped from the overseer. *Would* it work?
"Shoot, it done burnt out!" lamented Briley.
"Hold on. Give it time."
"Aww, it ain't gonna. Let's just run--."
Then, suddenly, POP! POP! POP!
The overseers and tappers sprang from their shanties and tents, hollering and trying to make sense of what was going on! *"It came from over yonder, boys!"*
"Who's out there!"
"Check them tents!"

While the men broke the fog of sleep and got their bearings and began to shine lanterns into tents, True and Briley proceeded to fetch their homemade oars and, on tiptoe, slipped out the other way, to Briley's boat.

319

They commenced paddling downstream, careful not to make one slosh or take one careless breath. After they reached the Apalachicola, they let her drift. Only then did they exhale.

Those drops of water would carry them home.

***

November, 1935

Back at the old homeplace. *Ain't a tin of food in the house.* True fetched his pole. Caught a fish for their supper. Cooked him outside.

Back at their old routine.

At first, Briley thought he'd work six months and save for the marriage license. But he couldn't wait! He was talking about marrying Efola before Christmas.

Out on the bars, they sweated and watched the finishing touches go on the bridge. The ramp into town. The test car driving out on what locals now called the "Long Bridge." The state road people turning the swingbridge—open and closed. They scraped by, looking at that symbol of hope with everyone else.

One person was missing from it all, True felt. A part of him who wasn't there—the brother who was gone. True wondered what Gibby would have thought about all this. If he'd still want to get on with Demo George like he talked about. That—and he missed Harlowe.

On the 11th day of the month they celebrated the opening of the bridge. The papers played it up big! And, indeed, it was a "big doins," with the Governor motoring down to cut the ribbon. The State wanted tourists to come and spend money and this completed what the brochures called the "Gulf Scenic Highway!" Locals were proud of it and thought it meant a brighter future for the county. True and Briley stood among the hopeful crowd. They watched Egg Brown drive onto the bridge—the first to cross from Eastpoint to Apalach.

***

January, 1936

True forgot it was his birthday—Briley had them oystering like their life depended on it. Out early. Stay late. Do, whatever odd jobs they could get in the evenings. But Harlowe sent him a letter wishing him a fine day!

Later that week they took off long enough to get to the Methodist Church in Apalach. Briley in a storebought suit. True cleaned up to be his best man, putting on Foss' coat and necktie.

Briley sure looked uncomfortable at the front of that church, his hat-line like a half-painted wall where the sun baked him red as a boiled shrimp below the brim. True thought his uncle may feint in that starched collar!

In walked the bride.

Folks, of course, commented and gossiped in the pews.

"Oh, that's a nice dress!"

"He's marryin' really late in life!"

"Twenty-six!"

"Well, he is a hard-worker. Orn'ry, but a good worker."

"Oh, ye-ess, that's purty dress!"

Briley got out the "I do" before the preacher finished.

"Efola Santino, do you take this man to be your lawfully wedded husband?"

True never saw Briley so nervous, and where he wasn't talking! But, Efola said *yes!*

Briley kissed her without making her fall, and out the door they went, Seago revving his Ford, waiting to carry them to their little "honeymoon house" at Commerce and Forbes.

It wasn't long before Briley asked True to follow him over. "I need you to come work with me, boah."

"What's this?" asked Lexie.

Briley took his hat off. "I need Ol' True, heah. Oysterin's better. We can do all right with the two of us!"

"You're gonna send home money, ain't ya son?"

True nodded.

"And you stay out of them pool halls! That's a place where you can get in trouble, hear?"

"Yes'm."

Then, True collected his fishing rod and his other shirt. Climbed in Briley's Model T. He waved to Florie and Foss Jr., but there wasn't time to do much looking back.

In the rented house, the married folks had one bedroom, Efola's brother had the other. True slept on the sofa couch. And every day before dawn, they walked down to Marks Brokerage, beside which Briley kept the boat. *Git back to work.*

True would run them out into the Bay. Squeeze tongs. Pull. Do it again. Fill the hold and put in at Water Street where they'd hoist the oysters up in a bucket.

Day-after-day. To True, it was a season that knew no changing.

If he felt restless, he'd walk down to the Ford dealership. Look at the cars. Walk down to the *Dixie*. Listen to the gunfire from the Western playing. This week it was a Harry Carey picture.
I sure wish he'd come back.

Part IV

SIXTY-FOUR

February, 1936

Clouds rolling in. Sawgrass dancing, the cool wind's rush like a breath from above. The first raindrops plopping one-by-one on a glassy River. Birds fluttering off before the sky really opened up. Then the downpour. Rivulets flowed down the street toward the river. It "talked" over the roof above True's head. The sound was comforting. A good omen. *We can use it,* thought True.

***

"Well, I'll be darned."
It was rare Harlowe should receive a telegram. A.T. Perkins—bossman of the Apalachicola Northern—had sent it!

He slept on one train. Then another. Finally, Ol' 150 backed in to town. Harlowe looked out at the ground rolling by—the whitewashed fences and tin roofs of home.
On the platform, under the lightbulbs—familiar faces.
"Howdy, boys! Doc!"
Seago, Twiggs, and Murrow were there to meet him.
"Pratt!"
"Good to see ya!"
They all sawed his hand. Piling in to Seago's Ford, they carried him to "The Grill"—the restaurant that had opened on the corner, in Sangaree's old funeral parlor.
"You gonna love this place, I'm tellin' ya!" Seago promised.
They sat down by the window.
A girl brought around the menus. "Why, Mr. Pratt!"
"Evie. You're all grown up and married now. Makes me feel like an old, old man."
"Oh, hush! You ain't old! Good to see ya, hear?" She smiled at the others. "I'll be back to take your order."
Seago put a nickel in a slot machine. "If I win a quarter, I'll go see a picture show!"
He gave it a yank. It came up sevens. "Hot damn!"
Harlowe thought he recognized the slot machines—some of "his" eleven. The good times "got going" after Pender was appointed and the Tallahassee politicians legalized gambling in '35, it seemed.
"What are your plans, Pratt?" asked Murrow.
"I'm on a job for the railroad."
"We can't convince you to run for office?" asked the Doc.
Harlowe shook his head. "I think I'll try this a while."
"We sure are glad to have ya back!" Seago exclaimed.
"Yes, all of us," Murrow agreed.
Evie returned. "All right, what can I get y'all?"

Harlowe boarded the afternoon train to St. Joe, meeting with Mr. Perkins at the company offices there. Once he got the run-down, and had supper, he rode the train to River Junction. He soon identified the wily fellow who was thieving from freight cars up the line. The affair was kept quiet on order from Perkins. The latter appreciated the manner in which Harlowe avoided publicity—the last thing Alfred du Pont, the new owner, wanted.

Then came work for the Seaboard Line, catching the elusive safecracker that had hit depots up north. Again, Harlowe handled it without notoriety. Then came discrete matters for paying clients whom Seaboard bigwigs sent his way.

Harlowe was making enough money to move back into his house and buy a 'new,' second-hand Model A. The salesman at Anderson Ford vouched she'd do sixty on the straightaway!

His home he whitewashed, fresh. He fitted locks on every door—he'd have no more contraband props posed on his property! He even purchased a little piece of land near the Bay City Lodge—someone might want to build on it one day!

Harlowe liked to walk down to the waterfront before he left on the job. Today, he watched the *Mary D* going out. Watched the bridge swing around. Watched her glide though, heading for the pass. Looked until she faded to a speck.

More tourists were coming now. Harlowe noted the tags from Tallahassee. Georgia. He got going. On the "Long bridge" he waved to True and Briley, tonging yonder.

True waved back, wondering what kind of case his uncle was on! "Hey, listen at this," said Briley, interrupting his thoughts. Briley always had a story. True wondered if he'd ever run out. "Listen at this!" he'd say, and he'd commence telling another.

***

May, 1936
Harlowe looked in at the easy chair in the display window at Gorrie Furniture, at Market and Avenue D. "Hello, Mr. Harlowe!" said the salesman.

"Howdy, Pat."

Harlowe continued down the sidewalk to the Grill. He nodded to Pender in the back corner (his cronies seated with him).

Murrow occupied the usual window table. Harlowe joined him. "Howdy, Doc"

The smalltalk petered out and the Doc turned to what he really wanted to discuss. "The people want you back, Pratt."

"Oh, I don't know, Doc. I've--."

"Wouldya at least consider it?"

"Well, if the people want me—I don't know that they—."

"They do. No one will run against you. You've only to worry about Pender."

"Even if I took a notion to—well, I ain't put my name in. I haven't paid the filin' fee."

"Some of us took care of that for you. You'll be on the ballot if you tell us!"

Harlowe held out his hand. "All right."

Gentle shadows stretched their arms up Market Street. The whistle blew at the sawmill. The men walked home—and Harlowe walked the town.

Could he be Sheriff again?

He looked out at the river, its unchanging genteel pace. Listened to the freight train—Engine 301—coo-ing like a dove, through the low-country, toward the iron bridge. Smelled the *Riverside's* coffee drift down Water Street. Water lapped and lines creaked on the shrimpboats, a forest of nets and rigging and booms poking up over the docks, the fellows mending their nets as men had for centuries. The sun settled behind the trees that embraced the western oustkirts of town.

This's why I'll do it. This place. These people.

***

August, 1936
A hot summer. But at least it rained. Harlowe's detective work kept him away a lot, True reckoned. He was too busy working, wouldn't have got to see Harlowe anyhow.

True's season continued. Leave before sunrise. Oystering. Doing odd jobs. Come in to sleep on that couch. Lying in bed, he'd hear a car drive over the grating on the bridge—more than probably it was Harlowe.

The election was far off—like Christmas! Too far off to do any good today!

It was far off for Harlowe, too. He blew a tire coming home. He patched it, but it was so hot the patch melted off before he traveled a mile and he was on the side of the road again!

***

Harlowe stopped at Tommy's store.

He thought back to that night. *Wind howling. The men gathered there.*
He went in.

"Well, how are ya, Pratt!"

"Howdy! Howdy Miss Crock."

"We sure are glad to see ya!"

He looked around. *He could still see the faces. Birch's. True's.*

"What have you been up to?" they asked.

He told them—never quite losing sight of that night.

"Well, I reckon I better head over to my sister's."

"Ya stop by again, hear?"

He nodded.

"Goodbye, Pratt," said Mrs. Crock.

"Bye, now."

Harlowe took True and the little ones fishing at 17 Mile Beach. Harlowe let True drive the Ford.

"You're doin' fine, son. Nothin' to it. Now ease 'er into high. That's right. You've got the hang of it, son!"

True smiled. Harlowe was glad to see the boy's confidence grow.

Later, they joined Murrow at the *Riverside.*

"You might try giving a talk. At church, at least!" advised the Doctor.

Harlowe loathed campaigning. He wasn't one to stand up at Battery Park and 'speechify.' "If they think I do a good job, then they'll vote for me," was how he thought.

"Would ya at least try?"

"I'll think about it, Doc." The last time he made a speech, at the Episcopal Church, he forgot to thank half the folks he ought to! He was so nervous he'd say *damn* or *hell* or something like that!

At that, Andy Wing walked in—the retired Captain.

"Come join us."

"Sure, Pratt!"

***

It wasn't election season without a mullet fry. Seago had his kettle bubbling. True helped him cut up taters for the pot.

Ira Brewer had a nose for free food. He cast a glance at True. "How-you?" Looked yonder at the tables. "It ready? How-you, C.A.?"

Seago's sweaty eyelids didn't raise from his knife-work. "Oh, I'm finer than frog hair split four ways." He dead-panned in such a way you couldn't tell if he was on the level—or slightly mawking Ol' Ira. Seago turned the other way. Tasted his slaw. "Ummmh! Ummmh! That's *purty damn good,* son!"

"Cornbread—in a ball?" asked Ira.

"Yes, son. That's for fryin' up my momma's cornbread, right there,"

Huff brought his kids to eat. The commissioner 'talked up' Murrow. Baseball and politics.

When everyone had gone, True helped the jailor and Harlowe clean up.

"Last one," said Harlowe.

"We got it."

"Good night, Mr. Seago," said True.

"All right, boah, be good!" said Seago.

***

Sunday night. The weather turned cool and damp—forty-eight hours to the election. Harlowe walked by the courthouse. Stood there looking at it. He'd spent a good part of his life there.

Then he heard an organ—and singing. Somehow, he found himself walking toward it. Found himself looking up at the little white church on 9th.

He listened at the door. Looking in, unseen. Families, together, in pews. The doorframe buzzed with their voices, the organ. *"How firm a foundation..."*

Go in? How would they look at me—a divorced man?

Yet, somehow, the rough waves inside his mind grew smaller. *No matter what happens tomorrow.*

***

Election day. Pender was speechifying. Harlowe watched the men oystering. He thought about Gibby, not so much about the votes. Out yonder, men were trying to tong up something useful. Cull out the junk. *We'll see.*

He drove to Panama on a job for Mr. Perkins.

When he returned, he found Murrow and Seago waiting on his porch. They shook his hand—and informed him he'd won!

"You back! Now things'll be back the way they oughtta be!" Seago declared.

"Well, that is if ya want the job."

"Hell, yes!"

SIXTY-FIVE

January, 1937

On a bitter cold afternoon Judge Clary swore him in. True made it to the judge's front porch just in time to see.

Later, at the Armory, Tennie Buckles won the "Miss Apalachicola" beauty contest! True just got a glimpse of her as she was crowned and made her procession to Cleve Crumley's waiting taxi.

Harlowe walked to the Courthouse, alone. The roof-peaks and chimneys, poking up over the trees, beckoned like lost kinfolk. It looked a little sweeter to him. Even the streaks of dirt, sweat on the red brick, the faded paint were beautiful, like the lines on the face of a beloved friend.

He turned the worn knob. Breathed the courthouse smell—old varnish and paper. The hall was silent, hours after quitting time. He looked down it. The doors that represented each department in the county: Superintendent of Public Instruction. County Assessor of Taxes. Supervisor of Registration. Clerk of Court.

He climbed the stairs. Felt the bannister rubbed smooth by the grasp of many hands. Enjoyed the familiar pop and creak beneath his shoes.

He looked in the courtroom. All the pews. The clock. He walked past the heavy door to Judge Clary's chambers.

On the sign which jutted from the wall, Pender's name remained.

Yet, he was home.

He opened the door. Pender had repainted the walls, but the room was, otherwise, unchanged. The same cypress half-paneling. Fireplace. Heart-pine floorboards. But, missing were the old rolltop and table, Pender having supplied his own things. Harlowe set his shotgun in the empty rack. Got a fire going. Set out to determine *why in the hell* the telephone was out of order! It was dark by the time he got it *cut on.*

Across town, the wail of the evening train advanced, and the fire had, at last, taken the chill off. Harlowe settled on the floor. Reading his notebooks. There wasn't a scrap of paper from Pender on Gibby's case.

He pulled out the photo of Gibby and the redfish. "Allright—now we can get after this thing."

***

True finally got the motor started. Then beating a path out to the oyster bar, they worked from a frosty dawn to a sun-soaked afternoon.

Most of those hours Briley filled with complaining. "Havin' your old lady madatchu ain't what you wohnt, son. 'You ain't got the house money,' he decried in falsetto. 'What's the point gettin' wired for 'lectricity when we caint afford to cut it *own*?' I have a drink now 'n then, I like my cigarettes, an' go see a ballgame. She thinks I done spent the money but I ain't! T'weren't there to start with!"

True smiled.

"When we wed, I couldn' buy a hummin'bird on a string for a nickel! I hate to admit it I ain't any better off now, not by a damn sight! Now, it was good to hear about Ol' Pratt. I know you happy about that."

True nodded. He had hope again.

That afternoon, True made sure his shirt was clean and his hair combed for the trip over to St. George. He asked Briley if his tie was straight and he left on the skiff.

It took an hour, and he had to fix the motor twice, but he made it. Tennie hardly looked up from her magazine. "Oh, you came? Where are'ya taking me?"

He walked beside her to the skiff, too timid to put his arm around her. She did all the talking, about things she wanted to do when she could get away from here. She'd packed a picnic basket and let him take her to Dog Island. Purple flowers grew on the dunes. And he sat with her, there, on that lovely, secluded spot.

"I *am* glad to get away from Mother," she admitted.

He nodded.

"My life revolves around that light. I hate it. Totin' those damn buckets of oil!" She opened up to True about things he thought she didn't say to anyone, like she trusted him. And that made him like her all the more, like he was close to her, where he wasn't close to anyone, expect Harlowe.

"I'm glad I won Miss Apalachicola. But," she shrugged her shoulders. "I'm still here."

He looked in her eyes when she talked to him. They were green, tinged with firey bursts of amber. Her hair was dark, her skin like porcelain, inheriting the features of the Greeks on her Mother's side.

Finally, he got the nerve and kissed her. The feeling nearly took his breath from him, like running a distance, not being able to breathe and feeling light-headed.

She grinned at that. "Oh, I've been kissed before. Lots."

She pulled him close, kissing him back. It was something for her to do besides darn socks and help her Mother, but she soon turned her attention to the food they'd brought. When it was gone, she decided, "I'm bored, take me home."

He did. True was at her feet. Anything she said was fine with him.

When she told him she was moving to Apalach to finish her schooling, he was in heaven!

***

Seago was alarmed. "Y'sure you wanna go nosin' around up theah?"
"I have no choice," Harlowe concluded. "I have to go."
"The deal with the neighbor?"
"What bothered Whittle, what got him sent to Chattahoochee...was more than an argument over a fence!"

Harlowe knocked on doors again. But couldn't find anyone who knew what Junior had done.
Harlowe found Whittle's nephew at his store. "Was there anyone else who might know about the argument the old man had?"
"No. I can think of no one."
He returned to Doctor Harvey's office in the yellow-brick, six-story building. "We both know Whittle wasn't crazy. Did he tell you somethin' about the Cory boy?"
"You have no right coming here!"
"Did you sign off on his commitment?"
The old doctor turned red, shook his fist. "I will not violate the confidences of-of any patient!"

***

The fog lay heavy over Indian Creek. Harlowe heard something. Sounded like a man moving along the bank.
Harlowe had been checking the area after reports of a campfire, but saw nothing in the walk back here.
Suddenly, something splashed in the water.
Harlowe peered into the rising mist. It was a gator.
The fog was thick as a wool blanket.
He worked his way along the bank. The show emerged a tree. Moss hung from them like funeral shrouds. He heard footsteps. He ran.
He found a spray of roses left on the crooked tree branch.
He found no trace of whomever left it.

***

February, 1937
A man, tall, shuffling, stopped behind a pinetree. He proceeded to the next tree, watching Little Foss pitch one last ball. Then the little Fulton boy, Butterbean, and the rest scattered— heading home for supper.

With the last kerosene lamp extinguished, it was as dark as a tomb in Eastpoint.
Harlowe was watching. Sitting in his automobile.

331

He was there too. Watching R.J. Williams walk to the outhouse. In the darkness.

He crept toward it. Then, froze. *Headlights!*

***

Harlowe turned around at the Williams place, letting his headlights caress the trees.

***

Heart pounding, the man retreated, slipping back into Tate's Hell, the old tapper's road, his Ford.

All the children home now, Harlowe left to meet the *Save Time.*

***

"Yeah, Cap'n. He sure did. He done hired me as a mixer at the plant," said Jeter.

"Good," Harlowe replied.

"Ya want I should keep my ears open, report back to you anythin' I see, is that it?"

"That's right."

CLICK.

***

March, 1937

Harlowe was on the roof-ridge of Mrs. Slocumb's chickencoup.

Wiped his brow and glanced toward the Bay. Out at the building clouds.

Mrs. Slocumb looked up from her clothesline. "I wanna thank you men for doin' this. Maybe they won't get loose so much?"

"Yes, ma'am!" they both replied.

True handed him up the new shingles. He hammered in the nails.

True rolled out the chicken wire. He thought his uncle was happy. He sure seemed to be.

Presently, a few raindrops fell, large and heavy. True felt them and smelled them.

True smiled. He was glad to have his uncle back.

***

Harlowe sat with them a while. He owed them that on their yearly visits—Gibby's birthday. Aubrey's and Lillian both wore their finest for the trip to the courthouse. It was still simple clothing. Made from flour sacks. They looked as shattered, broken, as the first night, Harlowe thought. Only, now, they seemed smaller, more fragile, with the appearance of wrinkles, strands of gray not present at last year's meeting.

They talked about Gibby and Harlowe listened. Kept the coffee coming.

They were happy for a moment, even talking about that last day. "Gibby said it was a good time to catch a fish. The moon was right, he didn't wanna miss it!"

But their smiles both faded quickly again. Mrs. Birch looked Harlowe in the eye. "Can I ask you straight out?" She seemed much older, like the bones of an elderly woman showing through on a still-young face.

"Yes, ma'am?"

"Will the ones that done this to my Gibby get punished? I know they will one day, but I mean here in this world."

"I believe they will.

"We appreciate ya," said Birch.

"Thank you so much," said the woman.

Harlowe refilled her cup. Her hands reflected the years of intricate sewing she'd done—the onset of arthritis.

"Y'know I have little, but I'm happy," said Birch. "I don't need money, I just love oysterin', my fam'ly." He looked down for a second, the pain of Gibby's being missing from that family didn't need mentioning.

"We are blessed," said Lillian. Neither would ever know abundance, but they knew contentment nonetheless. They took great pride in their section, in making a living on the water.

"We've been married twenty-five years and we never raised our voices at each other," said Mr. Birch.

Lillian nodded, her eyes closed in reflection. "That's a fact."

"Well, I think it's wonderful. I wish some of my 'customers' would learn from you," said Harlowe. They all chuckled at that.

"I wish we could give you more to go on," said Mr. Birch.

"Aubrey, don't worry with that. You've done given me every name that could possibly be of help."

"Well, I hope so, Pratt. I feel like I oughta—I sure wanna do somethin'."

"I've probably mentioned this before, Shureff?"

"Yes, ma'am?" Even if he had heard it, he'd let her speak until she was ready to go home, and he'd listen to whatever she had a mind to say to him.

"I've tried to think about folks he mentioned. Anyone he'd described. There's a bunch of 'em. He made friends so easy."

"Everybody liked that young'n," said Harlowe.

"I've given you ev'ry one. I keep thinkin'...did I let 'im down—somethin' I shoulda looked out for—like a storm comin' or a snake? I reckon you never git done thinkin' was there somethin' more ya coulda done?"

"I reckon you don't."

"Have you ever been able to find out about Mr. Whittle?" she asked.

"No, ma'am. No more."

Judge Clary walked by in the hall. He looked in and said, "Hello. Good to see ya, Aubrey. Miss Lillian."

"Howdy, Judge."

"Is Pratt, any help to you all?"

She told the judge, "He's Gibby's voice—all these years."

"That means a lot," Harlowe said. *It meant more than anything.*

SIXTY-SIX

May, 1937

May, when the last puffs of Spring coolness lingered.

After working all day, Efola sent True to the Nichols' store.

It was bright inside. White walls. The green counter that had been there all his life.

"Can I he'p ya?" asked the clerk.

True handed the woman the list. "My, you've grown tall, True!"

He blushed a little.

"I knew your deddy. You favor 'im." She ran the hamburger meat through the machine. Wrapped it in paper. Finished boxing up the canned goods. "Y'know, your deddy was such a hard worker! You almost as tall as he was!"

True nodded. Tipped his hat, "ma'am."

"Bye, True."

The day ended with the menfolk—they let True tag along—gathered around the radio at the *Riverside*. They could get the fights now! And folks hung on the announcer's every word!

Harlowe got called away. Outside, things were whispered in his ear. But it wasn't a secret long. A young white girl named *Mae* was "attacked." That meant, *raped.*

A colored boy done it.

Harlowe pulled up in his Ford and called to the Negro, Robert Hinds. A scared sixteen-year-old emerged. Stood there shaking on his mother's porch.

"'You best git in,' is what your Uncle said. And the boah walked right over and climbed in the car an' Pratt carried him to the jailhouse. True, I wouldna b'lieved it if I hadna seen it!" Seago explained. "And there he sets."

True looked down the hall, timidly. He saw Hinds slouched in the corner of his cell, hugging his knees, tears streaming down his copper-colored cheeks. True thought he was about the same age.

The clerk of court burst in. "Pratt, there's fixin' to be trouble. The men are on their way here!"

Scarcely he'd said this, screeching around the corner came two Fords. They squeaked to a stop and eight men got out. True looked out. They were millworkers, rough customers, more than a little Who-Hit-John

335

warming their insides. They advanced on the door of the jailhouse, hoopin' and hollerin.'

The sky was deep blue and pleasant. These events did not seem real.

"We wan' 'im! We'll do what needs done!" And many profanity-laced things were hollered.

True saw Harlowe step in front of Seago and Brewer—the only men he had—and face those big men, standing in the doorway.

"He's a prisoner now. And he'll see Judge Anderson presently!" Harlowe told them.

The men continued to holler and demand Harlowe turn Hinds loose.

Harlowe said no more.

He never looked away. And, somehow, the men began to walk away. One by one.

True was amazed. *That look.* Harlowe backed those men down with only the look in his eyes, his few words hanging over like they'd come from Moses or Robert E. Lee!

The Fords pulled away. Seago nudged him, "Hot damn! J'see it True? Like somethin' in a *pitcher,* son! I b'lieve ol' Harry Carey couldna--."

"Ain't over yet," Harlowe cautioned, pouring himself a cup. He looked concerned. *But,* True realized, *he ain't sore at the men.*

When he walked back to the cell, and told Hinds he was all right, True saw he had no animousity there, either. No anger. *"He always leave a man his dignity."*

But as midnight approached, and more drams were drunk, another crowd grew. A larger, noisier one. Three men wouldn't hold them for a minute when they boiled over.

Harlowe's thoughts went back to the Forehand posse. *We had a trial. That's what has to be done now.*

Harlowe phoned Briley. "I want you to carry True home."

He did. And, True heard, by the time the crowd entered the jail—and gazed in befuddlement into the empty cell—Harlowe and the prisoner *was clear to 'Panama.'*

Harlowe got home fuzzy-headed for not having slept. Glanced toward the River, the fast-moving clouds billowing up. Storms could come up fast.

For a moment, he watched the grey clouds, rolling across the Bay like smoke from a speeding locomotive. *It looked that that in 'twenty-seven.*

He checked locks on the stores. Came in. The smell of the rain mixed with Claudie's soap in the bathroom. Pratt fell asleep to the drumming rain.

***

Friday. The children slept on the porch. Marlene. The boys.
I could just reach in and grab the boy!
Suddenly, the hounds started yapping! The gray figure bolted for the woods.
C.P. was roused. "Shutup-Damn-ye!" he hollered at the dogs.
A trembling man listened from the pine. *I needed this. I've got to have it. I'll be back soon.*

***

Harlowe found tire tracks on the old tapper's road.
He leaned back in his Ford that night. Watching.

***

Saturday, R.J. Williams, who was seven now, dipped his canepole in the water, off the old ferry dock.
It was getting dark.
The figure dressed in gray emerged from the trees. Moving toward the boy.
He grabbed Mack.
The boy welped.
True dropped the armful of stovewood and picked up the ax, running down there.
The fellow bolted—running headlong into the woods.
True ran to the store to phone Harlowe.

Harlowe rolled off the ferry. Raced up the old road to the Williams' place.
Birch and Quick had their shotguns. They'd come back from the Sumatra Road in Quick's mule-drawn cart. They hadn't seen anyone!
True told Harlowe what the man looked like. "Tall fella. Broad-shouldered. No, sir, I didn't see his face. Well, he had something on his face. A baseball catcher's mask."
"Can ya tell me anything else you remember about 'im?"
"No, sir. Happened so fast! He was tall—like a ballplayer."
"Good, son. Could you sell what color the clothes were?"
"Gray. Britches and 'is shirt."
"It looked like a catcher's mask?"
"Uh-huh. Best I could tell, sir. Run fast as a deer!"

Harlowe, toting his shotgun, walked into Tate's Hell. The saw palmetto was thick, man-high. Ahead, the tangle of shrubs grew taller, darker, like the walls of a maze.
He passed through, sideways, down an impossibly narrow hogtrail.

It grew quiet, beyond the range of the Williams' barking dogs.
Toting his shotgun, he walked along.

There were a hundred places to watch and hide, at every tree, behind every mass of vines, the darkness pitch-black.
Through that difficult country, coming about three miles since he'd left the farm, he reached the tapper's road.
He eased toward the treeline, looking down the road.
Suddenly, something moved. It was a moccasin. He saw its fangs. And before he could react, it was striking at his leg. It got his boot. He hit it with the butt of his gun.
It struck again. He weaved to avoid it. Fired both barrels and killed it.

He walked another quarter of a mile and, there, in the sand, he saw a rut, where a car had "dug out." The tires left little trace in the sand. They looked like the tires on his own Ford!

Seago picked him up, out on the Sumatra Road. They drove north, checking. Near Whiskey George Creek, he saw more tracks in the sand, as if the fellow pulled over for some reason. There were no footprints so the fellow hadn't climbed down from his automobile.

They drove back to the farm.
Twiggs was drinking coffee on Mrs. Williams' porch as Harlowe walked up.
R.J. huddled with his mother.
Harlowe asked him, "Did you know the fella?"
"No, sir!" said the scared boy.
"Evuh see 'im before?"
"No, sir."
Harlowe questioned the Williams men. *"We ain't seen nobody!"* they said.
"What about you, son?"
"Hell, I was here—we all was!" said Denny.
"They was here all evenin'," promised Mother Williams.

C.P. Williams and Birch had come back by now. "We looked everywhere," said C.P.
Mr. Quick, and Mr. Daughtry and several other men came, with their guns.
"Whatever you have to do, Pratt, we're behind ya. All of us. We done talked it over."
"Thanks boys. I can use ya. Look after your homes, families. I'll tell ya what I want you to do later own. I'm goin thisaway."
He walked down to the old ferry dock. Rechecked the ground with Twiggs.
"We gonna have to patrol through here a lot more," Harlowe told him.
"Two of us?"
"Yeah, I know." Harlowe waved his arm back toward the folk gathered at the Williams' farm. "We can have Quick and the other men help."
"Okay."
Seago nudged Harlowe's arm. "He's goin' for the li'l boys? What kind of feller we lookin' for?"
"I dunno. The doctor-books have a word they use, 'pee-doe-phil-ya.'"

Seago cussed. "All I know is I'd like to git 'im in my sights! The hell with all the fifty-cent words—there's only one thing y'can do with a rabid dog!"
"Well, we've got to *find* the dog."

***

Marlene sat on the porch, snapping stringbeans. Harlowe walked over to her. She looked smaller and more childlike than her age, thirteen years old, would suppose.
Harlowe squatted down to talk to her. "You sure are a fast worker."
"Thankya."
"Say, I was wonderin' if you were around when--."
"She ain't seen nothin'!" spat C.P. "I thought I toll you to fetch stovewood? Git up from thar and git to your chores, girl!"
C.P.'s been drinking, thought Harlowe.
"Ain't ya asked enough questions, Cap'n?"
"Maybe. I'll see ya around, C.P."
"Ya, I expect you'll keep chasin' ghosts!"
"Well, I believe he's flesh and bones, this fella."
The man staggered closer. "Sonofabitch! Y'got any ideas?"
"A few."
"A'ight Cap'n. Keep 'em close to the vest. Hey, don't miss the ferry!"

***

Two o'clock on a moonlit night. Harlowe had his thermos and his coach gun on the seat.
He saw a glint of light. Then someone run. He chuckled—it was a kid getting up to use the outhouse.

The bugs finally went to sleep as dawn neared. Quick went home, but Harlowe was still watching.
Night after night it went on, but the man didn't come back.
Harlowe would head to the office, his hip pockets dragging.
"Y'reckon he's an *athaleet?*" asked the jailor.
"Maybe."
Harlowe checked it.
He talked to men on ball teams—Tallahassee, Moultrie, Albany. To men who coached high school teams in the Panhandle and in Georgia.
He even reintervieweed the ballplayers who'd come to town that week in '27.

Junior Cory had played baseball, Harlowe remembered from the annual. His neighbor on Pensacola Street thought he was home all night, the night before last.
Down the street the older lady told them, "I dunno. He likes to drive places, he told me. Takes little drives up in Georgia. The open country!"

Harlowe sat down the street watching him, Friday and Saturday night, but the fellow never left his house. It felt like dragging all day, hoping you catch something—only to find the net empty one more time.

Harlowe watched. And dug up half the county.
The men in Eastpoint kept a fire in a barrel at the intersection, brought food for Brewer, spelled him when he needed to sleep.
Pratt was out there many nights, his car backed into the tapper's road. Commissioner Huff chided him, "You're fixated, Pratt! I'm gonna tell ya, poking a hornet's nest isn't good for our county! This does no one any good!"
Harlowe told True, "I'll keep doin' it until they vote me outta office."

***

June, 1937

Seago run his launch, the *Barbara Jean,* toward the middle of the Bay. It was calm and hot, blue sky as far as a man could look. Harlowe and True came along.

Out in the middle, Seago turned the wheel, taking her up into a little cove locals called the "Big Bay." It was hemmed in by sawgrass marsh. Not even the rustle of the wind could be heard in there. It's so quiet the silence has a sound! Felt heavy on their ears. Like being wrapped in a nice heavy quilt, soft and soothing, like you could hear the blood flowing in your head.

"I imagine he'd come up here," thought True.

Seago baited his line.

Harlowe looked all around.

"There's a bigun' in here. Ol' Pauley said he got away," Seago explained. The jailor put a whole crab on his line. A big redfish could swallow it whole! He dropped the baited hook and the crab settled to the bottom.

True baited his with a piece of crab. He waited, but didn't get a bite from the ol' Red.

Suddenly, Seago gave a holler and jumped, nearly tipping the boat! "I b'lieve I got 'im!"

He tugged at the fish. "Hot damn! He's a big'n!"

Seago pulled and pulled. True remembered how excited Gibby was the day they took the skiff up here. *"There's a big ol' redfish in here! Ol' boy that's friends with my daddy let 'im get away. I ain't gonna let that happen,"* said Gibby.

Gibby felt the strong tug on the line and got busy. A redfish was biting! "Look at 'im fight, True!" The boy pulled and pulled to get him aboard the little rowboat. True had to help lift him. "Thanks, True. Les' put 'im in this sack!"

Gibby dropped another crab. Then another one tugged at his line. This one was particularly strong. After he got the fish aboard the rowboat, he dropped another piece of crab...

"Look at 'im, y'all!" Seago cried.

"He sure is big!" thought True.

"Is it the one you was after?" asked Harlowe.

"Nah—but he'll do! *Son!*" The big man lay the fish on the sack. "He's too big for that sack! Hot damn, I love this!"

"Gibby loved coming out heah," said True.

Put on another crab. Seago dropped line again. Leaned back in the boat. And caught another one! "Ain't as big, but sho' is a good'n!"

Then True felt a tug! "Pull 'im!" said Seago.

The fish splashed vigorously at the surface! "He's a Bull Red!" cried Seago, grabbing the net. "Damn! He's too big for the net!"

True fought him in to the boat.

"He's just a floppin'—damn, he's a beaut, son!"

They motored in. "He woulda come thisaway," said Harlowe, talking up over the motor. Harlowe tried to see if he could see it through Gibby's eyes—those last hours. The trees on the shore got bigger. An automobile grew recognizable. The old chimney from Elmer Smith's bar.

"Would he get in an automobile with a stranger?"

"I reckon he would—to get to ride in one!" True answered. "Gibby would talk to anyone. If you come a stranger y'left a friend."

Harlowe thought about that, sadly. Waved his arm. "The storm could have tossed that skiff out theah."

"It was off the bluff when you found it?" asked Seago.

"Yessir."

"Reckon he grabbed him 'fore he secured it?"

"Could be."

Seago steered to Cat Point, as Gibby might have.

"No one saw him come in and where. No one saw his tracks," said Harlowe.

Seago cut the throttle as they rounded the Point—and saw the Birches' roof.

"Would he leave with a stranger, you reckon? What kind of man?" wondered Harlowe.

"Someone who talked fishin' or huntin'," thought Seago.

"Or baseball," said True.

SIXTY-SEVEN

August, 1937

Twiggs resigned to Captain a boat in Carrabelle. Harlowe began interviewing men for his replacement.

Brewer wanted his cousin, Danny Santino, to get the job. Harlowe told him, "I reckon I'll talk to these men, and I'll decide on the best one." He put on his impossibly ancient spectacles, his signal for Brewer to quit pestering him.

Harlowe shook hands with the last man who had inquired—a fellow who kept store in Sopchoppy but had kin nearby. The man left, but then Harlowe heard someone coming softly up the stairs.

"True! Good to see ya, son! Pull up a chair."

True sat down. Harlowe pulled his chair close to face him. "What can I do for ya, son?"

"Shureff, I come to ask you for that job, sir." True said it just as he'd rehearsed.

"I see," Harlowe replied, as if he wasn't aware True would be coming. "Now, you are a little young. And you don't have any experience."

"Nosir," True admitted. He tried to get a read of the Sheriff's legendary poker face. Harlowe was being especially cagey, and it was killing him not knowing what he was thinking. "I'm seventeen-and-a-half. I-I know this is what I wanna do."

"Well, there's no uniform. No automobile. No salary. Work outside in the heat, the rain, and cold. It can be dangerous. If ya do the job right, not everyone's gonna be happy with you. Sometimes *nobody's* happy with ya." He paused, letting the words sink in, the worst of what law enforcement had to offer, in case his nephew should be dissuaded. "You have a shotgun, but you'd have to provide your own handgun—if you was to get the job. Might take you a while, savin' up."

"Yessir." *'I caint tell if he's trying to talk me out of it or not,'* True thought.

He kept on with it, keeping True in suspense. "It ain't like what you read in stories. Sheriffin' ain't a glamorous life."

"Nosir." True thought he was going in with a realistic understanding of what life as a sheriff's deputy in Franklin County would be like. It was the job he dreamed of for so long. He knew he wouldn't get rich, and there'd be times he might wish he was back shucking oysters. But he wanted this!

Harlowe seemed to think about it carefully, his hands resting on the arms of the oak chair, looking at True.

"You've grown into a big fella, what about six-two now?" he asked, already knowing the answer.

"Yessir." True *had* grown, his muscles were solid from working outdoors every day. Harlowe reflected on the decision for what felt like, to True, a long time. The ticking of the clock echoed like thunder off the bare, plaster walls and floors. True never knew the tick of that clock, the passage of each second, to have such magnitude! He was on the edge of that old chair. Harlowe seemed to sense his anticipation. Looked the boy squarely in the eye.

"You can have the job, son." He gave a grin. Extended his hand. True nearly leapt to his feet and shook it.

"Wanna think it over?"

"I don't have to think on it none. Yessir, Shureff, I want it!"

"That's fine, son. You can start tomorruh." He clapped True on the back. "I always figured to make you my deputy."

True nearly floated out into the street he was so happy.

True looked up to his uncle all his life. Now, to be working for him! True felt his life was really beginning!

***

True woke early. Before Briley and them occupied the bathroom, he shaved, combed his hair. Put on a clean workshirt. Foss's necktie.

He thought back to when he was little, when Harlowe asked him, *"Has Gibby mentioned any new friend? Anything botherin' 'im?"*

"No, sir."

Now, True hoped he could help Harlowe—and keep his promise!

No sooner had he climbed the backstairs, Harlowe swore him in and shook his hand and now he was a deputy-sheriff!

"How do ya feel, boah?" asked Seago.

"Caint hardly believe it. I'm a *puhlease* man!*" True pronounced it the same as he would his former profession: *'oyster* man.'

Harlowe poured them each a cup. The large room may have been spartan, but Harlowe always had a pot of coffee going. He'd returned his old roll-top, table and chairs, too. The telephone and gunrack comprised the rest of the furnishings. True had known these things since he was an infant.

Harlowe spread out papers browned with age. They went through Gibby's case, from the beginning, every detail.

"So, what next?" asked Seago, loosening his necktie.

Harlowe refilled their cups.

"No one's seen anything since that night at the Williams'."

"Y'may not solve it n'less he comes back!" thought Seago.

Harlowe replied. "Well, I believe it comes back to Tallahassee—what was done to Mr. Whittle."

"Uh-huh?"

"Somethin' happened with the son—that's nevuh been cleared up."

"I agree, ya gotta at least look at 'im," Brewer acknowledged.

"And we're gonna find the body," insisted Harlowe.

True bought a second-hand Colt, but he lacked handcuffs. Seago knew where everything was in the courthouse, and True decided to approach the jailor about a pair. He stood at the door, a little nervous. The big man sat there behind his paper in his spectacles, reading and listening for the phone. "What can I do for you, young man?" he asked, not looking away from the sports page.

"Mr. Seago, I was wonderin' if there were any more handcuffs?"

"Come on in heah!" Seago led him over to the little closet. He found an old box, behind a clothestree. "Let's git you a set of handcuffs of your own."

He handed them to True. "Ya need somethin' ya jus' ask C.A.! You know how to work 'em?"

"Uncle Pratt's been showin' me."

"Come on."

Seago pulled up chairs. Handed the set to True. "Show me."

True locked one on his wrist and unlocked it again.

"A'ight. Go on and oil 'em. They need it." He tossed True a rag. It didn't matter if you were sitting in an office with him, on a boat fishing with him, or sitting beside him in a church pew. If he wanted your attention, he'd nudge you with his elbow and go, "look here." That was how he talked. And thusly he nudged True's knee: "Look here," he began, and as True oiled the old steel, the jailer swore the boy to secrecy and proceeded to tell True a story about the first man he ever handcuffed.

***

They'd passed the last house in Eastpoint. Harlowe pulled off the coastal road into the brush.

"That's Sonny Brewer's land," cautioned Seago.

Harlowe walked toward the woods anyway. "Boss, I don't think Sonny would likeya diggin' up his land!"

Harlowe plunged the shovel anyway.

True watched, wide-eyed.

"All right, boys. If a squirrel's buried here I wanna know," said Harlowe.

"A' ight, here we go," said Seago, hopping down with his shovel. "You comin', T.K.?"

The men poked all over the place, a little farm squeezed by Tate's Hell. Entangled saw palmetto fronds formed a wall seven feet high, impassible except the narrow hog trail leading into 'Hell.'

They worked around vines as thick as rope.

It felt snaky, to True, like little snaky eyes were watching. The oaks had arms like gray snakes which added to the feeling. Made True shiver.

They checked this ground too.

That's when True found it—a spot where the earth was depressed. "'Bout about five feet long—theyuyh!" They dug it out with their hands.

"Nothin'."

Undeterred Harlowe moved them yonder.

They worked to the sounds of a fiddling insect band. "Ooh. I'm burnin' slap up!" cried Seago.

Harlowe handed him a canteen.

Brewer scoffed. "Ten-thousand places to hide a body; gators coulda got it and scattered it. Ain't no tellin'. The Resurrection will pull in them bones, 'fore we will!"

As the woods turned grey in the dusklight, they sweated and were savaged by mosquitos—and found nothing.

It was dark when they loaded up, bugs swarming in the headlights—as if to say they'd won, and the secrets buried here belonged to them.

SIXTY-EIGHT

Apalachicola—September 1937

True walked by the Fuller. Belle Jenkins leaned out, "Mornin' Mr. True! Come in heah n' have some coffee!"

He did. "How y'likin' yo job?"

"Jus' fine," he said. And he couldn't help telling her that Tennie moved to Apalach with her mother and sisters, anticipating Mr. Buckles' retirement from the lighthouse corps. "They bought a home near Chapman High on Avenue E. She'll finish hah skool in town! But, I-I'm too shy to talk to her."

"Naw. Y'can do it."

He thanked her for the coffee.

"You be careful, now."

Later, True walked toward Tennie's house. Turned around three times before he worked up the nerve. Then he marched up to her porch, where she sat, snapping stringbeans. She talked to him like that day on the beach. Finally, she looked over and smiled. "Take me for a coke?"

He felt like he was floating over the ground. All the way to the fountain at Buzzett's. Kids went there after school for an ice cream or a coke. They found a place at the counter. A nickel coke was a lot on his pay, but he didn't think twice! "Oh, that's good!" she said, finishing her glass.

At that, the whistle hollered at one of the seafood houses.

"Kinda makes me think of Gibby. He used to like to watch the boats. Wanted to captain one--."

"Where are you taking me after this?"

"I dunno. Down by the--."

"Oh, let's go to a dance!" He thought he might could scrape up the money to get there.

And that was how it started.

Tennie worked at the A&P after school, and True would somehow scrape up enough money he could meet her after she got off work.

Friday, nervously, he tried to get his tie on straight, looking in the reflection of the window.

"Tennie Buckles you say? Damn, son, she's the prettiest gal in town!" Seago exclaimed.

True smiled.

347

"That dark curly hair, like one 'o them Greek goddesses."

"Like what?" Brewer retorted.

"Them Greek goddesses—aint ya read no mythology? Helen of Troy, son!"

"What the hell you talkin' about?" said Brewer.

"Books, son. And I ain't talkin' 'bout comic books."

Brewer scoffed. "Ah! I'll see you boys."

After Brewer had gone, Seago nudged True. "Her face's jus' like a statue. I'm proud o' you, boah!"

Seago leaned forward. "She give a little kiss, huh?"

True blushed.

"Yeah, she did! Come on, son! I tell ya it's them quiet ones ya gotta watch!"

***

Seago read the *Times*. "*Huff Recognized by Women's Club.*' Hmm. But they won't run the story about Gibby—the anniversary?"

"Nope," replied Harlowe. He looked at True, "Where they might help they're nowhere around."

The phone interrupted.

"Took me long enough, eh!" Jeter cackled.

"That's all right—did you check on it for me?"

"Yeah—toldya I would. Y'sittin' down?"

"Yeah."

"A'ight. Now, his son caused Ol' Daddy all kinda problems. Lamar put him in a place for *alkeyhaulics* down in Daytona. Oh...'round nineteen-n'-twenty-seven!"

"Is that right?" asked Harlowe. He looked over at True.

"C'n ya b'lieve that—a place like 'at where they try to cure a body of drinkin'?" They might as well attempt to cure a man of breathing, so far as Jeter was concerned.

"There's a private sanitarium in Daytona. That's the one?"

"Hell, I dunno. Ain't got no interest in that—not in any such!"

"When did you say he was sent theah?"

"I don't know the month, now. 'Round the time y'interested in."

"Who told you?"

"Look here—I got my friends I talk to. You got your'n. Now, I got to go."

"Wait a minute."

"Ya want me to moveover?"

"Yeah."

"A'ight."

"Soon as you can."

CLICK.

"He hung, up," said Harlowe. "All right. Before we go any *fu'ther.*
Somethin' I gotta say."

True nodded.

"This is li'ble to be ugly. I got into a hornet's nest with his daddy. They
won't roll out the red carpet for us if we come at the son."

"Yessir."

"All right."

Harlowe drove. The hood of the car swung around as he turned on Market
Street and headed for the bridge.

The bridgetender waved. Harlowe waved back. True looked out at the
boats coming in from the oysterbars, Briley's among them. Only a few
days ago he would have been out there with them. He didn't look back.
This was his new life—one different from Foss's.

The MotoMeter out front. The hum of the tires. It would be a fine outing—
yet this was for a purpose, True knew. US-319 ran up through the
National Forest. They drove along for miles before Harlowe spoke—adding
to the gravity True felt.

They passed a building with a pagoda roof just south of the tracks. Signs
said, "Green Derby, "Bowling," "Dancing."

"It's really a night club, True." That meant refreshments of the "hi-test"
variety—not strictly legal in the Capital City. "Alkeyhaul and 'other
things'," Harlowe explained, meaning prostitution. "Place across the street,

theah, serves lickuh, also." True had noticed the "High Hat" (the new name for the old blind tiger).

"We gotta be careful, son. Men who run this town don't take kindly to outsiders nosin' around."

True nodded. It was his first time visiting Tallahassee. Coming up, it seemed like the ends of the earth! The Capitol dome loomed up the hill as they neared downtown.

True read from the phone directory, *"Cory Concrete is the second largest employer in town, after Elberta Crate."* Cory still resided on Gadsden Street. "He'll be at his office," thought Harlowe.

They got back in the car. Drove out Gaines. Turned down the Lake Bradford Road, heading for the silos.

True noted the letters, **C-O-R-Y.**

They walked down the hall to the office, removing their hats as they approached the secretary. "Mornin', ma'am. We wanna see Mr. Cory."

It was the same gal—she looked at them, crossways. "May I ask what this is about?"

They told her and she led them back. "Lamar" hadn't aged noticably. He'd added a photo or two.

He smiled. "Mornin', boys! Please have a seat."

The small talk concerned fishing, the construction business, Lamar as gregarious as anyone you'd meet.

"I really enjoy my trips to your county," he told them.

Harlowe produced the photo of Gibby. "I'm looking into the murder of this little boy."

Lamar looked. His countenance changed, ever so slightly, Harlowe noticed.

"I know nothing about it. I wish I could help you, but I've told you everything I recall."

"Your son was theah. He left your party, sometime, didn't he?"

"Why shouldn't he? Just what are you *driving at,* Mr. Harlowe?"

"He did go off alone, then?"

"He may have. But I don't think so. You didn't answer my question—why is this important to you?"

"I think he...saw somethin' out theah."

"No. He woulda mentioned it if he had."

"He went off on his own, now isn't that right?"

"No, when we were through fishing, we all went home together—before sundown."

"When you or your son were in Eastpoint, last."

Lamar crossed his arms. "A few weeks ago, for me. I'll have my secretary send you the information."

"All right. I appreciate it."

"You'd have to ask Junior when *he* was down there, last. It's been some time. He's rather busy."

"Okay."

Lamar smiled—a little forced, Harlowe thought. Lamar held out his hand, affably. "I hope I can get down to your county soon—do a little Gulf fishing. I hope I see you fellas."

"Yessir. Goodbye, sir."

They walked to the car. "True, did you notice his face, when I showed him the photo?"

"No."

"Watch a man's face, son. His hands. The way he sits. That'll tell you a whole lot more than his words."

True nodded.

They drove to the grammar school on Calhoun, where Junior taught. Harlowe walked down the hall. There were photos of the schoolteachers on the wall. Junior was the only man. Harlowe looked at the faces in classrooms. Innocent. Eager. *First day of school for these young'uns!*

He got to the corner. Tucked behind it. He watched the principal walk down the hall, stopping at Junior's classroom. The younger man hurried down the hall to use the telephone. His face reddened. His hands shook.

Harlowe slipped back to the car. "In the time it took for us to drive here, he's gettin' a phone call from Daddy."
True nodded.
'All right, we wait."

351

The bell rang. Junior hurried to his Ford V-8. Drove downtown.

They tailed him down the sidewalk, on Monroe. Harlowe spoke out of the corner of his mouth. "Use the *winduhs*. You can stop and light your cigarette. Act like you're browsin.'"

Doing like Harlowe showed him, hats on low, they'd followed Junior Cory five blocks, and the latter hadn't noticed!

People passed them by without noticing them. Like they were *invisible.*

True recalled those days in Miss Hazelwood's class. Reciting. Ciphering. Copying the blackboard. He never got to finish school. *Maybe this is where school really begins!*

They watched Junior enter the Surprise Store. Glanced in the windows as he browsed. They paused in the display alcove, watched him come out. True saw Junior fling his cigarette down. *Seems like somethin's botherin him.* True looked over at his uncle. *He seen it too.*

It's getting dark. Junior crossed Adams Street.

They approached the windows of Yon's Hardware store. "Look in the reflections son." Harlowe barely moved his lips. He lit a cigarette. Handed True the pack. "Y'see it?"

In the reflection of the plate glass was a Ford—it had pulled to the curb across Adams. "He sure seems like he's lookin' thisaway," said Harlowe, out of the corner of his mouth.

"Yeah," True whispered.

Junior went in the store. They kept going. True used the reflection from the sewing machine store's windows. Saw a hat leaning out of that car! True tossed his match away. *He's lookin' thisaway.*

Harlowe saw it too. "Come on, True!" Quickly, Harlowe led him around the corner—turning down College. They ducked behind the bricks. "One of Ledbetter's men."

The car backed out on Adams. Crept along the street, like he was looking. He was, Harlowe realized, looking at some girls.

He grinned. "He's not interested in us." They walked back to Monroe, toward the automobile showroom. No deputies in the reflection. The Cadillac salesman peered out at them. Saw True's hat and coat and went back to fiddling with the blotter on his desk.

The big church on Monroe glowed. Yellowish lamps. And the colors of stained glass.

They approached Redfern's (formerly Maxwell's). They watched Junior get back in his car. People were coming in and out, paid them no notice.

In the traffic, True lost Junior. "Take Pensacola. I believe he's headin' home," said Harlowe. True followed the quiet road of bungalows and trees. "Just up the road theah."

"I see 'im," said True.

Junior's Ford was in the driveway of the bungalow, a modest house, freshly-painted, and close to the Women's College.

True pulled to the curb, where they could watch it.

It grew dark.

The lights went out. He hadn't gone to see his father.

SIXTY-NINE

Tallahassee, Saturday, 9:00 a.m.

Junior backed out of his driveway. Unusually, he wore a ball cap—most men wear fedoras.

"All right. Let's see where he goes," said Harlowe.

True started the Ford. Pulled out to follow. "Give 'im plenty of line, son."

True let Junior pull away some. Kept several carlengths as the car proceeded downtown.

"That's good, son."

Junior turned onto Monroe. Passed by the Capitol. "Ease up a little. That's right."

The fellow pulled in to Byrd's baseball supplies on South Monroe. They could see Junior was wearing baseball trousers.

They parked across the street, watching in the rearview mirror.

The man emerged carrying ball gloves.

When he pulled away, they followed.

"Am I doin' all right?"

"Just keep doin' what you're doin'," Harlowe said, True staying well behind the newer car.

Junior turned onto Bloxham, stopping near the Centennial Field grandstand.

Little boys ran out to his car.

"He's coaching those boys," said Harlowe.

Junior began exercises on the field with those eight kids. They seemed happy. It seemed normal. What could be more normal, more American, than *baseball?*

"You almost feel like a nut, a heel, to challenge this young schoolteacher."

True nodded. Presently, he added, "them boys are all 'bout Gibby's age."

"Yeah."

Harlowe and True approached the man cutting grass in the outfield. "Say, you know that fella over theah?"

"Sure, that's Junior Cory—he started a league for poor boys in the city. Real nice thing, ain't it?"

"Yessir. Thankya," replied Harlowe. They sat in the car, watching the young teacher pitch to the small boys, some of which wore overalls, some lacked shoes. They seemed happy to get to play.

Junior carried some of the boys back to their homes across the tracks. He chatted with the father of the last one, at the back stoop of an apartment house on Gadsden.

Junior proceeded home. After dark, he appeared on his porch. Looked both ways down Pensacola, and got in his automobile.

He turned down Gaines. Then Lake Bradford. Pulled into the lot of the concrete plant.

"Up theah."

"I see 'im," True replied.

As they passed the plant, they saw another car tucked behind the office—Lamar's La Salle.

True pulled to the shoulder, just past the plant. "Move up a ways, True. We can take that sidin.'"

They got out. Walked along the tracks. Reached the corner of that office. They heard loud voices. It was pitchdark—the only light came from the window of the office.

"I told you, stay home and keep you damn mouth shut!" Lamar shouted.

"Mother won't like the way you're speaking to me!" said Junior.

"I don't give a damn, this time, boy! You'll do as I say, or you'll find yourself in jail—I can't get you out. I won't!"

The younger man hung his head. "All right."

Junior walked back to his car. Drove home. Went to bed as his father had ordered.

They saw the light go out.

"Let's go. We've seen all we're gonna see tonight," said Harlowe.

They met Daughtry and Birch at the tapper's road. "See anything, boys?"

"Not a damn thing."

Harlowe took True to the *Riverside* for supper. Everyone was talking about Jimmy Bloodworth. The kid who made it. They listened to him play on the crackly radio.

Mr. Nichols, too, in white apron, leaned against the doorframe, fanning with a newspaper.

"The national pastime," said Seago.

"It angers me someone would distort that. Use it to lure them younguns," said Harlowe. "We used to play with scraps from the sawmill. We didn't all have fathers, but we had men that we could look up to. It meant somethin' besides jus' knowin' we were poor."

SEVENTY

Monday

The rain dripped through the roof of the jail.

"Good fishin' for catfish," said Seago. "If ya don't mind getting' wet. Hang 'im by the head from a nail on a tree and cook 'im outside—umm-umm! Y'all fixin' to leave?"

Harlowe nodded. Got his shotgun.

***

The dripping clouds hung low over the city.

Junior's old teachers at Leon High wouldn't talk. "Ledbetter's blockin' us." Harlowe nodded to Sackett's car down the street.

True started the car. "Where to?"

***

Two hats approached. Jeter looked out from behind a pile of trash. The trash dump by Centennial Field had heaps of garbage—little hills to hide amongst.

When they were close enough to recognize, Jeter popped out. "H'dy, Cap'n!"

Jeter looks like he expects something, True thought.

"I haven't any money for liquor," Harlowe told him.

"Then maybe I ain't gonna tellya what I found out." Jeter had got on Lamar's crew, spreading concrete.

"Let's hear it," said Pratt.

"Bootleggin.' That's how he made his money—*'riginally."*

"Go on."

"They say Cory run a boat—when they first had Prohibition. Freighted the stuff in at Magnolia Bluff."

"I'll be darned."

"He was pals with Pender—for sure! That's why Pender's instinct was t'stop yer damned nosin' around that night."

"Yeah."

"Y'can be sure Ledbetter he'ped on this end."

357

"Coverin' for the boy, then?"

"What the hell d'ya think? Yes!" Jeter pulled a crumpled newspaper clipping from his pocket. "See this? This is what you're up against. See, it's time for the High Sheriff's yearly moonshine raid!"

Harlowe read it.

"Ledbetter gits his name in the paper. That fella loses a little this month, but he's back in bidness for the rest of the year. Ledbetter gets a li'l fee for his trouble. That's how it is in Leon County—why don't ya get wise to yourself and quit bein' so damned righteous—what's it got ya?"

Jeter nearly fell over. "Pratt, I need a bottle, now. Real bad." He wobbled on his knees. "Please."

"Don't let me down," said Harlowe, the rain dripping from his hat.

"Ya done a lot fur me, Pratt. I ain't forgit it."

"All right. Anything else?"

"He's got a lot of people in his pocket. Ledbetter's gotten used to havin' money. Just bought that five hunerd acre farm west of town."

"Yeah."

"He's not gonna let ya jus' shut off the spigot. Lamar an', ah."

"Uh-huh?"

"T'tell ya the truth, I'm a little riled."

"Whaddya mean?"

"They don't think too much o' me—at that job. Talk to me like I'm so much white trash. Mother didn't raise no trash, now! I'd like to say somethin' to that foreman. Sure thinks he's smart."

"Let 'em think you're dumb. You're no use to me if they know you're listenin' in."

Jeter cussed. "I don't like the way they talk to me!"

"I need your eyes—not your mouth."

"Bah! I love you too, Pratt—I sure do! I'll have ya somethin' big for long, heah?"

***

Tuesday. "Sackett's got a man watchin' the road," Harlowe said. "Let's take Highway Twenty into town."

While Junior Cory was in his classroom, they waited on Gadsden.

Lamar emerged from his home, later than usual. Harlowe closed his watch. 11 a.m.

The La Salle went by them.

"Allright, Let's go," said Harlowe.

True swung out behind it. In front of the Capitol, Monroe funneled down to two lanes. True kept the horse-drawn ice wagon between them as Cory hung out his arm, made a left down Lafayette Street.

They passed the row of gray shacks at the city limits. Pretty green farms began, then—five blocks from the Capitol dome. They turned onto the "Tampa Highway," a narrow, concrete lane that terminated, eventually in that bigger city to the South. There were no other cars in between them, so True—as Harlowe taught him—hung back.

Five miles out, Cory began to slow. Turned down a dirt trail. True pulled to the shoulder. Cattle were grazing aside the road, and looked back at him.

A dusty sedan sped by, leaving town, the hum of tires carrying far down that lonely road until it was gone and they were there, alone.

They got out. Walked into the trees. When they reached the edge of the woods, they could see the twine and stakes for the foundation of what would be a large ranch house overlooking the edge of Lake Lafayette.

Lamar stared out over the twine, a king surveying his posessions.

They followed him back to town. He swung over to the Blue Line Lunchcounter on South Adams. The place looked depressed. Lights out. One man eating chili in the corner. Lamar sat in back. Minutes passed— he looked like he was waiting on someone.

Harlowe hung around by the window. The waitress refilled Lamar's coffee. Presently, the lawyer, Mr. Smalley, walked in. The two men had a hushed, but intense conversation.

Junior's old neighbors, at Gadsden Street, offered nothing but superlatives about the family, and the boy.

"Never an ounce of trouble outta him! I've known him since he was a little fella!"

Harlowe got behind the wheel. Turned South on Gadsden. True noticed Harlowe look up at the mirror. They'd crossed Call Street. "That Ford's still back theah. One o' Ledbetter's men—Mealer."

Harlowe turned the wheel quickly, going up Park Avenue. He turned South on Monroe, put a truck in between him and Mealer, then turned onto College, then Meridian, going into the labyrinth of cross streets, the Model A heeling over in the turns. He skidded to a stop in the driveway of an apartment. Harlowe looked back with a satisfied grin as the deputy's car proceeded haplessly on College.

True marveled at how easily Harlowe gave him the slip!

They picked up with Junior's current neighbors on Pensacola Street.

"Nice enough fella. He ain't in trouble now, is he?"

"No, sir. Just lookin' for some information."

"I can't say one bad thing about him," said the man.

The next house. "Oh, he's a fine fella! Why, he's a father figure to them boys who lost their pappy!"

"Oh—why, that would be Young Lamar Cory, you speak of! Such a fine fella!" gushed an elderly woman.

"I know for a fact he carried them boys in his automobile to all the games. And carried 'em home. Such a good man!" said another.

"Junior started the baseball league for poor kids. Never had anything like that," said the lady next door. "He's so dedicated to the students."

"He even bought them equipment when they couldn't afford it!" said the man across Pensacola. "He helps the elderly people on Sundees, with their yards!"

When Harlowe asked if Junior was home at certain times in late May (when they'd tracked a man in Tate's Hell) the neighbors got sore. "What's this about?" asked the housewife down the block, her hand going to her hip. When they told her they were just looking for information, she shooed them to the door. "You have your nerve prying into his affairs!"

"What is it you wanna know about Junior?" asked an elderly lady.

"Well, what can you tell me about the boy?"

"He's a nice fella. Real nice."

Harlowe asked about his absences the last week of May. She slammed the door and hollered at them, out the window. "He's a fine young man. You oughta be ashamed of yourself, snooping on him!"

Yes, how could *you question him?* He was a picture of normal, all-American looks, like he'd stepped out of an ad for suits in the paper.

They took Highway 20 out of town. Harlowe looked in the mirror, grinned. No one was there.

***

Harlowe took the train to Daytona. He found a lap-sided-and-gingerbread Queen Anne on Beach Street with a small sign by the door: "PRIVATE HOSPITAL & SANITARIUM."

He opened the door. Found a desk with no one sitting behind it. After a long wait, an aloof nurse emerged. "Yes?" As he explained who he was, her face had one position—a frown. It looked more stern as she raised an eyebrow, "Oh, we cannot tell you that! Our patients' records must remain private!"

"Can you tell me if you had such a patient here?"

"Just a moment!"

She disappeared down the hall—entering a side door. She emerged after a quarter hour. "Yes, he was a patient here. Now, if you'll excuse me?"

"Jus' one more question, ma'am. I'd like to know when he was admitted?"

"I cannot divulge that information!"

***

True creased the *Democrat* to the bit about Junior's youth league—they'd listed the names of the boys.

Harlowe and True found a lean-to apartment in back of the house. It was noisy by the tracks. The rattling trains, the crate and box factory.

They knocked. Said who they were. Mrs. Cotton bade them in.

Hats off, they perched in a tiny living room-kitchen-bedroom. "Oh, he's a godsend, that man—he even picks up the boys for practice!"

"Ma'am?"

"Ya gotta holler over this train! Wait til it's past! Where was I?"

"You were sayin' he picks up the boys?"

"Yes, sir. Picks them up—right in front of the house! Even helps them with their homework! My husband died, so it's been wonderful having help. I've ever heard him say anything out of the way. Never."

361

"Next one is 309 East Gaines," said True. They found a peeling, wooden house, the walk overtaken by weeds, a listing outhouse in back. They stepped over empty cans on the porch. Knocked.

"Don't look like nobody's home," thought True, looking in the windows. Harlowe could see in the front window. And agreed.

They drove to the intersection of Lafayette and Boulevard, a swath of red clay mud, finding a rooming house the years had not been kind to. They crossed the porch—a collection of rotting planks and flaking paint. Harlowe rapped on the screen door. A radio blared *Gang Busters* from inside. "Jus' come in! I'm listening to my program!" hollered an old man.

The screendoor protested their entry. A palmetto bug raced between them as they walked down the hall. The man in the chair—the landlord—didn't look at them or speak any further—his ear was to the cabinet, trying to hear the show. He motioned down the hall to the woman standing beneath the solitary lightbulb, talking into the payphone.

The hall reeked. Scribbled phone numbers filled in the lighter spots of peeling wallpaper adjacent the phone. The woman doodled a flower while she gabbed, wedged between the "blower" and the stairs.

"Sure, Phil, that'll be fine!"

She looked over at Harlowe. *"Just a minute,"* she mouthed.

"Say, I gotta go Phil. Yeah. You'll pick me up—okay."

They took their hats off. Introduced themselves.

"Oh, so that's it."

"We jus' wanna talk to ya."

"About what? I haven't done anything."

Harlowe explained it was about Cory. "Maybe we can talk inside?"

But she was already sore. "What's he done? Why are you *skulking* around?"

"We're just lookin' for some information."

"Same as accusing.' Look, my old man left. Need I say more? Mr. Cory is nice to my kid—he's been swell!"

"We're not accusing anyone, just trying—."

"He has his methods and he's a great coach. He's trying to do all he can for the boys—."

"Miss, if you'll--."

"You got some nerve!" She aimed her cigarette at Harlowe's feet. Her heels clicked down to her door which she banged shut.

True read their list. "Elzie Parramore."

They found the apartment on West St. Augustine Street, mere blocks from the Capitol, a muddy, dirty street lane of woodframe apartment houses, shacks occupied by dirt-poor whites. Standing water reached out from the street to nearly cover the yard of the house.

A naked child stood in the doorway, crying. A barefoot young woman was hanging dingy laundry next door.

They walked around, through the mud, to a back apartment.

No one answered.

"Next one. A father this time. Typewriter repairman."

They stopped at the corner of St. Augustine Road and Gadsden Street. "That's it—the roomin' house." The back stoop was soft underfoot. What wasn't rotting was gray-weathered. The capitol dome loomed over the roof, the dingy sheets and nightshirts on the line, over the sour smell of chickens that confronted them.

They entered. Found the apartment to the left.

"I can't do much for my boy," said Mr. Newlin. "But baseball's something for him to believe in! Young Mr. Cory is a great coach. A leader! He's doin' all he can for the boys!"

"Yessir, but--."

"Just what are you trying to do? He's a young teacher and people are jealous and try to cause trouble for him! He has his methods. He-he's a great coach!"

It was the same every family they visited.

"He's a fine fella. Does so much for the youngsters!"

They went back and talked to the man they'd missed on Gaines. Same refrain! The man was put out that they were suspicious of the coach!

"He's Florence Nightingale and Lou Gehrig all rolled into one," said Harlowe, as they got in the car.

"Yeah."

"It's bewilderin', True, the people actin' so. Like you caint question 'im."

"It sure is. Like they're all readin' from a script."

"Yeah, like recitin' a creed or somethin' in church."

It *was* like a religious devotion. Harlowe heard of preachers holding sway over folk like that—Elmer Gantry types. Harlowe had met his share of hucksters, snake oil salesman, but this was different. Maybe harder to contend with. He was exploiting what the parents felt over their boys getting a chance to play ball and get an education they otherwise couldn't afford.

Harlowe and True sat in the car as Junior Cory dismissed the children at the grammar school.

The kids walking up the street, past Harlowe's Ford.

"Let's go."

True pulled from the curb, following Junior.

They took side streets West, keeping Junior's car in sight, block after block.

"Only one man to look out for at night."

True nodded. Ledbetter only had on deputy on duty after sundown.

True pulled to the curb down the street from Junior's bungalow. He yawned. It would be a long night.

***

They talked to the parents of Junior's former students, from 1935, on. It took some doing just getting a list—a young mother who lived on Franklin Street, was—after they explained about Gibby—very helpful.

"Next one. Mrs. Young. 303 S. Boulevard Street," said Harlowe.

"Another roomin' house."

They walked down the dimly lit hall. The landlord was snapping peas, sitting on a stool in back. His bangs fell over his eyes like a sleepy terrier. They told him who they were looking for. "Is this her apartment?"

He nodded.

True knocked. The sound of little kids playing and someone running a sweeper on the floors filled in the void. True knocked again. "The boy should be in school," Harlowe reckoned. No one answered.

"Won't do ya no good to beat on it—she's at work," said the landlord, barely looking up from his basket.

"Yeah? Would ya happen to know where she works?"

He shook his head.

True found out, from another lady in the building, that Mrs. Young worked at the New-Way Laundry—612 S. Copeland.

The press hissed. Machinery droned. The place was steamy and confining. "Oh, hello! Picking something up?" hollered the man at the counter.

"Well, I was wonderin' if you could help me. I understand Mrs. Young Works here."

The man nodded to the washers. They walked past as a man, eyes nearly closed, squeezed a steam press on a pair of britches. It banged and hissed loudly.

Mrs. Young was about thirty-five, stout, her mouth a small straight line on a square face. They introduced themselves.

Her brown eyes revealed surprise. "Apalachicola—I've never even been there."

"We just have a few questions about your son's coach."

She shook her head. "Some kind of trouble?

"No. Just lookin' for a little information," said Harlowe, giving his easygoing grin.

"Your son is seventeen now?"

"Sixteen."

"He was in Mr. Cory's class when he was first employed as a schoolteacher?"

"Yes. It's been a few years."

"Nineteen-hunnerd-and-thirty-five?" Harlowe knew Junior began teaching the 7th grade then.

"Yes. Finley was twelve when they met. What's it all about?"

"What kind of man is Mr. Cory?"

"Oh, he's a great man. The boys set a lot of store in him."

"Coachin' and all?"

"Yes, baseball—it's been a wonderful thing for Finley. And many of the boys from poor families."

"Have you known him to act unusually in any way?"

"No," said she.

"Have you had any concerns that Mr. Cory has acted in any way to hurt Finley or the other boys."

"Certainly not."

"Has your son had any difficulties?"

"No, he's an excellent student. Gets good grades. He's a good fella," she said. "There's nothing wrong a 'tall."

They thanked her and walked out. "Whaddya think, son?"

"She seemed honest."

"Ya notice her chest rise and fall? How she's breathin'?"

True nodded.

"When I asked her if her son had any difficulties, she lied. Notice all of 'em lost a parent? Mr. Newlin is a widower. Mrs. Young's husband left her."

"He's goin' for them that lost a parent," realized True. Like an animal preying on a wounded critter.

"None of 'em well off. He knew that."

Produce in bins. The doors open, on account of the heat. At Byrd's grocery a man in a work apron stocking shelves greeted Harlowe. Harlowe walked in. Approached the counter which had a cooler below. He asked the boy working there, "Do you know Mr. Cory?"

"He was my coach. Couple years ago. The best I ever had!"

Harlowe thanked him. Left. Located Junior in the stands, watching the ballgame at Centennial Field. Final game of the season. Versus Thomasville.

***

At last Mr. Raines had returned to his office. At least his light was on. Harlowe and True walked in the side door that led up to the offices. They climbed the polished staircase to his door. O. C. RAINES STATE ATTORNEY. Harlowe paused. He knew if he wanted any help from the prosecutor, Raines had to be *convinced*. The old man had been the prosecutor for the entire circuit, for years, and he could be as immovable as the old brick church on Monroe when he wanted to be.

He knocked.

Raines gruffly summoned them back.

True's heart beat a little faster. Raines was an intimidating presence to him.

The old man rose, shot his eyes at True. "Are you old enough to be a deputy?" he spat.

Harlowe accepted the chair offered. He lay a draft subpoena in front of the man.

The prosecutor examined it and grunted. "Let me see if I understand this. You want to get your hands on the boy's sanitarium records?"

"That's right."

"I'm not going to do it. I won't put that boy's momma through that. It was a drowing accident—that you have down there." He shoved the subpoena back at Harlowe.

True looked at the prosecutor and back to Harlowe.

"Don't we owe somethin' to the other boy's momma?" asked Harlowe.

True watched Raines's face flare with anger. "What do you mean by that?!"

"I mean we owe Miss Birch somethin'," Harlowe replied.

Raines jabbed the desk. "You have my decision."

Raines' secretary walked them out.

"I do hope you gentleman have a good day."

True smiled. "Yes, ma'am, you too,"

"Bye, now," said Harlowe.

Harlowe turned to True after the door clicked shut. "Ya know who that is, son?"

"No."

"Her maiden name's Cory. She's Lamar's sister."

True shook his head.

"It's a company town, son. It hasn't changed much...since Sheriff Jones and the convict leases."

***

Raines was on the phone with Lamar.

"I jus' don't understand it. Is he tryin' to railroad my son?" asked Lamar. "Can't you call him off?"

367

"I've tried. He's stubborn. He's got no education, but he sticks to his guns!"

A woman's voice came on.

"This is Junior's mother!"

"Hello, Miss Julia."

"Don't let him go after my boy, Owen."

"This isn't going anywhere."

"Thank you, Owen."

***

They found Judge Bill Anderson stirring a sauce in his kitchen. He lived in a small house on Beard Street. Some thought Anderson mighty young for a judge. First elected in '32, after but a few years as a Leon County judge, he rose to the circuit court. Some thought he didn't look like a judge, either. More like a wrestler, burly, with a stack of thick dark hair. He struck an intimidating presence in court; but now, by the stove in his bathrobe he was downright friendly, thought True. So maybe the man put on a little of that seriousness with his robe? He'd taken over Johnson's small county docket, so he'd "ride circuit" when the local courts were in session, travelling from his Tallahasee residence, to Crawfordville, Apalach, etc.

"I'll take over, dear," his wife told him. "Shoo!"

"Why don't you boys come in here," Anderson said, beckoning them to the living room, which doubled as his study, brown volumes of the Southern Reporter sharing space with Mother Goose and Mary Poppins. The room seemed oddly small with Anderson perched on the easy chair in the corner.

Harlowe laid it out. "Am I off base, Judge?"

Anderson read over the papers. Threw back his tumbler of scotch. Kept reading, raising an eyebrow at the conclusion. "It seems clear-cut to me, Pratt."

"Well, Mr. Raines is again' it."

"Oh? He wouldn't give you the subpoena?"

"No, sir."

"Raines being Raines?"

"If he says somethin' he thinks it's law."

"Yeah. It isn't simply a difference of opinion. Or a debatable point-of-law. What you're up against is a man that has taken the mantle of the law unto himself. When he makes up his mind it's as if he's walked down the mountain with stone tablets. When he says no, why, you can't even question it! He invokes the authority of the church, and he's so used to going unchallenged he thinks anyone who disagrees with him is a heretic! Or a moron!"

Harlowe nodded.

"Not everyone can stand up to that."

At that, the telephone jangled. Anderson walked down the hall to answer it and it became apparent it was Raines himself on the line! They could hear him barking at Anderson from the hall.

The judge replaced the receiver, calmly. Returned to the room. "He gave me an earful!" Anderson looked down, twisting the cap on his fountain pen.

True thought, *we're sunk!*

Then Anderson looked up. "Raines is the state attorney—but he isn't king! We still have a constitution," growled the former fullback. "Y'want me to sign?"

Harlowe nodded.

A twinkle in his eye, True watched him scrawl his John Henry on the paper. Handed it to Harlowe. "We'll make Raines mad—but he'll be more mad *with you!*"

"Yessir."

Harlowe folded the subpoena. "Thankya, judge. We 'preciate ya seein' us."

"Not a'tall."

***

They drove all night. Harlowe handed the paper to the nurse. Presently, she returned with the file.

True looked at Harlowe. The latter nodded. Junior was admitted four weeks after Gibby went missing!

However, the records only showed vague entries, such as, "Dr. counseled patient."

Or nearly unreadable jottings about alcohol treatment.

"Three sheets of paper," remarked True.

"That is all we have!" insisted the nurse.

"Well, may I see...Dr. LaFaye?" Harlowe asked, reading the name off the first page.

"Doctor LaFaye is no longer with us," she answered, robotically.

"Have you any idea where he's gone?"

"I haven't. I heard he retired from the practice."

"Yes'm. May I speak to the doctor in charge?"

"I'm sorry, sir. He isn't here and I haven't any idea when he'll be back."

"All right. Let's go, True."

They caught up with the Doctor who ran the hospital, in a Seabreeze restaurant. "He sure seemed flustered," Harlowe declared.

"He sure did."

SEVENTY-ONE

Montgomery, October

Spotless sidewalks. Immaculate public buildings. In 1928 Lamar sent his son, to the Starke School on Houston Street, three blocks from the Confederacy's first White House. Harlowe and True parked. Walked down the long hall to the commandant's office. The latter received them in his book-lined study. "Junior was a model student, here. No misconduct whatsoever," he told them.

Harlowe nodded.

"One thing does stand out, though."

"Yessir?" Harlowe asked.

"He was involved in a terrible wreck returning home from the school. Nearly died. Train derailed near Foley."

***

They followed Junior home from the grammar school. The door of his Ford didn't close all the way—frustrated, he grabbed the handle and slammed it. He paced beside the car, hands on his face. "He's wound up tighter than an eight-day clock," Harlowe thought.

***

Two days later. The automobile sped toward the coast at midnight. It was the only car on the Sumatra Highway.

Near the old tapper's road, it slowed.

Is that a car? Backed in there? He locked up his brakes. His heart pounding, he palmed the lever into reverse, sand flying as he turned around, his foot to the floorboards.

***

Harlowe saw the headlights. Threw it in gear. Spun tires as the Model A swung out onto the highway.

He bounced over the dip, nearly coming out of the seat.

The car shuddered on the washboard, but Harlowe kept his foot to the floor.

Ford V-8. Maybe a '37. *He's weaving all over the road. Like he's drunk.*

Mile after mile they raced past the pines, parallel with the desolate tracks.

While he gained on the fellow, Harlowe couldn't quite catch the newer car. He'd kept the taillight in sight. Couldn't read the tag! The driver was alone. *The back of a head.*

***

He's still back there. Shall I just stop? No—I'd be ruined!

His eyes were more blurry, the rum catching up with him. He weaved and swerved. Finally those two glowing headlights got smaller.

***

They neared Sumatra. The other fellow skidded on the soft sand. Harlowe could just about read the bouncing numbers now. The first two were "13". *That's Leon County!*

Something went "BANG!" Harlowe wrestled with the wheel, managing to keep the car straight as it plowed into the ditch and slid on the flat tire. He got out to look. Got out the jack. *Damn!*

SEVENTY-TWO

October, 1937. The next week.

They went to see Mrs. Parramore. She let them talk to Elzie. Harlowe was sure nothing had occurred with Cory.

He looked at True. "I'm glad that boy is unharmed. But, damn, it's like pullin' in an empty net."

They drove to see Mr. Newlin.

No answer. "No lights on around the other side," said True.

"He has mail in the box."

True looked in the window. "Looks empty."

The landlady cracked her door. "They's gone. Lit out yesterdee."

"Did Newlin say, why?"

"No."

"How did he seem--."

"Didn't pay attention—he paid me."

CLICK.

They drove downtown. Split up to talk to the shopkeepers. Met at the dump.

"I talked to the man at the fillin' station theyuh."

True nodded.

"Said they left, didn't say anything."

"I tried the A&P. Accounts paid in full over theyuh. Pulled his young'un from skool. Paid up, cash money."

"What does that tell you?"

"They bribed 'im," said True.

Harlowe told Seago, when they returned. "Damn—another one? Looks like they plumb got away with it," said Seago. "You goin' home?"

"Yeah."

***

Brewer left his position by the tapper's road. He'd watched all night. Fighting heavy eyelids he reported to Harlowe. "I saw nothin', boss."

True phoned. "Junior was home all night."

"We'll pick back up with 'im tonight," said Harlowe.

Harlowe talked to folks in Eastpoint about keeping up the watches. They were ready for tonight.

The telephone was jingling when he got back to his office.

"This's Tommy—T.K. was over heah, tryin' to git ahold to ya."

"Did he say what it was about?"

"He saw a fella on the Old Ferry Dock Road."

They ran down the stairs. Seago climbed in back. They crossed the bridge running as fast as the Ford would go.

They found Brewer crouched on the side of the road. The sun had set to treetop level, and he was examining something in the shadow.

"No footprints. I drove up the road, theah. Saw the boy in the treeline. I hollered at him—he took off runnin'."

"Back into the woods?"

"Into Tate's Hell, yessir."

Brewer turned to Seago. "He run from me—fast. Thataway."

"Show me," said Harlowe.

Brewer got in. They drove to the Fulton property line. "Right heah, yes."

Harlowe checked for footprints. Saw none. He walked back to the treeline, then stepped through the vines, into the woods. "He sat there a spell. See that impression in the weeds theah?"

True nodded. The stranger was watching the house. Just sitting there. It made the hair on True's neck stand. "You can see the back door from here, easy—where Florie and Little Foss sleep."

"I know it."

"Want I should send for a dog?" asked Seago.

"Yeah."

Seago ran to his Ford. Raced away to phone for one.

It was Wednesday—and *daylight*. Harlowe cussed.

Toting his coach gun, Harlowe entered Tate's Hell, True behind him with his Remington.

Into the labyrinth. Harlowe stopped at a Y formed by the gap between huge saw palmetto and two hog trails, each leading further into the woods. He looked down them. Then noticed something. Took a step closer to examine it. A single strand—from a spider—stretched across the trail at shoulder height. "Look here." He pointed to where the rest of the web had been torn down. "He went thisaway." Harlowe pointed down a narrower gap that branched off to the right.

They moved through the gap. It was darker, the sun dropping midway down the pines now.

Harlowe stopped where the trail dead-ended at wall of saw palmetto. Carefully, he looked each way. It was light enough to see down the trail a ways, but dark enough half a company of men could be hiding among the black titi.

He went right. Ahead, odd tracks crossed the trail. In the black mud.

"Whaddya think, son?"

"Them's deer hooves."

"Yep. They run right across here." They run from thick woods and shrubs, across the trail, into the thick woods again. "What else y'see?"

True pointed to some pine straw that had been disturbed. "Deer wouldna done that."

"You're right. He squeezed through theah. An' went on."

They kept going. It grew darker. The foliage thicker. The sun had retreated further. *A bad hombre could be hiding close enough to touch your sleeve, you wouldn't see him until he had ahold of you!* True realized.

True pushed a branch aside, carefully, while he stepped over a fallen limb, vines grabbing at him as he threaded his way in. *This place could swallow a man whole!*

There's no sign of the stranger. Only more leaves and twigs and vines to push through. It's dead quiet. So quiet he could feel it in his ears—his pounding heartbeat as loud as a foundry.

They kept on. It seemed like miles.

Harlowe stopped. Pointed at something. More pine straw the man had run through.

They couldn't see but a yard at a time, the woods were so thick. Harlowe listened for any sort of movement.

They eased to small openings in the vines and brush where they could look. In some spots they had to move sideways, squeezing through tree trunks and palmetto.

Suddenly there was a snap! Loud as a gunshot! Like someone took a step!

Harlowe, fearing an ambush, went still, and True did likewise.

Neither could see past the scrub. The big pines were perfect hiding places and the bad man could pick them off easily if they moved!

They heard running, boots crashing through saw palmetto!

They ran after the sound, dashing from the cover of one pine to the next. Harlowe then True.

Harlowe motioned for him to stop. *Listen!*

Heck, y'hear somethin', but ya caint see where it's comin' from! He can see us, but we caint see him! True realized.

"Stay back, True!" And Harlowe took off running, headlong now, bullets be damned! True tried to keep up. He didn't know Harlowe could run so fast!

But it wasn't enough. The other fellow's faster!

True never caught a glimpse of him!

Finally, Harlowe halted, out of breath.

"He's gone!" Harlowe gasped. "No tellin'...where he went. Y'see 'im?"

True shook his head.

"He took off like a deer."

It was nearly dark. They could only see in gray. True noticed his uncle had been cut by the vines. Was bleeding.

Just then, True heard something behind him!

He took cover, aiming the shotgun at the sound. *Where'd it come from?!*

Harlowe got behind a pine. Swung the side-by-side at the shadow. "Git them hands up! An' come out!"

The shadow seemed to move.

Then disappeared.

Suddenly, something brushed True's leg! *What the hell!* True nearly fell to the ground as he brushed him, knocking True off balance, the black bear lumbering back into the darkness!

Harlowe grinned.

True caught himself on the tree but hadn't caught his breath.
"Yeah...caint say I was evuh tripped...by a bear!"

They followed the path taken by the human. Torn vines. Small clues as to his course. True felt eyes watching with every step, but whatever man or critter it was, now, he did not know.

Another quarter hour or half hour passed. It was hard to gauge. *"Where are we, exactly,"* True wondered. *"Are we lost?"* They were deep in the woods, further than True had ever been.

"We're headed East, I believe."

They worked their way through to a gap. It was True that noticed them: The ruts the mule teams used—years ago.

They followed them out to the Sumatra Road. They'd reached the highway. But it was miles from where Harlowe thought. They headed south. "Well...maybe someone'll pick us up," thought Harlowe.

True nodded. The road was lonesome. Only the sounds of the crickets. The sky had cleared, the moonlight making the sand below their feet oddly white. "Might be a while for we see a car."

After a quarter hour, they saw headlights. Two round eyes. The car crept along in low gear, toward them. *Who's that?* wondered True.

"It's C. A.!" Harlowe exclaimed.

The jailor pulled his Ford alongside. "Whachy'all fight a panther?"

"We sure are glad to see you!" said Harlowe.

"I'm glad to see y'all!"

Then, arriving from Estiffanulga, was the man with his dog.

"Let's look up the road," said Harlowe. They piled in and Seago drove them north, toward Sumatra.

"Stop at the old loggin' road."

The dog was barking in the car behind them. Harlowe shined his light.

"Y'want 'im to put the dog out?" asked Seago.

"No, he's gone. In an automobile," said Harlowe.

"Damn."

***

True walked his "beat." He listened to Greek words flowing out of the kitchen of the *Riverside.*

Mrs. Slocumb, watering her flowers, called "Good Morning!"

Her roses made the side of her house seem like a ticker-tape parade of yellow and pink.

"They sure are pretty!"

"Thankya! I'm right proud of those!"

An old black gentleman in striped shirt and spectacles swept in front of his store on "The Hill," stopped to wave to him.

***

Two gray hats turned up Junior's walkway. The brims shaded the men from the hot sun. The hats had an ominous appearance, like approaching storm clouds, thought Junior, peeking out the window.

"The neighbor lady saw his car was gone during the relevant time," said True.

"He has no alibi," Harlowe declared.

They knocked.

No answer. True knocked again. Junior's heart thumped in his chest.

"We gotta catch 'im," said Harlowe. "We'll sit out at the county line ev'ry night if we have to."

SEVENTY-THREE

Apalachicola—October, 1937

Sunrise. Ticking motors of oysterboats. Baking bread mixing with the salt-air.

True walked along 4th Street, past the Fuller. Cheerfully, Belle Jenkins called from the door of the kitchen. "Good mornin'!" She tossed True a hot biscuit. "Y'have a good day, now! Be careful!" said the old colored woman.

"Yes, ma'am!"

He walked down Market Street. Mr. Fortunas stopped his car to say hello.

True liked making the rounds in Apalach.

***

The patients being led through the corridor gave True a chill.

The nurse unlocked the door. "Please, this way."

She led them down a hall to a small office. Elston thrust out his hand. "Hello Harlowe!" His other hand held a Camel, of course. "Sit down, boys. Sit down."

"Doc, I got a question you might could answer."
"Yes—what is it?"
Harlowe explained about the sanitarium.

"That's often a euphemism," Elston explained.

"Uh-huh."

"People are sent away because of a psychiatric problem, but it's more palatable to label them a drunk than nuts—or a sex fiend, a sex deviant, as the case may be."
Harlowe nodded.
"I would like to bring in Dr. Cotillard. Do you mind?"
"No, sir."
At that Elston reached for the phone. "Cotillard! Elston, here. Yes, could you come to my office? Good."
The young psychiatrist appeared, presently.
"He was fourteen, you say?" asked Cotillard.

"Yessir. Fourteen at the time o' the disappearance."

"Certainly is shocking, so young," agreed Cotillard.

"Could a boy that age do something like that?" Harlowe asked.

"Well, I think so. Capability, from a psychiatric point of view, may form. Strength and size being present, why, age may not be a decisivie factor in the least."

"He was a husky fella."

"This really bothers you, doesn't it, Pratt?" asked Elston.

"Well, you look at his life. He obeys the law. Follows the rules. No marks against him, helps everyone. Somewhow, *it almost convicts him.* I know it caint be so, and *that's* no proof, but it's like hiding a conterfeit bill in a stack of good ones, you wouldn't even be looking for it."

"The crime is in the 'absence,' it's hiding in plain sight in what looks normal and good," said Elston.

"Yes," agreed Cotillard.

"There are medical problems that go hidden for years that way. Then all of a sudden—." Elston snapped his fingers. "And you hear it said, 'No one saw it coming.' Cancer. Heart conditions. And now, psychosis."

The psychiatrist adjusted his glasses, reflecting on the problem. "Oh, yes, and in the situation you describe, this 'absence' makes the job of the detective so much harder, combining his job with that of the psychiatrist, perhaps."

***

They parked near the Caroline Brevard School. Presently, the younger Cory climbed in his coupe. Motored away.

He sat down at the counter at the Seminole Café. 104 ½ South Monroe. Alone.

Driscoll was I nthere. He'd put on weight, Harlowe noticed. The moonshiner lay money on the table in back. Began to leave. Suddenly, he stopped and clapped Junior on the shoulder. Harlowe read the man's lips. *"Don't worry, boy."* Harlowe nodded to True who slipped out the back, to the alley. Presently, Harlowe paid for his coffee, folded his paper and left.

He found True by Fain's Drug. "'Don't worry, boy.'"

"That's what he said?"

"Yep."

5:00 p.m. The teacher was still grading papers. He stayed late. Went to bed early.

When they returned to Apalach, Harlowe found a letter on his desk. Opened it. "Junior attended the men's college," said Harlowe. "I wrote the

Sheriff down theah. This says, 'Lamar Cory, Junior has no record of arrests while attending the university and there are no 'unsolved' crimes regarding missing boys in Alachua County.'"

SEVENTY-FOUR

Apalachicola, October

Hard times were getting harder.

Sheip's closed. Its smokestacks loomed, silently, over the town, as jarring as a funnel cloud.

Harlowe heard his friend, Ed, was leaving Apalach, rather than wait and see if its doors would open again.

Harlowe wiped his brow. At least he had the benefit of a second man again, a jurisdiction as vast as his.

He assigned Brewer to Carrabelle. The latter wasn't happy about the move, but Harlowe kidded him a little. "It'll give you some experience for when when you run agin' me."

True would work the Western end of the county. Harlowe was already sending him on calls.

***

You don't see too many new cars in Apalach, the curbs lined with black Model T's, interrupted, on occasion, by a tourist parking something with a brighter hue. Likewise, T.K. Brewer's REO was a little newer, shinier than the typical, looking as smart as his tailored gray pinstripe. His Daddy's store had 'hung on' and the man had ambition. People thought he looked like a sheriff—in the mold of Gentleman Bill Ledbetter.

Brewer tried to warn Harlowe what he was contending with. "Lamar's an important man. You don't want him getting' aggravated with you!"

Harlowe was listening, Brewer thought. But he didn't seem convinced. "Boss, you caint prove it was the boy! This case will—we'll all catch hell for it, if ya keep on. C. A., y'see it, donchya? That there ain't enough on 'im?"

"I don't see the State's Attorney bringin' that to a grand jew-ree, no, sir."

"There's more to it," Harlowe insisted. "I know it."

"They own that town. Lamar and them," warned Seago.

Brewer smiled when he saw the paper—his name on the front page. He showed Seago and Harlowe.

"DEPUTIES RAID STILL."

"Carrabelle, eh?" asked the jailor. Everyone knew Brewer's family "interests" were safe in Apalach and Eastpoint.

"We oughtta do more of it, boss! Let folks know what we're doin'! Matt-of-fact, there's a still on the island," Brewer believed.

Harlowe wasn't enthusiastic. "Go look if you wanna go."

***

The back door of the Floridan Hotel. They saw Junior use it. Harlowe and True followed up the staircase.

Harlowe eased to the corner where he could get a look down the hall. It's s narrow, low-ceilinged, like the passageway of a ship. Junior receded down the red carpet until he found Room 312. He tapped at the door. Was admitted.

They heard the elevator stop. Footsteps on the carpet. A prosperously rotund man in light gray suit. He grew bigger until Harlowe recognized the face of the Governor. He stopped at 312. The personable voice of the one who answered the door was known to Harlowe, also—Lamar. The door clicked behind them.

True followed Harlowe, silently, to the door. They couldn't hear what was said through it. Just muffled talk.

Harlowe stepped out onto the fire escape, leaving True to watch the hall.

It was stuffy in the rooms. Consequently, the windows were opened. Harlowe eased to the iron stairs on the fire escape. Crouching under them, he was able to listen to the talk drifting from Room 312, without drawing attention from below. The politicians' voices carried.

Harlowe recognized that of Senator Thurman Ensley, who represented Franklin and Liberty Counties.

Lamar Senior clicked his lighter open for the latter.

"Hmph, fine cigar, Lamar—mighty fine."

"Like I told you fellas, it's nothing compared to what I have planned—if everyone plays ball."

"Sure, Lamar."

"Plenty of money for me. And a little left over for Senator Thurman Ensley!"

"Don't forget about me," said the governor.

"I ain't."

"So you wanna get Junior into law school? That shouldn't be too hard," said the Governor.

"Yeah, and in a few years he runs for the House," said Lamar. *"And we have another man we can rely on."*

"It's all fallin' in to place," said Ensley.

"It's a cinch! Junior practices law a few years, gets his name out there. We'll get the papers t'play 'im up, good. Get those dirt-farmers and shopkeepers t'vote the right way. And he's in."

"Your daddy's pretty smart," said the Governor.

"Yessir."

The crowing drifted out to Harlowe's ears.

"Congratultions, Bill! So long, Bobby!"

He heard the others say their goodbyes. Harlowe moved behind the door, watching though the crack. The Senator left from the sidedoor on Call, below him.

Harlowe descended the fire escape. Hid behind a car in the alley. Watched Lamar get in his La Salle.

True heard Junior say, "so long!" Slid back to the corner of the hall. When Lamar left, True went out the back way. Found Harlowe in the car.

Harlowe had a little note. "Found this. He said to meet him at the dump." Harlowe tore it up.

They proceeded to the spot near the municipal power station. Listened to the hiss of the boilers. No people in sight. Harlowe checked the mirror— no one following. He turned into the dump.

Jeter scurried out from behind a pile of ash.

"All right. What can you tell me?"

"Git me a beer an' I tell-ya!"

"Come on."

"Driscoll-n'-Lamar's thick-as-thieves—Driscoll will do anythin' Lamar tells 'im to!"

"Go on."

"Lamar's *good* friends with the shureff and the state's attorney."

"I know that."

"Lamar paid for the Guv'ner's inaugural barbeque! Betcha didn't know that! Lamar he'ped Ledbetter during the last vote—he coulda bought two Cadillacs from Mr. Proctor over theah!"

"Okay."

"If ya think that's somehtin' there are rich folks outta town who he hunts with. New York. And so on. Real money!"

"It fits what Collis' wife said—about the Tallahassee man being powerful," Harlowe reckoned.

"Y'may not want to mess with Lamar."

"Yeah?"

"Tol-ya 'bout 'is bootleg days. He woulda killed a youngun if he got in his way."

"Yeah, what have ya heard?"

"Nothin' definite. Heard Lamar took a shot at a rum-runner—out in the Guff. The boy 'horned in' on 'is bidness."

"Lamar has had people killed. I have no doubt," said Seago. "Y'remember that lawyer keeled in the wreck in Sopchoppy?"

"I remember," said Harlowe. "Car stalled on the tracks, killed the man and his galfriend."

"There's talk he was Lamar's lawyer and that car didn't stall," Seago replied.

They found the October 1926 newspaper. *"G.F.&A...Overland car...Sopchoppy...1926 ...tragedy."*

They went to see the engineer when his train stopped in Carrabelle.

"I sure thought it was odd. Didn't see the driver movin' a' tall!" The engineer threw his hands up. "That was about the time Sheriff Jones was removed. A lot of things happnin' then. Bootleggers. You name it!"

"Yessir?"

"I didn't ask too many questions. I'm just an ol' train driver, you understand. What do I know about automobile accidents? But it sure didn't seem to add up!"

"Yessir."

The man was still troubled by the wreck. "There was no time to stop, boys—even runnin' thirty miles-an-hour, y'need a quarter-mile!"

***

Harlowe and True went upriver. Uncle Tiny was cleaning some channel cats. "I jus' come out to guidefish, now. Make me some money—off these Yankees!"

They laughed.

"Otherwise, I don' come to town."

"You used to run a boat for a fella."

"Didn't know you knowed about that! Yeah, I used to run a boat. Them boys' brought in rum liquor to the island. They had a fishin' smack I'd sail for 'em. Take it in to the island. Then they had someone else tote it to Eastpoint where they had 'em a car waitin'. Didn't do it too long."

"Why's that?"

"I don't like workin' for someone else. Wuddint long before I got crossways with this ol' boy—you know 'im."

"Lamar?"

Tiny nodded.

Harlowe asked him about the lawyer.

"He had that feller keeled, sure. He ask me to do it. Now, if someone needs killin' that's one thing. This feller had a wife and a sick young'un. Lamar wuddint too happy with me after I said 'no' to that deal."

"Did Foss work for 'im?" asked True.
"Some. Maybe yo deddy took a few secrets to 'is grave. He ain't keeled no one, I can tell ya that—might make ya feel a fair piece better."

"You know anything about Lamar and Pender?" asked Harlowe.

"I know some things, but I don't wanna git keeled. I done told ya enough. Ya foller the scent where ya think it goes."

***

Lamar looked through the Redfield scope, sighting in on him. Lining up the sights on his heart, as he stood there unawares. *"My, he's a big fella!"*

Lamar breathed. Squeezed the trigger. The report crackled. It sounded oddly remote, like he was somewhere watching from afar. Time slowed. Lamar's heart beat much faster than the passing seconds.

The buck ran, thinking he wasn't mortally wounded. But the .30-06 bullet had pierced vital organs, and after a dash into the saw palmetto, the big fellow fell with a thud. The report, the hoofbeats subsided, it was dead silent in the pinelands near Whiskey George Creek.

Cory ran to see! Called to his colored man to help him carry the big boy home!

The Negro paced off the shot. "Dat's two-hunnuhd yahds, Massa Lamah! Yazzah, he sho' is a beaut!"

SEVENTY-FIVE

October, 1937

Sheip's lights came back on, the mill cutting furniture, board lumber. The town was glad to have it.

The phone rang—Jeter.

"Y'hear? Up by Whiskey George creek—kilt a buck at two-hunnerd yards. It's in the paper up heah. He's a good shot, son."

CLICK.

They got in the car. Headed North. They tailed along as Lamar went to inspect a new road. The outdoorsman wore khakis. Slouch hat. Harlowe could see he also had a rifle in the backseat.

They were pouring between Quincy and Tallahassee. Lamar had the contract to reroute US-90 on a straight shot, West. Harlowe and True slipped back through the woods to their car.

True looked over at Harlowe, as if to ask, *'What next?'*

"Well, I b'lieve it's time we talk to *Lamar Junior.*"

They parked in front of the school. Walked down the hall. Right into Junior's classroom. He looked up from the papers he was grading, startled.

Harlowe lay the photo on his desk. "Gibby Birch. From Eastpoint. Eight-years-old."

"He looks about eight, I suppose. What's this about? I'd like to help you, but what has this to do with me?" *This fella is cool,* Harlowe saw. *Didn't miss a beat.*

"The boy went missin' right after this photograph was taken."

"That same boy? My goodness!"

"You were theah when this was taken. You've been avoidin' us. We'd jus' like to talk to ya about that boy."

"I'm afraid I don't—I haven't been avoiding you. I'd be happy to help you, if I knew what it was you were after."

"You know where we're from?"

"Why, yes. I imagine you fellas had a long drive. You drove all this way to speak to me?"

"We were in the area."

"I wish I could help you fellas, I'm sure I don't know anything that would be of any use. Nothing I can recall—perhaps you can refresh my memory about what it is you're wanting to know."

"You were there with your daddy. The boy showed off his fish to you and your friends, theah."

"Where?"

"Indian Creek."

"Well, you may be right. You see, my father used to take us there—fishing. Before he expanded his business, and before my brothers and I started playing baseball—at Leon High. Does that help you, Mr. Harlowe?"

The latter nodded.

"Now, the boy I don't recall. He may have showed us the fish. That's certainly possible."

"That's your father, theah."

"Yes."

"He remembered the boy."

Cory shrugged as if to say, *'Well, there you have it.'*

"Do you like children, Mr. Cory?"

"If I didn't I'm in the wrong profession. Sure, I like children." The man was unflappable—looked Harlowe in the eye throughout. "I still don't know what all this is about, Mr. Harlowe. I'd like to help you, but I'm not sure I can. Now if you would tell me how I'm supposed to fit in this, maybe I can clear it up."

"You'd like to clear it up, then?"

"Sure—like I said, I want to help if I can! I've no reason not to, I just don't know this boy, never saw him after he told us about the fish, and I know nothing more about it."

"You spoke to him then?"

"Yes, I assume so, based on what you said. I'm sure he ran along afterwards. I don't recall any child spending too much time with us—not this one or any other."

"This little fella." Harlowe held up the photo. "I think you talked to him. You talked to him about baseball. You talked to him about fishin'. You befriended him. He walked with you and your daddy down to the Bluff."

"If that were so I'd tell you. I've no reason to lie to you, Mr. Harlowe."

Harlowe looked at the childrens desks. They were too small to sit in. He pulled a chair from the corner, sat astride it. Looked at Junior. The latter confidently smoothed the paper on his desk. "Is there anything else I can answer, Mr. Harlowe?"

"Yes. Your property bordered Whittle."

"Yes."

"You did somethin' you shouldn't have—Whittle called you on it."

"No. Now, I'm very busy, as you can see."

"Your friend Mr. Driscoll caint erase what happened."

"I don't know any Driscoll. I don't know him."

"Oh?"

"I mean, I know who he is, is all."

"You've been to Whiskey George?"

"I've hunted there with my daddy."

True's eyes went back and forth from Harlowe to Junior, like a tennis match. He couldn't get a read on the teacher. He certainly didn't reveal anything, True thought.

Jr. almost seemed to be enjoying this conversation. "Something else, Mr. Harlowe?"

"Uh--." Harlowe scratched his chin. "You're not a bad fella. 'Cause I know it bothers ya. I saw the flowers you left. Maybe you're ill. Maybe there's a way to get better. If ya come clean, I'll help ya. Do all I can for ya."

"Mr. Harlowe, thank you—but, I'm in no need of help."

Harlowe crossed his arms. "I'm gonna find out. I'm patient."

They walked back to the car. Got in.

Harlowe turned to True. "He done it."

There was no doubt in Harlowe's eyes, True saw—he nodded.

"I'm gonna need your help to get 'im, son."

***

Hoyt Conway walked into the room at the Floridan. "Harlowe's here right under your noses. Two or three nights a week."

Ledbetter and Raines cussed.

"I tell ya I never trust a quiet man," said the State's Attorney.

Ledbetter jabbed his cigarette. "If he says anything, why, they'll believe us."

"I'm jus' tellin' ya," said the shamus.

"He has an obsession with this," said Raines. He sounded like he was describing a disease.

"If I was murdered I'd want him on the case," said Conway. "I'm tellin' ya, I wouldn't mess with Harlowe. Don't let that country house builder business fool ya. I saw him up close when he was workin' for the Seaboard line. You think he's dumb, then watch out, he's got ya." He made a movement like hooking a fish.

"Bah!" Raines scoffed.

"He must have an angle. What's he think he'll gain?" Lamar wondered.

"He thinks it gets him votes. He thinks it helps him with those people down there," said Raines.

"Maybe find a way to...live with Harlowe," said Conway.

"Get him to see the light," said Raines.

"Naturally I'm not going to beg him," said Lamar.

"Naturally." Lamar grinned, understanding they were talking his language—money.

***

October, 1937

The Yankees battled the Giants in the World Series. The radio at the Riverside blared the announcer, the plink of the bat. Harlowe leaned against the wall outside, where it was cooler, listening through the screendoor.

Hot, he carried his coat back to the jailhouse. No breaks in the case. And that was Conway's car parked down the street.

***

The phone rang—Ledbetter. The small talk seemed to be leading to a point, and it did. "You're really lookin' in to him—the schoolteacher? Why, he's *Lamar Cory's* son!"

"That makes no difference to me," Harlowe replied.

"I admire that, Pratt. I really do. Stop by see me at the house, hear?"

***

They sat in True's car, watching. The door opened. The teacher emerged.
"All right. Here we go."
True mashed the starter.
Cory backed out his driveway. A moment later, True eased out from the curb, following the newer Ford to a house on Georgia Street. Junior rang the bell and a woman in a pretty dress climbed in his car with him.
"He has a girl?" wondered True.
"It sure looks thataway."

They followed Cory out of town, toward Lake Lafayette.
Out in the country, the darkness was broken by a glow of lights, strung along a driveway. Junior turned down it, finding the end of the line of cars which stretched from the highway to the sprawling new ranch house at the end.

"Housewarming party," reckoned Harlowe.
Another car slowed and pulled off from the highway. "That's Ledbetter."
"Yeah," said Harlowe.
"Let's go. I reckon that's all we're gonna see tonight."
They drove back. Hungry children stood in open doorways, in shanties by the tracks.

They slipped past Sackett's car. Sped toward home.

***

"Junior Cory's Mother never leaves the big house on Gadsden."
They rang the bell. No answer.
Deputy Durfee pulled up in his car. "No one's home," he told them.

***

November, 1937

"JR. CORY ELOPES"

County commissioner Corbin Huff dropped the paper on Harlowe's desk.
He gave him a look, As if to say, *"You're a fool for pokin' the hornets nest.'"*

Seago held it up.

"Yeah, I know," said Harlowe.

"He makes the paper. Gets sympathy. You're suspectin' 'im, but the paper plays it up how nice a feller he is."

391

"We talk to 'im and four weeks later, he's getting married."

"That too!"

***

True walked "his beat." It was a cold, clear night. He could see his breath. Mr. Sangaree, the barber, greeted him.

"Howdy, Miss Hilda!" The telephone operator was going home. "Have a good evenin', True!"

Kids drove past. "Hey, Mr. True!"

He walked along Market Street. The covered sidewalk, awnings, down the block, made a tunnel. He looked out to the end, and a full moon. Walked to the corner, stopping by the penny scale at Creekmore's.

He passed beneath the old Ruge Canning offices, closed now, on Water Street. They were cotton warehouses a hundred years ago.

The freight train bellowed. Mixing with the sounds from the picture show and the machinery of the ice plant as he walked along.

***

People won't talk. "Ledbetter's blockin' us," said Harlowe.

Behind the city incinerator, Jeter waited, half-lit.

"Got a cigarette?"

Harlowe handed him the pack.

"Thanks. Lamar and them got their first road work with no experience—none whatever."

Harlowe handed him a match. "Yeah?"

"I'm tellin' ya—Lamar never poured so much as a driveway! But somehow he got 'im the State Road contract!" Jeter took a drag with shaky hands. "They set him up with it—his daddy worked at the road department, see? That's how Lamar walked in and got 'im that contract."

"Go on."

"This thing goes back years. His father—he come up with the Guv'ner, y'see?"

"All right."

"He set up that big operation usin' money he made from Prohibition. He paved the Tampa Highway." Another puff. "Outta town."

"Yeah."

"He done cut the new highway through Eastpoint, y'know that."

Harlowe nodded.

"Then he starts repayin' the favors. Gives Ledbetter and Raines money for their campaigns."

Harlowe nods.

"Then Lamar gets his *sister* a job with Raines."

"Right."

"Y'know Huff bought all that Vrooman land, *knowin'* Lamar got the contract to pave the road through Eastpoint! So, the State pays Huff top-dollar for the land. And they pay Lamar—who Huff and them lobbied on behalf of in the first place! It's all *woven* togethuh. Y'caint beat these fellas. Play in their league and they'll grind ya up like rock at his plant. Y'caint beat 'em!"

"I'm gonna try."

"Why don't ya get wise to yerself—an' let it go? Lamar cain do whatever he wohnts—or pay to have it done! Y'caint win, I'm tellin' ya!"

***

"They done sewed it up tight, then," said Aubrey.

"Like a spider's web," Lillian added.

"Yep.

"He's got his friends up theah—that's all it takes. It ain't about workin' hard to git somewheres, like our kids in Franklin County got to do," said Aubrey.

Harlowe nodded.

"Just git rich out of thin air 'cause of who they know. Another feller works his whole life an' don't earn enough to buy ground to git buried under or leave to his youngun. These kind can pick up the phone and git their youngun a city job. Am I understandin' it?"

"Yep."

"It ain't right," said Birch.

"Well, I reckon that's what we're up against," said Harlowe.

"Folk are scared, Pratt. Of the 'ghost.' The 'gray man'—some of the youn'ungs call 'im."

"Yeah," Harlowe replied. It seemed to stop. The 'gray man' hadn't returned in weeks. Harlowe was glad. He was angry. He was tired. All at once.

Huff dropped by. "I'm tellin' ya as a friend, things'd be easier for ever'body—includin' you—if ya stopped dredgin' up trouble!"

"Let sleepin' dogs lie, eh?"

"Ye-ess. It can only hurt our section!"

Meanin' it would hurt the business you stand to do if no one rocks the boat! Harlowe thought.

"We wohnt those Tallahassee folks to come an' spend their money! We don't need a fight!"

After he left, Seago told him, "Huff's encouraging Pender to run again."

"I know it."

***

December, 1937
Junior's Leon High classmates didn't know why he went to military school—then returned. *"It was just never discussed."*

Others flat refused to talk.

"I reckon they caint block us in Gainesville," said Harlowe.

They left at 2:00 am. Arrived on campus to find college boys in ties sitting under oaks, studying. Having breakfast at the dining hall. The fellows were about to take their finals.

They walked into the red-brick administration building. Found Junior's photo on the wall. "Class of '35."

They talked to Junior's old professors. They all liked him. "He never spoke of any trouble. He never gave us any concern," said one.

The Dean stated, "Junior was just a good fellow. Almost nominated class president. He was quiet, at first, but really opened up and did well. Almost popular, I'd say!"

"Anything unusual at all?"

"He almost *dreaded* going home. I know he went home for the summer the first year—in 'thirty-one. Then, after that, he always worked here. As bus boy. Odd jobs helping his coach. Practicing."

The Coach, at the ballfield, confirmed it. "Got a game tomorrow. Playing Kentucky! Sure I remember him—best relief pitcher I had!"

They asked if he recalled anything unusual.

"One thing, maybe."

"Yessir?"

"Just a feelin.' But it seemed like Cory never wanted to go home! The summer of his freshman year, he returned to the campus early. Walked up and asked for as much work as I could give him. All four years, he did that! Like he just wanted to stay busy. Why, he'd stay out here for hours, practicin'!"

"He evuh say why—anything about how he got on at home?"

"No." The coach stepped back, dodging a fly ball. "Say, will you fellas excuse me? Got to deal with that! Hey, what's the matter with you fellas!"

Coach wheeled about, returned. "Yeah, seemed like he dreaded goin' home—but why, I don't know. It stood out. Most of the fellas wanna go home and take it easy! Anything else you fellas wanna ask me?"

"Did Cory ever mention Eastpoint?"

"No. He never mentioned anything about any trouble, or anything in your part of the state. But I thought he was glad to get out from under his momma's thumb."

"Go on."

"Nothing definite, you understand, just what I surmised."

"Any other difficulties he mentioned?"

"No, sir. Other than a comment or two about his mother, I never heard him mention anything, well, unhappy. He was always joking and funloving. But I sensed something was off with his mother."

"Did he ever let on what it was?"

"No, he didn't. Anything else?"

"Nosir. I appreciate it. Good luck tomorrow!"

In Gainesville and Tampa they tracked down classmates the instructors identified as friendly with the boy. They were all the usual sort of things: *"Nice fella." "Swell!" "Generous to a fault!"*

***

True drove Harlowe's Ford. The bells clanged, the traffic light turned red. The gates flopped down. True eased to a stop as he waited for the bridge to swing round for the *Maria* to come through. The gates were raised. True let out the clutch, the car picking up speed. Gulf Breezes flowing in the windows, he crossed the 'long bridge.' Yonder, Aubrey Birch tonging—the last man out on the water.

True turned down the road to Cat Point. Passed Egg Brown's long chicken house. The fence. Stopped at the path to the schoolhouse.

He looked through the pines. Kids were playing baseball on the floor of pine straw. *Just as we'd done.* True looked back into the woods. *Is 'he' hangin' around—the 'gray man'?*

The oysterhouse looked more frail, whiskered. True went in and said hello to Bingham. The old man still worked in the same spot, as if bolted in.

Then McCannon burst inside. *He must be ninety by now.* "Looky here—I know what you're after. You're liable to get in a lot of trouble, hear?"

"Sir?"

"Y'know what you're doin'. Git on home!"

True told Harlowe about the odd interaction.

"No, son. He didn't do it." Harlowe handed him more papers to serve.

***

At night, True watched the road into Eastpoint, taking his turn sitting at the old tapper's road in Harlowe's car.

You thought all sorts of things trying to stay awake. He thought about that instant where black began to turn to grey, and then a few moments later where you could see things in *shades* of gray, but it was before your eyes could distinguish the actual colors of things. *Why wasn't there a name for that? It isn't night. It isn't dawn.*

Sometimes Harlowe would sit with him. It was nice to have the company. Harlowe's thermos of coffee.

Today, in that grayness just before dawn, they checked up the road, and the old terpentine roads the "Gray Man" apparently knew well.

It was quiet. Cool. No new tracks.

"We run 'im off."

"Ever since we talked to him, he's stopped. I reckon we stopped him comin'. But it may be harder to catch 'im," said Harlowe.

***

The telephone was jingling when he walked in.

"I've a call from Tallahassee, Shureff. Person-to-person, long-distance."

"Thankya, Miss Hilda."

No greeting, just, "When can I come home, anyhow? I'm tired of this dry county bidness!"

"I need ya theah."

"Aww, c'mon, Pratt!"

"This is reducin' your sentence."

Jeter cussed. "Anywho, I got somethin'!"

"Yeah?"

"The boy's roamin' all over in his automobile. Whenever he ain't keepin' skoo! Wearin' a grin like he's in the catbird seat!"

"Where—"

"Don't know where he goes! I ain't followin' 'im! Ya send me some money?"

"We'll see."

"Bah! I love you too. Bye!"

***

True went to see Tennie after work. The kid next door said that she had left with her mother and sisters to spend Christmas in Atlanta.

SEVENTY-SIX

December, 1937

The tally calls echoed in True's ears.

"Git back to work, boy!" hollered the overseer—only it was Foss's *voice.*

He lunged at True with an axe-handle. True froze like a tree!

"Ah!" True bolted upright on the couch. Heart pounding, he blinked. Got his bearings. *Just a dream!*

He dressed. Walked down to the River. Watched George's new boat going out, until she was out of sight. *Gibby woulda liked that. Never got his chance.* Mrs. Slocumb's rooster crowed and he walked to work.

When he got in, Harlowe had a job for him. "What should I be a-lookin' out for, boss?"

"Well, any case that's similar to this one. I had a job for the Seaboard Line, once. We were tryin' to find this fella who robbed safes—depots up and down the line. He was smart enough or lucky enough he didn't leave us a trail. Just like the fella we're after. So, I started lookin' other places. *Find his crimes—find him.*"

True nodded.

"He's done it some other time, son. We know Junior likes to roam. We have to roam too. Check every card in their files. *We have to do our homework to catch 'im, son.*"

"Yessir."

True boarded the train. He checked files on up the Apalachicola River valley to Columbus and Atlanta.

He'd show Junior's photo. "Do you recognize this man?"

No one did.

True walked from depots to sheriff's offices and little police stations, Harlowe's words driving him on: *He's done it some other time.*

"I wonder if I could take a look at your record books right quick," he'd say.

They'd raise an eyebrow at his youth. His lack of a badge. But when he told them who he was and showed his appointment letter, they believed him. He seemed too homespun to be making it up. Or they felt sorry for him, a skinny kid in workshirt who'd come all this way.

He looked for missing boys. Anything like a kidnapping.

One town after another. Many remembered Harlowe. *"Oh, the Sheriff didn't come this time?"*

"No, ma'am."

He looked at paperwork until his eyes crossed. Town after town he found nothing useful. True found a report of a missing boy in the paper in Quincy. The sheriff had no file on it.

The secretary dumped out her ashtray. "Oh, Eddie come home last year!"

True walked into the Tallahassee courthouse. Ledbetter wasn't around. The ol' gal allowed him to look! *Missing persons? Children?* There were two sheets of paper on file. None on young boys.

Sackett called the girl over. "Who's that?'

True's back was turned, at the cabinet; he recognized the voice.

"Oh—I dunno," replied the secretary.

"Well, we better--."

When they looked back, True was gone.

***

Christmas Eve, 1937

True stepped down from the train. Walked to the office. Reported to Harlowe—who gave True the rest of the night off. True would have rather stayed!

He walked along Market Street, past stores which had, in this Depression, managed to scrape by and keep their lights on.

Down the sidewalk as the last glow of sunset faded. He could take in the scene of shoppers and pretty things, but not be seen. True found it comforting, being invisible, just as he had in his boyhood. He was just a fellow under a hat, blending in like that lightpole. Here there was a peace he didn't know in Christmasses 'back home.'

The store windows were bright, their wreaths welcoming happy customers, the sky adding a touch of clear violet over the rooftops. True looked down Avenue E, in the cool, quiet night air, admiring how pretty it was. Even the lightbulbs at the Standard Oil station seemed brighter, Christmas Eve.

Each window told a happy story. A boy was getting a new baseball glove. A young couple paid for their meal at the Louis Café, and walked home arm-in-arm. Storeowners closed up and turned out the lights, content to make a little money today.

True lit a Chesterfield—he'd start back to Briley's house, but there's no hurry.

SEVENTY-SEVEN

January, 1938

"The gal Junior dated in college?"

"Yeah?"

"I have a name," said True.

They motored to Jacksonville to find her.

Harlowe turned down Bay Street. "She works at the Merrill-Stevens shipyard," said True. "Up there." A tugboat wailed a signal. Sparks flew from the welders on the ship sprouting up behind the building. They entered the office. Found Miss Garland working as a stenographer.

"Yes, sir. I enjoyed dates with him at first. Then he got strange when I didn't want to go steady."

"Oh?" asked Harlowe.

"Yes! Just really funny about it. 'You *got to,*' he said. 'I was counting on it!' he says. Like I turned him down for a job, or something."

"He evuh rough with you?"

"Onetime he and I argued and he held me down until I listened. I told him I didn't like it. Junior acted funny and, well, he just wouldn't start the car when I told him I had to get home. He got a very odd look, but finally he started the car."

"He's married now. Do you know the girl?"

"No—she seems lovely, but I don't know her. His father told him he needed to or else is what I heard. His mother tried to ruin it. But they eloped and his dad helped. Did I help you—I'm afraid I don't have much to tell you other than what I've said."

"You've helped us more than you realize. We appreciate it."

"Sorry you had to come all this way."

"That's all right. We tried to reach you on the telephone but couldn't get through."

"Oh, that darn party line!"

"Yes ma'am. Well, thanks again."

"Bye!"

"Goodbye," said they.

***

The telephone rang. Harlowe had just drifted to sleep.

"What will it take to come to terms?"

"Who's this?"

"A friend of important people. You interested?"

Harlowe hung up.

***

"Take me out," she said.

True walked to her house. She emerged in black gloves to her elbow. A matching floppy hat. A smart skirt and suit jacket with big buttons.

A ticket's fifteen cents at the *Dixie*. He bought her a hot dog for five cents. And he was broke again.

Afterwards they walked along. Tennie trawled her pocketbook lazily, her heels clacking on the sidewalk. Looking in the windows at Austin's.

"This store's a joke!"

"I've always liked it. When it was Montgom'ry's, Uncle Pratt would bring me here. Y'really don't like it?"

She laughed. "Oh, it's not so bad I guess. Let's go in!"

A girlfriend saw her. "Hey, Tennie!" She waved Jenny over. "Oh, I like your hat!" Tennie put her hands to it, turning left and right, showing it off like models do. True looked at rods and reels while the girls fell back to the suits.

"Do you even like him?" Jenny asked.

"Well. Maybe I'll make him into something interesting," Tennie replied, running her gloved hand over the suit sleeve.

They giggled.

***

"Sure, I'll cover for my son when he gets in trouble," said Cory. "I can't have him in trouble. He's my boy!"

"No one blames you, Lamar," said Raines.

"I, uh, I'm gonna get him into politics like I can't get into—I like the gals too much!"

Ledbetter laughed. Raines looked the other way. "Anyhow, Junior is married now. He's fine. His wife knows he can't drink and she'll watch

401

him. That sheriff down there is just *obsessed* with going after him, because of me."

"Yes," growled Raines.

"Thinks he can make a name for himself if he arrests a son of mine. But he has his price—and we'll soon settle this."

"Uh-huh?"

"He's got to see that he can do well if he plays ball. He's got his position and he'll have money. He'll see reason—I'm sure of it."

"If he doesn't, we'll break him," said Ledbetter. "Why not call in Slats O'Dell from Panama City—he's good at digging up dirt—you want a divorce he'll make your sainted grandmother look like a whore."
Driscoll had been silent until now—sipping his drink at the window. "Why not hire the fella from Miamuh. I can send for 'im—end the Harlowe problem."
"I don't know, Obie. *A sheriff,* Obie! I'm not sure we can sweep that under the rug!" said Lamar. "I think that goes too far."
"I of course don't know what you're talking about," said Raines.
Lamar laughed, slapped Driscoll on the back. "We'll work it out without a sledgehammer."

***

March, 1938

A papermill opened in St. Joe. Now Apalach's largest employer was out-of-town.

Just after sunrise, they watched a steady stream of Fords and Chevrolets heading that way.

True learned a classmate of Junior's—both at Leon and the university—now lived in Haines City. They drove down and found the Bollinger residence not far from a big citrus plant.

Porch across the front. Gleaming white trim.

"Please come in. We are about to leave for dinner. But we can talk for a minute. Sit down, won't you?"

Harlowe and True folded into the stuffed chairs.

"Care for a drink?" asked the man. He had two highball glasses. He handed one to the wife.

"No, sir."

"Very well." He kept the other glass. Sat beside the woman on the davenport. "You know, Junior and I weren't exactly friends. Junior was a loner-type. In high school, I mean. He didn't talk much. Didn't really 'fit in.' Both June and I were in his class—at Leon."

The woman nodded. "That's right. Mr. Harlowe."

"Was that your experience too, Mrs. Bollinger—he kept to himself?"

"Why, yes. I agree with what my husband said, he was a loner. Until his senior year, maybe."

"Oh?"

"Well, he lost weight and hit some home runs and became more popular. Before that he was, well, a 'nothing.' I hate to say that—."

"But it fits," said Mr. Bollinger.

"Was he Tall and husky in those years?"

"He was a big fella for his age, in the ninth grade," said the wife.

"Tubby, I'd say," said the man.

"The boys sorta caught up with him in height. But he was more heavy-set," explained the woman. "Until the last year or so, like I mentioned earlier."

"Yes ma'am. He was picked on a little, before that?"

"Well, gee, I guess a little. He didn't have too many friends when he was a sophomore, and I guess the kids did give him a bad time."

"Junior was much less *introverted* in college," said the man, pronouncing the word like a disease. "He was well-liked in Gainesville."

"He'd lost weight and all. He was curly-haired and handsome—if you want a woman's opinion," added Mrs. Bollinger.

Bollinger drained his glass. "Y'sure I can't get you boys a drink? You, you're kind of a quiet one ain't ya?" he asked True.

True nodded.

"You mentioned he changed his appeareance some, Mrs. Bollinger. Would you say he became more popular afterwards?"

"Why, yes."

"Lamar tried to encourage him to socialize. Go with him on hunting trips abroad. His mother wouldn't allow it.

"He was shy of women, I'd say," added the woman. "I'm not sure he went on dates—when he was in college I mean."

"No?"

"Not seriously, anyhow. I recall maybe or two dates he had. Not sure with whom," said the woman, looking at her husband.

"He had to go home. To Mother. Couldn't go on dates!"

"He had to get home...to his mother?" Harlowe asked.

"Yes," replied Bollinger. "If he didn't have practice he had to go home to her."

"Could you...elaborate on that?"

"His mother—there is only one word."

"Yessir?"

"Domineering."

"Oh?"

"Yes, domineering. His father was much more easy-going. Dare I say, *passive.* His mother was just what I said."

"Yes?"

"Domineering."

"How did he get on with his daddy—him bein' 'passive,' like you said?"

"I think Lamar was disappointed he wasn't more like him—things came more naturally for Lamar," answered Bollinger.

"Mrs. Bollinger, did you know his Mother and Daddy?"

"Oh, I didn't know them."

"My understanding is his father covered up for a lot of things he'd done— all his life." Bollinger took a cigarette from his case. Hanging from his lips, he added, "He couldn't have people talking, now, could he?"

"Would you recall any of the details?"

"My gosh, you're talkin' back in the Twenties—before the Big Crash! That was a long time ago."

"Yessir."

The man took a drag on his cigarette. Loosened his tie. "Gee, I suppose it was just the feeling I had. I cain't tell you specifics—maybe if you had somethin' to jog my memory?"

Harlowe leaned forward. "The Easter break from classes...in nineteen-hunnerd-and-thirty-two."

"Okay..."

"Do you recall whether he went home that week?"

"Let's see, that was our Freshman year? Now that, I recall—distinctly!"

"Uh-huh?"

"I remember his father picked us up in his car."

"Yessir? Anything else stand out?"

"One thing...when he got back, he wouldn't say anything about what he'd done."

"That was unusual?"

"Yeah, even for Junior."

"Is there anything else, unusual, you remember?"

"Say, there was this one-time—Senior year—Cory was a little tight and talking more freely, y'follow?"

"Sure."

"He said his father wanted to send him to a military school—Texas A and M. And he actually wanted to go. But his mother wouldn't hear of it."

"Do you know why, Mr. Bollinger?"

"Don't know! I only know they had a helluva row over it, his parents. 'You'll ruin the boy,' said his daddy. I'll never forget the way Junior explained it. Like he was talking about another person, not him, yet you could tell it really bothered him."

"Yessir."

"She didn't want him to go far from home, that may have been the reason."

"But you think Junior actually wanted to go?"

"It's funny, but I think he did. Almost like he felt he needed to be punished for something."

"Oh?"

"I can't put my finger on it. Just what I felt at the time. He kept talking about discipline and regimine. It sounded like hooey to me. He sure didn't give his old man any trouble in going, from what he said that night in particular! I sure woulda if my pop had wanted me to go there."

"Yeah?"

"Sure! Military school is for the birds! Gainesville was the bee's knees—shindigs every Friday night and I'd hitchhike to Tallahassee to see my girl every other Saturday. Couldn't do that at that Texas monastary."

Harlowe grinned. "I reckon not. And you say his mother wouldn't hear of it—what did he say about it?"

"I can't recall exactly, just something about him being far from home. Junior had a helluva time convincing her not to take a place in Gainesville and, well, oblige him to move in with her! He told her none of the fellas would have anything to do with him if she pulled that! I'm surprised the kid made it like he did, with an old lady like that."

"Yeah?"

"He's a swell Joe!"

"Is that right?"

"Why, sure! None better than that egg! Salt-of-the-earth is the stuff he's made of! But 'no thanks' to the old lady."

***

True learned another of Junior's High School classmates, Dan Tooley lived in Denedin. They drove down to speak to him. He asked them to meet him at a Scotland Street address. He opened the door with a trowel in his hand. "Come on in, fellas."

"Sure. We appreciate ya talkin' to us like this."

"Oh, I don't mind! I'm not sure if I can help? Back this way—I-I'm finishin' up the bathroom."

The man got on his knees to spread cement. "Junior was a nice fella—always wanted to help people. I didn't know him *real* well. Hope he's all right."

"We're lookin' for some information. It's been told to us that Junior Cory hunted and fished around Eastpoint sometimes...and may have had friends along."

"Well, I'd say that's correct."

"That sounds familiar then?"

"Uh-huh. Uh, say, ya mind handin' me that?"

"Sure." Harlowe handed him the bucket.

"I was with him on some of those trips. We weren't exactly friends. But we went along, some of the fellas and I."

"Do you recall one trip in September nineteen-hunnerd-and-twenty-seven?"

"Is that around the time the boy went missing?"

"What do you know about that?"

"I remember hearing about it once we got home—from one of those trips. It was the last week before school. We didn't stay long, on account of that. But I recall hearing about the little boy once school resumed. The fellas were talking about it. Teachers too."

"Junior Cory was on that trip?"

"Yes."

"Where?"

"Oh, along the coast—the Sound."

"Near Eastpoint?"

"Yes, on someone's land. Then we moved to a creek. Don't recall the name. We thought the owner would run us off, so we moved."

"Was it Indian Creek?"

"Why, yes, it was."

"How long were y'all there?"

"Most of the week. Fishin' wasn't too good. Some of the fellas went back to the Sound and fished. Then, we broke camp and moved—we set up near Sumatra."

"When was that?"

"Well, later in the week."

"Go on."

"We was of a mind to try the creek up there. Two or three of our classmates."

"How long did you stay?"

"I believe it was just the last day. We had to get home."

"Was Junior with you?"

"I don't remember what he was doing. Doesn't stand out. I wish I could remember but it was ten years ago."

"About what time did y'all break camp and head home?"

"It woulda been before the storm. Around three o'clock, I suppose." The man daubed on more cement. "Can't be sure."

"Was Cory with y'all?"

"Gee, I can't remember. I'm not sure what you mean."

"Well, did y'all ride togethuh? Y'all come in more than one automobile?"

The man straightened. "As a matter of fact, we did. We had three automobiles. Junior had one." Tooley grinned. "Old Tin Lizzie!"

"Who'd you ride down with?"

"Come to think of it, I rode down with Junior! His father had a big Packard and there was one other Ford."

"Who did you ride home with--."

"Lemme see, now. I remember! I didn't ride with Junior, I rode back with his father!"

"All right. Did Junior leave with the group."

"Why, no, he didn't, come to think of it! He stayed behind for some reason."

"Mr. Tooley, do you remember anything else unusual about that trip, the way Junior was actin', anything?"

"No, sir. Nothing, far as I know."

"But you do remember he stayed on?"

"Yessir. And now it's coming back to me. We commented that we hoped he wasn't caught in the storm. The weather was quite nasty later that night."

"When y'all were at Indian Creek, did you see this boy?"

Harlowe showed him Gibby's photo.

"Nah, don't remember him."

"Did Junior leave camp by himself when y'all were down there?"

"He may have. He and his dad took their fishing tackle and left the group. The other fellas and I stayed by the creek. Didn't catch much!" said Tooley, smoothing the cement.

"Would you know the names of the other fellas?"

"Sure, I can give them to you."

"Much obliged, Mr. Tooley."

"Yeah, don't mention it."

***

"Git your shovel, son," said Seago.

Brewer cussed. But he fetched it. Hopped into Seago's car when the latter drove to pick him up.

A rattlesnake was sunning himself along the banks of Indian Creek. They passed him by, careful not to disturb the six-footer!

"Let's check this area good, boys," said Harlowe.

They began poking and turning ground. No one lives there. It's a pretty spot to fish and camp.

"Jus' 'cause he camped heah, don' mean he buried heah!" protested Brewer, angrily wielding the shovel.

"I b'lieve I hit somethin'!" cried True.

They got down on their knees. Dug it out. "It's a bone!"

"C. A.—whaddya think?" asked Harlowe.

The big man examined it. "Deer bone."

They kept going, as the creek meandered toward Tate's Hell. They found nothing but old campfire ashes and a crushed tin can.

Back into Tate's Hell there was a pond. Harlowe started them on the banks of it.

"Why we gotta check 'is pond?" asked Brewer.

"In case he was put theah."

"No one evuh comes through heah, boss!"

Harlowe waded the pond, checking with his stick.

They moved on to the hogtrail. Past a coal-black oak.

Humid. The sun going down and cottonmouths coming out. True could almost feel them slither. He shivered as he stepped over the entangling roots and vines. The back of his neck crawled with the thought of snakes, with the bugs that were brushing his head, the scary hiding places in the black trees all around.

True stopped. "Hey, the ground's kinda soft heah!"

"Yeah, it's right low. Somethin' was buried here," Harlowe said.

They went down six feet, Harlowe explaining what Collis had said.

They spent the next three hours digging. Finding nothing.

Up the Sumatra Road, the spot Mr. Tooley identified as the campsite, they searched too. Working shovels and sticks. Sweating. Brewer lamented, "We out here half the night and ain't found nothin'!"

Harlowe thought about Seago's newspapwer article, about Judge Crater. *"So many places a man can fall, or get put."*

He sighed. "All right, boys. We can go."

It was pitch-dark when Harlowe got home. He poured a glass of milk. Listened to the train leaving.

Presently, there came a knock at the back door.

"I seen your light on."

"Come on in. That's all I have to drink, but help yourself." Harlowe nodded toward the bottle.

"I'm good," Aubrey replied.

Harlowe told him he'd been looking up the road.

"You really leavin' no stone unturned."

Harlowe cut the lamp on in the living room. Birch folded himself on the divan. Harlowe borrowed Claudie's chair, facing him. The younger man just sat there, silently. "You all right, Aubrey?"

The latter shook his head. "Naw. It hit me hard today. I had to come over to Apalach. Jus' thought I'd stop in."

Aubrey looked faraway. "I miss 'im. Days like 'is. I was lookin' into doin' a little shrimpin'—and it made me think of all he's missed. I'm a'ight now. I don' wohnt Lillian to worry."

"You can telephone Tommy's store, if ya wohnt to."

"Nah. It's a'ight. I'll git on the ferry an' git home." He reached for the door. "Thanks, Pratt."

Harlowe held out his hand. Smiled. "For what?"

SEVENTY-EIGHT

April, 1938

"I'm bored—I'll call true!" said Tennie.

Jenny looked surprised.

"What? If he'll take me places, why not?"

"I thought y'didn't like him that much."

"He'll do for now."

True picked her up. They walked 'uptown.'

True was happy walking aside her.

Tennie glanced over at the fellow in a new Ford. Imagined herself riding in it.

True fed her at Louis'. They walked to the show. He paid for the tickets.

"Buy me a candy, willya?"

He reached in his pocket.

"I like-ya when you're light and gay! Not that serious, 'Lawman True'!"

***

Jeter rang. "Look here, I ain't got much money for the phone. Lamar's been braggin' he gits what he wants in this town. That he cleaned up this mess right well. You figure the rest."

CLICK.

Harlowe looked at True. "All right—we're goin back up theah."

Junior looked in the store window. Down the sidewalk whistling, not a care in the world. *He doesn't know I'm tailin' him. Like I'm invisible,* True thought, proud he learned to do it the way Harlowe showed him. His hat on low, he blended in among the people shopping and tending to business.

Junior went in to the Elks' Club. A deputy's Ford came around the corner. True cut down to Adams, walking quickly. He looked behind him the next block. The car crept along.

True walked down to Bloxham, ducked into the hobo jungle along the tracks. Brown shanties. Crate-shelters. Men, women, children—whites—living there. If you could call it living.

A gaunt dog looked at him and ran. True peeked out to see the Deputy's shiny car dash away.

True followed him again, Saturday morning, as Junior walked down Monroe Street. True followed him all week and Junior hadn't left town.

***

Jeter watched Lamar Senior drinking beer, flirting with the gals at the Green Derby.

"Deacon Raines" somehow put on blinders to Lamar's "tomcat" behavior. Lamar could do no wrong in the prosecutor's eyes. Though, othwerwise, he could scarcely approve of the row of Jax beer bottles lined up in the back corner booth. Jeter chuckled. To Raines, the law was black and white— except for friends and kin. Jeter finished his beer. It was his turn to bowl.

***

When he got up she was the first thing he thought of. Sitting in Harlowe's car, alone, he imagined her beside him. When he fell asleep he drifted off with Tennie on his mind. He saw himself running for sheriff. With her as his wife, there's nothing he couldn't do!

On their date he bought her a banana split at Buzzett's, ice cream and whip cream piled beautifully in a white dish. Tennie polished it off. Started on the soda he'd spent his last nickel for.

She yawned. "I like to never git to sleep last night. Darn cousin of mine is stayin' with us!"

He walked aside her, past the stores. She looked, longingly, at a dress in the window. "I want that. What do you want, True?"

"Maybe run for sheriff one day. Maybe settle down. Own a little farm."

Tennie got a bored frown. "Pish-posh to that—take me home."

***

Next day, True watched in the mirror of the Ford, Junior got out of his car on Park Avenue. Turned the corner, up Monroe.

He entered the F&T restaurant. True glanced in the doorway.

Ledbetter flirted with the waitress. Like she hung on his every word. His cronies gathered around him.

Ledbetter's new Stetson lay on the table.

He didn't acknowledge Junior, as the latter sipped his coffee, at the counter.

As dusk neared, Junior walked the town, looking in shops. True followed, glancing in the doorways, open as it was sultry tonight. Junior walked down to the tracks on Adams. Watched some boys playing ball, yonder.

***

It was the first Birthday meeting where True sat in.

Mr. and Mrs Birch were hurting the same as the first night, True saw.

Gibby's mother wanted to talk about him. They let her.

"Gibby loved being on the water. Hunting. Fishing. Either one. He smiled so big—loved everything about it! Y'couldn't help smile when ya around him. He made you laugh, made you feel good even in midst of hard times."

"He'd want to fish so much I had to tell 'im, no son, we caint go out every night!" added Aubrey. "When I couldn't, he'd go find True n' pester him!"

Mrs. Birch patted True's arm. "He'd find you n' wouldn't take no for an answer!"

True laughed. "No, ma'am!"

They were a shell of their younger selves. They appeared smaller, much older, True thought.

Harlowe poured coffee. They remembered their son, brother.

***

Junior drove home from a nice dinner with his wife. White jacket affair.

"She seems like a nice gal," thought Harlowe.

The Ford V-8 pulled into the drive. True pulled in behind it.

Junior looked up. *Startled?* True wondered, as they approached.

"Jus' wanna talk to ya," said Harlowe.

"Would you excuse us, darling"

The woman smiled. Went inside as instructed.

Junior took a seat on the porch swing. *Confidence,* True thought. The teacher made an expression as if to say, "And?"

Harlowe put his foot up on the step.

"Y'know ya did a bad thing."

"Mr. Harlowe, I don't know what you're referring to. You have the wrong idea about me." *He's calm. Hands in his lap. Leg crossed,* True saw, noticing the things Harlowe taught him to study.

413

"I can tell you pretty much everything you did, son."

Junior looked at him curiously.

"You saw 'im on the skiff. Waited for him to come in at the ferry landin'. You talked to 'im about fishin.' Baseball. You got him in the car—he thought you were a friend."

"No."

"When you drove past the road to Cat Point, he tried to get way. He fought you. He hollered. Maybe you got scared—I know you were young—fourteen. Weren't much older than he was. He hollered and you hit him."

"No."

"You choked 'im. Maybe you didn't mean to. But you were scared. Then...you buried him."

"None of that is true! It-it's a horrible thing to say!"

"You set his boat adrift. Make it look like he'd got caught in the storm. That was smart. But not enough. You buried 'im where he might git found."

"No."

"Buried 'im along the road, didn't ya?"

"No, Mr. Harlowe."

"Your daddy sent ya to Daytona—four weeks later. We both know why."

"I drank too much. I got into daddy's bourbon—I was fourteen and forgot myself. You said yourself I was fourteen! That's all there was to it!" True noticed his fidgeting—pulling at his trouser crease.

"I'll find the answers. I'm patient," Harlowe vowed. Junior got up. Shut the door behind him without further reply.

True started the car.

"What do ya think, son?"

"You were getting' to 'im. I noticed his hands—was like he didn't know what to do with 'em."

"That's good, son. I believe you're right."

***

June, 1938

Saturday night, True and Tennie had a double-date with Briley and Efola. "It's nice to ride someplace—and get outta here!" said Tennie.

They went to the dancehall at Carrabelle Beach.

True couldn't dance the fast dances. He bought Tennie a coke—she pouted a little less. "Now that you graduated High School, what are your plans, Tennie?" someone asked her.

"Anything to get away from here!"

***

"Let's find my brother," said Harlowe.

"All right, bossman," said True.

They found Jeter by the tracks, near the Colored College.

The bottle protruded from his pocket when he slumped against a tree.

Jeter almost passed out against the pine!

Harlowe nudged his brother—who mumbled something profane.

"How's that?"

"Oww—my head hurts. Y'woke me, damn ye!"

"Don't cuss me 'cause you're hungover," said Harlowe.

"Sorry! I could use a beer—y'bring me one?"

"Whaddya have for me?"

"This fella that works for 'im from time-to-time."

"Yeah?"

"He tol' me some things...while ago."

"Go on."

"He done tol' me somethin'—now, I need some money, Pratt!"

"What did he say?"

"Said Ol' Junior made some comments. That he'd done somethin' bad."

"Somethin' bad—is that all?"

"Yeah."

"When did he make that comment?"

Jeter began to fade out. "Wake up," said Harlowe, giving him a nudge with his boot.

"When?" asked True.

415

"Not long after the li'l feller took missin'.'"

"What's his name?"

"Emerson."

"Where's he at, now?"

"Ledbetter got 'im in 'is jail."

After he was released, they went to talk to Emerson.

They found the skeletal figure sleeping in the city dump.

"Good afternoon'! Good afternoon'!" the man said, loudly.

They asked about Lamar.

"I used to run with Lamar, sure. Had a fallin' out."

"Yeah?"

The man squinted at them, could hardly sit up. "I apologize I've already had me a sip or two."

"You were sayin' you were friends with Lamar?"

"I come up with 'im...in Quincy. Him and his uncle. Played cards with them boys, hunted with 'em, everythin.' 'Til the bank foreclosed on me."

"You know Junior Cory?"

"Sure! Knowed 'im since 'e was so high! He's a-uh-schooltreacher now."

"Yessir." Harlowe asked him about the incident with Junior.

The man was hesitant, but answered. "Yeah, I said that—sure did."

"That's what I wanna know."

"Okay—I'll tellya. 'Bout ten years ago, we got to passin' the jug around one night—and somethin' happened I ain't never forgit."

"Go on."

"Well, one o' the boys built a bonfire, we're settin' around, ya know? I hear Junior Cory talkin'–starts cryin'! Says he done something real bad! His daddy bull-rushed 'im, snatched 'im up outta that chair, put him against a tree 'n told him he best 'shut-the-hell-up.'! Done poured out the whiskey. Threatened all them boys—well, me too!"

"Threatened ya?"

"Yessir. He proceeded to say that we'd be in a lotta trouble if we mentioned it. We best go and forgit it!"

"When was this?"

"When the young'un said all that?"

"That's right."

"Hell, ten years ago if it was a day! But I remember clear as anything."

"Can you narrow it down?"

"Well, lemme see. You know, bossman, we were drinkin' out theah 'cause it was Christmas!"

"Yeah?"

"Uh-huh. And Junior was about fourteen."

"Christmas of twenty-seven?"

"Damn, I guess it had to have been! Yeah, that's when it was!"

"You're sure what he said?"

"Uh-huh. 'I done somethin' really bad. I hurt someone.' I swear that's it, damned word for word."

"Okay."

"Never seen Lamar get rough with that boy before—he got 'im up outta there, an' he flat sure didn't want nothin' more said!"

"All right. We appreciate it."

They walked away. Rain fell on one side of Bloxham. It was sunny the other. They reckoned Emerson told the truth. But lies from Lamar and his son would be weighed more credible in the courtroom up the street.

***

"Well, Howdy, Pratt!" said Seago.

"Any mail come?"

"Lemme check the box right quick!"

The men talked it over. "You caint use 'im in court," said Brewer. "None of it.

417

"I know it. Unless I find the body," said Harlowe.

Seago handed a postcard to True.

They continued to talk.

True read the card from Tennie.

"I have gone to Atlanta to visit my Aunt Margarites."

She hadn't said anything. Didn't said goodbye. Her card doesn't say when she'd be back.

True walked down Market Street to the bridge. Not a single car went by. *Maybe Tennie's right to wanna leave. Caint give her much, here.*

He watched the men tearing down houses—making room for a new courthouse. He enjoyed a cigarette. The seagulls laughing.

SEVENTY-NINE

Tallahassee—August, 1938

"You insisted I come here, Mother," said Jr. Cory.

"I made all this for you!"

"I don't want stew, Mother!"

"Yes, you do."

"Fine—I'll eat!"

True heard them—standing by the fence.

The fellow got in his car. Whether he was sad or enraged True could not tell. He pulled away from the curb, slowly. Following Jr.'s Ford. He saw the latter turn down the Old St. Augustine Road.

True hung back, no other cars on the upaved, lonely road through plantations, woods East of town. It was like a tunnel, with a canopy of trees, and clay bluffs on either side. Once or twice, True lost him as the latter descended a hill or rounded a corner.

Finally, the road entered flatter country. True saw Junior turn down a two-rut trail that ran along a corn field.

It was an area True didn't know. Junior proceeded about a mile-and-a-half and stopped. Then pulled off the road into woods.

True stopped and eased up the trail as slowly and quietly as he could, afoot. Got as close as he dared.

The car had stopped up on a hill, in a clearing covered in broom sage.

True slipped through the woods, to an oak, close to Junior's car.

Junior got out. Stood by the fender, as if he were transfixed on something in the distance. True looked yonder and saw, up the hill were ten ancient columns, and chimneys equally narrow and soaring, all that remained of a grand house.

Silence prevailed upon the field. Melancholy rested heavy between the columns, where lovely rooms occupied by gentlemen and ladies, pianos and talk of the price of cotton had once wafted in the air with the scent of wysteria. And Junior gazed out there, oddly.

Then, got in his car and left.

True told Harlowe, when he returned.

"What is the significance of the place?" Harlowe wondered.

***

They drove out Tennessee Street. The boy's alma mater had moved to a brand-new three-story building since Lamar Cory, Jr. matriculated. Up the front steps ascended Harlowe and True. Classes hadn't resumed. They walked down the empty hall to find the principal, Mr. Reeves.

He was thin, in a grey suit which made his shouders seem wider, bonier. "Oh, Junior Cory was a fine young man, well-mannered. He followed all the rules and was a helpful fellow," said the principal.

"No trouble with 'im?"

"Oh, no! Not in the least. He was a good ball player, after his junior year. A magnificent runner."

"Yessir. We know about that."

"Say, I hope nothing's wrong."

"Just lookin' for some information."

"I'll help any way I can, of course."

"We appreciate it."

Harlowe asked about Junior's absence.

"He left school before Thanksgiving. Was gone, oh, three months. No, come to think of it, he didn't return until his Junior year."

"Have you any idea why?"

"That, I do not know." The man's face blanched, True noticed.

"I'm not aimin' to cause you any trouble, Mister Reeves. I got a little boy missing in my county."

"That-that's terrible, Mr. Harlowe, but I've said all I'm going to. Good day, Mr. Harlowe, Mr. Fulton."

They returned to Harlowe's car.

True looked at Harlowe. "He knows somethin', True."

They got back late. Eastpoint was pitch-dark. The lights of the Gorrie Service Station glowed ahead. Then the bridge and home.

***

"Oh, there you are. Say, will you buy us a coke?"

True had walked to the depot to meet Tennie. He fetched her bag, and Tennie's friend Jenny found them.

"Gee, everything is the same as when I left," Tennie said, glancing in the store windows as they walked past. "What have you been up to?" she asked, absently.

"Workin.' Made me a little money with Briley. I-I missed you." He leaned in to kiss her cheek.

"Hmm." At that, she leaned away to look at a dress in the window.

They headed for Buzzetts. "Did you like Atlanta?" True asked.

"Oh, it was swell! Interestin' people. Suppers in fine homes. Parties all the time. Something to do every night of the week! Say, will you buy us a banana split, honey?"

Friday, after Tennie got off work, True spent his last dime at Buzzetts, buying her a "float." She sipped it absently. She seemed bored. Nothing he said made any difference.

Rex Buzzett was working there now. He looked at True, and back to Tennie. "Y'want another'n?"

"Yes, please!" said Tennie. True still oystered part-time. He pulled up the rest of what he'd made this week.

Saturday, Tennie was with her friends when a salesman came by. She flirted with him on the porch. Then, he asked her out.

"Umm. Sure, I'll go!"

Jenny could hardly believe it.

He grinned. "Okay—I'll pick you up tonight."

She looked up at him, dreamy-eyed. "Okay!"

After he pulled away, Jill asked, "Say, I thought y'had a date with True?"

"Well...I had. True *is* kinda cute. And maybe I can push him to be something--."

"And take *you* somewhere," interrupted Jenny.

"That's right! But he's not ready yet. And he hasn't a Clark Gable mustache nor an automobile like this *gentleman.*"

Marlene Williams was helping her dad deliver melons on the wagon.

She looked over at Tennie and the salesman.

"Would you *believe* that heifer?"

"What's that, Marley?" asked C.P.

"Oh, nothin', Deddy."

"Let's move along, then."

Mrs. Buckles stepped out on the porch. "Is that salesman gone? What are you smiling about so, Tennie?"

"Why, I got a date—with a man who's a good talker."

"Oh," she said, sadly, "you oughtn't do him thataway, Tennie."

"Aww, I'm just having fun! I'll patch things up with True n' go back to the soda fountain next week."

Tennie shot a glance at her friend. "Don't look so shocked, Jenny. I want a man to date me up right 'n take me places!"

Jenny and Jill laughed. "Tennie Buckles, the 'Louise Brooks' of Apalachicola."

"I like fellas with class and I like to get tight once 'n a while. What of it?"

"By *class* do you mean, 'dough?'" asked Jill.

Tennie shrugged.

She stood him up again after that. True heard talk. She was going with a drummer from Eufala—who owned an automobile.

"Why walk when you can ride." True heard the gossip at Buzzett's.

Briley and Efola had gone dancing. "We'll see ya, True."

The door banged shut. True was lonesome, but he had no place to go. What better than walk the town?

He enjoyed the lights, seeing the couples together, crowded tables at The Grill. Seeing people, together, happy, somehow you don't feel so lonesome. Maybe it's like watching a movie. Just hearing talk. You didn't feel so alone.

He looked through the window a moment. He walked along and glanced in other windows, lights bright, folks smiling. He listened to the music and laughter drifting from the pool hall as he stood at the doorway, looking in. He walked by the *Dixie,* heard the end of the newsreel. Saw Mr. and Mrs. Clark eating a hamburger at the Louis Café, sitting by the window, talking. The Huffs sat in back and weren't talking. A fella bought popcorn for his girl, off the cart outside, the pair rushing inside hand-in-hand before the show started.

The door shut behind them. Lonesomeness hit him again.

He walked back down Market, which was deserted with the stores closed. He looked in the windows at the Gorrie Furniture Company, the suites of furniture set up like rooms in a nice house, ready for some family to enjoy.

He found himself at the old pavilion at Battery Park. Abandoned and quiet, he stood at the rail, looking out at the Bay. He smoked. Thought about the stories Lexie told them about this place; the elegant dances when she was a little girl, the lovely dresses and music. She lived with Uncle Pratt then, after her mother died. True pictured the people filling the floor, the music, the scent of the Magnolias, the Gulf breezes. He thought of that through another cigarette or two.

He awoke at dawn, on the couch. Stepped over his aunt and uncle's shoes and things. Walked down to watch the shrimpboats going out.

He woke up Briley. And they oystered all morning, Briley hungover and snarly.

After they got back, he walked. Past Harlowe's house. Along the tracks. There wasn't one other person around. He ached for Tennie.

She's been to Atlanta. Knows these fellas who've done so well! That always had all the right words to say! he thought, sadly. *I never seem to have the words!*

Gibby could talk to anyone. I never had to say much when he was around. He'd always come get me to fish or play ball. Carried me along like we was paired horses!

True used to look at the Fords at the W.O. Anderson agency, every day, but he hadn't been over there for awhile.

"Well, I'll walk up there and say hello to Mr. Willoughby, anyway. I certainly caint afford no car."

He walked down Market—that's when he saw her! A roadster—sidemount spares, yellow body, black fenders! *A whole lot like the one the couple from Atlanta had that day! Or my old toy!*

He stood by her. Got lost in shiny paint and nickel; until Willoughby startled him. "Y'like that one, True?"

"Uh—yessir."

"Caint seem to sell it! Boss wants fifty bucks for 'er. Firm!"

It took the rest of the day to scrape up the money, and a promise to pay the balance in a week, but True drove away in her.

Pulled up in front of Tennie's house. She sat on the porch filing her nails. Bored. "Hey, Tennie! I got a car now—thought maybe we could go for a ride."

She barely looked up. "That old breezer—why, what would it do to my hair?"

"I can put the top up."

She jumped up. "No foolin'! It's really yours?!"

"Yes."

She climbed in. "Where are ya takin' me?"

"Louis' and the *Dixie* in style!" When they'd spent all his money they sat in the car, watching the lights cut off, one-by-one. Tennie leaned back and looked up at the stars.

"I wanna go places. And have plans every night of the week. With friends, with people who are part of it. I want to be a part of it all. I wanna be somebody! And get somewhere!"

"Sure."

"Say, look at that new Chevrolet, Mr. Taunton got! You oughtta get one, True. Buy it on installments—easy as pie!"

"Yeah. Might do that."

***

The noise of the canneries. Belts whirring. The smell of fish. The gritty feeling. True got paid for his oysters and walked to the courthouse. Gasoline money didn't come easy. He had to save some for Saturday night.

They waited for the bridge to turn. A shrimpboat inched her way through.

Harlowe said they had a call in Carrabelle. They found the house near the tracks. Harlowe got out. "Wait by the car, heah?"

Harlowe talked to the man about shrimping. He spoke gently—for the fellow had a baby under one arm, a revolver in the other! "Yeah—I know Taranto—good man."

"Yeah."

The boy's as tense as a piano string! Harlowe thought. "Now, I can understand why you'd steal from Ol' Tuckah. Ol' boy's a snake!"

The man grinned. Started talking about Tucker's scallywaggin' ways. Finally, he handed Harlowe the baby.

Harlowe exhaled. Nodded.

The man let the revolver fall from his hand. "Good, son."

He hung his head. "Yeah, I done it. And...I stole that lumber from the mill. I jus' wanted t'tell ya that."

"Okay."

True eased over, cuffed him.

"What now?"

Since he'd stolen more than $50 in lumber it was a felony. "You'll be bound over for the circuit court, when the Fall term commences," Harlowe told him.

True studied Harlowe's every step. Harlowe noticed that True moved in to cuff him—without words.

Folks greeted them when they walked into The Grill. They sat down and the folks adjacent said, hello, too.

"Good to see y'all," replied Harlowe. Doc. Murrow joined them.

"Have you a seat and I'll git a menu," said the waitress, Evie.

True didn't say much after Carrabelle! He downed the coffee, gratefully!

While Harlowe was away, True handled the night shift the first time. That meant working the county, alone.

He drove to Harbeson City. And all the way to St. Theresa.

Tired, the lights of the Gorrie Service Station beckoned. Last stop before the long bridge—and the man had coffee! The attendant sat there, fanning himself with the *Democrat,* when True walked up. "Hey, True!"

"Howdy."

"Yeah, have some coffee. Cool ya off! Lonesome tonight, ain't it?"

True nodded. Sipped. Somehow scalding liquid *did* relieve the heat.

"Yeah, pretty quiet. Only all-night station in the county. What a job, eh? I reckon, it keeps me outta the cotton patch."

"See-ya!"

***

Harlowe stood outside the house on Gadsden. He wanted another look. Junior's old room was the one that looked out into Whittle's yard, according to the old gardener. *So close.*

Then, Harlowe imagined the Eubanks boy walking down this sidewalk on his way home from school.

EIGHTY

August, 1938

Seago emerged from the outhouse, squinted at the sun, and moseyed on back. Harlowe heard him on the stairs. "I'm gonna tell ya, son, T.K.'s making folk mad in Carrabelle, the way he struts around like a bandy rooster," said he.

"I know it."

"T.K. doesn't want to be out theah. Thinks he's got a better shot at gittin' elected if he's in Apalach, bein' seen!"

"Yeah."

"Whachya gonna do?"

Harlowe thought about it. "I could send True over theah. Y'reckon he's ready?"

"Reckon he is. Bossman, you like a good mother hen fixin' to let the boy go on his own—checkin' and makin' sure he's ready to fly!"

***

True took a bed in the rooming house. If someone needed him, they'd ring the payphone at the gas station up the road. The owner would come wake him up.

True worked alone. He'd be without help if trouble arose, no radio to call for help. It felt good knowing Harlowe had confidence in him. Harlowe told him, "County never provided us a badge. Sheriff Waltham used to say, 'Boah, yer gun is yer badge!' Speak with authority and people will listen. Don't let 'em see you scared. You've got a good head on your shoulders—I know you'll use it."

Friday night, True dropped off Tennie. After *Rich Man, Poor Girl,* he had barely enough gasoline to get back to Carrabelle.

Saturday night, True listened to the clanging piano and cussing which spilled out of the pool hall.

A drunk approached. Big as a bull. True wasn't sure if he wanted help or wanted to fight. "Someone done stole my car, y'hear me?"

"Yessir."

"They done stole it!"

True helped him look. There weren't many places it could be in Carrabelle. "There it is, Mister!"

The man left it by the hotel, right across the street! He squinted. "Oh, there it is! Thankya, son."

True got the man home. He began crying as True helped him to his door—about these hard times. And his wife went from hollering to crying, too, seeing her man was drunk again!

"Y'all git some sleep, things'll look better in the mornin'!" True told them.

Next day, Seago stopped by. "You wohnt some coffee, boah?"

Seago bought him one at the restaurant. And today's *Democrat*. "Look here—feller caught a four-hunnerd-pound Tarpon out in the Guff, Saturdee. Know who it was?"

True shook his head. "The fish or the man?"

"Ha-boah! That's good! Nah, it was Lamar, son!"

"Yeah?"

"Listen at this--." At that, a man burst in, approached True and bade him come out to his automobile.

"My sister in the car, theah!" True saw her in the backseat. She was crying some. Her face swollen. He walked over. "What happened, Miss Ella?"

"Well, y'know how Tick gits!" she whimpered. "Yesterdee, I carried 'im to 'is job. I thought that was the end of it, but when he got home, he was still mad at me. I don't know what I done to make him so mad!" She started crying more.

True listened to her tell her story, in between sobs. She kept getting close, with whiskey on her breath. He kept leaning back to no avail.

"I know I shouldna thrown the pie at 'im. Didn't mean to hit 'im with it!"

"Is that when he hit ya? On your face, theah?"

"Naw—he didn't hit me then! I threw a dish at 'im, 'cause he cussed me! Mr. True, ain't no one gonna set there'n cuss me!"

"Yes, ma'am."

"What's gonna happen to 'im? I don't wohnt'im to go to jail n' lose 'is job. He's got a good job at the mill!"
"I understand."

"I feel better talkin' to you! Y'kinda calmed me down, y'know?"

"Yes'm."

True got the brother to go home. And found the 'other half' on the porch down the street, smoking and pacing.

The man bowed up on True. "Boy, whachu wohnt! I'll whip yo' ass!"

True remembered what he'd seen Harlowe do, how to talk to people.

"H'dy, Tick—you remember I used to fish with yer son?"

"True—True Fulton?"

"Yessir!"

True got Tick's side of it, the woman waiting in Seago's car.

Seago got the man a rag to daub the pie out of his hair. "I feel better talking to ya, Mr. True!"

Seago walked the woman to the porch and the couple apologized to each other.

"Y'all through fightin' now? 'Cause next time one of ya is gonna have to see Judge Clary."

"We through fightin', we all made up now!" the woman beamed. "We like you! Ya listened to us. Don't like Mr. Brewer—he don't listen! He come up here, mean, and hateful!"

"Listen, ya know wha' else?" Tick slurred. "Y'don't talk down to us, neither. Y'want a snort, young fella? Whaddabout you, C.A.?"

"That's all right, Mr. Crutchfield. Y'all git some sleep, now, heah?"

It was back to checking the highway—looking for wandering cows—waiting for that payphone to ring. True thought about the article. *That fella, gettin' his 'pitcher' made. That fish—that should be Gibby when he was forty and married! Gibby won't get the chance.*

EIGHTY-ONE

August, 1938.

Even in Carrabelle, Tennie was the talk of the town with her photos.

"She done went to Panama to git her *pitcher* took. She's givin' them out like salvation tracts," said Twiggs. Dakie Orr showed True one of these glamor shots!

The beauty queen was being talked about in Eastpoint, too. Marlene's sisters mentioned the photos. "Oh, how pretty Tennie is!" remarked Glen and Runt.

Marlene cocked an eyebrow. "Oh, y'mean the 'Queen Heifer'?"

True went by to pick up Tennie. She wasn't home! Driving back to Carrabelle, he saw her going into the dancehall—with the drummer.

Monday, coming up the stairs, True overheard Seago. "He's fun for her right now, but she don't mean to be no wife! She was runnin' around with the salesman Fridee--."

True stammered, "G-Good mornin'."

Harlowe patted his shoulder. "Y'ready, son?"

True drove. *Uncle Pratt hasn't rubbed it in, nor questioned me.* True was glad his uncle did that for him. "Where we headed, today, boss?"

True found out it was more watching, Harlowe had in mind.

***

True was in Apalach for a trial. After it was postponed, he walked uptown. Listened to the laughter, the singing and chanting of the colored shuckers on Water Street.

On Market Street, he neared the A&P. The doors were open for the air. His heart beat a little faster, since--.

"Hey, True!"

He stood in the doorway, smelling Eight O'Clock coffee from the grinder. Tennie was grinding it for a customer. "Howdy, Miss Key," said True.

After Tennie waited on the woman, Tennie threw her arms around True. "I have been awful to you! I want to...make it right! For starters, have a cup of coffee—on me!"

Raines' secretary phoned. "Could you meet with him this afternoon?"

"Yes, ma'am."

They drove to the Capital City. The woman smiled. Held the door for them.

They entered, and Raines lay into Harlowe from the instant he settled on the chair.

"No body—no evidence of anything but a drowning and you come up here, like you're investigatin' the Lindberg case! Have you nothing better to do down there!" Raines reared back in his chair. "Understand something, your authority stops at the river—no one elected you sheriff of Leon County! Now before you interrupt—I'm tellin' you it's better you just listen—if ya wanna make it worse, go ahead!"

"Mr. Raines, I have a summary of the evidence. It's typed." Harlowe lay the bound pages, more than an inch thick on the desk. Raines cast a disdainful glance and kept on. "Keep botherin' the Corys and get ready for a lawsuit! Don't expect me to get you out of it!"

"All right. I'll take the responsibility."

Raines glared at him for an instant, before uttering a dismissal. "I'm through. You can go." At that, his secretary showed them out.

True started the car. Harlowe shut the door. Looked over at his nephew. "I'm not gonna quit."

True nodded.

When they got back, Seago ran out to them. "Whad'jall do? Raines is fired up! Son, I heard he cussed you up and down! Heard he told Ledbetter, 'Harlowe oughtta stick to buildin' houses!" *The big man had his sources,* True knew.

It bothered True, Raines saying what he did. Harlowe patted him on the shoulder. "Don't worry about him, son—means we're on the right track!"

***

Today, it wasn't 'watching' Harlowe had in mind.

They drove up in True's car—which wasn't known by the deputies. When Ledbetter's men went home, True staked out Junior's bungalow. Sat in the car, like before. But, while Junior and wife ate their steak supper at the Silver Slipper, Harlowe stepped out onto the running board. "Wait for me, hear?"

He disappeared into the dark backyard. And went inside the house!

The back door was mighty easy.

What am I looking for? Everything.

He opened drawers. Looked under the bed. Climbed into the attic. The house was tidy and well-kept—a credit to Mrs. Cory. Baseball trophies lined a shelf. Baseball equipment filled a small closet in the hall. Beside the bed, a Bible lay opened to the fifty-first Psalm. The only unusual thing he found, perhaps, was a new camera the teacher had purchased. He carefully returned it to it's box. Slipped back to True's automobile.

"Let's go see Driscoll, right quick," Harlowe said.

And Harlowe got in Driscoll's apartment like an old cat burglar.

EIGHTY-TWO

October, 1938

Harlowe had them along the Sumatra Road, poking into woods dense as a wall!

"I caint imagine he'll want to go on," whispered Brewer.

Seago shrugged.

"Boss, it's gittin' late!" cried T.K.

"All right, boys. Let's go," said Harlowe.

"Where?" said Seago, hoping Harlowe meant 'home.'

"Up *a ways.*"

They piled in the automobiles. Seago was telling Brewer all about *Pals of the Saddle*—until Harlowe told True to stop, just before the bridge at Whiskey George Creek.

True got out of the car, quickly—eagerly. Brewer moved like Prissy on an errand. Harlowe looked back. "Boys, I appreciate you comin.' We gonna do this one more time. Then, I b'lieve we'll have it."

Brewer didn't know what to make of that! *Had the old man jumped the tracks?* "How will-ya know it's him even if we find somethin'?" he wondered. "I mean the State's Attorney done said—."

"I know it'll be him," Harlowe insisted.

"Smoke, True?" asked Seago.

"Sure."

Harlowe led them past an elbow of the creek, upsteam. Through a treeline. Onto a little, low spit of land in the crook of the next elbow—the creek doubled back on itself like a snake. They commenced digging, poking sticks into the ground.

They worked up a sweat without finding a thing. Then, out of the blue, Seago gave a holler! "Look here—b'lieve I got somethin'!" Harlowe ran over. They all got down on their knees, digging by hand.

"Damn. Just a tin plate!" cried Brewer. Deflated, they got up. Started a new area.

"What's wrong?" asked True.

"I tore my britches!" said Seago. "Sho' did!"

They kept on. It was near six o'clock. They crossed a path of twisted roots. They were hard to distinguish from snakes—until the real thing moved!

True's skin crawled at the cottonmouth gliding across the path, the refracted rays of sunlight glinting off its back. The thing was thick as his arm. Uncomfortable grayness settled into the treeline—as dusk approached.

They reached the next elbow, and clearing, the creek turning this way and that. The ground was low, soft, covered in wiregrass. Sweating, arms aching, they cut it up, searching out its secrets as if hunting for treasure. *Never knew a night this damn loud!* Seago thought. A cacophony of fiddles and jew's harps from an orchestra of bugs assaulted his ears. "Got to stop. I'm slap wore out!" he cried. He wiped his brow and neck, but wiping did no good in the humidity.

Brewer got them aside for water and whispered, "What's he aimin' at— some kinda revival meetin'?"

"I dunno," answered Seago. "I reckon he wants it *bad.*"

Seago looked at True. "I tell ya what, he's stayed after it. You can be proud of yo uncle!"

Harlowe started poking into the next elbow. "Son, he don't know when to quit!" Brewer whispered.

They moved back toward the road, to a small clearing where tappers had shanties at one time. It was obscured from the road, a secret room in the pines. They poked the ground. In between the saw palmetto.

Brewer called out to Harlowe, yonder. "Do we have-to go own? That's all this, here, by the road! We ain't found nothin'!"

Harlowe looked right at him. "Keep on—the whole clearin'."

Reluctantly, Brewer and Seago moved back toward the remains of the shanties.

To a low area carpeted with pine straw. A lone pitcher plant, oddly in bloom this late, grew in the corner of wall still standing.

They found nothing buried, but tree roots. Harlowe struck out and he knew it!

Brewer tossed his spade in the car. Rolled down his sleeves.

"All right, fellers, y'all have a good night," said Seago, fixing to crank his car.

Harlowe kept digging the low spot, stubbornly. True brought the lantern over and tried to help. *Down deep to nowhere! I feel sorry for 'em!* Seago thought. The big man almost got his shovel and went back, but suddenly they stopped.

"True?" asked Harlowe.

The boy went white. Nodded.

Seago's jaw dropped. "Son-Sonofabitch!" He dashed toward them. "T.K., come *look at this!*"

Brewer ran. "I'll be damned." *How'd Harlowe know?*

"Shine that lantern down *heah,* C. A!"

"I'm comin, Shureff!" Seago had run back for the lantern. Was trying to get it lit!

Down in the hole was a jumble of bones!

True, was wide-eyed as an owl in a lighting storm. The first skeleton bones he'd ever seen! He shivered—the shadows seemed to move, the moonlight made faces ghostly. Now the train whistle moaning—so damn loud it seemed like she was on top of them! And, they reckoned these were a child's bones, and they damn well might belong to his friend!

They dug, carefully, with their hands. True and Harlowe, handed a leg bone and an arm bone up to Seago. Jumbled up with the leg bone and dirt was a rotted scrap of burlap. "A sack?" Seago wondered. "Uh-huh—sho' is!"

"No one owns the land heah," said Brewer. That jungle hemming in the area from three sides was part of Tate's Hell. "You'd have-to wohnt to get back heah—would have-to know the area."

There were little finger bones. Carefully, they handed them up.

"I'll be darned!" whispered Seago.

"You was right—all along!" declared Brewer.

The sheriff clapped the dirt from his hands. "T.K., would you, kindly, fetch Doc Murrow?"

"Huh?"

"And Mr. Hickey."

"Huh?"

"I want you to go find Doc and the photographer. Carry 'em back heah or ask 'em to come, presently. Notify Judge Evans if you can find 'im." *"If he ain't half-lit."*

Brewer thought it odd about Murrow, Hickey, but he climbed into Harlowe's Ford. Sped off to do as he was asked.

"Take a break, son." Harlowe handed the boy a cigarette.

A half-hour passed. Harlowe didn't know how he'd get the county to pay for it, but he wanted more than his word. "They won't get to sweep this thing away like a damn sandcastle on the seashore," he told Seago. Mr. Hickey climbed down from the car. Harlowe led him to the grave. The photographer man looked terrified! "I ain't never taken pictures like 'is."

"It's a new experience for me too, R.P. You think you can get a couple right heah? And take one back a little fu'ther—that area, theah?"

"Uh-huh. Where the hole is and the pines behind?"

"That's right."

"S-sure, Pratt."

"All right. You got enough bulbs?"

"Y-yeah." Shakily, he put one in. Snapped a photo. Swapped the bulb and flashed another. Again. And again. Finally, he'd shot a dozen.

"Thankya, Mr. Hickey. You done good."

The man was happy to go!

Murrow arrived in Crumley's taxi; the doctor zigzagged through the pines, the colored man aside him with a flashlight.

Harlowe nodded to True to continue. Carefully, True cleared more dirt with his fingers. And there was another layer of bones! "Tarsal bones. Humerus. A pelvis," Murrow identified.

Doc looked at what they'd laid on Harlowe's coat. "Pratt, I'm afraid I can tell you no more than what you can see yourself. It's a child. You can see that from the size, length of the femur and so forth. How he died is somethin' you'll need to know."

"Well, I'm just thinkin', just thinkin' you understand. But I wonder if a doctor from Riverside Hospital in Jacksonville, might be brought in."

"Yessir?"

"You need someone who knows more than I do. A fella who can look at these bones and give ya something that'll help catch who did this."

"Dr. Elston?" suggested Seago.

"Certainly, if he's available," agreed Murrow. "Even if he couldn't come Doctor Elston could suggest who to telephone, having himself worked at Riverside."

"We'll phone him. T.K., what did Judge Evans say?"

"He didn't wanna come! He wuddint drunk, he just said, 'no need.' He'll git up with-ya!"

"All right." Harlowe looked back at the hole. "Keep siftin', True."

"Yessir."

True sifted with his bare hands, through the dirt and fragments of bone.

"No buttons in theah?"

"Nosir. No clothin'!"

"He prob'ly wuddint wearin' no shirt!" thought Seago.

"Gibby only had on his britches 'n 'spenders, mos' likely," True reckoned. "And that funny hat."

Doc handed a cigarette down to True. "Thankya, Doc."

The men held their feeble lights. In the weak glow that spilled into the hole, True was able to distinguish bone from tree roots. He stayed down there, handing up the pieces to Harlowe, one at a time.

"Got somethin'!" True handed it up. A strip of leather from the bottom! "His 'spenders. Made of old plowline. One side—I don't see the other." True dug deeper just to be sure.

True looked at it. Looked back to the pile of bones. Back to Harlowe.

"Yessir. Well, we know it's him, son," said Harlowe.

Doc looked at the article. "Appears to be fully intact."

Harlowe looked at each of them. "I appreciate you boys comin' through and workin so hard. I caint tell ya enough."

They moved the pieces, the makings of a macabre puzzle, putting down a tarp in the trunk of Crumley's taxi.

True was give out. Harlowe had to help him out of the hole. Walked him to the taxi. He sat in the front seat, silently, while the others loaded his friend's bones in the trunk. They had to hand carry them for the automobiles couldn't come through the trees. *Gibby was just parts like a car in a shop. Best not think of it.*

Harlowe closed the trunk. The doctor looked over at him. Harlowe nodded. He could only say it low, *"Always knew I'd find 'im."*

"We can take the...remains to my office...uh, they'll be safe there. Then you need to get some rest—you all do!" Murrow declared.

"All right, Doc."

"Skeered ya, huh?" Seago whispered to True.

True swallowed. Nodded.

"You 'n me both! Standin' theah, y'all comin' up with them bones! Hell, I felt my heart beatin' out my chest!"

"Hold on. We got some more diggin' boys," said the Sheriff.

"What?" spat Seago, wiping sweat away. "What the hell we lookin' for now?"

"Britches. No clothin' found with 'im. Don't that strike you as odd?"

"I dunno, maybe the worms done got it—done eat it up after how many years he's been down there."

It didn't pay to argue. "All right, bossman," Seago relented, handing a shovel to True. They dug down another foot. They saw nothing. "Y'want us to keep goin'?"

Harlowe shook his head. "No—let's fill 'er in."

True rode with the bones back to Murrow's office. First thing in the morning, they notified the coroner. Judge Evans was fit-to-be-tied, but he came anyway. Harlowe and the others had gathered in the examining room, Harlowe leaning against the counter.

Evans had a hangover. Consequently, he was particularly ill-tempered this early in the morning. However, when he saw Aubrey he reined in some of his displeasure. "More than likely you just disturbed a nigra burial grave!" he said, softly.

Harlowe responded, "With no head?"

Louder, screechier, he retorted, "Y'should give the bones a respectful burial! And go about your business! The bones display no indications of violence. Don't you agree, J.S.?"

"Well, not so's I can determine."

"Animal coulda got the skull—I see no reason to make more of it! Nothin' more can be done!" insisted the lawyer.

"Aren't you gonna order an autopsy?" asked Harlowe.

"I just told you! There's no need o' one. No sign that indivdual—whomever he was, died an unnatural death."

Harlowe knew, from being informed by Miss Hilda, that Evans had already phoned the State's Attorney. He leaned forward. "No inquest?"

"Who'd testify? To what end? It's undetermined. Person unknown. John Doe. That's how I'll sign the death certificate. Good, day, *gennellmen.*"

"Certainly a jew-ree ought—" protested Brewer.

"I am not required to summon a jury! The Sheriff knows that—Pratt?"

Harlowe looked disgusted. "Yeah, no one can make ya."

"There's no cause, Pratt! Y'can see that?"

"Sure, Judge. You've made up your mind."

Birch had held his peace until now. "Ya ain't gonna call a jew-ree? Why the hell not? If it were Cory killed down heah, you'd call them *jew-roars!*"

"I don't want any hard feelings. After our investigation, here, there's not one sign of criminal agency!"

"How's that? Someone done stowed away a youngun out theah an' nobody knowed about it, ain't head nor jaw with it, nor marker, how can ya say it ain't no crime?" demanded Birch.

"I've made my decision, Aubrey. The law give me no other choice! Now, if you find something else, why—you boys understand."

They all looked at him. Birch was thoroughly appalled. Evans washed his hands of it. Officially, he had. *Now he can go back to bed and get to the bar at the Gibson by 2:00.* "Sure," said Harlowe.

Harlowe lit a cigarette as Evans drove away. "What do you think, Doctor?"

Murrow studied the bones on his examination table. "Pratt, I disagree but I don't know enough to argue with 'im."

"Go on."

"I mean no disrespect to Judge Evans. But, I declare, he may be mistaken, heah."

"Yes, sir?"

"You see this area, heah? It may be a trauma—an injury."

Birch nodded.

"What do you recommend, Doc?" asked Harlowe.

Murrow accepted a light. Puffed and mulled. True looked at Harlowe and back to the Doc.

"I believe you ought to send for—well, it's my opinion that we should telephone Dr. Elston and ask him to come d'rectly! I think there must be a thorough examination of these remains for determination of cause and manner of death. That is my recommendation, sir."

"Well, I take that recommendation, sir. And I'm glad to do it."

"Evans' gonna be peeved," Seago cautioned. "You didn't ask him nothin' about sending for the pathol'gy doc."

Harlowe looked at the old doctor. "With these polticians we have heah, it's better to say your 'by-your-leaves' than beg for permission."

Murrow smiled. "If it suits you, I will telephone Doctor Elston immediately."

"Fine, sir."

***

It was baking hot at the depot. Their quaint little railroad was, as always, late.

The "3:10" from River Junction backed in at a quarter-of-four! Murrow wore his white straw fedora and shirtsleeves to meet his colleague. Elston, also, wore a summer hat and had worked himself into a foul mood from the hot train ride.

They had to work around the elected coroner without riling him. Quietly, they put Elston in a car. Whisked him to Dr. Murrow's office.

Elston cussed the heat in the examining room. Began to look at the bones. "You boys did a fine job collecting and cleaning."

"Yessir," replied Harlowe.

"You think y'can tell somethin' just from these bones?" asked Brewer.
"Oh, yes," replied Elston. He wasn't even rough when he answered.
"How did you fellas come to find the remains—where?"
Seago answered. "Well, Pratt—the Sheriff—was just *fit to be tied!* We were out there, all evenin', hadn't found a *damn* thing! 'Well, boys, you can go on,' he says. We was fixin' to leave, then he commenced to jus' *flailin'* the shovel! Dirt flyin'! But ain't come on a damn thing! He plum wore hisself out—had t'quit then!"
"Yeah?" asked Elson, getting his bag open.
"Then True come back n'started to he'p 'im! Both of 'em kep' on. I'll be damned if True, theah, hit somethin'!"
"This was along the Sumatra Road?"
"Yessir."
Elston nodded. He was quiet for several minutes, analyzing the bones, looking at certain among them under a surgical loupe.

"You were, correct, Dr. Murrow. Broken hyoid. He was choked. That suspender may be your instrument."

"Yeah, Doc?"

"He may have choked him with it, and that's how it was deposited with the bones. It seems to me the body was moved—the sack, the way the bones weren't in line and so forth."

Seago and True looked at Harlowe.

"I reckon Gibby tried to fight 'im off and he killed him," Harlowe declared. "Couldn't take the chance o' gettin' caught."

They were all sickened by the story the evidence told.

Elston scoffed at the coroner's paperwork. "'Undetermined,' horse feathers!" His language got stronger the more he went on!

"You reckon the state's attorney will take it to the *grand jew-ree?*" wondered True.

"He's got to." Harlowe looked pale. "What...that young'n went through—it bothers me."

Evans was consulted by telephone. "I don't find cause to change the record. I disagree it shows foul play—y'said yourself, the skeleton wasn't intact, that it was likely moved. No, I won't change it."
"The matter is conclusive!" protested Elston.
Harlowe and Murrow tried to calm the latter. He was hopping mad by the time Evans hung up.
They drove to the Gibson Inn. They had a seat at the bar. Scotch was poured for the doctors and Seago. The coffee in back suited Harlowe. Murrow enjoyed a Chesterfield, Elston the rest of his Camels, smoke clouding the comfortable, mahogany-paneled room as the men talked. An hour passed. They, as men who had experienced politics, had questions that answered themselves. And they had answers that offered only more questions. And they had the same answers and the same questions as when they walked in. But it did good for men to talk it over, sometimes, enjoying tobacco and their drink of choice.

The Birches joined them. "There is no doubt. I've seen this kind of injury many times," Elston explained.
"You reckon, now, they'll call a grand jew-ree?" asked Mr. Birch.

"Will the state's attorney pursue it?" asked Mrs. Birch. "Can you persuade him?"

"We're sure gonna try."

***

They met at the Floridan.

"Don't call it murder. It ain't murder," said Raines.

"*Did* he kill the kid?" asked Hoyt Conway.

"If we admit it's murder, we look bad," said Ledbetter. "We could be embarrassed. 'Why didn't we do anything sooner?' they'll say."

"Don't build it up," said Huff. "It'll blow over. If you fight with 'im, you give 'im what he wants, get his name in the paper! Let him alone he'll get tired and quit."

Raines got up. "Harlowe isn't a detective. All he's ever done is catch a few chicken thieves and, uh, jail a few coloreds down there. It's not murder if *we* say it's not."

"Pender won't comment either way. If he's asked," said Huff.

Hoyt Conway chewed his pipe. "I talked to the editor, O.C. He's got the word that any stories on this would be be viewed as mighty unfavorable."

"You think he'll play ball?" asked Ledbetter.

"He'll play ball."

Raines was grave, "This is a good place to live. We have good people here. Harlowe would have people thinkin' there's a madman loose! Now I gotta worry he'll turn up out here on Mun-row interrogatin' people. They'll wanna know what I'm doin," said Raines.

"I know, O.C.," said Conway.

"We're not gonna call it murder if it hurts the people of this town, we're here to protect," said Raines.

"Can't he be reasoned with?" asked Lamar.

"Money? He's too stubborn," said Ledbetter.

"You know, coming to an understanding is the shrewd thing. Better to have a man with part of the action, than have him outside," said Conway.

"I agree," said Lamar.

"If he wants to be stubborn—why, we can make things pretty unpleasant for Mr. Harlowe," said the private dick.

***

Huff started cordial. "I know you've always done a fine job for the people of this county, an' uh, we all appreciate that. But this thing with Tallahassee. You spend countless hours on a case that the state's attorney believes was an accident! Hell, the boy probably run away and joined the circus!"

"I checked on that. Maybe if one was in town that week, he coulda got ideas. There wasn't one."

"What you trying to do? What will satisfy you, Pratt?"

"I mean to arrest the killer."

Huff's face got red. "You mean Cory? This is a damn mess, Pratt! I'm tellin' you this is bad for this county!"

True came in the, wide-eyed. "Don't worry about that, son. He and I never gee-hawed."

Harlowe talked to the tappers at Green Point, some of whom had been there in '27. They recalled nothing unusual going on at the gravesite in all those years. One last thing he had to check before they saw Raines.

Then they had to wait two more days. Raines' secretary informed them that the prosecutor and his wife had to go out of town on a family atter.

They climbed the stairs to the latter's office. "Harlowe. You come all this way, let's hear it."

Harlowe told him about the bones. "It was murder. An' I can prove it."

"The coroner's jury didn't call it murder."

"No, sir, they didn't. They left it undetermined. They didn't have the remains at that time—we have 'em now."

Raines jabbed his finger at the desk. "Your coroner hasn't amended his findings. He felt these bones were older than a decade. You want me to try a case where all the defense has to do is call Evans?"

"Elston can explain that. He's had pathologist trainin.'"

"He's a nuthouse quack. Jury won't buy that."

"Doesn't it strike you as odd these bones are the same size as Gibby and no head? And put just miles from where Junior was campin'? Right there, we have the suspender just like the ones Gibby wore."

"Conjecture. Opinion. Suspenders like a thousand other farmboys. Everythin' you're comin' up with's useless."

"That broken hyoid bone—surely, *that* isn't useless," said Harlowe.

"If you want to do it you don't need me—arrest him! But get ready for Mr. Smalley to get it thrown right out of there!"

"Supposin' you put somethin' into tryin' the case, it wouldn't get thrown out."

Raines went red and jabbed his finger at them. "I've had about enough of this foolishness. Keep bringing it to me, I'll keep telling you the same answer. I won't prosecute it! I know what I have to prove to a jury and how to do it without someone like you tellin' me how! I've been doing this since you were still scrapin' for oysters!"

They walked out to the sidewalk in front of the bank. True looked at his uncle, wide-eyed. "Ya caint pay attention to him, True. He's just thataway."

True nodded.
"Let's go, son."

Harlowe lit a cigarette as they drove home. *Manner of death—was it naïve to think it's a question of medical fact, or the verdict of a jury, rather than a political calculation? Deciding we had a killer around wasn't good for the people who run things. It might upset folk. Then again, it might implicate the wrong folk.*

***

They told the Birches about the meeting. "It ain't important then, what happened to Gibby! "Our son don't matter!" Aubrey reasoned.

"We're from Eastpoint 'n don't matter!" added Mrs. Birch. "We don't count as much as his fam'ly—one o' their families up theah!"

"It's like my son is nothin' more than gravel they mix in the concrete and have 'em a new road! Jus' bury us underneath."

The pain on their faces—True shuddered at the sight.

EIGHTY-THREE

November, 1938

Junior opened the door for the boy to get in. They drove to the teacher's bungalow. Cory led him to the door, the child holding his schoolbooks. Harlowe spun the wheel over, pulling across Junior's driveway.

He looked over at Junior. The latter looked back—closed the door. Mrs. Cory peered out the window, a bewildered look on ther face.
Harlowe and True sat there, watching through the front windows as Junior helped the boy with his lesson.

***

Harlowe entered his kitchen—telephone jingling in the hall.
Her voice was raspy, like she was in poor health—or a lush. "I have some information for ya. About the missin' boy. I'll be at the tourist court."
"Who is this?"
"Jus' git here—it'll be worth your trouble I promise-ya!"
CLICK.
Harlowe parked on De Soto Street. Hat low, he walked in the back way to Lake Ella. There was a small boy fishing at the lake. No one else around. Harlowe walked around the stone cabins, over to the "log cabin" indicated. There was no car in front. He slid along the back wall to the window. Looked in.
They've set a girl in there. Practic'ly neck-ed. She was lying on the bed, looking up at the ceiling, smoking. Bottle on the table. He looked around the corner and saw a new business-coupe yonder—the Private Dick was there, no doubt with a camera ready to go to work.
Harlowe high-tailed it out of town.

***

Junior brought the boys home, Harlowe and True were there, again.

"What if he calls Ledbetter?" True asked.

Harlowe got a 'look.' "I hope he does."

Harlowe knew this couldn't go on much longer. They couldn't always be there. Junior sat by the window, the shade up. His wife was his alibi! They were too! But Junior would find the right time, when there were no witnesses.

***

Magnolia Bluff—where he'd found the boat. Harlowe parked at the foot of the bridge, looking out over the water. It was hard not to feel dejected. Ledbetter had assigned two cars just to watch Harlowe, with instructions to stay on his bumper the moment he entered Leon County. A Tallahassee reporter was poking around Apalach. Trying to dig up dirt—thought Seago.

The man approached Harlowe. In the shadow behind the courthouse. "Mornin.' Can I...do somethin' for ya?"

"Oh, good morning! I'm Jim Coughlin—with the *Democrat?* Say, I would you sit for an interview? Maybe we can cover some of the cases from the old days."

Harlowe shook his head. "Why not run somethin' that would do some good?"

"Like what?"

"Gibby Birch."

"Is something happening?"

Harlowe told him a great deal had happened—and Harlowe figured this was the one time any reporter took an interest—might as well tell him they'd found the body. "You can Talk to Mr. and Miss Birch—half a dozen people."

"I'll have to speak to my editor about that."

Harlowe nodded.

"If what you're saying is so, why hasn't a grand jury been called?"

Harlowe said, "We hope there will be. We're askin' Mr. Raines to do just that."

Even the *Apalachicola Times* hadn't mentioned the bones. The "black-out" on Gibby's case continued.

***

One more time—they watched Junior's house. Through the window. Watched him drop off the boy, like they were cattle dogs watching a coyote.

It was dark. Hot. The crickets chirping as they changed a flat south of Tallahassee. A car slowed—Sackett's Ford. He pulled in front of the De Soto. Got out. "Howdy, Pratt—True! Saw y'all. Thought I'd have a friendly word with ye. Y'know ridin' around here, doin' what you doin'—it's not very neighborly. Some folks' are startin' to get aggravated with that. We're all friends, so I'm gonna let it go. But I wanna tell ya—Lamar's a good man. I went to skoo with 'im. We won't have ye you makin' trouble for 'im—or any decent people."

"I ain't aimin' to make trouble—but I'm gonna find out what I wanna know. And I'm gonna arrest the murderer and anyone that helped," said Harlowe.

"Why, there ain't no murdruh, heah! Y'think we'd let one jus' run around town—you're crazy," he said softly.

"Well, I reckon the jew-ree ought to decide that, Royce."

At that, two more deputies pulled up. Surrounded the car on the jack.

Harlowe looked at True. *Stay still.*

True nodded.

Sackett jabbed his finger. "You ain't gonna arrest nobody in this county. Keep drivin' by 'is house, and I'll arrest *you!*"

Durfee bowed up on True, trying to provoke him. "That goes for you, too, boah! Hey, boah, ya gonna let me push ya?" The man pulled out his handcuffs. Grabbed True's wrist. "I'll put ya in jail!" True shoved him back.

Harlowe saw the man in the shadow. Saw the shotgun. "Get back, True."

True was red with anger, but he stepped back.

Sackett stood in the glow of the headlights, making his face yellowish, pale. "Now, we've known eachother a long time, Pratt. But keep on, someone's gonna get hurt. I hate that, but you leavin' me no choice."

***

Mr. Couglin phoned Raines. Ledbetter was in the office.

Raines hung up and cussed. "He wants to ask about the Birch case!"

"Talk to Merritt. Get him to run a story that puts an end to this."

"What'll he say?"

"He can write...how Harlowe's been drunk during the daylight hours! N' Sundee! After that, y'think there'll be any sympathy out there for him—all them church ladies and such?"

Raines got a look of disgust on his face–Harlowe imbibing like that–even though they'd just made it up.

The State's Attorney summoned the local editor, Merritt Campbell.

"Oh, it is a very nice view from this office!" said the editor, crossing the room.

"Sit down."

"Thank you. I'm curious about this Birch case. My reporter was down there—piqued my interest."

"I know you called about it, but there's nothing to it, Merritt. The Birch boy had a history of runnin' away."

"Oh?"

"As the state attorney I was elected to be a minister of justice, to stand for the law—*to do right*. That individual, has forgotten what he was elected to do—if he ever knew."

"Sheriff Harlowe?"

"Yes, Merritt. He's trying to make a name for himself on a tragedy. It's a sad thing, but I think the boy is still alive."

"Yessir?"

"He run off."

"That's what you've determined?"

"Things like this happen, all the time. My, uh, nephew ran away for several years. He wrote his mother he had joined the navy. An' I, uh, I have nothin' but sympathy for the Birch boy's mother. There's no sign of foul play, and it's unfortunate Harlowe would say the things he does. It's irresponsible."

"There's talk—there's talk in Apalachicola—that Harlowe thinks this is being swept under the carpet, by yourself and Sheriff Ledbetter. Is there some reason not to pursue a serious crime like this?"

"I don't know where he gets that. Why, the sheriff and I work night and day to solve them."

"There's no truth to it then."

"There's nothing to any of these claims of his. Now, I must be going. I've a case in Wakulla County."

"Of course. Could you comment on that later in the week?"

"Sure, come up and see me and I'll tell you all about it. Good to see you, Merritt."

***

Today's *Democrat*. Seago swatted it with his paw. "Can ya b'lieve this? They all but call you a carpetbaggin', scallywaggin' drunk, Pratt!"

"No mention of Gibby a'tall," said True.

"I'm not surprised," said Harlowe.

447

"'Some consider Sheriff Harlowe's actions lawless, bordering on vigilantism.' Why, it's all lies!" Seago cried. "Aubrey had the right idea—take 'im out in the boat, put 'im where he'll never be found!"

Harlowe walked the hall of the courthouse. He patted the pistol in his coat. He usually didn't notice the weight of it against his chest.

I can end this. The way it's going, True or one of my men may get hurt. Wind up on the side of the road somewhere.

No, you said it before. That ya wanted a trial so everyone would know what happened, everybody see the Cory boy was guilty. Harlowe believed in the law–he saw it work in the Forehand case where they stopped a lynching and tried the killer. And in the Hinds case of late.

True found him, later, on the bank of Scipio Creek. They watched a frog flick his tongue and get a fly. They stood at the boundary of civilization and wild land. Maybe it wasn't a clear boundary. Law on one side. Justice the other.

"No, we're gonna do it within the law. So everyone can see a man like that don't just get by with it. It's worked before, and we ought to let it work now. We got to believe in that."

True nodded.

"You don't have to come with me, son."

"No, I wohnt to."

"All right. We got to be smarter about it."

They got in the car, passing the Cory truck pouring concrete for the new courthouse—up the ramp to the bridge.

Ledbetter's men were prowling Tallahassee.

They spotted each of the cars. "See that one, True?"

"Yeah."

"There's Hoyt Conway—by the hoe-tell."

They drove Seago's Model A—so far it hadn't been spotted.

They reached the grammar school unobserved.

"It's set to rain," said Harlowe. The final bell, they followed Cory home—his student riding beside him.

Mrs. Cory wasn't home, they saw.

True's heart beat fast. Matching the beating rain.

Harlowe slipped over to the house. Looked in the kitchen window, raindrops streaking down the glass. Junior sat at the table, helping the boy with his arithmetic.

The downpour began. Harlowe ran back, got in the car with True.

They followed until Junior dropped the boy at his apartment.

True noticed the car following, then.

A Ledbetter man. "Kinda late for him," thought True.

"Don't stop," said Harlowe. They sped down 319—into the darkness.

***

Ledbetter had a man at the county line, by the dam. Another waited near Junior's house.

"It's no use. Let's go, True." They took US-90 through Quincy.

Then raced South. Sped along until they were clean through Sumatra.

Suddenly, a rifle shot cracked the night air. Bullets whined just shy of the windshield. *In an instant he was in France. He was on the Sumatra Road. France. Sumatra.* "Lean on it, True!"

True shoved the throttle to the floor—the car lunging forward.

Another shot! A bullet pinged Seago's fender.

Leaning over the wheel, True kept his foot to the floor until they made the Franklin line.

They got Seago and Brewer. Loaded Winchesters. Went back up the road with eyes peeled.

In the daylight they walked into the flatwoods. "No casings—no nothin'," remarked Brewer.

"About what I expected to find," said Harlowe.

Harlowe talked in hushed tones with Murrow in the parlor of the old house. Doc thought Harlowe looked exhausted. "I haven't enough to make Raines call the grand jew-ree. Risk to my men is too great. I don't wanna get one of 'em killed. I have to stop," Harlowe admitted.

It sickened him. He knew Junior would roam again. Would hurt a child when the eyes come off him. *Harlowe could see him now. Looking back at me. His coy half-smile. Closing that door—knowing he's won.*

EIGHTY-FOUR

Christmas Eve, 1938

Tennie promised to walk to the *Dixie* with him. He knocked, but it was Mrs. Buckles who answered. "Oh, I'm sorry, True. She left—not more than a quarter-hour ago. Would you care for some coffee? It's cool out there."

"Sure. Thankya."

He sat. Had a cup with her. "Well, I better go," he said, after he'd finished it.

"It was so nice you visitin' with me, True. I hope to see you again soon!"

"Yes'm."

True walked along the sidewalk—uptown. There was a comfort in the quiet, yet a painful lonesomeness pulled at him at the same time. He liked the decorations, the wreaths, the glow of the streetlights. It was getting dark now, turning cold.

He heard a voice he recognized, and looked over. *She doesn't see me, but there's Tennie climbing into that Chevrolet with Angie and the Rackliffe boys! Tennie's no fifth wheel, they're double-dating.*

True looked at the fishing rods in the window of the Western Auto, trying not to let another cold teardrop roll down his cheek.

***

"Huff's got his hackles up about somethin'," said Seago. "Oh, hello, commissioner!"

"Uh-Mornin.' Pratt, we'd like to talk to you, first."

Harlowe walked with him, down to the basement of the courthouse.

Seago found True, outside. "I'm gonna tell ya. He ain't no friend of your uncle's, now." All they could do was wait.

Harlowe faced the commissioners, alone in the chair. They'd been stirred up to a froth.

"Three-dollar toll calls! A whole page of long-distance calls. The county caint afford such expense!" Huff really raised the roof. *One of his better speeches!* Harlowe reckoned.

"How many days were ya in Tallahassee?" another commissioner wanted to know.

Harlowe told them.

451

"You're causin' trouble we don't need!" Huff snapped. "The guv'ner has hired a private detective to look into your actions!"

"I've nothing to hide," replied Harlowe. "He'll spend more time tryin' to discredit me than they ever did on Gibby's case."

"We need tourists—not investigators," said the other commissioner.

"And for a case the coroner said was an accident!" remarked Huff.

"What have you got to say, Pratt?" asked the older commissioner at the far end.

"We've traveled as cheaply as we could and got this close to solving it. If you vote this in, you'll about cut all I get."

"Let's vote." They proceeded to raise hands. They wouldn't reimburse Harlowe's long-distance telephone bill. Or his mileage. But they spared the money he got to run the jail—at the urging of the older gentleman. "Uh, we've voted, and my message to you is, get back to work—on our county's bidness and no more!" Huff admonished.

Harlowe sensed Pender's hand was in this. The latter angling for a run in '40.

In the hall, Huff shoved eviction papers at Harlowe. "Uh—I need ya to serve these, Pratt."

"Yessir."

Seago was coming down the stairs, then—True behind him. The jailor looked at Harlowe. *Yeah?*

Harlowe told him.

"Damn skinflints," muttered Seago.

Harlowe looked at True. "Not much we can do—on the other."

***

True got home. Changed in time to pick up Tennie. True was beat. He oystered part-time and did odd jobs to keep gasoline in the car.
He forgot about being tired when Tennie started kissing him, parked on Bluff Road. Abruptly, she stopped. "Say...can I ask ya somethin'?"
"Sure."
"Weel," she said in a little voice. "Can we see the new picture at the *Dixie?* Pwease?"
***

Harlowe sat by the road in Eastpoint. It always gnawed at him that the man could come back. He'd drive back across the bridge and it would gnaw at him and he'd turn around. *Was it an obsession?*
He looked out over the Bay. The wind was hot and swift.
It's fixin' to storm.

Part V

EIGHTY-FIVE

January, 1939

Harlowe shingled the roof for the Sheip's—127 Bay Avenue. Cashed the check at the bank. True bought his first suit-of-clothes that matched. Second hand. And a fedora that still had some of its shape left in it.

And they could pick up the case again.

The Williams girl, Marlene, flagged him down as he was leaving home. "Boy, that sure is a nice suit!"

"H-hey, Marlene, whachya up to?" True replied.

"Oh, nothin.'"

She made smalltalk—not what she wanted to talk to him about.

"Well, it's good talkin' to ya. I gotta get goin'. I have a, uh, date with Tennie."

He seems so happy about it. "You know she--."

"She what?"

"She's only gonna do you wrong--." Marlene put her hand over her mouth. She was never one to hold back what she was thinking, but she knew she'd gone too far.

"Well, I gotta be goin'. See ya, Marlene."

He checked files in police stations. Sheriff's offices. He showed the photos to folks in parts of Florida tourists never saw. They'd shake their heads, politely, tell him they were sorry they couldn't help.

Driving along, he went over what Harlowe told him. *Similar crimes. Missing children. I'm interested in anything that could show Cory done this before.*

The local sheriffs and chiefs let him look, but True wondered if he really would *know it* if he saw it. After four thousand miles and a set of recaps, he hadn't!

The last one was the worst, it took him nearly two days of legwork to hear, "Oh, that that little fella's home. That paper shouldn't be in there!"

He crossed the Georgia line chasing another one. Only to find the lost boy had turned up after the report was filed, and no one notified the Meriwether County sheriff.

He looked at Harlowe's list. Drove to Marianna. Talked to peanut farmers. Hog farmers. To women working in a sewing factory. To people in places that weren't on the maps.

He crossed off Marianna. Took US-90 to Chipley. He showed a picture of Junior at the feed store. He showed the photo at the brick-factory. Showed it to boys picking oranges. No one knew the face.

He waited on the train to rumble through the little downtown, there. Parked beside the courthouse. Dashed up the steps. His shoes echoed down the polished hall. He stopped at the door that said, "Sheriff's Office." Opened it.

"Ma'am, I'd like to see the Sheriff."

The lady barely looked up from what she was doing. "He ain't here just now."

True explained what he was there for. The lady looked up only to shoot him a curious glance. Then she vanished behind another door.

She returned, presently, a man with her this time.

"Jus' what'r you a-huntin' fur?" he asked.

True explained.

"Go on and let 'im look," said the fellow. True didn't know who he was.

The woman led True to wooden cabinets which lined a small corridor. He started through the drawers stuffed with papers.

People passed by in the hall, curious about the stranger. "What's he here fur?" they whispered.

"Why, he's huntin' a paper."

"Yeah?"

And, sometimes, the same lady would ask him again, what it was he was looking for. "A lost child paper, arrest card, anything," True explained.

"You awful young aint ya?"

He was a stranger, a curiosity. It almost made him laugh, but it was oddly tiring just looking through paperwork. He closed the drawer. Rubbed his eyes. Shook his head.

"Where you headed next?" asked the woman.

"Oh, Graceville, I reckon."

"Good luck with that," she dead-panned.

One last drawer. His eyes felt like they were filled with sawdust. *Last one. Hope I have money enough to make Graceville and back!*

He opened it. *Nothing...Nothing...Wait...Hold on!*

"Lost boy...picked up by Patrolman Everly...child returned to mother in Tallahassee."

And the name—Finn Young. Where've I seen that?

Then it occurred to him. *That's it!* True nearly leapt with the paper!

He jotted it down. Closed his notebook. Wheeled about for the door!

"Y'find somethin', son?" asked the man there.

True turned around. "Yessir—thanks! Bye, now!"

True had to find a payphone. Didn't see one in Chipley. He raced on to Cottondale—screeching to a halt at the depot. Dove in the phonebooth. Dropped a nickel. More change for Apalachicola. "I found it! Missin' boy— he run away from Tallahassee!"

Harlowe was elated. "That's fine, son!"

"Picked up in Chipley! Finn Young—Finley Young—I remembered the name from the ballplayers—he's one of the boys!"

"Yeah—I remember the name," said Harlowe.

EIGHTY-SIX

Harlowe read it over as they drove—an automatic rifle between them.

"The boy's name is Finley Young. Y'say there's no record of it at Leon County?"

"Not that I saw," said True. "Run away in thirty-seven."

Harlowe had given True the BAR rifle. They'd used them as light machine guns at Château-Thierry. *"Tote it with a round chambered—any time we get near Tallahassee,"* Harlowe had said. They were at the City Limits, now. As evidenced by the butterflies in True's stomach.

They turned onto Boulevard. A dark void. No streetlight.

The screendoor groaned. Down the hall, the landlord fussed with the sink in the bathroom, a cigarette hanging from his lips. He shined with sweat, cussed the wrench. "Yeah?"

"We're lookin' for Mrs. Young."

The landlord didn't answer. True saw the door was ajar. Looked in the gap. "She's gone."

Harlowe looked about. He opened the chiffarobe—it was empty save a few mothballs. He looked at the bed and the roll-away contraption the boy slept on. The sink had a drip, loudly plopping the rust-stained bowl.

Across the hall, the door cracked open. They asked the woman about her neighbor. Her face puckered. "What she's up to, I wouldn't know. Her, a divorced woman. That is something I don't approve of, sir—and I don't associate with people who live—*that way!"*

Harlowe tipped his hat. "Yes, ma'am."

They found her in Tifton, getting off work at the cotton mill.

Her fair skin flashed pink.

"Whadya want with me?"

"It's about Finley, ma'am. We jus' wanna talk to ya—we have our car, can we drop you someplace?"

"Well...it beats walkin'."

True held the Ford's back door ("suicide door") for her.

She was guarded—and curious. Settled in the back seat. She looked at True, as he drove. Studied Harlowe.

"Whadya want with Finn? He ain't done nothin'."

"No, ma'am. It's about when he was found over in Chipley."

"Oh, that. He run away's all—nothin' more to it."

"He just up and run away—he had no reason?" Harlowe asked, gently.

She looked out the window. "Why, boys jus' run away sometimes—they don't need a reason!"

"Now...he must have had a reason, hadn't he?"

She didn't answer.

"Mrs. Young?" He looked out at the road, then back. "I think he had a reason. I think you know there was somethin' wrong—somethin' to do with Mr. Cory."

They'd reached her house on Jay Flowers Road. Her face was bright red. "Thank you for for comin'—but we have no need of help—I'm sure you can do some good somewhere else, but my Finn doesn't need help!" She flung the door shut—practically ran up the walk.

***

Jeter dropped the bucket. Lamar looked over at him. "He any good?"

"He's O.K," said the foreman. "Dipso."

Jeter began washing the cement truck.

A car pulled up and Lamar walked over.

Jeter put down the hose. Slipped back around the office. In the new Olds sat Bill Ledbetter. "Look ya know I'll back you, Bill. And O.C.," Cory promised. "But I may need you on my deals; they're bigger than ever, these contracts. I don't want people nosin' around, you understand."

"Sure."

"I need you to 'run interference'—y'know, like football. That's something we'll have one day, *football.*"

Ledbetter seemed astonished. He knew Lamar had pushed through a few projects at the Women's College—but football seemed a little 'out there.' "Y'think so? The gals are gonna play football then?"

"Ha! The gals! I'm tellin' ya, in ten years' time when we have a school for *men and women,* we'll have football. Maybe I'll build the damn stadium."

"You been drinkin'?"

459

"No, I mean it, Bill! Think of the new hotels, *subdivisions*—maybe two or three! And I'm gonna build 'em. As long as no outsiders cause trouble, why, we can have us a damned kingdom here!"

***

They parked behind Leon High.

Took the stairs stairs to to the second floor. Mr. Dukes was the Young boy's teacher. "Yes, his freshman year. He was a fine student. Very bright."

"You were the boy's teacher at the time he ran away from home?"

"I was. I understand he's move. Is he all right?"

"Yessir. Have you any concerns?"

"No. I haven't."

"Any about him running away? I wonder if he mentioned anything botherin' him."

"No. He never discussed it, but--."

"Yessir?"

"I recall something else that was odd. It may not mean anything. You see, he was an excellent ballplayer, but he didn't want to go on team. His classmates begged him to; he really acted *funny* about it!"

"Funny how?"

"Like he was afraid."

"When he ran away—and came back—did you question the boy at all?"

"I asked him about it. He wouldn't say anything to me. He came back from the Panhandle and just threw himself into his studies. I could sense there was something wrong, but I didn't—I didn't follow up. I was busy. I was new. Perhaps I should have. Pat Holliday was his best frien. He's a senior, now. You may want to talk to him."

They found the senior working his afterschool job—delivering telegrams.

"Did Finnley say anything about why he ran away?"

"No, sir. I was surprised he ran away. Dunno why. His mother and daddy seemed real nice! But--."

"Yeah, son?"

"Things seemed to fall apart. His folks split up. His momma was...drinkin'—dunno know if that was so, but that's what I heard."

"Did it seem like somethin' was botherin' him?"

"Well, sir. He seemed to change. Stopped playin' ball! I live for baseball—I couldn't imagine not wantin' to play! He never would say what was bothering him. He gave up his spot—would been first-string catcher."

"This was before he ran away?"

"No, sir—after. I jus' thought it had something to do with his folks splitting up."

They got back in the car. "He's a good student, shows promise as a ballplayer, an' he suddenly runs away. Why?"

"Junior Cory," True reckoned.

Harlowe rubbed his chin. "Yeah. But you know what a good defense lawyer might say. *Something wasn't right in the home all along. Folks split up.*"

"*Reasonable doubt.* Unless he wohnts to add somethin'."

"Yeah. Sure like to talk to 'im and find out, wouldn't you?"

"Yeah."

***

They met Jeter at the dump. "Yeah, that's what I heard. N' I been a-workin' at the new ranch, too. Paintin' and such."

"Yeah?"

"I seen your buddy, Driscoll, out yonder. I hear he gave that gal money to leave town."

"Anything else?" asked Harlowe.

"Nah—done told ya. I could use a li'l beer money, now."

They pulled up in front of the Young's duplex—company housing for the Tifton Cotton Mills. "Well, at least y'didn't pester me at work," she said, throwing scraps to her little dog. "I've answered all the questions I'm going to—I have to fix supper."

True noticed she had two girls, playing in the yard. The woman looked over at them, then back to the lawmen. "Come in. Away from little ears."

She lit the stove. Got out a pan for the beans. "Nothing happened to my son."

"No, ma'am."

"You're crazy—y'think I'd stand for that for one minute?" She opened the can. Dumped it in the pan.

"The boy never mentioned what was done to him?" Harlowe asked.

"Huh-who says anything was done to him? I told ya--."

"We believe it ties in to a missin' boy—our missin' boy from Eastpoint."

"I know nothin' that would help you."

"Has Finley seemed upset by anything? Have ya noticed a...change in 'im?"

She didn't answer. But the way she stirred the pan gave him an inkling.

"What about when the Deputy in Chipley brought him home, did he say anything then?"

She started pouring biscuit batter into a pan.

"Mrs. Young?"

She nearly dropped it. "Please, let us alone! You'll make trouble for us, and I want no part of it!"

"You let 'em run you out? You gonna let 'em--."

They heard someone coming up the walk. True saw it was an older boy—walking home from an after-school job. He looked sixteen; thin, darker hair than his mother. Same nose and mouth. "Don't say anything to him," Mrs. Young whispered.

Harlowe nodded.

"My son's doing well here. Don't spoil it for him."

"Yes, ma'am."

"Hello, son! These men are from the mill—just--."

"Just checking on some tools gone missin'."

"Oh," said Finley.

"Come on, I'll show you to the door."

She shut the door behind them.

"What about the other boys—still on his team, in his classroom?" asked Harlowe.

"I can't help ya! I can get the boy into a trade school job at a factory—he'll be all right. What can you offer him? You'll ruin him, that's what!"

***

Newlin's neighbor was home from his WPA job. "Sure, y'can talk to my son."

Harlowe spoke to the boy, Ollie. He was Jack Newlin's best friend.

"Nosir. He never said nothin' to me. I ain't heard from him. I--."

"Yeah, son?"

"Wouldya tell 'im I said, hello, if y'find 'im? I miss 'im."

"I will, son."

The boy indicated Jack's great-grandmother lived on West Madison.

They found the old woman drawing water from the well behind her rented house. She had no electricity nor running water, and it appeared none of her neighbors did either.

"H'dy, Miss Newlin."

"I caint see ya—*who's there?*"

Harlowe tipped his hat.

"I'm Pratt Harlowe. This is my nephew. I wonder if we might talk to ya."

"What's this about?" "Yessir?" she asked weakly. She clutched the bucket, terrified.

"We ain't gonna hurt ya, ma'am—jus' wanna talk to ya."

"What about?"

"Your grandson, Mr. Newlin, and his boy. We were wonderin' why he left town so sudden."

She teared up. "I ain't in trouble with the law, now am I?"

"No, ma'am. You're not in trouble, neither is your grandson. Would ya know why he left the way he did?"

"I dunno," she sobbed. "He seemed skeered."

"Yes, ma'am? Scared of what?"

"I don't know, sir! Somethin' skeered him's all I know. I better say no more. I don't like what goes on in this town sometimes. With people who run things."

"Who?"

463

"I don't know," she whispered. "They in the shadahs—with no faces I can see."

"Yes, ma'am."

"I jus' know my grandyoungun and his boy--."

"Yes, ma'am?"

"They didn't look like they wanted to go. He tells the boy, 'You caint fight these people!' Skeered me to hear 'im talk like that."

They had to stop for the train whistle screaming. She continued. "He said, 'there's no happy endin' for us.' They packed up. Said, 'Granny, we can make the midnight train.' Last I saw 'im—and my great-grandyoungun."

***

On Boulevard Street, another elderly lady in a small house. She'd been a neighbor to Mrs. Young, across the street.

They removed their hats. Knocked. Explained who they were.

"Oh, you fellas are lawmen?"

"Yes, ma'am."

"Come on in, then—it's about Mrs. Young, you say?"

"Yes, ma'am."

"Is there anything wrong? You're the sheriff wheah, now?"

"Franklin County, ma'am."

"My! From all that way down yonder?"

She had them sit in her small front room. Poured coffee.

"Did she mention any trouble?"

"No. No, I couldn't imagine she'd be in any trouble—she was a sweet girl. Lovely children."

"Did you know about her boy running away?"

"Ye-ess," drawled the sweet old lady. "So sad. The boy just needed a father; her husband--."

"Yes, ma'am?"

"Well, I hate to say it," she whispered. "They split up—her man left her!"

"He ever come around?"

"I don't believe he has ever come to see those children!"

"You say, they've move up to Georgia?"

"Yes, ma'am."

"And that there may have been more to the boy runnin' away?"

"Yes, ma'am. That's what we're tryin' to find out."

"Well, she never said. But I did notice somethin'—that the boy didn't want to go to school. She had to make him go. I just thought it was somethin' boys do. Maybe there was somethin' wrong—I'm very concerned now," she said.

A Ledbetter man turned the corner.

"I think its time we get outta here, you reckon?"

True started the De Soto.

***

Jeter carried his sack of beer through the courtyard to the front door of his apartment. He went in. Downed the first bottle.

At that, a shadow crossed his window. A man in a hat.

Someone's at the back door? Is that the knob turnin'?

He'd locked it. He crept barefoot into the kitchen, got a knife.

Tap-tap-tap. *Damn.* He looked out the front door. *Pratt!*

Jeter opened up. Motioned Harlowe into the little arched vestibule. "I came in the backway—from Calhoun."

"Y'like to skeer me t'death!"

"You didn't show up at the dump."

"I wuddint feelin' too good, damnit!"

Harlowe shot a look at the empties on the floor.

"You ain't got to tell me, a'ight? They're gonna do something to ya. Don't know what. But they're gunnin' fur ya."

They heard the freight train passing, yonder.

***

Under a naked bulb, they found Mrs. Young doing piecework, in her kitchen.

She didn't look up. "You're a stubborn man, Mr. Harlowe."

"Yes'm."

"I can't tell you anything today I couldn't tell you two days ago." Her hands were shaking, True noticed. He could see that Harlowe noticed it, that she was really frightened.

"We can help you--."

"Y'can help me by lettin' this go—please."

A train whistle blew. They left.

***

True drove along, thinking. He'd heard about Huff summoning his uncle, the county commission grilling him. There were no secrets in Apalach.

True didn't know about politics, but he knew Harlowe was getting pressure. Despite how long he'd been sheriff, his uncle could not defy Huff and the commission for long. It grieved True, knowing this thing was so important to his uncle. *Well, it's important to me, to Mr. Seago. But I'm not sure Uncle Pratt has anything else—nothin' else to live for!*

He'll solve it. I got to he'p!
The sun glowed its last before it ducked below the Bay, as if someone moved a switch, highbeams-lowbeams-off. Leaving a crisp, clear purple sky. The lights glowed at the Gorrie Service Station, against the darkness of Eastpoint, the violet expanse of the Bay.

True turned around, heading back along the highway toward Carrabelle.

Ahead, there, was a car on the side of the road. *Was she broken down? Well, I've come half-a-mile from Eastpoint; reckon, they walked back to the service station?* He slowed to look at the Model T. He saw shadows. *Is that two men inside?* He was nerly alongside, now. *A fella and a young woman. Oh, they're just neckin'.* True mashed the accelerator to go on. *Wait!*
It was unmistakable, even in the dim mirror. *He hauled off and hit her!*
True slowed. The man drew back to hit her again. The car rocked when he swung. *Popped her, good! Hell—this* was *going to be an easy night.*

True swung the car around. Stopped. Ran toward the Model T. "Hey, fella, hold on! That ain't no way to treat a gal."
True shined his flashlight in the window.
The girl's shirt was torn open. She was very young.

True smelled liquor on the man's breath. True recognized him: Brannon Williams—C.P.'s brother.

"Hold on, partner," said True, interrupting the man's belligerence. True shined his light across the seat. It was the little Williams girl—Marlene. *Damn.*

True's eyes went to the empty bottle. The man's red, flushed face. The man's niece trembling, her shirt torn clear to the fourth button. It didn't take much of a detective to put it together.

Brannon swung the door open—all 250 pounds of him getting out. "Look here, this ain't nothin'—she sassed me, and I slapped her for talkin' back."

"Why's her shirt torn?"

"She's hard on her clothes. What's it to you, anyhow?" He took a step toward True.

"Take it easy," said True.

"You take it easy. You don't tell me nothin', boy, you hear me! I'm fixin' to go home."

At that, headlights approached—C.P. and his boys in the battered Overland car.

C.P. stomped down from the running board. "What's goin' on here?"

"I found your brother heah...with your li'l girl."

"She sassed me. I's givin' her a ride home! We's comin' back from Carrabelle."

"If Marlene sassed him, he can hit her. Ain't nothin' that concerns you!"

"I b'lieve maybe there's more to it. Maybe I'll just carry him to the sheriff's office until we straighten it out."

"You ain't doin' a thing to my brother!" C.P. roared, jabbing at True. "You aint fixin' to carry him to jail! Or noplace!"

Brannon shoved Marlene by the shoulder. "Y'see what you caused, girl? Damn you!" He was built like a brick outhouse. He looked like he wanted to slap the girl. And clean True's clock. And he could damn near do it in one swoop.

True knew *Harlowe* wouldn't let him. He swung, landing a solid left hook on Brannon's jaw.

"Boy, I'm gonna beat your ass!" He rubbed his jaw—like he'd had a bad shave—and took a step toward True.

True hit first. He hit him again and again, the man doubling over as Fulton slammed his fist into his gut, then twice into the man's cheek. Butterbean—the fat cousin—had arrived by then. He bowed up on True. Cussing him. Grabbing his shirt. True wasn't having it. "Y'want some too?" He lay into Butterbean and sent him running down the road.

Marlene's daddy had stayed by the car the whole time, but now it was his turn. "Y'ain't got no right to hit my brother! Or my nephew! I'll be callin' Pratt first thing in the mornin'!"

True just looked at him. C.P. turned, then, getting in the car with a slam of the door, while two of the boys helped Uncle Brannon back in his Ford. Marlene looked up at True with big eyes, and mouthed the words, "thank you!" as the car pulled away.

True nodded, uncomfortably.

The beat-up vehicles rattled away, the occupants each—except one—giving the young lawman their sourest looks.

True rubbed his sore right hand; he'd split his knuckles hitting that hard-headed old buzzard.

That night, Marlene prayed. "Lord, watch over him. I like him a whole lot."

***

In the morning, True slinked into the office like a dog that just ate a pie off the table Thanksgiving. He thought, sure, he'd be fired!

But as he walked in he found Harlowe grinning. The latter replaced the handset on the receiver.
Harlowe tried not to laugh. "What in hell did you get yourself into last night?"
"Am-Am I in trouble?"
Harlowe glanced at True's knuckles. "Hell no, ol' Brannon deserved everything you gave 'im, and then some."
True was relieved. "I thought you'd be mad, sir."
"Mad, hell, I don't care what they say." He poured a cup. "Here."
"Thankya."
"You know, I looked at C.P. Williams as a suspect."
"Yessir?"
"C.P. didn't do it. I looked at all them boys, actually."
True thought the coffee did him good; he finished his cup while the sheriff sat, quietly at the window, looking off yonder.
"Ida done one thing different though."
"Yessir?"
"Ida used the butt of the shotgun—saves your knuckles."
True grinned.
At that, they heard someone coming up the stairs.
"Maybe that's another Williams coming to complain," Harlowe whispered.
"Very funny."
It *was* a Williams. Boy's clothes and straw-colored hair under a hat, but too little to be one of the boys. It was Marlene! She stepped up to True. Handed him a bag of oranges. Then ran off, back down the stairs in her bare feet.
"I reckon she swiped 'em from her daddy," said Harlowe.
"Yeah...I reckon she did. Real nice oranges."
"Son, you can take what I know about women, and it wouldn't fill this ashtray. But I think that gal's sweet on ya."
"Aww, she's just a kid. Why ya think she's stuck on me?"
Harlowe waved a match to his cigarette. "Way she looks at ya."
"I didn't notice anything?"
"Watch the eyes—they'll tell ya."

True nodded.

"Women wanna feel safe. And you protected her last night. She ain't likely to forget it. That's somethin' that gal's probably never had before."

"Yeah—what do-we have goin' on today?" asked Fulton, trying to change the subject.

"Pretty little thing," said Harlowe.

True nodded weakly.

Heavier feet on the stairs now—Seago's. "That little gal's something else! The other day I come around the corner an' heard her givin' Jimmy Kemp what for, son! She just come by me, swingin' her arms and hummin' a tune."

Harlowe nodded to the oranges.

"Oh—y'oughta take her fishin with ye!" offered Seago.

"I-I'm takin' Tennie to see a show," said True.

Thankfully, Harlowe sent him to serve some court papers—and he left.

The phone rang. Jeter.

"Look here. Driscoll used to spend time in Quincy. Heard he had him a galfriend over theah. I say *had*. They parted ways. Had 'em a knock-down-drag-out."

"She's not feelin' too kindly toward him, I imagine."

"Ha! I'll say!"

"Where do I find her?"

"You figure it out."

Harlowe found her working at a cigar factory. "Driscoll paid those fellas to beat up Collis."

"Y'know that for a fact?"

"Yessir, I was there. Don't go spreadin' it that I toldya, now!"

"No, ma'am.

"Beat's me!"

EIGHTY-SEVEN

January, 1939

"Hello, boah," said Seago. "I see the gears a-turnin.' You plannin' somethin.' Uh—you ain't quittin' areya?"

True held out the ring. "I-I'm thinkin' 'bout askin' Tennie to marry me."

"Son! You tell yo' uncle?!"

"I caint find 'im."

"Ain't no tellin.' Ya know your uncle."

They got in Seago's car and, presently, found Harlowe

"Your nephew's got somethin' to tell ya."

"You ain't quittin'?"

"No, sir. I'm askin' Tennie to get married."

"Well, that's wonderful, son! Y'all will be wantin' a house, I expect. Maybe you an' me can get started on one, if ya find you a piece of land."

"I sure appreciate that."

"When ya gonna ask her old man?" Seago wondered.

"Soon as I can git over theah."

They shook his hand. "I'm happy for you, son," said Harlowe.

"Good luck, boah!" Seago exclaimed.

***

The lightkeeper put on his uniform coat and hat to make it official. "You sure have my blessing, son! And I mean it, I think of you as a son already. But you've talked to me enough. You'll want to get back to Apalach, I'm sure!" said Buckles.

True thanked him. Trekked back across the island to the dock. Got the motor going—though not as fast as the butterflies racing in his belly, the long, wet ride back to Apalach.

Tennie was in her room, a copy of *Look* on her knees.

She didn't look up. True went to one knee—what Seago said he should do.

"Tennie, will you let me have your haa-nd in mairge?"

She looked up, curiously. Then laughed.

"What's funny?"

"Say, that's a funny gag! That's really good, True!"

"Y-yeah."

"You really *can* be funny at times! You looked dead serious! Where are you taking me tonight, huh? A show?"

"Sure, we can go see a show."

"Wait...you really *meant* that. Marry you and live here?" She shook her head. "That's sweet of you, but I can't. I-I'm surprised. We're friends and all, but not—I thought we were just friends!"

"I thought that--."

"Yes?"

"I thought that you--."

"Look, we were just havin' fun, True! Why ya wanna act so serious?"

"Is there someone else that's asked ya?"

"No."

He nodded.

"Look, I'm gonna be a nurse. I wanna live in a city. I want to experience the world, see shows and brightlights, everything bright and gay! I wanna have fun!"

"We can have fun—togethuh."

She stood. "I don't wanta be tied down, not here. You're a good fella, but there's so much more waiting out there for me. Dances, parties, going places. Things I haven't experienced, things I dream about and wanna do. You and I jus' don't want the same things right now."

True looked away.

"I am fond of you—and I appreciate you asking." She put the ring in True's hand.

He stared at the water for a long time before he got up and moved along.

True worked harder, trying to distract himself. He kept to his routine. He heard a week later that Tennie's father took her to Chattahoochee on the train, and she began her nurse training at Florida State Hospital.

He felt sadness inside every time something reminded him of her; it was pain like someone died. Chattahoochee may as well have been the other side of the moon.

The sheriff tried to keep his deputy busy, serving papers, anything to keep the young fellow's mind off the girl from the island.

Seago's words reverberated. *"He's fun for her now, but she don't mean to be no wife."*

"I'm just a diversion for her. That's how it started, I was a break from her chores, hauling oil up to the top."

EIGHTY-EIGHT

February, 1939

True stopped to watch the men building the new courthouse across from Briley's house. Then he went inside.

"Hey, True!" said Efola.

Uncle Cullen clapped him on the shoulder. "Hey, boah!"

Thye sat down to supper, Briley and Cullen tearing into the food like hounds. While reaching for the squash, Cullen shot a glance over at True. Like Foss, his eyes were black beads. His looks were similar, though craggier, with a pine-bark complexion. "Hear Tennie thought you couldn't support no wife."

True nodded. Cullen was blunt, but he spoke the truth. Rumor was Tennie had talked to her parents about the proposal, and said as much.

"I can get you a job over there. With me. Have ya somethin' steady." Cullen meant the paper mill.

"I'll think about it."

"There's a future in it. I'm tellin' ya. Ol' Wylie Sapp's workin' with me now."

Briley chimed in, "So's Ira Brewer—he got 'im a job theah. Jus' got promoted too."

True thought about it for a few days and was on his way to ask Cullen to talk to his bossman when he heard: Everyone in town was talking about Tennie. "J'hear? She's goin' to nursing school in Chattahoochee!"

True walked up to her porch, crowded with friends and well-wishers. "Gee, I'll be busy, True. I just won't have time for a beau. We'll still be friends though. Sorry, I gotta get the phone. Bye, True!"

True wandered to Panama City. A little sandpiper kept him company. Scurrying about at his feet, running from a breaking wave. Searching for something. Then running from the next breaking wave. True fell asleep on the sand.

***

April, 1939

Harlowe looked in the mirror. Scratched a razor over his face. That old man looking back at him—it didn't match what he felt. Recently turning *fifty,* the clock had gotten ahead of itself, surely! He laughed—Cussed— Turned out the light.

Gibby would be twenty-years-old, thought True. Another birthday meeting. They were more sullen, knowing Lillian was on her back stoop crying and couldn't stop.

They took Harlowe's boat upriver.

They passed the train bridge. The water bronze, quiet. "He loved to fish up here. Hunt these islands," True said.

"Saint Mark's Island?" asked Seago.

"Yessir," said True. "Gibby shot a buck deer, yonder, on that bank. He'd tie off, heah. Caught 'im a bass right heah."

Seago and True were pulling in the catfish.

Harlowe had no luck. "Never been a good angler," he said.

"We'd come up this way. As far as the wind would take us," said True. By now, they reached the Pinhooks, deepest spot on the Apalachicola.

"When he felt his line bounce, he'd holler, 'look here!' Get so excited he'd nearly fall out the boat! I remember 'im, plum wore out from pullin' them fish, he'd go to sleep in the boat!"

They started back. "He'd wanna show his fish, show 'em to folks when he come in, reckon?"

"He'd wanna show everybody," True replied.

Harlowe nodded.

"Y'see Marlene?" asked Seago.

True got bashful. "Well, yeah. Last week."

"I know it. I saw her talkin' to ya. She likes you, boah."

"H-How do you know?"

"'Cause when y' said somethin' she laughed."

"It wuddint that funny. I ain't funny like T.K. or Uncle Briley."

"Or me."

"Y'all can tell one story after another, have folks in stitches, but my mind goes blank like Miss Hazelwood callin' on me. Somehow, she likes what I say."

"I'm tellin' ya," said Seago. "Don't take no Sherlock Holmes. Her face just lights up when you're around."

***

June, 1939

True drove out to Carrabelle Beach, early. He walked the shore, alone. Looked out over the Sound. Stood by the dancehall, quiet at this hour. *Got to help Uncle Pratt. It's better than thinkin' about tennie. She's out theah somewhere—with someone.*

Harlowe sent him to watch Mrs. Young's house. If Driscoll was threatening her, Harlowe wanted to know.

***

Marlene *put up* her older sister's glamour magazine. Went outside to feed the chickens and collect the eggs as she did every day.

Her brothers, one by one as they left for work, tossed their clothes at her. She had the tub filled and had commenced to scrubbing.

Some of her galfriends stopped by on their way to town. She poured them coffee. They chatted while the pie baked in the oven. "You still dreamin' about True?" asked Laurie.

Marlene shook her head.

"You never was a good liar. Look at you!"

"Ol' True won't know what hit him," said Della.

Hush!

"Look at her smile," said Laurie.

***

True's landlady knocked. "Oh, almost forgot, a lettuh come for you."

"From Tennie!" True tore it open. "She's askin' me to come see her!"

He read it over and over. *"We could get married when I graduate…you can get a job with the chief, we can start over together and have fun."*

So it was 'back on!' True spent all the money he had to drive to Chattahoochee to see her each week.

***

Seago came to see True. Bought him a coffee. Opened the Saturday paper. "My goodness. Tennie—I, uh."

"What?" asked True.

"Well, I, uh. I hate to--."

True took the paper. *"Tennie Buckles to wed...*plans to quit nursin' school. Will soon be Mrs. Robert Duff!"

"I'm sorry, boah."

True handed the paper back to the big man. "What's the rest of it say?"

"Well, just that there'll—well, this talks about the big doins they got planned. You sure? I mean, it's a rich man that owns restaurants. Son, I'm sorry."

True's face drained. He walked out.

Seago told Harlowe about it. "I'm sorry, Pratt."

"Ain't you fault. Hell of a way to find out—read it in the paper. She never said anything?"

"I reckon not. Anyhow, I got some more 'good' news fur ye."

"Oh?"

"Ol' Pender. He's been takin' his lunch every day with Huff—over at The Grill."

"He's just bidin' his time."

Six months after Gibby disappeared, Pender opened the Gulf gasoline station on Avenue E, across from the Chapman School. Huff opened his hardware store around the same time. Recently, the former sheriff founded "Pender Oil Distributors" on Water Street. Both men had done well, indeed, since that day.

"True?"

"He took off. I looked for 'im. Didn't see 'im no more," said Seago.

At the *Riverside*, the men listended to Joe Louis vs. Tony Galento. Harlowe came in. Sat beside Seago. "Y'look beat. Y'find 'im?"
Harlowe nodded. "He's out in the woods."
"What, he wouldn't come back with ye?"
"No."

***

June, 1939

Harlowe put on his spectacles. Opened the letter. Presently, came footsteps in the hall and little taps at the door. A little blond figure had made them. There, in a flower-print shirt she'd made out of a flour sack, stood Marlene Williams.

"Escuse me, Shureff. Is True around?"

The little gal had become quite pretty. She wore her brother's hand-me-down jeans rolled up several times. The home-made shirt was probably the best one she had. She looked tired. "Hiya, Missy. You walk across the bridge?"

"Half-way. My cousin carried me the rest."

"Have a chair, Missy. He took off. True, I mean."

She flopped on the chair. Rolled her sleeve up. "He took off?"

"Yeah." He got up to get the coffee pot. "We caint sit here without coffee."

"No, I suppose not."

"I tried to talk to him. He wouldn't say anything a' tal. I ain't never seen him like that. He went out in the woods. Won't come back."

Marlene nodded, sadly. "What do ya reckon can be done about it?"

Harlowe looked across the cup, thinking. "Well...sometimes, a man just needs to be alone. Sometimes he needs to see what he's got his mind fixed on ain't no good fur him."

"I understand. Sorta. I know why he's—well, maybe it's none of my business, but—."

"But you wanna help him."

Mr. Pratt's a quiet man, but his eyes show he understands a lot, she thought. "Yes." She sipped the coffee, grateful to have it. C.P. told her to 'git outside and git her chores done' before she could have any this morning.

"I hope you can help him," said Harlowe. "I sure could use 'im!"

She smiled. Then wondered, "But you think it'll jus' take time—how long?"

"I don't know, Missy."

She went away, sad—down the stairs.

Then he heard her running back up.

"There's got to be *somethin'!?*"

"Well...I reckon maybe there is."

She knew what she was going to do now. She gave a mischievous grin. "Well, I gotta git home to start on my chores. Thanks, sheriff!"

"For what?"

"For list'nin'!"

477

A plan in mind, she was already out the door, her barefeet tamping down the stairs and out the door. Marlene had a unique way of swinging her arms when she walked—fast. There she went, across the courthouse yard and down Tenth Street!

Harlowe smiled. He was happy True had someone—although the boy might not know it yet!

***

Marlene went home to do her afternoon chores.

Her Daddy barked questions at her. "Where have y'been? Y'git the tobackey and things?"

"Right here."

"Where y'been?!"

Her plan would have to wait.

***

Harlowe found True, half-drunk, on the bank of Whiskey George Creek.

"The little Williams gal was askin' about you."

True didn't look up.

"I was hopin' you'd come back with me. I sure could use you, son."

True just stared blankly over the creek.

***

Marlene stood in front of the mirror. With her hat on and her brother's hand-me-down flannel shirt, she could pass for a boy. She had freckles on her nose and skinned knees. She took a bath. Combed her hair down. Imagined herself in a lovely dress. *I might even be purty.*

The shadow fell over her bed. Just a band of light marked the floor through the crack of the door from her mother's kerosene lamp. Marlene got on her knees in the darkness. "I know I ain't nothin' glamorous. But

Lord, could y'make him just look at me? Just one time?" Tears came. "Just one time, Lord—please!" She read from her mother's bible and prayed on it.

Next day, she got her morning chores done early. All Eastpoint was talking about how True 'got a drunk on.'

"You ain't goin' up theah? Deddy'll have your hide!" warned Runt.

But that pretty, mischievous smile, meant there was no dissuading Marlene.

She saddled Victoria, riding the mule up to Whiskey George. The mouth of the creek opened to a wide rivelet that flowed past peaceful savannas of wiregrass and cabbage palms, and into the still, onyx pools that hemmed the top of the Bay.

She looked over there, sadly, seeing him, a ragged scarecrow swilling moonshine by a cabbage palm that jutted out at an angle over the creek. "True!"

He squinted at her, up on that mule. She hopped down in her boy's shirt and baggy dungarees.

True muttered to himself, something she couldn't make out. He held a fishing pole in one hand and looked down at the end of it in his hands. "What are you doing?" she asked, almost in a scolding tone, like the one she used with her brothers.

True shot her a surly, drunken look.

"The way you got that line outta the water, you aint gonna catch nothin'. Here, let me see it." She grabbed it and sat down beside him.

He didn't answer. He wobbled, staring blankly at the jar of 'shine. The place was as silent as the inside of a bank vault. So peaceful. *No wonder he'd come here.* She looked at him. "What are y'thinkin' about?"

He just shook his head.

"Y'got to be thinkin' about somethin'. Talk to me."

He finished the jar, then flung it where several others had met their end.

"Talk to me."

"There's a lot inside, I reckon."

"Sure, there is. Tell me."

"I can't put it in words—don't know how." He fought back the feeling in his throat, he fought getting choked up.

"You loved her."

He looked away. And nodded.

"I know you did. I reckon you still do, or you wouldn't be carryin' on so." She put her hand on his shoulder. He stared ahead. Gritting his teeth—lest tears come to his eyes.

"I know it, because I watched you. I saw the way you lit up when you talked about her. I know how that is, how good that is. Your ol' friend Marlene knows."

His eyes squinted and he nearly toppled over. She caught him by the shoulder and laughed. "Do you know who I am? You awake?"

He nodded. "I know y'didn't like her."

She let out a sigh. "It ain't that. I saw she'd hurt you. I done told you that. I wish it weren't so. I have lay awake many nights wishin' it was me that was hurtin', my heart breaking to think of how she's hurt you."

He looked at her, not sure what to think. She touched his shoulder again. *She's soft, warm*, he thought.

"I reckon this ain't a good time to tell ya, but I'm tired of watchin' you get hurt, a-tearin' yourself up for someone that don't keer about you. An'—."

"Your cousin told me t'other day, wha' you said, 'bout likin' me," True slurred.

Marlene's face flashed red. "Well, he shouldna said nothin'. But I reckon it's time to let it all out in the open. Yeah, I like you. I love you. I ain't too proud to say it. I ain't too proper to wait to say it at the right time. Everyone in the county knowed it but you, I reckon."

"I guess I just didn't—."

"You didn't notice me. I was just a kid! But if you looked at me, you'd see I ain't no kid!"

"I see that." Marlene was seventeen, and beautiful, even in her hand-me-downs.

"Really? Even with all that moonshine you've been drinkin'?"

True nearly fell on his face, laughing. "Nah, you beu'ful."

"You're a mess, True Fulton." Her hand went to her hip. "You sure can't hold no liquor."

"I know."

"No, I reckon not. You smell worse than a horse stall."

He shook his head, grinning and laughing. *She really speaks her mind. Her eyes are pretty. Never noticed how blue they are. Or are they green?*

He looked back to the water.

"Deddy said he seen a big ol' redfish up here in this creek. Maybe we oughta move up a-ways."

True didn't answer. He had that blank, pickled stare, his head bobbing like it was too heavy for his neck.

"Ooh! Now, look here, I done caught you a fish! A big'n too!"

She tugged him in and held him up, proudly. "If you can walk, we'll take him home and cook him for supper. I hope you'll sober up some 'fore my deddy sees you. You're a *sight!*" At that, she tossed him the striper. He flailed his arms to catch it, squatting to his knees before he got a hold of it.

She laughed at him. "My deddy just might shoot you, comin' up to the house like you are—you look more like a bear than a man." She brushed his whiskers with the back of her hand.

He leaned on her shoulder, trying to walk. It was awkward, the petite girl trying to hold up a six-foot-two-inch man. He stopped—to look. "Yes, the sunset is pretty. An' peaceful." She rubbed his shoulder with her soft hand.

"Can you climb up on ol' Victoria?"

He nodded, reaching for the horn of the saddle, but missing it, nearly falling on his face. "My goodness, True Fulton! Here, I'll he'p you. True Fulton, you get done with this pinin' over that Tennie Buckles, you hear me?" She found his rye whiskey and threw it away. He looked at it, sadly, as it settled into the blanket of pine straw on the ground, the remaining contents, seeping into the dirt. He nodded. "Yes ma'am." He saw double, looking at her out of squinted eyes.

She threw his hat at him. "Yes, ma'am is right! I'm gonna get that heifer off your mind, True Fulton. You'll see. Won't be long before you're lookin' at me the way you used to look at her. Only it'll be more, 'cause I got a whole lot more personality!"

"I can see that."

"Oh, you can see me?" She held her fingers up. "How many are there?"

True tried to focus but could manage no better than a drunken squint. "Careful. Don't fall off," she said, laughing.

She kissed his cheek.

"Don't get to used to that—until were merrit."

"Married? What?"

True blacked out after that. True tried to remember later, if he really had proposed marriage. *I don't believe I said anything whatsoever on the ride*

481

back! He heard wedding music and it troubled him some. He thought his memory was clear on that point. But time blurred together. The next thing he remembered was seeing the lantern glowing at the Williams' house.

C.P. built boats—when he was sober. The bones of one rested alongside the home. Her mother and younger sister had supper ready. Her whole family ate like hungry bears tearing into the trash bins behind the hotel in Carrabelle. True couldn't eat more than a mouthful, his head was spinning and he was still drunk.

Marlene put him in the big bed in the back room of the house, where sick people lay. He looked up at the ceiling, the work he'd done. He went to sleep with her sitting on the bed, holding him close to her. She got up as soon as he dozed off, going to help her mother with the dishes.

"He's not going to stay here eatin' me outta house and home," said Mr. Williams.

"Why, it's only for tonight," said Mother Williams.

In the morning, Harlowe came to see him. "I'm glad you're back from the dead, son. I can use you!" Fulton sat up. Shook his uncle's hand.

Harlowe noticed True was pale as a sheet. "Missy, is this boy eatin'?"

"Yessir. He's had bacon and eggs. Didn't do him much good, though. He's been a-throwin' up."

"I'm better now!" said True.

"Hmm."

"What is it, shureff?" asked Marlene.

"Well," replied Harlowe, scratching his chin. "I's just wondering how folks would view a lawman that looked like he'd served a few months in jail." True's clothes were stained with sweat and dirt, his hair matted. He smelled as bad as he looked.

They laughed. "I must look a sight," said True.

"Well, y'might shave. And, Missy, reckon you could get 'im a bar of lye soap?"

"Yessir, and I'll fetch him the basin and water."

"Good!"

"I'm 'bout ready to scrub him down like an infant!"

True frowned. "I can wash just fine."

Mother Williams looked in. "Marlene's been funnelin' coffee down his gullet, like water through a fish."

Harlowe gave a grin. Marlene refilled his cup. "Much obliged. I'm glad you two got togethuh. Everybody always said you were right for each other." Marlene smiled with satisfaction at that.

Marlene brought True a razor and a bowl of water. Held the mirror for him to scrape off his beard.

I never noticed her smile before, how bright it is, True thought.

"There's clean shirts in the 'chester drawers,'" said Marlene. "One o' my brothers'll fit ya."

He put one on. She hugged tightly, her head against his chest. He held her and it was a nice feeling, but he didn't say anything. She sighed. "I know it's bad, but I jus' wanna see ya all the time!"

She turned him loose. "But I know you got work to do—git out there an' git to your sheriffin' and I'll always be here, a smile on my face when y'git back!"

"All right."

She shook his hand roughly. Gave him a peck on the cheek. "I reckon it's all right. Seein' we're engaged now!"

"Huh?"

True finished shaving. Ran out to get in the car with Harlowe.

"Mighty glad to have you back, son," Harlowe declared.

True waved to Marlene. They were on the road—to Tallahassee.

EIGHTY-NINE

June, 1939

Their first "date."

The way she looked made his heart beat a little faster: White shorts and checky shirt. Her hair, which she'd washed and parted to the side. The beautiful girl had been there all along, underneath the dirt, tomboy clothes. She shut the door. "I'm excited to ride in your car! Nicest one I've evuh rode in!"

"Thankya."

They drove past the dairy. Out of town.

They parked along the road. Walking along the quiet shore at 17 Mile Beach. Talking. *She seems interested in what I think. Isn't in a hurry to* get somewhere. *She seems happy—like she's* already somewhere. *Coming here in my old car. Just water and sky. And me! It cost me twenty cents' gas to get here, but she looks at me like I'm Clark Gable!*

Her smile was like the sunrise. He looked into her eyes—they were warm and sparkling like the Gulf in the summer, the way the water beckons you to dive in and forget everything else! Where might these feelings take them if he let himself fall?

He answered by pulling her to him. Still a little shy, it wasn't a long kiss.

"I was hopin' you'd do that. I was...waitin' and waitin'." She'd already begun to lean back in. Her lips touching his, light as a butterfly. Then, pressing against his like they'd merge. He was diving in, with her, into that other world. Everything else above the surface faded in significance. Time stopped. Even the air from above wouldn't do. He'd stopped breathing. She breathed something new into him. Her soft lips, her touch, pushed out everything else, like she'd become part of him, down to his soul.

He'd never felt a kiss like that. *It was very much different than—what was her name, now?*

Had it been a minute-or-five-or-sixty? Finally, they separated. "Don't git too used to that," said Marlene, playfully. "At least not until we get merr'itt."

A simple date. But it's enough, True realized. *I'm enough for her! We're enough for each other.*

Then she got a worried look. "Daddy will expect me."

She swung her bare feet in the car. And she seemed smaller, more vulnerable than before, riding back, the rain peppering the windshield of the car.

***

Marlene came up to True's chest. She fit perfectly, for walking along their arms around eachother. He liked how she talked about books she read. And what a big sense of humor she has!

The sunset across the Bay was the prettiest one yet, True thought, their arms around each other, as they looked across toward Apalach.

"One of my favorite things—as a boy—was when Uncle Pratt carried me fishin,'" True told her. "Out theyuh."

She held him close to her, her head resting on his chest.

***

July, 1939

"Lamar's got the town—up theah," said Seago.

"Well, he's fixin' to get some more," said Harlowe. He nodded at the Cory Concrete trucks going past the windows of The Grill.

"He got the contract to pave the runway for the Army," said Murrow. Indeed, the airfield had buildings sprouting like weeds, out past the dairy.

"Don't see why the army needs a base heah—ain't likely we'll be in another war—and I don't see one comin' heah less'n its over oysters!" said Ed Jones.

"Huff will be happy to sell to the soldier boys, anyhow," said Seago. "How you like bein' retired, Doc?"

"Fine! Jus' fine!" Murrow had sold the old mansion. Irene Tucker was converting it to a boarding house.

"We found out more about Junior's mother. That she went to his Scout camp and pulled him out. Lamar wanted him to be around boys his own age," said True.

"She *hovered* him!" Seago surmised. "Well, I got to go?"

"Where ya goin,' C.A.?" asked Harlowe.

"Goin' see the Gene Autry *pitcher,* son!"

Marlene hurried so she'd be ready to meet True. She toted in double the stovewood. C.P. barked, "Ya dropped some, gal! Git the hogs fed while yer at it!"

485

"Y'wanna go see a *pitcher?*" True asked.

"Well...we might could pack us a picnic basket and go to Lafayette Park," thought Marlene.

So they sat on a blanket. Looking out over the water. A flash of red lit up the sky over the Bay.

"Look at the heat lightning!" said Marlene.

It cost nothing to set out a blanket. And it had cooled some near 11 pm. The reds, purples, and oranges alternating above were magnificent.

True loved sitting with her—every minute was good. And she liked him—just the way he was. He could hardly believe it! He didn't want to jinx it!

They were lying on their backs, looking up as the stars came out.

"My goodness, how bright they are!" she said.

They walked back to True's car. "Something worries you," she said.

"This thing—has almost broke Uncle Pratt. That he hasn't solved it."

"I think he'll solve it. And you know something,' I think he won't do it without you."

He nodded. Looked away.

"Gibby was *your* best friend."

He nodded.

"He was like a brother. To you," said Marlene.

"Yep."

"You miss him."

A tears formed in his eye. He rubbed it away.

"Talk to me."

"I'm just—I don't always know."

"Yeah? Don't always know what, baby?"

"Don't always know what I ought to do next. Or even what to think."

"Yes."

He nodded.

"Some things make ya wannna cry. They do me too," she said.

"Somethings make me wanna cry."

"But ya don't."

He shook his head.

"And now?"

"You come along."

"Yeah, I come along." She winked.

"Feeling you next to me makes me feel all right."

She kissed his cheek.

"You make me feel…"

"What do I make ya feel?"

"I dunno. Shoot. Y'make me feel…special. Never felt that before," he said.

"I feel the same thing. No one's every looked at me like I'm beautiful. Or fought for me. You treat me like a delicate flower. And it's so sweet." At that, she planted a kiss.

***

July, 1939

"Teachers get the summer off," said Seago.

"Yeah," said True.

They saw the Cory's motor in to town, in Carrabelle. And Lamar was driving a new LaSalle—bright red.

"I'll let the bossman know," said Seago.

Father and son took a room at the hotel. True looked in the window of the lobby. Lamar was treated like the Governor coming to town!

"He caught the biggest tarpon last year. He'll do it again, more than prob'ly!" said the desk clerk.

"Red snapper, Mr. Dobkins—that's what I'm after!" said Lamar, slapping the man on the back. He winked. "But I wouldn't turn up my nose at a tarpon!"

True watched. He parked the De Soto behind trees where he could watch them leave the hotel.

He saw them walk to the waterfront, and step on the *Kingfish,* a cabin cruiser for hire. Both Cory's toted nice rods and reels.

A colored boy toted bait from the little store on Marine Street.

True phoned from the payphone at the filling station up the street.

"All right. Keep watchin' 'im."

Seago learned that the owner of *Trouble*—one of Apalachicola's yachts—wanted to come and challenge Lamar to a little friendly competition. The other yachtsman in Apalach, didn't want to be left out, so they let it be known they were coming.

And the word spread about the little competition.

Carrabelle's mayor, not to be left out, made a speech in front of the movie house. "Perhaps, one day we'll have tournaments like they do down south." He shook Lamar's hand and gave him the key to the city. They looked out at the five yachts tied in the harbor. "It wasn't quite Miamuh or Lauderdale but it sure is something!" said an old-timer.

Early the next morning, engines burbling and boats bobbing on their lines, the mayor and Commissioner Huff made more speeches. True watched the spectacle from afar. It ended with the odd chugging of a much older vessel—the *Barbara Jean!*

Seago tossed his line to the man on the dock. "I don't wanna miss this!" he cried. True saw that with him, was Uncle Pratt!

Junior walked over. "Good Mornin', Mr. Harlowe."

"Mornin'."

"I came here to go snapper fishing."

"Good luck."

Seago hollered for True to hop on. "They ain't gonna wait!" he cried.

The boats shoved off. Motors gurgling as they made their way down the Carrabelle River, out to the Gulf.

Seago tried to stay out of the way of the faster cabin cruisers. *Kingfish* led the way. As the waves began to spray, the captains of the *Sea Dream* and *Countess* opened their throttles and left the *Barbara Jean* in their wakes. The *Southwind* and the *Trouble* passed them, likewise, like they were dragging anchor.

Not to worry! The weather was perfect. A light breeze, the water not too rough, and the sky endless—and they could follow the bigger boats to a good spot!

The water was deep, and green, under the keel, the boat gently rolling, occasional spray touching True's cheeks.

Presently, they saw the *Kingfish* and the *Trouble,* slow to idle, ahead. And True saw Junior and Lamar reach out with their rods and reels.

"Looks like a good spot, boys!" said Seago. He moved in and cut throttle, also. The boat rolled and they all baited their lines and let them drop to the bottom.

Harlowe looked over. The men from Tallahassee were pulling in fish after fish!

There was no cabin, hence no shade, on the *Barbara Jean*. Seago hat a big straw hat. Harlwoe and True sweated under fedoras. Though visibility was unlimited under a lovely deep blue sky, the air was hot, and heavy to breathe even before nine o'clock.

They heard arguing from the *Kingfish*.

"Your mother isn't here...can I have a moment's relaxation without having to--."

Harlowe looked at True. "Couldn't make out the rest. I reckon Ol' Lamar's caught in the middle between his wife and his son."

"Yep."

"Could almost feel sorry for the ol' boy." Harlowe baited his line again—a fish had taken the bait, but was too smart to let himself get hooked!

True and Seago each caught a couple small bluefish—still snapping as they pulled them up—but hardly big enough to keep.

Then Seago felt the weight on his line and cussed. "I got one, boah!"

He hauled up a red snapper that must have weighed thirty pounds! He hollered so that the men on the *Trouble* thought they might be sinking!

Seago baited his line again. "Whachya gonna do if ya win—with the money?"

"I dunno," thought True, not feeling anything but the weight of the rig at the moment.

"Get you a nice rod and reel, with that money!" said the jailor.

The other boats had spread out, only the *Kingfish* was close enough to see clearly. Harlowe cast his line—hearing the holler come from the *Kingfish*.

"Lamar musta hooked him a big'n," thought Seago.

They fished another hour, Seago and True both caught decent-sized snapper. Harlowe felt a bite. "Pull 'im!" hollered Seago.

"I'm tryin' to!"

"That was your line breakin', bossman."

"Lost 'im."

Then Seago got another one! Bigger than before.

The boats started coming in toward sunset. The men hung up the fish. And when they measured, Lamar had got the biggest red snapper!

He posed for a photograph. Harlowe and True hung around the edge of the crowd. "He's the best fisherman, hunter, prob'ly the best shot in the area!" someone said.

"Who?"

"Why, Lamar!"

A newspaper photographer flashed a photo, too, Lamar smiling broadly for the camera. There behind him, was his son, who had caught a decent size bluenose.

Just not quite out of his daddy's shadow, thought Harlowe. *The boy doesn't look as 'at-ease' with himself as Lamar.*

Junior noticed him, by the *Barbara Jean.* He walked down to Harlowe, extended his hand.

"Catch anything?"

"Not a damn thing," Harlowe replied.

***

September, 1939

"Yo uncle workin' me like a rented mule!" Seago lamented. "Paint the sashes, paint them
bars on the winduhs."
"You goin' to the ballgame?" asked True.
"Hell, yes."

And the Apalachicola team beat the Tallahassee boys that night! The first time in ages. Henson Jamieson cinched it with a home run in the ninth innning.

NINETY

September, 1939

They waited on Mr. and Mrs. Cory to get home from a party. Presently, the teacher pulled into his driveway. Cut his lights.

Harlowe got out of the car. "Evenin'."

"Uh-good evening. May I help you fellas?"

"Mr. Whittle. Your neighbor. He knew the way you acted around those younguns. He threatened to do somethin' about it. You and I both know it."

Jr. shut the car door. "That isn't true. Would you excuse us, dear?" He tried send his wife inside; she stood there, her mouth open in astonishment.

"Your daddy had the old man committed."

"I know nothing about that," said Jr., backing away.

Harlowe put his foot up on Jr.'s running board. "When you look in the mirror sometimes you caint stand to be around the fella lookin' back at ya."

Jr. backed up to the hood. Then his porch. "Go inside, dear," he said. He stumbled backwards to his door. One half of him in the light. Other half in darkness.

"When's the last time you were in Eastpoint, Mr. Cory?"

"Fishing with my father. Six months ago."

Harlowe nodded. That was true.

"Is there anything else, Mr. Harlowe? You—you fellas may come inside if you like. Have you any other questions?"

"One or two."

"Why don't you come in?" He led them into their small, tidy front room. They sat in the chairs and davenport. They looked at him. While it was warm, the young man seemed to be sweating more than Harlowe or True. He picked up his lighter. Put it down, for his hands were shaking. He opened the window. "Would either of you fellas care for a cold drink?"

"You and your dad move it?"

"M-Move what?"

"The body."

"No, Mr. Harlowe. I did no such thing. Say, would you fellas mind if I got a Coke? You sure you don't want one—just over here in the icebox."

"No, thanks," they answered.

"I'll get it dear," said his wife. Her eyes were like saucers. They heard her open the ice box and pop the cap off the bottle. And drop the bottle. Shattering it. Then her footsteps clicked back. "I-I'll get another."

"It's all right, dear." She sat beside her husband then.

"You came back by yourself in the car and took him. You couldn't he'p yourself. You pulled him in the car. Did...things...to him. An' you knew you couldn't let 'im just run home and tell what you'd done so you killed him and buried his body. Isn't that right, Mr. Cory?"

"That-that's a terrible thing to say. I *couldn't* hurt any child. Just *couldn't.*"

"Couldn't you?"

"No, sir. That's a horrible thing you're accusing me of!"

"Yessir. And it bothered ya. I can see it bothers ya now. It bothered you so much you took to the bottle. Isn't that what ya did?"

Jr. looked at his wife. Nodded. Looked back. "I haven't done anything wrong, Mr. Harlowe. Now, you'll have to excuse me. It's late. I must go to bed." A distant train whistle carried through the open window.

Jr. comforted his wife, who was crying now. "See, now, you've upset my wife. None of this is true. It's all a mistake, and you'll find that out."

Harlowe's ice-blue eyes bore through him. "I'll figure it out. I'm patient."

"Good evening, Mr. Harlowe. Mr. Fulton. I'm sorry I cannot help. You have my sympathy, though, for the work you're about. I can only imagine what the boy's family must be enduring."

Harlowe reached for the doorknob, looking back at Cory with those piercing eyes.

"Did you own a car when you were in hah skool?"

"My daddy wouldn't have allowed that. Goodbye, Mr. Harlowe."

"I'll be seein' ya."

They got in the car. Harlowe looked at True.

"Yeah."

The lights went out in the living room.

Jr. gave his wife a brandy. Put her to bed. Downed the rest of the bottle. Their car was still out there. He thought of phoning his father. He looked back—it was gone. Jr. passed out on the kitchen floor.

***

The City policeman was emphatic. "Sure, I'm sure. Junior had 'im a car, then. He couldna been more'n fourteen, fifteen years old."

"All right," said Harlowe. "We're talkin' nineteen-hunnerd-and-twenty-seven?"

"Yes. Junior had a Ford at that time."

They walked out of the police department onto Park Avenue. Harlowe turned to True.

"He lied to us. That's one more piece."

Harlowe got along fine with the city officers. A motorcycle officer pulled up. He nodded down the street—a deputy was parked there, watching Harlowe. The man shrugged, "Welcome to Tallahassee."

***

Harlowe moved True back to Apalach. He moved his things—they barely filled the passenger seat of his car—back into Briley's.

They slipped into Tallahassee. Harlowe and True watched at the fence—Junior coaching the young boys' league at Centennial Field.

"He ain't a bad coach," thought Harlowe.

Jr. saw them. Waved. When practice was over, he came over to them.

He smiled. "Mr. Harlowe—Mr. Fulton."

"You ready to tell me, son."

"If I had something to tell. Fine group of boys, aren't they?"

"Yessir."

Harlowe leaned his arms on the fence. Spoke low. "You lied to me. About Driscoll. And about your car."

"I was scared."

"Of whom?"

"Driscoll. He'll do anything my father tells him to."

"Why lie about the car? Nothin' incriminatin' in that."

493

"I suppose not."

"Except if you didn't want to admit you had a Ford in Eastpoint that night. You had one, didn't you?"

"Yes. But you said yourself it's not incriminating to have a car. I didn't do anything, Mr. Harlowe. You gotta believe that."

"You're pretty level-headed when you need to be—jus' like your daddy."

"My daddy's very smart."

"How's your momma?"

"She's well."

"Yeah?"

"Have you spoken to her? She tell you what a good boy I am?"

"No."

"Mother and I don't always see eye-to-eye. You wouldn't understand."

"My mother died—when I was their age." Harlowe nodded to the children. "So I understand not havin' one.

"Not having a mother. Yes—that's it isn't it? You think if yours hadn't died you'd be happier? Maybe she'd have taught you things a boy should know?"

"Maybe. How about you?"

"I guess we'll never know. Goodbye, Mr. Harlowe."

The man held out his hand. Harlowe took it. The fellow ran to pick up equipment.

"There's a fella who didn't know which way to go," said Harlowe. "Y'could almost feel sorry for 'im. Caint get loose of momma's apronstrings. Or outta daddy's shadow."

"Yeah."

They walked back to True's car. "Notice what he said about a mother to teach her son? He knows he isn't normal. He's wishin' he had a mother or someone to mold him the right way."

True nodded.

"Don't be in a hurry when you're talkin' to a man might be your murd'rer. Let 'im talk! He'll talk his way into the jailhouse."

At that, Ledbetter's men moved in, screeching to a halt by the trash dump.

Another Ford screeched behind those—Ledbetter himself.

The High Sheriff began pleasant enough, asking of things in the county, and True's momma.

Ledbetter, though developing a trace of jowels, still had that All-American square jaw, that newspaper-ad smile and haircomb. Tailored suits and Stetson hats to match.

He put his foot on the running board. He certainly saw the BAR, but didn't comment. His eyes were looking down the road, when he said, "I'm telling you to lay off, Pratt. You didn't even give me the courtesy of saying you're here. I'm gonna let that go, 'cause we're friends. But as your friend, I'm giving you some good advice—let Mr. Cory be. Just let 'im be."

"Uh-huh." *Courtesy. With you blockin' us at every turn? I'll be damned if I sit around while you 'hold court'!*

"So long, Pratt. When y'have time, let's go quail huntin.' It's good huntin' out at the farm."

It was dark when they got home. True pulled in to Harlowe's drive.

"All right, bossman."

"See you tomorruh."

True nodded.

"I 'preciate your help, son. Goodnight."

He paused as the sound of the car trailed off down the street.

***

True was up early. Walked by the Fuller. The kitchen door was open. He got ready for Mrs. Fuller to toss him a biscuit. *That smoke. Somethin's wrong!*

"Miss Fuller!" At that, flames erupted from the doorway. "Call the fire department!" True hollered, throwing his coat over his head and leaping through the flames and black cloud of smoke. Into the kitchen. He couldn't see. Or breathe. He felt someone on the floor. "Miss Fuller!" he gasped. He threw a tablecloth over her. Drug her by the shoulders.

Somehow, he managed to get her—and himself—out the door. He tore the singed tablecloth from her, lay her carefully on the ground. Tore off his own coat that was smoldering at the sleeves. He tried to holler—but couldn't' stop caughing. No one was around! He didn't know the oysterman who lived next door ran to Battery Park to summon the fire department.

The bell clanged! Volunteers, still putting on their clothes, pulled up on the truck.

"Miss Fuller!" True cried. She coughed. She was alive!

"We got her, True!" The men wrapped Mrs. Jenkins in a blanket and rushed her to

Doc Weems.

True, dropped to his knees, coughing. He felt the heat from the fire even out in the street. The firemen poured it on—hoping the flames didn't jump the breezeway to the hotel.

When it was over, it sat steaming, the window and door openings black with soot, the roof gone, burned up like paper. But the Hotel still stood.

Mrs. Jenkins died of smoke inhalation a few days later.

Spartan had that ragdoll look True had seen before. Harlowe and True stood beside him at the funeral. Sat with him in the empty parlor of the hotel.

***

October, 1939

They couldn't follow Junior. Ledbetter had his men out. They could only get occasional reports from Jeter.

"Junior has them younguns over to his house—and their parents. His wife cooks for 'em. He's a saint, if y'hear folk talk," said Jeter.

News arrived from Chatthoochee. Tennie hadn't got married after all. She was back at nursing school.

A letter arrived for True. He recognized the handwriting. He could smell Tennie's perfume. He walked up to the trash can on Market Street. Dropped it in.

NINETY-ONE

True looked over at the Lewis State Bank as they drove past.

"Raines will still say it's circumstantial," said Harlowe.

True shook his head.

"Let's keep diggin'. Just one more piece and we got it sewed up."

They tried until they were blue in the face. It felt the same as digging for bones, only it was mental exhaustion now, always dodging Ledbetter's men.

***

"Someone here to see-ya, True," said Efola.
True looked out—it was Tennie! "Hey!" She batted her eyes. Touched his arm. *"Weel,* I was in town, thought I'd say *hewwo."* She'd heard about True and Marlene. She leaned close. "Y'wanna go to Buzzett's?"
True declined. She frowned. Said something smart. Her heels clicked down the sidewalk.
But Tennie spread it all over town that they'd gotten back together.

The talk made it to Eastpoint. True found Marlene doing her chores. She turned away her face. "If ya wanna go back to her I won't beg. I'm startin' to walk away now. You can stop me or let me walk away. But you'll have to decide."
Gently, he turned her head. "If ya want that I understand." Tears welled at the corners of her eyes.
He kissed her. Held her.
"No more Tennie?" she asked.
"Tennie who?"

That night they danced the slow songs at Carrabelle Beach.
Clarinet—Benny Goodman-type-stuff.
Then the fiddle played—fast.
"Two-steppin'! Here, lemme show you," said Marlene. "Like this! Who said y'couldn't dance, boy!"
"They're fixin' to close," said Briley. "Meet ya outside."
People were leaving but Marlene looked at True. "I don't want this to end."
True really didn't want to. He wasn't much of a dancer and was still kind of self-conscious about it. But he did. She closed her eyes and smiled.
She seems so happy. I'll keep dancin' all night if she wants to. That smile.

The band was packing up. They kept going anyway, Marlene humming the waltz.
People watched. Pointed. True didn't care.

***

Christmas Eve, 1939

Their little town was so pretty at Christmas. Wreaths and red bows adorned the light poles and doors. Colored lights—the first of their kind in Apalach—were draped over the top of the store windows. White lights, like bright orbs, glowed at intervals down Avenue E. Heyser Chevrolet even had bows on the cars!

They walked along, Marlene and True, looking in the windows at Gordon's Department store. Just enjoying the feeling of it. The happy sounds.

True had his arm around Marlene. Her wool coat fit her closely. His hand rested in the curve of her small waist. She felt warm and safe.

Up Market Street past A&P and its display windows. The Dime Store. And Buzzett's—they had their Santa Claus in the window that waved, like they did every year, but it never got old. Sangaree's Barber Shop, the Ladies Hair Salon, Laniers Jewelry Store, were all decorated joyously.

True enjoyed watching Marlene and how happy it made her, doing this. He liked looking in Marlene's eyes better than what was in the windows—they looked more blue-green in the light of the display cases. They were always changing, like the Gulf or the sky.

At the corner, Creekmore Drug had its special things in the windows. Next door, on Avenue E, was the Pool Hall, and after that Rice Bros. Grocery which had "Toy Land" upstairs. They were all little stores, with friendly people and would have made another Rockwell scene. Finally, the town's Bank, lovely with wreaths and bows in the windows of the stately old limestone building.

They crossed the street. The *Dixie* glowed with its many bulbs, the place brighter and more cheerful than usual with its added decorations and color. They passed the busy Louis Café, walked down to Zingarelli's, which had toy soldiers and decorations in the windows.

They doubled back to Austin's, to look in the biggest display windows in town. Mannequins dressed up in blouses and hats. A sewing machine. A rod n' reel.

The bell tower of the Methodist church and the white lights down Avenue E were a part of the wonderful scene as well.

And so was Demo George's store, and finally the Nichols' store! "And that is *downtown* at Christmas!" Marlene declared. "I reckon it ain't big as New York, but I have everything a girl could want!" She leaned in for a kiss. He was happy to cooperate. They were happy, enjoying this time together.

He liked every minute, just walking, looking in the windows—although, usually, he didn't care for shopping. This being their first Christmas together, they couldn't afford to buy a single thing in *"them winders,"* but they had each other.

Last stop—the *Riverside,* for coffee, looking out at the water silvery and cool.

Then she got quiet. "Deddy'll expect me."

***

After work each night, True brought his tools to a little house in Two Mile— out by the dairy. The landlord described it as a 'sawed-off-shotgun,' it was so small.
True lay new flooring. Patched the roof and plaster. Cleaned up the overgrown brush. He kept it a secret until he could ask Marlene to marry him.

Harlowe let True work on the house. He drove north.
Stopped. Jeter dashed out of the woods and climbed in. "Listen at this. I got somethin' big on your buddy."
"Yeah?"
"Raines."
"What about him?"
"I know he and Lamar fixed Whittle. Fixed him good, y'see? Raines was paid—made a big donation to his church afterwards."
"How do you know this?"
"Rumormill!"
"I need someone who can testify."
"I don't deal in that business—no hearsay rules in a bar!"
"Yeah."
"Might wanna be careful—I keep tellin ya." Jeter shook badly—Pratt didn't know if it was the shakes or fear. "Y'don't question men like Raines. Y'question and maybe y'wind up in Chattahoochee too!"

Harlowe had talked to the Corys' housekeepers over the years. None would talk this year either. *Looks like 1939, too, would pass without a conclusion.*

NINETY-TWO

January, 1940

It's record cold!

True watched the bridge swing round, clearing the way for the barges coming downriver. He could see his breath. And the breath from stoves and exhaust stacks.

He watched the tug chugging by. The bells on the bridge subsided, and the cars went through.

He helped move Harlowe's desk into the new courthouse. Down to the office on the long first-floor hall.

There would be no new jail. "Tallahassee knows best!" Seago quipped.

They dragged Harlowe's trailer away, to pick up another load. Seago nodded to the Chevrolet advertisement covering the side of Gordon's Department store. "Right theah to remind ya your car's no good—jus' when ya fixin' to go someplace." He nudged True in the ribs, "C'mon now ya makin' all that money, go on 'n gitcha one o' them new Shiverlays!"

True smiled.

"I wanna go see that new *pitcher, 'Gone with the Wind!'* Whydoncha come with me, boah?"

***

Harlowe located Driscoll's old galfriend, working the switchboard at the telephone exchange in Thomasville.

"Dunno know what their beef was," said she. "Jus' heard them cuttin' up...laughin' about the beatin' they gave the boy."

"Collis?"

"That's who we been talkin' about, ain't it?" They hit 'im so hard, they like to kill 'im!"

She denied knowing about Whittle or Gibby.

They thanked her. As they walked out, the other operators were talking about *Gone With the Wind.*

"That Rhett is a good-lookin' man!" said one.

The other looked over at True and giggled when he blushed.

***

Marlene was on a ladder, picking oranges. "Ain't what they show on postcards—the girl lookin' glamourous!" She climbed down. Gave True a kiss.

"What brings ya this way?"

He got down on one knee. "No, no, True."

"Huh?"

"I ain't dressed right—look at me!"

She had on baggy pants. A sweatshirt. "Y'look fine!" he said, taking out a little ring.

"Ya wanna get married to me? I'm a handful."

"I'm askin'."

"Well—you ready?"

"Yes, ma'am!"

She took his hat and put it on her head. "Are you *sure?*" She was laughing. Pulling him close to kiss him.

Mr. Williams assented to the marriage. "I'll go along with the marriage so long as she will he'p out from time-to-time," he'd said. "He'p with the pickin' and washin'."

***

The orange afternoon sun made the new building glow—like a Greek temple.

Harlowe filed his paperwork to run for re-election.

At the barbershop talked turned to politics-and Gibby's case-and back.

"Y'think he knows who done it?" asked one man.

Seago looked at True and Brewer. "I tell ya what, no one ever worked harder to solve one. He ain't stopped no matter what they say."

"No, he don't give up easy, I'm tellin' ya," said Sangaree.

Like driving that truck! True imagined.

It wasn't just the Sheriff's Office which moved—Lexie took a room at the Old Raney House. True's siblings would attend Chapman.

Lexie told True, "now, you be careful. Y'can get in trouble over theah."

True nodded.

He fastened his necktie. Picked up Marlene. They piled in Seago's Ford.

Rounded up Briley and Efola. "Here's my share o' gasoline money," said Briley. "Nothin' left for candy!"

Squeezed in the little car, they motored to 'Panama' to see *"Gone With the Wind."*

***

The cement plant idle for the night, Lamar stood high on the catwalk looking upon his operation. Ledbetter came in the back way. Looked around.

"Up here, Bill!"

The Sheriff climbed the ladder. "Y'feel like a king up here?"

Lamar took a swig of bourbon. "Sometimes I wonder, can I get high enough? I wonder if it would be better to let go. Let Junior face what he's done. But what would I tell his mother?"

"Y'said you had a problem—urgent?"

"We got a problem. All this time he's had his brother up here."

"You're kidding?"

"No. The question is what do I do about it?" Lamar looked down into the mixers. Into the stone bin. "In that hopper is very fine stone dust. When it goes into the mix it's the stuff progress is made of. As it sits, here, it's finer than flour. He'd be buried in it, he'd suffocate in minutes."

Ledbetter shivered. "He slipped, eh?"

"Yeah, that's it. But he's the brother of a sheriff, Bill."

***

"Reminds me of my brother—that Rhett Butler," said Briley.

True nodded. His arm hugged Marlene a little tighter. Soon Briley and Seago were asleep. And he drove along US-98 in silence.

***

Harlowe's telephone was ringing when he walked in.

"Hello."

"You don't know me, Mr. Harlowe. But I can do something for you."

"Oh?"

"I'll get right to the point. What could you do with three-thousand dollars? Hear me out, now. You could pay off that mortgage at the bank. Yes, we know about that. You could live good. Enjoy life. Settle down with someone. What man likes to be alone? Just say the word."

Harlowe didn't say anything. *Do I know this voice?*

"Hello. Hello? I said three thousand."

"Who is this?"

"Think about it. I'll be in touch." CLICK.

Harlowe told Seago about the call.

"Damn—three thousand!"

"I'm just a country sheriff. What are they so skeered of?"

Brewer told them, "I went to a little git-together and Ledbetter was there. He seems like a reasonable fella. Pratt, maybe if ya could just ease up, things would be a tad easier."

Brewer left after that. "He wants your job, Pratt," said Seago. Harlowe knew that, True realized, seeing his expression.

Harlowe, looking out the window, nodded. "I know."

***

The wedding was in three days. Marlene heard the girls talking about Tennie. *"She said she could have True back whenever she wanted!"*

Tennie's beautiful. Dark hair. Tall. Graceful. Dressed beautifully. She could have been a movie star—a model for the newspaper advertisements anyway. Marlene looked in at Mother Williams sewing the wedding dress in the kitchen.

"It sure is a purty dress, girl!"

She helped Marlene put it on. Marlene got the mirror. It fit good, the dress she designed, her mother had sewn. "Y'think True will like me in it?"

"You know it!"

High shoes. Marlene tried to walk in them. "You look like that ol' funambilist Charlie Blondin!" said Mother Williams.

"Oh, momma!"

The big woman held her belly she laughed so hard. "I'm sorry, baby—caint he'p it!"

Marlene balled her fist. "Well, I'll tell you, I'll practice until I have it down pat!" Then she laughed, too.

***

Seago drove up in a Chevrolet! True put his hands on his hips. "Son!"

"Howyalikethat? Heyser gimme a deal on 'er. Give ya the first ride, seein' it's yer birthday!"

***

Taylor's place—110 South Monroe. The clack of the billiards balls, the rustle of conversation, and sounds of a Carter Family record. It all swirled together with the cigarette smoke.

"Hot damn!" Jeter just sunk the yellow "Nine."

Then he saw Durfee come in. The man was big. Looked like he wanted to hurt someone—Jeter knew that look. Had seen it in his stepfather enough. And he looked about—like he was waiting on help. "Hey, watch my beer, buddy!" Jeter told the barkeep. "Gotta take a leak!"

Jeter sauntered back to the toilet. The window was like a postage stamp. He stood on the filthy toilet. Slipped through like a squirrel diving through fence slats.

NINETY-THREE

January, 1940

The Sheriff picked up True. They joined Seago and a bunch of friends at the latter's house.

The men passed a jar around. Everyone was having a big time, but True was nervous. "W-what time is it?"

"Ten minutes of two," replied Harlowe. "We got time."

True couldn't get to the church soon enough; he was afraid he'd miss the wedding! He exhaled when, Seago pulled up in front of the little white church.

The preacher smiled. Held out his hand. "We won't start without you, son."

"Thankya, Dr. Reynolds."

"It's a fine day for a weddin'. And I'm proud to be the one marryin' you two! We'll get started soon."

"Yessir!"

Mother Williams was helping Marlene get ready in the church office. "Your hair's goin' every which way!" At that, the older woman wet her finger with spit. Patted it in place. "That'll hold ye!"

"Mommy, I do wanna feel purty when I walk down that row."

"You are! You're a purty li'l bride."

"You think so?"

Her mother nodded and checked the seams one last time.

Marlene's sisters were fussing about something, nearly coming to blows.

"Oh, no, this is my inning!" said Marlene. "Y'all settle down!"

Then the door opened.

"Who's there?" asked Marlene.

"You're the most beautiful thing I've ever seen." It was True!

"You ain't supposed to see me! Git back outside!" Turning towards her brother, "Now Denny, I done told you to keep him outta here!" Her older brother had forgotten. He'd already got knee-walking tight on the moonshine provided by the elder Williams. Denny had on an old-fashioned collar and necktie and could barely stand up.

Marlene slammed the door. She smiled at the compliment though. Stepped back and looked at herself in the mirror. She surprised herself.

505

The door swung open again.

"What in the world? Who is it *now?*"

It was her father—drunk, but still nosy. "What are you women up to?" He made no pretenses about his imbibing.

Mother Williams shoo'd him out. "Why, we're jus' getting' her ready, Deddy."

He grunted. Left to claim another jar of 'shine.

The church was crowded with kinfolk. Light from the big stained-glass windows bathed the aisle like a rainbow.

Denny, snatched off his collar. The piano clanged.

C.P. "herded" her in—his words. Marlene wobbled a bit in her high shoes.

"Ya'll hush," she whispered, catching Butterbean and the boys snickering from the pews.

Dennie tried to hold up Lonnie. "You've been drinkin' moonshine with Deddy. Shame on you!" said Marlene, swatting his arm. Folk in the audience laughed at the little blond scolding him.

She made it to the altar—opposite True.

Dr. Reynolds held his prayer book.

Her smile, True thought.

Marlene's eyes met his. She closed them, enjoying the moment she'd waited for all these years.

The pastor said things neither of them heard, until he called Marlene's middle name, "Beatrice." Cousin Butterbean chortled for all to hear.

Marlene shot a look in his direction.

"Is there anyone that objects to these two getting' married? Speak up or hold your peace!"

Dr. Reynolds looked around the church. Everyone looked toward the back—it was just Runt coughing.

True, then, noticed Harlowe in the back pew.

Marlene flashed a warning fist at her snickering cousins.

"Fine! I now pronounce you man and wife. You may kiss your bride, son!"

Marlene looked into True's eyes. Their lips met. Her warmth, her life, was all-encompassing.

Up the aisle they came—now married folks!

Butterbean flung handfuls of rice. "Hey, ya gonna feed us?"

"Yeah, Cousin," replied Marlene.

Harlowe shook True's hand. Marlene hugged the sheriff.

They dashed to Seago's new car—leaving in style!

The reception was at Harlowe's house.

Marlene spent most of the afternoon serving her family. Carrying plates of food to her brothers and daddy. They had one heaping plate after another, Marlene working harder than a waitress at a truck stop. It started raining and she was running between the kitchen and the living room and porch where everyone gathered. Finally, True had enough. Harowe winked at him and True dashed to his car. Pulled around the side of the house, the De Soto jangling with the cans and all kinds of things folk had fastened to its bumper.

He revved the motor. "Hey, darlin'. Wanna go for a ride?"

She wiped her brow. "I don't ride with strangers, Mister!"

"We won't be strangers by the time we get theah!"

"All right. But I don't let men pick me up, you understand. I don't want you to get the wrong idea about me!"

He flung the door open and she dove in. Her brothers were hollering for more food as True threw the car in gear. Dashed up the street. "I feel like we're eloping now!" she exclaimed. "Wait, where are we going?"

***

Jim Mealer stopped at a payphone at the filling station north of Tallahassee. He'd got to where he couldn't sleep nights—knowing what he knew.
Mealer took one last drag on the cigarette. Counted the change in his hand.
I've enough to phone Harlowe.
A car approached. His heart pounded. He held his breath until it passed.
Bill's really scarin' me. Tellin' Lamar he'd help him get rid of Harlowe's brother! Not a whore or vagrant—his brother! They're plannin' it, now! But, mostly, it's that damned paper sack that bothers me! I saw it settin' on his desk. I knew it was bad business. I knew where it come from. I was there when Lamar come by Bill's house! Lamar was upset. I could see that. They closed the door and talked the longest time. Bill took the rolled-up blue jeans and hat, then. Hid it in the closet! Then he wound the Victrola and laughed and cut up all night. After I saw it on his desk—well, I never saw them things again after that!

507

And Raines. He filed the commitment papers on Whittle. Finagled it so he'd never get out. I heard Bill braggin' about it!

Mealer took the earpiece off the hook. *"I can end this—give Harlowe what he's been lookin' for all these years."*

Then Mealer thought, *what about my job? I got to keep it.*

He hung up.

***

It was pouring as they turned up 24th Avenue and stopped. Marlene looked at the cute little place. The fresh paint. Shutters. The trim lawn. She nearly cried. "Y'mean this is ours?"

"Uh-huh."

He carried her things—Marlene's old canvas bag—up to the front porch.

True lit the stove and the hotwater heater. Marlene washed in the bathroom until a pipe broke, water spraying. Water rolling over the floor like a rising tide. True, shivering, tried to fix it. Then the roof began to leak, dripping on Marlene's head—every place she moved, holding the lantern for True.

Finally, without saying a thing, she grabbed a blanket and headed for the door. True looked up from the tub. "Hey, where you goin'?"

She hollered over the beating rain. "Out to the car—git yer shirt off and come on!"

She dashed through cold raindrops large as bullets. Dove in and slammed the door.

He looked on, his eyes going back and forth between the inch of water in the bathroom and his young wife—who was obviously mad—camping out in the car.

She rolled the side-curtain down. "We're having our dadgum weddin' night! I don't keer where it is, we're having it! So you best git over here!"

He ran. Barefoot through the mud. That cold rain made him gasp for breath by the time he climbed in. "Dry off with this towel!" said Marlene. The car was cozy with the side curtains drawn. She soon got him a lot warmer—True forgot all about the plumbing and roof!

***

Ledbetter kept up his image as a family man. He'd get drunk out at Lamar's ranch!

Lamar was feeling pretty high, too. "Damn it, I can't understand it! I thought we'd be able to reach him. Why, everybody has a price!"

"Apparently, he's too dumb to know his," replied Raines.

Cory looked over at Ledbetter. The latter shrugged. "I tried, Lamar."

"Why, I spend more money on a party than these oystermen make in a year! Damn it, I can't understand why Harlowe won't come to terms!"

NINETY-FOUR

February, 1940

Jeter was hiding. But he thought he'd left a bottle at the apartment. *Go git it and run—better panhandling down South!*

The old bindlestiff crept in. Rummaged through the kitchen until he found it—there's two fingers of booze left! He tucked it in his coat. Then, saw the face in the window. Pressed to the glass. A big face.

Jeter cut the light. Locked the door. Hollered at the sound of the man trying the knob. "Whachu want, boah? I gotta knife—I'll cut you one!"

The man forced the door open without any trouble.

Jeter flopped out a window. Dropped the bottle. Ran headlong for Calhoun Street.

At that instant headlights flashed. Jeter jumped on the sidewalk. The car swerved toward the curb, bouncing over it. Jeter dove into the hydrangeas. Thought for a second the fender grazed him.

It was a fairly new, gray coupe. The driver backed up, flinging grass. Jeter ran again, cutting down Georgia Street.

He heard the car accelerate behind him.

Then, out of nowhere, "Ahooooga!" A model A Ford, swerved in front of the newer car. Brakes screeched. Bumpers rattled together. Jeter ducked behind a tree.

The Model A had slid off against a tree.

The driver of the gray car backed up, tires screeching. It mowed down some shrubs and disappeared.

Jeter ran over to the Model A—Pratt's!

"Didn't recognize the automobile, did you?"

"No," said True. "No tag on it."

Both tires were flat on the Ford. The radiator was busted.

"Why didn't you stay put like I told ya?" said Harlowe.

Jeter cussed.

"He come down Calhoun Street, theah?" asked Harlowe.

"I reckon. He come at me. I turned the corner."

"It was a Pontiac," said True.

Jeter nodded. He was breathing hard—still scared.

"We saw ya right when he swerved at you again," said Harlowe.

"He come right up to my winduh—so I run," Jeter explained.

They went back to the apartment to look.

"You said he come up to your winduh. What did he look like?"

"Big fella—didn't git a good look at 'im."

"Well, that's just fine!" said Harlowe.

"Don't git mad with *me,* Pratt!"

"Now…I got a look at 'im when he was drivin'.'"

"Well, tell us!"

"Caint I hav-a bottle?"

"C'mon!"

"Your buddy—Driscoll."

Harlowe went outside, looking at the lock that had been forced, the window. Harlowe squeezed between the bricks and a tree. "Look here."

"Poison ivy!" said Jeter.

"Well, see how it's been disturbed? He touched it when he squeezed through to look in the winduh."

"This fella got into it!" said True.

Jeter said, "Be careful, ya got your arm in it, Pratt!"

Harlowe found Ledbetter at the F&T. "I'm glad you ain't hurt, Pratt. Hittin' the tree like 'at."

"That's missin' the point. Someone nearly killed my brother."

"Nearly killed your brother? Why, I had not idea, Pratt! Royce, what have you heard?"

"I didn't know sheriff. If he wohnts to make a report, we'll look into it."

"It was a gray Pontiac. Tried to run him down."

"Run you down?!" asked Ledbetter, looking at Jeter.

"Mighta been these colored boys," said Sackett. "They may have thought Jeter was movin' in on their shine operation. I hate to say that about your brother, now. I got it on good authority from a fella I trust—his nigra help stumbled on this still. Well, I didn't wanna make too much of it—Jeter

511

bein your brother and all—but it was in an area Jeter has been seen from time to time."

Harlowe knew Jeter couldn't run a still—he'd be dead if he had that much to drink. "We appreciate that, but we know who it is," said Harlowe.

"Who?"

"Obie Driscoll, that's who!" said Jeter.

"He'll swear to it right now," said Harlowe. "I'm gonna ask you—will you arrest him?"

"Pratt, I haven't enough evidence to charge anyone—if he wants to come down and make--"

"It was Driscoll, and you know it."

"I feel terrible about what happened, but I got to have proof! It's awful dark out there, and you said yourself it wuddint his car!"

"He operates a nineteen-and-thirty-seven Hudson," said Sackett.

"Sure." Harlowe scratched the rash that was beginning to form under his cuff.

Ledbetter gave assurances. "Truly, I am sorry about all this. Royce will look into it. If I hear something I'll call ye!"

"I'm aim to find 'im—any objections?"

"No, Pratt."

***

It was good coming home to Marlene. Seeing her smile, took away most of the tired.

She hugged him so tightly. She didn't know if it was so he wouldn't slip away or so she could just become part of him or because that was the closest she could get and that made her feel good. He didn't seem to mind.

Marlene lit a cigarette for him. Put it to his lips.

"Thankya, darlin."

She fixed supper for him. It wasn't much. They had two plates that they ate on and washed for the next meal. It didn't matter that they hadn't money. The had each other, True thought, as they washed the dishes and as he watched her comb her hair and get ready for bed.

She looked back at him in the mirror. She loved him so much she ached when he wasn't around. Both had rotten childhoods She could see maybe that was why he wanted to be a lawman, almost like he wanted to protect people, protect property, *'cause he never had that.*

Neither of us had much of a family life. We are our own family now!

The house, despite leaks and drafts felt as cozy and warm as a mansion.

The light in her eyes keeps me warm, thought True.

NINETY-FIVE

Next day.

She'd let him sleep a little. The sun woke him. He realized she wasn't there. She'd introduced soft things into the house. He smelled bacon frying. He found her outside, working in her rolled up blue jeans. The yard bloomed like a garden.

She looked up at him. Now she had her own home. Small and empty of furnishings, maybe, but filled with happiness and love. "Here, I'll finish fixin' your breakfast."

True kissed her. Waved. Drove down to the end of 24th Avenue to look at the water, like he did each morning. Down Bay Avenue to look at the blue house. On to the courthouse.

Harlowe had plenty for him to do.

***

Judge Anderson, though it was late, read the papers and signed the warrant. If it wasn't already clear, Anderson empowered him to arrest Driscoll anywhere—even in Leon County.

Problem was, no one had seen Driscoll in twenty-four hours. Seago said he hadn't showed at his apartment.

Harlowe and True, drove Leon County, hunting for him.

***

Raines phoned Judge Anderson. "You can rescind that warrant. You ought to rescind it!"

Anderson replied, "You are not king, O.C."

And hung up on him.

***

The Tallahassee paper's headline: "Cory Concrete Wins Bid for Runway." "For the Army Air Corp base in Tallahassee," said True.

"Let's go."

They drove north on the Thomasville Highway.

Ledbetter flagged them down.

They stopped, cows grazing on the side of the serene country road. Blue sky. Birds chirping. They met between the cars.

"What are you going to do, Pratt?"

"I'm gonna arrest Driscoll on witness tamperin'."

"I heard he left town."

Harlowe looked Ledbetter in the eye. "Bill, you better find 'im. 'Cause if I find 'im I may kill 'im."
Ledbetter went white. "Okay, Pratt." True was wide-eyed.

They tried his usual haunts. Pool halls. Alleys. Places True had no idea existed.

"The gun store, on Adam Street, theah," said Harlowe.

True went in. Came out. Shook his head.

"The hotel on Park," said Harlowe.

They climbed the dingy staircase. A woman answered when Harlowe knocked on the third-floor room. She barely had clothes on. Harlowe handed her money. She looked at Harlowe and True and back. "I'm buying somethin' else," he said. "Where's Driscoll?"

She looked in his eyes and shivered. "Ain't seen 'im. Not in three days."

No one had seen hide nor hair of him.

They approached his wife, sunning in the yard of the apartment. "Have ya seen 'im?"

"No, sir."

"Has he got any kinfolk in town?" asked Harlowe.

"Me and the kid are the only ones he's got," replied Mrs. Driscoll. "Some family."

"Ma'am." They tipped their hats. Walked back to the car.

At the depot, they found the man loading packages on the Railroad Express truck. He was middle-aged, broad shouldered, and mahogany skin. "Why, Mr. Pratt! How' do sah?"

"Mornin', Travis!"

"Good Mo'nin! How you is, Mistuh Pratt?"

"Just fine. Travis, you remember my nephew, True?"

"Yazzah, Mistuh True! I's glad to see ya! Last time you all was catchin' brim—and I had caught me some crabs off da dock."

"Yeah, that was a good day."

"It sho' was Mistuh Pratt. Would ya keer to step in my office, sah?"

They followed him around the other side of the freight car, out of view.

"How you like workin' for the line?"

"I likes it fine, sah. Bossman like me. I git the work did. H-How's Mistuh Moye's fam-leh?"

Moye was a railroad policeman murdered up the line. "Jus' saw Mrs. Moye and the kids. Thankya for askin.'"

"Yazzah. Mistuh Moye a good main. I remembers 'im."

"Travis, I wanna ask you somethin'."

"Go right ahead, sah."

"Mr. Tompkins runs things pretty good."

"Yazzah. He do!"

"Travis, I wanna ask ya somethin'."

"Yazzah?"

"Ya seen Driscoll?"

"No, sah, Mistuh Pratt. I ain't been through heah, No, sah. Dat's da truth."

"Y'know he works for Lamar?"

If Travis could have gone white, he might have. "Lamar—now he a pow'ful man."

"The son?"

"I-I hear things. Y'gonna get yo'self hutt, Mr. Pratt! I don' wan' no part of dis heah."

Harlowe nodded.

"Y'always fair tuh me. I tell you dis. I see him....trine talk to chirren. Why? He got no bidness wit em! Now, dats all I know."

After dark, they drove down to the Green Derby. The neon sign flashed, "BOWLING." "Dancing" and "Dining" were lit up in white light. The lot was packed, music spilling from the dance floor. "That's his Hudson yonder," said True. "In the back, theah."

Harlowe nodded.

True went inside. Harlowe watched with the BAR. A few minutes later, True returned. Got in. "Told 'em I'm his cousin. Bartender said, 'he ain't been in. He left 'is car. I'm sure he'll be back for it.'"

"All right."

Over the music, they heard crying. True got out, saw a woman sitting on the running board of Driscoll's car! "Y'never can drink right!" her male companion berated.

"Don' yell at me!" she squealed.

"Aww shut up! Ya always start blubberin' when y'drink!"

The man opened the door of the Hudson.

True approached. "Hey, Mister, ya know the fella that owns this car?"

"I dunno. Can't y'see I got my hands full, buddy?"

"Ya know the owner, ma'am?"

She snifled. "Obie Driscoll. Seen him here a few times, why?"

"Y'know where he is?"

"No. But he has a sister—why don't y'ask her?" the woman said. "Her name's Willy."

True tipped his hat. "Ma'am."

"Oh, quit cryin'!" hollered the man, as True walked back to the car.

True got in, told Harlowe.

They drove up to the farm off U.S. 90, east of town.

"We're lookin' for your brother—is he here?"

"No,"

"Has he been here?"

"Ain't seen him."

"I think you're lyin'."

"I don't keer what you think."

True glanced toward the barn.

"Naw, y'caint look in the barn. I'll call the law to ya, I mean it!" she spat.

A car pulled up, then. Chief Deputy Sackett's. He portly man stamped over. "What're you doin'?" he asked, his jowels shaking.

"I have a warrant for her brother." Harlowe held up the paper.

"I done told these fellers he ain't been here. An' I don't know where he is!"

Sackett smiled. "Maybe he took a vacation."

Harlowe was sure Driscoll was holed up somewhere. He'd had Mr. Seago and Jeter watching the train station, the Tampa Highway.

"Let's go, son."

True slipped through the woods, to the lean-to barn.

In a few moments he emerged. Ran back to the car.

Shook his head.

"Damn."

They met Ledbetter at the Standard Oil. "I'm looking for 'im too! We caint find him!"

Harlowe was angry. "We call ourselves lawmen—that's got to mean somethin'. If you caint deal with the situation, you should ask the govunuh for help!"

Ledbetter got to shaking, his lip quivering. "You're threatenin' my family!"

"What about their family—the Birch family?" Harlowe replied.

True was wide-eyed.

"I think he tipped 'im off," said Seago, after Ledbetter pulled away.

"We ask for his help and this is how he does," said Harlowe.

"Could be anywheres by now, boss," said Seago.

"You really think he helped 'im?" asked True.

"I figured he would," Harlowe said, sadly. "But I had to do that for what we got to do. Ledbetter won't go to the guvunuh on this. *He'd* look bad."

True talked to Willy's neighbors, at the next farmhouse.

Harlowe returned. Got in the car. "Ol' boy over at the store saw a Pontiac come through heah, yesterdee."

"Yeah?" True looked down toward the country store and house, yonder.

"He saw the car turn up the road, theah. Toward the little farm."

True started the car. They turned up the road. The old place was abandoned. "Foreclosed on," Harlowe said.

They approached the old house afoot. Guns drawn.

True, holding the BAR. Harlowe flung the barn door open. There was the Pontiac—but not him.

NINETY-SIX

Chattahoochee—later that day.

The driver of the Trailways coach mashed the starter. The diesel groaned and turned over. He'd let her warm up as the passengers boarded. A lady with large present wrapped in paper. A salesman in blue suit. An old couple. Cars passed, heading for the Victory Bridge. The red and silver bus would hasten across it, presently.

Driscoll staggered out of the men's room. Blinked his bloodshot eyes— tucked his shirttail—climbed aboard. Down the aisle. Looked the woman up-and-down. *Good, the big seat in back ain't taken.* He headed for it. Smirked. *Bus is leaving in five minutes—I'm in the clear! They'll never catch me!* The brochures promised the "Old Spanish Trail" run all the way to California!

Driscoll saw a hat. *Damn, someone's already sitting there.* The man looked up. *Damn—Harlowe!*

He didn't have to guess what Harlowe had wrapped in his coat—aimed at his belly.

"Let's go"

Driscoll turned around. "Where?"

"Takin' you back to Apalach." They got an odd look from the driver as they reached the door. Driscoll saw True and Seago across the street. He looked at Harlowe. Saw his eyes. *There's no point running!*

True clicked the cuffs on. Cuffed in front, it resembled some form of praying if one didn't know better.

He had a nice, light gray suit, but it was wrinkled. The man had a "long" belly. He'd boozed and caroused himself to jowels and a paunch, rather like a well-dressed hog. Harlowe nodded to Seago. "Roll up his sleeve."

Seago did. "Damn!" Driscoll had a blistered poison ivy rash all over his forearm.

"All right, let's go." They shoved him in Seago's Chevrolet. True got in aside him.

Seago pulled out onto Ninety.

The man glanced over at the asylum. Cussed. "Y'takin' me to Apalach?"

"That's right," said Harlowe.

"Y'makin' a mistake, boys!"

"Maybe."

Driscoll's fat face slanted to a sly grin. "Save y'self the trouble, y'get me down theah it's just a pleasant outin'. My lawyer'll have me out 'n half-an-hour 'n I'll be eating oysters at the Grill! You know Mr. Smalley? Jus' watch! You're outta your league!"

"We'll see."

Mr. Hickey pulled up. Had his camera. True led him back to Driscoll's cell. The photographer took a picture of Driscoll's rash-riddled skin. "Mr. Raines won't have to take our word for it," said Harlowe. "Thanks, Mr. Hickey."

"So long."

"Y'have a telephone in this place? I wanna make a telephone call!" said Driscoll.

"I wanna know who you workin' with."

"Hell—I work for myself. Always have."

"You collect the money for Ledbetter. Cory too. Moonshine—and other things."

"I've nothing to do with any moonshine. Not in years. I'm an honest man."

"No, your Ledbetter's 'bagman'—ain't that the word, True?"

"Yeah."

"You're crazy."

"We hear you been spendin' money pretty good. Where'd you get it?"

"Workin'."

"Doin' what?"

"Tradin' this or that."

"You spent nearly a thousand the last week you were in Tallahassee. What were you tradin'?"

"Sold some things."

"Come off it, you ain't worked in years."

Driscoll grinned. "You'll try to bluff it out. But you'll lemme go!"

"We'll see."

"They won't let ya in the front door with what you got—you'll never touch anyone in Tallahassee! Them that run things are a whole lot smarter'n you!" said Driscoll.

They heard the phone ring, across the yard.

Seago ran to answer it.

Came back. "Ooh, he's hot! Wants you to call 'im."

Harlowe looked up from his desk. "Who?"

"Raines. He's foamin' at the mouth!"

They walked to the office. Harlowe reached for the earpiece. "Yes, ma'am, I'd like to place a call to O.C. Raines, person-to-person."

It was a moment before the operator rang back. "I have Mr. Raines, Sheriff."

"Thankya. Hello?"

"You have no authority in Leon County!" barked Raines.

"I asked Sheriff Ledbetter's permission. I got a warrant signed by the circuit court," Harlowe replied.

"Would you transfer him to the jail in Leon County?"

"Nosir. He's in my jail, that's where he's gonna stay."

"You made your arrest. Who you gonna get to prosecute it?"

CLICK—Raines hung up.

"Get me Mr. Campbell," Raines growled.

The secretary had the party, presently. "Hello, Merle. Listen, ah, I know you wanted a comment on the arrest. I'm still lookin' into some things, and I hope you'll hold the story. Yes, Harlowe. I wouldn't like to see this aired out before we look into it. Goodbye."

***

"The Tallahassee paper didn't cover the arrest," said Seago. "Just looked."

Judge Anderson scheduled a bond hearing at Smalley's instistence. Harlowe carried the moonshiner to the courthouse in his car.

Harlowe sat him down at the defense table, in irons.

His mouthpiece hollered and danced. But Anderson denied the writ of habeus corpus. "Motion's denied." The big-time attorney usually got his way—started to get up. But he knew not to press Anderson too far—he settled back in his seat. Swung his hand over to silence his bewildered client.

Harlowe put him back in the car. Nodded to True. "I expect the Court will call a grand jew-ree, shortly."

***

February, 1940—the next week.

The phone rang. *Mrs. Young!*

"My son is...*despondent.* That's the only word for it."

"Yeas, ma'am?"

"I have to help him, do *something* for him! You were right, Mr. Harlowe. I-I didn't protect him."

"Y'caint blame yourself, ma'am."

"Will you talk to him?"

"Yes, ma'am."

"This is no life living in fear. Like we're dogs and they can bring us to heal when they holler."

"No, ma'am."

"If he testifies I wanna know we'll be safe. Can y'promise me that?"

"We'll come get you."

They met her at the Tift Theatre.

True opened the back door of Harlowe's car. She got in. Harlowe and True sat in front, the BAR between them.

"I'm scared-terrified! I feel someone's watching me. I know you got him—I heard about it!"

"Driscoll?"

"Yes, sir."

"You know, he caught me walking home from work one night. Say, you got a cigarette?"

"Sure." He lit it for her.

"Thanks," she said, taking a long drag.

"Yeah. He caught me walkin' home from work. Shoved money at me. Told me I'd better leave town. Said, if I didn't, my girls had to walk the streets! Mr. Harlowe, I just wanna earn a living, take care of my children! These fellas—well, I jus' never ran up against this sort of thing!"

"Yes, ma'am."

"I'm still getting telephone calls. Someone phones and hangs up!"

523

"Even after he went to jail?"

"Yes—I-I'm scared, Mr. Harlowe."

Harlowe nodded.

"I knew he did something to my boy—Cory, I mean. I didn't know how bad it was. I went to the sheriff about Driscoll. He wouldn't help."

"Ledbetter?"

"Yes. He told me no one would believe us! That maybe I *oughtta* move— the sheriff said that! I had no choice, then."

"Yeah."

"You got another cigarette?"

"Sure."

"I had to work. Mr. Cory offered to take the boy to practice. Tutor him. That's how it started."

He preyed on that. Their being poor, Harlowe thought.

"I don't know what happened, not all of it. He'd never talk about it. Don't know if he will!"

"He's *despondent?*"

She teared up. "He sits in the backyard—staring off at nothing!"

"Mrs. Young, I'll do everything I can for 'im."

"Thank you—y'think he'll be all right then?"

He smiled, reassuringly. "Yes, ma'am. Come on, Lets go get your kids."

Finley got in the car. "Why are we going? What about school?"

The girls were cying, having to leave their friends.

They fell asleep, outside of Bainbridge, exhausted.

***

Bottles covered the table out at the ranch.

Pender said, "I plan on runnin' again, boys. Filed the papers."

"We're goin' to deal with Harlwoe, and when we do, why, the coast'll be clear to you getting another term," said Ledbetter.

"I want it so he'll never run again," said Raines.

"You think it'll work?" wondered Ledbetter.

"The guv'ner's got O'dell diggin' up dirt," said Sackett.

"He needs to work fast!" growled Raines. "I heard Harlowe was nosin' around over there at the Floridan Hotel! And he's still botherin' Junior. What if the boy cracks?"

"We just got to make this whole thing goaway, thats all there is to it," said Lamar. "We all stand to do well if I can get these military contracts. There's a war comin'—that's money to be made, boys! I *can't have* a scandal!"

***

Mrs. Young awakened as True pulled up in front of the Fuller. She blinked—taking in the old wooden hotel.

"Y'all are safe heah," said Harlowe.

True carried one of the girls. Harlowe carried their bags. The white desk clerk showed them to their room. "The *Dixie Sherman* it ain't. But we change the sheets every week!" said he.

Mrs. Young nodded. Following along.

"Bath's just down the hall. Well, good night, ma'am."

"The hotel has a kitchen—well, it's almost finished," said Harlowe. "Y'all can eat theah until you get on your feet."

She tucked in her girls. Saw to it that Finley had a blanket.

"Don't you worry ma'am. Anyone comes here'll have to get past Ol' True, theah."

The young deputy looked fearsome in the light of the hallway. Shotgun and hat.

Harlowe came, later. "I'll spell ya." He took the chair, coach gun across his lap.

NINETY-SEVEN

March, 1940

She felt safe in his arms, walking with him, sleeping beside him. She had to tell him so, the words couldn't be held back. Pressed against him, kissing his neck. "I feel so safe with you!"

He didn't know what to say. Just held her tightly.

She had the life she wanted, now. More comfort than she'd ever known.

"Thank you, Lord, you let me have him as my husband. I didn't pray for anything close to this, but here it is just the same. I just hoped maybe he'd settle down and try to love me—after Tennie. But he looks at me like I'm the thing in all the world that makes him happiest. The only girl in the world. He holds onto me the way I hold onto him!"

He held her until she fell asleep. He lay there, listening to the night. He liked having her close to him, touching him so softly. How she fit under his arm, tucked in close to his heart.

She just goes right to sleep on me, like a cat. She said she felt safe with me. That made me feel funny. She loves me. I hope I can love her like she deserves.

She has the yard like a garden with flowers blooming everywhere.

Her laughter. The sound of my new home—Paradise.

***

The scent of orange blossoms flowed in the windows on the bridge, as he drove Marlene to Eastpoint. "I'll do the washin' True. Y'can pick me up this afternoon?"

"Sure, darlin'."

True went to relieve Harlowe. "The ladies from the church brought some clothes for you and your girls, on the bur-ah theah," said the Sheriff.

"Thank you."

"Howdy, son."

They went out on the porch.

"The boy say anythin'?" asked True.

"No."

That night, True went to the Nichols store with Marlene. The breeze puffing against the screendoors. The glare of light against the white shiplap walls. They were the only customers. The store about to close. Rain about to fall.

The lady at the counter wrapped up the hamburger meat. Smiled. "I watched you grow up, son."

Marlene hugged her and they went home, happily.

***

"How bad can—how bad can it be for Finn? No one in my family has ever been in a courthouse except for me—and that on drunk ch—that's what happens isn't it?"

"Yes, ma'am." Harlowe explained what would happen in a trial.

Mrs. Young's eyes moved back and forth as she contemplated, and off to the furniture, the pieces bearing scars that looked like worry lines. It was as if he were describing medieval procedures or the rules of society on Mars, court trials were something foreign to her.

"It sounds rough."

"I won't lie to you, Miss Young, it can be."

"I'm worried, terribly, about my son." Her fingers moved all around the coffee cup, nervously, as if she was trying to find a grip on all the problems of the world in that cup.

"I understand."

"I don't know if he'll talk about it. He hasn't told me anything. But when I mention Mr. Cory, he goes all to pieces. He still isn't the same, he just isn't my happy boy! It's like this dark cloud hangs over him!

***

The room darkened with the approaching storm. Finley switched on the lamp.

The boy was holding a model aeroplane he'd made.

Harlowe sat facing him, talking to him. But the boy wouldn't say anything.

Harlowe looked at the model, carefully lettered, "U.S. MARINES." It appeared to be Finley's only possession. His sisters started school, at Chapman. The elder boy refused to go.

Mrs. Young said Finley got rid of his baseball penants and things. But he held onto that model. "You like aeroplanes, son?"

Finley kept looking out the window at the raindrops.

Harlowe went out, finding Mrs. Young in the kitchen, helping out. "Least I could do," she said. "I can't get a thing out of him, either, Sheriff."

Harlowe went back in. "Like aeroplanes?"

"Yessir."

"I see the markings. You like the Marines, son?"

"Yessir. I-I used to wanna be a Marine."

"It's a fine outfit. You'd be a good one—coulda used ya at *Château-Thierry!*"

"Yeah? Say, no foolin', you were in the Marines?"

"Yeah—joined up. Didn't know no better, I reckon. Nah—I liked it. Kinda runs in the fam'ly. My uncles were Marines—for the Confed'racy. Granddaddy was one o' those boys at Tripoli."

Finley wondered about that scar—where Harlowe had his hair parted. "You were in France, saw trenches and all?"
"Yeah."

"Gee!"

"Son, why did you run away? Son?"

"I wanted to get away from *him.*"

"Okay."

"Wanted to get clear."

"From Cory?"

Finley nodded. "And from his town. I didn't care what happened to me. Just wanted to go where I wasn't ashamed any longer. Just started walkin'."

"I understand. Kinda long walk to Chipley."

"Yeah! A couple truck drivers felt sorry for me. Picked me up. Rode with a couple sows one time."

Harlowe grinned.

"I wanted to keep going."

"Where were ya aimin' to get to?"

"Didn't matter. Just wanted to *go.* Have you ever felt that way?"

"Yeah, son."

"No foolin'?"

"I rode the trains some. Went all the way out to California feelin' thataway."

"What brought it on?"

"Lost my wife. Then my job."

"Oh. Wow."

"You don't have to be ashamed, son. Cory has to answer for what he done. But you've nothing to feel sorry for."

A tear rolled down the boy's cheek. He wiped it away, looking at the "MARINES" bi-plane in his hands.

"He wanted me to help him. That's how it started. He drove me in his car, out past the city limits. He told me he'd let me lay out a new ballfield—a place for the fellas to use. Anytime they wanted. The poor kids. He promised me we'd build it the way I wanted. But he stopped the car and there was nothing there. We walked around and there were no tools. I'd never been out there before. There's just old chimneys there, old columns from a big house that isn't there anymore. Part of an old plantation or something. No house, just columns and chimneys is all."

"All right."

"Mr. Cory pointed to where home plate would be, a little dugout. Then it started to rain. He had me get in his car. He kept talkin' about what it would look like, there'd be lights and everything and what it would mean to the boys who had less than me, and I was gonna help. He said I was his best player and I could help with the fellas who had less than I did. And then—uh. That's where—." The boy fought back the tears. "It was dark and--."

"Okay."

"It rained harder an' harder. He said if I yelled no one'd hear."

"Go on."

"Then he—he—that was the first time it happened." The boy looked down in abject shame.

"It's all right, son."

Finley looked up with an utterly lost look on his face.

"It's all right. You're a brave fella."

Finley told him Cory had taken him there more than ten times.

"He told me I was a great ballplayer. Out of all the kids, I'd make it to play for a college. And he'd help. He'd say the other poor boys, this was just something for them to do, but for me, well, I'd play for a university, maybe even professionally. He filled my head with that. It made me sorry to question him, when he was looking after me so, and he was my pal. But he wasn't. I knew it, and he had me so scared, so afraid he'd kill me—or he'd tell everyone. Don't you see?" Finley was sobbing now, losing the effort to fight the tears, his face in his sleeve.

"Yes, son." It both enraged and nauseated Harlowe.

"Mr. Harlowe, there's something else? Something else that made me scared."

"Yes, son?"

"He said, if I said anything about him, he'd kill me. *'I'll kill you like that other boy—and I'll get away with it.'* That's what he told me."

"That other boy—did he say who he was?"

"No, sir. Just that he'd killed a boy several years ago—a boy who tried to get him in trouble."

"Did he say who he was, where this was?"

"Only it was out of town, that no one would ever find him. Oh, and he said he knew places to hide a fella and get away with it."

"Anything else?"

"No, sir."

"All right. The old plantation house—you could show me?"

"Yessir."

The boy quieted some. And they spoke of school. Despite everything, Finley made good marks. And he promised to attend—tomorrow.

"You're a brave young fella. Woulda liked to have had ya with us in France," Harlowe declared.

Harlowe walked downstairs. Mrs. Young was drying dishes. She looked up at him.

He nodded.

The dish slipped from her hands. "Oh, God. Dear God!"

Shards of glass scattered across the floor. Harlowe helped her pick them up. "Sir, I'm scared for my son. This man is--."

"I know."

"I trusted him. I trusted him with my son!"

"It's not your fault. You caint think about that."

"I suppose not. I need to think about what comes next—what was it you said?"

"The *grand* jew-ree."

"Goodbye, Pratt, and thank you!"

***

"Evenin'," said Harlowe.

Murrow stepped in. True poured.

"That helps, some, duddint it?" thought Seago, hope glimmering in his eyes.

"You know it," replied Harlowe.

Seago clapped True on the back. "That's a jam up job you done! Huntin' them files—findin' that report!"

"You did good, son," said Harlowe.

"What the Young boy said, why, I think that clinches it," reckoned Murrow.

Later, Harlowe spoke to Finley in his room, tried to narrow down the dates certain things occurred. "Yessir, seventh grade. Eighth. And ninth—you see he came to Leon High to help their coach. That's why I quit the team. I couldn't get away from him." Harlowe wrote a statement for Finley to sign.

NINETY-EIGHT

March, 1940—the next day.

"Yes, this is it," Finley told them. "He'd park there."

The bones of the old mansion, columns like weathered bones, vine-covered chimneys, the oaks with grey whiskers, made True shudder.

A myriad of emotions flashed across Finley's face, like the changing of a motion picture screen.

"You all right?" asked Harlowe

"Yessir."

"Anything else you remember, son? Anyone who might have seen you in his automobile?"

"My old boss. At Byrd's grocery."

They drove downtown, and Harlowe got out to do some checking.

Presently, True met him at the spot Harlowe asked him to. He pulled to the curb and Harlowe climbed in. "I was talkin' to the man at the store over theyuh."

"Byrd's?"

"He confirmed Finn worked for 'im making deliveries, in nineteen-hunerd-and-thirty-seven."

"Yeah?"

"Harlowe looked back at the boy. "He said Cory was all the time pickin' you up from the store and he'd wait outside. Backs up what you told us."

"It sure does," said True. "Where to, boss?"

"Let's run him home."

***

They were invited for supper at Briley's. Marlene put on a new dress she'd made and combed her hair. But she was still not ready. "True, can you find my good shoes? I might woulda been ready but I had to got the stove to light and I forgot to iron--."

"It's okay, baby." He handed her the shoes from the bedroom.

"You're so patient with me," she said. And—"

"Yeah?"

"Iwas gonna say I wonder where you get it from—but I know. Just like your uncle." He smiled. "Yeah."

***

They parked on Monroe. Seago sat in the car, as Harlowe and True walked into the bank, climbing the stairs to Mr. Raines's office. The secretary led them back. Raines didn't get up.

"*'I'll kill you like I did that other boy,'*" Harlowe repeated.
"Where is the witness?" Raines growled.
"He'll testify at the grand jew-ree, but I caint give you his location just yet. He's scared of the Corys—with good reason."
"There's no reason to be scared of the Corys—they own the concrete business. I've known Lamar—*for years*. He's one of the finest people in this town. And you wanna go after *his son?*"

"There's no question Junior was in the area at the time Gib-beh went missin'. His schoolmate, Mr. Tooley told us that Junior stayed behind. We got the Orr boy sayin' that he saw Junior. Here's his statement."
Raines frowned. "Go on."
"Lamar and Junior are both familiar with Tate's Hell. Both hunted theah. They know the old tapper's roads." True lay the newspaper clippings on the desk.
"That's it?"
"We have a sworn statement of a man who heard Junior say he done something terrible, got upset over it."
"He's upset about *what?* Did he mention the Birch boy by name?"

"This was three months after Gibby was taken."

The prosecutor scowled. "Your connection to the Birch boy is *tenous*—weak! Who did you say the witness was?"

"Emerson."

"You can have ten Emerson's and it won't get you to first base! He's *sorry*," spat Raines. Sorry was the worst thing he could call someone in his mind. "The jury—decent citizens of this town—won't believe a word he says. He was convicted of four crimes—by me!"

"Liquor offenses, Traffic offenses, 's all."

Raines peered at Harlowe way down the tip of his nose somewhere. "Crimes!" he growled.

"He's an old moonshiner, 's all."

"Y'might as well call in my nigra fieldhands to tesify. Cory can afford the best lawyer in town, bring 'em up from Miami! This isn't some nigra chickenthief you're dealin' with. He won't roll over and plead guilty, he'll make a fight of it!"

"I don't keer if he hires from *Miamuh,* and Clarence Darrow himself, he's guilty. Have the fight and you'll win! It ain't just Emerson. We have *Gibbeh* in the photo!"

True set it on the desk. "He and his daddy admitted bein' around the boy. Junior talked to 'im. He knew 'im."
"That may be, you have a bigger problem with the Court, in case you haven't realized it."
"Yessir?"
"I *told you no case, in this state,* has ever been tried without a body!"

Harlowe stood. Took a book from the shelf.

"What are you doing? I've been practicing law for forty years! I don't need *you* to tell me what the law is!"

Harlowe slid the book in front of him.

Raines scanned it. *"The Supreme Court...1888...State v. Jos. Anderson...Charles E. Abbe...going towards the bay...body has not been found."*

"I'm just a country sheriff...I ain't tryin' to tell ya what the law is, but I...*believe* that's a precedent.

True was wide-eyed.

Raines shoved the book away. "Anyone can parrot a book! How will the court rule? You can't prove it's *that boy's* bones! There wasn't any blood found down there or anything to suggest violence! Unlike your *Anderson* case, there! Tire tracks for a Ford automobile *is all you got!*" He said the last bit like he was talking to the filthiest whore on her way to a home for unwed mothers.

"We have quite a bit more if you'll listen. We have Finley Young. What was done to 'im. What Junior told 'im. It's as good as a confession."

"You waste my time with this other boy—well, you can't charge Cory with the Birch boy's death and then *sit there and tell the jury* about *some other crime* you think he's committed!
You need it in simple terms so you can understand it? *You can't prove your case by tellin' the jury he's done it before!* Anyone who's read law for a week knows that! You don't get to parade this thing about another boy in front of the jury—why, Judge Anderson would *put you in jail* if you attempted to bring it up!
Harlowe retrieved another volume. "You're the lawyer now, and a damn fine one. I'm just a country sheriff, so you tell me if I'm wrong. But don't Florida courts follow the *English rule*—the jew-ree gets to hear about the other crimes, if they're relevant to the case?"

Raines snatched the book. "Twenty-four Southern, four-seventy-four. *Roberson versus State.* I've read that!" he snapped. "So? It's still a big *if* that Anderson will *find* it relevant! I say no." Raines slammed the book. True was amazed!

"It's theah, in the opinion, Mr. Raines. I'm askin' ya for that boy's Mother and Daddy."

"Even if Anderson let it in, only his statement about doing something to that other boy would be admissible!"

"Fine."

"That's, *if* you believe it. He never reported it! I say the jury won't believe him!"

"Why's that?"

"The kind of home he's from. Divorced mother. Up against the word of a *respected* teacher!"

"'Cause he's *white trash?*" interjected Harlowe.

"I'm not sayin' that! Don't put words in my mouth!"

"Will you call the grand jew-ree."

"No!"

"What about the charges for the Young boy?"

"In all you're *readin'*, I'm sure you've come upon the *statute of limitations?*"

"Yessir. I understand that applies to the earlier offense—in nineteen-hunnerd-and-thirty-five. Not for the incidents in the eighth grade and so on."

"No!" barked Raines.

Raines, the self-renowned teetotaler, looked at Harlowe with particular disgust, "are you still *drinkin'*, Harlowe?"

The sheriff looked at True. "Come on, son."
True started the car. "Reckon Judge Anderson will help us?"
"He might could," answered Harlowe.

***

Judge Anderson offered them a seat in the livingroom. Mrs. Anderson brought them coffee; they made small talk while the kids played in the hall of the cozy house. The topic did turn to the reason for the visit. "Raines thought the bones weren't enough to establish a corpus, is that it?"

"Yessir."

"I can't prejudge a case, you understand, so I take this purely as a question of black-letter law."

"I'd like to know if I'm not on solid ground."

"Before you move ahead—with something, generally speaking?"

"Yessir, that's what I mean."

"Are a skull and bones without direct identification, sufficient to establish corpus?"

"Yessir. That's the problem we're havin'." Harlowe referred to the case precedent.

Anderson smiled. "I would have loved to have seen Raines' face. You shoulda been a lawyer, you would have been a damned good one." Anderson opened the books, scanned the decisions. "I agree with you, what you have, in addition to the circumstances, proves corpus delicti—at least enough to go to the jury."

"All right."

"On the 'English Rule,' courts are reluctant to use it. The fear is that we'd convict a man on account of the *other* crime. But yours explains motive— *powerfully.* I'm inclined to allow it in. What's your next step? Perhaps I shouldn't ask."

"I'm gonna force his hand."

NINETY-NINE

Later that day.

True pulled up by Junior's house in the De Soto. They saw the boys playing ball. Parents in the living room. "He's got a crowd of witnesses," said Harlowe.

They dashed down a sidestreet. Avoided Ledbetter's new Oldsmobile lurking on Adams.

Harlowe talked to Finley at the Fuller.

"I understand," said the boy.

"You tried, we know you did!" said his mother.

"And I'm gonna keep tryin.'"

"I appreciate what you've done for me," said Finley. The boy got a funny look on his face.

"You all right?"

"Can I ask you something? Just you, I mean."

"Sure, Finn."

"I'll leave you to it," said Mrs. Young.

"Thanks, mom."

After she'd gone downstairs, Finley tried to find the words. "Well, how do you put it behind you? When something happens? I'm not sure I can."

"I know one thing, son."

"Yes, sir?"

"It takes time."

"One thing really bothers me. I'm not sure what--."

"Yeah, son?"

"I'm not sure what kind of man—I'm not sure I can be a man. Well, now. Gettin' married. Everything."

"Sure, you will, son. You'll be a good man." Harlowe patted him on the back. "We may see you a Lieutenant of the horse marines, before long!"

True dropped off Harlowe. In the porchlight, Harlowe looked thinner. His coat hanging off him. True knew he was trading repairs for gasoline.

***

Marlene watched True sleeping. *"He's so gentle with me. What went on in his home must have been horrible. He won't talk about it, but I see it in his eyes."* She teared up. Held him tighter.

In the morning, she left to do for her daddy, her brothers, as she did twice each week. True didn't like it, but he didn't say anything. He kept silent, only to come home and find Marlene exhausted, mashing out hamburger meat for their supper.

"I'm so tired, True. But I gotta go back tomorruh!"

"To do the washin'?"

"Uh-huh. I'm so tired of it, but there's nothin' to be done about it."

"You don't have to keep going over theah. I know he's your daddy, but it's gone on enough. You can quit."

"I can?"

"You sure can."

He looked serious about it. Marlene was shaking, like she was in trouble, or soon would be—but happy too, like a bird freed from a trap. "Okay."

They slept late. Heard a door slam. And cussing. True looked out the blinds. C.P., Denny, Lonnie! "Girl, you got chores to do!" hollered C.P.

Marlene dressed hurridly. "I gotta go!"

C.P. beat on the door.

True opened it. "She's stayin' heah."

"She's my daughter and I told ya--."

"She's *my* wife."

Marlene's daddy jabbed at True's chest. "I'm gonna whoop yer ass, boy."

True felt like a squirrel in that doorway, C.P. big as a bear! *Be like Uncle Pratt that day at the door,* he thought. "You can whip my ass but she ain't goin.' You boys can wash your own damn clothes."

When the brothers got to the porch, True picked up a hammer. "Ya'll can git the hell off my land, right now!"

C.P. backed up. The boys backed up.

"Go on. Y'all git the hell outta here!" True hollered.

Marlene watched from the window—she'd never seen True get mad!

They took off, dirt flying. True lit up. "Damn, no good sons-of--."

Marlene planted a kiss on him.

"What's that for?"

"I love you!"

"Y-ya want a cigarette?"

She pulled him inside. "C'mon, that kiss ain't all I'm gonna give you."

***

On the radio at the *Riverside,* Joe Louis knocked out Johhny Paycheck

Harlowe had spent hours questioning Driscoll. Still wouldn't talk.

Harlowe paid for his coffee. Carried some in a jug, down to the Fuller.

"I can take over, now. Here, have some coffee."

"Thanks." True poured some. Enjoyed it. "Quiet tonight."

"Yep."

"Well, goodnight."

"Goodnight, son."

Harlwoe heard his car crank. Heard the gears whine down the street.
Jeter was staying there, too, but likely had a drunk on by now. Would be
little good with a firearm. He poured another. Lay the gun across his lap.

***

March, 1940

He looked in the window of the jail. Harlowe's hat. *"Damn, he's made it easy, the fool's sleepin' on that bench!"*

The man aimed the shotgun. Squeezed. The gunshot, the glass was like
an explosion. The hat flew.

He pumped the shotgun. Fired again. *"Cut 'im in two, that time!"*

Suddenly, he felt cold steel on his neck. *"What the hell!"*

"Lookin' for me?" said Harlowe. "Let's go."

Harlowe marched the fellow—whom he didn't recognize—back toward the
cells. Seago, come runnin' in his underwear. "Best fan him down," said
Harlowe. "See if he's got anythin' on 'im."

Seago slammed him against the wall. Patted him down. Pulled a knife off him. "I ain't got nothin' else!" spat the man.

Seago come up with a screwdriver. "In 'is boot."

Harlowe pocketed it. Looked at Driscoll. He was wide-eyed. It was clear he knew the new prisoner!

Seago shoved the new man in a cell. Slammed it.

Harlowe pointed his automatic at the man's head. "They caint help you. Your friends." The man began to whimper. "You got one chance to tell me what I wanna know."

The man stared at the little gun. *Liquor's wore off. It's me hooked, now!* The muzzle stared back like a window into his own grave. "All right! All right!"

"What's your name?"

"Judd Fallon."

"Who sent ya?"

"I dunno?"

"Then you're no use to me."

"All right! They paid me! Ledbetter let me out of his jail. Said both my arrests would be forgotten! A fella paid me. I got drunk! And I come down here like he said."

"Who was the man?"

"He wore a mask. But I recognized him. He works for Lamar Cory. At his plant."

"You were gonna kill me and get your buddy out?"

Fallon nodded.

Harlowe put the gun to Driscoll's head, next. The man looked like a cow led to slaughter. "You're gonna tell me everything I wanna know. You can go right now, or it might go easier on ya if ya talk. You ain't got but two choices."

"I'll talk. Can I have a smoke?"

True arrived, now. Mrs. Seago had phoned him.

"Let's start with Collis Hutto."

Driscoll nodded. "Bossman paid him to shut up. He knew where the boy was buried."

"You moved his body?"

"Yeah. I done that. Back off the road, theah."

"Whittle?"

"Yeah. He was behind what was done to the old man. Raines did the paperwork, got Whittle sent to the nuthouse. They knew Whittle knew. They shut him up."

"Raines get paid for it?"

Driscoll took a long drag, his hands shaking. "Yeah. O'course not for hisself! He's too pure. Used it to rewire the lights at his church."

"What about the money for Whittle's house?"

"Oh, you know about that? Raines and the other lawyer wangled it; they split the house money. Prob'ly went to a stained glass winduh."

"Lamar paid Mr. Newlin?"

"Yessir. The Concrete Company paid him a check a thousand dollars, although he'd never worked for the comp'ny in any capacity."

"And Kern?" harlowe asked.

Driscoll nodded. "We paid him."

"Hoyt Conway involved in it?"

"Lamar hired him. Raines hired him. Same difference."

Harlowe looked at True.

Harlowe lit a cigarette. "What about the Eubanks boy?"

"Huh?"

"Y'might as well tell us all of it, son."

Driscoll hung his head. "We paid his momma to leave town. We shut him up, too."

"Who was it took a shot at us on the road?"

"It wuddint me! I don't know who done that. But I know Lamar had it done. He ain't above payin' to have things done." Driscoll nodded toward the other man's cell, and cussed.

The three lawmen walked out. It felt like a long day on the water, but finally they pulled in the net on the money catch! "We've got it, True. We've got it."

At dawn they drove to Eastpoint. Aubrey was warming up the boat motor. Lillian was on the back porch, crying. "She's been like 'at two days, Pratt. Close to his birthday and all."

They told the Birches what had happened.

"I trust you, Pratt," was all she could say.

***

Raines met Lamar on the side of a deserted Thomasville Highway. "You heard?" asked Lamar.

"You're a fool lettin' that man out. A two-bit thief like that! I don't know what you expect me to do!" Raines barked.

"I know."

"Idiotic! I could expect that from Bill, but not you."

"I shoulda used the man from down south."

"You try to get cheap, now you got what you paid for."

"Y'think he'll talk?"

"Better call the governor now. Not wait. If Harlowe goes it doesn't matter what he knows. Fallon's been convicted of half-a-dozen crimes—by me. We have that workin' in our favor. Even if I have to call a grand jury, they'll believe what I tell 'em to."

***

They drove north, rifles loaded. They pulled into town at sundown.

They talked to Junior on his back porch.

"Driscoll told us...everything," said Harlowe.

"That on the level?"

"Sure."

"Your daddy had Driscoll come clean up. Your daddy knew Whiskey George, those old shanties. Driscoll didn't clean up the clothes—you kept those, didn't you?"

The man blanched. "I didn't do anything to the boy!" The teacher's hands shook as he tried to light his cigarette. He realized it and pocketed his lighter. *Yes, I kept the clothes until my father found out and got rid of them! I don't know why I did that!*

"Y'wanna make a statement?"

"I-I don't mean to be rude, but we've an engagement. I need to get ready for it. If you've no more questions—?"

Harlowe and True stood. "No, we'll be going, Mr. Cory."

"Good night, Mr. Harlowe."

"I'll be around."

They got in the car. "He's feelin' the pressure, True."

***

A night off. And for the first time in a month, they could afford to eat out. They walked in to the Grill. "How y'all doin," said Marlene.

"Hey, Marlene! Hello True!"

Evie brought their menus.

Marlene looked around happily. "I reckon I'll try that big fish sandwich," said Marlene.

ONE-HUNDRED

April, 1940

They met at the ranch. "Governor won't act yet," said Lamar. "He doesn't want to have this thing blow up in his face. Feels like he needs more before he can remove him. Afraid one senator or another might ask questions."

"You tell him about Fallon?" asked Ledbetter.

"No. Not yet."

***

The State's Attorney drove down in his automobile. It was a rare occasion for him to visit the county outside the term of court. Mrs. Birch poured him coffee at her kitchen table.

Raines looked about the tiny matchbox-like home. "Thank you for the coffee. I believe Sheriff Harlowe has gotten your hopes up. An, uh, there's no proof of anything he says. If I had it, I wouldn't hold back for a minute."

"Yessir?"

"I hope we can end all this, and not, uh, ruin anyone over this."

"My husband is out on the water—workin' like he does every day. We're hard-workin' people. I can tell you, that's not what we wohnt—to ruin' nobody. We don't want to cause trouble for nobody. We wohnt the feller that keeled our youngun to git what's comin' to 'im."

"I haven't finished, Mrs. Birch. What I started to say is we all want that, but we must have evidence. Harlowe has got you worked up for nothing."

"Today is my son's birthday—or it woulda been." Mrs. Birch handed Raines her son's photograph. "We're not educated people, Mr. Raines, but we've seen what all the Shureff has on this, and b'lieve it was Junior Cory that done it."

Raines' mouth opened like a cottonmouth. "You only know what Harlowe tells you. You may not realize it, but he's out for himself in this—he's facing an election in the Fall. Tell me, would you even recognize Cory if you saw him?"

"Nosir, but that don't make no difference if he done what he done! He didn't stop by and *visit* with us!"

Raines jabbed his finger. "Don't get coy with me! I'm tellin' you we have to have proof before I charge someone—anyone! Your boy run away—he'd done it before! Now, it may be more comforting to believe someone took him. But I'm tellin' you, you'll be a lot better off if you don't listen to Harlowe about all this!"

"No, sir, I don't believe my Gibby run off. I knew somethin' was wrong when he didn't come in."

"You *knew*. I'll tell you what *I* know. Your boy stowed away on a riverboat, just a few months earlier!"

"Boys will do things like 'at! But he was comin' home for supper, Mr. Raines! He wouldna missed my fried chicken."

"Fried chicken! I'm tellin' you the *evidence* shows he drowned or run away. You're being very foolish!"

"I don't know why you're bein' ugly to me, Mr. Raines, but I know my son ain't a runaway. I'm his mother and I know somethin' about it!"

"I've told you, no one did anything to your boy!" Raines growled. The State's attorney was used to his word being law. And this oysterman's wife should dare question *him?*

"He run off before, and you had no idea where he was. I'd say you don't know *everything* about your boy. You sure your husband didn't beat the boy, and that's why he run off?"

"Nosir, it ain't, and I think y'better speak to my husband when he gets back."

Raines didn't wait.

He shook his finger at her. "There *was* no kidnapping! You're going to get yourself in a lot of trouble, young lady!"

"Trouble—for what, sir? For askin' you to call the jew-ree?"

"This case will never be tried—hear me when I say that!"

"Then maybe we do it ourselves. *Somethin's* got to be done!"

"If your husband or anyone else takes the law into his own hands, *I'll indict him!*" Raines growled.

"Don't you worry about Aubrey! I might do the job myself, Mr. Raines!"

"You'll drop this or bear the consequences!"

At that, Raines got in his Ford sedan, and raced back up US-319.

***

"He come in here when I ain't home. Talked to my wife like she's trash!" Aubrey protested. Harlowe could see steam rise from his head. The air was humid, foggy, and Birch was hot!

"What a *nasty* old man!" cried Mrs. Birch. "I don't know much about the law, but I see you're up against it, Pratt!"

"I'm just an oyster man. Here's a rich Tallahassee fella. I either shut up, or they crush us like a pack of cigarettes!" said Aubrey.

"Ye-ess, just exactly!" Lillian agreed.

"I'm mad enough to ride up there!" Aubrey was usually so mild mannered, but Raines had been particularly nasty to Lillian, and Harlowe knew it wouldn't' take much and Aubrey and his cousins would be on their way.

"*I'm* goin' up theah," said Harlowe.

***

"You don't have it, Pratt. You'll never have it. Mrs. Birch is a *hysterical* woman—an' she's got her neighbors riled up. That's what's driving this. But it's not good for anyone *but you!* I tried to explain to that woman that we needed evidence. Not your useless theories. She wouldn't listen. And I won't do this because she wants to be the talk of the town down there. Nor because you want to win votes!"

"Nosir, you're wrong about Mrs. Birch. She's a good woman."

"I won't go around and around with you. I've been doin' the job you shoulda done. And I have facts. I asked you while ago—how do we know this boy boy didn't run away?"

Raines held up a paper. "Sheriff Ledbetter *took time off* from what he's doing to look into this. The Birch boy has run away *more than once.* His parents had difficulty controlling him. All a defense attorney would have to do is call Bill and your case gets dismissed. These are *facts* I've given you—that he was a runaway who didn't mind his parents."
"Gibby was an innocent child. He didn't deserve what happened to him."
"That was not my meaning," Raines retorted.
"There is one other thing. Those people were having marital problems in twenty-seven. Birch left her and went to Harbeson City."
"He worked at the sawmill there—for a week. He didn't leave Lillian."
"Let me finish. Birch was a drunk and his aunt was worried about Mrs. Birch—and the boy. I have the paper right here." The old man held up the letter if it were Holy writ. "This woman describes Birch being found in a state of drunkenness—the day of your 'kidnapping.' 'She was crying and taking on, I thought maybe he hit her,'" Raines read aloud.
"Go on."

"This is his own family saying this! 'He has a temper. I seen him put welts on the boy.' This is Birch's aunt, Eunice."

"I don't believe there's any truth—."

"My man uncovered it."

Harlowe showed the paper to True. "Slats O'Dell, eh?"

"He talked to the aunt. He also found out some more things about your friend Birch."

He lay an affidavit, signed by P.T. Daughtry, detailing Aubrey's moonshining activities. "Pretty sure there's a crime in there, Harlowe." Raines seemed to take considerable pleasure in saying this. "You should have been looking closer to home."

"We have a boy murdered. Folks can twist things around and make Aubrey look bad, or anyone look bad if they want to, but it doesn't change the facts in front of ya."

"Hold on, Pratt. Not only your 'shine runnin-friend. Your Mrs. Birch isn't out of this yet."

"How's that?"

He opened another file. "She didn't cry. Any normal mother *would have.*" Harlowe thought of every time he stopped to check on Lill. The blank look on her face where she didn't know how she'd go on another day. How she sat at her back door, crying her eyes out alone. *"Horse manure.* If you had--."

"I'm tellin' you, I *won't* charge him. You've nothing but your assumptions. You don't *know* it's his skull. May as well go to court on women's intuition."

Raines help up another file. "In case you don't know, it's my name at the bottom. I was elected prosecutor over the circuit," he said, jabbing his finger toward the window. "Not you. It's my name on all of this. See my name on the door there? Where it says, *'State Attorney'?'* That means I'm the one who decides. If you can't understand that get someone who can explain it to you. Now, I've had to clean up the mess you made—this is the *nolle prosse* for Driscoll. Keep holdin' him if you think you can, but I won't be tryin' 'im! The same goes for Cory. This is a good town and I'm going to protect it from you. I won't have you railroad one of our people!'"

"A *grand jew-ree* would indict, and you know it."

"If you're moronic enough to arrest Cory, get ready to try it yourself because I won't. I'll see to it the chief judge turns him loose."

"I'll ask the judge to appoint a lawyer to try it."

"You think they'll go against what I tell 'em? Any of 'em? They won't go without me. They'll laugh you out of the courthouse. Then get set for a lawsuit. His lawyer will take everything you got. If somehow it ever got to a grand jury, I'd tell them everything we found out about Birch. I'd tell 'em it's an accident and that'll be their verdict. And another thing—you may have decided to let Birch go, but I won't let him get away with breaking the law. I'm not bluffin'." He shoved a paper across the desk. With dates and times Birch carried moonshine into Leon County. *Affidavit from Aubrey's cousin, Thad. Ledbetter had been busy after all. Do you ever know someone for certain? I reckon not. Not everything, but I know Aubrey is not a violent man,* Harlowe thought.

"How would that woman get along, with her husband in the State Prison?"

At that Harlowe stood abruptly and walked out, True trying to keep up.

Harlowe got in the car. He looked eviscerated. "A State's attorney and a sheriff."

He looked True in the eye. "We done solved it. And they gonna do somethin' like that? It's pitiful. Let's head home."

Harlowe went to work on the "new evidence." Presently, he phoned Raines with his findings. "Thad Birch will say anything if you buy him a jug. Everyone in Carrabelle knows it."
"I've heard enough."
"Eunice Birch has dementia. Doc Weems will swear to it."
Raines cussed. "I've made my decision!"
CLICK.

The drove to see the Birches at their home. "To say he just run away, it just so hurtful," said his mother. "And to say Aubrey was drunk an' beat us? That's a a lie!"
"They say I beat 'im? They swore that and everythin'?" Harlowe could see that thought pained Aubrey. "And they say I carried moonshine?"
"Thad stood by his statement," said Harlowe.
Aubrey was surprised. "I don't know why they'd say that—any of 'em."
"They don't like us, that side of the family. They've been in trouble with the law. You know that," said Mrs. Birch.
Harlowe nodded.
"Like they say, there's 'the Birches,' and then there's the 'damn Birches,'" said Lillian. "Cousin Thad is one o' the 'damn Birches.'"
Aubrey nodded.

"Thad is no good. He worked the turpentine still at Green Point—when he did work. I ain't carried no shine in fifteen years, I swear to you," said Aubrey.

"All right. I'm gonna look into it," said Harlowe.

"Now, I ain't forgot this other thing. I done lied to protect Aubrey? I didn't cry, so I's in on it, is that it? What the hell kind of man is Raines?" asked Mrs. Birch.

"Lill."

"No, Aubrey! This ain't right! I'm of a mind to—maybe a woman shouldn't talk this way, but if I shot Cory and if they rigged it so I was convicted, a momma lookin' out for her son, so be it."

"Lill!"

She looked out over the sawgrass. "I know, Aubrey. Thankya, Pratt, for standin' up to that man!"

Harlowe looked out, too. The edge of civilization and wilderness, law and justice. Maybe the courthouse could work. He still had hope. He didn't want to be lawless to stop lawlessness but he would if he had to.

Harlowe told them Raines hired a private detective to dig up dirt on them.

"On you, too, Pratt?"

"Yes, ma'am. Me, and my deputies."

"I don't understand it! To come against our little county like this!" declared Mrs. Birch.

***

They discussed it further at The Grill. Seago showed them a copy of the Tallahassee paper. The article cited, *"anonymous sources that state that Franklin County Sheriff P.K. Harlowe has been observed drinking on the job."*

"Y'know how Mr. Raines goes own an' own about 'doin' right,'" said Seago. "But he just flat *refuses* to do right."

"I know it," replied Harlowe.

"Why don't you see the Guvunuh?" asked Murrow.

"Yeah, Pratt, maybe we can slide in there and see 'im. Talk to 'im when Raines ain't a bug in his ear, git 'im to see!" reckoned Seago. *"Then* I'm all for just goin' and gittin' Cory and hang 'im from the nearest tree. I know you ain't for no lynchin' but there are times that call for it!"

"We got the judge still, don't forget that. If we can get the laws to work, that's what I aim to do."

"You ougthta go see that editor, Pratt! *Set 'im straight!"*

"No, sir. They'd only find something I said one way and make it look like I meant t'other. I quit drinkin' a long time ago. People that know me, know that. Boys, I thought there was a chance that reporter would have some intergrity...and...gumption. That was my mistake."

Harlowe saw Doc Murrow off at the station. Shook his hand.

The governor met with the Apalachicolan.
The old man sat across from him at the old mansion.
"I am concerned about what you've told me, Doctor. I will speak to the Attorney General about the matter, in the morning."
He rose. Extended his hand. "Say hello to your wife for me, J.S."

They met Murrow at the station when he returned. Three days past without an answer. They waited. They met at The Grill.

"You still haven't heard from anyone?" asked Murrow.

"Not even a postcard!" said Seago.

"Well, you tried, Doc. I 'preciate it," said Harlowe.

"I appreciate it so much, now," said Birch.

***

Seago found Harlowe in the office, early. "Pratt, he's already tryin' to git the Guv'ner to suspend ya."

"Yeah?"

"You know who." *Raines.*

"He never got that hot about the killin', did he?"

"You right, Pratt! It's a damned shame. But what I'm getting' at is—they'll remove ya agin'. I'm tellin' ya."

"Go on."

Seago held up the *Democrat*. "Raines walked in with this in his hand, I guaran-damn-tee ya. 'Malfeasance!' 'Spends considerably more time building houses than he does on his official duties.' 'Misue of funds.' 'Running his business out of the courthouse!" And it keeps on. 'Harassing people out of his jurisdiction to win votes.' You oughtta sue for slander, boss!"

"In a Tallahassee court?"

"I know—but they plumb lied! They write this stuff without even settin' foot in this county. I ain't seen a reporter in town have you, True?"

"No."

"Ummmh-mmmh!" Seago decried.

Harlowe winked. "Yeah, I ain't built a house in ages."

"What I jus' told ya ain't all they is. They comin' after ya. Guv'ner says he may ask Raines to call a grand jew-ree, *for you!*"

***

The next day.

"They done it again, boss!" cried Sego. "Listen at this. 'A disassembled still, half-pint bottles, and full bottles containing intoxicants were found on Sheriff Harlowe's property, in an old lean-to.' You want me to go on?"

Harlowe shook his head.

"Where'd they get that, bossman?" asked True.

Brewer came in. "They were pokin' around your land on the Bay City Road."

"Well, you didn't have no still theah!" gasped Seago.

"That's a big story! We can prove that!" said True.

"It's hard to compete with the newspaper, son. Once they deliver 'em, they never take 'em back," asked Harlowe.

"Whaddya think will happen?" wondered Seago.

"I imagine the Guvunuh's lookin' at it."

Presently, Huff summoned Harlowe to the commission meeting.

He had a warning: "Sheriff, some of us are concerned your 'visits' to Tallahasee will upset some of our neighbors to the north. Tourists bring money. We stand to have more businesses open here. Good for the county. So we don't need to upset those people!"

He didn't have to say his "Gorrie Service Station" and little tourist cabins in Eastpoint were doing a fair trade with the travellers.

The other commissioners wanted to know how often he'd been in Tallahassee recently.

Huff held up today's *Democrat.* "And this's shockin', Pratt! That you'd be involved in illegal liquor-makin'—you a lawman!"

True looked at Harlowe, seated like a witness under cross-examination. Under pressure that would crack most men, Harlowe replied, "I'll see it through."

ONE-HUNDRED-ONE

The next day

Junior's wife arrived home from church, finding Harlowe sitting on the porch, in the dark.

"Mr. Harlowe, why—my husband isn't here."

"Yes, ma'am."

"You know there's something wrong. I can help your husband before it's too late."

"I still don't know what this is about, really! I know my husband hasn't done anything."

Harlowe told her about Gibby. And about the other boys. He hated having to tell her about the matter. "I don't want to hurt you, Mrs. Cory."

"Well, you are hurting me—both of us. Don't you see there's no way he's done anything? If I thought that, I wouldn't—do you think id stay married to him for a mimute if he was capable of such things? He's a good man, Mr. Harlowe. Now, I think you'd better go!"

"Yes, ma'am. I'm givin' him a chance, Mrs. Cory. He can help himself now. I'll do all I can for him. But times' runnin' out."

"I appreciate it, but I intend to protect my husband. You think I'm foolish?"

"You seem like a nice woman."

"Then let me take care of him."

"He'll do it again, Miss Cory."

***

Harlowe went to relieve True at the Fuller.

Spoke with Mrs. Young. "Food all right?"

"Yes, sir, it's fine," she replied.

"Good."

"Finn said you'd wrote a letter for him—about getting into the Marines."

"Yes, ma'am."

"I really appreciate that. He seems better. He seems to like school."

"I'm glad to hear it."

"I do have one complaint."

"Yes, ma'am?"

"I have to work!" said she. "We can't depend on charity."

"Yes, ma'am." He tipped his hat. Left.

Seago came to watch, then.

"He reminds me of an older Harry Carey. Oh, I hope he didn't hear me say that!" said Mrs. Young.

Seago laughed. "He *is* like an old cattledog, always watchin' over the town."

"Yes, he is, isn't he?"

Seago didn't mention that Harlowe had run Slats O' Dell off, earlier, when the latter was snooping around the Fuller. "Responsibility comes first, and its sad. Now for me, fishin' comes first!"

She laughed.

"He's sad?" she wondered.

"He's had his share 'o sadness."

The next day, Murrow and Harlowe came to see Mrs. Young.

Murrow said, "Sheip's mill has need of a secretary. We was thinkin' you might be interested. We've also found a little place for rent, near the skool."

"Y'all have done this for me? Why—you barely know me?"

"Isn't that what bein' Christian means?" asked Murrow.

***

Junior got home, finding Harlowe waiting in the living room. "Mr. Harlowe's here," said his wife.

Cory Smiled. "Hello, Mr. Harlowe! How are you?"

"I'm all right. The Birches aren't so good."

"How are--?"

"They're hurtin'. You can help them."

"I wish I could."

"You can get it off your conscience. I'll treat you fairly."

"I know you would. Would you care for a drink?"

"No, sir."

"Cigarette?"

"Thankya. Have you many friends?" asked Harlowe, accepting the smoke.

"No—Bill and Royce."

"Driscoll's been talkin'. It's only a matter of time," said Harlowe. Junior held the lighter for him. "Thankya."

"I can't admit to something I didn't do." Harlowe noted a Colt .45 on the table in the hall. A bottle of cleaning solvent, beside it.

Harlowe said goodbye to the man and his wife. Stepped out onto the porch.

At that, Durfee pulled into the driveway.

"If he's botherin' ya, I'll arrest him!" said the deputy.

"He's not bothering me," said Junior. "He's okay. It's all right."

Harlowe met True on the road, at sunrise.

"He showed no reaction. See what he does."

True nodded. He waited. The fellow left school at 3:00 pm.

Walked down by the tracks, past the shanties.

True watched, remembering Harlowe's words. *"Payin' attention to things."*

He noticed a wiff of smoke in the air. Ran toward it. Saw Junior kneeling in the trees, trying to burn something. The teacher put more leaves on it. The flames spread. He ran.

True dashed to the flames, kicking the camera and photographs from the fire.

"I wanna upchuck seein' something like that, Uncle Pratt. Camera's ruined, but some o' these snapshots--."

Harlowe took them. "He may have been doin' something as I sat outside in the car, all those parents in the front room. I let him get by with it, True!"

Harlowe looked at the burnt photos—clearly Junior and a child. "You did good, son!" He clapped him on the shoulder. "Good detective work."

Harlowe jimmied the back door of the teacher's house. He and the Missus were having dinner at the Silver Slipper. In the smaller bedroom, there was more baseball stuff than before,   photos of Ruth, Gehrig, Alexander, things a boy would be drawn to.

There was a big heavy chair in the corner.

He almost missed it! That odd lamp—*art moderne* and quite large. *Something funny about it. I'll be darned. It opens. He set the camera in theah!*

He found True. Got in the De Soto. "Gibby woulda fought. Now he has an easier way. He's got their trust. He's set that camera up. They don't know what he's up to—swept along with it. I'm with you—It's enough to make a man sick," said Harlowe.

Harlowe coughed—a deep cough that maybe someone with pneumonia had.

"You a'ight?" asked True. *Harlowe seems exhausted, his voice frail. Hands seem to tremor.   Getting older.* It made True shiver.

He nodded. "I wanna arrest 'im before practice tomorruh. He ain't gonna hurt another youngun."

ONE-HUNDRED-TWO

Eastpoint—the next day.

They met by Gibby's grave, the cars pulled in facing the headstone. "He killed a boy in our county and thinks he can get by with it." Harlowe shook his head. "Nosir. Take along an extra box of cartridges and keep your eyes open. Let's go."

They weren't surprised that the speech was brief. True got the impression Harlowe would never stop if it was the last thing he did.

Harlowe reached for the car door.

"It could be dangerous. He's armed. His daddy's armed," said Seago. "Might have help. Maybe we oughtta--."

Harlowe looked at Seago—True—then back.

"Maybe Brewer oughta come?"

"I need him to mind things heah."

He looked at them. True nodded.

Finally, Seago, exhaled. "A'ight bossman." They pocketed ten extra rounds of buckshot. And sped North.

They met Judge Anderson at First Baptist Church. "No one would think to look for me here," quipped the jurist.

They sat in the pews. Harlowe handed the judge the typed affidavit. "I'm no lawyer, now. I wanna know your opinion—would the case hold water."

"When your uncle says, 'I'm no lawyer,' watch out," he told True. "He knows more law than some of the faculty at the University of Miami law school."

They all felt the gravity of the moment. In the sanctuary with high ceiling, the organ, the pupit. Finally, Anderson looked at them. "You got him."

Anderson signed the warrant they'd prepared. "What about Raines?" asked the judge.

"We see him next."

***

"He can't see you," said the secretary.

"He'll have to see us," said Harlowe. He flung the door open.

"What do you want! What the hell are you--."

Harlowe lay the singed photos before him. "Junior had a camera in the house theah. He had them to his house, the boys."

Raines looked sickened. "Go on."

True saw a chink in Raines' armor for the first time.

"He done it to three boys. An' Giib-beh," he said, drawling out the name. "I've told ya about the evidence on the murder."

The State's Attorney balked. "You'd upend this town with a circumstantial case—this would be a contentious trial—how would that help the Birches if it's an acquittal?"

"You've got no choice," said Harlowe, his voice strong.

"Whaddya mean?"

"I got Driscoll spillin' everythin'. You give me Junior or I can keep goin' on 'is daddy."

"A jury won't believe Driscoll—they'd say he lied to save his neck!" roared the prosecutor.

"We've laid out evidence to keep a stenographer busy for a week, Mr. Raines. But if that ain't enough, I'll play it the Tallahassee way. True?"

"Sure." True opened the case of photos and lay them before the lawyer.

They clearly showed Ledbetter—with a buxom young thing at her house trailer.

"That's the trailer park at Mun-row and St. Augustine, Mr. Raines," True advised.

Raines seethed with anger. "I know where it is!"

"Well, we know all about that eighteen-year-old gal and how Bill wrecked his car drunk and settled through your law firm." True watched the two men. It was like a movie showdown. The country sheriff *had* the prosecutor, and the latter knew it.

Raines' voice seemed to go on octave deeper. "You know *nothing!*"

"We know about the false petition on Old Man Whittle."

Raines cussed.

"Easy, Deacon. We have proof of what I'm sayin.' Ev'ruh bit of it."

Raines glanced at the affidavit and shoved it back. "You believe anything Driscoll has to say you're a fool!"

"He sure seems to know a lot about the goins-on in the Cory Comp'ny."

"None of that would be admissible!"

True looked over at Harlowe. Mr. Raines, we know you got cash money— enough for a good train robbery—from Lamar. When that lawyer was killed in nineteen-hunnerd-and twenty-six."

"We have the man who came to kill me," said Harlowe. "Fallon."

Raines turned white.

"Yeah, one other thing. Eff-Bee-Eye's lookin' into some of Lamar's road contracts--."

"What?"

"Now that Lamar has a bid to pave those runways for the Air Corps, they wanna see if he's on the up-and-up. They wanna talk to *you.*"

Raines was beside himself. "How do you know this?"

"I've talked to those Eff-Bee-Eye boys."

The prosecutor stormed down the hall to the empty office. He picked up the extension and phoned his friend. Lamar.

"They have me over a barrell!" Raines growled.

"Election coming. Got to think of that. It didn't help you, before. But it will hurt ya, now."

"Sonofabitch, I know it!"

The prosecutor retired to the lavatory. Ran cold water. Hot water. Wiped his face with a towel. He was shaking. Near crying. Harlowe eased down the hall and heard him in there.

Harlowe shoved the door open. Stood behind the tall man grasping the sink. He looked like a tall pallbearer. The power he had could not prevent the decay, the grayness that showed on the man's face. "You always say 'do right.' Seems to me it's a lot easier on a fella than trying to hold back the flood like you are now."

"What do you want?"

"I want you to carry this to the grand jew-ree. For the murder, and what was done to Finley!"

"All right! Now get out!" he hissed. He signed the warrant, *approved!*

Harlowe and True ran down to the latter's car.

They told Seago.

"What about Ledbetter?"

Harlowe looked at C.A. as if to ask, 'what *about* him?'

"All right, Let's go," said Harlowe. They got in the cars. BAR and shotgun next to True. Harlowe had his automatic. Seago drove his car, shotgun and Winchester rifle beside him.

They drove down Calhoun to the school.

"He's already left. Why, he went home, I imagine," one of the teachers advised.

"He just said he had an emergency. Not quite twenty minutes ago," said another.

"Thankya, ma'am. We'll try his house!"

True put the De Soto in gear. Raced up the hill. He flung the car onto Pensacola. Seago screeched tires, behind trying to keep up!

The traffic wasn't helping, loping along with no sense of urgency. "Lean on it, True!" True swung around a sedan, accelerating as fast as his car would go. They slid to a stop at Junior's home.

Mrs. Cory let them look. She was sniffling. "My husband isn't here. He-he left ten minutes ago. He received a call. He said he was going down to Wakulla Springs. I told him, please don't go!"

They raced down US-319. Along the wall of trees which marked the beginnings of the Apalachicola National Forest.

They didn't see another car. Then, suddenly, ahead from the trees rose a plume of smoke.

"Down along the G. F. & A., right-of-way!" said Harlowe.

True kept his foot to the floorboards. "Over theah, True!"

True slammed on the brakes. He turned off, toward the column of smoke, at the Bloxham Cutoff crossing. A train had stopped, dead!

They lept from the car. Hopped on a train car, and down the other side. "Down yonder!" They ran toward the train engine. Smoke billowed over them, making Harlowe cough. Flames poured from the twisted wreckage of a Ford coupe crushed between the steam engine and the tracks!

The engineer came running with a fire extinguisher. "Y'all, he's still inside!"

Harlowe looked. "Yeah, he is!" The flames were spreading. They had to hurry! They tried to pull the door open. It wouldn't budge! The engineer poured the bottle on the flames to keep them at bay. But they were lapping all around the passenger compartment. True and Harlowe both pulled on the door as hard as they could.

The flames were spreading over the roof. "She may blow!" warned the train driver.

"Stand back," said Harlowe. He took the fire extinguisher and busted out the window.

They got the door open. Pulled Junior out. Seago had to help drag him and lay him on the track. As soon as they'd done that, they were hit with the blast of heat from the gas tank exploding beneath the Ford, the entire car aglow.

Harlowe felt junior's chest.

"We got t' stop the bleedin'!" cried the engineer.

"No, we don't. He's dead," said Harlowe.

"I musta drug 'im a quarter-of-a-mile," reckoned the engineer.

The freight train hissed and puffed behind them. The flames popped at they consumed the car.

The men didn't say anything. They stood watching until an automobile pulled up—Ledbetter's.

"I's comin' 'round the bend, n' I seen the car! I shoved the brake, jus' no way to stop," said the engineer. He was shaking and upset. "It's like he stalled—jus' settin' there!"

"Damned shame," said Ledbetter. "Squeezed to death! You caint beat the train!"

Harlowe and True walked with the engineer. Let him sit on the running board of True's car. "Coulda swore I seen another car backin' away!"

"See what kind?" asked Harlowe.

"Nosir, I didn't."

True looked at Harlowe. They had no doubt about that phone call. "They were his friends, Bill and Royce--."

"All nice and neat," True reckoned.

Harlowe let out a sigh. "Yeah."

A doctor arrived in a taxi. Ledbetter slapped him on the back. They politicked and waited for the fire engine and, not long after, Junior was deposited in the back of a hearse.

***

True turned down the road to Cat Point.

Hugs. Tears. Mrs. Birch held onto them for the longest time.

Birch shook Harlowe's hand. "He got what was comin' to him—for what he done. Thankya."

"We prayed the Good Lord to watch over you, an' he'p you, Pratt," said Mrs. Birch. "Do you see his hand in this, all these years?"

He nodded. "Yes'm. I do."

They drove over the bridge—the sun going down, the water like liquid silver. Colors turning. Peaceful.

Doc Murrow flagged them down by The Grill.

He had a telegram.

Harlowe worked the envelope open. "From the Guvunuh. *'You are hereby suspended.'* *'Failing to enforce the liquor laws...state liquor agents found evidence of a moonshine still'*...so forth and so on." Harlowe handed it to Seago.

"Boss, I—*damn.*"

"Well, it ain't the first time," replied Harlowe, giving a grin.

The big man flushed red. "You was framed, boss. Caint ya fight it?"

Brewer walked up.

"This is to authorize you to take over the responsibilities of Sheriff P.K. Harlowe who I suspend today until I have time to consider this matter."

Brewer was alarmed. "Boss, they arrested two nigras, they say was he'pin' ya! The revenuers say you guarded while them boys loaded the 'shine. It ain't true! I don't want the job that badly."

"We know the real reason for this!" said Seago.

"Boys, there'll be a trial," said Harlowe. "I aim to make a fight of it. Coffee?"

They sat around the table. Talking about all the ups and downs of the last ten years. "Ten years," repeated Harlowe. "Hard to believe it."

He shook True's hand. *Was it goodbye? Was it thanks?* True didn't know.

"I-I'm sorry to see you go. Ya taught me everything I know."

Harlowe grinned. "If you wanna shrimp, we might could go in on a boat—I know where there's one for sale."

True nodded. Left with Seago and the Doc.

Evie approached with her coffee pot. "Warm you up?"

Harlowe nodded. "Thankya, Evie."

ONE-HUNDRED-THREE

Sunday.

Seago tossed him the *Democrat*. "Just come on the truck! You're on the front!"

"Harlowe Suspended"

Harlowe turned the page.

"Page four, boss."

Harlowe turned the pages. *"Railroad Accident Takes Life of Beloved Schoolteacher."*

"Tied up nice and neat," said the jailor.

"Well...justice can take many forms," Harlowe declared. "Whaddya think about Ocala? I can write a lettuh to the sheriff down theah."

"For True?"

Harlowe nodded.

"You wohnt that boy to succeed, donchye."

"Yep."

***

"Sheriff, Finn has a lightness, a brightness about him now. That cloud has lifted from him. No matter what is said, you did that for him."

"I'm glad to hear that, Miss Young." Harlowe bent his hat to her.

He heard the organ as he walked down the street. He found himself by the door of the church, listening. *"...Jesus paid it all, all to him I owe!"* The organ buzzed the glass. Made the hair on his neck stand.

Harlowe found himself walking in. His legs were moving but it felt like someone else was walking. People turned to look at him.

They stepped out into the aisle to shake his hand.

Dr. Reynolds took hold of his shoulder and wouldn't let go.

Harlowe looked back at the congregation. Ira Brewer. Huff. Seago. True and Marlene. They were all there.

When it was over, Lexie hugged him. It was the first they'd spoken in ages.

After services, Seago fried fish and they lounged on his porch.

Suddenly someone came up the street cussing and hollering. Jeter! He was toting the biggest Bull Red anyone had seen of late.

"My, goodness!" exclaimed Seago. Everyone gathered around Jeter. He was red-faced and happy.

"Caught him o'er the flats, boys."

"Dadgum!" said Seago.

"True, you an' Pratt oughta come out with-me sometime!" Jeter slurred.

"Maybe we will."

"You a good fisherman, I know. Pratt never was a good angler!" said Jeter. "He'll catch a little trout or sumpin'—not no big 'Red. Nosir, he never did catch a bigun!"

True looked at him. "Didn't he?"

THE END

**

If you enjoyed this book please leave a review on Amazon! --author